ROYAL

REBEL

Praise for HEATHER FROST

"*Royal Rebel* is everything I love about romantasy—
epic world-building, swoon-worthy romances, and an
emotionally complex plot that's as intricately layered
as the characters and world. I can't get enough of this
brilliant 5-star read and Frost's masterful storytelling!"
- One Book More (Julie) on *Royal Rebel*

"Readers of this series are like tortured souls in need
of a happy ending, but still longing for all the twisted
things that can happen in the span of a chapter.
Mind you, the whole story is just *terrific!*"
- Darkest Sins (Silvia) on *Royal Rebel*

"Enchanting, thrilling, and captivating, *Esperance* drew me
in from the first page and didn't release me until the last.
...Frost has a winner on her hands here!"
- Author Rebecca Zanetti on *Esperance*

"I can't get enough of Heather Frost's books. They're
all so layered and immersive with brilliant characters,
twisty plots, and the most swoon-tastic romances.
...Completely un-put-down-able!!"
- One Book More (Julie) on *Esperance*

"Everything was perfect about this book. If you haven't started reading the [series] then I have no idea what you are doing. Perfect for those who love royals and Sarah J. Mass."
- Thindbooks on *Royal Spy*

"*Royal Spy* is a gripping story with strong, powerful characters. Excitement, betrayal, love with every turn of the page in this heart pounding adventure. I couldn't put it down!"
- Min Reads and Reviews (Mindy) on *Royal Spy*

"Frost has outdone herself with her irresistible characters and fascinating backdrop of Eyrinthia. This is a must-read for any fantasy lover!"
- Author Ashley I. Hansen on *Royal Spy*

"Heather Frost is a force to be reckoned with! ...So many twists, turns and puzzle pieces, it truly makes Frost one of my favorite authors!"
- Author Sarah Hill on *Royal Spy*

"Heather Frost can write complex characters like nobody's business! ...[This] series is a hidden gem that I want to shout from the rooftops. If you are a fan of fantasy, this is a series that you need in your life."
-Book Briefs on *Royal Spy*

"This is a story that completely captured my attention from the very beginning and didn't let go the whole way through ... I've been craving a book like this."
- Getting Your Read On (Aimee) on *Royal Decoy*

ROYAL REBEL

FATE OF EYRINTHIA · BOOK 4

HEATHER FROST

Summary: Grayson is back in Ryden to rescue Mia, and Desfan is about to become serjan of Mortise. The danger in Eyrinthia continues to grow as the threat of war looms.

Paperback ISBN: 978-1-959122-03-6

To all my Grayson fans—this one is for you.

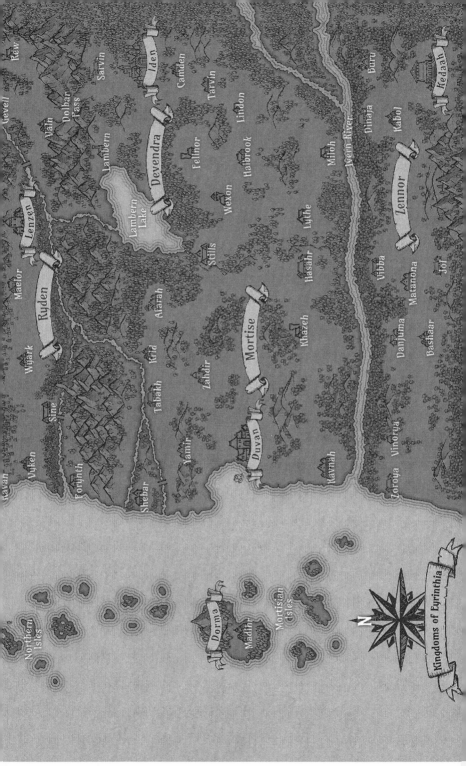

CHAPTER 1

MIA

SILENCE RANG IN MIA'S EARS, NEARLY AS SHARP as Grayson's screams had been last night.

Fates, she had never heard him scream like that.

She sat beside him on the cold stone floor of the cell, grateful he'd finally managed to fall asleep and escape the pain.

Tears stung her eyes, and her fingers dug into her crossed arms. The pressure kept her grounded. Kept her breathing. Kept her from falling into one of her panics. It kept her from banging on that locked door until Henri Kaelin himself came, so she could smash the glowing lantern into his face and make *him* burn.

A tear tracked down her cheek. She had never felt so helpless. So useless. Not during the shipwreck that had stolen her life, or during her nine years of imprisonment. When Grayson's father and brothers had entered the room, she knew it was going to be bad. She'd thought for one horrifying moment that Henri had come to hurt her.

She wished he would have hurt her.

Mia's ears roared, and the horrific memory swallowed her.

"What is that?" she'd asked, her fingers strangling Grayson's hand in hers.

Henri's soulless brown eyes flicked to her. "A reminder. Grayson can choose who will wear it."

Grayson stiffened. "Me," he said, his voice clipped. "Not her."

Mia's heart pounded. She didn't know what was in that vial. She only knew that it was bad. Very bad.

And, once again, Grayson was protecting her.

"You'll prove your choice by not fighting it," Henri said to Grayson, his words echoing strangely in Mia's ears—as if all of this was happening far away. Or like she'd been swallowed by a roaring ocean. "If you attempt to remove it before it has run its course, she will receive the same."

"I understand."

Mia glanced between Henri and Grayson, and fear made her throat almost too tight for breath. "Grayson . . ."

He didn't look at her. His focus was solely on his father. "She doesn't have to be here. I won't fight."

"For her sake, I'm glad to hear it."

Her body was still bruised from Carter's crushing hold. She'd fought, but he'd held her firmly while Grayson was forced to kneel before his father. When Tyrell followed Henri's orders and rubbed that white powder on Grayson's already injured jaw, all she could do was scream as Grayson's entire body went rigid.

Horror washed over her as she realized what that powder was. *Flame's Breath.*

Memories of a younger Grayson came to mind. He'd entered her cell one day, agony twisting his face as he'd cradled his burned fingers. His mother had left a white powder on his quill as a reminder to be vigilant, because danger lurked everywhere—especially from his evil parents.

Grayson still carried those scars on his fingers. And now, they would mark his face.

She'd struggled futilely against Carter's restraining arms. Sobs wracked her, but she'd been utterly helpless. She couldn't even hold Grayson while he was tortured.

At first, he'd tried not to make a sound, but he hadn't been able to burn silently.

When it was finally over, Grayson breathed raggedly on his side, his body drenched in sweat. His bleeding fingers clutched the sharp grooves in the stone floor, and his upturned cheek was bright red along his jaw. *Fates, his jaw . . .*

Her stomach had heaved, but she'd swallowed back bile. She was shaking so hard, she didn't know how Carter still managed to hold her.

Henri had straightened. "I trust that will serve as a reminder of your failure. I think a night in this cell will also help. You'll receive nothing for the pain. Only seek help if infection sets in." With that, he strode from the room. Peter was on his heels, and Carter finally released Mia so he could follow.

Her legs trembled, barely holding her as she darted to Grayson's side. She crashed to her knees, her hands fluttering uselessly before she grasped his shoulder. "You're all right," she whispered, throat pinched and eyes stinging. "You're going to be all right."

Grayson's breaths were labored and rattling. His teeth were clenched, his gray eyes fixed on her. The agony in them broke her heart.

Her free hand stroked dark locks off his sweaty brow. "I'm here," she breathed, blinking rapidly as she tried to banish her tears. "I'm right here."

A boot scuffed behind her.

Tyrell.

Grayson's pained gaze snapped over her shoulder, and she felt his entire body tense, preparing to spring. To attack the one who tortured him, or shield her as he always had? She honestly wasn't sure.

She tightened her hold on him. "Don't move."

He stilled, though tension still thrummed through his bunched muscles. His sharp gaze didn't leave Tyrell.

Mia looked over her shoulder, following Grayson's stare.

Tyrell stood there, the thick leather gloves that had protected his skin from that accursed powder dangling from one hand. His dark hair—so like Grayson's—was also falling across his brow, casting his eyes in shadow. His expression was locked, but his shoulders were low. "What can I do?" he asked her.

There were so many things she wanted to say. She wanted a physician for Grayson, though she knew he couldn't bring one. She wanted Grayson moved to his room—that also wouldn't happen. She wanted to hit Tyrell. Scream at him.

She thought, in this moment, he would let her.

"Leave," she said, her voice cracking.

A muscle jumped in Tyrell's cheek.

She hated what he'd just done. Hated that he'd hurt Grayson so deeply—so permanently. Even still, a voice deep inside whispered that he'd had no choice. None of them did. Not here.

Grayson's stiffness mounted. Mia squeezed her eyes shut. "Please, Tyrell," she begged. "Go."

Silence. Then a whisper of sound as Tyrell left.

When the door closed and locked behind him, Mia opened her eyes and twisted back to Grayson. He was watching her, his body shaking.

She didn't look at the burn. She wouldn't—not when he was staring at her like that. She knew how self-conscious he was of his scars.

He didn't speak. She doubted he'd be able to without horrible pain. Even from the corner of her eye, she could see the ruined skin along his jaw was mottled, covered in blisters that bubbled across the deep cut.

She wanted to comfort him, but she didn't know how. She didn't dare move him, even to cradle his head in her lap. She couldn't bear the thought of causing him any further pain. All she could do was twine her fingers through his and hold on.

Time passed. She didn't know how much. She stroked his hair and squeezed his hand. She pressed close to his body, so he would know he wasn't alone.

Eventually, Grayson shifted, and she helped roll him onto his back so he could be more comfortable. Even those careful movements made him flinch. He sucked in a breath when he turned his head. And even though he clenched his teeth, his nostrils flared and his gray eyes flooded with misery. Moisture had leaked from his eyes, and she brushed the tears before they could dash down his cheek and fall into the raw wound.

She couldn't take away his hurt. She couldn't even ease it. She could do nothing but hold his hand until eventually his ragged breathing turned less sharp, and finally his rigid body slumped in sleep. She could tell the rest was not deep, but it was a reprieve.

With Grayson unconscious, she finally studied the damage to his face.

The burn was on his right side, swollen and angry. It followed the cut his father had given him. That slice went deep, hitting bone, and it spanned nearly the entire length of his jaw—from below his ear, almost to the point of his chin. The blisters that mottled the edges of the cut made it clear that Tyrell had rubbed the powder into it, making the wound larger, the damage deeper. The redness of the burn spilled over onto his cheek, and a little under his neck—places the powder had touched. Those places, she thought, would heal in time, like the burn marks on his fingers from years ago. But his jaw . . . Would it ever heal? Would he even have feeling along the worst of the burn? Would he be able to fully smile?

Fresh tears clouded her vision, and she forced herself to stop. He was alive. That's what mattered. Everything would always be all right, as long as Grayson still breathed.

The night dragged on in horrible silence. Grayson slept.

Mia did not.

If Henri had wanted them dead last night, there was nothing either of them could have done. If he'd given Tyrell a knife instead of the powder, Mia would have had no choice but to watch Grayson die.

She had lost nearly everything in her life, but Grayson was the one thing she knew she couldn't survive losing. They had to leave. No matter the risk, they had to escape.

Grayson had said a boat was waiting for them at Porynth. From studying her maps, she knew where the port city was. It would take them about three weeks to get there, and Grayson had said the ship wouldn't wait much beyond that.

A ship.

A shiver wracked her, but she forced that particular fear away. She had more immediate concerns than stepping back on a ship. Besides, they wouldn't make it to Porynth in time to catch that ship. They were locked in a cell, with no idea how long Henri would keep them there. And even if they were released soon, Grayson needed time to heal. They couldn't leave right away, which meant the ship would be long gone. They—

The lock for the door grated.

Grayson jerked awake at the sound and instantly rolled. Breath hissed out of him, agony fracturing the sound, but he didn't stop moving until he was crouched in front of her, angled toward the door. The muscles in his shoulders bunched, his body coiled for a fight.

Mia's heart pounded. She braced a hand on Grayson's back as the door swung open.

Tyrell stepped in, not bothering to close the door behind him. The lamp in the cell had burned low, and the torches in the corridor behind him were blinding. "Father wants you in the courtyard," he said without preamble, his tone clipped.

"What about Mia?" Grayson's voice was guttural, roughened by sleep and a little slurred—probably because he was trying not to move his mouth too much.

Tyrell's lips thinned, his eyes darting to Mia as he answered his brother. "She can remain in your room, or wherever she chooses to be within the castle."

Grayson said nothing, but Mia stood, her eyes on Tyrell. "He can't go anywhere. He needs to rest."

"Orders have been given." Tyrell looked to Grayson. "I don't know where we're going, but Father said we'd be back by nightfall."

"We?" Grayson asked in a low growl.

"Peter, Carter, and the both of us." Tyrell paused, then added, "Mia will be safe. Fletcher will guard her, and I can put some of my men on her as well."

Grayson pushed to his feet. Mia was quick to grasp his hand, though he was surprisingly steady. He squeezed her fingers as he faced Tyrell. "We don't need an escort."

Tyrell snorted. "Perhaps you shouldn't dismiss me until you know you can make it up the stairs."

Mia's heart rate quickened as Grayson stiffened beside her. "I don't need anything from you."

Tyrell's eyes narrowed. He looked nothing like the Tyrell she'd befriended these past months. Even after their fight, when things were uncertain between them, he'd never felt so distant and cold. And Grayson . . . the animosity emanating from him was understandable, but so potent it was strangling.

Mia took a small step forward, still holding Grayson's hand.

The two brothers looked at her, and her cheeks warmed. Being the sole focus of both Tyrell and Grayson Kaelin was unnerving. "There's no need to fight," she said, hating how quiet her voice was. "Please."

Adding that word seemed to have a special effect on them—they listened.

Tyrell led the way out of the cell, and Grayson moved just slightly in front of her, their hands still joined.

No one said anything as they trekked up the stairs and through the quiet halls of the castle. They passed several servants and guards, all of whom stared at Grayson. One maid even gasped.

Grayson tensed. He believed his scars made him lesser; that

they made him ugly.

Mia hated his scars, but only because of the pain they represented. Grayson was beautiful to her—he always would be. She wanted to attack anyone who ever made him feel any different.

She scowled at the maid, and the woman hurried away.

When they reached Grayson's room, they all paused at the door. It took a moment for Mia to remember she was the one with a key. She released Grayson's hand and dipped her fingers into her pocket, overly conscious of the fact that Grayson and Tyrell were both watching her. It made every movement feel stiff and awkward.

Once she'd fitted the key in the lock, Tyrell spoke over her head. "I'll get Fletcher and be back for you."

"Fine," Grayson said—also over her head. "But I don't want your men guarding her."

Tyrell's jaw flexed. "Mia's safety is more important than your pride."

Grayson's brows lowered dangerously.

Mia twisted the door open and faced them. "Please don't fight."

"We're not," Tyrell said. The *yet* was heavily implied in his dark tone.

Grayson's eyes narrowed. "Mia, go inside."

Please had clearly lost its power. She crossed her arms over her chest and tried a different tactic. "There's no point in fighting. It will only bring Henri's attention back to us."

The two youngest Kaelin princes eyed her, but she refused to back down—or acknowledge the silent message they were both sending with their hard expressions.

Logic alone would not work on them. She sighed, and let

honesty ring in her voice. "If you hurt each other, you'll only be hurting me."

Tyrell's teeth clenched.

Grayson looked just as unhappy. He breathed out slowly and took Mia's hand, tugging her into the room without another word.

Tyrell remained in the hall. When Mia glanced back at him, a fissure of emotion cracked in his eyes as he stared after her.

Grayson closed the door.

Mia swallowed roughly. Her voice was low as she said, "I'm not in any danger from him."

Grayson met her gaze. "You said you weren't sure if he was still your friend."

That last word was spoken heavily, not that she could blame him. And he was right; she didn't know what relationship she and Tyrell had now. He had declared his love for her, and she'd told him there could only be friendship between them. He'd lied to her about sending her letter to Grayson, and she'd yelled at him. He'd saved her from Mama's abduction attempt—then Grayson had returned.

Things were complicated with Tyrell, but she knew one thing, so she repeated it: "He won't hurt me."

The hard planes of Grayson's face revealed nothing, but a hundred questions lurked in his eyes. He didn't voice any of them. She'd told him she wasn't ready to talk about what had happened between her and Tyrell, and she knew Grayson wouldn't press.

But, fates, he looked exhausted. And he was clearly in pain.

"I'm sorry," she whispered, her eyes darting to his jaw.

His expression locked. "You have nothing to apologize for," he said, his words a little rough as he tried not to move his newest scar. "What happened in that cell had nothing to do with you."

But it did.

He wouldn't have even been in there if not for her. He'd come back to Ryden to rescue her. And that burn ... he'd taken it for her. Grayson had allowed himself to be tortured—without being restrained—so she wouldn't have to wear that burn.

Her heart squeezed painfully. Fates, it was always the same with them. He sacrificed everything for her, and she could do nothing to protect him.

"Mia?"

She startled from her thoughts. Grayson watched her with concern, his head ducked slightly so he could catch her eye.

Moving slowly, with infinite care so she wouldn't jostle him, she wrapped her arms around his waist and eased herself against him, her cheek pressed to his chest. "Thank you," she whispered.

His arms locked around her shoulders, pulling her even closer. "For what?"

"For protecting me. Again." Her voice broke, but she forced herself to continue. "I'm sorry you had to. I'm sorry your father hurt you again, because of me—"

"No." Grayson leaned back, one hand shifting to curve against her cheek. His thumb grazed her jaw, coaxing her to lift her head. "There's no guilt for you to carry. My father has never needed an excuse to hurt me."

Henri didn't need an excuse, it was true. But he'd been hurting Grayson and manipulating him for years by threatening her. That truth was inescapable, and it hurt.

I'm your weakness.

She couldn't even make herself say the words, and that

made her a coward. But resolution burned in her heart. *I won't always be your weakness.*

Grayson studied her, his gray eyes unwavering. "I would make the same choice again," he told her. "To protect you, I would do it again—a thousand times, without hesitation."

She felt those words to her soul. Her eyes stung. "I don't deserve you."

He exhaled sharply, the sound disbelieving. "Fates, you're . . ." His voice drifted, as if he couldn't manage to find the words to describe what she was. Something in his gaze changed. Solidified. He leaned in, and her stomach fluttered.

He pressed a soft kiss to her lips, the gentle contact making her heart race. She didn't dare kiss him like she yearned to; she didn't want to cause him pain. But her mouth moved with his, following his lead. The brush of his lips was coaxing. Comforting.

Warmth flooded her veins, and her pulse kicked. Her fingers curled in his shirt, keeping him close. She had lived without him now, and she never wanted to do so again. New urgency filled her. A desperation to make him understand just how much she loved him. How much she needed him.

Grayson deepened the kiss, and Mia sucked in a breath as his fingers knotted in her hair. He turned, guiding her until her back pressed against the door. His chest rose and fell against hers, both of them breathing quickly.

He changed the angle of their kiss, and a shudder went through him.

Afraid she'd hurt him, Mia jerked back. "Careful. Your jaw—"

"I missed you," he rasped, emotion tangling in his hoarse voice. "So fates-blasted much."

Her heart clenched. "I missed you, too. But I don't want to hurt you."

He made a sound in his throat. "You aren't hurting me," he assured her.

Her face heated, but she couldn't stop her smile.

Grayson kissed one corner of it, and the simple action made her chest swell. "I couldn't breathe without you," he whispered.

The admission caught her off-guard, melting her. Before she could respond, he claimed her mouth again.

She tried to move with care, but Grayson only grew more insistent. Almost frantic, like he worried she would vanish.

The same desperate edge rode her, but she didn't want him to aggravate his wound. She pulled back. "Tyrell will return soon."

Grayson stilled, just as she'd known he would. But instead of drawing back completely, he set his forehead against hers, their heavy breaths mingling. His eyes squeezed shut. "You're right. We don't have long, and there are things we need to discuss."

She pressed a final kiss to his unmarred cheek before he eased back, giving her space. She grasped his falling hand, refusing to lose all contact with him.

He squeezed her fingers.

"Are you well enough to go with your father and brothers?" she asked.

"I'm fine."

Obviously, he wasn't *fine*, but she knew what he meant. He didn't have a choice, so he would force himself to be fine.

She pursed her lips. "I can ask Devon to—"

Grayson shook his head; a grimace sliced across his face, so he abruptly stopped moving. "It's not worth it."

"You need a physician."

"My father gave orders. I need to follow them. It will make getting out of here easier." He glanced around the room, clearly noting some of her things scattered among his own belongings. A sketchbook on his otherwise neat desk. A dress discarded over a chair in the corner. Some paintings propped against the far wall. "Pack whatever you need, but only one bag. The nights will be cold, so pack something warm. We leave tomorrow night."

"Tomorrow?" Fates, that was too soon.

"We can't delay," Grayson said. "The *Seafire* won't wait forever. When I get back tonight I'll sneak into the kitchen and get supplies."

She forced aside her unease at how quickly things were happening, so she could focus on his plan. "You won't need to steal everything," she said. "Before you came back, I was planning to escape."

He froze. "You what?"

She bit her lower lip. "I was going to come to you in Duvan. I got maps from the library. I gathered food and blankets. I even asked Tyrell to teach me how to ride a horse."

His focus remained trained on her. "You were plotting an escape?"

He seemed quite stuck on the idea. "I needed to come find you. I didn't want Henri to use me against you ever again."

Grayson's unreadable eyes softened. "Thank you. I have to admit, though, I rather hate the idea of you trying to escape on your own."

"To be perfectly honest, I didn't like the idea either. But I needed to reach you. Especially because you were in Duvan, and . . ."

"I was with Desfan."

Her brother's name punched her with painful force, and she couldn't hide a wince. Her family, her life before . . . all of it had been obliterated by the pain of Papa's beatings when she was seven years old and newly imprisoned. Fear, panic, and even guilt had kept it at bay ever since. Sometimes she dreamed of home, but they were such painful dreams, they were really nightmares. Usually they were just visions of a life she'd never have again. A father who held her. A mother who sang to her. A sister who played with her hair. A brother who taught her to swim.

The knowledge that Grayson had seen Desfan, and spoken to him . . . it was almost too much to comprehend. Her feelings were too complex to sort through. Grayson had been in Mortise—in the palace that had once been her home. He knew who she was; a secret she'd held for nine years, because the truth was too painful, especially since her *caretakers* had beaten her whenever she talked about who she really was.

Grayson had figured out the truth. And he'd gone to Desfan—her brother. Desfan had sent Grayson to bring her home.

Home. She didn't even know what that was anymore. Not with their parents dead, and Tahlyah, too. And Desfan didn't know the truth. He didn't know Mia was responsible for their sister's death. That horrible night, she'd lost Tally in the water. No matter what reassurances Grayson had given her when she'd admitted her deepest secret, she knew it was her fault Tally was dead. Desfan would never forgive her when he learned the truth.

Her heart pounded, and panic spiked.

"Mia?" Grayson stepped closer, his voice pitched low. "Are you all right?"

She pinched her eyes closed and took a deep breath, ignoring the tightness in her chest. Denial had saved her so often during the past nine years, and she clung to that now. She couldn't think about Tahlyah, or Desfan—she couldn't think about who she'd once been.

The tension inside her settled. She opened her eyes and met Grayson's worried gaze. "I never did make a solid plan for getting out of the castle, but we can use the supplies I gathered. I suppose we may need more, since there are two of us."

It was clear Grayson didn't want to follow her subject change, when she remained troubled by something. But—as always—he deferred to what she needed. He glanced around the room. "Where are they?"

A small knot tightened in her chest. "Oh. They're in Tyrell's room. Under his bed."

Grayson shot her a look.

She hurried to explain. "After Tyrell killed Papa, he carried me to his room. It was closer than the physician's ward, and I was . . ." *Dying.* Probably best not to tell him that; not when he was looking at her so intensely. "I was hurt very badly," she said instead.

A muscle ticked in Grayson's jaw.

Mia continued quickly. "Tyrell let me have his room while I healed, and then I was quite settled there, so I stayed."

"But you moved to my room later?"

"Yes. Tyrell and I . . . we had a fight."

Grayson's throat jumped as he swallowed. His voice was painfully measured. "Did he hurt you?"

He'd asked that before. She gave him basically the same answer, because she really didn't want to dwell on this right now. "Not physically."

Something sparked in Grayson's eyes—something she couldn't interpret.

She hurried on. "I don't know if I have enough supplies for both of us, but I can get into Tyrell's room while you're gone and bring everything here."

"I don't want you taking any risks."

"There won't be any risk. Tyrell will be gone with you, and any guard will know I used to stay in there—I'll tell them I left something behind. They'll let me in. Trust me."

"I trust you," he whispered.

She felt a comforting weight in those words. "Thank you." She hesitated. "I still hadn't managed to get warmer clothes, or a cloak, or tent. I read that snow can come early to Ryden, so I wanted to be prepared."

"I'll secure everything we need when I get back. I can sneak into the laundry to find a thick cloak for you."

Mia shifted on her feet. "Or . . ."

One questioning eyebrow lifted.

She swallowed back her hesitation. "We could ask for Fletcher's help. And his wife—Rena. She's worked in the castle for years, and—"

"No." His tone was even; uncompromising. "We can't risk telling anyone our plans."

"Grayson, just listen to me." She squeezed his hand, her voice low and intent. "You're not at your full strength."

Something flashed in his eyes.

Fates. That probably wasn't the best thing to say. She changed tactics. "You told me the ship in Porynth will only wait for three weeks. We can't delay, and there's too much to prepare. You can't do it all, and neither can I. If we're going to leave tomorrow night, we need Fletcher's help. And he can fight, if it comes to that. He's not truly loyal to Henri. We can trust him."

She could see the indecision in his eyes.

He was considering it.

She pressed harder. "Henri knows how close they are to me. He'll think they played a part in our escape, and . . . I can't let them be hurt because of me. Please."

His mouth tightened. "Fletcher could be on the grounds at night without rousing suspicion. He could get horses from the stable." Something they clearly wouldn't be able to get on their own, though it would speed their journey. Grayson's gaze turned calculative. "We could each take a different route out of the castle, and meet outside the city with the horses and supplies."

"Rena used to work in the laundry," Mia said, not even trying to hide the eagerness in her voice. "She could get clothes, boots, and blankets for all of us."

Grayson eyed her. "It could work."

"I can talk to them while you're gone."

"No. Wait until I'm with you. Just in case."

In case Grayson didn't believe in Fletcher's willingness to help them, and he had to silence the old guard.

She hated the mental image that inspired, but she agreed with a nod. "We should bring Devon, too."

His expression turned long-suffering. "Mia—"

"You're going to need him. And I've known Devon for years—he hates Henri, just like the Fletchers do. None of them would betray us."

Grayson exhaled thinly. "Fine. We'll approach him tonight, with the Fletchers."

She swallowed. A voice whispered she should be done, and

not push him any further. But . . . "I think we should consider asking for Tyrell's help."

His expression closed down. "No."

Her stomach lurched. "I think he'd come with us. And he would be an asset."

"No."

"I know you don't trust him, but—"

"I can't ever trust him," Grayson cut in, his words as sharp as blades. "Especially not with you." Pain sparked in his hooded eyes. "Mia, he *beat you*."

She winced. "I know. I remember."

"Then you can't believe for one second that I'd ever trust him with you."

"I know you two have a horrible history, but he's not who you think he is."

"I know *exactly* who he is," he argued. "And I would never trust him with your life."

"He saved my life while you were gone. Twice."

"And I'm grateful for that. Truly. But I can't trust him. Not with you. Please don't ask me to."

Mia looked down, her thoughts racing. Tyrell had terrified her once, so she understood Grayson's distrust. But the Tyrell she knew now was not the same Tyrell who had beaten her. Grayson didn't know this version of Tyrell—just as Tyrell didn't know the version of Grayson that she did. Both brothers were fierce, deadly, and unflinching, just as they'd been raised to be. It was only with her they showed a gentler side; a vulnerability that came through trust.

She wanted to fight for Tyrell. But, deep down, she felt a whisper of doubt. He *had* betrayed her once, with Grayson's letter. She might dare to trust her life with Tyrell, but she wasn't sure she trusted him enough to risk Grayson's. Not when the brothers were such bitter enemies.

She didn't want to leave Tyrell behind. But she'd resolved to leave him once before, hadn't she? At least this time Henri couldn't blame him for her disappearance; it would be clear she'd left with Grayson. Tyrell would be all right. He'd be angry she'd left, and hurt—the thought made her chest ache—but she didn't have another choice.

"All right," she whispered.

Grayson's fingers touched her chin, coaxing her eyes back to him. His were full of love and promise. "I *will* get you home," he said. "Everything you've had to endure here . . . I swear, all of this will be behind you soon."

She didn't know why, but his words—meant to be comforting—brought a strange chill to her skin.

CHAPTER 2

GRAYSON

GRAYSON TOOK SLOW, MEASURED BREATHS THROUGH his nose. The right side of his face was an inferno, but as long as he didn't move abruptly or stretch the burn, it was only a throbbing agony. He'd been talking too much, which had pulled at the wound.

Kissing Mia probably hadn't helped, but he had no regrets on that score. After being separated for so long, he'd needed her in his arms. Needed to feel her mouth against his so he could finally *breathe*.

His newest scar would be impressive. He knew that, even if he hadn't been able to study the damage yet. He wanted to. He wanted to know if it looked as terrible as it felt. But he didn't want Mia to see him looking, so he avoided the mirror by the wash basin while he got ready to meet his father and brothers in the courtyard. Whenever Henri summoned them all together, bad things followed. At least Mia wouldn't be left in the castle with any of them. Especially Tyrell.

Grayson picked through his old weapons, grimacing at his options. His best weapons had been taken when he'd been thrown into that cell downstairs. He didn't know if or when he'd get his sword back, or his favorite daggers. While their loss was the least of his worries right now, he still missed them. His weapons were a part of him, and he hated being without their familiar weight.

Buried among his old weapons, he spotted a worn pair of black leather gloves. The sight made him pause.

When Imara had packed his things in Duvan, she hadn't grabbed his gloves. He'd gotten used to not wearing them, but in this moment, knowing he had to be the Black Hand one last time . . .

He lifted the gloves and tugged them on, then belted on some knives. When he stood, Mia handed him a clean shirt. Grayson murmured his thanks as he carefully shrugged out of his bloodstained one. He could feel Mia's eyes on him, her worry like a physical vice around his lungs. Seeing his scarred body probably wasn't helping.

I can protect you. That's what he wanted to say. He wanted to reassure her that he was strong enough to keep her safe. He was stronger than Tyrell.

He didn't say a word, because there was a knock on the door.

Mia moved to answer it, but Grayson caught her arm. "Let me."

"It's probably Fletcher or Rena," Mia said quietly.

"It might not be." Grayson tugged the clean shirt over his head, careful not to let the fabric brush the right side of his face. He pulled the hem down as he strode to the door.

Three people stood on the other side of it. Grayson noticed Tyrell first, since his brother was the biggest threat. But since he hung back, Grayson took in the others.

Fletcher stood in front, the old guard's eyes rounded as he took in Grayson. "Fates," the man breathed. "You really are back."

An unfamiliar woman hovered beside Fletcher. Grayson assumed it was his wife, Rena. She had graying hair, and light wrinkles around her eyes and mouth. She was pale as she stared at his jaw, her lips parted in shock.

Grayson's grip tightened on the door's handle. He spoke directly to Fletcher. "Keep Mia safe while I'm gone."

"Of course." There was pity in the man's eyes as he stared at Grayson, along with a hundred unspoken questions.

Grayson twisted to Mia, who'd come to stand beside him. He brushed her cheek with the backs of his fingers. "I'll return as soon as I can," he whispered.

Her eyes battled worry, but it was clearly not for herself. "Please be careful." She darted a look at Tyrell. "Will you watch out for him?"

Grayson clenched his teeth.

Tyrell's eyes were as dark as ever, but he tipped his head in answer to Mia's question, his attention not leaving Grayson.

They were two predators, circling each other. Waiting for the other to make a fatal mistake. Searching for an opening. Salivating for blood. Fates, they'd been here before. So many times. But never quite like this—not with quite so much to lose.

Not with Mia standing between them.

"We should go," Tyrell said. "Father won't want to be kept waiting."

Grayson bent, ignoring the ripple of fire across his jaw as he brushed a kiss against Mia's surprised lips.

From the corner of his eye he saw Tyrell twist away.

The predatory beast in Grayson growled in satisfaction.

When he drew back, Mia's lips were pursed, her expression troubled. "You don't need to torture him," she murmured.

Those admonishing words shredded something inside him. He hated that Mia had seen his pettiness. More than that, he hated himself for deliberately using Mia to hurt Tyrell.

He also hated that her words—spoken with a pang of hurt—meant she *did* care about Tyrell.

His gut clenched. "I love you." Fates, the words shouldn't sound so desperate.

Mia gazed up at him, and he didn't think he imagined the edge of censure there. "I love you, too," she said softly.

Thoroughly chastised, he swore to himself he would never use Mia like that again. It didn't matter if it hurt Tyrell—not when it hurt Mia, too.

He stepped into the hall, ignoring the stares of the Fletchers. They made his skin itch. He strode after Tyrell, who must have been measuring his steps carefully, because Grayson caught up with him at the top of the stairs.

As Grayson made to pass him, Tyrell said, "Don't. We need to talk."

"We really don't."

Tyrell matched Grayson's pace, keeping them even as their boots clipped down the stone steps. "This concerns Mia's safety."

His spine stiffened. "Is that a threat?"

Tyrell gritted out a curse. "I'm not the one endangering her."

Grayson spun to face his brother. Tyrell tensed, but didn't

strike, so Grayson also checked himself. His fists opened and closed at his sides, and they stood glaring at each other on the otherwise abandoned staircase. "I'm not a threat to Mia," Grayson finally growled.

"Aren't you?" Tyrell's words were as sharp as the knives they both carried. "You're clearly not sane. You've held a blade to Father's throat twice now, and you're bristling with so much rage, I'm not convinced you won't attack Father when you see him."

Mia was the only thing holding him back on that score. If he didn't need to get her safely away from his family and back to Desfan, he would have killed Henri already.

"You've fallen out of his favor," Tyrell continued. "We all know it. He blames you for Liam's death, whether it was your fault or not. If you so much as twitch in a way he doesn't like, he will punish Mia."

"You're not telling me anything I don't already know," Grayson said, his voice pitched low. "I've lived with that sword hanging over me for years."

The skin around Tyrell's eyes tightened—probably at the reminder that Mia had been in Grayson's life far longer than she'd been in his. "She doesn't know who you really are, but I do. And I'm telling you, if you put her life at risk, I *will* kill you. That way, Father won't have any reason to punish her."

Grayson edged out a bladed smile. "You would like that, wouldn't you?"

"She'd be better off without you."

"You think she'd be better off with *you*?"

Tyrell glared. "At least I wouldn't let her suffer. I'm not stupid enough to rebel against Father."

"You're his slave."

"I'm his soldier. And because I serve him well, Mia has thrived. She got out of that cell because of me. She's been happy. Safe. She hasn't been a prisoner. I gave her that, Grayson. What have you given her? Years in a windowless cell. Fear and panic. Caretakers who hurt her—tried to kill her."

Grayson's body was wound with so much tension, he couldn't breathe. "You have no idea what you're talking about."

"You might have convinced Mia that you're something other than the Black Hand, but you and I both know you're not. And as long as you can't control your anger and your impulses, she's in danger. Don't do anything that could cause her harm, or I will end you. That is your warning, and the only one I'll give."

Grayson's teeth ached, he was grinding them so hard. "Are you done?"

"No. Because as much as I hate you, I think you care for Mia. It might be in your twisted way, but you do care."

He could barely hide his snort. The irony of Tyrell speaking those words to *him* . . .

Tyrell ignored him. "I'm giving you a chance to prove it. Distance yourself from Mia. Let Father see that distance. Let her be under my protection, at least until Father's anger with you has passed."

"Your plan is utter rot. He knows I would never turn away from Mia."

"So you won't consider trying? Not even for her sake?"

"No."

Tyrell's dark brows slammed down. "She doesn't belong to you."

That was a kick to the gut, because it was true. Not in the possessive way Tyrell meant it—Grayson knew he'd never owned Mia; if anything, she'd owned *him*—but the reality that he wouldn't be in her life once he got her back to Mortise hit him hard.

He'd known his fate before he'd left Duvan. Desfan had done nothing to hide it. Once Grayson returned Mia to the palace, he would be arrested for his crimes against Mortise, Devendra, and Zennor. It didn't matter that he'd ultimately betrayed Liam, or that he'd been coerced in the first place by Liam's threat to kill Mia. In the end, that hawk-sent message had called for Mia's abduction, rather than her death. Grayson still wasn't sure why his brother had lied to him about that. Threatening to kill her was more compelling, of course. And if Liam knew who Mia was, it made sense he wouldn't want to kill her; he would have wanted to use her.

Regardless, Grayson knew he would stand trial beside his brother, and he had no illusions as to how that would end. He would be executed for his crimes—at the very least, imprisoned for the rest of his life.

He couldn't think about this now. Getting Mia home safely was all that mattered. And part of that meant keeping Tyrell away from her.

He stared at his brother, his voice pitched low. "She doesn't belong to you, either."

The air between them pulled taut. The stairway was still empty of anyone else. They were alone—completely. Injured as he was, Grayson honestly didn't know if he'd win if Tyrell chose to pull a knife.

But he would certainly try.

Tyrell's jaw worked, then he folded his arms across his chest. "Mia has claimed us both. Neither of us have to like it, but we do need to accept it. That means I won't kill you—unless I have to."

Grayson didn't verbalize the same promise, even though he knew he would honor it. For Mia. "Are we done?"

Tyrell's mouth curled derisively. "I don't know what she sees in you."

Grayson's eyes grew slitted. "Fates only know how you managed to manipulate her into forgetting the fact that you beat her. But I assure you, I will *never* forget."

A ghost rose in Tyrell's eyes. "Neither will I."

He bristled, though he wouldn't have been able to verbalize why; Tyrell's guilt just felt wrong.

Grayson turned on his heel and continued down the stairs. Each step reverberated pain across his face, and he knew riding a horse was going to be excruciating.

Tyrell followed, and when they reached the bottom of the stairs he said under his breath, "I'm sorry."

Surprise—and wariness—pierced him. "For what?"

Tyrell's gaze dipped to Grayson's cheek. "For a lot of things."

The unexpected words stole every thought from his head. He had no response.

He watched Tyrell's expression harden, determination etched in every line of his face. "For her sake, I won't fight you. But let me make this clear—I am fighting *for* her."

Tyrell's words continued to ring in Grayson's ears as they entered the courtyard. It was autumn in Ryden, and the morning air was crisp. Snow capped the steep mountains to the north, and while the pines remained green, the other trees that dotted the lower hills and castle yard were turning vibrant shades of red, orange, and gold. Some had already browned, and he knew death was coming for the other leaves as well. The sun blazed in a blue sky with hardly any clouds, but the heat didn't quite make it to earth. Despite the chill in the air, Grayson knew his shiver came from the men standing in the courtyard.

Henri stood near his bodyguards, his saddled horse waiting behind him. Grayson's father was a handsome man, with rich brown hair and a confident stance. The strong planes of his face were unbroken by scars, and he wore an emerald green tunic that looked very much like a soldier's uniform. He also wore his golden crown, decorated with emeralds and rubies. For all the excess that Queen Iris eschewed, she had never said anything about that heavily jeweled crown.

Peter's tunic was similar to their father's, though the dark green fabric strained over his shoulders. He'd been training while Grayson was gone. He also wore a gold crown, thinner and less decorated than Henri's. It marked him as the heir to the Rydenic throne. He was already mounted on his horse, and he flicked an impatient hand at the servant who had just handed him the reins. The signet ring on his forefinger caught in the meager sunlight—twisted snakes with ruby eyes. Grayson was very familiar with the bruising weight of it.

Beside Peter, also astride his horse, was Carter. The second oldest Kaelin prince had thick dark hair that brushed his shoulders, and his long, thin face made him look rather like a weasel. He was not as physically strong or as intimidating as the rest of them, but he had a knack for poisons that made him indisputably dangerous. He caught sight of Tyrell and Grayson first, and he murmured something to Peter.

Peter twisted to look at them, and Grayson didn't miss

the play of emotions across his oldest brother's face. The quiet speculation as his eyes slipped between Tyrell and Grayson—arriving together, which was unusual. The hint of satisfaction as he studied the burn on Grayson's face. The twitch of his lip that betrayed his annoyance with Grayson. *That* look promised retribution.

Grayson had not accomplished the mission Peter had set for him in Mortise. He'd wanted Grayson to abduct Princess Imara and bring her to Ryden so Peter could marry her and force an alliance with Zennor.

I was never going to bring her to you, Grayson thought as he stalked down the castle steps. Not even before he'd met the princess, who had unexpectedly befriended him. His allies in Eyrinthia were few, but he knew Imara Buhari was one.

Peter's eyebrows drew together, as if he could read Grayson's defiance.

When Henri turned toward him, Grayson forced his face to go blank. Because out of all the nonsense Tyrell had spewed in that stairway, one thing was true: he couldn't afford to show any rebellion to Henri, or Mia would suffer.

So he became nothing. Nothing except the Black Hand. A beaten dog who returned to his master's harsh hand again and again, no matter how painful the abuse. One day, Grayson would bite back.

But not today.

Henri's mouth curved into a slow smile as he regarded Grayson's newest scarring. "Mount up," he ordered.

Grayson's horse was waiting with a stable hand. The boy looked terrified to be so close to the Black Hand's horse—let alone the Black Hand himself—but he only flinched a little when Grayson took the reins from him.

Mounting the horse proved to be less painful than expected, the practiced motion hardly stretching his cheek at all. But the burn still throbbed, and the chill air sliced against the open wound. Grayson only breathed a little sharper, not letting any other sound escape his clamped lips.

His horse tensed beneath him, as if sensing his pain. Grayson brushed his fingertips over the animal's neck, and the horse settled.

The hairs on the back of his neck lifted. Feeling eyes on him, Grayson straightened slowly, his head turning carefully until he spotted his mother standing on one of the second floor balconies that overlooked the courtyard. With one hand on the stone railing, Iris peered down at him, a slight smile tipping her lips. Her gray eyes were unreadable at this distance, but a chill raced down Grayson's spine.

She thought he'd killed Liam. She thought her control over Grayson was complete. She had no idea he'd betrayed her—that Liam still lived, locked in a Mortisian cell. He'd lied about Liam's death for several reasons. A strong one had been so he could use his mother as an ally.

Now, pinned by her stare, he wasn't sure he wanted anything from the Poison Queen.

"It's time for each of you to learn your role in the great war," Henri said, drawing Grayson's attention. The king of Ryden was seated on his own horse, his fist wrapped around the reins as he surveyed his sons. "We ride to Northland Barracks."

Just the name of the military outpost threaded unease through Grayson. It was primarily a place to house an army close to Lenzen, where soldiers could also receive further training. Everyone who served in the king's military spent time stationed there, including each of Henri's sons.

The camp was brutal. Rations were strictly limited to teach moderation. Soldiers were sent into the mountains to live for a week with nothing but their sword to teach them resourcefulness and endurance. Impossible games of war were played to remind them that not everyone survived battle. Excuses were found to punish them so they would learn the futility of defying authority.

Grayson had spent varying amounts of time at the camp over the years. When he was fifteen, Henri had decided he'd learned enough, and he was no longer required to go. He hadn't stepped foot in Northland Barracks since.

Henri and his guards led the way to the gate. Peter followed next, leaving the other brothers to nudge their horses into line. Grayson took up the rear, dread curling low in his stomach. His unease increased with every mile they travelled north. A biting wind funneled down from one of Lenzen's many canyons, but that wasn't what chilled him.

Whatever waited for them at Northland Barracks, it wouldn't be good.

Two hours of riding later, this was confirmed. In fact, it was so much worse than he'd feared.

As they rode into the valley that held Northland Barracks, Grayson's blood ran cold.

Thousands of uniformed men ran drills and milled about camp. The drills weren't new; men had been training here long before Grayson's birth. But the ranks had easily tripled since he'd last been here, and that was just the men.

Then there were the boys.

Sectioned off from the rest of the army was a camp for the youngest soldiers Grayson had ever seen. Some of the boys looked to be as young as eight years old—perhaps even younger. They wore emerald as well, but their uniforms weren't fitted. Why bother to do that, when it was clear their sole purpose was to fill out the ranks, surprise the enemy, and then die on some battlefield of Henri's choosing? It was clear from their gaunt cheeks that Henri barely deemed them worthy of the food it took to keep them alive.

Grayson's gut rolled. There were at least a thousand boys down there—probably more.

Commanders shouted orders, and soldiers of all ages came to attention, most looking fates-blasted terrified.

The Kaelins rode into the heart of Northland Barracks, passing tents, training grounds, cooking sites, and finally wooden outbuildings that housed the higher ranking officers and meeting rooms. When they finally stopped and dismounted, Grayson eyed the men and boys that filled the camp.

Fates, those boys. They were bloody and haunted, with swords that were too big for them. They stared at the Kaelins like they were seeing their own deaths.

They probably were.

When Grayson looked at his father, it was just in time to see Henri grin.

CHAPTER 3

CLARE

CLARE WOKE SLOWLY. AWARENESS SEEPED IN AS gradually as the morning light that crept around the pulled drapes of the room.

She was in her bedroom, which was attached to Serene's suite. The room was small, but no part of the Mortisian palace was plain. Even this maid's room was decorated with painted landscapes, fine linens, and soft rugs.

Murmuring voices drifted through the closed door. One sounded like Serene, though Clare couldn't make out any specific words. A low but booming whisper—that was Wilf—was followed by a smooth, deep voice—Cardon.

Clare's cheek pressed against her damp pillow. Her throat stung, both inside and out. The tears had made her throat raw, and the shallow cut from Michael's blade ached. The Devendran rebel had tried to kill her, because he blamed her for Eliot's death. Latif had killed Michael to defend her, and that still made her head spin.

Latif had been her abductor once, though he'd been blackmailed by Prince Liam Kaelin to do so. A prince who had *also* tried to kill her last night, though he'd thought she was Serene. He'd ordered Latif to kill her, but Latif had only pretended to stab her. Fates, remembering that moment brought back every bruising ache on her body; she'd fallen down several stone steps in the prison when Liam had kicked her down the stairs. And none of that had been the worst part of last night.

Her eyes burned. Fates, she didn't want to remember the worst part.

Warmth radiated at her back. The strong arm that draped over her waist kept her secure against a hard chest that rose and fell . . .

Bennick.

Clare's breath caught, and memories from last night flared.

Miss Ellington, I regret to inform you of an unfortunate incident.

Her fingers had gone numb. She'd dropped Commander Markam's letter.

It has been my task to check in with your brothers during your absence.

Bennick had grabbed her, his face pale and his eyes sparking with alarm.

On my most recent visit, I learned there had been a fire in Lower Iden. It destroyed most of the homes on your street—including yours. I'm afraid your brothers and their caretaker were inside, and there were no survivors.

Denial, sharp and fierce.

She could see Thomas and Mark—only thirteen and ten— smiling at her.

She had become the decoy for them. She had left them safe in Iden with a caretaker, and she'd recently asked for Serene's help in bringing them to Duvan. They couldn't be *gone*.

But they were.

She had no family left. She'd lost Eliot, and now . . .

She hadn't realized she'd started crying until Bennick had gathered her into his arms. "I'm so sorry," he'd whispered. "So, so, sorry . . ."

So many tears, then. Her body had shaken with them. Her breath broke with them.

There in the princess's sitting room, Clare's heart had shattered.

Bennick had pulled her onto his lap as he sat on the nearest chair. She buried her face in his neck, and her fingers clenched in his shirt. She sobbed until she thought her lungs would burst. Bennick had rubbed her back, his fingers skimming her spine, his other hand buried in her hair, keeping her pressed close. His strong arms were all that held her together.

When Serene, Cardon, and Wilf had entered, Bennick softly told them what had happened. Their shock and compassion were almost too much to bear, and Clare was grateful when they soon disappeared, leaving her alone with Bennick.

When her tears finally faltered due to exhaustion, he'd carried her to her room and laid her on the bed. She'd grabbed his wrist before he could fully straighten. "Don't leave me," she begged, her voice ravaged from all the tears she'd cried.

Bennick leaned in, his blue eyes intense as he stroked away the tears on her cheek. "Never."

He hadn't left.

He was still here, in her bed, holding her. Both of them were on their sides, her back to his chest. He was curled around her in a protective, comforting embrace. His low, even breaths stirred the loose strands of her hair, and one bent knee pressed against her leg. They both still wore their clothes from last night; Bennick had only removed their shoes and his weapons before he'd joined her.

This wasn't the first time Bennick had held her through the night. On Syed Zadir's ship, after a nightmare, he had offered the same comfort. That didn't lessen the intimacy of this moment, though. Not just because of the physical reality of sharing a bed, but the vulnerability of sharing her grief with him.

She pulled in a slow, wavering breath. It was morning. The sun had risen, and her brothers were gone.

It seemed unreal. Wholly wrong.

Bennick's breathing changed—thinned. He stirred, his arm pulling her even closer. His head angled, ducking until his stubbled jaw gently scraped against her cheek and his mouth pressed a tender kiss against her neck, just below her ear.

Warmth spread through her hollow chest, and her eyes burned.

"I love you," he whispered, his voice rough with sleep.

The first words he gave to her, the morning after her world ended. She couldn't think of a more perfect gift.

She slid her hand over his, which was flat against her stomach. She didn't trust her voice, so she just pressed her hand against his, trying to ignore the slight crookedness of her fingers, which Salim had broken so many weeks ago.

Bennick pressed his forehead against the nape of her neck. Silence grew, but it wasn't empty.

Beyond the bedroom door, the voices grew louder. The outer door of the suite opened and shut, and silence once again descended.

Bennick's thumb moved in slow, soothing circles against the soft material of her dress. She never wanted him to stop. She never wanted to move from his arms. But this moment couldn't last forever.

"I need to prepare for the coronation," she whispered, her voice thin and scratchy.

Bennick's hold tightened. "You don't have to go. Serene said last night that she'd go herself. You can take all the time you need."

She didn't remember Serene saying that, but she certainly believed the princess had. Even though Serene didn't always show her true self to the world, the princess of Devendra was fiercely protective and remarkably kind.

"Even if I don't go," Clare said, "*you* need to."

Serene was down two royal guards; Dirk had been killed during Ryden's attack at the betrothal signing, and Venn was still missing. He and Vera had parted from Bennick and Wilf in Krid, a city in northern Mortise. They should have arrived at the palace before Bennick, Clare, and Wilf had—but they hadn't. She prayed to the fates Venn and Vera were all right. She couldn't lose anyone else.

"The coronation isn't until this afternoon," Bennick said quietly. "I don't need to go anywhere yet."

They both knew that wasn't necessarily true. After the three-fold attack last night, there had been chaos in the Mortisian palace. Clare could only imagine that chaos was still being felt this morning.

Her thoughts flickered to Imara, who had been stabbed in the leg. *Fates*. She'd been so consumed in her own grief, she'd almost forgotten that. Hopefully Serene had been there for her cousin during the night.

"The coronation may not even happen today," Bennick said. "From a security standpoint, it wouldn't be a bad idea to delay."

Silence stretched once more. Bennick's love for her was a warmth that settled all around her. It gave her peace when all she wanted to do was scream.

Her lower lip trembled. "How long?" she asked, her voice cracking.

He knew what she was asking. His arm flexed as he drew her impossibly closer. "With the fastest messenger, it would have taken at least three weeks for the letter to make it here."

Thomas and Mark had been dead for more than three weeks.

Her stomach pitched, and she blinked as her vision blurred. "I should have known," she rasped.

Bennick made a soothing sound in his throat as his lips brushed the back of her neck. "You couldn't have known, Clare. Don't invite more pain."

Her lungs seared with the pressure of holding back tears. "I don't know what to do."

She couldn't even bury her brothers, because they'd turned to ash. Her baby brothers were gone, and she was in an entirely different kingdom.

Bennick kissed her shoulder, keeping her tethered despite the storm that was trying to tear her apart. "You don't have to do anything, Clare."

They remained on the bed for nearly an hour before Clare asked, "What will everyone think of you spending the night in here?"

"They'll think I care about you."

She frowned a little. "You don't sound concerned."

"I'm not."

"We're supposed to keep this a secret."

"I know." Bennick's thumb was still tracing circles, though his hand had shifted so the soothing pattern was drawn against her side. "But all the bodyguards already know."

She jerked in his arms. "They *do*?"

He only tucked her closer. "It's fine. Apparently they guessed the truth before we even left Iden. They won't betray us. They know I'm still dedicated to protecting Serene."

He sounded so calm, her anxiety settled a little. "We still need to be careful. What about Serene, or Bridget?"

"After last night, they've probably guessed, if they hadn't already figured it out."

She craned her head around so she could eye him. "If the king finds out, you could lose your position." Or his life, if Newlan decided to interpret Bennick's actions as treasonous. Technically, King Newlan owned her; she'd pledged her life to him in her service as the decoy. Until she died, she was nothing more than Newlan's servant. Now that he couldn't threaten her brothers, there really wasn't any punishment she feared—except what he might do to Bennick.

"He's in Iden," Bennick said. "And if word did make it back to him . . . I'm not sure how much I care anymore."

That made her stomach tighten. Before she could express her concerns, there was a soft knock on the door.

Bennick kissed her cheek, then gently rolled away. He rose

on the other side of the bed and crossed the small room to the door.

He opened it only a crack, but Wilf's gravelly voice traveled easily. "Is she still sleeping?"

"No, but she's resting."

Wilf grunted. "I asked Bridget to order food for her."

"Thank you."

"Cardon and I can attend to everything. You stay with her. She shouldn't be alone."

There was an undercurrent of old grief in Wilf's words, and Clare's broken heart fractured a little more. Wilf had lost his wife years ago, and he'd mourned her deeply—and not always well. He'd drunk to excess, gambled away most of his coin, and lost his position as captain of Prince Grandeur's bodyguards.

"I won't leave her," Bennick said, assurance in every word.

Clare pushed up from the bed and walked with bare feet to join him at the door. Bennick watched her, something like caution in his gaze, but he opened the door a little wider so she could see Wilf.

The giant towered over them. It looked like he hadn't slept much, either. There were wrinkles in his uniform, and his pox-scarred face was hard. His eyes, when they met hers, went soft. "I'm sorry for your loss, Clare."

She dipped her chin. It was the only acknowledgement she could afford at the moment. "Is the coronation still happening?"

Wilf frowned. "I haven't heard anything official yet, but everyone seems to be proceeding as if it is."

Bennick glanced at her. "You're not going."

She knew she wasn't up to pretending to be Serene right now, so she didn't push that. But she did hold his gaze as she said, "You need to be there. Serene needs all of you." Bennick's mouth opened, but she overrode him. "It will ease my mind to know you're with her. Please, Bennick."

He didn't look pleased, but he nodded.

Clare pulled in a deliberate breath. "I would also like a moment to change, and I think you should do the same."

Bennick hesitated.

Wilf rumbled, "I'll stay at her door."

Bennick finally gave in with a sigh. "All right." He reached out and squeezed Clare's hand. "I'll return soon," he promised. Then he was gone, leaving the princess's suite for his own room, which was located down the hall.

Clare missed him instantly.

Wilf rubbed the back of his neck. "Is there anything I can do?"

She shook her head. "I don't think so. But thank you."

He hesitated, then pulled her into his arms for a tight embrace. "You've been landed far too many blows, my little defender," he whispered roughly. "Don't ever feel like you need to weather them on your own. You've still got a family. You have all of us."

His words hit deeply, because she knew he spoke from personal experience. She squeezed him as tightly as she could. "Thank you, Wilf."

In response, he kissed the top of her head.

CHAPTER 4

DESFAN

"I REFUSE TO CANCEL THE CORONATION," DESFAN SAID.

From across the desk, Karim—his bodyguard and best friend—glared at him. "I'm not asking you to cancel it. I'm asking you to delay it until we can clear the palace of any possible lingering threats."

Desfan scrubbed the heel of one hand against his aching brow. He hadn't slept all night, and now that morning light beamed through the only window in his office, he was feeling the loss of sleep acutely.

He wasn't about to change his mind, though. "You've helped Arcas oversee the search," he said. "There haven't been any recovered prisoners since midnight, and no other insurgents have been found."

"They could still be hiding somewhere." Karim's thick arms were crossed over a broad chest, and his mouth was tight. He wasn't happy.

Desfan didn't blame him. He wasn't happy, either.

Last night, Amil—a fates-blasted traitor, as it turned out—had helped wreak incredible havoc during the banquet. Instead of celebrating the coming coronation, his court had been under attack. Lives had been lost; he still didn't have the final count. Princess Imara had been stabbed. Her blood was still trapped in the grooves of his fingernails, even after scrubbing his hands in a wash basin. His heart clenched, remembering the panic and fear that had choked him as he'd carried her from the room. They'd hidden in the kitchen pantry, of all places, and he'd held her and prayed to the fates that she would be all right. The wound had been deep, and he'd treated her the best he could, and he'd kept her awake and talking.

He'd *kissed* her.

His chest tightened, and he had to shove the memory of her soft lips aside. He was betrothed to marry her cousin, for fates' sake. He had no right to kiss Imara.

He'd done it anyway. And pushing aside his guilt was nearly impossible, because he couldn't stop reliving that moment. It had been far too brief, but that stolen kiss was branded on his soul.

It was the last thing he should be focused on right now, all things considered.

He'd spent the night walking among his wounded soldiers, praising them for their bravery. He'd also visited with nobles injured during the feast. He'd tried to comfort them, and he'd mourned with them for the loved ones they'd lost. He'd reassured those who were unscathed, but frightened. And every hour, he'd stepped into Imara's suite to check on her.

Once the physician had given her medication that kept her blissfully asleep, she hadn't stirred. But her maid, Hanna, was constantly at her side, and so was Princess Serene. The blade had torn through flesh and muscle before hitting the bone above her knee. The physician was quite confident her life had been saved, though infection could still set in. They wouldn't know the full extent of the damage—or the permanency of it—until Imara was well enough to attempt walking.

If he thought too long and hard about her condition, Desfan lost sight of all else. And he couldn't afford to lose sight of anything right now. He was about to become the serjan of Mortise. Duty, tradition, sacrifice for his people . . . that was his future. That was what he must embody.

Which was why the coronation could not be postponed.

Karim still glared at him. He wore the clothes he'd worn last night—as Desfan did—and he didn't seem to notice the wrinkles or the dried blood. He was so agitated, he hadn't even taken a seat for this meeting, despite the thick bandage on his thigh. He'd been hit by a crossbow bolt.

Serai Yahri—the only other person in the room—was seated on the edge of one of the chairs across from Desfan. The old woman looked weary, though her jaw was tight. She was the head of the council, and her steel gray hair perfectly matched her attitude. She and Desfan had not always seen eye-to-eye, but he had come to respect her. He thought she may have come to respect him as well. She'd remained uncharacteristically silent during this meeting, though.

Karim seemed to have no trouble filling the quiet. "The damage to the treasury will take weeks to fully catalogue, but nearly a third of the prison was emptied last night. While we caught many before they could flee, too many are unaccounted for. They could be hiding anywhere in the palace. Not to mention the men Amil brought in; they could be in the palace still, hoping to attack during the coronation. So, please—for once in your life—listen to me and do *not* go through with the coronation today."

Desfan sighed. "Karim, don't exaggerate; I've listened to you before."

His friend's eyes narrowed. "When?"

He flicked a dismissive hand through the air. "We'll have a veritable army guarding the throne room. The coronation will be protected. But it must happen. To delay would show weakness. Fear. And a disregard for tradition. That is not the Mortisian way." He leaned forward, cutting off Karim before he could argue again. "I know you want to search the entire palace again, and that's fine. But I won't postpone the coronation."

Karim growled in his throat.

Finally, Yahri stirred, shifting her hold on the cane planted in front of her. "Desfan is right."

Desfan's eyebrows shot up. "You think I'm right?"

She gave him a look, but didn't bother responding to that. "We cannot cancel the coronation. The people have been shaken to the core. If we do not follow tradition and crown Desfan this afternoon, there will be unrest."

Karim's dark brows pulled together. He faced Desfan. "Your new crown won't do anyone any good if you aren't alive to wear it."

That was a fair point. But even if he did die, he wouldn't be the last Cassian to sit on the throne. Desfan had once believed he was the last of his family, but Meerah still lived.

The truth of that still stunned him. His little sister, who he'd thought dead for nearly a decade, was *alive*. She was a prisoner in Ryden. And he'd sent Grayson Kaelin, of all people, to bring her home.

He still wasn't entirely sure he'd done the right thing in trusting the Rydenic prince. Especially since Grayson had already betrayed him once.

Not many people knew Meerah was alive. He, Karim, and Yahri knew, as did Liam Kaelin—who was in a prison cell below them. Imara—who didn't seem to care that Grayson had betrayed her, too—knew as well, along with Serene and her decoy, Clare. And the princess's bodyguards.

Fates, that was actually a lot of people. Desfan had no intention of letting anyone else find out, though. The truth was too precious, and potentially dangerous. Until Meerah was safe in his arms, Desfan wasn't going to trust anyone else with the knowledge that she still lived. They had too many enemies, and he refused to increase the risks to his sister.

He just prayed he hadn't sent an enemy to rescue her.

Yahri's lips pursed. "Karim does bring up an important point. The line of succession will need to be addressed."

"Meerah is my heir," Desfan said at once.

"If she returns and is able to wear the crown, yes," Yahri said. He didn't have a chance to question what she meant by that, because she continued. "But since you can't tell anyone about her yet, we need to think of the people. Until you're actually married to Serene, there is no promise of an heir. You should publicly announce your chosen successor, until such a time as you have a child. In the event of your untimely death, the successor you name could also serve as regent until your child is of an age to sit on the throne."

He glanced toward Karim, who immediately cursed. "No.

Absolutely not." His friend actually looked a little pale, which made his words sound less fierce. "I will give my life to protect yours, and anyone who bears the Cassian name, but I will *not* carry your fates-blasted crown."

Yahri's mouth twitched. "Karim is an admirable man, but he's not a possible choice. You need to select someone with noble blood. A distant cousin, perhaps."

Desfan frowned. "Do I *have* a distant cousin?" His parents had each been the sole child in their families, and Desfan didn't know much about his grandparents or their families. It had probably been discussed in his lessons as a boy—which he'd been atrociously terrible at paying attention to.

"Of course you have cousins," Yahri said. "They're just quite distant. I'll consult with the genealogical charts in the royal library, and we'll locate the most ideal candidates. You can make a selection from there." Her expression turned contemplative. "I know the Sifas have old ties to the Cassian line, and I believe our newest council member does as well."

Karim's brow wrinkled. "Razan?"

Yahri tipped her head. "Serai Krayt has a very old name, and the oldest families in Mortise have a tendency to have overlapped somewhere with the Cassian line."

Desfan cracked a smile. "Karim, you may have a chance at the throne after all."

Karim scowled, but Desfan swore there was a touch of pink in his cheeks.

Yahri released a slow breath. "All of this, of course, can be addressed another day. I think for now, the best thing we can do is make sure everything is set for the coronation. And Desfan, you really ought to sleep a little before the ceremony. It's quite long, and you'll be standing for most of it; it wouldn't do for you to fall over." She rocked and pushed up from the chair, her grip on the cane tightening. "I'll see to the final preparations." With that, she started for the door.

Karim crossed in front of her and opened the door, his chin jerking in a silent order to one of the guards in the hall to accompany the councilwoman.

When Karim closed the door, Desfan spoke first. "How's your leg?"

"Fine."

If Karim was bleeding out, he'd probably say the same.

Desfan rolled his eyes. "Please sit down."

Grudgingly, Karim did, though his arms remained crossed. "You're risking your life for a ridiculous ceremony."

"It's not *all* ridiculous. I do get a large crown out of it."

"Cut the wit, Des. This is your life we're talking about."

"I know. But the people need a serjan today."

"They also need one tomorrow."

He sighed. "I have every intention of living out the day."

"So thought many a dead man."

"You're always so pessimistic."

"And you're an aggravating optimist." Karim's eyes narrowed. "War is coming. No one can deny that now. Not after the attack we suffered from Ryden during the betrothal signing."

"I firmly intend to fight for Mortise for as long as there is blood in my veins," Desfan said. "But not all fights are on the battlefield. I need to win the trust of the people. I need them to believe that I'm more than the rebellious child I was, or the man who kept sailing away from his responsibilities. I need to show them I'm worthy of the crown. I need to do this."

Karim's mouth thinned, but he didn't argue. Instead, he said, "You're like my brother."

Desfan felt his face soften. "I feel the same."

"Then you have to understand, if something happened to you . . . If someone got past me . . . Fates, Des, that's not something I could live with."

Karim was not often vulnerable. Neither was Desfan, really. But the two of them had been through a great deal in their years together. Hurting Karim was not something Desfan ever wanted to do.

But he couldn't change his mind. Not about this. "Everything is going to be fine," he said.

Karim's jaw worked briefly. "I haven't decided if you'll have five guards, or fifty. But you will accept whatever I decide."

"Done." But almost immediately, he lifted a finger. "Except you can't be my guard today."

The temperature in the room chilled. Karim's expression iced over. "Excuse me?"

Desfan gestured to his leg. "You're injured."

Karim's glower was impressive. "If you're parading yourself in front of a room filled with fates-blasted people who might want to kill you, you're doing it with me at your back."

"You heard Yahri—most of the ceremony is done while standing."

"Then I'll wear comfortable boots," he snapped.

Desfan muttered a curse. "You're impossible."

"*I'm* impossible? You're a stubborn, royal idiot—"

"What other kind of idiot could a royal be?"

"—but wherever you go, I go," Karim continued, ignoring him completely. "There is no discussion. That's it. The end." He shoved up from his chair. "Now, do you want me to escort you to your room to rest, or do you want to check on Imara again?"

Desfan huffed as he stood. "You know, you're bossy enough you *could* be serjan someday."

Karim didn't bother to respond to that. He just wordlessly led the way to Imara's suite, knowing that's where Desfan needed to be.

Desfan slipped into Imara's bedchamber, following Hanna. The maid had informed him that Imara had finally opened her eyes about an hour ago. Princess Serene—who'd spent the night at her side—had spoken with Imara for a few moments before the Zennorian princess had once again fallen asleep. Only then had Serene's bodyguards been able to convince her to retire to her own bed for a much needed rest.

Desfan's relief that Imara had finally awakened was expected; the bite of jealousy he felt at not being the one beside her when she first opened her eyes was decidedly wrong.

His pulse skipped when he looked around Hanna and beautiful brown eyes met his.

Imara was awake. She was lying under a colorful quilt of red, gold, and sapphire. Her ebony skin seemed a little sallow, and her long braid was loose and messy. Still, she'd never looked more beautiful.

She was alive.

When she smiled at him, he couldn't help but grin back. Thank the fates she was still breathing; Eyrinthia would be a darker place without her.

"Don't you have somewhere to be?" Imara asked blithely. "A

coronation, perhaps?"

"They can't very well start without me. Besides, it's not until this afternoon." Desfan crossed the room and sat in the empty chair beside her bed. Bright sunlight poured through the open windows, and the crash of distant waves was punctuated by the cries of seabirds.

"Where is Karim?" she asked.

"In the other room."

"How is he?"

"He's fine."

Imara lifted one eyebrow. "Are those his words?"

A smile tugged at Desfan's lips. "How did you know?"

"It sounds like something Karim would say."

"True. But I promise, he's all right."

The bedroom door clicked faintly as Hanna left them alone.

Desfan's heart suddenly beat a little faster, but he tried to hide that as he asked, "How are you feeling?"

"A little peckish. Hopefully Hanna's gone for breakfast."

His mouth quirked. "I meant your leg."

"Oh, that." She waved her hand. "It's well on the mend. Barely hurts at all."

"I doubt that." His brow furrowed. "I'm sorry, Imara. I—"

"Please, spare us both. Unless you want to thank me again for saving your life, let's not talk about last night." She smoothed a hand over the quilt on her lap, suddenly intent on the colorful pattern.

It could have been his imagination, but her cheeks seemed to have a hint of color now. What part of last night was she thinking of? His pulse quickened as he thought of *his* favorite part.

He cleared his throat. "Has the physician been to see you

since you woke?"

"Yes, he left just a few minutes ago. He's been most attentive." Her eyes narrowed on him. "Quite possibly too attentive.
I'm sure there are others in more need of the royal physician's
expertise, but it seems he's been under orders to check on me
every half hour."

He didn't bother to feign an apology. "I needed to know you
had the best care."

Her eyes softened. "Thank you, Desfan. Truly. But my father
won't go to war over this."

"That's reassuring. But I had other motivations."

Her breathing thinned.

His own lungs suddenly felt too tight as he waited for her to
say something. Anything.

Her lips pursed. "You're a good friend, Desfan."

Fates. Her words seemed to draw a line in the sand, but the
way she said his name . . .

He was far too tired to have this conversation. He didn't
even know how he *wanted* this conversation to go, so why did
he feel a cut of disappointment that she'd merely called him
a *friend*?

He was betrothed to Serene Demoi, not Imara Buhari. He
had a duty to fulfill. An alliance to secure. He should not be
looking at Imara's lips, wishing he could kiss them again.

He needed to stop looking. *Now.*

He shifted in the chair. "Considering you saved my life, I
owed you the best possible care."

"I would tell you I won't let you forget it," Imara said, "but
you keep bringing it up, so I can't very well be the one to
remind you."

"I will never forget." The taste of fear had been sharp on

his tongue, had knotted his insides when he saw that knife plunge into her leg. The bleeding alone could have been fatal, but just knowing the agony she'd endured—was still suffering—pierced him deeply. She'd come back to help him. She had refused to leave him behind, and she'd paid dearly for that choice.

Imara reached out and touched the back of his hand. "You have enough to worry about, Desfan. Don't torture yourself over this."

Her skin was soft. Warm. Darker than his, and completely mesmerizing. He stared at their hands, watching as her fingers slipped away.

He nearly gave into the urge to snatch them back.

"I'll be fine, you know," Imara said, settling back against the pillows. "Although I don't think I'll make it to your coronation."

"Of course not. You're not leaving this bed until the physician allows."

She pulled a face. "Regardless of how quickly I heal, he says I'll need a cane—for a while at least." She gave a half-smile. "Yahri and I will start a new fashion. Canes will be all the rage in your court, just you wait."

"I'm sorry."

"Don't be sorry. You'll be the serjan—I'm sure you can have one, too."

A laugh burst out of him, but he shook his head. "I don't think I'll be able to afford one."

Her smile dimmed. "Is it so bad?"

"It's quite bad," he admitted. "But they didn't get everything." The coffers had never been so empty, though. If debts were called in, they would be in trouble. And with war on the horizon, he had expenses to consider. Soldiers required coin—an army required a great deal more.

Imara lifted a single shoulder. "I suppose that means no solid gold cane for you. You might also want to skip the jewels and keep it plain."

"That hardly seems like something fit for a serjan."

She chuckled. "Just find a Zennorian artisan to decorate the cane with khalmin. You can pick any color of ink you want, and the designs are breathtaking."

He enjoyed seeing her joy as she teased him. "Do you have any color recommendations?" he asked.

"Well, colors have meaning. You want to pick the perfect one." She tilted her head, studying him intently. "Blue."

"Blue?"

"Yes."

"That doesn't seem a very powerful color."

"Red means power, but it's also linked to violence and aggression. That's not you. Blue, though . . . Calm. Steady. Fair. Strong." She nodded once. "Blue suits you."

Suddenly, this didn't feel like teasing. He stared at her—the soft curve of her cheek, the rounded point of her small nose. She was perfect. The fact that they were both betrothed to others did not negate his feelings.

He swallowed. "Imara . . ."

Her spine straightened and she ran her palms over her lap again, smoothing the already smooth blanket. "Serene told me you came by often last night. You must not have slept much."

The abrupt shift in topic was defensive. She'd sensed the change in his tone, and she didn't want to talk about what had happened between them last night.

happened between them last night.

He needed to talk about it. Maybe not right now, but soon.

She was watching him, waiting for a reply. "I didn't sleep much," he said. Not at all, actually.

She frowned with obvious concern. "You can't very well fall asleep during your coronation. You need to go get some rest." When he opened his mouth, she raised her hand. "Don't make me talk you into it. Serene already tried to argue about leaving me, and I managed to persuade her."

He smiled slightly. "She may be more stubborn than I am."

"*May* be?" Imara's eyes rounded. "Serene's more stubborn than everyone in this palace combined."

That surprised a laugh out of him. "I think you're probably right."

"Desfan Cassian, one thing you need to know is that I'm *always* right. Now, go get some sleep. Yahri will never let you hear the end of it if you yawn in the middle of your oaths."

He wanted to stay with her, but she was obviously still tired, and he didn't want to wear her out. Besides, she did have a point. Yahri would never forgive him if he made a fool of himself and the Cassian name during the ceremony.

He rose. "I'll be back to check on you after the coronation."

"Be sure to wear your crown," she said, curling a loose tendril of dark hair around the back of one ear and not quite meeting his gaze. "I can't wait to see it."

He didn't like the tone in her voice. It sounded . . . distant.

And distance was the last thing he wanted from Imara.

CHAPTER 5

MIA

A KNOT HAD LODGED IN MIA'S GUT WHEN SHE'D watched Tyrell and Grayson leave together. Even hours later, that knot hadn't loosened.

She prayed to the fates they wouldn't attack each other.

As soon as the Kaelin brothers had disappeared from sight, Fletcher's head had cranked toward her. "What happened to him?" the old guard asked, his eyes wide.

"His father."

Fletcher muttered a curse as he shoved a hand through his gray hair. Beside him, Rena looked sick. "That man is no father," he growled.

No. Henri Kaelin was many things, but he was not that.

An image of her own father came unbidden to her mind. A large man with broad hands and an even broader smile. A deep voice that resonated throughout a room—or her chest, when he'd held her close. A laugh that was so beautiful, the mere ghost of it had Mia's eyes stinging.

Her father was dead. She hadn't been able to truly process that fact when Grayson had told her, but it hit her now.

Her father was dead.

When she'd first been imprisoned, she'd cried so hard for him. She'd screamed for him. He hadn't come, of course. He hadn't even known she was alive.

She'd stopped crying out for him a long time ago, but her heart was screaming now. It wasn't fair. After nine years of imprisonment, she was so close to the possibility of returning to Duvan, but she would never see her father again. He'd died only a handful of weeks ago—which seemed especially cruel. It wasn't the worst part, though.

Her father had died because of her.

Grayson had told her the serjan's health had been poor for years before he'd heard the rumor that one of his daughters might be alive. The shock of that news had sent him into a seizure, and he'd collapsed. He'd never recovered.

He loves you, Grayson had said of Desfan. *He asked me to tell you that.*

Maybe Desfan hadn't put it all together yet. Perhaps he hadn't realized their father's death was her fault.

But he would.

Mia had too many deaths on her conscience. Her father, Tahlyah . . . When Desfan learned the truth, he would hate her.

Her chest felt too tight. Her breaths were thin and sharp.

Fletcher touched her arm. "Mia?" Concern hung in his eyes and layered his voice.

She shoved the thoughts and memories away before they

could strangle her. "I'm all right."

He didn't look like he believed her.

Rena cleared her throat, the sound tentative. "Perhaps I can draw you a bath, and we can get you in a clean dress."

Anything to get them both to stop looking at her like she was only a strained breath away from breaking. "Yes. Thank you."

The bath had helped, as had changing into a clean dress. Rena had combed her hair and twisted the long waves into an easy knot at the back of her head. Feeling more settled and in control, Mia was able to approach Tyrell's door with something almost like confidence. Fletcher shadowed her, though of course he only thought she was going to retrieve a few things.

A single guard watched Tyrell's room, and it was someone Mia recognized, though she couldn't remember his name.

Before she could address him, an unfamiliar voice called out from behind her. "Lady Mia?"

She turned and saw a young boy step gingerly toward her. "Yes?" she asked, thrown by the title he'd given her.

The boy's tongue darted nervously over his lips. "Excuse me, but I have a summons for you." He held out a small card.

Mia's brow furrowed, but she murmured thanks as she accepted it. She had no idea who it could be from—all the Kaelins had gone with Grayson.

The words on the small card came into focus, written in a precise script, though it was clearly done by a female hand.

Mia,
Come to my garden for tea.

There is so much for us to talk about.
Queen Iris Kaelin

The card shook a little in Mia's suddenly cold hand.

She'd been wrong. Not *all* the Kaelins were gone from the castle. Grayson's mother was still here, and she'd just summoned Mia to her poison garden.

Mia's heart thudded as she entered the queen's poisonous realm. The queen's men who guarded the entrance to the private garden made it clear Fletcher would not be allowed in with her, so she alone followed the young boy into the secluded inner courtyard.

The walls were high and the area was filled with plants in the early stages of their seasonal death; the autumn air chilled Mia's skin, even though the noonday sun shone overhead. The smell of light decay and still-flowering shrubs tickled her nose.

Behind her, the door to the garden closed. Knowing Fletcher could no longer see her caused a shiver to run down her spine, but she forced herself to follow the pebbled path in front of her. The small rocks bit through the soft soles of her shoes.

The garden might have been beautiful, if Mia didn't know who it belonged to. Or that everything she looked at could probably cause pain or death. As it was, walking through the well-tended space lifted every hair on her body.

The queen waited in the back corner of the walled court-yard, seated at a wrought-iron table. Though Mia had never seen Grayson's mother, there was no mistaking her.

The queen's posture was exact and her dress was immac-ulately white. A pale lavender sash encircled her waist, and her long brown hair was gathered into a braid that trailed over one shoulder. Silver hair touched her temples, and there were a few fine lines around her eyes, but she was surprisingly pretty. Nothing like the horrible crone Mia had pictured when Grayson spoke of his mother. She wondered if the queen's beauty was what had fascinated Henri first, or if he'd been drawn to Iris for another reason. She couldn't imagine those two awful people felt love, even for each other.

Iris's gray eyes were an echo of Grayson's, and they were trained on Mia's approach. Her expression was smooth, re-vealing nothing.

Mia fought to keep her own emotions from showing, but those falcon eyes surely caught the slight hitch in her step as she hesitated beside the table.

She refused to bow to this woman.

Queen Iris's slender eyebrows lifted slightly. "Do sit down, girl." Her voice was cool and precise, and brooked no argu-ments.

Mia sat in the empty chair across from the queen. The table between them was far too small; she was careful to tuck her feet slightly under her chair, so they would have no chance of brushing Iris's. A steaming teapot sat on a tray with cups and saucers. The bright pink flower arrangement on the table did nothing to make the scene less threatening.

Mia kept her hands in her lap, unwilling to touch anything at the table.

Iris glanced at the hovering boy. "Leave us."

He eagerly darted away.

The Poison Queen studied Mia in silence. The hum of insects was the only sound, other than the rustle of leaves as a cold breeze teased the trees around them. Beneath the table, Mia's fingers twisted together, but she kept her back straight as she stared at the queen. It was unnerving to look into her cold eyes—so strikingly familiar, yet horribly foreign at the same time.

It was a relief when Iris looked away, her attention falling to the teapot. "Do you like anything with your tea?" she asked, lifting the steaming kettle.

"I don't want tea." Her voice only wavered a little, and she was proud of that.

Iris glanced up as she poured her own cup. "Are you sure?"

"Yes."

The corner of the queen's mouth lifted slightly, but the flatness in her expression belied any show of amusement. "Grayson has told you all about me, I suppose. Or perhaps Tyrell did that?"

Mia didn't respond. She watched as the dark liquid streamed into the white porcelain cup, her heart beating too fast.

"You're not what I expected," Iris said, watching the tea fall and the steam rise. When she set the teapot aside, she deftly lifted the small pot of honey. "You're passingly pretty, but I really can't understand how you've managed to bewitch two of my sons."

Mia said nothing. The queen's jab was petty and needed no response.

Iris stirred the honey into her tea with a smooth, practiced motion. "Shall I call you Mia, or do you prefer Meerah?"

Hearing her full name was jarring. Not only because it came from Iris, but because she hadn't felt like *Meerah* in years. The truth of who she was seemed to be attacking her from all directions lately.

Of course, Iris glanced up just in time to see Mia's unsettled reaction. The queen's lips eased into a smile. "I wondered if you'd even remember that name. You would have been a small child when you last heard it. That's one mystery cleared up, then." She blew delicately on her tea. "Carter was the first to tell me about you. Of course, we only thought you were Tyrell's new mistress. You ended up being so much more than that. Did you tell him who you were?"

The question was direct enough that Mia knew she had to answer. "No."

"And what about Grayson? You've known him much longer. Does he know who you are?"

Instinct screamed to lie, so she did. "No."

"Hmm. It must have been strange for you—having Grayson in Mortise. Knowing he would walk the halls of your childhood home, and that he would speak to your brother."

Her words were needles in Mia's skin.

Iris's eyes lit up, as if she sensed Mia's pain and relished it. "Are you sure you don't want a cup of tea? You look like you could use some refreshment."

Her throat was dry, but she refused to drink anything the Poison Queen offered. "I'm sure."

The queen shrugged and lifted her cup again, taking another measured sip. "My condolences on the death of your father." She paused, peering at Mia over the rim of the cup. "But perhaps you didn't know? Since Grayson doesn't know who you are, he had no reason to tell you what's been happening in Mortise."

Beneath the table, Mia's fingernails dug into her palms. *Say nothing.* It was clear the queen only intended to play with her. Hurt her. If she didn't engage—if she showed no emotion—this might end sooner.

Iris settled back in her chair. "You don't look surprised. Did you know of your father's death, then?"

Her jaw stiffened, but then she found herself saying, "Grayson mentioned it."

"I'm a little surprised by your lack of emotion. When a girl loses her father . . ." A shadow crossed her face. "Well, that pain leaves a deep scar. But perhaps you felt like you already lost him all those years ago. Or maybe you blame him. Fathers are supposed to be able to fix everything, yet he never came for you. That had to have hurt."

Mia's pulse was thready. She forced herself to take a breath, and the overly-sweet scent of the pink flowers filled her lungs. "I never blamed my father for my imprisonment," she said. "I only ever blamed your husband."

Iris chuckled. "Is that supposed to be your attempt at a barb? Oh, you silly girl. You'll have to try harder than that if you hope to survive around us Kaelins."

"I know very well how heartless *you* are," Mia said, her voice edged.

"What makes you think you know me?"

"Grayson has told me all about you. Tyrell has told me things, too. I can't imagine what sort of mother could do the things you've done to them." Mia wanted to stop, but the words kept pouring out of her. "You're a monster. You've tortured all your children—turned them against each other.

And you never once thought to stop your husband from imprisoning a little girl."

"Interesting," Iris murmured. "Go on."

Mia's breaths were shallow, and her heart skittered in her chest. She spoke through gritted teeth. "I was in a cell for nine years. I was a *child*. I was *beaten*. And you did *nothing*."

The queen angled her head. "My inaction bothers you?"

"Yes."

"Why?"

"Because mothers aren't supposed to hurt children. Their own, or anyone else's." Fates, why was she saying these things? She knew Iris didn't have a heart. There was no point in drawing this conversation out, or exposing her wounds—wounds she hadn't even fully realized she carried.

Iris's expression was impossible to read. "What would you say if I told you I didn't know the truth about you until last night?"

"I wouldn't believe you."

Iris set down her cup. "I'm going to be truthful with you, Meerah. You can choose to believe me or not—it makes no difference to me. But the first time I heard your name was when Carter told me Tyrell had a new mistress. A mysterious girl who appeared seemingly from nowhere. I was only mildly interested at the time, and I had other things on my mind, so I didn't investigate you as I should have. Then Grayson returned from Mortise, and Henri decided it was time to tell me what he's been plotting all this time." Her lips pursed. "The truth is, I didn't know you were living under my feet all these years. I wish I'd known, but I didn't."

"You wouldn't have done anything to help me."

"No," she agreed. "Henri often keeps his secrets, as I keep

mine, but this was a startlingly large secret. I admit, it bothers me. What bothers me even more, though, is that Grayson had you—this secret—for years, and I never knew. It makes me wonder what else Grayson might be keeping from me."

"Maybe you should worry about what else your husband is keeping from you."

Something flickered in the queen's eyes; it looked alarmingly like excitement. "If you're ready to taunt me, you're ready to answer my questions."

Her words made Mia's scalp prickle, but she didn't have time to think about why.

"Do you love Grayson?" Iris asked.

The abrupt question was surprising, but the answer fell out of her at once. "Yes."

Iris made a sound in her throat. Disgust? "Grayson was not meant to be loved. He is not meant to love in return."

"He's worthy of love. And he's more capable of it than you could ever know."

Iris raised one dark eyebrow. The move was startlingly like Tyrell. "I understand how Henri has used you to motivate Grayson, and I can't argue that he's reached great heights because you lived under threat. But some part of me wonders if you are a sickness inside him. If you are eating away his strength, leaving a hollow foundation that could prove his undoing. A weakness that will destroy him. I suppose time will tell."

Weakness.

That single word cut so deep, Mia sucked in a breath. Her shoulders felt incredibly heavy, but instead of sinking into her insecurity, she lashed out. "You're a hateful, evil woman. A horrible mother."

The fine lines at the corners of Iris's eyes deepened. "You know, I never wanted daughters. Thankfully, the fates granted my wish. I was given five strong sons. Each bred with a purpose. Grayson was raised to take orders. He was born for war, trained to withstand all pain."

Heat flared in Mia's cheeks. "He wasn't trained. He was *tortured*."

"And he has withstood it all. His scars are a thing of beauty."

"You're a monster," Mia bit out.

"No. I merely gave birth to one." The corner of her pink lips lifted. "Five, actually."

Mia's rage was hot, but oddly muted.

Iris grew contemplative. "You defend Grayson so fiercely, but do you even know the things he's done? What he is? He's a legend. A nightmare. His name carries a terror that brings men, women, and children crashing to their knees. In the other kingdoms, his name is whispered for fear of summoning his demonic presence. *That* is who you love."

Mia's skin felt too warm. "Grayson is no monster."

"He's a killer."

"Only because he was forced to become one." Her chin lifted. "You will never change my opinion of him."

"You are so naive. It's a miracle Grayson doesn't already resent you, but someday he will. How could he not? After everything he has suffered for you, he has every right to curse your name. If you died, I think a part of him would be relieved. Because once you were dead, Henri would have no more reason to hurt him."

Mia stiffened. The words cut deeply, because they followed her own thoughts and fears. He may indeed resent her one day, for all he'd suffered because of her—all he'd had to do.

She was his weakness, and everyone grew to despise their weaknesses.

Devastation hit her. Grief tried to drown her. Her head swam with the smell of those flowers.

Iris drew back slightly in her chair. "Are you manipulating Grayson?"

"No." The answer just fell out of her.

"You have no desire to use him for some purpose?"

"No."

"Do you love Tyrell?"

"I—I care about him." Fates, what was wrong with her? Why was she answering these questions?

"Are you manipulating Tyrell?" Iris asked.

Guilt soured in her belly. "Yes."

The queen leaned forward in her chair. "How are you manipulating him?"

"I—" Mia clamped her mouth shut.

"There's no use in fighting it," Iris told her softly. "The faersin in your system will continue to lower your inhibitions and you'll be compelled to answer me honestly. You will want to please me above all else."

Mia's stomach dropped. "But . . . I didn't drink anything."

"It wasn't in the tea. It's coated on the flowers you're breathing."

Her eyes darted to the pink flowers on the table. The sickly-sweet scent turned her stomach, and she tried to push out of her chair, but her arms and legs trembled, unable to hold her up.

"Faersin weakens the body along with your mental and emotional defenses," Iris explained. "At the moment, your body probably feels very heavy. You won't be able to walk away, even if you wanted to. Which I assure you, you won't. You'll want to answer my questions, and you won't lie to me."

Panic clutched her chest, but even that felt terrifyingly muted. "But . . . you . . ."

"You think I'll be impacted?" Iris tapped her nose. "I applied Savint Oil before this meeting. I'm quite unaffected. So, tell me—how are you manipulating Tyrell?"

The supplies under the bed. The escape plan—

"Escape," Mia whispered. Her voice trembled, but the words still came. "I want . . . to escape."

"And you thought Tyrell would help you leave the castle?"

"No." Tyrell would never have helped her escape. Not if it meant losing her. Would he come with her if she and Grayson asked? She honestly didn't know, but doubt crept in. Was that the faersin? Or just the overwhelming fog she suddenly felt?

"How did you plan to use Tyrell, then?" Iris asked.

She didn't want to answer, but she couldn't hold onto her reticence. ". . . Use him. I thought I could use him."

"Ahh . . . I think I'm beginning to truly see you, Meerah. Did Grayson tell you anything about Liam's death?"

It was another sudden shift in questioning, and it made Mia squirm.

Liam wasn't dead. That was a lie Grayson had told his father in the hopes of gaining his mother's help—fates, she couldn't betray Grayson to the woman who had ordered Liam's death in the first place.

But her mouth opened, and she had to say something.

Partial truths. She needed to share only partial truths.

Grayson had told her about the lie. He hadn't told her *how* he'd professed to have seen Liam die. "N-No. He didn't tell me about Liam's death."

Iris's eyes narrowed. "But he mentioned Liam's death?"

"Yes." He *had* mentioned it, when he'd told her it was a lie. Mia could feel herself compelled to clarify, but Iris asked her next question before she could speak.

"Why didn't you tell Grayson the truth about who you are?"

The change in subject was just as abrupt as before, and it shocked words out of her before she could try to rally her thoughts. "I couldn't."

"What do you mean by that?"

Tears stung her eyes. "I couldn't tell him the truth. It only brought pain."

"Because of the beatings you received as a child?" Iris asked. "Henri told me how he ordered your caretakers to make sure you didn't talk about your past."

Mia's voice cracked. "Yes. I couldn't even think about who I was."

"So you never told Grayson."

It wasn't a question, but she responded anyway. She wanted to explain everything to Iris. "No, I didn't tell him. Most of the time, it didn't even seem real. Who I used to be . . . I'm not her anymore. Meerah is dead."

"That's quite a statement. *Meerah is dead.* What makes you say that?"

"I'm not her anymore," Mia repeated. "And Desfan . . . he'll hate me."

"Fascinating," she mused. "Why do you think he'll hate you?"

NO! A voice inside her screamed. *Don't say anything. Don't give her anything—*

"It's my fault," Mia said, her voice breaking. "I killed Tally."

Iris's head tilted. "Who is Tally?"

"My sister."

The queen's gray eyes shined brighter. "You killed your sister?"

"Yes." Mia pinched her eyes closed. She could feel her fingernails digging into her palms, drawing blood. "I let go of her. In the water. She was so scared, and I let go of her hand."

"Did you do it on purpose?" The intrigue in Iris's voice made Mia's stomach roil.

"No." Her face was wet. When had she started crying? She wanted to brush the tears from her cheeks, but it would take too much effort to lift her hands.

Iris was silent for a moment. Then, "Killing is a choice. You didn't kill your sister, Meerah."

The words lacked emotion, which didn't exactly make them comforting. But they surprised Mia enough that her eyes opened.

"You didn't kill your sister," the queen repeated. "You just let her die."

The off-hand words were blades that raked her skin. Her breath hitched and her vision blurred. "I didn't mean to."

"Intentions rarely matter. Not where actions and consequences are concerned." Iris fingered the rim of her teacup. "Prisoner, or princess?" she murmured. "That must have been a confusing puzzle for a child. Once, you had everything your spoiled heart ever wanted. Then you had nothing. Darkness. Isolation. Pain. That became your whole world. And you lost yourself. The princess truly is dead." The corner of her mouth lifted wryly. "Excuse me; the *seraijah* is dead."

Her tone was mocking, but Mia couldn't disagree.

"You're barely worth anything to Mortise now," Iris continued. "You're broken, Meerah. You're no longer the person you were born to be. You wouldn't even know how to fit in there, would you? Your brother, certainly, would be better off without you."

A voice deep inside Mia—so deep, it had been silent until now, even in the midst of her doubts—roared in rebellion. And yet, with the floral scent in her lungs and her head feeling so heavy, she couldn't argue. Iris was right. Of course she was right. Why would Mia ever doubt her? Her words made sense.

Perfect sense.

"You could have purpose, though," Iris said. "And not just the purpose Henri has picked for you. You could be great, Meerah, if you chose to serve me."

"S-Serve you?"

"Yes. You have two of my sons ready to obey your every whim. I simply ask that you be their confidante. And then you will report to me everything they're thinking, everything they do. Wouldn't you like to help me?"

"Yes."

No! a deep part of her screamed.

Fates, she was so confused. She couldn't think.

Iris smiled gently. "Good. Now, I've learned through experimentation with Jazarah that the effects of the faersin can become difficult to manage. The head can become so clouded, you're not fully able to answer my questions anymore—or that you'll stop telling the truth in order to tell me what you think I want to hear. I think we've reached that point." The queen stood.

Jazarah, Mia thought belatedly. *Who is that?*

"She's Peter's mistress," Iris said, even as she bent to retrieve something from behind her chair. Had Mia spoken aloud? "She doesn't always remember everything we discuss here,"

Iris continued. "I imagine you won't, either. But she knows enough to give me reports. To whisper in Peter's ear what I want her to say." Iris smiled as she straightened, holding a small wooden box.

Mia tried to smile back at her, but she wasn't sure if she succeeded. Warning flared somewhere inside her at the sight of that box, but she didn't know why.

The queen placed the box on the table. "Some people have the ability to naturally fight off faersin. Considering how this conversation has gone, I very much doubt you do. But I must be sure. You understand?"

"Yes."

"Good." The lid of the box was fitted into some sort of groove, which meant it had to be slid aside to open. As Iris pulled the lid to one side, Mia was finally able to see the contents.

Inside was a creature Mia knew well. Her parents had always warned her to be wary of scorpions.

"This fascinating creature is from your homeland," Iris said. "The venom won't kill you, but the sting will hurt. A lot. The site of the venom's entrance will swell and turn red, but that will fade. So will the possible numbness. You may experience a fever if it stings you more than once."

Inside the box, the sand-colored scorpion skittered on its eight legs, the large pincers clicking once before it froze, the segmented tail curved forward over its body. The stinger was raised high, as if sensing a threat.

Mia sensed the threat, too, but she was unable to react to it. She was trapped, just as the scorpion was.

Iris slid the lid mostly back into place, leaving only a small gap. "Put your hand in the box," she said.

Mia's clouded mind didn't question the order, but her fingertips barely lifted on her lap. "I can't."

"You can. You can force yourself to do this for me." Iris's fingers brushed across the top of Mia's head, stroking her hair. "Do it now."

Mia wanted to please her. She truly did. But her muscles were unresponsive.

"Do it," Iris said again. "Prove that you will do anything I say. Your desire must override everything else. Fear, pain—even the fact that you've been drugged. You need to push past all of this and do what I say."

A shiver wracked Mia. Sweat beaded her brow. Her arm trembled. Then, slowly, her hand lifted.

"Good," Iris encouraged softly. "Just a little higher."

Inside the box, she heard the scorpion skittering. It shuffled and clicked in the darkness of its wooden prison.

Instinct shrieked for Mia to stop moving, but she couldn't. Her fingers brushed the open edge of the box, and then her hand slipped into the narrow opening.

There was a light graze over her fingers. Then the pincers clamped down with a horrible pinch, breaking skin, and the scorpion struck. The stinger stabbed into the back of her hand and agony burst.

Her body jerked.

Iris patted her shoulder. "Thank you, Mia. Now, leave your hand in there until your guard comes to fetch you."

The pincers had latched on and wouldn't let go. The scorpion struck again. And again.

Mia gasped as pain ripped through her hand. She whimpered, and her fingers twitched, but she didn't remove her hand from the box. She'd been told not to. She would obey.

She didn't remember why she had to—she just knew she did.

Besides, she was too tired to lift it.

The queen walked away, her white skirt rippling against the pebbled path.

Mia didn't really register anything other than pain until Fletcher wandered into view. His confusion gave way to horror when he saw her sagging in the chair, her throbbing hand still in the box.

"*Fates.*" Fletcher dove for her.

He jerked her swollen hand out of the box and yanked the scorpion off her. Tossing it back into the box, he scooped Mia into his arms and strode away from the table.

Tears tracked down Mia's face as she laid her cheek against Fletcher's shoulder. "I did it," she whispered, her words slurring, her heart pounding erratically. "I kept my hand in the box."

Fletcher swore again, the sound strangled. She didn't know why, but he seemed afraid. And angry. Horribly, furiously angry. "Hold on," he gritted out. "Just hold on."

Mia floated out of the poison garden in Fletcher's arms.

Then she just floated.

CHAPTER 6

GRAYSON

GRAYSON STOOD IN THE MAIN BUILDING OF Northland Barracks, his feet shoulder-width apart, his arms crossed over his chest. His fingers dug painfully into his arms, but nothing was as painful as the throbbing burn on his face. Sweat beaded his hairline and upper lip. His skin felt flushed. He hadn't eaten in far too long; perhaps that's why he felt slightly faint. Or maybe it was just being in this place, remembering the days he'd spent here as a child. The military camp had always been a place of horrors, but now . . .

Those boys.

They weren't soldiers. They were terrified children. But Henri didn't care. Of course he didn't. He'd given the orders that had brought them here. Those boys weren't here voluntarily. They'd been taken. Ripped from the arms of their mothers, probably. Perhaps their fathers had been coaxed to enlist with promises they could serve with their children, though Henri would never actually have allowed such a thing. No, the fathers would have been separated from their sons almost immediately. They would have been told that, if they trained well, they would see their sons again before the battle.

This radical expansion of the army could mean only one thing. Henri was closer to declaring war than Grayson had thought.

Desfan, Imara, Serene—none of them knew what was coming. None of them knew how vast Henri's army had become. This valley was filled with soldiers.

"This is only a fraction of our troops, of course," Henri said. The king stood at the head of the long table, where maps were spread. The Kaelin princes stood around the table, the only other occupants in the room. Grayson forced himself to listen. To watch. He tried to memorize every mark on the map, even the ones he didn't understand. Liam had taught him tricks and had honed his skills, and he used all of them now. Especially his least favorite—patience.

There was nothing he could do for those starving boys outside. Nothing he could do to stop his father from gleefully telling them his plans.

But he could listen.

Henri waved to the map sprawled in front of Tyrell. It showed Dolbar Pass. "I have troops already stationed here. They will invade Devendra from the north. I will lead them, with Peter at my side."

Peter didn't look surprised. He'd already known.

Of course he had.

Henri glanced at Tyrell. "What do you think?"

Tyrell stood across the table from Grayson. He hadn't said a word, and his face was an inscrutable mask. "It's an impressive force. Why wasn't I told?"

"You didn't need to know," Henri said.

Tyrell's expression tightened, just a little. "I'm in charge of training your soldiers."

"Yes. But you couldn't personally train them all. The men you've been training for the last year have made their way here, and elsewhere, to train others using your methods. But I would like you to assist now in training the boys."

Tyrell's mouth flattened. "Most of them couldn't even lift a sword."

"I expect you to change that." Henri braced his hands on the table and leaned all his weight on his arms. "They don't need to be elite. The sight of them alone will confuse an enemy and pull on their compassion. Then, with their guard lowered at a critical time, those boys have a chance of killing at least one enemy before they're put down. You'll teach them how to do that."

Grayson watched Tyrell closely, but his sadistic brother merely nodded. There was no spark of glee or anticipation, like Grayson would have once expected. In fact, there was no emotion at all.

Henri regarded them all. "Nothing spoken here will leave this room. Is that understood?"

They all murmured assent.

Henri pushed off the table, his golden crown glinting in the light from the nearest window. "My entire reign has built to this moment. You have been prepared for this all your lives. There is no room for failure. No place for hesitation or doubt. It is finally time for the great war. What my father once failed to do, I will now accomplish."

His eyes slid to Grayson as he continued. "Liam's death creates some issues, but we will adapt. For now, I want you to focus on your individual tasks. Each of you has been assigned an army to command. An experienced commander will serve at your side, but *you* are the standard the people will gather under. Your names are legend, and it is in your names that the soldiers will fight for me and for Ryden. Be sure they fight well."

Unmistakable warning lived in those words.

Henri continued. "The commanders you will serve with have been training the majority of your forces. You will meet them after we're done here. The attacks will, of course, focus on Devendra and Mortise. I had planned to leave Zennor for now, but Peter has some designs for Zennor that have intrigued me."

Grayson's eyes slid to Peter, the fine hairs on his body rising. He knew Peter had planned to marry Imara, but was he planning other things? Regardless, Grayson had been right to warn Imara; Peter might send someone else to abduct her, since Grayson hadn't done it for him.

Henri was still speaking. "When the war is won, Peter will sit on Devendra's throne under my leadership as High King of Eyrinthia. When the day comes that he's needed back in Ryden, his future son will take over the Devendran throne."

The king looked at Carter. "I want you to lead a second army into Devendra, entering here." He tapped a map, showing another mountain pass to the west of Dolbar. "Your targets will be the military outposts here, and here, which will also secure the Devendran-Mortisian border. When these battles are won, Zennor will crumble easily. You will reign as king, answering only to me."

Carter's eyes glittered.

Henri shifted his gaze to Grayson. "You will lead the attack on Mortise by ship. Your focus will be Duvan. You will take the heart of Mortise and secure the coastal strongholds while Tyrell will lead another army over land, hitting Mortise here, here, and here." His finger drew back from the cities he'd highlighted, looking at his two youngest sons. "Both of you will have a chance to prove your worth to me, and to Ryden. The one who serves me best will reign over Mortise."

Tyrell stood a little straighter. They had been raised on competition, and Henri had just presented the biggest prize yet: a kingdom.

Grayson didn't move, and his expression remained unchanged. He wouldn't have wanted to be a ruler, even if he wasn't planning to escape.

"There is another prize of sorts," Henri said, and when he began to smile, Grayson's stomach dropped. "I have held in reserve a bit of leverage I can use over the Mortisians—their ruler, in particular. It has been a closely guarded secret and will continue to be so. But it is time all of you knew of her."

Grayson's mouth ran dry. *No, no, no . . .*

Tyrell had stilled completely, his gaze fixed on Henri.

"Her?" Peter asked, his brow furrowed.

Henri's attention moved between Grayson and Tyrell. "I have in my possession the youngest princess of Mortise, Meerah Cassian. She has been thought dead for nearly a decade, but in reality, she has been my prisoner."

Grayson's pulse thundered, but still his expression was locked. He didn't know how to react. His father was watching him, clearly reveling in divulging this revelation. He didn't know Grayson already knew the truth.

Tyrell didn't seem to be breathing.

Peter's eyes narrowed. "Where is she?"

"Oh, I've kept her close." Henri's amusement was obvious in the sardonic twist of his lips. "Some of you have gotten quite close to her."

Tyrell's jaw cracked. "Mia."

Peter shot his brother a look.

"Yes," Henri confirmed.

"Who else knew about this?" Peter demanded.

Henri threw a sharp look at his heir, who instantly tempered his expression. "No one. I only told your mother last night. No one else needed to know the truth, until now."

"Why now?" Grayson asked. His voice was heavy and rough from disuse.

Every eye went to him, but he didn't care. He had eyes only for Henri.

The king's eyes lit with perverse pleasure. "Because it's finally time for her to be useful. And I must say, she will do an even better job than I dared imagine."

Grayson's fingers dug deeper into his arms.

"What are you planning to do with her?" Tyrell asked.

"She will serve multiple purposes in the coming war," Henri said. "And I'll use her any way I see fit. But the endgame has always been clear. At the conclusion of the war, after Mortise has been conquered and their newly crowned king is dead, Meerah will be given to either Tyrell or Grayson—whichever of you wins the Mortisian crown."

Grayson's pulse thundered in his ears. He could feel the mask on his face crack.

No.

That was the only word in his head, and it was absolute.

Tyrell viewed him from across the table.

Grayson's hackles rose and his eyes narrowed. *Over my rotting corpse.*

He didn't need to express the sentiment verbally—Tyrell's jaw firmed.

"Why?" Carter asked. "Wouldn't she serve more of a purpose if you used her to break Mortise? Send her piece by piece to her brother until he surrenders the country without a fight."

A growl vibrated in Grayson's throat before he could think to swallow it back. Every eye snapped to him; Tyrell's were black.

Fates, Grayson needed to keep his mask in place. Betraying emotion in front of his father and brothers would only bring him—and Mia—more trouble.

Henri chuckled softly. "I've considered such a thing, Carter. When I first got her, I nearly did just that. I knew Saernon would buckle easily. It would only take her smallest finger, and he would have bowed before me. But his people would not have done so; the Mortisian council wouldn't have allowed it. In the end, I would have only gained Saernon's head. So, no. The girl is more useful alive and in one piece." He eyed Grayson, all amusement gone as warning took over his expression. "For now, at least."

Peter's calculated gaze was steady. "By putting her on the throne, you're giving the Mortisians a Mortisian queen."

Henri tipped his head. "Exactly. They'll be less inclined to rebel. Especially because their queen was once a princess they thought was lost forever, but was saved by my mercy." His smile grew as he studied Tyrell, then Grayson. "Whichever of you serves me best will win a crown, a kingdom, and a wife. So serve me well."

It wasn't long before Henri dismissed them to meet privately with the commanders they would each serve with, while he went to inspect the forces.

Grayson was currently awaiting the arrival of Commander Zaden in an otherwise empty office. The features of the room were plain, befitting a military barracks. There was an un-cluttered desk, some wooden chairs, and a locked cupboard against one wall. The starkness of the room was in complete contrast to the chaos in Grayson's head.

It had been horrible enough that his family knew about Mia. That Tyrell had *paraded* her in front of them. But now they knew who she really was. The speculative, greedy light in Peter's eyes as they'd filed from the room made Grayson's hollow stomach churn.

We're leaving. It's going to be all right, because we're leaving tomorrow.

None of his brothers would have a chance to touch her.

Especially not Tyrell.

Fates. It all made so much sense. Why Henri hadn't argued Grayson's attachment to Mia all these years. He'd *encouraged* it, in his own sick, twisted way. And it made sense why he'd pushed Tyrell toward her, too. Somehow, he'd known Tyrell would want her.

Henri always seemed to know.

Grayson fought a shudder. He didn't know if it was caused by his thoughts, or the fever he suspected he had.

Without warning, the door opened, and Grayson stared as Captain Reeve entered the room.

The man's presence was unexpected. Grayson hadn't seen the young captain since he'd left for Mortise. Reeve was a few years older than Grayson, with a strong jaw and handsome features. His uniform fit him well, his eyes were iced with a fervor that came only from a soldier desperate to prove himself indispensable. Months ago, when they'd gathered taxes from the remote villages in the northern mountains, Grayson knew Reeve had been sent to spy on him. To judge his loyalty to the crown. He had nearly caught Grayson when he'd helped a widow and her two young children escape arrest. Grayson had also saved Reeve's life on that trip. At the time, he'd wondered if it would change anything between them. Create a sense of loyalty, or even a debt.

Looking at him now, Grayson doubted it.

Reeve pushed the door closed and inclined his head. "Prince Grayson."

"I'm waiting for Commander Zaden," Grayson said, forgoing any greeting.

"I know," Reeve said. "I'm supposed to meet with him, too. I've been appointed to First Captain in his army."

Grayson's eyebrows lifted. "That's quite the advancement."

Reeve's gaze strayed to the flaming side of Grayson's face. "Did the Mortisians do that?"

"No." Grayson didn't expound. Partly because he owed this man nothing, but mostly because talking hurt, and the pain seemed to be building.

Reeve straightened. "How do you find the king's armies?"

"Younger than expected."

Something sparked in the young captain's eyes. "There will

87

be no mistaking the victor in the coming war," he said.

"I remember how much you've looked forward to this war."

"Yes. My grandfather would be proud of my command."

He probably would have been. The man had been a hero in the infamous Battle of the Sine years ago. In reality, it had been a massacre of innocents; an entire city had been condemned for unknowingly harboring Mortisian spies. No one had been allowed to live.

Reeve shifted his weight. "There are rumors sweeping the camp. About you and Prince Liam. They say he died in Mortise."

Grayson said nothing.

Reeve must have read confirmation in his silence, because he swore and shook his head. "It's lucky you escaped." His eyes darted again to the burn on his face.

Grayson gritted his teeth. He didn't like the staring. "Do you enjoy serving under Commander Zaden?" he asked, forcing himself to speak. Anything to distract Reeve.

"Serving under him is a privilege," Reeve said at once. "He's a hero. That he chose me to be First Captain . . . It's a huge honor."

It almost sounded like he was trying to convince himself, which drew Grayson's attention. There was a sense of disquiet about Reeve, and it dampened his old zealousness. He looked a little less like the perfect soldier Grayson had known. Whether it was due to the treatment of the young boys outside or a disagreement with Zaden's reputed brutality, Grayson didn't know.

Or maybe Grayson was giving him too much credit.

In the end, it didn't really matter. It wouldn't change anything. Reeve was First Captain, and he would resolutely follow that path. He'd dedicated his life to this. He wouldn't stop now.

"Fair warning," Reeve said. "Zaden will not accept anything less than complete loyalty. Try to make sure there are no . . . incidents."

He was clearly talking about Grayson defending the Hogan family. What Grayson *didn't* know was if his words were a threat, or if Reeve was actually attempting to warn him.

Before Grayson could decide, Commander Zaden entered the room.

Reeve stiffened to attention, and Grayson straightened his spine. Not in respect, but in an effort to look stronger than he knew he currently appeared.

Commander Zaden was older than Henri by at least a decade. Despite his mounting age, he had no sign of a gut. He looked fit, capable, and assured. His silver hair was trimmed short and his blue eyes were cold as they took in Grayson. The man had scars on his weathered face, and everything about him seemed hard.

He let the moment draw out for an uncomfortable moment before he bowed his head. "Prince Grayson."

"Commander."

Zaden kicked the door closed and crossed the room with heavy strides, claiming the lone seat on the other side of the desk. That left Grayson and Reeve to settle in the chairs across from him.

"Your reputation is strong, Your Highness," Zaden said, no real deference in his tone. "So strong, in fact, I almost forgot how young you are." He tipped his head toward Reeve. "Obviously, I have no trouble utilizing talent wherever I find it—young, old, it doesn't matter to me. I just want to know you're good at your job, and that you'll do it. That being said, your father has told me several things that concern me."

Reeve shifted in his chair, obviously uncomfortable.

Grayson couldn't care less about that. He reclined in his chair, allowing his Black Hand persona to fully take over. "What exactly did he say?"

"He said you sometimes lack focus. However, he didn't think that would be a problem in this case."

Because he was dangling Mia in front of him—and Tyrell.

Grayson wanted to clench his teeth. Instead, he let his head tip to the side, ignoring the flare of pain as his raw skin stretched with the movement. He regarded the commander coolly, and he kept his voice cold as well. "What seems to be your problem with me, then?"

"I don't trust a man without first knowing his passion. The men I like best have a passion for war. A passion for winning. Somehow, I don't think that's you. So, what is your passion, Black Hand?"

Grayson smiled thinly. "Serving my father."

He didn't know if the man believed him, but he finally nodded once. "See that your passion doesn't fade." He straightened in his chair. "Commander Weller and I have discussed at length our strategies to bring Mortise to its knees. He and Prince Tyrell will do this by land, while we attack by sea. The fight will be bloody, but we will succeed. There is no other option."

"When do we attack?" Grayson asked. He should gather every bit of information he could to report back to Desfan. Fates knew the Mortisians would need every advantage.

The commander lifted one shoulder. "When the king commands. Commander Weller and Prince Tyrell will act first, taking down each city along the coast and neutralizing their ports. They will burn their ships before they can launch while we will make our way to Duvan. Once we have taken the city, we will march on the strongholds and larger cities in Mortise, moving east toward the Devendran border—which Prince Carter and Commander Groves will have fortified. Are those objectives clear?"

"Yes," Reeve said at once.

Grayson merely nodded.

"Good." Zaden leaned forward, his forearms braced on the desk. "While the king hasn't given an exact date for this attack, I believe we can expect our orders before the year's end."

Grayson silently cursed. Desfan was not ready for this—not with his father so recently dead, and certainly not against the numbers Henri had raised.

"The attacks on Mortise will be launched first," Zaden continued. "Desfan Cassian will call for Newlan Demoi's aid, which the king of Devendra may or may not give. If Demoi does uphold the newly signed treaty and send soldiers to Mortise, it won't matter. Before they have a chance to arrive, Mortise will be ours. And by the time those troops turn around, they will find Devendra has already fallen to us Ryden well. They will have no choice but to surrender." Commander Zaden shrugged. "Tactically, the invasion plan is flawless."

Grayson had to admit, it did seem that way. The bolt of terror he felt was definitely unwanted, but he couldn't help it. By taking Mia to Mortise, he was taking her to a future battlefield. Not that he had any other options, but . . . *Fates*. What if he managed to escape with Mia, only for her to fall under Henri's power again? If he conquered Eyrinthia, that's exactly what would happen.

Henri couldn't win. Grayson wouldn't let him.

He just didn't know how to stop him.

"Until our orders come, we will continue to train our soldiers," the commander said, ignorant of the way Grayson's pulse had spiked. "Prince Grayson, I've been assured you will join us weekly. I think the boys in particular would benefit from seeing you around the camp. I have struck the fear of the fates in them, but you will inspire even greater fear." He smirked a little. "I've been encouraging my men to spread tales of your exploits. The boys are terrified of you—as are the men. They train harder for me, because they fear your retribution. I want you to further that whenever you come to visit." The man stood. "They're anxious to meet you, I'm sure. Let's not disappoint them."

Grayson spent the next two hours inspecting the army his father had assigned him. Too many were children, and all shied away from him, their faces pale and their fearful eyes darting.

Grayson said nothing. Not when the commander barked at them and made them jump. Not when one boy failed to lift his sword, and the commander kicked him in the ribs. The boy had wet himself before the blow even landed.

Zaden had saved the disciplining of several new recruits to be done very publicly with Grayson present, and he had no choice but to stand there and watch as six young boys were whipped.

Rage pulsed inside him, and he wanted nothing more than to intervene. Every muscle was coiled with a painful level of tension. But as each lash cracked against skin, Grayson knew that opening his mouth would do nothing. Their punishment would be increased, or Mia would be punished as soon as they returned to Lenzen, or his father would throw him back into prison. He couldn't risk any of that. He wasn't just protecting Mia, or himself. Mortise and Devendra needed a decent warning before this war started. That was larger, more important, than anything else.

It did not take away the guilt he felt when those boys screamed.

After the whippings, King Henri appeared, stepping out of the crowd with his guards. The soldiers—both young and old—who had gathered to watch the punishment stared at the king with varying expressions of awe and terror as he walked among them.

Henri stopped just in front of Commander Zaden and Grayson. "You are the future of Ryden," the king said to the rapt crowd, his voice deep and resonating. "You will pave the way to victory. Your ferocity will lead to the destruction of our enemies. You will be impervious to pain. You will not fear sacrifice. We will crush those who oppose us. We will no longer remain huddled in the snowy mountains of our homeland. We will conquer Mortise and Devendra and enslave all survivors. Lands and estates will be given to the deserving warriors in my army, regardless of rank or station. Ryden will know a new age of victory and prosperity!"

The commanders in the army led the cheer, and the soldiers joined their voices—some more strongly than others. Beside Grayson, Reeve shouted with them, and Grayson's blood chilled at the roar of sound. He didn't join the cheer. His jaw was immovable, his eyes so dark no one bothered to reproach his silence.

Liam had known. About the boys, about the increasing size of Henri's army. As the spymaster of Ryden, he had to have known. He knew the danger Henri posed to all of

Eyrinthia—Ryden included. That's why he'd made plans to bring down their father. He'd been trying to stop *this*.

Grayson hadn't agreed with Liam's methods, but in that moment, he wished his brother was with him. Liam was the only other person who could understand what it was like for a son to defy King Henri Kaelin.

Standing in the middle of a cheering army, Grayson felt wholly alone.

Much later, when he finally made it to his horse, Grayson rechecked the saddle out of pure habit.

Footsteps approached, and from the corner of his eye, he saw Tyrell striding toward him. His brother was bristling with too many emotions. Anger. Confusion. Hurt.

"Did you know?" he demanded, his voice a low hiss.

Grayson faced him. "Know what?"

Tyrell's eyes flashed with irritation. "About Mia. Who she was."

"You heard Father. No one knew."

His nostrils flared. With a muttered curse, he turned toward his own horse.

As Grayson resumed tugging the fastening straps, the words he'd been holding for hours finally came out. "No matter what games our father plays, Mia will never be yours. I will never allow that to happen."

Tyrell's hands paused; he'd been checking his saddle as well. When he twisted to meet Grayson's gaze, his eyes were dark. "She's not yours to control."

"No. But I will protect her from you."

Tyrell's expression darkened. "Careful, Grayson. We're heading into war. Nothing makes the fates so thirsty for blood as a battlefield."

Grayson gave his brother the cool edge of a smile. "Is that supposed to be a threat?"

Tyrell didn't get a chance to answer.

Carter, Peter, and Henri joined them. Grayson swung up onto his horse, the burn on his face throbbing and his vision blurring briefly as pain swelled.

By the time his sight cleared, Henri was also mounted, and he ordered them to move out.

Tyrell wheeled his horse around, moving to ride on Carter's far side.

As far from Grayson as possible.

Grayson didn't miss the flash of satisfaction on Henri's face as he glanced between his two youngest sons.

Hatred for his father spiked. He had forced Tyrell and Grayson to become rivals over the years, driving them with meticulously planned tortures and forcing them to engage in violent fights. But this was a fates-blasted nightmare. He'd put Mia between them, manipulating all three of them. Because, as much as Grayson hated to acknowledge it, he knew Mia's feelings for Tyrell were real. She cared about him. And Tyrell wanted her. He wasn't going to stop wanting her once Mia and Grayson escaped.

He would come for her.

Grayson wanted to protect Mia—always. But he wasn't going to be able to protect her from this.

In the end, he was going to have to kill Tyrell. He knew it, and Tyrell had clearly reached the same conclusion about him. And no matter how that final confrontation played out, Mia would be hurt. Which meant neither he nor Tyrell could ever truly win.

CHAPTER 7

DESFAN

FOLLOWING MORTISIAN TRADITION, DESFAN STOOD at the doors of the throne room, greeting the men and women who had come to witness his coronation. Though he'd only managed to snatch a couple hours of sleep, he wasn't tired. His stomach rippled with nerves, and an anxious, restless energy thrummed through his veins as he smiled and welcomed the seemingly endless parade of witnesses.

Karim stood at his shoulder, a full row of guards just behind him. That wasn't strictly following tradition, but Desfan didn't argue. Frankly, he was afraid Karim would hit him if he protested.

It was impossible to see the end of the line, because it extended beyond the palace walls. He only saw who was next when they stepped through the outer door and into the corridor. The procession had begun an hour ago, but he knew he was nowhere near done.

In the throne room, music played for those who had already greeted Desfan. He hoped there was enough room for everyone who had come. Invitations had been sent out soon after Serjan Saernon's death, and while many nobles had arrived weeks ago, some of the faces Desfan saw were new. He tried to memorize names and faces, but it was always a relief whenever he saw someone he knew—until he saw Princess Serene.

Guilt pierced him, though he managed to keep his smile in place. "Serene."

"Desfan." She tipped her head in a slight bow. "I wanted to thank you for taking care of Imara last night."

Heat touched his cheeks. "Of course. She saved my life."

The corner of Serene's mouth lifted. "She mentioned that. But truly—thank you. You protected her, and insisted that she receive the best care. I'm in your debt."

"Nonsense." He wasn't sure what else to say. He knew he would have to tell Serene that he'd kissed Imara. But before he did, he wanted to speak to Imara about things. Until that happened, things were bound to feel strained between them. Thankfully, Serene didn't linger.

After she'd disappeared into the throne room with her guards, Desfan greeted several members of the council and their families, including Ser Anoush and his son, Arav—who was a little younger than Desfan, and a rather arrogant young man who had taken an instant dislike to Grayson. Right behind them came Ser Sifa and his son, Ranon. Ser Sifa often aligned with Ser Anoush on council matters, though his personal grievances against Ryden had ensured his hatred of Grayson and Liam, even before the Rydenic princes had betrayed them. Ranon, on the other hand, had become a friend to Grayson. Desfan felt a little guilty seeing him now, because Ranon had been asking for a meeting ever since Grayson's arrest. He suspected Ranon wanted to visit Grayson, since he—like most people in Mortise—thought Grayson was in a cell with Liam. Obviously, a visit wasn't possible, so Desfan had been avoiding the Mortisian nobleman.

Ranon greeted him respectfully, and Desfan was relieved he didn't bring up Grayson. Then again, his father was standing right beside him; Desfan didn't imagine Ser Sifa appreciated Ranon's friendship with the Rydenic prince.

As Desfan greeted Ser Sifa, he was reminded of Yahri's desire for him to choose an heir. It wasn't something he wanted to do. Naming another heir while Meerah still breathed felt wrong. Regardless, he knew he had no intention of naming Sifa as his heir. Distant relation or not, Sifa was far too quick to anger; especially where Ryden was concerned.

Then again, that may not be such a bad thing, with war looming.

After the Sifas moved on, Razan Krayt approached.

Karim stiffened beside Desfan, but Razan only glanced at him as she stopped in front of Desfan. Instead of just clasping his hand as everyone else had done, she gave his fingers a comforting squeeze. It was a silent show of friendship, and it loosened some of the tenseness that had built up in his shoulders. "Thank you for coming," Desfan said.

"I wouldn't have missed it." Her mouth twitched up at the corner. "In fact, I think I'd lose my seat on the council if I did." She looked at Karim, and Desfan could practically feel her nervousness. "How is your leg?"

"Fine." His tone was short, inviting no further questions.

Razan's spine straightened. She tipped her head, saying

nothing else before she walked into the throne room.

Desfan eyed Karim. "You need to tell me what's—"

"No."

"But—"

"There's nothing to say," Karim bit out lowly. "Nothing has changed between us."

Desfan made a scoffing noise in his throat. "That's a load of rubbish. You were inseparable during the fight last night. Even if I have to tie you down, I'll—Thank you for coming, Serai Nadir."

Tamar Nadir had a small smile playing about her lips as she stepped forward. "I feel as if I'm interrupting a good conversation."

"It will keep," Desfan said, while Karim snorted irritably.

Tamar was a middle-aged widow who lived on the border, close to Devendra. Desfan had come to truly respect her. Not just for her unwavering support for peace with Devendra, but also for the kindnesses she had shown Serene and Imara.

Tamar Nadir's smile was not quite as bright as it had been when she'd first arrived at the palace. Desfan knew that she and Dirk—one of Serene's bodyguards—had grown very close, and she clearly still mourned his death. Desfan wanted to allow her the time and space she needed, but he was also anxious to meet with her.

"Did you receive my missive?" he asked her.

"I did." Serai Nadir's curiosity was obvious in her gaze. "Am I to be told the nature of this meeting you've called me for?"

"I would value your opinion on some matters," Desfan said.

"That's quite vague, but I suppose I'll find out when we meet." With that, she bowed and also disappeared through the open doors of the throne room.

The next face through the door was very familiar, and Desfan couldn't hide his grin. "Avao!"

Karim's grandfather beamed as he stepped forward, breaking all sorts of traditions as he grabbed both Desfan and Karim in his long arms and crushed them to him. The man had grown older, but seemed as strong as ever. "Boys, it's been too long."

Karim grunted as he clapped his grandfather's back. "You're the one who chose to sail to all the southern islands."

"Yes, well, I wasn't exactly getting any younger." He tugged back, his eyes skimming both of them. "Fates, you've both grown even taller!"

That was doubtful, but Desfan still smiled as he clasped the man's shoulder.

Avao Tarn had been a fixture in Desfan's life from his first breath. The man had served as Farah Cassian's bodyguard, and he'd been like a grandfather to Desfan and his sisters. Through a twist of the fates, Avao hadn't been aboard the ship that had carried Desfan's mother on her final journey—it was the only reason he was still alive. And thank the fates he was. If he'd died that day, he never would have known his own grandson existed. He hadn't met Karim until the twelve-year-old boy had shown up on his doorstep, needing a home.

If Avao hadn't been alive to take Karim in, then Desfan never would have met his best friend. He couldn't even imagine what his life would be like without Karim.

Desfan grinned at Avao. "I didn't know if you'd receive the invitation. We weren't sure where to send it."

Avao's old eyes got a bit of a twinkle. "Ah, well, the fates knew I couldn't miss this. And, luckily, I was able to find passage on a ship with an excellent captain."

The next man in line stepped through the door and Desfan's lungs froze. Emotion lodged in his throat. "Captain Seveh."

The captain of the *Phoenix* smiled. "Hello, Desfan."

Seveh was as tall and thin as Desfan remembered, although he had several more gray hairs at his temples. His beard was just as short and neatly trimmed, also touched with silver. He wore his official uniform, though it was a little sea-worn.

Desfan didn't care. This man had helped pull him from the darkest part of his life. He owed Seveh for so much. Not caring who might be watching or whispering, Desfan stepped forward and embraced him, the knot in his throat growing hot.

Seveh held him tightly. His voice was a little rough as he said, "I'm sorry about your father. He was an incredible serjan—a good man."

"He was," Desfan said. Saernon Cassian had not always been a perfect father to Desfan, but he had done the best he could. In the end, that was all anyone *could* do. And if Saernon hadn't sent Desfan to sea with Seveh and Karim . . . Well, Desfan didn't want to think about what sort of man he'd be today.

When Seveh drew back, there was a sheen of moisture in his eyes. "Fates, you've grown into your own. I'm so proud of you, Desfan."

The simple words meant far more than Seveh could ever know. Desfan's chest expanded. "When I sent your invitation, I didn't think you'd be able to make it."

"Yes, well, we were on a fairly tight schedule to make it work, but we refused to miss it."

"We?" Desfan looked past Seveh and saw a good portion of his old crew peeking through the door, all of them dressed in their best.

Jershan, the first mate, scratched at his missing ear as he smiled. "I'll forgive you for not sending fancy invitations to *all* of us."

"I won't," Siv, the rigging master griped.

Desfan laughed. He greeted each man from the *Phoenix*, and he didn't even wince when Siv pounded his back with his massive hand. Their reunion in the hall was exuberant, and Desfan didn't care if people in the throne room heard the commotion.

"Little grumpy you, becoming the serjan," Jershan chuckled. "What a thought!"

Jayiv—the ship's physician—grinned. "Ah, the stories we could tell about you."

"At least wait until the feast," Desfan begged. "There will be plenty of wine, so maybe people will forget everything you say."

Jershan's eyes widened. "We're invited to the feast?"

"Of course!" Desfan lightly punched his arm. "Just don't sing any vulgar sea shanties in front of the nobles."

"There's no other kind of sea shanty," Siv huffed.

Captain Seveh cleared his throat. "Perhaps we should let Desfan get his crown, now."

The men grinned and shuffled into the throne room. Seveh was the last to leave, and he gave Desfan a final approving nod before following his crew.

Avao remained with them, a frown on his face as he looked at Karim. "What's wrong with your leg?"

"Nothing," Karim said.

Avao looked to Desfan, and he felt compelled to answer. "He got hit with a crossbow bolt last night."

Karim glared. "I'm perfectly fine."

Concern flooded Avao's face, but before he could say anything, Serai Yahri stepped out of the throne room. She wore her ceremonial council robes and the green fabric shimmered with gold thread. Her cane tapped the stone floor as she approached. "Avao," she greeted, her voice uncharacteristically warm.

"Amna," he returned with unmistakable affection, along with a slight bow.

Karim blinked.

Desfan's mouth twitched.

Yahri looked to Desfan. "We're running behind. Finish your greetings quickly."

He nodded, because arguing with Yahri wasn't worth it.

Yahri turned to Avao. "Will you escort me?"

"It would be my honor." He stepped forward, though he did pause beside Desfan. His voice was a low whisper as he asked, "Is he all right?"

"He will be," Desfan returned, just as quietly.

Avao's mouth thinned, but he let it go. Then his voice dropped further. "I would speak to you privately when you have a free moment. Without Karim."

Desfan's eyebrows pulled together, curiosity pricking him. "Of course."

"Thank you." Avao turned to Yahri and offered his arm.

As they walked away, Karim frowned at Desfan. "What were you whispering about?"

"I'm not sure." It wasn't exactly a lie, since Avao had told him nothing.

Before Karim could press, the next person stepped forward to greet Desfan.

The throne room was filled near to bursting. The glowing sun slanted through the tall windows that were opened to the sea breeze and the wraparound balcony that edged the elegant room.

The coronation ritual was long, and Desfan's mind wandered. Not aimlessly, though. As he stood before the crowded throne room, listening to Yahri recite the ceremonial words, he felt the stirrings of old doubts and fears. He remembered past mistakes and shames.

He wasn't worthy to wear his father's crown. He was a failure. A pretender.

He'd been focused on so many other things leading up to this moment, he hadn't actually considered what he was about to do. He was about to swear oaths to Mortise. He was about to sit on that throne, until the day he died. Every breath he took for the rest of his life would be as the serjan. Everyone in this room would be looking to him. War was coming, and he would be expected to lead, to have all the right answers. And if he failed, people would die. Fates, even if he *succeeded*, people would die. The magnitude of what he was about to do terrified him.

Then he looked out over the room. He saw Avao. Razan. Seveh, and the rest of his old crew. He saw Serene, watching him with quiet confidence. He thought of Imara, who believed in him.

None of them viewed him with fear or doubt. All he saw was hope, pride, and joy.

Karim stood with him, closer than any bodyguard probably

ever had to a serjah about to be crowned Serjan. Yahri stood before Desfan, speaking with surprising gentleness.

In that moment, Desfan felt a warmth so intense, it brought tears to his eyes. He felt his father standing with him. He could feel his mother, almost as if she'd taken his hand. And Tally was there, and even Mia, though he knew she was not lost to him in the same way. His family surrounded him, their presence filling the room.

He was not alone.

When Yahri asked if he would serve his people unfailingly, he swore he would.

When she asked if his reign would be fair and just, he made a promise to everyone in that room—and beyond it—that it would be so.

And when she asked if he would give his life, breath, blood, and soul to Mortise, he vowed he would.

Yahri asked him to kneel, then she placed the heavy crown on his head.

When Desfan rose and faced the applauding crowd, he did so as Serjan Desfan Saernon Cassian, Ruler and Caretaker of Mortise.

CHAPTER 8

SERENE

THE FEAST TO MARK DESFAN'S CORONATION WAS more celebratory than Serene would have imagined, considering it had only been last night that many of the people in this room had been attacked. But the people of Mortise, she was coming to realize, were resilient. And they rarely let anything interfere with a good party.

Serene sat at Desfan's side during the meal, though they barely had a chance to talk. And once the meal concluded, the nobles began to mingle.

She didn't feel like talking to anyone. She was exhausted after sitting beside Imara for most of last night, and she was anxious to check on her cousin again.

Around her thumb, she twisted a simple silver ring. It had belonged to Dirk. She had never learned the story of its significance; she'd never bothered to ask him where he'd gotten it, or why he always wore it, and he'd never shared. Dirk had been private, but unfailingly kind.

Fates, she missed him. It felt like she'd been missing him for an eternity already, but he'd only been gone for a month. He'd been her bodyguard since her birth, and the grief of his loss was a constant weight on her heart. It was a familiar pain, reminiscent of what she'd felt when she'd lost her mother. From that experience, she knew the pain would never truly end; time simply dulled it sometimes, allowing life to creep back in. But the loss was always there. The grief became a part of you.

From across the room, Desfan stole a glance at her. Concern was in his gaze, as well as a silent question.

A part of her remained upset with him for letting Grayson out of prison. Liam and Grayson were responsible for Dirk's death, and she didn't think she could find peace until both Rydenic princes paid for what they'd done. But she didn't blame Desfan for doing whatever he deemed necessary to save his sister, even if that meant sending the Black Hand to rescue her.

Justice would wait for Grayson—if he ever came back.

Desfan was still watching her.

Serene shook her head a little and forced a smile. It felt thin, but the new serjan must have accepted it, because he didn't leave his conversation with Serai Essa and Ser Anoush.

Serene was proud of Desfan. He'd been undeniably hand-some and regal during his coronation, and the throne room had hummed with charged energy. When he'd spoken his vows, his words were full of strength, hope, and duty. Any doubts she'd once harbored about Desfan's ability to rule Mortise were laid to rest in that moment. He would be a good monarch; perhaps even a great one. She was lucky to be engaged to him. She knew that.

She just didn't feel it.

Her attention wandered to Cardon, who stood near her. He was observing the room, his gaze intent. His brown hair was neatly arranged, and his dark blue uniform fit his sculpted body perfectly. A pale scar cut diagonally across his right cheek, and it caught her eye as it always did. Not because it was an imperfection—it wasn't—but because it reminded her of the day so long ago that they'd saved each other. She'd been fourteen, but her young heart had fallen into his hands that day.

He just hadn't known it at the time.

Wilf stood on her other side, and it was feeling his gaze on her that made her straighten.

She couldn't stand alone any longer, and she certainly couldn't allow herself to stare at Cardon. She'd avoided even being alone with him since she and Desfan had signed the betrothal agreement, and she couldn't let herself become distracted now.

So, even though she didn't feel like approaching anyone, Serene surveyed the room. Spotting Tamar Nadir, she moved forward with Cardon and Wilf trailing behind her.

The middle-aged Mortisian woman looked beautiful as always as she sipped a glass of wine in the corner, overlooking the festivities. When Serene reached her, Tamar dipped into a curtsy. "Princess Serene."

"Serai Nadir," Serene greeted, following the woman's lead in the formalities, since it was a formal occasion. Despite that, they'd become friends while staying at the widow's manor, and on their journey to Duvan. "I hope you're well," Serene added.

Tamar's smile was a little strained. "As well as I can be."

Serene's heart felt suddenly heavy. Tamar and Dirk hadn't had enough time to explore the love that had been growing between them. "I'm sorry."

"So am I," Tamar said gently. "For both of us."

Serene glanced down at the ring on her thumb. She spun it once with her forefinger, then removed it and held it out to Tamar.

The woman blinked, but her confusion fled once she touched it. Holding it with her fingertips, her face softened. "Dirk's ring."

"I think he'd want you to have it," Serene said.

"This ring meant a great deal to him. I never saw him without it." Tamar fingered the silver band, moisture shining in her eyes. "This is a kind and beautiful gesture, Princess. Truly. But I cannot take this from you. He loved you so much. In many ways, you were like a daughter to him." She passed the ring back and wrapped Serene's fingers around it. Squeezing gently, she said, "Keep it. And perhaps one day, give it to your son or daughter. Let his legacy live on in the future he dedicated his life to protecting."

Serene's throat grew tight. She fisted the ring, the metal digging into her palm. "Thank you."

Tamar's smile wavered with emotion. She leaned in and pressed a kiss to Serene's forehead. It was an almost motherly gesture, and Serene hadn't felt that kind of comfort or affection in far too long.

As Serene slipped the ring back onto her thumb, Tamar asked, "How is Princess Imara?"

"Awake and alert. We don't know yet how lasting the damage

will be."

Tamar sighed. "There have been too many tragedies lately." Her eyes drifted across the room, and she almost smiled. "I'm glad today was a victory."

Serene followed her gaze and found Desfan had moved away from the two council members, and he was now laughing with a group of his sailor friends.

One of Desfan's greatest strengths seemed to be his personable nature. Whether he was talking to sailors or high-ranking nobles, he seemed perfectly at ease.

As Serene watched, one of the sailors linked arms with Desfan and Karim and began belting out a song. The man sang horribly off-key, but Desfan joined in almost at once, and the other crewmembers followed suit. Karim—after a shake from Desfan—began to sing as well.

Serene and Tamar weren't the only ones looking on as the new serjan sang with his old crew. And, Serene was pleased to note, she didn't see any looks of disapproval. Then again, she didn't see Serai Yahri.

Razan moved to stand on Tamar's other side, her lips twitching as she followed their gazes to the singing men.

Desfan was grinning, and even Karim was smiling now. Fates, the bodyguard was handsome. He should smile more.

Tamar looked at Razan. "How goes your attempt to win back the illusive Karim Safar?"

Razan lifted one slim shoulder, which sent a ripple through the shimmering fabric of her scarlet sari. "Progress seems to come and go like a wave."

The men hit an excruciatingly high note, and several nobles winced.

Razan chuckled. "Considering the fact he's singing, Desfan

probably convinced him to drink something, which means I might make a little more progress tonight."

Serene had seen some of the interplay between Razan and Karim since the woman had arrived in Duvan. She'd been recently appointed to the Mortisian council, and it had quickly become clear that she and Karim had a history. Serene didn't know their full story, just that they'd met years ago, and they hadn't parted on good terms.

"I thought you were making real progress after that dance you shared at Eyrinthia's Ball," Tamar said to Razan.

Serene's cheeks warmed as she recalled that night. She was suddenly very aware of Cardon, though he hadn't moved any closer.

"That dance wasn't quite as loving as it may have looked," Razan said, a bit dryly.

Tamar laughed. "Oh, he looked quite angry. But then, so did you. And any dance with high emotion is interesting, at the very least."

"I suppose you're right," Razan admitted. "It was . . . interesting."

Serene met Razan's gaze. "What exactly is keeping you apart, if I may ask?"

She bit the inside of her cheek. "It's quite a long story. The important parts are, years ago I found myself on the *Phoenix* with Karim and Desfan. Karim and I grew quite close. The only problem was, I betrayed him and Desfan."

Serene's eyes rounded.

Razan nodded. "I'm sure that comes as a surprise, considering everything."

Yes, like the fact Desfan had appointed her to the council.

The Mortisian woman fingered the long stem of her glass.

"I didn't think I had a choice at the time, but my betrayal put them both in danger. Desfan forgave me. Karim did not."

"He cares for you," Tamar said. "Anyone can see it."

"Except for him," Razan muttered.

"Oh, he's perfectly aware of how he feels. That's probably what has him so tied in knots." Tamar patted Razan's arm. "He'll come around. Just keep trying."

Razan blew out a slow breath. "It's hard to face his continual derision and dismissals."

"Love can overcome any obstacle, and it is worth any headache or heartache." Tamar's soft words rang with sincerity and experience. The woman had lost a husband, but she had still opened her heart to Dirk—only to lose him, too. The fact that she could say those words—feel them so deeply—was a testament to her strength.

One of Desfan's sailors called out for Razan to join them in singing, and the young woman moved to do so.

Behind Serene, the air stirred, then Cardon's voice was at her ear. "I was just told the physician is on his way to see Imara, if you'd like to be present for his visit."

His soft breath warmed her skin, and the memory of his mouth on hers made her fight a shiver.

If only love *could* overcome any obstacle.

She said her goodbyes to Tamar, then turned to see Cardon hadn't moved back. The long scar on his cheek jumped as his jaw clenched.

She realized belatedly that he must have heard every word of their conversation, and it was beyond obvious that his thoughts had wandered to their stolen kiss on the beach as well. She'd run from the ball that night, and Cardon had chased her—then he'd kissed her senseless. They hadn't spoken of it since that night.

Thankfully, they couldn't discuss it now, because Wilf stood only slightly behind Cardon.

As they walked to Imara's room, Serene asked Wilf about Clare. Her friend had lost so much since becoming her decoy; it was heartbreaking to see her lose her little brothers as well. There was love between Clare, Thomas, and Mark—unlike Serene's relationship with her own brother. Grandeur was threatened by her, and probably wanted her dead. There were times she missed the boy she'd grown up with. The little brother who had followed her around the garden, or begged to play with her in the nursery. But after everything that had happened—everything he'd done and *not* done—she didn't know if she would truly mourn his death. Certainly not like Clare mourned her brothers.

Something about that broke her heart.

They reached Imara's suite, and the Zennorian princess's guards allowed them in. Serene proceeded into her cousin's bedroom, leaving Cardon and Wilf in the sitting room.

The physician was talking to Imara in low tones when Serene entered the room. Imara looked far too tired, and the physician appeared concerned.

They both looked up as Serene stepped toward them. "What's wrong?" she demanded.

"Nothing," Imara said at once. "He's only telling me what *might* be wrong, but nothing is actually, currently, wrong."

"You were stabbed," Serene said, folding her arms as she reached the side of the bed. "That was decidedly wrong."

"Princess Imara is correct," the royal physician said, a bit gently. "I was merely preparing her for some of what she might face during her recovery." He turned back to Imara.

"The important thing is to not overdo anything, especially at this stage. You must follow my advice and give your body time to heal."

"Thank you," Imara said with a smile. "I'll heed your advice."

The physician smiled in return. Fates, no one could withstand Imara's sweetness—and the Zennorian princess knew it. Sometimes, she used it as a fates-blasted weapon.

When the physician excused himself, Serene settled into the chair beside Imara's bed. "What exactly did he say?" she asked, crossing one knee over the other as she leaned back.

Imara lifted an eyebrow. "You're doing your *imperious Serene* again."

"Imara."

Her cousin sighed and glanced toward the ceiling. "Fine. He said I may struggle to walk for the rest of my life—or not walk again at all."

Serene's lungs stopped working.

Imara's chin dropped, and she picked at a loose thread on her quilt. "He also said I could be fine, with barely a limp. We won't know until we know, so there's no point worrying about it."

Serene reached out and took her cousin's hand. "I'm sorry."

Imara shrugged, not looking at her. Then she tightened her hold on Serene's long fingers. "So," she said, her tone a little brighter. "How was the coronation?"

"It was very nice, actually."

"No one died, then?"

Serene's mouth twitched. "No."

"Good." Imara eyed her. "How does Desfan seem? Is he all right?"

"Yes. He actually seemed quite happy today."

"Good. I'm glad."

Something about her tone was wrong. Serene frowned. "Are you all right?"

Imara took a slow breath, not looking at her as she released her hand. Looking at the quilt in her lap, she said, "I kissed him."

Serene blinked. "What?"

Imara blushed, but she managed to peek over at Serene. "Last night, when we hid in the pantry, I . . . well, he kissed me. But I kissed him back. I think. Or maybe I didn't, and I just didn't stop him. It all happened so fast, I'm not sure."

Serene stared, unsure of what to think—what to feel.

Imara bit her lower lip, waiting.

Serene kept staring.

Her cousin's mouth pressed into a line. "Desfan," she said pointedly. "I'm talking about *Desfan*. Your betrothed? The man who just became serjan—"

"I know who you meant, I'm just . . . surprised." But maybe she shouldn't have been. Imara and Desfan had become friends quickly. She'd seen how at ease they were with each other, how frequently they exchanged smiles and confidences. She just hadn't realized her cousin had developed feelings for him, but it was clear she had. And—obviously—Desfan felt something, too.

"I'm so blind," she breathed.

"It didn't mean anything," Imara said in a rush. "Fates, how could it? It was just the moment. Both of us nearly died. Our emotions were high. He just leaned in and kissed me, and I—I really do think I may have kissed him back. But we were interrupted by Karim and Razan." She threw up her free hand in a staying gesture. "I promise, they didn't see anything. This will stay between us. There won't be any scandal—"

"Imara, I'm not mad," she said, interrupting the frantic spill of words.

Now it was Imara's turn to stare. "You're . . . not?"

"No." She wasn't sure why she was unbothered. Maybe because she didn't love Desfan. Or maybe it was because she loved Imara, and she wanted her cousin to be happy. It could have also been the fact that she'd kissed Cardon the night before her engagement to Desfan had become official—and, even now, she was desperate to kiss Cardon again.

She fiddled with the silver bracelet on her wrist. It was the hidden garrote Cardon had given to her for her fourteenth birthday, mere weeks after they'd saved each other's lives during a hunting trip that had taken a dangerous turn. Even though she'd been young, she'd started to fall in love with him that day.

Imara released a slow, tense breath, pulling Serene from her thoughts. "You're really not mad?" Imara asked, obviously disbelieving.

"No," Serene assured her.

Imara's eyes narrowed. "If I were engaged to marry Desfan Cassian and *you* kissed him, I'd probably slap you."

Serene's lips tugged into a smile. "Maybe that's because you actually have feelings for him."

Imara groaned and covered her face with both hands. "Fates," she muttered. "It won't happen again. I swear it. And I'll leave. As soon as I'm able. In fact, I'll have someone carry me out of here tonight—"

"You'll do no such thing. The physician said you need to stay in bed and not overdo anything."

Imara dropped her hands to blink at Serene. "How are you

so fates-blasted calm?"

"I'm not calm, I'm just not overreacting."

"Overreacting? You think I'm overreacting? You do realize I tried to tell you about this first thing this morning, only I thought—no, better to tell Desfan that you're going to *tell* Serene. That way, he'll be duly warned and prepared to face her wrath. Then I see Desfan, and I think—no, better just tell *Serene*, because talking to him about what happened is completely *mortifying*. So I needed to just find the courage and tell you."

Serene arched one eyebrow. "Am I really so terrifying?"

Imara snorted. "You know very well that you're terrifying."

She almost smiled. "So you haven't talked to Desfan about this?"

"No." She suddenly looked wary. "You're not going to march out there and confront him, are you?"

"No." Serene leaned forward, once again taking Imara's hand. "And I want you to forgive yourself. You're clearly berating yourself far more than I ever could."

"But—"

"I trust you completely, Imara. If you say you aren't going to kiss him again, you won't."

Imara's throat bobbed as she swallowed. "I won't."

Something in her quiet voice made Serene's heart clench, and she had to swallow back the question that wanted to surface. *Do you want to kiss him again?*

Serene didn't need to ask. Imara's feelings on the matter were painfully obvious; she hadn't even denied Serene's earlier comment about having feelings for Desfan.

"Will you do me a favor?" Imara asked quietly.

"Of course."

"Don't ever tell Skyer that I kissed Desfan."

Serene didn't know what she'd expected, but it wasn't that. And she didn't like the subtle fear in those words. "You still haven't told me enough about your betrothed," she muttered. The little Serene did know about him, she didn't really like. Imara had told her that Eilan Skyer was the leader of the Kabu Clan, one of the nomadic tribes in Zennor. His title was Warrior, and he had challenged his own father in order to become the clan leader. One of his titles was Sky Painter, because he painted the overhead trees—or the jungle's "sky"—with the blood of his enemies.

Not exactly the sort of person she could picture Imara marrying.

Her cousin glanced away. "It doesn't matter."

"Your happiness matters," Serene countered.

"I need to marry him. Things in Zennor . . ." She peeked at Serene. "They're worse than I've let on."

Imara had never looked so serious, and that alone made Serene tense. "Explain."

The Zennorian princess let out a slow exhale. "If the monarchy and the clans don't reach an understanding, Zennor could very well face civil war. Things are that tense. I should never have left, only . . . I needed to see you. I needed to have this last adventure, before I married Skyer. But as soon as my leg is healed, I need to return to Zennor. It's time for me to go home. Especially now . . ."

Her words drifted, but Serene understood. Now that Imara was developing feelings for Desfan, she couldn't stay.

Serene ground her teeth. "I hate this," she said.

A furrow pinched Imara's eyebrows. "What?"

"This entire situation. The fact that you have to marry a

stranger who clearly unnerves you. That Desfan and I . . ."

Imara said nothing into the silence. Not for a long moment. Then, "Desfan will make a wonderful husband, Serene. You will both be happy. I know it."

"What about you? Will you be happy?"

Imara smiled, and it was perhaps the weakest smile Serene had ever seen on her cousin's face. "Haven't you heard? Princess Imara is always happy."

CHAPTER 9

MIA

"THAT VILE WOMAN," FLETCHER GROUND OUT. "That horrible, evil *snake*—"

"Please stop," Devon cut in.

Mia sat on the edge of Grayson's bed, her head aching and her right hand throbbing. The spikes of pain had passed with time. Now, it was a dull agony, and her hand felt double its normal size. She'd been stung eight times by the scorpion. The pincers had cut into the skin of her thumb and middle finger. Fletcher had had to tear the thing off her.

Tingling had set in around each sting mark, but Devon assured her that wasn't a bad sign. Neither was the numbness or the fact that her heart still pounded, even hours later.

She wasn't sure if her head ached from the scorpion venom, or the faersin the queen had poisoned her with. Thank the fates her semi-paralysis and that sick need to please the queen had seemed to wear off quickly, once she wasn't breathing in the tainted flowers. The strange veil that had clouded her mind lifted soon after she was safely in Grayson's room, and the horror that had been dulled was exposed in full force.

She'd panicked, and Devon had held the salts to her nose and coaxed her to breathe through the attack, which lasted an eternity. She didn't think it was just because of her disturbing tea with the Poison Queen, but everything else as well. Her past coming back to haunt her. Grayson's torture—her help-lessness as he'd screamed. Being in the same room as Grayson and Tyrell when their hatred was enough to strangle the air in her lungs. Their desperate plan to escape. To go to a *ship* that would take her to Mortise—to Desfan.

You're barely worth anything to Mortise now . . . You wouldn't even know how to fit in there, would you? . . . You're broken, Meerah . . . You're no longer the person you were born to be . . . Your brother, certainly, would be better off without you.

The words felt jumbled in her mind. Were they her own thoughts? Or had Iris said those things? Fates, so much of their conversation was muddled. Missing. But the ache she felt was heart-crushingly real.

You're broken, Meerah.

Devon stayed with her through the entirety of her panic. His soothing voice and compassionate touch steadied her, and finally her panic eased. He treated the scorpion stings as best he could. He'd laid a bandage with ointment around her hand, and then periodically peeled it back to inspect the swelling.

At the moment, a slight frown pulled at Devon's mouth, his focus on her hand even though he'd just spoken to Fletcher. *Please stop.*

Mia peered at her old guard, who continued to pace the

room, his fury still white-hot. "You don't understand," he growled at the physician. "The queen is a fates-blasted—"

"Stop," Devon said again. "Or I'll ask you to leave."

Fletcher bristled. "You didn't see what she did to—"

"I know what she did." Devon's gaze lifted from Mia's hand, and for the first time she realized the physician's calm was not deep. His voice might be carefully measured, his ministrations gentle, but his eyes blazed as he looked at Fletcher. "I hate the queen for what she did. But your words aren't attacking her, they're agitating Mia, and that needs to stop."

Fletcher's mouth clamped shut. He looked to Mia, and his shoulders dropped. "I'm sorry."

Her tongue slid over her dry lips. "It's all right."

The old guard's face crumpled. "Fates, it's not all right. She hurt you. She made you hurt yourself. I should have moved faster. She walked out without you, and I . . . I knew something was wrong. She told me you were just finishing your tea . . ."

"It's not your fault."

Her tea with the Poison Queen had been horrific. Far worse than anything she could have imagined when she first got the summons. The scorpion hadn't even been the worst part. It had been the weight in her chest—the burning need to please Iris. She didn't think she'd betrayed Grayson in any way, or told the queen of their plan to escape, but . . . Faersin was terrifyingly potent. She'd been completely malleable, left vulnerable to Iris's non-existent mercy. The mere memory made her shudder.

"Rena will be back soon with some food," Devon said softly, cradling Mia's palm as he draped the bandage over the back of her hand. "Having something to eat will help you settle. Are you still feeling the effects of the faersin?" Devon had known

123

the drug, once Mia had been able to tell him what the queen had used on her.

"I don't think so," Mia said. "I just have a headache."

"I have something that will ease that. I didn't want you to take anything while the faersin was still clouding your head, but it should be all right now."

Mia gratefully accepted the medicine, and after she swallowed it down, she regarded Devon. "When Grayson returns, can you please help him?" She quickly explained about the cut on his jaw, as well as the burn made by Flame's Breath. "His father told him not to seek treatment unless infection set in," Mia admitted. "I . . . hoped you might check on him anyway."

Devon's eyes were clouded, but he nodded. "Of course."

"What's going to be next?" Fletcher muttered. "Grayson is being tortured. The queen might have killed you. This place isn't safe. It never has been, but this is madness."

Mia pursed her lips. She'd promised Grayson that she wouldn't ave this conversation without him present. But . . .

She cleared her throat and said softly, "It's only going to get worse."

"Why do you say that?" Devon asked, at the same time Fletcher said, "It's because Grayson is back."

Mia shook her head. "No, it's because of who I am."

"Because of who you are to Grayson?" Fletcher tried to clarify.

She exhaled slowly. "That's only a part of it."

Wariness entered Devon's eyes. "Perhaps you shouldn't say anything more. I don't think the king would—"

"I'm leaving," Mia said. "Grayson and I are leaving. And I'd like both of you—and Rena—to come with us."

Devon pulled back a little.

Fletcher stilled.

The silence was strained, and Mia swallowed with difficulty. "I want you to come with us. We could use your help."

"There is no escaping this castle," Fletcher said, his voice a bare whisper—as if he feared even the walls might hear them. "Mia, even if you're not in a cell anymore, you're still very much a prisoner—"

"Arrangements have been made," she cut in. "We're leaving."

Devon's brow creased. "Where would you go? Nowhere in Ryden would be safe."

"There's a ship waiting for us. It will take us to Mortise."

"Fates, no." Fletcher took a step back, his hands lifting, his posture almost defensive. "You need to stop talking about this. We'll be executed for even *knowing* this—"

"Only if you stay," Mia said.

Devon's shoulders tensed. "Or if we're caught."

She dipped her chin, allowing that. "But the longer we all stay, the more likely we are to be hurt—or killed." She looked to Fletcher. "You have been a loyal guard and friend. Henri knows this. If I go, you will be punished. You know that."

Terror flickered across his lined face. "You're giving us no choice."

"I know. And I'm sorry. But I don't want to leave you here. I don't want your lives on my conscience."

"Grayson didn't want you to tell us this," Fletcher guessed slowly. "This is a risk for you—he wouldn't have condoned that."

"He was reluctant at first," Mia admitted. "And he wanted to tell you himself, but . . . I know you need time to consider."

Devon lifted one sardonic eyebrow. "Can we refuse? I have a feeling the Black Hand won't appreciate that."

"I won't let him hurt you. I know that, even if you don't choose to come with us, you won't betray us."

Devon exchanged a look with Fletcher.

The older man looked torn. "Mortise . . . It's a mad idea. What sort of life could we carve out there?"

"You would stay with me." Mia's heart suddenly pounded.

Fletcher huffed out a rough breath. "We'll all be fugitives—you and Grayson especially."

"I promise you would be safe with me."

"We'll starve," Fletcher argued. "Mortisians have no love for anything from Ryden—especially its people. We probably wouldn't even be able to find employment, or—"

"You would find employment," she said, voice growing more emphatic. "With *me*."

Fletcher's sigh was sharp. "Mia, you don't understand. You've been a prisoner all your life, but—"

"You will live with me at the palace in Duvan."

Fletcher stared.

Devon blinked. "What?"

Mia took a breath, her pulse racing. "My brother is Serjah Desfan Saernon Cassian. He might even be the serjan by now. He will offer a place to you, I'm sure of it. Or gold, if you would rather go elsewhere."

"The Mortisian prince is . . . your *brother*?" Fletcher sounded strangled.

Her fingers twisted in her skirt, her voice wavering a little. "I am Meerah Jema Cassian." The words fell flat. Probably because she wasn't sure if she *was* Meerah anymore.

Meerah is dead.

She shifted her weight on the bed, uncomfortable with the echoing thought. Her gaze dropped to her covered hand.

"I'm the last surviving seraijah of Mortise," she said, her voice quieter than before.

The room was utterly silent.

She could think of nothing else to say, so even though the silence was blistering, she kept her lips pressed together.

Nothing happened for several long moments, until Fletcher rasped out, "We're all dead."

She shot him a look, surprised by the raw edge in his voice. "What do you mean?"

"Mia, if you escape . . . if you return home . . ." Fletcher's eyes were a little wild, his face horribly pale. "Your brother will retaliate. There will be a war. Rydenic families will be slaughtered. And we certainly won't be welcomed into the castle—he'll kill us for assisting in your imprisonment."

"Desfan wouldn't do that." But hesitation gripped her. The last time she had seen her brother, he was eleven years old. Who knew who he was now, or what he would do? Certainly not her. She tried to set that fear and doubt aside. "I wouldn't allow any harm to come to you. You have protected me, and you would have aided in my return. You'll be rewarded."

Fletcher shook his head. "That's not how anyone would see it. I've been your prison guard for nine years—not your bodyguard."

"That's not how I see it."

He grimaced, his eyes uncharacteristically hard. "I never stopped them, Mia. I heard the beatings they gave you in the beginning, and I never spoke out. I stood on the other side of that door, and I ignored your cries for help."

Devon looked away, his body tense.

Fletcher was shaking. His words were a little hoarse as he said, "You were an innocent child, and I was too afraid to help you. I was a coward, and because of that, you suffered."

Her chest burned. "Fletcher, you couldn't have done anything. If you had interfered with the king's orders, you would have been killed."

"Yes," he rasped, the sound full of desperate agreement. "But I would have *done* something. Instead, I listened to your pain—your fear—and I did nothing."

"I don't blame you."

He choked on a hoarse laugh. "Of course you don't. You always think the best of those around you. You imagine our hands have been tied, but I held a key. No brother could overlook that. I am an enemy to him, in every conceivable way. I am *your* enemy. And yet you don't admit it, even to yourself. You see me as a victim. You see *everyone* as a victim. You love Grayson, for fates' sake!"

She flinched.

Fletcher was not done. "We can't go to Mortise. We'll be arrested. And if you return, a war will come—"

"There will be a war anyway," Devon interrupted. His gaze was firmly on Fletcher now, his expression grim. "We all know the king's great war is coming. But we have a chance to be on the right side of it. To do the right thing—finally, after all these years." The physician turned his attention to Mia, and she could read so many regrets in his eyes. "I will do anything I can to help you."

She reached out with her good hand and squeezed one of his. "Thank you."

Emotion rippled across his face. He stood, letting her hand slip away. He sank to his knees in front of her and bowed his head. "Your Highness," he whispered, his tone almost reverent.

Mia hadn't expected that. She wasn't sure how to react. Her cheeks warmed.

"Please don't," she said, her voice thick. "There's no need to do that."

Devon's head lifted, though he remained on his knees. "There is every need. You are the first royal I have ever wanted to kneel before."

Her eyes misted. "Thank you." The words were inadequate, but they were all she had.

The corner of Devon's mouth rose. "You have my loyalty, Princess."

From the corner of her eye, she saw Fletcher fall to his knees. He bent his entire body, his head bowed so low his forehead touched the floor.

Mia slid off the edge of the bed and dropped onto her knees in front of him. She was careful not to jostle her injured hand, but her other fingers stretched out to rest on his hunched shoulder.

He shuddered at her light touch.

Her heart clenched. "Please look at me, Fletcher."

"I can't."

He sounded so miserable. Her hold tightened. "I don't blame you. I never have."

"I blame myself."

"Then help me now," she begged. "Let me help *you*. Let's all leave this awful place behind."

Slowly, his head lifted. Tears shone in his eyes, and his chin wavered before he said, "I will speak with Rena, but I know she'll want to go with you."

The tightness in her chest loosened. "You'll come with me?"

His expression solemn, as if he were swearing fealty. "Yes, Mia. I will come with you."

Rena arrived not long after with a tray of food. Mia would have ignored the roasted potatoes, braised chicken, green beans, and still-warm rolls, but Devon insisted she eat.

They settled in the corner of the room, where Mia and Rena sat in the only two arm chairs. Devon fetched the wooden chair from Grayson's desk and offered it to Fletcher. The older man waved it away, choosing instead to stand beside his wife's chair.

While Mia ate, Rena was caught up on events. She was startled to learn the truth about Mia, but she wasn't resistant to the idea of leaving. "There's nothing for us here anymore," she said to her husband. "Not if Mia is gone. Not since we lost Thane . . ."

Fletcher's face tightened at the mention of their son, who had died years ago as a soldier. Fletcher nodded once, and the decision was final.

Devon and the Fletchers looked to Mia, like she was a monarch, and they were ready for a command.

Her mouth dried, responsibility suddenly weighing heavily on her shoulders. "We'll need to pack lightly," she said, repeating Grayson's words. "We'll be traveling to—"

"Don't tell us which port," Fletcher cut in. "We already know enough. You can tell us where we're going right before we leave."

It seemed like a wise precaution—one Grayson would probably have thought to take. It made her wonder if she should wait for him, but time seemed so limited, and the Fletchers and Devon were eager to hear the plan.

Forcing aside self-doubt, Mia began to share the ideas she and Grayson had discussed. Rena believed it would be easy enough to secure warm clothing and extra blankets from the laundry. "With how quickly the weather's turned," the older woman said, "no one will think anything of it."

Mia asked Fletcher about securing horses from the stable, and he nodded. "I can tell the stable hands that Rena and I are going into Lenzen to visit friends."

She wished she could ask Fletcher to take Grayson's horse from the royal stable, but that would be impossible; the old guard wouldn't be allowed to take a horse that belonged to a Kaelin prince. Even so, she hated to leave the animal behind. She'd visited him frequently in Grayson's absence, and he'd helped soothe the ache in her heart.

Devon spoke, interrupting her thoughts. "That will only get us two horses. We need five."

"We can purchase more in Lenzen," Fletcher said. "Grayson has coin—he gave me some before he left for Mortise . . ."

The plan continued to pull together as they talked. Mia almost mentioned that the plan was to leave tomorrow night, but she held back. Not because she didn't trust them, but because she honestly wasn't sure if it would happen. Grayson had been adamant about leaving then, but fates only knew what he'd had to do today, or how that might impact things.

Besides, precautions weren't a bad idea, even if she trusted everyone in the room.

Time passed, and Devon lit a small fire in the nearby fireplace as the room began to grow chilly with the oncoming night.

They were still discussing preparations when the door

opened and Grayson walked in. Weariness dragged at his shoulders and tension lined his expression. The burn on his jaw looked even darker and angrier than it had this morning. He paused when he saw Fletcher, Devon, and Rena in the room. A level of alertness flashed back into his gray eyes. Then he saw Mia, and his attention narrowed on the cloth bandage that enfolded her right hand.

He muttered a curse and strode across the room. "What happened?" he demanded.

"I'm fine," she told him.

Fletcher made a sound in his throat.

Grayson crouched in front of her, one gloved palm landing on her knee. The firelight danced across the unmarred side of his face, throwing shadows across the dips and hollows of his face. It only added to the intensity of his expression.

"I'm not in any danger." She spoke quickly, because it looked like he was ready to tear the room apart.

Devon's attention was riveted on Grayson's burn. "Fates," he breathed.

Grayson's only focus was Mia. "What happened?" he repeated, more darkly this time. The tendons in his neck stood out starkly and a muscle in his cheek jumped.

She supposed her words hadn't managed to calm him at all.

While she struggled for words, Grayson looked to Devon, his glare a silent command.

Devon's throat flexed as he swallowed. "She had tea with your mother."

Grayson's entire body locked. His gaze swung back to Mia, his voice rough and furious. "What did she do?"

Mia sighed. She looked over his tightly coiled shoulder. "Could you all leave us for a moment?"

They all stood. "We'll just be in the hall," Fletcher said.

Mia thanked them softly.

After they'd filed out and closed the door, she used her good hand to cup Grayson's unmarred cheek. His skin was hot to the touch. Almost feverish. Her heart broke. "Grayson . . ."

He set his hand over hers, pressing her palm to his face. "Please," he said. "Tell me what my mother did."

"I need you to be calm."

"I am calm."

He was *not* calm. He thrummed with barely banked rage and fear.

She had thought this would be easier if they were alone, but her throat felt horribly thick. The stings on her hand flared with remembered pain, and she fought back a wince.

She forced herself to take a breath, then she told him what had happened—everything she could remember, at least. The queen's invitation that had really been an order, and how she hadn't touched anything at the table, or had anything to eat or drink. Then she told him about the faersin, and the harsh lines of his face grew harder.

"I don't think I said anything that would hurt you," she said in a rush. "I would never betray you, Grayson."

He shifted her palm to his lips and kissed the base of her thumb gently. "I know," he murmured against her skin. "You were brave. Perfect. But what else did she do?"

Haltingly, she told him about the scorpion in the box.

Grayson's expression was strained. Fire burned in his eyes. He pulled off his black gloves and slowly—with infinite gentleness—peeled back the edge of her bandage. When her swollen hand was revealed, his breath hitched.

"It doesn't really hurt anymore," she said. "It's just sore.

Devon said the swelling should be much better by morning."

"*Fates*." His strained voice cracked against the curse.

She decided not to mention the panic attack she'd had afterward.

She shifted her hand into his hair, her fingers threading through the dark locks. "I'm all right," she told him. Soothing him somehow loosened the vice around her chest, and she breathed a little easier. "I'm all right," she repeated. "It's nothing." Nothing compared to what had been done to him.

"It's not nothing." He hadn't looked away from her swollen hand. His scarred fingers trembled above her reddened skin, but he didn't touch her. There was really nowhere *to* touch; the entire back of her hand was covered in the scorpion stings. "She was supposed to be my ally," he ground out, fury threading his voice. "She thinks I killed Liam for her. She shouldn't have done this to you."

"I don't think your mother is a very predictable person." She bit her lower lip. "How are you feeling?"

He stiffened, but his motions were extremely careful as he replaced the bandage on her hand. "I'm fine."

"The burn looks bad."

He winced.

She mentally cursed her poor choice of words. "It looks painful. Maybe infected. Devon is right outside. Your father did say you could see a physician if it got infected."

"Maybe later. We need to talk first."

She didn't like the tenor of those words. "What's happened?"

Grayson scrubbed the back of his neck, and the motion dislodged her hand from his hair. She let it fall to her lap. "My father took us to a nearby barracks," he began.

And the horror of the day continued.

Grayson told her everything he could about what he'd seen and heard at Northland Barracks, saying they both needed to remember every detail so Desfan could be told.

The picture he painted . . . those boys. That army. Henri's plans.

"He told my brothers about you," Grayson said softly. "Who you really are."

The revelation that all the Kaelins knew about her was unsettling, but she could tell there was more. "What else did he say?"

"He's pitted Tyrell and me against each other. Whoever serves him best gets you, and the Mortisian throne."

She felt the blood drain from her face.

Grayson took her hand, squeezing gently. "It doesn't matter. We're not going to be a part of this. We leave tomorrow night."

Her spine straightened sharply. "Oh, fates, the supplies. I never got them from Tyrell's room. I can go now—"

"No," Grayson cut in. "Not tonight. Please, I just . . . I need you right here. With me."

She didn't have the heart to argue with him. And, frankly, she was exhausted. She didn't want to leave this room—or him.

She nodded toward the closed door, where Devon, Fletcher, and Rena had vanished. "I told them the truth about me," she admitted. "And about our plan to escape."

Grayson sighed. "When I saw them all in here, I thought you might have."

"I'm sorry I didn't wait. I didn't tell them when we planned to leave, though, or where the ship is waiting."

"That's good. But I need to question them. I need to hear for myself that they won't betray us."

"I understand." And she did, even though she knew Devon and the Fletchers wouldn't betray them.

The fire crackled in the hearth beside them, and the comforting sounds somehow amplified the silence that had fallen.

Grayson watched her, still crouched before her. Too many emotions churned in his gray eyes, impossible to interpret. But just his nearness affected her, as it always had. Her heart beat faster, and warmth spread throughout her body.

She leaned forward, setting a kiss against the corner of his mouth, as far from the burn as she could get. Her stomach fluttered as she gave into the desire that had been building since the moment he'd walked into the room.

Grayson responded at once, shifting his mouth so it fit against hers more firmly. His lips were warm, and the most intriguing mix of hard and soft. His familiar scent—spice and pine—surrounded her, granting her a peace she felt all the way to her bones. He was her safe harbor. He always had been.

She'd fallen in love with him when they were children, but the love she felt for him now was so much more. Deeper. It was everything.

She was in love with Grayson, and she knew that would never change.

His hand settled at the curve where her neck met her shoulder, and his thumb traced against the base of her throat as he deepened the kiss, once again taking it further than she would have dared with his injuries.

Her good hand moved to the back of his neck, her fingers sinking into his soft hair. This kiss wasn't as desperate or frantic as the one they'd shared this morning. This kiss was filled only with comfort. Love.

When he eased back, his eyes were intent. "No matter what

happens, I'm going to make sure you're safe. You're going to be all right, Mia."

It was the second time that day he'd said comforting words that didn't manage to quite comfort her. This time, at least, she knew *why* she hadn't liked what he'd said.

Her grip firmed on the back of his neck. "We're *both* going to be all right."

Grayson studied her, then slowly dipped his chin. "We will be."

CHAPTER 10

GRAYSON

MORNING LIGHT CREEPED AROUND THE EDGES OF the closed drapes. Grayson had barely slept, even with the strong medication Devon had given him last night to help with the pain radiating from his jaw.

With his back flat against the bed, he glanced beside him, where Mia still slept curled on her side. She had turned toward him in the night, her bandaged hand between them on the mattress. Her rich brown hair was tousled against the pillow, and even though she still wore her dress from last night, she looked completely comfortable. Peaceful. Beautiful.

He ached to touch her cheek. To brush that stray curl from her neck. To wrap himself around her so nothing could ever hurt her.

He stayed where he was.

They had slept in the same bed before, but this time it felt

139

different. Knowing who she was . . . *Meerah Cassian*. A seraijah of Mortise. Desfan's sister. All good reasons to keep his scarred hands off of her.

But there were other reasons.

We're both going to be all right, she'd said.

We will be.

His promise had been absolute. He would be in chains when all of this was done. All that waited for him in Mortise was a cell. He also knew his execution was likely; he'd deceived Mortise, Devendra, and Zennor, even if he hadn't actually helped Liam in the end.

Mia didn't need to know any of that. Not yet. And when it was time . . . he would make sure she understood he would be fine, no matter what his fate was. Because as long as she was safe, he *would* be all right.

He'd greedily taken her offered kisses yesterday, but he shouldn't be selfish and steal more from her. Not when he knew they would eventually be separated.

He might be the Black Hand, but he was not that cruel.

So he didn't touch her. He didn't brush away that curl on her neck. He kept still on his side of the bed, and he waited for her to wake.

She did so slowly. A shift in her body. A grimace as her hand bumped against the pillow. Then her eyes blinked open, and slowly she focused on him. Her mouth eased into a small, sleep-heavy smile.

"How is your hand?" he asked softly.

She glanced down at it and flexed her fingers. "Better, I think. It feels less swollen." She looked back at him. "What about you? Do you need more medicine?"

His jaw was on fire. The medication Devon had given him

must have worn off. Last night, after they'd invited Devon and the Fletchers back into the room, they'd talked for the greater part of an hour. Finally, Grayson had relented and let Devon examine him.

He'd battled self-consciousness as Mia had hovered, but Devon seemed to sense that. He'd asked Mia to wet a cloth in clean water, and she'd seized on the task and hurried to the basin of water across the room.

Devon had lowered his voice. "The burn is bad. Flame's Breath causes lasting scars." His chin dipped toward Grayson's fingers. "The vividness will fade in time, as you know. The damage along your jaw, however, concerns me. Your flesh was burned inside and out because of that cut. I'm afraid the pain will be bad for a long time, and infection has certainly set in. I need to clean it, and that's going to hurt. A lot."

Grayson kept his voice pitched low. "Not in front of Mia."

Devon's mouth tightened, but he nodded. "That would probably be best. I can tell her we need to go to my office in the physician's ward."

"Can this wait until morning?"

"It shouldn't."

Grayson glanced at Mia, who was wringing out a wet cloth on the other side of the room. "I don't want to leave her right now," he said quietly. "Not after what she went through today."

Devon sighed, but clearly understood. "First thing in the morning, then. In the meantime, I have some powerful medicine that will dull the pain. It's one of the queen's concoctions, actually. I don't recommend its use often, because it can be addictive. But it's probably the only thing strong enough to make a difference right now." Devon stepped over to his bag. "I only have a little of it, but I'll try to get more. It's a rare blend, because it contains an expensive Zennorian drug called olcain." He held out a small packet to Grayson. "Take only a pinch of the powder. Put it under your tongue, and it will dissolve quickly. You should feel the effects almost instantly. Use it sparingly—only when you truly need it. Otherwise, you should use the milder medication I left with Mia."

"Thank you," Grayson said, tucking the packet into his pocket.

"No need to be brave," Devon said. "Take some now. It will help you sleep. I expect you to come see me first thing in the morning."

Now it was morning, and Grayson didn't want to move. He didn't want this quiet moment with Mia to end. Just lying beside her brought more peace than he had words to express.

She was still curled on her side, looking at him.

He realized she was waiting for an answer, so he forced a thin smile and hoped it was reassuring. "No, I don't need more medicine yet." That was a lie, but he wasn't about to tell her how bad the pain was.

Mia shifted, moving until their arms brushed. She set her bandaged hand on his chest and rested her head against his shoulder.

He couldn't resist draping an arm around her waist and easing her closer. His heart beat faster, and he wondered if she could hear it—feel it.

After a long moment, Mia sighed. "I should go. Tyrell always trains men in the morning, so I can get into his room easily."

Grayson's spine stiffened against the mattress, and he tightened his hold on her. "I'll come with you."

"No. You need to see Devon. He said he wanted to do a thorough examination first thing in the morning."

"It can wait."

She drew back enough to look at him. "No, it can't. You need to take care of yourself."

Devon had said the same thing before leaving last night, but he'd added in low tones, "You can't take care of her if you're dead or incapacitated with pain."

That thought was what made him finally acquiesce. "You'll take Fletcher with you."

She nodded.

There was a knock on the door, and Rena announced herself through the closed portal.

Mia sat up, and so did Grayson.

Fire ripped over his jaw, and he had to clench his teeth to keep from making a sound.

Mia slid off the bed, calling out, "Come in."

The maid did, and she looked a little cautiously between them. Grayson could tell he made Fletcher's wife nervous, but he was used to that.

Rena curtsied haltingly toward Grayson, then more fluidly for Mia. "Shall I summon breakfast?" she asked.

Mia looked to Grayson. "Would you like to eat before visiting Devon?"

"No." He was in too much pain right now to eat, even though he was starving; he'd barely eaten anything Mia had handed him last night. "I'll go see him now."

"All right," Mia said. "We'll have breakfast once you're back."

Grayson held her gaze, his focus intense. "Be careful."

Her face softened. "I'll be perfectly fine."

She wouldn't even see Tyrell, he reminded himself. So he tipped his head and made his way out of the room. Fletcher stood in the hall, silent and alert.

They exchanged nods that spoke volumes, and then Grayson stepped away. He didn't head for the stairs that would take him to Devon, though. Instead, he stopped by Tyrell's room to assure himself his brother was indeed gone. Once satisfied, he made his way to the physician's ward.

His movements were stiff, and he was careful not to move any more than necessary—especially his neck. Because whenever he shifted, it sent a stab of pain to the roaring burn on his face. The pain was somehow worse than yesterday, and he wasn't sure how that was possible. His hands shook, and his breaths came out shallow and taut. He hadn't made it far before he paused in a shadowed alcove and pulled out the packet Devon had given him last night.

He took a pinch of the powder with trembling fingers, and the bitter taste permeated his mouth as it dissolved under his tongue.

But the pain eased.

He found Devon's office rather easily. It was tucked in a high tower in the physician's ward, and a guard easily directed him.

Grayson knocked on the closed door, and it soon swung open. "Prince Grayson," Devon said. "Come in."

The room was small, and a bit cluttered. A bag was on the unmade bed in the corner, with clothes stacked around it.

"You shouldn't let anyone else see you packing," Grayson said.

Devon closed the door. "Fair point." He stepped around Grayson and flicked a blanket over the pack and clothing. Then he faced Grayson, his expression carefully neutral. "I know you see me as the weak link."

The unexpected words made Grayson stare.

Devon crossed his arms over his chest. "I'm not Fletcher;

you haven't known me for half your life. But I've been taking care of Mia for years. I'm loyal to her."

"I know." If he hadn't been, Grayson would have killed him last night.

Devon let out a slow breath. "You don't remember me, do you?"

Confusion swirled inside him, and he frowned.

The physician smiled faintly. He looked oddly resigned. "It's all right. It was a long time ago. You were maybe five years old. You were hurt. You came to the ward, and I helped you, even though all of the physicians were ordered not to attend the princes unless it was a matter of life and death." He shook his head slowly. "You were a little boy, and you were in pain. I was incapable of turning my back. Of course, the king found out."

"He didn't kill you." The statement was somehow a question.

"No, but he made an example of me. And his punishment was . . . fitting." Devon's throat bobbed as he swallowed. "He disliked my compassion, and he wanted to rob me of it—or at least make me suffer for it. He demoted me to the prison, where I've spent years tending the people he tortures. And while I've eased some of their suffering, I have watched many more die. Taking care of Mia . . . that has been my only true reprieve. I would do anything for her."

Grayson didn't question the man's devotion. He didn't particularly like how strongly people seemed to feel for Mia—especially when that person was Tyrell—but he couldn't deny that Mia was just that way. Anyone who spent time with her became devoted to her. Including Devon, apparently.

The man's chin lowered. "I tell you this so you know I'm loyal to both of you, so long as you have no designs against her."

Grayson had no idea how the conversation had turned to this—Devon, needing reassurance of *his* loyalty to Mia—but he answered honestly. "Mia means everything to me. I would cut my own throat before harming her."

Devon nodded, and that was the end of it. He turned to a side table, which was riddled with bottles, small mixing bowls, and a chipped mortar and pestle. He lifted a small leather pouch and handed it to Grayson, the drawstrings tightly closed. "I mixed more powder for you. Olcain is hard to obtain, but I raided the ward last night. I forgot to warn you, but there is a possibility of severe headaches as the drug leaves your body. If that happens, resist the urge to take more to treat the headaches—they are a sign that your body is relying on the drug too much. Now, you should take more before we begin the cleaning."

Grayson nearly told him that he'd already taken some in the corridor. But the pain was still there, and he couldn't afford to let his body betray him. Mia needed him strong, now more than ever. So he took another pinch of the powder, and Devon got to work.

Peter ambushed Grayson on his way back to Mia.

The oldest Kaelin prince didn't actually manage to surprise him, he just appeared suddenly before him. And with Carter at his side, he issued a sharp order. "Follow me."

Grayson wanted to refuse, but a fight wasn't worth the effort, and he didn't want to risk rousing suspicion.

He trailed after his brothers, moving to a rarely-used sitting room on the first floor of the castle. Once inside, Carter remained by the closed door, and Grayson followed Peter to the center of the room. When Peter abruptly twisted to face him, Grayson's dulled senses couldn't react in time. Peter's fist slammed against his freshly cleaned burn.

The blinding pain sent Grayson to his knees. A ragged gasp echoed in the room. His entire face throbbed, despite the potent drug that swam through his veins. He felt a trickle of blood from where Peter's ring had dug into the raw, freshly cleaned cut. The agony was indescribable; he couldn't breathe.

"Stay on your knees," Peter said evenly.

Grayson's ears rang. His vision wavered, then came into sharp focus. His fingers dug into the simple braided rug. Nausea swam in his gut, but he forced himself to breathe through it. And as he did, he felt the heat of his rage. A fury that he'd forced down far too many times. He knew he couldn't risk retaliating; Mia wasn't safe, yet. But something in his very soul refused to stay down.

Not this time.

He rose slowly, uncurling from the floor until he stood before Peter, stretched to his full height. His brother was the oldest Kaelin prince, but he was the shortest; he had to look up slightly to meet Grayson's gaze.

Surprise flickered through Peter's eyes, followed by a flash of fear.

Menace and threat both emanated from Grayson, but he said nothing. Did nothing. Just glared at Peter, his fists clenched at his sides.

Tense silence stretched. Then—slowly—Peter's lips curved into a satisfied smirk. His thoughts were as clear as if he'd spoken them: he didn't think he needed to fear Grayson, because he thought he could control him. *Use* him.

He was wrong. He just didn't realize it yet.

Peter folded his arms over his chest, clearly showing silent acceptance of Grayson's refusal to kneel. His voice was unconcerned. "You failed me in Mortise. It was a simple task, Grayson. What happened? Why didn't you bring Princess Imara to me?"

"I had no opportunity to abduct her," Grayson said, his voice dark.

"Failure is failure. And it's something you've done a lot of lately. You're not quite living up to your fearsome reputation, are you?"

Grayson didn't bother to respond. "What are your plans for Imara?"

"Oh, the princess will still be mine. But because of your incompetence, I'll have to deal with some mild inconveniences first. Never fear, I'll make you clean up your mess in due time." Peter took a step back. "I want you to win Mortise."

The words came out of nowhere. Grayson blinked. "What?"

"I want you to win father's challenge," Peter explained. "I want you to have the Mortisian crown. I want you to win Mia."

The sound of her name on his tongue made Grayson's protective instincts flare. He hated the easy way he said it. The familiarity, as much as the intrigue. He hated thinking that Mia had ever been in a room with Peter—that she'd been *alone* with him.

Peter didn't seem to notice Grayson's tension. His expression had turned musing. "Perhaps I should start calling her *Meerah*. The lost little princess . . . no wonder she fascinated me from the first moment I saw her. She's just full of secrets."

He concentrated back on Grayson. "Tyrell wants her. I can't decide if he actually cares for her, or if he just wants to steal what's yours. But he will fight hard for her, and he's already fought dirty."

Grayson's spine stiffened.

Peter's lips twisted into a smug smile. "There are many things I could tell you. A lot happened between them while you were gone. But if you want to know what I know, you must give me your allegiance."

"I don't care what you know."

"You say that now, but . . . did you know Tyrell gave her gifts? That she slept in his bed? Did you know he dressed her in beautiful clothes and tried to pass her off as his mistress?"

Grayson tensed. He couldn't help it.

Peter's smile stretched wider. "Did you know she wrote you a letter, and he said he sent it—but instead he kept it? He read it, Grayson. Her words for you, and he kept them. He stole them from you, and he lied to her about it."

Grayson knew Peter was trying to rile him, but, fates it was working.

"Did he hurt her?" Grayson asked through his teeth.

Pleasure sparked in Peter's eyes. "He certainly touched her, but I doubt he ever hurt her. He was trying to win her affection. And she was falling for his lies, Grayson. I saw that with my own eyes. I helped put a stop to that when I showed her the letter he'd lied about. And I can continue to help you, if you help me."

"Help you with what?" He told himself he was asking not because he'd ever consider accepting Peter's help, but because he needed to know his brother's plans.

"When the time comes, I'm going to need someone to help

me take care of a few people. I want that someone to be you."

Carter snorted from his place near the door. "He couldn't even manage to kill Princess Serene. I could—"

"Your particular skills will be useful, Carter," Peter cut in. "As we've already discussed. Now, stay out of this."

Carter bristled, but remained silent.

Peter turned back to Grayson. "My plans for Zennor are coming to fruition. But there will be some loose ends when all is done. Some rather dangerous ones. When I call you, I want you to eliminate them."

Though his face still throbbed from Peter's harsh blow, Grayson forced himself to remain focused. "Who do you want me to kill?"

"I'm not going to burden you with any details yet. Just be ready. In return for your service, I'll make sure Father chooses you as the ruler of Mortise. You will get Mia, and Tyrell will get nothing. Do we have a deal?"

If Grayson were truly a spy, he might consider putting off leaving Lenzen, in an effort to try and learn something vital from Peter. But he wasn't a spy—not really. His only true goal was getting Mia out of here tonight. So he merely bowed his head. "We have a deal."

Peter stepped closer, and it took every bit of willpower Grayson had not to let instinct take over and attack him.

"I will allow you only one failure," Peter said, his tone laced with warning. "And you already used it on Imara. Fail me again, and I will make sure you're there to see Tyrell sit on the Mortisian throne, with Mia as his wife. *That*, Grayson, is a promise." He turned on his heel and stalked from the room without looking back.

Grayson twisted to face Carter, who watched him with

banked wariness. "Mother asked me to give you a gift."

Rage blasted through him at the mention of the queen. What she'd done to Mia . . . Grayson's skin felt too tight, and his pulse thudded in his ears.

Carter's brow furrowed. "Aren't you going to ask what it is?"

"No. I don't want it." He didn't want anything from his mother. He prayed to the fates he and Mia would be gone before Queen Iris tried to corner him to learn the details of Liam's death.

He didn't trust himself to be in the same room with his mother right now.

Carter's lip curled. "I don't know what she sees in you. What *any* of them see. Father, Mother, Peter . . . they look at you, and somehow they don't see the rabid dog you are. If I could, I would eliminate you."

Grayson's brutalized face throbbed. After everything, his temper rode dangerously close to the surface, and the powder Devon had given him swam in his veins, making him feel strangely invulnerable. And that, perhaps, made him reckless.

He took a step forward.

Carter—predictably—shrank back.

When Grayson smiled, he knew it was not a good smile. "Do you ever wonder what they see in you?" he asked.

Carter's face tightened. "I'm loyal."

"You're weak. Pathetic. Malleable. Everyone knows it."

Carter's hands fisted at his sides. One forefinger was shorter than the other because Peter had cut off the tip years ago. That was the day Henri had made his rules for the Kaelin brothers: no killing, and no severe maiming. Only scarring was allowed.

"At least I'm reliable," Carter said. "The others all come to you because they think you're the strongest of us. But I know that relying on you is a mistake."

"Why don't you warn them, then?"

Carter only glowered.

Grayson's cold smile stretched wider, and he ignored the flash of pain along his jaw. "Ah. You *have* warned them. They just don't believe you. Or, more likely, they simply disregard you."

"I don't trust you," Carter said, his voice thin. "You should watch your back."

He really should. He should let this go. Playing with Carter did nothing—not when he and Mia were leaving.

That didn't keep him from stepping closer. He didn't stop until he was right in front of Carter.

To his brother's credit, he didn't fall back this time.

Grayson kept his voice low. "We both know you're too cowardly to ever stick a knife in my back—or even slip some poison in my food. You're too afraid that the others would find out, and you'd be next."

Color rose in Carter's cheeks. "You're not invincible, Grayson."

"No. But my weapons are sharper, more direct, and much more deadly than yours. You should remember that."

His older brother visibly seethed. "One day, the others will see what I do, and you will no longer be useful."

Grayson stared at him. Saw the mix of hatred and fear in his eyes. "I never wanted to fight," he said quietly.

Surprise twisted Carter's face, along with a spark of confusion.

To be honest, the admission had surprised Grayson, too. But he found himself continuing, "I didn't want to be like any of you. But when I resisted, all of you tortured me. So I learned, and I learned well. I am what you made me. It's not my fault if you don't like the nightmare I've become."

Silence stretched. Grayson wasn't entirely sure what he saw in his brother's eyes now. It couldn't be regret. It couldn't be shame. And that spark—there and gone so fast he barely saw it—could not be longing; a wish that their pasts had been different.

Carter shifted, his voice a little edged as he said, "Mother secured your weapons after Father had you thrown in prison. She asked me to return them to you."

Ah. The Poison Queen's gift. Grayson had almost forgotten.

"They're in my room," Carter continued. "Follow me." He turned on his heel and marched to the door.

Grayson trailed after him. And though he didn't expect an attack, he let his hand rest on one of his belted daggers.

CHAPTER II

MIA

Mia stood back as Fletcher knelt to retrieve the supplies she'd hidden under Tyrell's bed. Her hand truly felt much better this morning, but Fletcher had insisted. While he pulled things out, Mia scanned Tyrell's room.

She hadn't stepped foot in here since the night of the king's birthday, when she'd fought with Tyrell. Rena had come back to retrieve her things, but everything else looked the same. There was a chair by the window—Tyrell had placed it there so she could see outside while she healed after being stabbed. A book was lying on the chair, and though she couldn't see the spine, she knew it was *Soren's High Seas Adventure*—a book she'd handed Tyrell when he'd taken her to visit the castle library. And in the far corner on a low table sat Tyrell's hand-carved Strategem set. The black queen was missing, because he'd given it to her.

155

Emotion tightened her throat and she glanced away—only for her eyes to snare on a red ribbon lying on Tyrell's bedside table.

She recognized it at once. It was the ribbon he'd tied around the small box that had held the queen piece he'd given her. He'd pocketed the ribbon that night, she vaguely recalled.

He'd kept it.

She didn't know why, but that made her heart clench. She reached for it, letting her fingertips glide over the satin ribbon. She couldn't quite release it, even when Fletcher had dragged out the two bags from under the bed and stood.

Outside the bedroom, the main suite door opened with a loud bang.

Mia twisted toward the open bedroom door, the silk ribbon clutched in her hand as Tyrell stalked in.

His face glistened with sweat and his dark blue shirt clung to every ripple of muscle on his torso. The long sleeves were shoved up his forearms, and his dark hair was ruffled—by wind, training, or his own fingers, Mia wasn't sure.

He looked caught in a rage, but he halted abruptly when he spotted Mia and Fletcher. His eyes cut between them, then he took in the bags at their feet. Surprise flashed across his features. "You're coming back?"

The hope in his voice made her wince. "No. I just needed to get the last of my things."

Hurt slashed across his face—then his expression closed off. His chest lifted on a heavy breath, and some of his earlier tension returned as he met her gaze. "Where is Grayson?"

Mia's throat was horribly dry, but her palms were sweaty. "He went to see Devon. His wound was infected."

Tyrell shifted back a step and pushed a hand through his

dark hair. The nervous motion made him seem younger than he was. Vulnerable. "Can I please talk with you?" he asked softly. "Alone?"

Mia bit the inside of her cheek. They were leaving tonight—this might be the last time she ever saw Tyrell. Her hold on the ribbon tightened, and she glanced at Fletcher. "Will you wait outside for me?"

He didn't seem particularly happy about it, but he lifted both bags and moved for the door. As he slid through it, he cast a quick look at Tyrell.

The prince ignored him. His attention was solely on Mia.

The main suite door clicked shut a moment later. Silence drew around them as they stared at each other.

Finally, Mia whispered, "You kept the ribbon."

Tyrell's eyes changed. She wasn't sure how; they were still hard, but maybe they were a little softer as he stepped through the doorway, fully entering the bedroom.

Her heartbeat quickened at his approach, but she didn't move.

He stopped near the corner of the bed, keeping a few paces between them. "Yes, I kept it." His tone said more than those simple words conveyed.

She moved slowly, setting the ribbon back on his bedside table. Her voice was heavy as she said, "I kept the queen."

There was a long pause. "I didn't know if you would," he whispered.

The air was thick with words unsaid. Emotions unnamed. Fates unknown. If Grayson didn't already have her heart . . .

But he did.

That didn't ease the pang in her chest as she faced Tyrell. "I'm sorry," she breathed.

His entire body jerked. "Don't." He sounded strangled.

Her breath caught. "Why can't I apologize?"

"Because saying you're sorry feels like you're really just telling me goodbye."

Fates, he didn't know how right he was. Her eyes stung. "I'm not saying goodbye, I just . . . I need to apologize. I'm sorry for the way I reacted that night. For the things I said to you. I didn't mean them. I was just hurt and angry."

Tyrell looked away. A muscle feathered along his clenched jaw. "I deserved everything you said."

"No. You didn't. I was cruel."

He still didn't look at her. "I betrayed your trust. It's my deepest regret." He huffed, the sound dark and heavy. "And I have a fates-blasted mountain of regrets, so that's saying something. But what I did hurt you, and it pushed you away." His hands clenched. "I don't know why I break everything I touch, but I suppose you're right. I'm incapable of love."

"I never should have said that—it was wrong. You have a beautiful heart, Tyrell."

He laughed once, the sound hard and edged. "Nothing about me is beautiful, Mia. Or good, or redeemable."

"I disagree."

His shoulders tensed. "If I'm so good, then why did I ruin what was between us?" He didn't give her a chance to answer before he muttered, "I hate myself for what I've done to you—to us."

"Don't," she begged softly. "I don't hate you. I forgive you."

He flinched, and tension coiled in his shoulders. His breath rattled out of him as he cursed. "Fates, I wasn't prepared for this. For you. I ran up here because I'd been told Grayson was skulking at my door . . ." Finally, he looked at her, and his eyes burned with a fire so intense her breath stalled. "I came ready to fight him, and now you're standing here telling me you're sorry and you forgive me, and all I want to do right now is kiss you. I've been wanting to kiss you for so long it *hurts*."

A fracture tore through her heart. "Tyrell . . ."

"Don't worry, I won't. I know you don't want me to—and that kills me." He shook his head. "I'm sorry for ever hurting you. That first time, and that last time. I lied about your letter to Grayson because I'm a selfish coward, but I swear I never meant to hurt you."

"I know." Her voice cracked, along with something inside her.

She had never seen Tyrell look so vulnerable. Lost. Shattered. And for the first time, she realized what her leaving would do to him, and that broke her heart.

She crossed the space between them in long, rapid strides. His eyes widened, but that's all she saw before she wrapped her arms around his waist.

The embrace clearly surprised him, but he didn't hesitate to hold her in return. He crushed her to him, his arms trembling as his head ducked beside hers. He held her like she was the only thing that mattered in his world.

She held him tighter, burying her face against the hollow of his throat. "I'm sorry," she whispered, her voice wavering as her first tear fell.

He couldn't know what she was apologizing for. Not really. But his arms clenched around her, bringing her impossibly closer.

For a long moment, they simply held each other. A desperate embrace that gradually eased into one of comfort.

He broke the silence when he whispered, "I don't want you

to go."

She froze. Her heart tripped. Fates, had he guessed—?

"I don't want you to go back to him," Tyrell continued, his warm breath teasing the sensitive skin behind her ear. "He's going to keep you away from me. I won't know if you're safe."

She sighed, pressing her forehead against his chest. "I'm safe with him."

His head shifted; his chin grazed her temple before settling on top of her head, and his arms tightened across her shoulder blades. "There's an empty room just down the corridor. You'd be close enough to both of us, but you'd have your own room. You don't have to stay with him, Mia. Especially now, when our father is still so angry with him."

She sighed and tugged back.

Tyrell's arms tensed, resisting her pull. Then he let them fall, and she drew back. Not completely, just enough that she could face him. Her hair had fallen forward, so she raised a hand to push back a curl from her cheek. "Tyrell, there's—"

He grabbed her wrist with a sharp curse. "What happened to your hand?"

She followed his gaze to her hand, which was covered in the scorpion stings. The puncture sites were still red, though the swelling had gone down.

She exhaled slowly. "Your mother ordered me to have tea with her yesterday. There was a scorpion. I'm fine."

The look he cut her was so much like Grayson's last night, under other circumstances she might have laughed. Instead, she ducked her head until she managed to catch his gaze. "It was horrible, but I'm all right. You and Grayson don't need to avenge me."

His expression tensed. "Are you in any pain?"

"No. It's just sore now."

His grip eased immediately, but he didn't release her. The pad of his thumb brushed the soft skin of her inner wrist and she fought a shiver.

"I hate everything about this," he whispered.

She didn't think he was just talking about her injured hand. Unsure of what to say, she remained silent.

They stood so close. He smelled of crisp outdoor air, sweat, and the spice of his soap. And when he peeked up at her through long, dark lashes, she couldn't look away. "I know who you are," he said.

She stiffened—an ingrained reaction, nothing to do with him. His tone was soft, and he touched her carefully.

Mia forced herself to relax. "Grayson told me what Henri said."

Tyrell searched her face. "Why didn't you tell me?"

"Because there was nothing to tell. I'm not her anymore." *Meerah is dead.*

You're broken, Meerah.

Tyrell's throat flexed as he swallowed. "Did you tell Grayson? Did he know?"

"No." It was only half a lie; she had never been brave enough to tell Grayson the truth; he'd had to learn it on his own, in Mortise.

Tyrell stared at her. Maybe believing her, maybe not. His full lips pressed together. "I don't care who you are. You don't have to be Meerah. You don't have to be anyone but yourself."

She wanted that to be true, but she didn't think it was. Soon, she would be going home. She would have to face her past. The demons there. The expectations of her brother, and her people.

Unless she was rejected. Desfan may not want her in the palace once he learned the truth about Tahlyah's death. Or if he decided to blame her for their father's death.

Her emotions were becoming too much. She shoved all of that away as she met Tyrell's gaze. "Maybe you're right," she said. "We only ever have to be who we are."

The words hung between them, feeling surprisingly profound.

She studied Tyrell, just as intently as he watched her. Instinct had her place a hand against his chest, and she could feel the pounding of his heart. "I care about you, Tyrell," she whispered. "I need you to know that."

The angles on his face sharpened. "That's sounding like another goodbye."

She didn't deny it. She lifted onto her toes and placed a soft kiss against his cheek. When she drew back, she said, "You're a good person."

His eyes clouded. "That only proves how blind you are." There was no heat in the words; just a statement of fact.

Mia gave him a small, almost sad smile. "You *are* good. You just lost sight of that for a while."

His eyes burned with intensity. "He doesn't deserve you, Mia. Neither of us do."

"You both deserve so much more than you think."

He set his free hand against her waist, as if he sensed she was about to pull away and he needed to keep her close. "I'm not going to stand by while he puts you in danger."

Her palm was still braced against his chest; her fingers tightened. "Grayson's not putting me in danger."

"Of course he is. The mere act of being near you puts a target on your back. He's always been dangerous, but after

Mortise . . . he's different. Can't you see that? He's unstable. Volatile."

"Grayson would never hurt me."

Tyrell made a sound in his throat. Probably disagreement, but he dropped that and tried another track. "My father will hurt you if Grayson steps out of line. We all know it, but Grayson refuses to do anything about it. All you need to do is agree, and I can get you distanced from him. Just enough that my father won't have reason to hurt you."

"Your father never needs a reason for what he does. And you don't see Grayson clearly—just as he doesn't see you clearly."

"I see him just fine. He'll put you at risk. It's only a matter of time."

"Grayson didn't hesitate to take that burn for himself. He didn't struggle. He endured that for me." Her stomach twisted sharply, and she couldn't stop her grimace.

Tyrell's jaw tightened. "I didn't want to do that."

"I know. You didn't have a choice."

There was a long moment of silence. They were still standing so close. Her hand was still on his chest, and he still held her waist.

His voice was strained as he said, "Promise me you'll think about taking that room."

She didn't have the heart to hurt him more than she already had—and would. "I'll think about it," she whispered.

He relaxed a little. "Thank you." His chin dropped and he leaned in until his lips brushed her forehead. The kiss was soft and brief, but his mouth hovered against her skin as he said, "After you left that night, I searched for the queen. When I couldn't find the blasted piece, I thought you'd thrown it into the fire."

Just like his mother had destroyed the rest of his first Strategem set; the black queen had only survived because Tyrell had held the piece in his fist, shielding it from Iris's disgusted fury.

Mia pulled back to meet his hooded eyes. "I would never do that."

His eyes dipped to her lips.

There was a knock on the outer door—probably Fletcher, worried about her.

Mia dropped her hand from Tyrell's chest.

His hand tightened on her waist, keeping her close. Then, one finger at a time, he let her go. His fingertips left a haunting touch, and then there was only space between them.

"Thank you, Tyrell," she said. "For everything."

He didn't respond, just watched as she stepped around him and left the room.

Fletcher didn't ask any questions, and she didn't offer any of what had just passed between her and Tyrell. The old guard simply followed her back to Grayson's room. He put the two bags of supplies just inside the door, and then he moved to stand guard in the corridor, leaving Mia alone.

She was a little relieved Grayson hadn't returned yet. She needed a moment alone.

Nervous energy vibrated through her. She fiddled with the pebble at her throat; the necklace Grayson had given her before he left for Mortise. It was her most cherished possession.

She knew she wouldn't be able to take much with her to Mortise. Most everything she had would have to be left behind.

But she couldn't leave everything.

She crossed the room to the wardrobe in the corner. There,

tucked in the back, was the wooden box she'd put Tyrell's queen in. She pulled the wooden piece out, her fingers running over the intricate grooves he'd carved when he was younger, along with the newer embellishments he'd added later. She searched the wardrobe until she found a thin leather cord, which she tied around the queen so she could hang the piece around her neck.

Two necklaces. Two men she loved, though in different ways.

Her gaze caught on one of her sketch books, and an idea formed.

She went to Grayson's desk and found the letter he'd written her before he'd left for Mortise. She set it carefully aside to pack in her things, and then she found a blank sheet of paper, quill, and ink.

She wrote a letter, folded it, and tucked it into the front of her sketchbook, which she set on the desk.

Feeling more settled, Mia stood and started to pack.

CHAPTER 12

CLARE

CLARE BREATHED IN DEEPLY, PULLING THE BRINY sea air into her lungs. She was glad she'd agreed to walk on the beach with Bennick this morning. Getting outside of the palace, away from the concerned and pitying glances of her friends . . . It was nice to be able to just walk with Bennick.

This stretch of beach was private, walled in as part of the palace grounds. It was beautiful. Before coming to Mortise, Clare had never seen the sea. She only wished her brothers had had a chance to see it, too.

Bennick was beside her, their hands joined. No one else was on the beach, probably because everyone in the palace had been up half the night celebrating Desfan's coronation. She hoped Desfan could also sleep in, but she'd been around royals enough to know that such a thing was doubtful. He probably had a full schedule of meetings today.

She hadn't known Desfan long or well, but what she'd seen, she admired. She'd never thought to have something in common with him. He'd lost his family, just as she now had. She hoped, one day, she could display even a measure of the strength he seemed to exude.

For now, avoidance was her preferred method of coping. So, after a long time with no words between them, she asked Bennick, "Did I hear Cardon say you have a meeting with Karim Safar today?"

"Yes, along with Kiv Arcas. They'll be discussing some additional security measures, and I'll hopefully get an update on the palace searches that are still being conducted." Bennick's forehead grew lined. "A lot of the Devendran rebels were killed the night of the attack, but I'm sure many escaped."

"None have been found hiding in the castle, though. They probably left that night."

"Probably," he agreed. But a shadow remained in his crystal blue eyes.

Clare said nothing, though her thoughts raced. Bennick didn't know that the rebels who had attacked the palace weren't the only Devendran rebels. There were two factions; one was the group her brother Eliot had belonged to—the ones who had tried to kill her so many times—and the other was led by Serene. She did so largely in secret; only the most high-ranking rebels knew she was their leader. The rest of the rebels simply knew they wanted her on the Devendran throne.

While Clare had assisted Serene and her rebels on occasion, she hadn't accepted the princess's offer to officially join their ranks. The potential risk to her brothers had felt too great at the time. Now, she wondered if she *should* join. Serene would make a much better ruler than Newlan or Grandeur.

Bennick touched her arm, drawing her from her thoughts. "We should head back."

She nodded, and they wordlessly turned and started toward the palace.

"My meeting with Karim and Arcas shouldn't take long," Bennick said.

"Take your time." She felt a little guilty that she'd been selfishly keeping Bennick so close. He had many responsibilities, and he needed to feel free to do them. "While you're gone, I think I'll write to your father," she said. "He might have concluded his investigation by now, and I'd like to ask him about Mistress Keller. I don't know if she had any family, but if she did, they should be informed."

"I'm sure he's already taken care of that," Bennick said. "He's efficient at his job."

That was true enough. Commander Markam had always taken his career seriously. Unfortunately, that dedication did not extend to his responsibilities as a father or husband. Bennick's relationship with the commander was not good, and that was before he'd learned that the infamous assassin—the Rose—was his father's illegitimate son.

Zilas was out there, somewhere. Probably still in Mortise, and certainly just as determined to kill her and Serene. Killing the princess was for his professional pride. Killing Clare would simply torture Bennick, and that was reason enough to drive him. Jealousy, hatred, and a fierce desire to turn Bennick against the commander—it had twisted Zilas's soul.

Family. It could be complicated, messy, and sometimes terrible. It could bring the greatest joy, and the most soul-crushing heartache. In the end, family was everything. Especially the family one chose.

"Bennick! Clare!"

They both tensed and looked across the beach, up the steep stone staircase that led to the palace.

Wilf was halfway down the steps and barreling toward them.

Clare's stomach plunged.

Bennick gripped her hand as they darted toward the steps. Running on sand wasn't easy or quick, and by the time they reached the base of the stairs, Wilf was already there.

He was breathing hard, but his eyes were bright. Clare was shocked to see not panic or alarm, but relief etched on his pox-scarred face. "They're here," he said, breathing hard. "Venn and Vera are here."

Clare burst into the princess's sitting room. Vera was nowhere in sight, but she immediately spotted Venn. His long black hair was secured at the back of his head in a messy knot, and his clothes were dusty and wrinkled. When he twisted around and saw her, his brown eyes sparkled and the corner of his lips tipped into a grin.

She was in his arms before she even realized she'd thrown herself at him.

Venn crushed her to his chest, laughing. "Fates, I think it's safe to say you missed me."

Clare buried her face in his chest, her throat so tight she could barely get any words out. "I've been so worried about you."

He snorted. "*I* was fates-blasted worried about *you*. You're the one who was abducted!"

"And you vanished."

Venn surprised her by pressing a kiss to the top of her head. "Vera and I took a little detour, that's all."

"Clare?"

Venn's arms loosened, and Clare twisted to see Vera standing in the doorway of Serene's bedroom with a tearful Bridget. Clare had never seen Serene's head maid look so emotional, but she touched Vera's arm almost with reverence, as if she were afraid Vera might disappear again.

Clare understood. She felt the same as she stared at her friend. Vera looked as travel-worn as Venn, her light blonde hair falling loosely around her shoulders, but she was here. She was *alive.*

The last time Clare had seen Vera, she'd been running into the Mortisian night after Clare had helped her escape the mercenaries who had abducted them. Salim had snapped Clare's fingers in retribution, and in the end it hadn't felt worth the sacrifice. She thought Vera had been hunted down and killed.

But she'd escaped. She'd found Venn. And now, she was standing right in front of her.

Tears stung Clare's eyes, and Vera's own shined as the two women rushed to embrace. A sob caught in Clare's throat, and Vera burst into tears as she clutched her tightly.

Fates, the two of them had been through so much together. They'd walked through hell together after Salim had abducted them, and they were finally together again.

Something deep inside Clare settled as she held her friend, and eventually her tears slowed. "Fates. I'm so glad you're all right," she breathed.

"I'm so sorry I left you," Vera managed through her tears. "I'm sorry Salim hurt you. I—"

"It's all right. I'm just so glad you're here—that you're alive." Clare tugged back so she could meet the younger girl's gaze. "Where have you been?"

Vera released a strangled sort of laugh, tears still slipping down her cheeks even though she was smiling. "It's a long story."

Across the room, Venn and Bennick embraced, clapping each other on the back. When Bennick withdrew, Wilf stepped forward.

Wilf wasn't a particularly affectionate man, and Venn in particular usually irritated him, so Clare was surprised when Wilf grasped Venn's hand and hauled him in for an embrace. "Glad you're all right," he grunted.

Venn's shoulders loosened. "Thank you, Wilf. It's good to see you."

Wilf released him and turned to Vera. He was infinitely more gentle when he took her hand, and he didn't pull her any closer. "I'm relieved that idiot managed to keep you in one piece."

Vera smiled a little, though Venn made a scoffing sound. Clare felt another jolt of surprise when Vera wrapped her arms around Wilf—a man who had once intimidated her. "It's good to see you, Wilf."

Bennick stepped to Clare's side. "I think it's time we heard what happened to you both," he said.

"We should find Serene, then," Venn said. "It will be easier to tell this just once."

"She and Cardon went to visit Serai Yahri," Wilf said.

"Serene wanted to know how she could best help after everything that's happened."

A furrow grew between Venn's dark brows. "From what Vera and I have heard, things have been continuing in the usual fashion for you all. Attacks, would-be assassins, rebels, and the like."

Bennick made a sound in his throat. "Unfortunately, yes. And there's probably more you haven't heard."

"Fates." Venn's expression turned grim. "I'm afraid our tale isn't going to improve things."

Wilf shifted back a step. "I'll get Serene and Cardon. In the meantime, Bennick and Clare can tell you everything that's been happening here."

———————————⟨⟩———————————

"Fates," Venn said into the brief silence that fell after Bennick stopped talking.

Wilf had not yet returned with Serene and Cardon. Bennick and Clare had briefly shared how Clare had been rescued after losing her in Krid, and their journey to Duvan on the *Seafire*, Captain Zadir's pirate ship. They also told them about Dirk, as well as the events leading up to Desfan's coronation.

Bennick, who sat in a chair across from them, glanced at Clare. She knew what he was silently asking; he wanted to know if she was ready to tell them about her brothers.

Her heart clenched. She gave a slight shake of her head.

Bennick's eyes softened, then slid back to Venn. "Desfan is starting his rule with some challenges. Unfortunately, as this is Serene's future kingdom, we're definitely sharing in them."

Vera, who sat between Clare and Venn on the long settee, let out a slow breath. "I'm so glad you're all right, Clare. But poor Imara. And Dirk . . ."

Venn swallowed, his eyes going hard. "We'd heard about Prince Liam and Prince Grayson's attack during the betrothal signing, but we didn't know about Dirk."

"He's buried on the palace grounds," Clare said softly. "If you'd like to visit him."

Venn's jaw was tight, but he nodded.

Vera set a hand on Venn's knee. Without hesitation, he rested his hand over hers.

It was a simple gesture, but it communicated so much. Despite everything, warmth spread through Clare's chest. She was glad Venn and Vera had resolved things between them; they'd both been miserable when Vera had pushed Venn away.

The door to the suite opened and Serene swept inside, followed by Cardon and Wilf. Everyone rose from their seats, and Serene threw her arms around Vera. "Thank the fates you're all right," the princess said. Then she hugged Venn. "We've all been so worried. Desfan sent out men to try and locate you."

"We had to make a slight detour," Venn said. "It took a little longer than expected."

Serene stepped back. "Tell us everything."

Once everyone was settled, Venn began their tale, with Vera chiming in occasionally. Clare knew they were leaving some details out, but she wasn't worried—she could get the story of their rekindled romance later. For the moment, she listened as intently as the rest of them while Venn told them how he and Vera had left Krid only to stumble upon three young

Devendran children in desperate need.

The love Venn and Vera felt for the children was obvious, and Clare felt a flicker of fear for their fates, since they weren't here. But that fear was quickly assuaged when Vera assured them the children had been returned to their father—a man named David Holm—and they were all safe in Salvation, a refugee camp for Devendrans that had been established outside the walls of a Mortisian city called Zahdir.

As their story unfolded, it quickly became clear that things in Eyrinthia were dire.

Refugees were fleeing Devendra to escape the Hunt, an organization led by Prince Grandeur. The military group specialized in apprehending anyone suspected of rebel activity or association. Arrests, torture, wrongful imprisonment . . . the stories turned Clare's stomach.

Venn and Vera also told them about the animosity they'd witnessed—and experienced—between Zennorians and Devendrans. They'd heard rumors that many refugees who fled into Zennor's northern jungles were never seen or heard from again. The Devendrans they'd met on the road were extremely distrustful of any Zennorian; even Venn, who was only half-Zennorian, and been attacked for nothing more than his lineage.

The more they spoke of Salvation—the camp that should have been a refuge—the more Clare felt herself pale. It hadn't been a sanctuary at all, but a trap used by the Hunt to capture any rebels who had fled to Mortise for safety.

"We rid the camp of the corrupt leaders," Venn told them. "And we left a good man in charge, named Zander Fellnor. But I carry a letter from him to you, Princess, and to the serjah—well, *serjan*, now. Zander is asking for assistance."

"Of course," Serene said. Her expression was inscrutable, but Clare knew her well enough now to see her tension, as well as her racing thoughts. "I will personally talk with Desfan and plead our needs."

Our needs. Once again, Serene was proving to be a devoted princess. Those refugees had fled Devendra, but she still considered them hers.

Cardon muttered a curse. "How can Grandeur do this?"

"He's changed," Wilf said, his voice a deep rumble. "He isn't the boy he once was," he continued, his words reminding them all that he'd once been Grandeur's bodyguard. "He's taken on his father's fears and anxieties."

"That's not exactly what I meant," Cardon said. "He's breaking laws laid out in the Garvins Treaty. Conducting a military operation in a foreign land—especially without the approval of the reigning monarch—is strictly forbidden. It's grounds for war."

"I don't think Grandeur cares about breaking any laws," Venn said, his expression darkening. "The prince has condoned torture of innocents and torn apart families. I don't know if he's mad with power, or just simply mad, but he must be stopped. I don't know how much the king knows of his activities, but Newlan must be informed."

"I'll write to my father," Serene said.

"You need to tell him everything," Vera said. "Including the fires."

Clare jolted at that word. "Fires?"

"Yes," Venn said. "We heard the story more than once. Zander's own family suffered the same fate. His son was arrested on suspicion of being a rebel, and he was killed during his interrogation. While Zander took care of affairs, his home was burned to the ground—with his son's wife and child inside. Zander can't prove it, but he knows the fire was set by the Hunt. According to what we've heard, they set fires as warnings or retribution for anyone suspected of rebellion—and they do it on Grandeur's orders."

Clare's heart was no longer beating. Her lungs were locked.

Vera glanced at her, concern in her eyes. "Clare? Are you all right?"

Bennick was kneeling in front of her in the next moment, his hands gripping hers.

"What is it?" Venn demanded. "What's wrong?"

Serene swallowed. "We recently learned Clare's home was burned. Her brothers were inside, and . . . there were no survivors."

CHAPTER 13

SERENE

"He killed them because of me," Clare whispered.

Serene watched her as they stood on the balcony of her large suite. The sun was setting, and it was the first moment they'd had alone since Venn and Vera had shared what they'd learned during their travels.

David Holm's name had hit her hard—he was one of her rebels. Thank the fates he and his children were all right, despite everything they'd been forced to suffer.

The Hunt . . . James had told her weeks ago that Grandeur had formed the Hunt, but she hadn't realized how evil their actions were—or how widespread of a problem they'd become.

They'd set fires to homes, killing everyone inside . . .

Her stomach was in knots, but she tried to keep her tone level. Controlling her voice, her reaction—it was all she could control right now. "We don't know that for certain."

Clare pulled her eyes from the glittering sea and put her back to the stone railing. Looking at Serene squarely, she said, "Grandeur ordered that fire to be set. I know it. He doesn't trust me; he hasn't for a while. He thinks I betrayed him for you."

Serene tried not to wince, though she didn't think Clare even noticed the accusation in her words. Her decoy was many things, but never cruel. No, she was just stating fact. It didn't occur to her that she could be blaming Serene for this.

Fates, if Grandeur had done this, then it *was* her fault. She'd convinced Clare to be her spy. To feed information to Grandeur. To push his paranoia. To see how far he would dare to go, or how hard he might dare to strike.

She supposed she had her answer now.

She swallowed hard, feeling sick. She'd never meant for this to happen. She thought he'd strike at her, not Clare. Not two innocent boys.

Serene strived for calm. They didn't know anything for certain. "We don't know the results of Commander Markam's investigation into the origins of the fire. There could be—"

"Grandeur killed my brothers to punish me," Clare bit out. "Even if Commander Markam learns the truth, do you really think he'll share that with me? Or will he protect the Hunt and the prince?"

Serene's shoulders fell. Of course Commander Markam would protect Grandeur. Protecting the prince was protecting the crown—something the commander had taken oaths to do at all costs. The Hunt might be a new faction of soldiers, but it was still part of Devendra's military. The commander would protect them, too.

"I need to send someone else to determine the truth," Clare said. "To find proof that Grandeur did this. Someone who has no ties to Devendra, or the Hunt—or the rebels," she added, as if she'd read Serene's intention to offer.

She wasn't offended that Clare didn't want one of Serene's rebels to look into things. She could understand Clare's need for someone with no biases to determine the truth.

"Do you have someone in mind?" Serene asked.

"Yes. Latif."

Her eyes widened. "The man who is currently in prison for abducting you and agreeing to kill you?"

"He was blackmailed by Prince Liam," Clare said. "And Latif said he was never going to kill me."

"He said that *after* he was arrested."

"True, but he did save my life in the prison the other night—twice. I trust him. He's a man who wants to redeem himself by doing something good, and he's loyal to me." Clare met Serene's gaze. "Will you ask Desfan to release him?"

She let out a slow breath. "I don't know if Desfan would even consider it, Clare. He has many reasons to hate Latif."

"I know. But I need him. Please, Serene."

She wanted to protest, but the way Clare looked at her . . . This woman had lost so much. Too much of that had been in direct connection to being Serene's decoy—and her friend.

She couldn't deny her this. Not when it could bring Clare a measure of peace. "I'll plead your case," she said. "I'll ask tonight." She'd sent a message to Desfan immediately after getting Venn and Vera's report, and her future husband had offered to see her before dinner.

Clare's tense body relaxed slightly. "Thank you."

Serene wanted to say more. Apologize. Thank her in return,

for all she'd done. But she struggled to find the right words.

Clare's voice was lower as she said, "What are you going to do about Grandeur?"

Her hands rolled to fists at her sides. "I'm going to stop him. I'm going to steal his crown. I'm going to make him face justice for every crime he's ever committed."

Clare looked at her without blinking. "I want to help you do that. All of it. I want to be one of your rebels."

The words caught her off-guard. Clare had hesitated before to become fully involved as a rebel. But that had been to protect her brothers. Without them . . .

Still, this was a weighty decision—a treasonous one.

"Are you sure?" Serene asked.

"Yes." There was no doubt or hesitation in Clare now.

The princess nodded once. "Then we will make him pay. Together."

Clare's eyes cleared a little, shining with new purpose.

Serene felt the familiar weight of responsibility. Clare wasn't the only one relying on her these days—and time wasn't on her side. Everything in Eyrinthia felt like it was breaking. Serene wasn't sure how to fix things, especially since she was stuck in Duvan.

She wanted to visit Salvation, and help the refugees there. She wanted to find out what had happened to all the Devendrans who had vanished in Zennor. She wanted to talk to James and consult with him on how their strategies needed to change in order to protect the rebels and their families.

She wanted to go to Zennor and counsel with her uncle, King Zaire Buhari. She could use his wisdom. And while there, she would seek out Ivar Carrigan. Her father's cousin was a man with many enemies, but Serene trusted him completely.

Clare had once asked about Carrigan, and Serene had said she hardly knew the man. That had been a lie, but she was used to protecting him.

Fates, she could use his advice. Because even though she knew it was reckless, she burned with the desire to return to Devendra right now and take the throne from her father. She wanted to bring justice to him and her brother for all their crimes.

While she was wishing for impossible things, she also wanted to stop the war with Ryden before it had a chance to start, ensure Imara's happiness, and find herself a future with Cardon.

In short, she wanted far too many things, and she was only one person.

At that thought, Serene blinked and refocused on Clare.

Her mind began to race.

Serene met Desfan in his office. They were alone; Karim and Wilf stood in the hall outside, and she didn't imagine there was much of a conversation happening between those two.

Serene told Desfan everything Venn and Vera had learned about Salvation and the Hunt.

Desfan scrubbed a hand over his face. He looked weary. Far too weary to have only been wearing the crown for one day.

"I knew of the increase in refugees," he said, gesturing to the pile of letters on his desk. "But I hadn't heard anything of this camp."

"According to Venn, the Hunt may have suppressed any messages that tried to reach you, in order to hide what they were doing." Serene passed over the letter addressed to him. "This is from Lord Zander Fellnor. I believe he'll be asking you for aid and protection."

"I will do everything I can for them," he promised.

"Thank you."

"You're welcome," Desfan said. "Fates . . . I can't believe Prince Grandeur has overstepped so far in Mortise. Our alliance is still new—what made him think he could operate the Hunt within Mortise?"

"I don't know. I do ask that you don't strike out at Devendra—at least not yet. I'll be writing to my father to determine if he knew what Grandeur was doing. If he didn't know, I will make it clear that the Hunt must be stopped and that my brother must be punished. If my father knew . . . Well, I'll make it clear that Mortise will have every right to retaliate."

Desfan grunted. "I'll have to inform the council about this, but I can wait to do so until we receive word from your father."

"I would appreciate that delay." There was no need to publicize what had been done, until fault could be determined. The peace between their kingdoms was far too tentative for that.

Serene took a breath. "I want to go to Zennor."

Desfan's shock was obvious. "Why?"

"I want to learn the fates of my people who ventured into Zennor for aid and vanished. I also want to consult with my uncle on several matters that concern all of us—Devendra, Mortise, and Zennor. I think it's vital that all of us are united to face the threat Ryden poses."

"I agree," Desfan said. "But, Serene, you can't leave. We've signed the betrothal agreement, but my people need to get to know you before the wedding. The peace isn't secure yet."

"I've considered that," Serene said. "Luckily for me, I have the ability to be in two places at once."

He leaned back in his chair, his brown eyes thoughtful. "Your decoy, Clare Ellington."

She nodded. "I'm a trained diplomat, but Clare has a natural affinity for connecting with people. She will do a better job than I ever could here. She has already agreed to act in my stead to help build unity with the people of Mortise."

"Meanwhile, you'll be free to go to Zennor."

"Yes. I'll travel anonymously, so as not to ruin the illusion Clare will be weaving here. I know Mortise and Zennor have healthy trade relations, but you have no military obligations to each other, which could make the coming war with Ryden complicated. I would like to speak to my uncle and attempt to broker a stronger alliance between your two kingdoms."

"I would love to have Buhari's men on our side," Desfan said. "But you aren't officially a Mortisian yet—not until we marry. You can't negotiate for us."

"I can at least begin talks."

He shook his head. "You have no official capacity to do even that."

"Then appoint me as your delegate."

Lines appeared on his forehead. "That's not exactly following tradition."

"Perhaps not, but it *is* an option." When he said nothing, she leaned forward. "It's the *best* option, Desfan. My uncle adores me, and he'll listen to me. I can persuade him. And if all three kingdoms are united . . ."

"You think we might intimidate King Henri enough that he

won't dare attack?"

She lifted one shoulder. "I don't know. But it's worth a try. Even if it doesn't work as an intimidation tactic, it will give us an edge in the war with Ryden."

Desfan sighed. "I can't argue that."

Serene hesitated briefly. This was the part she wasn't sure how to address, but she went with her gut. "There's something else I would like to discuss with my uncle—Imara's betrothal."

Desfan stilled. "Why?"

"Several reasons. For one, I don't like the sound of Eilan Skyer. For another, I don't like how Imara talks about him— which isn't often, but it leaves an impression. I think she's scared of him."

Desfan's gaze darkened. "Why would her father arrange a marriage with a man she's afraid of?"

"According to Imara, it's because relations with the clans are exceptionally bad right now. I want to believe there's another way to secure peace between the monarchy and the clans—even if it's just by the fact that war with Ryden is coming and they can't afford infighting."

"Do you think you could help negotiate a peace that doesn't require Imara's marriage to Skyer?" Desfan asked.

"I don't know," she said honestly. "I won't tell Imara of my intentions, because I don't want to raise any false hopes. But I'll do my best to ensure she doesn't have to marry Skyer."

Desfan tipped his chin. "I support you in this."

Serene studied him for a short, silent moment. "Desfan, I'm going to be very direct now, and I trust this will stay between us."

He suddenly looked cautious. "Of course."

"Our marriage was arranged strictly for political reasons. It's a fact I resigned myself to long ago, as I know you did. We don't love each other."

Desfan said nothing. No denial, but no agreement. Silence, in this case, was absolutely the safer political move.

Serene ignored the risks and continued. "I've been prepared to marry you for so long, I couldn't see any other option. Despite everything, I was ready to become your wife."

"Was?" Alarm edged into his tone.

"Yes. But I'm hesitating now. Not because I don't think we could make this work—we are both dedicated enough to our people that we could do this. But I now realize that by marrying you, I would be hurting one of the most important people in my life: Imara."

His face was inscrutable. "Serene—"

"You kissed her, Desfan."

He paled. His throat flexed. "Serene, I—"

"I'm not upset. Imara told me what happened, and I haven't been able to get it out of my head." She flipped up a hand. "Not the image of you two kissing, but the way she looked when she talked about it. When she talked about you."

Something flashed in his eyes. There and gone, too quick to analyze.

"I've watched you with her," Serene said. "And I've watched *her* with *you*. And while I think things are new and tentative between you, something very real is there. I don't want to hurt her by marrying you. Especially if there's another way. For all Liam Kaelin's faults, he was right about one thing: the coming war with Ryden has the power to create strong alliances between Zennor, Devendra, and Mortise—without the aid of an arranged marriage. If I can broker peace between you and my uncle, Devendra would be united by default because of the alliance shared with Zennor. And if King Henri marches on any of us, we will all be united against him—whether or not you and I are married."

Desfan ran a hand over his mouth and the dark scruff on his chin, his thoughts clearly racing. "No one can know we're contemplating this."

"Agreed." They had sacrificed too much to get to this point. Others had, as well. "Until things are settled between Zennor and Mortise—or until the war starts—we must remain engaged. We can't have even a whisper of rumor, or all of our efforts up until now will have been in vain." She paused. "You and Clare can continue to build the peace between our peoples, and I will do what I can in Zennor. I may fail, but I feel it's worth trying. Do you agree?"

Desfan studied her for a long moment. "Yes."

A thrill sparked in her chest, and the nerves in her stomach settled. "Good." She eyed him. "It's possible I could persuade my uncle to consider a betrothal between you and Imara, since that would arguably be a more profitable match to Zennor than her marriage to Skyer, but I will only try to arrange such a thing once I can ascertain from Imara that you are who she wants. I will not force her into anything."

"I don't want to force her, either," Desfan said readily.

"Then it's settled."

"When will you leave?" he asked.

"As soon as possible. The journey to reach my uncle in Kedaah will take about a month."

"Do you need any additional men?"

Serene shook her head. "I want to travel quickly and without drawing unnecessary attention. I'll only take two of my guards." She'd already chosen Cardon and Wilf.

Bennick, as captain of her guard, needed to remain here in Duvan, to solidify the illusion that Clare was Serene. Venn would also stay, since he knew the most about the situation in Salvation; if Desfan needed assistance or advice, Venn could provide that.

"I can talk to Captain Seveh," Desfan said. "The *Phoenix* is a fast ship, and he's still in port."

"Perfect. Let me know as soon as he's ready to sail, and I'll meet him at the harbor."

"What are you going to tell Imara?"

Serene exhaled slowly. "That I'm hoping to negotiate peace between Zennor and Mortise. I don't want to get her hopes up for anything more, especially when her focus needs to be on getting well. You'll keep a close eye on her, won't you?"

"Of course. And I'll lend extra guards to Captain Markam so Clare will be well protected at all times."

"Thank you." She clasped her hands on her lap. "I hate to ask something else of you, but Clare has asked me to speak on her behalf. About Latif."

Desfan's spine went rigid. "What about him?"

She quickly explained about Clare's brothers; the fire, and their suspicions that it may not have been an accident. She didn't accuse her brother or the Hunt outright, but she implied someone at the castle may have had a hand in it. Desfan listened intently, not interrupting—even when she brought up Clare's reasons for wanting to send Latif.

When she'd finished, the serjan pushed back from his desk and stood, pacing toward the window. One hand raked through his dark curls, but he said nothing.

Serene remained silent, letting him think.

After a long pause, he twisted back to face her. "I'm sorry for

Clare's loss. It's one that I unfortunately know well."

"And Latif had a hand in that," Serene said quietly.

The skin around Desfan's eyes tensed. "The man helped take my sister from me. He may have been following orders, but he did it all the same. Even when he came to my father, he didn't tell him the truth—that his employer had sold Meerah to King Henri. He just said there were rumors she might have survived the shipwreck. He was a coward. And his cowardice cost my sister—and my father and me—greatly."

"I know," she repeated. "But Clare says he seeks redemption."

"He deserves a noose."

Serene didn't respond, just let him process her request. She knew she was asking a lot. Too much, maybe.

Desfan blew out a hard breath, but his voice was surprisingly soft as he said, "I haven't actually determined his punishment. I thought I'd decide once Meerah returned."

"You wanted to wait for her opinion?"

He grunted. "That would be the more noble thing. But no, I wanted to wait and look in her eyes. Talk to her. *Know* her pain. Then I would know how much pain should accompany Latif's death." He reclined back against the wall, his arms crossing over his chest. His expression was suddenly distant. "When Mia was maybe four or five years old, she found a spider in her room."

Serene didn't know why Desfan was telling this story, but she listened intently.

"She screamed so loudly," he recalled. "And she just kept screaming. Everyone came running; guards, servants, my parents—me as well. Tahlyah was already with her. And that's actually what had made her scream so long and hard. Meerah's first scream was because the spider scared her. The others were because she didn't want Tahlyah to kill it."

Serene just watched him, saying nothing.

Finally, Desfan shook his head. "Unless my sister is much changed, she wouldn't want Latif to die. No matter the part he played in her fate." He met Serene's gaze. "If he is the only one Clare trusts to bring her the truth about what happened to her family, I will not keep her from the peace she might gain. Even if I'd rather keep Latif in a cell for the rest of his life."

"You'll pardon him, then?"

"Not exactly. Very few know his role in things, so I can avoid a formal trial. I will release him from prison if he'll do this for Clare. But when his mission is complete, he'll be banished from Mortise. That will be his punishment."

Serene rose and walked to him. "Thank you, Desfan. You're a good man. Far better than I once gave you credit for."

The corner of his mouth twitched. "I've never excelled at first impressions."

She smiled a little, stopping a pace away from him. "Yes, well, your reputation wasn't exactly spotless."

"No," he agreed. "For what it's worth, Serene, you've exceeded my expectations as well."

That settled a nice warmth in her chest. "If we do marry, I think we'll at least be friends."

Desfan took her hand. "Agreed. And if we don't marry, we will also be friends."

Serene squeezed his hand. "If everything works out as we wish and you're free to pursue Imara . . . will you?"

A light entered his eyes. "Yes."

This time, her smile was wide. "Good."

CHAPTER 14

MIA

RENA BROUGHT DINNER TO THE ROOM AS USUAL. She prepared Mia for bed, and then she made a show of retiring for the night, in case anyone was watching them. Fletcher went with her, as he usually did. Grayson dismissed the night guard, just as he had last night. Mia recognized the guard as one of Tyrell's men, and she knew the dismissal would be reported to him. Tyrell would have no idea that tonight would be different, though.

Mia was terrified of what the night might bring. Her only consolation was that they all knew to meet at Porynth Harbor, in case something went wrong. Grayson had told them the location over dinner, along with the name of their ship: the *Seafire*.

Nerves danced in Mia's belly, apprehension making her feel a little sick as she settled her thick cloak over her shoulders.

Grayson had foregone wearing his cloak. His longsword was secured at his hip, along with the rest of his daggers—two of which he'd carefully packed in his bag, warning Mia that the blades were coated in poison. He wore his signature black clothing, though he'd left his leather gloves on his desk. The blatant placement almost felt like a message to his father, or his family—or perhaps it was for himself.

He was done being the Black Hand.

Grayson hadn't said much throughout the day as they'd both packed. To be fair, Mia hadn't had much to say, either. Tension was thick in the air as they'd made the final preparations for their escape. She'd watched him surreptitiously as he'd picked through his things, choosing to shove only a few items in his pack. She understood the necessity of packing lightly; she'd be leaving behind books Grayson had given her, as well as sketches and paintings she'd done over the years.

Carefully folding a spare dress, she'd asked, "Will you miss anything?"

He had blinked, almost as if he'd forgotten she was in the room. "What?"

"Will you miss anything here? The things you'll have to leave behind?" This was his home, as horrible as it had often been.

He met her gaze, his gray eyes sure. "No. None of it matters—not as long as I have you."

Her heart warmed. "I feel the same."

He smiled gently, and they continued packing.

"I am sorry about leaving your horse, though."

He glanced over at her, clearly surprised. "Why?"

"I visited him often while you were gone. He . . . calmed me. He made me feel closer to you." Her head tipped to the side.

"Why didn't you name him?"

Grayson seemed even more surprised by this question, but he still answered. "Naming him would have shown that I cared about him."

And that could have made the horse a target to the other Kaelins.

"Did you ever name him in your mind?" she asked.

"I thought of him as *Horse* sometimes."

She pulled a face. "You can't call him *Horse*."

His eyes sparked with mirth. "Do you have a name in mind, then?"

Mia nodded. "*Vehrin Varah*."

His brow furrowed. "It's Mortisian, but I don't know what it means."

"The closest translation is 'gentle soul.'" Her cheeks warmed with sudden embarrassment. "I know it doesn't sound fierce, but he seemed that way to me. Soulful, kind, and valiant."

Grayson's expression softened. "It's a perfect name for him, Mia. Thank you."

There was an undercurrent of regret in his voice, and she instantly felt bad. "I'm sorry if this makes leaving him harder."

He shook his head. "I'm not sorry. He deserves a name."

Not that the horse would ever hear it.

Mia shook off the memory of that conversation. The present needed her focus, now.

It was time to go.

Wrapped in her cloak, Mia pulled in a slow breath, but her fingers still trembled as she tried to tie her cloak.

Grayson's fingers were suddenly there, gently working the thin ties for her. "It's going to be all right," he said quietly.

She let her hands fall. His nearness warmed her—not only

because she could feel the heat of his body against hers, but because she always responded to him this way. "Are you sure you're up to this?" she asked.

He nodded once. The burn looked as painful as ever, but he'd just taken more of the powder Devon had given him. The medicine seemed to alleviate the worst of the pain. He moved more easily, and even spoke more clearly.

She still worried about him.

He finished securing her cloak, but he didn't step back. His fingertips brushed her throat, and her heart rate spiked. Especially when he fingered the two necklaces there—the pebble and the queen. He didn't ask about the Strategem piece, but he must have guessed Tyrell had given it to her, because the lines in his face deepened.

He tucked a stray curl behind her ear and met her gaze. "Stay close to me. If anyone approaches, say nothing and keep your head down. Do you have your dagger?"

"Yes." It was secured at her waist by a plain leather belt. She'd never really practiced using it, though. Despite the training Grayson had given her since they were children, they'd avoided blades. Henri never would have allowed her to have a weapon. But once they were free and Grayson was feeling better, she would ask him to teach her so she could wield the knife with confidence.

Grayson leaned in and pressed a soft kiss against her lips. Fire ignited inside her, and it took all her willpower not to snatch hold of him when—far too soon—he drew back.

He shouldered his pack, and Mia did the same. He took her hand, and together they left his bedroom, slipping into the shadowy corridor.

They'd waited for the first bell after midnight, so the castle was asleep. They made their way on silent footsteps toward the nearest staircase. Mia's most inconspicuous dress was a dark charcoal gray, and the fabric whispered against her legs as they moved.

They saw no one, until they reached the base of the stairs. A patrolling guard glanced up at them, his tired eyes registering them too late.

Grayson dropped her hand and lunged. He had a hand clamped over the guard's mouth and a dagger in his heart before Mia could blink. As the guard sagged in death, Grayson dragged him toward the nearest shadowed alcove, then lowered him silently to the ground.

His dagger was streaked with dark blood as he rose, but Mia didn't hesitate to take his free hand when he reached for her. Grayson said nothing, and neither did she. They just kept moving.

Her heart pounded in her chest. She'd never seen Grayson kill before, and she was more rattled than she wanted to admit.

They reached the castle's laundry room, which Grayson had determined would be the least guarded way out of the castle. The direct access to the yard had been designed for the servants who had to haul water inside, but it would serve them well tonight.

The large room was deserted, as Rena had assured them it would be at this hour. Weaving their way around giant wash tubs and long tables stacked with folded linens, Mia began to breathe a little easier.

Their plan was working.

Outside, they stuck to the shadows as much as possible. They didn't run into any guards, which felt like a fates-blasted miracle. She glimpsed a few on the wall that surrounded the grounds, but they were looking outward. They didn't expect people to be sneaking *out* of the castle.

Devon would meet them at the back gate behind the training yard. He planned to bribe the guards there, while Grayson and Mia remained hooded in their heavy cloaks, pretending to be people Devon had treated. The training yard still stretched before them, along with several outbuildings, but Grayson didn't falter as he pulled her forward.

Mia had been on the grounds often enough these past weeks, but seeing the vastness of the night sky above them still gave her pause. For half her life, she'd been in a windowless cell. She was still adjusting to how large the world was—how small she felt when she was out in it. She tightened her hold on Grayson's hand, forcing her eyes away from the silver half-moon and the glittering sea of stars.

Her chest felt tight. Fates, she couldn't afford a panic. Not now. She drew in slow, long breaths as Devon had taught her, hoping to keep the panic from fully rising. Once they were safely away, she'd pull out the small jar of lavender salts she had tucked in her bag.

She remained close to Grayson as they skirted the training grounds, and her lungs strained as their pace increased. She knew her endurance was not as impressive as most. And even though her stab wound had healed, she still felt a twinge of discomfort. Her swollen hand throbbed dully. Despite her cloak, the night air chilled her.

Once they were beyond the wall, they would enter the nearby forest. The Fletchers—who would already be in Lenzen by now—would meet them at a place called Oland's Bridge.

The stone wall before them became towering the closer they came to it, until finally they rounded the last outbuilding in their path and the gate came into view.

Immediately, Mia knew something was wrong.

There were no guards. Devon stood alone, reclining against the gate, his shoulders sagging and his eyes fastened on them.

No. That was wrong. His eyes weren't fastened on them. They weren't fastened on anything.

A dagger had been driven through his throat, the hilt nearly lost in the shadows of night. And it wasn't the only one. There were at least three other knives, all buried to the hilt in his chest. It looked like the blades were long enough to have pinned him to the closed gate.

Mia sucked in a breath; pain, horror, and shock all hit her at once.

Devon was dead.

One of the only people in this entire kingdom that cared about her was dead, and . . . fates, it was her fault. She never should have asked him to leave with them.

Grayson went rigid, his hold on her hand strangling.

A shadow peeled away from a nearby tree. "I told you I'd be watching you, Grayson."

Mia's heart thundered. It was his brother, Carter. And he wasn't alone. Four more shadows stepped forward, moving to surround them.

Grayson didn't give them the chance. With blinding speed, he threw the dagger in his hand. It lodged in the stomach of the closest man, and he dropped to his knees. Still moving, Grayson threw another dagger—this one hit its target as well.

The other two men rushed forward, and Grayson drew his longsword to meet their drawn blades. Steel clashed as blows were exchanged, their movements so quick, they blurred.

Mia wanted to close her eyes. She wanted to cover her ears

and block out everything. The sight of Devon's lifeless body. The gasps of the dying soldiers. Grayson's grunt of pain, and then his snarl of fury.

Mia was frozen. She'd witnessed violence before, but this was different. Worse. Fiercer. Adrenaline rushed through her body, making her skin prickle.

A memory surged. She was a child, standing in the palace training yard, watching her father fight with his men. He was sparring, but she didn't realize that. She'd thought the fight was real—that those men were trying to kill her father. The men were large and they hit hard enough to draw blood. She'd started to cry.

Desfan and Tally had teased her.

Mother had given them stern looks, then she'd crouched before Mia and wiped away her tears. "None of these men are in real danger, my love. It's a game, nothing more."

This fight with Grayson wasn't a game.

As she watched, Grayson's sword slashed across the stomach of one of the two remaining soldiers, wrenching a death cry from him. Grayson's scarred face was a blank mask, but his gray eyes burned with intensity as his blade flashed in the moonlight.

Mia did not fear him. She could *never* fear him. But, in this moment, she understood why people did. She understood why they called him the Black Hand, and why Tyrell did not trust him. If this was the only side of Grayson people saw, she could understand their terror.

Peripheral movement snatched her attention as Carter took a quick step back. His round eyes were riveted on Grayson's furious battle with the remaining guard. He seemed to just be realizing that he hadn't brought enough men to contain

Grayson.

Not nearly enough.

The older prince jerked back another step, his mouth opening to call an alarm.

If Carter yelled for reinforcements and their escape was stopped, Grayson would be punished—again.

Mia would not allow that to happen.

She dropped the bag from her shoulder and darted forward. She hit Carter right in the abdomen, under his guard—a vulnerable place to hit, Grayson had taught her—and they both crashed to the ground.

A curse spat out of Carter. His sword bounced away and his elbow slammed into her back. Pain sparked, but that didn't stop her from reaching for her sheathed dagger. She didn't plan to kill him—only get him to surrender.

Carter's fingers dug into her wrist, and her swollen hand flared painfully. She couldn't stop her small cry of pain.

Carter bucked beneath her and they rolled, each of them grappling for her knife. He wasn't as strong as Grayson or Tyrell, but he was still larger and stronger than her.

A sick misgiving stabbed her. She was going to lose this fight.

They stopped rolling, and Mia gasped as Carter's weight smashed against her ribs. Sprawled on top of her, his boots digging into the ground, he wedged one hard forearm against her throat.

Mia gagged.

Carter's breaths were sharp. Fear was in his eyes, along with desperation. "He won't hurt me if I have you," he gasped. "He won't—"

Carter's head was jerked back, cutting off his words and baring his throat to the silver moonlight. His entire body was yanked off her, and Mia instinctively rolled away. She looked back just in time to see a dagger slice, and Mia's stomach pitched as crimson blood rained down.

Grayson's hand fisted in Carter's long black hair, and he released his limp brother with a shove. Then he stared down at her, his breathing even, his hands bloody.

Mia's throat burned.

The whole fight had lasted mere moments, but adrenaline still shot through her veins. Instinct screamed danger, even though Grayson was the only one standing over her.

Grayson, who had killed six men tonight without hesitation. One, his own brother.

Grayson's jaw stiffened. He bent and retrieved his long-sword, which must have fallen, and he hurried to sheathe it. Then he reached out a hand—the one not holding the bloody dagger. "We need to go. Someone will have heard."

She stared at his outstretched hand, then her gaze flickered up to his gray eyes. There was no regret. No pain. No fear. Nothing but resolve.

Her lungs burned. When she hauled in a breath, her whole body shuddered.

Grayson's mouth pressed into a line. He grasped her left hand and pulled her to her feet. She gripped his fingers, her body shaking. Concern was now etched into his hard face. "Are you hurt?"

Her chin was wet. She touched it, and her fingertips came away bloody. Some of the spray from Carter's blood. She swallowed hard, her stomach convulsing. "No." She wasn't entirely sure what she was denying. She wanted to deny everything she'd seen over the last few minutes, beginning with Devon's death.

Grayson squeezed her hand. She thought he wanted to say something—comfort her, or defend what he'd done—but instead he sheathed his dagger, still streaked red, and pulled her back to their dropped bags. He snatched them both up, and then he moved for the gate.

Mia averted her eyes from Devon's body.

Grayson paused only to grab Devon's pack, which was lying on the ground nearby, and then he dragged open the gate. It protested with a metallic squeal that made Grayson wince.

Once outside the castle walls, his hand still wrapped around hers, they ran toward the dark edge of the forest.

Mia hoped it would be deep enough to swallow them.

CHAPTER 15

TYRELL

TYRELL PROWLED DOWN THE DARKENED CORRIDOR, his hands clenched at his sides. Fear, denial, grief, hurt—all of that swirled in his gut, but it was too much to process. Too much to *feel*. So he focused on the strongest emotion: rage.

Grayson and Mia had been gone for an hour now, and every moment that passed felt like a blade twisting in his heart.

Peter had pounded on his door, jerking him from sleep. He'd spoken tersely, giving him just enough details to make Tyrell's head spin.

His head was still spinning.

He'd been given orders, and he'd obeyed, even though all he wanted to do was tear out of here.

Grayson had taken Mia.

Movement at the end of the hall caught his eye. Peter was prowling toward him, both of them silently arriving at the king's study at the same time.

Peter entered first, and Tyrell was right behind him.

Their father stood behind his desk, his hands planted on the smooth surface, his arms braced. His entire body trembled, and when he lifted his head to face his sons, Tyrell stiffened at the fury burning in his eyes. "Close the door."

Tyrell did as ordered. It was just the three of them in the room. Iris was with Carter's body.

Tyrell had never seen his mother exhibit raw emotion, but when Carter's lifeless body had been uncovered . . . The Poison Queen had gripped the edge of that table, and she had screamed.

Peter gave his report without prompting. "We have no direct witnesses, but from what I've learned, Grayson killed seven men tonight; Carter, one castle guard, the four guards at the gate, and a physician named Devon."

Tyrell's blood chilled. "Devon is dead?"

"Yes." Peter glanced at him. "I'm not sure if Grayson killed him or not, because the physician's death was different than the others. His body was staged; he was left hanging on the gate."

The image was horrifying. To know Mia had seen it—possibly even witnessed his death—made Tyrell grind his teeth. He didn't know Devon well enough to truly mourn him, but Mia would be devastated by his death.

Henri watched him closely. "You've interacted with the physician. During that confrontation, do you think he would have been loyal to Carter or Grayson?"

"His loyalty would have been to Mia." There was no question of that in his mind. But who had killed Devon? Carter, because he saw a traitor aiding in Mia's escape? Or Grayson, because

Devon had tried to prevent him from taking Mia into such reckless danger?

Peter made a sound in his throat, and Tyrell did not like the calculation—or the appreciation—that flared in his eyes. "Mia is small, but she's not one to underestimate, is she?"

Henri frowned at his eldest son. "What else did you learn from interrogating the guards?"

"The first ones to reach the scene immediately sent men to trail Grayson and Mia, and it looks like they headed for the woods, not the city. I sent men to pursue them."

Henri's dark gaze shifted to Tyrell, silently demanding his report.

As soon as Tyrell had been told about Grayson's escape, he'd been ordered to track down the Fletchers. His eyes narrowed. "Alun and Rena Fletcher are gone. They borrowed two horses from the stables and left through the main gate during the changing of the guard. They told the night guards they were visiting a friend in Lenzen, but they didn't specify who. I have men searching for them."

Henri said nothing.

Peter and Tyrell followed the king's lead, and silence burned the air around them. The quiet was dangerous, because it left Tyrell to his thoughts. Gave more space for his encroaching panic.

Grayson had taken Mia. She was gone. Not only that, she was with Grayson, who was so far gone in his rebellion that he had recklessly endangered her life tonight. He'd run away from the castle. He'd deserted Henri—deserted all of them. He may have killed Devon, for fates' sake, and he'd ruthlessly murdered Carter, who was the weakest of them all. Tyrell had seen the deep cut across Carter's throat; there was no sign of indecision, no sign of reluctance. Only brutal efficiency.

Grayson could have subdued Carter in any number of ways, but he'd chosen to kill him. That was a line none of them had ever crossed. Not Tyrell, even in his darkest moments. Not even Henri or Iris had killed their own blood.

But Grayson had.

His brother had snapped. Tyrell had seen the change in him, sensed the danger, but even he had not anticipated this.

Grayson had thrown his rebellion in Henri's face in the most flagrant, brutal way possible. And he'd dragged Mia into it.

"How did Carter know Grayson would try to escape?" Henri asked, his voice nothing more than a whisper. "How did he know which gate to watch?"

Peter's jaw tensed. "Mother told me she asked Carter to keep an eye on Grayson. Apparently, Carter offered gold to several guards in the castle to spy on Grayson and Mia, as well as those who have been closely affiliated with the girl—the Fletchers and Devon. There were reports of Rena Fletcher gathering extra clothing from the laundry, and the guards at the back gate noticed Devon lurking during the afternoon." He paused. "We'll probably never know if Devon decided to warn Carter of Grayson's plan, or if the physician intended to leave with Grayson and Mia. What we do know is that Carter paid the night guards to leave the gate, and he set a trap with his own men."

"He was a fool," Henri said, his tone low and unreadable.

Tyrell and Peter exchanged a short look.

Henri pushed away from the desk, his voice rising as he continued. "Carter has long wanted to prove himself, but he was ill-prepared. He should have told us what he suspected. Fates *blast it*!" He pounded the desk and Tyrell barely stopped his flinch.

That fury . . . it was aimed at Grayson, but it would touch Mia. Of course it would.

His stomach pitched.

Peter's voice was cool. "They can't have gotten far. We'll find them."

"Alive," Henri hissed. "I want them both alive." He looked to Tyrell. "You will lead the hunt."

Tyrell straightened. "As you order."

"Why bother to keep Grayson alive now?" Peter asked. "He's a rabid dog who should be put down. Surely we can't trust him again—not after this. He killed Carter. Fates, he may have even killed Liam in Mortise. He must be executed."

"I am king," Henri ground out. "And I *want him alive*."

Peter inclined his head. "Yes, Sire."

"I'll need more men," Tyrell said. "We must spread out." There were a thousand directions Grayson might go. The forest was wide and deep.

"Take as many as you need," the king said. "Just find them. Grayson knows far too much, and they are both infinitely valuable to me."

Peter looked to Tyrell. "You should search Grayson's room. There may be clues about his plan, or at least his destination."

Tyrell almost scoffed. As if Grayson actually *had* a plan. His brother wasn't thinking rationally, or he never would have taken Mia like this. But Peter's idea wasn't all bad, so he nodded.

Henri turned to Peter. "Return to your mother. Carter's death is a particular blow to her. I will be there shortly."

Peter tipped his head and left.

Tyrell stood alone with his father, who studied him closely. "You're angry with Grayson."

"Yes," Tyrell said.

"You're angry he killed Carter."

"Yes." There was no real love between any of the brothers. They were all monsters—Tyrell included. But Carter was so far out of Grayson's league in a fight, his death hadn't been fair. It had been murder. Vicious and cruel.

"You're angry he took Mia," Henri continued.

"Yes." His voice was a mere breath, but it vibrated with the intensity of his anger. The fear that had clutched him when Peter had first come to him swelled, impossible to crush.

Henri stepped forward, stopping only when he was directly in front of Tyrell. "Use that anger. Find him. Find *them*."

Tyrell's throat felt too tight, but he forced the words out. "Will Mia be punished?"

Henri eyed him. "If you bring her back to me, no. That will be your reward. But if someone else finds her first, I'll have no choice but to mete out punishment."

Tyrell's shoulders went back. He punched down his fear and gathered his anger into something he could use—a weapon. "I will find them."

When Tyrell closed the door in Grayson's room, his lungs constricted. Mia's soft scent was everywhere, and so were her things. She'd left her sketchbooks. Her paintings. There, hanging in the open closet, was the beautiful gown she'd worn the night of the king's ball. The night she'd fought with Tyrell and left him.

He pinched his eyes closed and ordered himself not to think. Not to feel.

He failed.

The pain gutted him. Mia was gone. She was out there in the dark, cold woods. She was alone with Grayson, who was going to get her hurt or killed.

Tyrell needed to find her before that could happen.

He forced his eyes to open and his feet to move. He went to Grayson's desk and instantly spotted the discarded pair of black gloves. Just the sight of them made his blood boil. He threw them aside.

Forcing himself to focus, he glanced over the papers strewn across the desk. He lifted one of Mia's sketchbooks so he could riffle through the papers. Nothing stood out to him, or screamed Grayson's intentions.

His brother would not find any safety in Ryden—but which kingdom would he choose?

Mia was from Mortise. Would he go there? They might find refuge . . . but they would also find Mia's brother. According to Grayson's report—if he could be believed—Desfan Cassian had a thousand reasons to hate Grayson. He had been an enemy to Desfan and Mortise. Of course, Grayson might think to barter for a safe haven with Mia, but he would have to know that Desfan would never trust him to be around Mia.

So, maybe they would go to Mortise, but maybe they wouldn't.

Devendra was a future warzone—Grayson wouldn't go there. Maybe Zennor . . .

Tyrell spotted a stack of books at the back of the desk. He set Mia's sketchbook aside so he could peruse the spines.

Maps, survivalist guides for traversing mountains . . . Were they going to go by land, then, and not by ship?

Tyrell spent the next half hour going through the entire room, but he found no other clues. He didn't know if the books truly indicated the path Grayson and Mia had taken, but he would follow them into the forest. He'd head south, toward the border mountains. He'd also send troops to Vyken and Kavan, just in case Grayson intended to escape via the sea. Perhaps he'd even send men to Porynth as well; it was farther south, but it was a large port.

He needed to pack. He needed to go after them.

For some inexplicable reason, he lingered.

Inside his pocket, the length of red silk ribbon burned. He'd snatched it up when Peter came to him, and he couldn't bear to leave it behind. Mia had touched it, just this morning. Somehow, it made her feel closer to him.

I'll find you, he promised. He could keep her safe. From his father, and from Grayson.

He moved toward the door, but the sketchbook on the desk snared his attention. He picked it up, fingering the edge. After a brief hesitation, he yanked open the bedroom door. One of his men in the hall straightened sharply.

"I want every sketchbook and painting in this room moved to mine," he said, his voice clipped. "Everything of hers. See it done."

"Yes, sir."

Tyrell strode to his room, the sketchbook still in his hands. Once he was in the privacy of his suite, he thumbed the book open. Almost immediately, he spotted the folded piece of paper just inside the cover.

His heart stopped. He unfolded the page and moved to the nearest window so he could read it by the light of the moon.

Tyrell,

I know you're going to be hurt when you read this, and I'm sorry for that. But there are things I need to say. Things I couldn't say when I was telling you goodbye.

I need to thank you. When you first came to visit me after Grayson left for Mortise, I was filled with so much dread. But you were a gift, even though that's not what your father intended. Thank you for your kindness. For everything you gave me. I couldn't take all your gifts with me, but I will always treasure the black queen you made, just as I will always treasure our friendship.

I know I didn't give you everything you wanted. I certainly didn't give you what you deserve. I hope, one day, you find someone worthy of your love. Someone who can give you her whole heart. For now, please know that you will forever hold a piece of mine.

I hate to leave you here. I wanted you to come with me. Maybe someday you will leave your family and Ryden behind. If you do, please come find me. I'll be so happy to see you again.

You are good, Tyrell. Don't let your father or anyone else – including yourself – convince you otherwise.

I pray that the fates watch over you.

My love always,

Mia

Tyrell's eyes burned. Mia's handwriting swam as his vision hazed. Her words echoed so deeply inside him, he knew he'd never be free of them.

I was telling you goodbye.

This morning, that's what she'd been doing. When she'd held him . . . Fates, he hadn't realized. If he had, he never would have let her go.

I hope, one day, you find someone worthy of your love.

You, he thought desperately. *There can only be you.*

I wanted you to come with me.

Even if that didn't tell him everything, he knew what it meant. She'd wanted him. She'd asked Grayson if Tyrell could come, and he'd said no.

Tyrell's hands shook.

Would he have gone? If Mia had asked him to leave with her, would he have said yes?

They'd never know, because she hadn't asked. Grayson hadn't *let* her.

Something in his chest clenched, too many emotions tangling in his throat.

You are good, Tyrell.

He didn't know what he was in this moment, but it wasn't *good.*

He wanted to rip Grayson apart. For keeping Mia away from him. For *taking* her away. He'd endangered her. He was out of his mind, and Tyrell needed to stop him. Grayson couldn't be allowed to hurt Mia ever again.

My love always . . .

When Tyrell folded Mia's letter, his tears had stopped. His hands weren't shaking anymore. His pain and fear was buried under one furious purpose: killing his brother.

Mia could only be safe—only be his—once Grayson was dead.

CHAPTER 16

GRAYSON

GRAYSON RE-TUCKED THE EDGE OF MIA'S cloak around her shoulder. She was asleep, curled at the base of a towering tree, using her pack as a pillow. She shivered as a cold wind skated through the trees.

He just felt numb.

Dawn was lightening the edges of shadows, chasing the deep darkness of night away. They were hidden near Oland's Bridge. The worn plank-bridge stretched over a narrow point of the Julne River, and it was a landmark in this part of the forest. It was used by hunters and woodsmen, though no one had arrived yet to use it.

Grayson sat beside Mia, his back against a large boulder and his ears attuned to the area. He disregarded the normal woodland sounds—the low rush of water, the hum and chirp of insects and birds, the breeze that fluttered the yellowing leaves. He listened for the snap of a twig. The rustle of a boot against leaves. The snort of a horse.

He heard nothing, but he did not relax.

There was no sign of Fletcher or his wife. That meant they didn't have blankets, horses, or bedrolls. They didn't have a tent. Grayson had given Fletcher the larger portion of his gold so he could purchase horses in Lenzen, so he and Mia had limited coin. They only had the food Mia had prepared for her escape, which wouldn't stretch as far with the two of them.

They couldn't keep waiting for the Fletchers, who might have been delayed or captured. It was possible they'd even betrayed them, and that's how Carter had known to ambush them at the gate.

Carter.

Grayson's hands fisted. He'd scrubbed them clean in the frigid water of the Julne last night, but he could still feel the blood on his hands. He'd scrubbed the blood off of Mia, too, and she hadn't said a word.

He pinched his eyes closed. He hadn't slept at all last night. He'd been keeping watch. He wasn't even tired. The medicine Devon had given him kept him oddly energized, even though it sometimes made his thoughts feel stilted.

Devon.

Maybe the physician had been the one to betray them. If so, he'd paid for his treachery.

The callous thought made Grayson wince. Perhaps he wasn't entirely numb.

He needed to stay numb. It was the only way he could keep moving. The only way to keep Mia safe. He'd committed to being the monster his father had forced him to become, because Mia needed him to be the Black Hand; it was the only way he'd get her safely to Desfan. He just hadn't expected to kill his own brother last night. He didn't even remember making that choice. Everything had been vividly sharp, and yet, his thoughts had blurred. He'd eliminated the danger. He'd gotten Mia out. His actual actions . . . He hadn't felt fully in control, even though his every move had been coolly efficient.

He knew he'd frightened Mia. He had seen the flash of fear in her eyes after he'd killed Carter.

In truth, he'd frightened himself.

Maybe he'd taken too much of the powder. But, what other choice did he have? If he didn't take it, the pain from his wound was too much.

If he hadn't been drugged, would he have killed his brother? He didn't know. But he had crossed the one line no one else in his family ever had—he'd killed a Kaelin. His mother thought he'd killed Liam, but . . . He had actually killed his own brother.

Carter had tortured him all his life. He'd threatened Grayson and bullied him. He'd been Peter's eager accomplice in so many abuses over the years. But all Grayson could see when he closed his eyes now was a younger Carter, smiling when he received a nugget of praise from their father. His eyes glowing with pride when their mother congratulated him on mixing a particularly complicated potion. The quiet calm on his face when he rode a horse, and the gentle way he'd pat the mare's neck.

And Grayson had ended his life. He'd had no choice, and Carter's death had been fast, but that didn't ease the ache building in his head.

He tugged his pack closer and found the powder. He took a pinch and placed it under his tongue to dissolve. The taste was bitter, but his shoulders almost instantly loosened. His clarity sharpened, the pain faded, and the numbness blessedly spread. He breathed a little easier.

He dragged Devon's pack closer, finally taking the time to sort through his supplies. He felt a twinge of guilt, going through a dead man's things. But they would need his supplies, especially if the Fletchers didn't make it.

A change of clothing, a purse with a few coins, a small knife in a belt. Fates, the man hadn't even been able to defend himself when Carter's men attacked because he'd packed his weapon. Grayson swallowed and continued to dig through the bag. Some jerked meat, hard biscuits, dried fruit. Not enough to last them long, but enough to get them a little farther from Lenzen. He also found a small jar with more of Mia's salts, and a thick lavender-scented candle wrapped in wax paper. There was also another packet of the powder he'd given Grayson, and assorted healing supplies, including a jar of burn ointment. It was labeled in a tight, neat script. Devon's handwriting, presumably.

All that remained of a physician named Devon.

Grayson's fingers tightened around the jar.

Mia stirred and sat up, keeping her cloak tugged around her shoulders. Her loose braid was mussed from sleep, and some dirt streaked her cheek. Her brown eyes found him, and he couldn't quite read the emotions in them. Pity? Compassion? Worry? "Did you sleep at all?" she asked, her voice a little roughened from sleep.

"A little," he lied. He set aside Devon's things and handed her the canteen he'd filled earlier.

She took it, shivering as she drank. The water of the Julne was always cold, even in summer. The river came straight from the northern mountains, slicing through a deep ravine. When it hit the valley, the river slowed and widened, breaking into several branches as it wound through the forest. It was somewhat of a barrier between southern Ryden and the capital, not that it saved the people who lived in the south from King Henri's laws—or the son he sent to enforce them.

"Fletcher and Rena?" Mia asked softly.

"They haven't made it."

She fiddled with the canteen's cap. "Maybe they were ambushed, too. They might have had to take a different route."

"Maybe."

Mia bit her lower lip, her eyes aimed down. "I shouldn't have asked them to come. And Devon . . ."

Grayson grasped her hand, and he must not be completely numb, because he felt a warm spark when he touched her. "What happened to Devon wasn't your fault."

"Wasn't it?" She lifted her head, and tears glittered in her eyes. "He wouldn't have been there if I hadn't insisted on bringing him with us."

"You didn't force him to do anything. He chose to leave." He squeezed her chilled fingers, keeping her gaze on him. "Mia, he loved you. He wouldn't want you to blame yourself for what happened."

Mia's lips trembled. "I can't believe he's gone. I can't lose Fletcher and Rena, too."

"We don't know what happened to them," Grayson said. "If they're able, they might still meet us in Porynth." If Fletcher *had* betrayed them, then no doubt a portion of Henri's army would be waiting for them, too. But he couldn't think of another place to run, and it was in the general direction of Mortise, anyway. If he decided going into the port city would be too dangerous, they could bypass it and keep going south. They didn't have enough supplies or gold for that, but Grayson would deal with that eventuality when—*if*—it ever came up.

The more pressing reality was that they couldn't make the entire journey to Porynth without horses. That would delay them too much, but they didn't have the coin to buy horses. He'd rather not interact with anyone, anyway—he wasn't exactly unknown in Ryden. Stealing horses would also draw attention, but that would probably be their best option. It was just so hard to think. At least the pain in his head had dulled.

"We can't keep waiting for them, can we?" Mia asked, breaking into his thoughts.

He raked a hand through his dark hair, ordering himself to focus. "No."

She nodded, though regret hung in her eyes. "They'll meet us at the harbor, like you said."

He didn't dispute her hope. "We'll need supplies eventually," he said, "but I want to keep to the forest as long as we can."

She shifted closer and wrapped a hand around one of his. "I'm sorry," she whispered.

He stared at her.

Her expression softened, though her grip on his hand tightened. "For what you had to do last night," she explained. "Carter . . ."

He tensed. "I didn't have a choice."

"I know." She watched him closely. "Do you want to talk about it?"

Fates, no. He remembered the first time he'd committed murder. His father had ordered him to take an old man's life, and he had. Soon after, he'd broken apart in Mia's arms.

He couldn't afford to break right now.

"Maybe later," he said. "We need to eat, and then we need to start moving."

Indecision wavered on her face, but she didn't argue. She passed him the canteen, and he drank deeply; they would refill all of them before leaving Oland's Bridge. While he unwrapped dried fruit and jerked meat, Mia reached for the jar of burn ointment he'd set aside.

"We can do that later," he protested. "You should eat."

"Let me take care of you." She twisted off the lid as she knelt before him. Her fingers brushed his heavily stubbled chin. Fates, when had he last shaved? It had to have been in Mortise.

He made no reply, just winced as the cold, slightly oily substance touched his skin. The scent was sharp and cool, and Mia's touch was infinitely gentle as she traced the balm over his burn, starting at the back of his jaw and moving across the infected cut. Despite the drugs in his body that dulled everything, he could feel every careful brush of her feather-light touch.

Her breaths were thin and shallow, matching his own. A furrow grew between her brows. "The blisters seem worse." She leaned in, angling for a better view.

He couldn't stop looking at her. The familiar curves of her rounded face. The deep brown locks that curled against her temples, loosened during the night from her braid. The warmth of her deep brown eyes. The softness of her pink lips.

He flinched when she touched the corner of his open cut.

She jerked back. "Sorry." She studied the wound with a frown. It was hard not to turn his face away. He'd stopped being overly conscious of his scars when he'd lost his gloves in Mortise, but feeling Mia's scrutiny brought all of his insecurities to the surface.

He knew the fainter marks on his cheek would lessen in time—like the scars on his burned fingers—but they would never truly fade. And his jaw would be an ugly mess for the rest of his life. He'd known he would never be handsome in the way his father was, but next to Mia's beauty . . .

It shouldn't matter. When all this was over, he would be rotting in a cell in Duvan. He wouldn't be with Mia. No one would see them together and think they didn't match.

They never *had* matched, even before his face was ruined.

Fates, the drugs were making him morose.

"Were there any other healing salves in the bag?" Mia asked.

It took a moment to realize why she was asking; a burn ointment wouldn't do much good for the gaping wound along his jaw. "I don't know," he said.

Her mouth drew into a line. "I don't know the best way to treat it."

"It's fine. It doesn't need anything."

She set down the burn ointment and reached for Devon's pack. She rooted around, finally pulling out another jar, a salve for cuts. Grayson doubted it would do anything to make the deep cut heal better, but perhaps it would help stave off infection.

This time when she leaned in to apply the medicine, he kept his eyes down, firmly on his rolled fists, pressed almost painfully against his knees. He wanted to know what she thought of his newest scar, but he refused to ask. Maybe a part of him dreaded knowing what she thought of it.

Her warm breath danced lightly across his skin as she worked with gentle fingers to tend his wound. When she was done, she prompted him to take more of the pain medicine.

He didn't tell her he'd already taken some, and as the powder dissolved under his tongue, Mia finally began to eat.

Though she must have been hungry, she ate slowly. Her eyes roamed the area around them, taking in the tangled limbs of the towering trees, and the leaves that were turning shades of yellow, orange, and brown. He knew Tyrell had taken her outside, but being in a thick forest would have been a new experience. She watched raptly as a squirrel dashed up a nearby tree, and her head turned at the call of a bird.

He had to prompt her to keep eating; they couldn't afford to linger.

When they'd both finished, they consolidated Devon's belongings into their own packs, so they'd have fewer bags to carry. After refilling their canteens, Grayson shouldered his bag. "We'll keep to the deer paths," he told her.

He'd grown up hunting in these woods, but so had his brothers, and no doubt many of the king's soldiers. He had to hope Henri thought he'd choose speed over stealth; that would keep the search concentrated on the king's highway, and not spread too deeply into the forest.

Mia's fingers wrapped around the straps of her pack, which dragged against her shoulders. Her expression was alert, but full of trust.

Even if it killed him, he was going to make sure this was Mia's first day of freedom—not her last.

Mia's stamina was better than he'd anticipated, but his own strength was flagging. They stopped to rest too frequently, but at least they hadn't seen anyone else.

His head pounded relentlessly, so the next time they stopped, he surreptitiously took more medicine to dull the pain. He didn't know why he hid it from Mia; there was no good reason.

As the aching in his head receded, Devon's warning rang in his ears. *Resist the urge to take more to treat the headaches—they are a sign that your body is relying on the drug too much.*

Grayson didn't know what else to do, though. He couldn't allow his body to register the pain right now. He needed to be alert. Focused. Ready to fight. Mia needed him. It became his mantra, which helped him keep moving. *She needs me. She needs me.*

He was growing more feverish, but there was nothing he could do about that. He kept walking. The air grew colder as night came upon them, and it felt good against his sweat-streaked skin, though Mia shivered.

He found a sheltered spot just off the narrow deer trail, among an ancient oak's many thick roots that protruded from the ground. Tucked between the large roots with their backs against the wide trunk, they were protected from the worst of the wind. Grayson spread Devon's spare clothes beneath them so they wouldn't have to sleep on the hard ground.

After they'd eaten a cold dinner, Mia reapplied the ointments to his face. When she touched his overheated skin, concern bloomed in her eyes. "Grayson, you have a fever."

"I think it's already dying down," he lied.

She didn't look convinced. When she urged him to take more of the powder, he did without hesitation, and his muscles relaxed as the medicine dissolved under his tongue.

Mia settled next to him, pulling her cloak around her as she rested her head against his shoulder. He hesitated only a moment before wrapping his arm around her, bringing her closer. She settled against his side, one hand pressed to his chest. It was the one marked by the scorpion stings. "How is your hand?" he asked, feeling bad he hadn't asked earlier.

"Fine. The swelling is down." She shifted against him, her body pressing closer—seeking warmth, he realized. "Without horses, do we even have a chance of reaching Porynth before the *Seafire* sails?"

"We'll reach some small villages soon. We'll get horses and other supplies there."

"Maybe there will be a physician we can visit."

He winced. "We can't afford to leave a trail."

"If you still have a fever, you're seeing a physician." Her tone was so final he didn't bother to argue.

And maybe it was the olcain powder in his blood, or the strange numbness in his head, but he found himself saying, "Peter told me about you and Tyrell."

She stiffened. When she pulled back enough to look at him, her expression was guarded. "What did he tell you?"

"He said you two were inseparable. That he gave you gifts. That you slept in his bed." He bit his tongue to stop the spill of words, but it was too late. His hurt and desperation were clear, even to him.

Color spread over Mia's cheeks, but her voice was firm. "Tyrell was a friend when I desperately needed one, and Peter only ever tried to ruin that."

"Like when he showed you the letter you wrote me? The one Tyrell promised you he'd send?"

Seeing her face fall, he instantly regretted starting this conversation.

"Tyrell isn't the person you think he is," Mia said. "He's had to bury everything good inside him so your parents couldn't hurt him."

Grayson's voice was a bare whisper. "Do you love him?"

"I do," Mia whispered, and his gut dropped. "But I don't love him in the same way I love you." She touched his chin, forcing his gaze to meet hers. "Grayson, I've loved you since I was a little girl. You're my best friend. You're the one thing in my life I've always been able to trust in. My light in darkness. That will never change." She took a breath. "I care about Tyrell. He's my friend. I'm sorry if that hurts you, but I can't change how I feel." She lifted his hand and brushed a soft kiss against his knuckles. "I know he's hurt you, and I know you've hurt him. But you were both raised by monsters. You both did what you had to do to survive."

And Tyrell didn't have you. Grayson didn't speak the words, but they stuck in his mind. Hadn't he often wondered what he would have become without Mia in his life? He could have easily become as ruthless and cruel as Tyrell.

"Tyrell said he loved me," she said, and even though Grayson had known of Tyrell's feelings for her, it still caused an ache in his chest. Mia seemed to sense that; her palm pressed more firmly against his heart. "I don't love him in return—not like that—and I told him that. He knows where I stand, and I need you to know, too. If there's ever a choice between you and Tyrell, I will *always* choose you. I don't want you to ever doubt that."

He could see the two necklaces she wore; the pebble he'd given her—the pebble that had brought them together—and the black queen from a Strategem set. He knew without asking who had given it to her.

"I love you," he told her.

She squeezed his hand, and his chest heated as she carefully set her lips against his mouth. "I love you, too."

Curled against him, it wasn't long before she fell asleep.

Grayson knew he should stay awake and keep watch, but he was exhausted, and Mia's warmth and comforting scent surrounded him. For the moment at least, she was his to hold. So he rested his unmarred cheek against the top of her head, and that was the last thing he knew.

CHAPTER 17

DESFAN

"SERJAN, I . . . DON'T KNOW WHAT TO SAY," Tamar Nadir stammered.

"Say yes," Desfan urged.

They sat in his father's office—*his* office, now. He'd probably need to redecorate for the space to actually feel like his. So much was changing; Yahri had insisted it would be disrespectful of tradition if he didn't take the serjan's quarters, so servants were currently moving his things into his father's suite. They'd packed away everything that had once belonged to his parents, setting it aside for him to go through later. He rather dreaded the idea—until he realized it was something he could do with Meerah, once she was home.

The thought gave him strength—he wasn't alone. And it wasn't the only positive thing for him to focus on, either.

Yesterday, he'd helped Serene discreetly make all the necessary arrangements needed to travel on the *Phoenix*. Seveh was sailing the southern patrol route anyway, so the ship would not attract any undue attention by taking Serene to Zennor. The princess and her two guards had slipped aboard the *Phoenix* along with other members of the crew earlier this morning. Only the most trusted guards and servants knew she'd left Duvan at all.

She and Desfan had discussed many reasons for why she needed to journey to Zennor, but none of them resonated as strongly inside him than the need to break off Imara's betrothal. He knew next to nothing about Eilan Skyer, but if Serene was worried... Well, that was enough to make him feel like his inherent resentment toward the man was completely warranted.

If Serene succeeded in all her goals, Imara would be free of her betrothal, and Desfan and Serene wouldn't have to marry. Desfan would be able to openly court Imara—something he hadn't dared to consider until Serene had put the possibility in his head two days ago. Now, he struggled to think of little else. Which was unfortunate, because many other matters needed his attention.

Like his current meeting with Tamar Nadir. Because—once again—he had council seats to fill.

Ser Zephan and Ser Ashear had both died weeks ago near the border. He'd only learned of their deaths when Serene had arrived in Duvan, and with all of the ceremonies for his father's funeral and the coronation, Yahri had said some allowances could be made for delaying filling their seats.

One of them would be filled as soon as Serai Nadir agreed to take it.

Tamar's frown drew deep lines in her brow. "I'm not a

politician."

"Perfect. Neither am I. And Razan isn't, either."

"I have no strong connections to any of the local powerful families," Tamar protested. "I've spent too many years living outside of Duvan."

"That makes your perspective all the more useful," Desfan countered. "I want more opinions—broader views. I also want someone with strong moral convictions, and I would especially like someone else who will advocate for peace with Devendra. Please, Serai Nadir."

She studied him for a long moment, her face revealing nothing. Then she sighed. "Do I have to wear the green robe?"

His mouth twitched. "Only while the council is in session, or at formal affairs as outlined by Serai Yahri."

"Do I have to live in Duvan?"

"You'll have a permanent apartment in the palace, but you may leave during breaks, and you may ask for a substitute if ever you need time away."

Tamar let out a weary sigh. "Very well. I agree."

"Thank you." He meant it. Tamar Nadir was a perfect choice for the council, but he knew it required sacrifices.

"I suppose I can see Yahri about any further questions I have?" Tamar asked.

"Absolutely. She's expecting a meeting with you as soon as you're able to arrange it. In the meantime, I'd like your advice on something."

Curiosity bloomed in her eyes. "Of course."

"Mortise has been through difficult times—my father's illness and death, my personal fumbles and shortcomings, and, of course, this new alliance with Devendra. Many vocally protested my betrothal to Serene, and though that matter is now settled, I receive letters daily from concerned citizens. They fear Devendra. Even though war with Ryden is coming, it's not a reality yet for most of Mortise. How do I help them see the benefits of this alliance? How do I help them not see Devendra as an enemy?"

Tamar considered his words. "You're working in very general terms, Serjan. You can't tell the Mortisians to like the Devendrans; that's too broad. Trust is built between individual people. So, if you wish to make Mortisians like Devendrans, you must get people to interact and connect on a personal level."

"That will take time."

"Yes," she agreed. "But it will be worth it. With your permission—and King Newlan's consent—I can begin to arrange dinners and other events along the border. And here, we can continue efforts with Serene's help. She has made great progress in your court already, so let her go into Duvan and mingle with the people in the city. She can shop in the markets, praise our craftsmen, and have dinners with the lesser nobility. She can even visit some of the orphanages you've set up in her name."

"These are excellent suggestions. I would like you to talk to Yahri about your ideas. Together, you can draft a letter to King Newlan. Meanwhile, I'll speak with Serene." Or Clare, he supposed. "Thank you, Serai Nadir."

She bowed her head, matching his formality, and they both stood. "If I can help heal some of the hatred between Mortise and Devendra," she said, "I will consider it to be my life's greatest achievement."

Desfan smiled. "Welcome to the council, Tamar. I'm glad you're with us."

"And I'm glad you're our serjan," she said, surprising him

with her sincerity. "I had great admiration for your father and his rule, so I mean no disrespect when I say I think you're going to be an amazing serjan. I think you'll do wonderful things for Mortise, and all of Eyrinthia."

Her words rendered him speechless, and continued to echo in his head long after she'd left.

He'd been in meetings since dawn, and now afternoon light poured through the window. He didn't know if Karim was still standing guard outside his office door, or if he'd taken a break and appointed others to watch him.

Desfan hoped Karim was resting. His friend had pushed himself too hard during the coronation three days ago, which was evidenced by his more pronounced limp. It had taken a few threats, but Desfan had finally managed to convince him to rest yesterday, and hopefully he was still taking things easy today.

Desfan only had meetings today, since there were so many things to catch up on after the coronation. All regular meetings would resume in a few days, which included council meetings. Before everything resumed, he really should interrogate Liam Kaelin. The Shadow of Ryden would have many secrets in his spymaster head, and truthfully, Desfan should have made time to interrogate him sooner. Liam had been in a cell for a month now. To be fair, it had been a very busy month; Desfan had been dealing with his father's death, settling his court after a myriad of attacks, and attending ceremonies to celebrate the late serjan as well as commemorate his own coronation. Not to mention, he'd learned the truth about his sister's fate, and was far more consumed by her rescue than anything else. In the end, he simply hadn't had the time to interrogate Liam. But perhaps that could work in his favor;

maybe now, after being so ignored, Liam would be more willing to talk—desperate for any sort of company.

Perhaps that was wishful thinking, but it was a tactic he should at least pretend he'd chosen, in case that earned him an advantage.

Maybe he'd visit Liam tomorrow, if he could fit it in amid all his other responsibilities. He was still waiting on the full report of the damage done to his treasury, but there were payments to be made, letters to read, another council member to choose—though Yahri had a couple of suggestions he needed to consider—and he needed to write to Lord Zander Fellnor. He needed to do what he could for the Devendran refugees in the camp called Salvation, and he needed to consider what action he could take against Prince Grandeur and his Hunt, without endangering the tentative alliance between Devendra and Mortise. Serene suggested a strongly written letter. Desfan had other desires, but a letter was probably the most tactful approach.

His next appointment knocked on the door, and Desfan smiled as Avao entered.

"Thank you for agreeing to see me so soon," Karim's grandfather said as he took a seat across the desk. "I know you must be extremely busy."

"I can always make time for you." Desfan leaned back in his chair, studying Avao. The man looked . . . worn. "Are you well?" he asked, worry rippling through him.

"These days, I feel older than the sea," Avao said honestly. "But I do think my travels have been good for me."

"I'm glad to hear that."

In the brief silence, Desfan nearly told Avao about Meerah. Fates knew the old man would be overjoyed to learn she lived, but he would probably feel helpless and fearful until she returned safely to Duvan. In deference to that, he decided to hold his tongue.

It was just as well, because it became instantly clear that what Avao had come to discuss was not a light subject. His features turned visibly grave. "Desfan, I'm not sure how to say this. Karim's mother is dying."

Desfan stared. "What?"

"She's fallen ill," Avao said. "I didn't know until I arrived back in Duvan, the night before your coronation. When I went to visit Azima, they told me she has a wasting disease. They sent a letter, but I must have missed it in my travels. The physicians at the asylum don't think she'll live much longer than a month or two."

Desfan swallowed—hard. He had never met Karim's mother, who lived in an asylum for the insane located in Duvan. Karim hadn't been to see her in years. Azima rarely recognized him, and when she did, she would either cry and beg him to take her home, or she would scream at him for leaving her.

Karim didn't often speak of his mother. He'd only ever shared the details of his childhood once, years ago, soon after he and Desfan had first met.

Avao swiped one hand over his weathered brow. "I don't know how to tell Karim. I know he isn't close to her, but . . . I know he loves her."

Desfan knew that was true, even if Karim had gone through times of resenting her, fearing her, and feeling ashamed of her.

"You don't need to be the one to tell him," Avao continued quickly. "That's not why I'm here. But I would like you to be with him when I share the news."

"Of course I'll be there."

Avao hesitated. "There's a chance he will refuse to go see her. I wouldn't blame him, but I think he should go. I think he'll regret it if he doesn't."

Desfan had to agree. No matter how tumultuous his relationship with his father had been, Desfan would give anything for a last visit—a chance to truly say goodbye.

"If he doesn't want to go, I'll talk with him."

Some of Avao's tension melted. "Thank you. I know it will be his choice, but . . . I appreciate you being there for him."

"When are you going to tell him?"

"I shouldn't delay much longer. Maybe tonight, if that will work for you?"

"I'll make anything work."

Avao tipped his head. "Thank you, Desfan."

"Of course." He rose from his chair when Avao did. He stepped around the desk and clasped the man's arm in a tight grip. "I can't imagine how painful losing your daughter must be. I'm sorry, Avao."

Sorrow deepened the lines of his face. "So am I. But we both know all too well that the fates aren't always kind." He shook his head as he dropped Desfan's arm. "I have lost Azima before. Many times, and in many different ways. I can only be grateful for the good memories I have of her. Focusing on them helps to outweigh the heartache. And I will always feel fates-blessed for Karim."

"I feel the same."

"I'm glad he's a loyal friend to you, Desfan. After the losses you've both suffered . . . Well, you're both very deserving of the friendship you share."

Avao told Karim about his mother after dinner. They were in Desfan's suite, in the sitting room where he had once spent hours with his parents and sisters, so many years ago.

Desfan sat close as Avao spoke to Karim in low tones. Karim didn't say much, though he did ask a few questions. *How long? Is she in pain? Does she need anything?*

Avao hugged his grandson, tears watering in his old eyes as he assured Karim that everything was taken care of, and her pain would be manageable for whatever time she ended up having.

A month or two. Short as a breath, really.

Avao asked if he would go visit her.

Karim said he would.

Avao asked if he wanted to accompany him to the asylum tomorrow.

Karim said no.

Avao's face fell, but he nodded understandingly.

Desfan watched the entire exchange, his heart aching for his friend.

Eventually, Avao left.

Desfan stayed beside Karim on the long settee, letting the silence stretch.

"I need to visit her," Karim finally said. "But I'm not ready yet."

"You have time."

"Not much."

Desfan touched Karim's tense shoulder. "I'll go with you, whenever you decide to go."

Karim looked to him. "You knew. He told you first."

There was no accusation—just a statement of fact.

Desfan still felt the need to explain. "He wanted me to be here for you."

His lips pressed into a line. "I have to sort through some things before I go."

"I know. Avao knows that, too. He's not disappointed."

"He looked disappointed."

"He wasn't."

There was a long pause, then Karim said, "The last time I saw her was two years ago. We stopped in port, just overnight. Do you remember?"

Desfan remembered. He'd stayed on the ship rather than visit his father at the palace. Karim had gone ashore, though he hadn't told Desfan where he'd gone.

"I took her flowers," Karim said, his voice almost flat. "Pink ones, because that's her favorite color. I was nervous. I didn't want to go, but I knew I should. So I did. And as soon as I stepped into her room, she threw a lamp at my head."

Desfan didn't know what to say, so he only squeezed Karim's shoulder.

"I thought maybe she was having one of her waking nightmares," Karim said, his voice still horribly even. "That maybe she thought I was a demon or some other monster, and that's why she was screaming at me. Then she called me Jahnu."

Karim had never spoken the name, but Desfan knew it instinctively. Jahnu was Karim's father. A man who had hit his wife and son before abandoning them.

"I suppose I look like him," Karim said, and for the first time,

Desfan detected pain in his voice.

"You're not him."

Karim's breathing thinned. "I abandoned her, just like he did."

"It's not the same."

"It is. He left her to her demons, and I've done the very same thing." He pushed to his feet, his hands trembling. There was a wild, almost desperate light in his eyes. "I need to get out of here."

Desfan stood at once. "I'll come with you."

Karim shook his head, but he didn't say anything when Desfan followed him to the door. They exited the suite and strode down the hall, Karim limping slightly. Desfan thought his friend must have a destination in mind, because he walked purposefully. It wasn't until they turned down a narrow corridor that Desfan realized where they were going—the gardens.

The moment they stepped outside, Karim walked faster. His limp was more pronounced as he moved closer to a run. Even though night had fallen, the gardens were lit by interspersed torches and moonlight. The air was sweet with the scent of flowers, but Karim didn't seem to notice that as he hurried down the pebbled path.

"Karim?" a voice called out.

Desfan and Karim both turned, to see Razan. She had a book in her hands, and she was just rising from one of the garden's many stone benches. A nearby torch perfectly illuminated the concern in her dark eyes.

Desfan tensed. A confrontation with Razan was the last thing Karim needed right now. "Razan," he began, but she didn't even look at him.

She dropped the book on the bench and crossed the short

distance to Karim. She was tall, but her head still had to tilt back a little so she could meet his gaze.

Karim was breathing too hard, but he said nothing, and neither did she. They just stared at each other.

Without a word, she wrapped her arms around his waist and tucked herself against him.

Karim's arms hung by his sides, and his chest rose and fell with each barely controlled inhale and exhale.

Then—shocking Desfan to the core—Karim's arms went around Razan's shoulders, and he crushed her to him, his head buried in her long dark hair.

When Karim's breath hitched, Desfan eased back a step. He turned and quietly headed back toward the palace.

Just before he went inside, he glanced over his shoulder and saw they were still locked in each other's arms. The torchlight flickered in the breeze, but even without that distortion, it looked like Karim's curved back was shaking.

Razan only held him tighter.

CHAPTER 18

CLARE

"You truly trust me with this?" Latif asked, his expression disbelieving.

The Mortisian man sat across from Clare in the princess's sitting room. Bennick sat on the settee beside Clare, though there was no doubt he was still a soldier at full attention. His back was straight, and he watched Latif with a gaze as sharp as a blade.

Bennick didn't trust Latif the same way Clare did, but he trusted her, and that meant more than she could express.

Latif was a middle-aged man with a face weathered from years on the sea. He had dark hair and brown eyes, which—at the moment—somehow managed to be both wary and bewildered. He'd been brought up from the prison, cleaned up, and then shown into the princess's suite. Despite the guards that had surrounded him, his confusion had been clear when he'd entered the room.

If anything, his confusion had grown as Clare outlined what she wanted him to do.

"Yes," she said, answering his question. "I trust you. And I need you." She clasped her hands on her lap and tried to explain her reasoning. "I can't go myself, and I need to send someone I know is impartial. If my suspicions about Prince Grandeur and the Hunt being behind the deaths of my brothers are correct, I can't trust Commander Markam's investigation to be truthful. I can't trust *anyone* from Devendra. I need you. If you do this for me, Serjan Desfan has agreed to release you from prison—but you will be banished from Mortise once you've completed this investigation for me."

Latif's throat clenched, but he nodded. "Kiv Arcas explained that before he brought me up here."

"Will you do it?" Clare asked. Her heart and lungs were frozen as she awaited his answer. If he refused, she didn't know who else to ask.

Latif still looked surprised that she would trust him, but he bowed his head. "I would be honored to do this for you, Clare."

Her shoulders relaxed. "Thank you."

Bennick cleared his throat, drawing Latif's eye as he spoke for the first time. "You'll be conducting your own investigation, but I'll give you a letter of introduction you can give to my father, or any member of the city guard if that becomes necessary. It can give you access to their investigation notes, or protect you from any questions they may put to you. You do not answer to them—you answer to me and Clare."

"Of course, Captain Markam." Latif hesitated. "If the prince *is* responsible for the fire . . . what should I do?"

"Don't attempt to do anything," Bennick said. "Bring whatever proof you can to us, and then your part in this will be done."

"And be careful," Clare added. "Grandeur is a dangerous enemy."

"I will take care," Latif assured her. "And I'll work as quickly as I can to bring you news. But I must ask . . . why do you think the prince may have struck out at you in such a horrific way?"

Bennick's breathing thinned. He wasn't looking at her, but she knew he was listening closely for her answer. This was a question he hadn't asked, but he'd clearly wondered.

She exhaled slowly, her eyes on Latif. "I told you about my brother, Eliot."

"Yes. He was a rebel, but he was killed." The man frowned. "Why would Prince Grandeur retaliate against you for your brother's crimes, if the king himself did not?"

"There's a possibility Grandeur did this on the king's orders," Clare said. "However . . ." She glanced at Bennick. His expression was carefully neutral, but his gaze was intent as he waited for her answer. "Before I left Iden," she said, "Prince Grandeur asked me to spy on Princess Serene."

Bennick stopped breathing. He hadn't known that.

Latif's eyes widened.

"I refused him," Clare quickly lied to both men. There was no way to detail the truth without revealing Serene's secrets, but it was important for Latif to know something of her history with Grandeur. "He considered this a betrayal, and he has not forgiven me. I believe his anger has only festered. The last time I saw him was during our travels to Mortise. He was upset with me still—worse than before. You must avoid him at all costs. Do not attempt to approach him or question him. I don't think he would hesitate to kill you."

"I will guard myself," Latif assured her. "And I will learn the truth of what happened to your brothers and their caretaker. You have my word."

There wasn't much more to say after that.

When they all stood, Clare took Latif's hand and squeezed. "Thank you."

Bennick handed Latif a pouch filled with coins. Serene had given it to Clare yesterday, before the princess had left for Zennor. It wasn't the only thing Serene had left her with, but it was the thing that had made Clare's eyes burn. "Thank you," she'd managed to say.

The princess's lips had pressed into a line. "I hope he finds the truth so you can find peace. Or vengeance."

Peace or vengeance. It would be her mantra. She prayed it would keep her grounded until she could learn the truth.

"What weapons are you most comfortable with?" Bennick asked Latif.

"Daggers," the Mortisian man said at once.

"I have some in my room you can take." Bennick glanced at Clare. "I'll help Latif on his way. Venn is just outside."

Clare nodded, watching as the two men left.

Once she was alone, she moved to the balcony, walking until she reached the railing. She set both palms against the smooth stone, warm from the morning sun, and looked out at the rippling sea.

Strange, to think Venn and Vera had returned only three days ago, and yet Serene had already left for Zennor. She'd taken Cardon and Wilf with her, and Clare already missed them. Bridget, Serene's head maid, was still fuming that Serene had left her behind, but the princess didn't want to draw unnecessary attention, and she had insisted Bridget needed to remain with Clare. This was partly because Bridget was one of Serene's rebels, and Serene was adamant that Clare have her assistance. Especially because Serene hadn't had a chance to speak with James, one of the rebellion's top leaders, before she'd left. Clare had been entrusted with a letter to him, and Bridget was under orders to help make sure Clare could get it to James whenever he was able to make contact.

Serene had spent half the night sitting with Clare, discussing what her role in Duvan should be, and which nobles in Desfan's court Serene had most recently had conversations with. Clare's stomach danced with nerves if she thought too long about the fact that she was slipping into Serene's shoes once more. She hadn't fully pretended to be the princess since Bennick had rescued her. She hoped her old skills would return, because she could not fail. Too much hung in the balance.

Having Vera back was a huge relief, though. Clare had missed her friend desperately, and she'd been so worried about her. They'd spent hours talking, crying, and smiling together as they'd exchanged every detail of their stories. Vera shared all about her reconciliation with Venn, and though she'd blushed a great deal, her smile had only grown. The two were firmly in love, and Clare doubted anything could come between them now. Vera also told Clare about the Holm children she'd mothered for weeks. Her love for those children was evident, as was her pain from missing them. Clare knew that pang of loss and longing, because she'd felt the same when she'd had to leave her brothers in Devendra.

Still standing on the balcony, Clare slipped a hand into her pocket and withdrew a mangled piece of tin. The toy soldier Mark had given her when she'd left Iden so long ago had been thrown into a fire by Salim and melted into an unrecognizable mess. The crumpled metal easily fit in the palm of her hand. She hated the fact that her brothers might have been thrown into a fire as well because of her actions. Fates, how would she ever live with herself?

She hadn't conducted any last rites or memorials for Thomas and Mark. She couldn't—not until she knew why they'd died. Until she knew the truth, she wouldn't be able to put them to rest.

Soon enough, she would know. Then she could find her peace with the fates, or seek vengeance against Grandeur.

The sea air lifted the loose strands of hair around her face. She drew in a deep, bracing breath, then let it out slowly. She slipped the melted tin soldier back into her pocket.

She didn't know how long she stood there, but it must have been a while, because Bennick returned. She knew it was him who stepped lightly onto the balcony behind her, because her body suddenly hummed. His scent of leather and spice surrounded her, and then his hand touched the small of her back as he came to stand beside her.

He said nothing for a long moment, just stared at the sea with her. "Why didn't you tell me about Grandeur?" he asked softly.

"I didn't see a reason. There was nothing you could have done."

His hand tensed against her back. "Were you afraid of him?"

"A little," she admitted. "But I told Serene about it. And then so much happened . . . I truly didn't think of how he'd asked me to spy for him until recently."

Bennick absorbed this, and she hoped he believed her. Finally, he spoke. "When Serene began making arrangements to bring your brothers here . . ."

"Yes," she said, though he hadn't really asked. "It was because I worried for them. But not just because of Grandeur."

Bennick's hand slid, moving to curve around her waist so he could bring her closer against his side. "I hope Latif finds the truth," he said. "And no matter what he finds, I'll stand by you."

She knew what that truly meant. If Grandeur and the Hunt *had* killed her brothers, Bennick would seek vengeance with her, even if that required standing against Prince Grandeur and King Newlan. And his father, if Commander Markam was involved.

She rested her head against his shoulder and wrapped her own arm around his back. "Thank you," she whispered.

In answer, Bennick's fingers curled more tightly around her side, and he pressed a kiss to the top of her head.

<hr>

Later that day, Clare wandered the physician's ward dressed in one of Serene's simple day gowns. It was dark purple with gold accents, the material gathered at the waist with a gold sash. Vera had pinned her hair up, and that was a relief from the Mortisian heat. The day was warm, and the rooms she walked were filled with people injured during the attack before Desfan's coronation.

She recognized some of the names from Serene's hurried introductions, but luckily the princess hadn't had a chance to get close to too many of the lower nobles. Clare sat with them, visiting briefly with everyone in the ward. She mourned with widows who had lost their husbands, and men who had lost their wives; she held children who were now motherless or fatherless. She asked the physician's staff what else she could do, though they were hesitant to put her to work. But a few of the more badly injured nobles needed assistance writing letters to loved ones, or having letters read to them, so Clare did that, grateful once again that languages came quite naturally to her. Her Mortisian wasn't flawless, but it was perfectly acceptable, and no one seemed to suspect she wasn't exactly who she pretended to be.

Bennick and Venn shadowed her, and every time Clare saw them standing together or talking in low tones to each other, her heart warmed. Thank the fates Venn and Vera had returned safely. She'd missed them both so much, and she truly didn't know how much more loss she could survive.

Being among the wounded was emotionally draining, yet also healing in a way. After being consumed with her own loss, it felt good to think of others in need and help where she could.

A girl of about three years old—who had mercifully been safe in her parents' suite during the attack—currently sat curled in Clare's lap, her soft cheek pressed against Clare's chest. The girl had whined when the physician had come over to check her mother's wound, so Clare had hurried to scoop her up. Bouncing her gently on her lap and telling her stories she used to tell Mark and Thomas had sufficiently distracted her. Before the physician was finished, the girl had fallen asleep in her arms.

When the physician left, the mother looked to Clare with a grateful smile. "Thank you, Your Highness. You have a tender way with children."

Clare continued to stroke the sleeping girl's dark hair. "She's beautiful."

The noblewoman's eyes shone, though there was sadness there. "Sidrah looks very much like her father."

Clare's stomach dropped. "Is he . . .?"

"Still alive, thank the fates," the woman said, though tears swam in her eyes. "But he isn't doing well. He has a terrible fever. They took him to another room . . ." She blinked quickly. "I was shot first, in the shoulder. When he realized we were under attack, he covered my body with his own. He was hit twice. The physicians don't know if he'll survive." She dashed a hand across her face, swiping away her tears as her voice broke. "Kashif didn't even want to come. He hates leaving Dorma. But I insisted we couldn't miss the coronation. I . . . I don't know what I'll do if I lose him. And Sidrah . . . I just pray to the fates he'll recover."

"I'll pray for him as well," Clare said, now rubbing the little girl's back.

The woman managed a wavering smile. "Thank you, Your Highness. That would mean a great deal to me." She took a full breath, and that seemed to help settle her emotions. "Apologies, I didn't mean to burden you with any of that. Especially not before we're truly introduced. I'm Ilah Hassan."

"It's a pleasure to meet you, Serai Hassan."

"Please, call me Ilah. It seems only right, since my daughter is currently sleeping in your arms." Ilah Hassan's gaze softened as she viewed Sidrah. "She refuses to stay with her nursemaid, so she's been spending most of her days and nights here with me. But I know she gets restless. She just hates to be away from me. And, in truth, I hate to be parted from her."

Clare thought of all the children she'd met today, most of them visiting their parents in the physician's ward. "Perhaps I can speak to Desfan about setting up an activity for all the children."

"That is most thoughtful of you, Princess. I'm sure the children would enjoy a diversion. And I know all the parents would appreciate it as well."

Clare stayed a little longer, but once Sidrah woke, she set the girl back on Ilah's bed and excused herself to give the mother and daughter some privacy.

When Clare turned, she was surprised to see only Venn standing nearby. She hurried over to him, her voice low. "Where is Bennick? Is something wrong?"

"Nothing's wrong," Venn said at once. "Karim came a few moments ago to ask Bennick to join him and the serjan for Prince Liam's interrogation."

Clare stiffened at the mention of Liam Kaelin. She'd only met the Rydenic prince once, but that had been enough. He'd been in the process of trying to escape the prison, and when he'd seen her, he'd assumed she was Serene and ordered Latif to kill her. Latif hadn't—obviously—but Liam Kaelin was not one of Clare's favorite people—and that was before he'd kicked her down the stairs. Liam hadn't orchestrated her abduction by Salim and his mercenaries, but he'd learned that Amil Havim had, and he'd used her abduction to his advantage.

Venn touched her arm. "You've spent hours here. Why don't you visit Imara? According to Vera's last conversation with Hanna, the princess is bored to the point of tearing out her hair."

Clare didn't need to be convinced to visit the Zennorian princess; Imara was her friend, and she could use some time with her. And, she thought, with one last look at Ilah and Sidrah, she just might have a task to combat Imara's boredom.

CHAPTER 19

DESFAN

DESFAN WASN'T SURE IF IT WAS A GOOD IDEA to interrogate Liam Kaelin right now, considering Karim's personal upheaval, but his friend insisted he wanted the distraction. And he did *not* want to talk about his mother, *or* about what had happened between him and Razan in the garden. Desfan had asked—twice.

Desfan led the way into the holding room in the upper prison with Karim and Bennick Markam right behind him.

Liam was already there, his wrists and ankles both shackled. He sat in a chair across a scarred wooden table, facing the door. Three guards stood behind him, and two more were in the corridor just outside. Considering who their prisoner was, it didn't seem excessive.

The Rydenic prince looked worse for wear. He was usually well-groomed and composed, but after spending weeks in the dungeon, his features were sharper. His brown hair was longer, and his facial hair had grown from artful stubble to full beard. Desfan had made sure he was fed well, but he hadn't been given comforts, and his worn and dirty clothing showed that.

"You're looking a little less cocky than usual," Desfan said. "I do hope you haven't been too bored down here. I'm afraid I've been too busy to visit. While your days may feel endless, mine fill all too quickly."

Liam's expression was almost neutral, though there was an edge in his brown eyes that Desfan had never seen before. "Where is my brother?"

Desfan pulled out the chair across from Liam, letting it grate loudly on the stone floor. He sat, and Karim and Bennick flanked him. He didn't look, but he assumed their expressions were appropriately intimidating. "Is the Shadow of Ryden feeling brotherly affection?" Desfan asked dryly.

Liam's jaw flexed, so quickly Desfan would have missed it if he'd blinked.

Desfan leaned forward, allowing menace to darken his words. "Let me assure you, I can relate."

Liam settled back in his chair, his chains rattling softly. "You know about Meerah, then."

"Well deduced." No part of his fury was feigned as he glared at the Rydenic prince.

Liam's response was to sigh. "If you expect me to apologize for not telling you about your sister, you'll be disappointed."

"Don't worry. I don't expect that sort of humanity from you." Desfan's gaze narrowed. "Your crimes are many and varied, but when you burn in hell, I hope you suffer the most for what you've done to her."

"I wasn't her captor."

"No. But you kept her from me. And I swear to the fates, if she dies because of that message you sent, I will annihilate you."

Liam stared at him unblinking. "I suppose you've been talking to *one* of your Kaelin prisoners, at least."

It was a less direct way of asking about Grayson, but Desfan could sense Liam was anxious to know about his brother.

He could use that.

He leaned back in his chair and folded his arms. "This meeting could determine the rest of your life. I suggest you think carefully on how much you'd like to cooperate with me."

"As entertaining as your threats are," Liam said, "I would appreciate you coming to the point."

Ah, there was a hint of Liam's arrogance. He hadn't lost his confidence after his time as a prisoner, but he wasn't as calm as he pretended to be. Evidence of that fact came from his first question about Grayson; the words had leapt out of him, unchecked.

He was checking himself now, but Desfan doubted his hold was strong.

Desfan almost smiled. "Grayson was quite willing to talk. He doesn't seem to feel any loyalty to you."

One eyebrow lifted. "Is that supposed to surprise me? Or is the goal to make me angry enough to turn on him?"

"Does it make you angry?"

"No." And, fates, he truly looked unaffected. "We're Kaelins. Betrayal runs in our veins just as much as sheer evil and selfishness. You may need to try a different tactic, Serjah." His eyes widened, with just an edge of mocking. "Oh—excuse me, you're probably wearing a new crown these days, aren't you?

Congratulations, Serjan. May you enjoy your rule—regardless of how short it will be."

"Who do you expect will kill me?"

"I'm not sure I'd dare hazard a guess; you have many enemies, and while they have varying abilities, men can surprise you. Like Amil Havim, for instance. I'm surprised he managed to rally such an attack against you. He brought in Devendran rebels and Mortisians against the alliance, and he managed to attack you, empty a considerable number of your prison cells, and raid your treasury—all in one devastating blow." He gave the barest hint of a smile. "Your guards talk."

Desfan would be having a stern conversation with them.

Liam wasn't done. "Amil is no longer a problem, of course, but you didn't see him as an enemy, did you? Even though he'd been working against you for quite a while."

"So I've gathered," Desfan said, a bit mildly. "But you knew all along Amil couldn't be trusted. You learned about him ordering Princess Serene's abduction at the border and you sent Latif—a man also known as Gamble—to collect her from the mercenaries in Krid."

Liam's head tipped to the side. "I'm not surprised you put that together, since Latif is here. I'm sure the coward told you everything he knew."

"He did," Desfan said, not bothering to correct his assumption that Latif was still a prisoner. "And it reinforced a narrative I frankly don't understand. Latif was ordered to kill Serene at the Rydenic border, in an effort to frame Ryden for her death. You also told Grayson that killing the monarchs at the treaty signing would irrevocably turn every kingdom against Ryden. But my question is, why frame your own kingdom?"

"You're asking, but you already know the answer. Grayson wouldn't have kept that part from you."

"You want to destroy Ryden."

"No," Liam said at once, surprising Desfan. "I want to destroy my father and the rest of my accursed family." He scratched one shackled wrist, and the chains clinked. His voice sounded a little less intense as he said, "While we're discussing narratives we don't understand . . . I was surprised when Serene showed up in Duvan, since she was supposed to be abducted by mercenaries. And I'm afraid I was so preoccupied with my own plans, I simply assumed Salim failed to capture her. But when I saw Latif the other night in the prison, with Serene dressed as a servant—well, I assumed it was Serene." His focus shifted to Bennick. "Until Captain Markam yelled *Clare*."

Desfan felt the air in the room change as Bennick stiffened.

Liam smiled faintly. "Tell me, Captain Markam, was it your idea to find a lookalike to play Serene? A decoy is rather ingenious. And I'll admit, I had no idea there was a double in place. You should take that as a compliment, since I generally know almost everything." He looked back at Desfan. "As you can see, I find ways to stay entertained in my cell." With shackled hands, he gestured toward his head. "There are a thousand different puzzles to sort out in here."

"I'm relieved you're not bored, Liam," Desfan said, his sarcasm clear. "Now, will you explain yourself?"

"You want to know why I want to destroy my father?"

"If you'd be so kind as to tell us, yes."

Liam snorted. "Clearly you haven't met my father, or you'd understand instantly. But then, perhaps you have an idea. The man bought your little sister, threw her into a windowless cell, and kept her there for nearly ten years."

Every muscle in Desfan's body went rigid. "I know your father is evil, manipulative, and a tyrant."

"Then you know some of what's coming for you. But let me assure you, my father is not an enemy you can beat. Not now."

"Explain that."

Liam made a scoffing noise in his throat. "The reasons are far too many to get into. But suffice it to say, you will reach a moment in the not so distant future when you will wish I would have succeeded in killing you, Serene, and Imara."

Desfan stared at him. "You're insane."

"I'm practical," Liam countered. "If my plan had succeeded, the armies of three nations would already be marching toward Ryden. Instead, you've spent over a month on parties and meaningless tradition. Maybe you sent letters to Newlan and Zaire, telling them what happened—or maybe Serai Yahri convinced you to wait until you got your new crown. But I assure you, you'll realize all too soon the danger Ryden poses. And when you're standing on a blood-drenched battlefield, surrounded by your dead, you will think back on this moment and realize, *Liam was right. It would have been better if I'd died.*"

His words lifted the hairs on the back of Desfan's neck, but he refused to show his unease. He also didn't know how much he could trust Liam—the man was being far too forthcoming. "Do you fear your father?"

"Yes," Liam said, with no hesitation. "If you don't fear Henri Kaelin, you're a fool."

"Why do you fear him?" Desfan pressed. "What do you know about his plans? What's coming?"

Liam leaned forward and set his chained hands on the table. "Where is Grayson?"

"If I tell you, will you answer my questions?"

"I think we can make an arrangement: an answer for an answer."

This wasn't a very good deal; Desfan had many questions, and Liam seemed to only have one. But if Liam was willing to play . . .

"I get my answer first," Desfan bargained.

Liam tipped his head. "Ask your question, then."

"Will you help me bring down your father?"

The prince's fingers curled, making fists on the table. "That isn't the question I expected."

"Yet, if you answer right, I'll get all the answers I need."

The corner of Liam's mouth twitched. "You're a gambler, Desfan. Tell me, do you think that was a good gamble?"

"Is that *your* question?"

Liam huffed a hard laugh. "I see no point in joining forces with you. When Grayson betrayed me, I lost my chance to destroy my father."

"If you help us, we'll stand a much better chance against him."

"Except you're not just fighting him."

Desfan straightened in his chair. "What do you mean?"

"Is that the question you truly want me to answer?"

He ground his teeth. "Yes."

Liam almost smiled. He tugged his hands off the table, settling them on his lap. "My father has been making inroads with some notable people in Zennor for the past couple of years. He's been discreet—he even kept his dealings from me. But I'm his spymaster. I discovered things. Peter has been involved as well, and it seems my father is willing to let him take the credit."

"You need to be more specific. Who in Zennor is Henri talking to?"

"I don't know everyone involved."

"Buhari?"

"No. The king is unaware of my father's maneuverings. But I believe there are members of the noble class, as well as the criminal elite, who have allied with my father. And there are factions within many of the clans who are siding with Ryden. What this means for you, Serjan, is that when war comes, you'll be facing enemies from the north and the south."

Desfan's fingers dug into his sleeves, keeping his arms crossed. His mind was spinning. This was disastrous. Made more so by the fact that Serene was on her way to Zennor right now.

Fates.

He needed to send her a message, but he had no idea when it would actually reach her.

"Where have you been keeping my brother?" Liam asked, his voice quieter than before.

Desfan didn't consider lying—he assumed Liam would be able to tell, and he wanted to support honesty between them. "Grayson isn't here."

A muscle in Liam's cheek jumped. Then he cursed with surprising heat. "You sent him to Ryden."

"He volunteered," Desfan said.

"My brother is an idiot," Liam gritted out. "You've sent him to his death."

"He seemed confident."

"That's because he's a fool. And when it comes to Mia, he'll risk anything—especially his own life."

"You would know—you exploited him by threatening her."

Liam just shook his head. "I expected you to separate us. I didn't expect you to send him to *Ryden*."

"He said he was my sister's best chance."

"He is, but that doesn't mean he'll succeed in rescuing her."

"Why?"

"Because our father will never let him or Mia go. And no matter what Grayson tells our father, he failed here. Which means he'll be punished. And that will probably mean Grayson won't have access to Mia."

Desfan tried not to let his anxiety show. "You seem to care about his fate."

Liam met Desfan's gaze, something like wariness in his eyes. "And you have a lot of faith in him. You do realize that, if he manages to escape with Mia, he won't come back here?"

His stomach—already knotted—clenched.

"You *do* realize it," Liam murmured, studying his expression. "More than that, you fear it."

It was time to move past this; if the subject didn't change, Desfan's thoughts would spiral. "Will you help me defeat your father?"

Liam said nothing.

Desfan's mouth thinned. "You gain nothing by being difficult."

"I see no reason to be particularly helpful. My fate is already sealed. You're either going to send me back to my father as part of some bargain and he'll kill me, or you'll put me on trial and then kill me."

"You plotted the assassination of three royals from three different kingdoms," Desfan reminded him. "Any punishment you receive is warranted. But I think you're missing the point."

The corner of his mouth lifted sardonically. "Please, enlighten me."

"Everything you've done was because you wanted your father destroyed. So help me do that now."

Something in Liam's demeanor shifted. His face hardened. "He's not the only one."

Desfan frowned. "What?"

"He's not the only one I want destroyed." Liam lifted his chin, his eyes calculating. "You're not going to win this war against my father, but there are other enemies you can kill for me."

"I won't be your personal assassin."

"No," Liam agreed. "But if you see that my enemies are your enemies, you'll kill them just the same. Not that I expect you to believe me, so I suppose you'll just have to do things the hard way. Did you figure out who was bringing olcain into your city?"

Desfan blinked. The swift change in topic made his thoughts jumble briefly. "A Zennorian drug master named Sahvi."

"Excellent. Make some inquiries about his acquaintances, and that should lead you to some of our mutual targets."

"The olcain problem is being handled by the city guard." And it was a problem Desfan had helped solve months ago when they'd arrested Jamal.

"I'm sure Yahri has been teaching you all about delegation," Liam said. "But I believe this is something you'll take a personal interest in. Haven't you wondered about the timing of it all? Why olcain began to pour into Duvan precisely when it did? Right when you were struggling as regent and Serene was on her way to you?"

"Are you saying Sahvi was making a political move with the

olcain?"

"That's one theory. Keep looking to see what others you find. And if you'd be so kind as to tell me when you start killing people, I'd appreciate it." His shoulders went back. "Now, if you'd excuse me, I think I'd like a little more peace and solitude."

"We're not finished," Desfan argued.

"I am," Liam said. "And I suggest you hurry along. You're living on borrowed time, Desfan, and I think you'll regret not finding the answers to this particular puzzle."

"Thank you for keeping your silence," Desfan said after the holding room door closed, leaving him alone in the room with Bennick and Karim. "I know that couldn't have been easy."

"I wanted to strangle him more than once," Karim admitted.

"Thank you for your restraint, then," Desfan said, his smile feeling weak.

"He's too valuable to execute," Bennick said, almost musingly. "He knows far more than he teased us with. Perhaps you should consider a deal in which he becomes a well-kept prisoner, rather than facing a noose."

Karim shook his head. "He must stand trial. That is our way, and the people will expect it. Your own king will expect it, after what the Kaelins nearly succeeded in doing to Princess Serene. And King Zaire Buhari will demand justice as well."

Bennick didn't argue.

Desfan rubbed a hand over his brow. "In many ways, he

shared more than I expected." Not that he'd been abundantly clear, though. "We won't resort to torture," he added, just to make that perfectly clear. The Garvins Treaty, signed by his ancestor long ago, protected prisoners from other kingdoms—especially royal ones. Desfan would not break those oaths, even if Ryden obviously had.

"We have time for further interrogations," Karim said. "Yahri believes we can keep the trial at bay until Grayson returns."

If Grayson returned. Fates, that was a depressing thought. He shoved it away so he could focus on the two men in front of him. "What were your observations during the interrogation?"

Bennick glanced at Karim, but when the Mortisian man gestured for him to speak first, the captain said, "I think it was wise to make him wait down here so long. He revealed more than he probably would have otherwise, though toward the end he reverted to old habits. He seemed genuinely worried about his brother."

"I thought at first it might only be anger," Karim said. "Or even just curiosity. But he *was* actually concerned. I'm not sure that bodes well for us."

"How so?" Desfan asked.

"It contradicts what Grayson told us. He painted Liam as an enemy; that he threatened Meerah and coerced Grayson to help him. While Liam didn't contradict any of this, I expected a different reaction from him. Why was he concerned for the brother he blackmailed—the brother who also betrayed him?" Karim lifted one shoulder. "It's possible Grayson lied to us."

That did nothing for Desfan's knotting gut.

"I think it also unsettled him that Karim and I were silent," Bennick said. "That was another wise decision on your part."

"Thank you."

Bennick tipped his head, but his gaze became more serious. "What was he talking about at the end? About Sahvi, and olcain?"

Desfan expelled a heavy breath and reclined against the table at his back, two hands dropping to grip the long edge on either side of his hips. "It's an old problem. Well, I *thought* it was an old problem. Olcain is a dangerous Zennorian drug."

"I've heard of it."

"Then you probably know it's highly addictive and very expensive. The streets of Duvan were recently flooded with it. Karim and I tracked down the source to a drug master called Sahvi, but since he's a Zennorian criminal, I satisfied myself with cleaning the olcain out of my streets and sending Zaire Buhari a letter, warning him about Sahvi's exports."

"Do you think Liam is just trying to distract us?" Karim asked.

"I don't think so," Desfan said slowly. He glanced at Bennick. "I would value your outside opinion. What do you think of Liam bringing this to my attention?"

"He doesn't have much to lose at this point," Bennick said. "He looked and sounded sincere. He wants you to share enemies, but he won't name them, because he knows you won't trust him outright."

Karim grunted. "Unfortunately, I think Liam did give us something worth looking into. If Sahvi is connected with the Zennorians he mentioned earlier—the ones allied with Ryden—then the olcain could have been a preliminary attack meant to destabilize us."

"I agree," Desfan said. "I'll ask Arcas for a report on any olcain activity in the city, and we'll start asking some questions."

"It's possible Imara knows of this Sahvi," Bennick said. "She might also have some insight into who in Zennor might have aligned themselves with Ryden."

It was a good idea. Desfan nodded. "I'll ask her."

"Thank you for including me," Bennick added.

"Of course. I prefer a more unified approach when it comes to Liam. He's a good liar." Besides, they were all facing the threat of Ryden—and possibly a faction in Zennor as well.

He wasn't wearing his crown at the moment, but he certainly felt the weight of it.

CHAPTER 20

IMARA

IMARA'S LEG THROBBED, BUT SHE ENDEAVORED to ignore that as she sipped tea with Clare. She was in bed—of course—and Clare sat in a chair at her bedside.

Imara had never thought twice about something as simple as walking. Now, trapped in bed and facing the prospect that she might not walk ever again . . .

The fear settled on her chest with all the weight of a boulder, and it worsened with every passing day. She was beyond grateful for the distraction Clare had handed her.

"I think we should do an afternoon at the beach," Imara said, her fingertips warming against the porcelain sides of the steaming teacup. "The children should get outside, and we can recruit some of the palace staff to help with games and food."

"That's a wonderful idea. We could teach them some Devendran and Zennorian games. I'm sure Venn, Vera, and Bennick would volunteer to help."

"And Hanna would be delighted, I'm sure," Imara said, loud enough that her maid—sewing across the room—easily heard. Hanna rolled her eyes, but Imara could see a smile play at her lips. She tried not to dwell on why Hanna looked relieved.

Imara had not been herself the last five days. It was easier to pretend when she had visitors, but when she was alone, she felt a shadow creep over her. And it wasn't solely due to her injury.

"I can make arrangements with Desfan," Imara said, firmly shoving all memory of that shadow aside.

"Thank you, Imara. I appreciate your help with this."

"Of course. It gives me something to do."

Clare glanced at Imara's quilt-covered legs. "Has the physician said when he'll let you try standing?"

"He'd like me to spend a few more days in bed. It's driving me mad."

"I'm sorry."

"Don't be." Imara took a sip of tea. "If anyone should be sorry, it's my cousin. How dare she leave?" Her tone was light, but in truth, she really *was* upset Serene had left.

Serene should be here, courting Desfan, and Imara should be the one headed back to Zennor. She didn't know when the switch had happened, but she was no longer content to hide from Skyer and her responsibilities at home. Perhaps it was getting injured and seeing how quickly life could change. Her father needed this alliance with the clans. He needed *her*.

A voice inside whispered it was something else that had changed her mind. *Someone* else.

Days later, she could still feel the press of Desfan's lips against hers. She could see perfectly the heat in his deep brown eyes. Her skin tingled, even now, remembering the touch of his callused fingers.

Fates. She gripped the teacup more firmly and threw out every thought in her head that contained Desfan Cassian.

She was doing that with alarming frequency these days.

". . . Desfan might."

Imara jerked and looked to Clare. "What?"

The Devendran woman eyed her. "I just said Desfan might have some ideas about what foods the children will like best."

"Oh. Yes. Good thinking." Heat entered her cheeks. She tried to hide it by taking another drink of tea.

Clare's lips parted, but before she could ask any questions, there was a knock on the suite's outer door. Hanna left to go see who it was, and it wasn't long before the object of Imara's distraction strode in.

Desfan wore a deep blue kurta today, and his thick dark hair curled over his brow. His intent gaze found her immediately, and when he smiled, the appearance of a slight dimple in his right cheek nearly undid her. His jaw was covered in dark stubble, and she knew exactly how it felt when it rasped against her skin. He was tall, broad-shouldered, and the most devastatingly handsome man she had ever seen.

And he was not hers.

"How are you feeling?" Desfan asked, his voice rich and deep.

Imara's hands shook a little, so she lowered her teacup to balance it on her good knee. "Better every day," she said, attempting a lightness she didn't feel.

Desfan's eyes softened in a way that was completely dangerous. "Good."

Her insides melted.

Bennick and Karim had entered the room behind Desfan, but Imara only noticed them when Bennick stepped closer to Clare. "Are you ready to return to the suite?" he asked.

She nodded and stood, offering to take Imara's cup.

She almost kept it, just for something to hold on to. But with the tremble in her fingers, it was probably safer to relinquish it.

Clare promised to return later, and then she and Bennick left. Karim wished Imara well, and then he also disappeared.

Hanna hadn't returned, which meant Desfan and Imara were alone. *Blast.*

Her heart raced, but she tried not to reveal any unease as she resettled against the mound of pillows at her back. She needed to say something—anything to fill the sudden silence.

"You aren't wearing your crown," she blurted.

His expression grew puzzled. "No, I'm not."

Her cheeks warmed, but she attempted to ignore that. "Well, I told you before the coronation that I wanted to see it. I'm beginning to think it doesn't exist—or you lost it." Fates, what was wrong with her? She needed to stop talking.

The corner of Desfan's mouth lifted. "I'll wear it sometime, I promise."

That charming grin could be her undoing. Imara cleared her throat. "How did Liam's interrogation go?"

Desfan stepped closer to the bed and lowered into the chair Clare had vacated. He was close enough she could smell his unique scent. Spicy citrus, with a hint of the sea. "Did Clare tell you about that?" he asked.

"She mentioned it."

Desfan raked a hand through his hair, tousling the curls. "It was . . . interesting. I actually wanted to ask you a few questions, if you feel up to it."

"Please." It would give her something else to focus on other than how much she wanted to run *her* fingers through those dark locks.

Desfan told her everything Liam had shared, along with the discussion Desfan, Karim, and Bennick had had afterward. Though he glanced over his fears about Grayson, Imara saw them clearly.

"Grayson will bring Meerah back," she said, her voice soft but sure.

Desfan exhaled. "I wish I could share your faith."

"You can trust him."

"Can I?" He shook his head. "Sometimes I think I trust him, and that's why I sent him. But maybe I only sent him because I didn't have another choice."

"You let him go because it was the right decision. Don't torture yourself over it."

His eyes remained serious, but the corner of his mouth quirked. "You make it sound so easy."

Imara couldn't control the impulse to reach out and set a hand on his knee. "When Grayson was preparing to leave, I forged a letter for him—in your hand."

He stared. "You—"

"Yes. I'm very good at that sort of thing. But before you decide to arrest me, let me finish." She took a breath. "I told Grayson to give it to Captain Zadir once he and Meerah were safely on board the pirate's ship. The letter instructed Zadir to take Grayson wherever he chose, and then deliver Meerah to Duvan."

Desfan's chest rose with a sharp breath. "You . . ." He didn't seem able to finish.

She increased the pressure on his knee. "He didn't take it, Desfan. I gave him a way out, and he refused it. He will save Meerah, and he'll return—just as he promised you. He'll have a cell, or a trial, or whatever else you dictate, because he loves her. There's no other explanation."

A vein at his temple pulsed. "I'm not thrilled you did that."

"I know."

"I should probably ask *how* you forged that letter."

"Or you could let me remain mysterious." She flashed a smile, but it faded quickly. She withdrew her hand. "I am sorry if my actions upset you, but please understand. Grayson is my friend, and he saved my life. I owed him the same favor."

"Your loyalty is admirable, but also reckless. What if he *is* an enemy?"

"You don't believe that. Not completely. Or you wouldn't have sent him to save Meerah."

Desfan had no response to that.

Imara smiled a little. "I see you're avoiding the fact that Grayson loves her."

He pulled a face. "The idea makes me sick, so, yes, I'm avoiding it."

"I think that's a natural reaction for an older brother."

He grunted. "Can I ask you some questions, now?"

"Of course. I don't know how much help I'll be, though. I don't know who in Zennor would ally with Ryden."

His expression fell. "You can't think of anyone?"

"There are members of the court who complain about my father's rule, but nothing so serious that it would lead them to commit treason."

"What of the clans?"

Imara sighed. "There has been some unrest among many of

the clans, but their issues are with the monarchy, and negotiations are taking place. Their roots are so firmly in Zennor,
I can't imagine them looking beyond the kingdom's borders
for allies." Frankly, they didn't need to; the tribes were filled
with fierce warriors.

Desfan studied her. "Your intended, Eilan Skyer—he's leading the clan negotiations with your father?"

Sudden nerves fluttered in her belly. She had to fight to keep
her face neutral. "Yes. But as I already said, their issues are with
the monarchy—nothing beyond Zennor concerns them."

"What complaints are the clans citing?"

"The usual things. They want a voice in the court, but they
don't want to be constrained by it. They want more land and
less interference from the crown."

Desfan's eyebrows pulled together. "Imara, just how bad are
things in Zennor?"

She bit the inside of her cheek. Should she be honest, or
diplomatic? She was talking to the Serjan of Mortise, after all.
Anything she divulged about her kingdom, he could choose
to exploit.

She released a slow breath and felt her shoulders loosen.
"My father would not appreciate me speaking so candidly with
you. But things in Zennor are not good. We are on the edge
of a civil war."

Desfan's mouth pressed into a line. "With the clans?"

"Yes, and their supporters. Some of the lower ranking nobles feel they will gain power by siding with the clans, and even
some of the monarchy's strongest supporters are vacillating
between which side to support. Once my father agreed to
Skyer's proposal for my hand, tensions eased. That's the only
reason I dared leave. But I need to return as soon as I can."

Desfan leaned forward, his arms braced against his thighs. "I appreciate your candor. Is there anything I can do?"

Imara shook her head. "The rifts must be repaired by Zennorians—the clans and the crown. But thank you."

"Do you think Serene will be able to help? She's renowned for her diplomacy."

"I'm sure she will try, but I'm not certain what else needs to be arranged at this point." Her marriage to Skyer would settle things quite permanently.

It looked for a moment like Desfan would say more, but instead he asked, "Do you know the name Sahvi? He's the drug master responsible for shipping olcain into Duvan."

"I'm sorry, I don't recognize the name. My father would."

"I wrote to your father weeks ago about Sahvi," Desfan admitted. "There has been ample time for him to send a response, but I've heard nothing yet."

"Did you specifically request a response?"

"No, it was more for his information."

Imara nodded once. "He's been so busy with the clans, I wouldn't expect a reply. But if you'd like, I could write to him and ask for his thoughts on Sahvi, and the threat he might pose to Mortise." She'd already sent one letter with Serene—an apology, more than anything, and a promise to return home as soon as she was able to travel—but she could easily write to her father again.

"I can write to him," Desfan said. He quirked his lips. "And I'll be sure to ask for a reply this time."

Imara's pulse thrummed in reaction to that casual smile. "In the meantime, will you be pursuing the olcain mystery from here?"

"Yes, but I'm not sure what new answers could be found. I

already investigated things once."

"Tell me what you learned before—it might help to say things out loud."

"All right. If you're sure you don't mind." When she nodded, Desfan straightened, his arms dropping as he resettled in his chair. "The olcain was being stored in warehouses belonging to Fang, a criminal who operates purely in Duvan. He hasn't been seen in the city since he tried to ransom me and Karim."

A laugh caught in her throat. "That sounds like a story."

Desfan grinned. "Oh, it is. Captain Zadir rescued us, actually—it's how we met."

"I want to hear this whole story sometime, but we should probably stick to the olcain for now."

He nodded his agreement. "Let's see . . . the olcain was brought in on ships owned by Rahim Nassar."

That name snagged Imara's attention. "The merchant?"

Surprise sparked in Desfan's eyes. "You know him?"

"I know *of* him. He created quite a stir whenever he visited Zennor. Some claim he's the most handsome man in Eyrinthia—definitely the most handsome Mortisian."

Desfan arched a dark brow. "That's new information, though I'm not sure how it's relevant."

All right, she was teasing Desfan. But only a little. Those rumors were quite detailed. "Rahim Nassar made quite a few strong connections among the nobility, and he was a favorite to have at parties. He rarely ventured closer to the capital than the midlands, so I never met him, but he was a successful, well-known merchant."

"He was in Zennor a lot, then?"

"Frequently." She suddenly brightened. "If you arrest him, can I be part of his interrogation? I'd love to see if the rumors are true."

Desfan rolled his eyes. "I don't know how I'll arrest him. I can't even gain a meeting with him. The men at his warehouse tell me Nassar has been in Zennor."

"A shame."

Desfan seemed lost in thought. "If Rahim Nassar frequented Zennor, that's how he could have met Sahvi. They may have created a partnership, and Nassar extended his smuggling business to include transporting olcain."

"He's a smuggler, too? Fates, he's getting more dashing all the time."

Desfan snorted, but made no actual comment. "I'll continue to pursue this. Thank you for talking me through things."

"Of course. What else am I going to do?" She paused. "Oh. I should mention, you're hosting a party."

His head cocked. "I am?"

"Yes. A very important one. But don't worry, I'll plan everything. I just need your permission to use the royal beach and make use of some of your servants."

"My staff is yours, as is the beach." He glanced at her covered leg. "Are you able to—?"

"Oh, the party isn't for me, so there are no worries on that front." She would miss seeing the children's fun, but the party wasn't for her sake.

"I'm intrigued," Desfan said. "Who is this party for?"

Imara smiled. "Your smallest subjects."

Imara was just drifting to sleep when the bedroom door brushed open. The sound was slight, but she still caught it. Frowning, she blinked into the darkness. The curtains were drawn, muffling the moonlight, but she managed to pick out the dark shadow at the foot of her bed.

"Hanna?" she asked, her voice heavy with sleep.

The shadow rounded the bed, and Imara's heart beat faster when she realized it wasn't Hanna. The shadow was far too large. It belonged to a man.

A man was in her bedroom.

She opened her mouth to scream.

"It's me," the shadow said.

Relief poured through her veins, though her heart still hammered from his unexpected appearance. "Jekem—you frightened me." But if her bodyguard was here in the middle of the night, it couldn't be for a good reason. She was instantly more alert, and she scrambled to sit up. Her wounded leg bent and she hissed in pain. "What's wrong?" she asked through gritted teeth.

Her bodyguard let out a slow exhale. "This was the best moment," he whispered. "I'm sorry."

She frowned, not understanding. *The best moment?* For what? It was late at night, and the room was pitch black. Why hadn't he carried in a lamp?

Jekem stopped beside her bed. Something in his sudden stillness sent a chill across her skin. "What's going on?" Despite her best efforts, her voice trembled.

"I thought there was a chance the fates would save me from this," he said quietly. "Our travels with Serene were not safe, after all. But Hanna told me today that you plan to return to Zennor as soon as you're healed, and I'm afraid I cannot let that happen."

Imara's fingers knotted in her quilt. She opened her mouth to call for—

His fist hit her temple.

Imara gasped as she fell to the mattress, her vision sparking. As she recoiled, her leg reflexively jerked, and tears stabbed her eyes as the stitches in her skin tore. She sucked in a breath to scream, but Jekem shoved a pillow in her face, pressing down hard.

The pillow smothered everything—her scream, her breath; sight and sound.

Panic attacked her. She thrashed on the bed, but Jekem only climbed on top of her, still pressing the pillow against her face with one hand while the other captured her wrists in a painful vice. She thought she heard him say something, but she couldn't make out the muffled words.

His knees dug into her sides as he straddled her. The bones in her wrists grated as he held them immobile in his fist, trapped above her head.

Her lungs burned. She squirmed beneath him, trying to buck her hips to dislodge him, but he was too heavy—too strong.

She was going to die.

No.

Desperation caught her. She dug her heels into the mattress and shoved. Agony sliced her injured knee, but she didn't stop trying to throw him off. She twisted her head back and forth, but the pillow remained in place. In fact, the pressure increased until she feared he'd crush her skull.

Her head pounded. Her ears roared. She screamed, but even she barely heard it.

The bedroom door banged open, and the weight on top of her vanished. Her trembling hands clawed at the pillow, tearing it away from her face.

She sucked in air.

Her body shook. She was covered in sweat. Her knee was an inferno of pain, and her cheeks were wet with tears she hadn't felt until now. Her chest rose and fell in heavy gasps, and her eyes darted around the room.

In the darkness, she could hardly make out the two shadows, grunting as they fought each other.

A pained hiss and a thin curse revealed Kaz's identity, giving a name to her rescuer—her senior bodyguard was fighting Jekem.

Imara's heart thudded, and she wanted nothing more than to run. But she couldn't. Her leg would never support her. Her throat felt raw, but she cried out for Hanna.

It was a pathetically weak shout.

There was a terrible, fleshy thud, followed by the crash of a body hitting the floor.

Imara whipped her head toward the shadows, where now only one man stood.

Terror flashed through her.

Then Kaz boomed out, "Hanna!"

Relief crashed into Imara. Her throat squeezed, and a sob cracked in her chest.

Kaz strode around the bed and dropped to his knees beside her. His large hands framed her face. "Princess? Are you all right?"

"He—he tried to kill me."

Her own fates-blasted bodyguard had just tried to assassinate her.

Kaz rumbled a growl. His fingers tensed against her skin.

Hanna rushed in, carrying a lamp. The single flame flickered weakly in the glass, but it was enough to illuminate the shock carved on the maid's face.

Kaz threw a look at her over his shoulder. "Get the physician. Tell him—"

Imara shrieked as Kaz suddenly threw himself over her. He grunted, but didn't get off her.

Hanna cried out as footsteps pounded. Glass shattered, and a gust of night air wafted into the room.

Imara gripped Kaz's shoulders. That's when she spotted the knife embedded in his arm.

She swallowed back bile as understanding dawned. That knife had been thrown at her, and Kaz had shielded her with his own body.

Kaz pulled back, his eyes narrowed on the shattered window Jekem had presumably just launched himself through.

Imara's fingers dug into Kaz's wrist, not that he was trying to move from her side. She looked to Hanna, who's mouth hung open. "Get the physician," Imara said, her voice far calmer than she felt. "And send for Captain Markam, please."

CHAPTER 21

BENNICK

BENNICK STOOD AT THE BROKEN WINDOW IN Imara's bedroom and looked down. There was no body.

Jekem had survived his desperate jump.

There were enough narrow ledges and balconies between here and the castle grounds, he could have scrambled his way down. A search was being conducted, and Bennick had sent Venn to alert the guards to watch every gate, but he had a sinking suspicion Jekem was already gone.

"I should have snapped his neck," Kaz said tersely. "I thought I'd rendered him unconscious with that blow, but ... *Fates*." His cursing continued as the physician tugged a needle through his torn flesh.

A chill snaked down Bennick's spine. If Kaz hadn't moved so quickly, the knife he'd taken would have hit Imara.

Clare stepped into the bedroom. She was wearing a long,

pale pink robe, the thin silk shimmering as she strode toward him. He wouldn't have disturbed her at all, but Imara had been shaken after the unexpected attack.

Clare's mouth was set into a thin line. "You need to hear this," she said.

Bennick didn't hesitate to follow her back into the sitting room. Behind him, the physician cursed, and Bennick knew Kaz had brushed the man aside to trail them.

Imara was sitting on the settee, her legs stretched out on the cushions and a pillow wedged behind her back. There was some bruising already surfacing on her face, especially around her nose and her temple, where she'd been struck.

Clare hurried to stand by Imara, her hand going to the princess's shoulder. "Tell them what Jekem said to you."

Before Imara could, voices sounded in the corridor. The door shoved open and Desfan and Karim strode in.

Both were clad in loose white shirts and sleep pants. Desfan's feet were bare, but he didn't seem aware of that. His focus was trained on Imara, and he went straight to her. He crouched before her and grasped her hand. His eyes burned as he took in the bruises on her face. "Are you all right?" he demanded, his deep voice vibrating.

The serjan was *furious*.

Imara stared at him, clearly taken aback. "Wh-What are you doing here?"

Desfan's eyes narrowed. "Your fates-blasted bodyguard just tried to kill you. Where else would I be?"

"Sir Grannard sent a guard to me," Karim explained to Bennick. "He knew we'd want to know."

Desfan hadn't looked away from Imara. "What happened? What did he do to you?"

"He tried to suffocate me with my pillow." Imara's throat flexed as she swallowed. "Kaz interrupted, and they fought. Then Jekem threw a knife at me, Kaz put himself in front of it, and Jekem jumped out the window."

Desfan flicked a glance toward Kaz, who was only half-stitched and still bleeding. Then he focused back on Imara. "You're getting ten Mortisian guards. Karim will handpick them."

"Thank you, Serjan," Kaz said quickly.

Imara's mouth snapped shut.

Desfan tightened his hold on her hand. "Your leg—"

"The stitches tore a little," Imara cut in before he could fully form his question. "The physician has already tended me."

Desfan didn't look relieved. In fact, he still looked livid.

Frankly, Bennick was a little surprised by the serjan's strong reaction to the attack. He and Imara were friends, clearly, but now Bennick wondered if the serjan felt more for the Zennorian princess.

Or he simply feared King Zaire's retaliation if his daughter was murdered in Desfan's palace.

Bennick cleared his throat. "Serjan, Imara was just about to tell us what Jekem said to her."

Desfan's intensity sharpened.

Imara took a steadying breath as she visibly gathered her thoughts. The petite princess looked even smaller than usual, and far more vulnerable than Bennick liked to see her. He was used to an Imara who smiled, joked, and viewed the world in a positive light. He hated that she'd been attacked—especially after she'd already suffered a terrible injury. "He didn't make a lot of sense," Imara began. "He said he was sorry, and . . . he actually sounded upset. Like he didn't want to kill me."

Desfan made a harsh sound deep in his throat, and Bennick agreed completely—there should be no compassion for the man who had attacked Imara.

"He said this was the best moment," she added, a slight waver in her voice.

Kaz stiffened. Karim and Bennick both turned to him, though Bennick managed to speak first. "Why was this his best moment to attack her?"

Kaz gritted his teeth. "Jekem took the lead tonight. I was off-duty. If I hadn't checked in before going to bed . . ."

"He said *sorry*," Clare whispered, sounding a little ill. "Why would a killer say that?"

"Could he have been blackmailed somehow?" Bennick asked, his eyes still on Kaz. "Did he have debts? Family that could have been exploited?"

"I don't think so." The bodyguard looked miserable, and not just because of his bleeding arm. Bennick could relate; failure of any kind hit a bodyguard hard. Even though Kaz had succeeded in saving Imara, she'd been hurt. And not even by a stranger, but a man Kaz had known well and trusted.

Betrayal had its own burn.

Imara was shaking her head. "He didn't sound desperate. He mostly sounded upset that he'd have to be the one to kill me. Like he thought my travels with Serene would have brought me to my death instead." She glanced at Hanna, who was wringing her hands in the periphery. "He said you mentioned my plan to return to Zennor as soon as I healed."

Hanna sucked in a breath, her eyes glittering with tears. "Fates, I . . . Yes, I told him. He asked, but—I swear, I wasn't part of this."

"I know," Imara said at once. "But Jekem said I couldn't

return to Zennor."

"Why?" Karim asked. The Mortisian bodyguard was generally a man of few words, but when he spoke, he made them count.

"I don't know," Imara said. "He didn't give me any specifics before he put a pillow against my face." Her tone failed to be flippant, because she shuddered.

Clare rubbed the princess's shoulder, her attention on Bennick. "Someone in Zennor doesn't want Imara to return home. Jekem was following orders—which means someone told him to make sure she didn't come back."

"But why?" Desfan demanded, reiterating his bodyguard's question.

"Someone doesn't want the clans to unite with the monarchy," Imara said softly. "It's not about killing me—it's about stopping my marriage to Eilan Skyer. It's the only thing that makes sense. And since he's a tribal warrior, I'm the easier target."

"Jekem won't get another chance to hurt you," Desfan said tightly. He looked to Kaz. "I want a full description of him distributed to the palace guards and the city guard. We'll find him. In the meantime, I need to know that her other guards can be trusted."

Kaz's expression was strained. "I trusted Jekem, so my opinion cannot be relied upon."

"Kaz has my full trust," Imara said at once. "So do all the others."

Desfan didn't look satisfied.

To be fair, Bennick wasn't, either. He looked to Kaz. "You and I will interview each of them tomorrow. And I would recommend you use the serjan's offer of additional guards to organize rotations so your men are never alone with her."

"This is insane." Imara scrubbed a hand over her forehead. "Jekem has served my family for years. I can't believe this is happening."

Clare squeezed her shoulder. "You can stay with me tonight—or however long you'd like."

"Thank you." Imara's gaze swept the room. "All of you."

"You need to inform your father about what happened," Kaz said. "The king must be warned. So does Skyer, in case he's in danger as well."

"I'll write a message first thing in the morning," Imara assured him.

"And I'll prepare a messenger to take it with all speed," Desfan said. "I'll include my own letter, assuring your father that you'll be safe here until this threat is handled."

Imara frowned. "What do you mean?"

The skin around his eyes tightened. "You're not going back to Zennor. Not while you're a target."

She tugged her hand from his. "I can't just hide here."

"Why not?"

She threw her hands up, exasperation pinching her tone. "These cowards don't want me in Zennor, so that's exactly where I should be!"

Desfan's mouth opened, but Clare broke in. "Perhaps this can be discussed later. If it becomes relevant at all." She looked to the physician. "She'll be unable to travel for a while, won't she?"

The man tipped his head. "Yes, Princess Serene. Weeks yet, I imagine."

Bennick caught Desfan blink once, and glance at Clare. The serjan wasn't used to having Serene's decoy in place, which meant he was more likely to make a mistake and reveal the secret.

No one else seemed to catch this moment, at least.

Imara leveled a look at Desfan. "Satisfied?" she asked.

"For now." He pushed to his feet, his attention going to Kaz. "Karim will speak with you in the morning about permanent additional guards, but tonight I want you to utilize the ones in the hall. I'll also get that window repaired first thing in the morning. Let me know if there's anything else you need."

"Thank you, Serjan."

Desfan turned to Imara. "Are we friends enough at the moment that you'll allow me to carry you down the hall?"

Imara glanced at Kaz, noting his bleeding arm. Then she looked at Bennick and Karim.

Desfan sighed. "Your father is going to want my head, seeing as you've nearly died twice while in my care. Please, let me do this so I have something good to tell him."

Imara echoed his sigh, but she relented. "Fine."

"Thank you." Desfan bent and scooped her up, infinitely careful with her wounded knee. Once Imara was gathered securely in his arms, with her elbow wound loosely behind his neck, Desfan strode for the door.

Karim followed at once. Kaz also tried to go, but the physician stopped him. "I really must tend to your wound, sir."

Bennick nodded to the tense bodyguard. "I've got her."

Kaz grunted, but allowed the physician to resume his stitches.

Clare asked Hanna to gather anything Imara might need, then she and Bennick left Imara's suite and headed down the hall toward Serene's room.

"Imara is more afraid than she's showing," Clare said, keeping her voice low so the guards stationed at the door wouldn't hear. "I can't imagine how it would feel to have one of your bodyguards turn against you." She paused. "Actually, I thought Wilf was trying to kill me once. But to truly experience that . . . Fates, it would be so hard to feel safe after that."

Bennick wanted to take her hand, but he resisted the urge; the guards could still see them. "We'll keep her safe," he assured her.

Clare glanced up at him, worry in her eyes. "This feels like what we went through in Iden, with Gavril. And again with the Rose."

Bennick sighed, unable to argue. Gavril had tried to kill Serene to stop her marriage to Desfan, and Zilas had been hired to do the same. Both men had nearly succeeded in killing Clare—and his half-brother was still out there.

Bennick knew it was only a matter of time before Zilas re-entered their lives. And since he knew what Clare meant to Bennick, she was his target just as much as Serene was.

"They're cowards," Clare said quietly. "Targeting women who have no choice but to follow the orders they've been given. It's terrible. I hate that Imara has to face this."

"She's not alone," Bennick said. "You'll be able to do more for her than any of us, because you've been where she is."

They were nearly halfway down the corridor before Clare said quietly, "I don't truly understand what it would be like to be forced to marry for political gain. But I do know some of her fear. I've been targeted, and I know how it feels to not be in control of your own life. To live, knowing your life isn't truly your own."

The words—so matter-of-factly spoken—made Bennick's heart clench. He hated that Clare felt like her life wasn't her own. He wanted to protest, but he couldn't. Unfortunately, there was truth in what she said. King Newlan would never let her go; not when he could still use her.

But the fates would rot before Bennick allowed Clare to feel trapped for the rest of her life.

CHAPTER 22

MIA

GRAYSON WAS *NOT* FINE.

It had been three days since their escape from the castle, and though Grayson kept insisting he was fine, he clearly wasn't. He kept rubbing his head, his eyes were unfocused, and his skin was feverishly hot, even though the air was chill. They stopped to rest with increasing frequency, even though she now walked with an arm wrapped around Grayson's back. As the day passed, he allowed her to take more of his weight, and his steps grew unsteady.

Panic tightened her lungs, but Mia didn't let the emotion attack her. Somehow, she was holding it back, though she knew she would have a breaking point.

Her grief for Devon flared. She wished the physician was with them. Fates, she couldn't believe he was dead. Had she ever truly thanked him for taking care of her for so many years? She couldn't remember, and it made her heart ache.

She wished the Fletchers were here. She wished she wasn't so alone, especially when Grayson suddenly staggered.

His weight was too much; they both hit the hard ground. Pain shot up from her knees, and she grunted as she fought to keep his head from knocking against the dirt.

He blinked blearily at her as she eased him onto his side. "Can't—stop."

Her eyes stung. "Grayson, you can't keep going like this."

His body was wracked by a terrible convulsion. The burned cut along his jaw was inflamed. Infected. Without help, he might die.

"Keep . . . going."

"I can't carry you," she said, her voice coming out a little hoarse. "And you can't keep walking."

Fates, what could she do? Grayson had said there were villages nearby, but they hadn't seen one yet. Surely they must be close.

Darkness was falling. Her heart pounded. She didn't know if he'd survive another night without help.

"Powder," Grayson said tersely, teeth clenched in pain. "Need. More."

She immediately reached for his pack and dug inside for the small pouch. She worried he'd been taking too much. That maybe it was the thing allowing him to push his body too far. But if more powder would help him make a final push . . .

She found the powder. There was less than she'd expected. She took a pinch of it, as she'd seen Grayson do, and put the medicine under his tongue.

He shuddered as it dissolved. But his eyes soon sharpened.

She pressed a kiss to his feverish forehead. "How close are

we to a village?"

"We can't . . . be seen."

"Grayson, you need help."

He didn't object, and that alone made her fear escalate.

He grimaced and pushed up until he was sitting, his shoulder pressed against a narrow tree beside the path. "We have to be near Edgewood," he said, sounding breathless and far too worn. But he spoke less tightly, and with more clarity. "We just have to keep following this path. Once we're there, you can hide in the woods and I'll find a physician if they have one, and food and horses."

"You can barely stand. I can go—"

"No."

"Grayson—"

"It's too much of a risk."

She didn't argue, because she didn't want him to exert all his strength on a useless disagreement. The burst of strength from the medicine wouldn't last long; soon enough, he would be in no condition to protest.

She stood, ignoring the bruises on her knees, the soreness in her feet, back, and shoulders. She helped pull Grayson to his feet, and they resumed walking. He didn't lean on her, at first. But within an hour, he was slumped against her, barely shuffling forward.

It was full dark now, though moonlight filtered through the canopy of leaves overhead. She heard the distant howls of wolves, and the fine hairs on her body lifted. *Fates, no.*

Then, through the trees, Mia spotted the yellow glow of lights in the distance. The village—Edgewood. A wave of relief hit her, and she gasped. "Grayson, we're almost there."

He let out a low groan, but she didn't know if he'd actually heard her.

The howling of the wolves hadn't grown any louder, so she dared to leave Grayson near a thick pine tree. She couldn't keep carrying him, and she needed to make sure the village would be safe for them.

He was so lost to his fever, his eyes barely fluttered as she stroked his dark hair off his sweaty brow. "I'll hurry," she whispered. "Don't move."

He croaked her name, and the sound was so broken, it tore at her heart.

She left her pack with him, taking only a pouch of coins. She checked the knife sheathed at her hip, her fingers trembling from the cold and from fear.

With a last look at Grayson, she darted into the village. It was a small settlement on the edge of the woods, with only one unpaved street. Most of the windows were dark. There was an inn in the center of town, with a wooden sign that creaked as the breeze made it swing.

She tried the door, but it was locked.

She felt the unsettling touch of watching eyes, but when she looked over her shoulder, the street was still empty, and she couldn't see anyone hovering in the nearby windows.

She forced her anxiety away and knocked on the door.

The sound was small. Timid, even to her own ears. Her already tight lungs tightened further. Panic was closing in.

She forced herself to breathe and knock again—harder this time.

Movement rose from inside the inn, and the front window lightened as footsteps approached. The lock disengaged and the door eased open, revealing a glimpse of a man.

He had dark hair, narrowed eyes, and a pinched face. "What

do you want?" he demanded, his voice low and gruff.

Mia's breath hitched. "I . . . Is there a healer in town?"

The man eyed her. "You hurt?"

"No, but my companion is."

The man glanced up and down the street. "What companion?"

"I left him at the edge of the woods." It was only when the words came out that she realized how they might sound—like they were fugitives, trying to hide.

Which they were.

Suspicion hardened his features. "No healer here," he said brusquely. "And we want no trouble." He started to close the door.

Desperation spiked, and Mia slapped her hands against the closing door. "Please! I have gold. I can pay you."

That gave him pause, and he looked her up and down with a little more interest. "How much have you got?"

"Enough for a room, food, and a message to be sent to the nearest healer."

Indecision danced in his eyes, but the internal struggle was brief; greed won. "I got one room, and I can send one of my boys to fetch Tobin—he's in another town, but he's the closest healer."

"Thank you. Could you come help me carry my friend?"

"Show me the gold first."

Mia hesitated, but she really had no choice. She opened the purse, and his eyes lit up.

"Just a moment," he said, before he closed and locked the door.

Agitation ran through Mia's body as she waited on the doorstep. Fates, she hoped she'd done the right thing. But what other choice did she have? Grayson needed help, or he was going to die.

Finally, the door opened and the innkeeper came out. He was dressed in worn clothes and a long, dirty cloak. He carried a lantern, and Mia saw the tarnished sword belted at his side. Right behind him came two young men, dressed similarly. The older one was probably around Mia's age. The other was perhaps a couple years younger. They both rubbed sleep out of their eyes as they studied her with interest.

"Lead the way, girl," the innkeeper ordered.

Mia did, though she was carefully attuned to the men who trailed her. Vulnerability clawed at her, but she didn't allow it to show in her posture. She walked with her shoulders back as she guided them toward the edge of the forest.

She was nearly there when a horrible thought struck her. What if they recognized Grayson? Alarm flashed through her, but it was too late—the innkeeper spotted Grayson.

"Fates," the older man muttered, lifting up the lantern for a closer look. "What mauled him? A wolf?"

The glow of the lantern cast harsh light against Grayson's scarred cheek and inflamed jaw. Slumped against the tree with his eyes closed, he looked almost dead.

Her heart stopped. She dropped to her knees, relief nearly overwhelming her when she realized he was still breathing.

She looked up at the innkeeper and his sons, who looked on curiously. They hadn't recognized him; if they'd known this was the Black Hand, they would have reacted. She took comfort in that, and fought to make her voice commanding. "I'll give you more gold if you ask no questions. Just help me get him inside."

The innkeeper's chin jutted out, but he nodded. He waved

at his boys. "Timothy, Garrett—bring him."

"Please be gentle," Mia said as she shifted aside. While the two boys grunted and struggled to lift Grayson, she gathered up their packs.

Grayson stirred as he was moved, but he didn't fully wake. His groan was filled with pain as his head dropped back.

"We'll take him through the back door," the innkeeper said. "Timothy, you'll ride to fetch Tobin."

The older boy only grunted.

The innkeeper led the way back to town. Mia walked beside Grayson and the boys who carried him. Soon enough they were inside, and Grayson was lowered onto a bed in an upstairs room. Meager light filtered in through a small window that overlooked the street below.

Timothy left to fetch the healer, and the innkeeper ordered Garrett to bring food. Then he faced Mia. "I'll take my gold now."

Anxiety surged, and she clutched the purse in a tight fist. She didn't know the worth of these coins; she'd been a prisoner for too long, and a child of a different country before that. Rydenic coins meant nothing to her.

The innkeeper watched her closely, and she could feel his curiosity growing. Along with his impatience.

She took a small handful of coins from the purse and set them in his hand. "This will suffice for now," she said. It took all her willpower to make sure it didn't sound like a question.

His eyebrows lifted, and she caught a hint of surprise. "You'll pay more later?"

Fates, she'd overpaid. "Yes," she said, trying to sound confident. "If you treat us well and give us privacy."

The man shoved the coins into his pocket. "Of course."

A brutal shiver tore through Grayson. Mia hurried to the bed and tucked a quilt around him. She glanced up at the innkeeper, who silently watched them. Her skin tightened. "I need to clean his wound."

The man stirred. "I'll bring you some things," he said, moving for the door.

"Thank you."

He paused, as if her gratitude was unexpected. Without another word, he left the lantern on the side table and stepped out of the room.

Mia closed the door behind him. She was relieved when she saw a lock, which she quickly twisted into place. Her heart hammered. Adrenaline had been flooding her veins for so long, she didn't know if her pulse would ever slow.

She didn't know what to do, or who to trust. She didn't know if she'd made a terrible mistake in coming here, but Grayson had needed help. He was incapacitated—completely helpless. It was her turn to protect him, and she felt wholly incapable.

She moved to the bed, and sat on the edge beside him. Sweat streaked his skin, and his face was twisted with pain. He was whispering something—a nearly soundless mutter. She smoothed the hair off his brow and leaned in to kiss him gently. "You'll be all right," she breathed. *You have to be all right. I can't lose you.*

He moaned, the sound low and trembling. "Needs me," he mumbled. "She needs me . . ."

Tears stung her eyes and she gripped his hand. "I need you," she told him. "I'm always going to need you. Please don't leave me."

His fingers twitched weakly against hers.

She prayed the healer came before it was too late.

CHAPTER 23

GRAYSON

GRAYSON'S ENTIRE BODY BURNED. FLAME'S BREATH licked everywhere—even in his blood. And while he burned, he saw Carter straddling Mia on the ground. Raising his knife for a killing strike.

Grayson was too far away. He wouldn't reach them in time. He still launched himself forward.

The blade flashed, and Mia's throat was cut.

Grayson's very soul wrenched, and he screamed.

A dagger materialized in his hand. He didn't hesitate to slit his brother's throat. Then he held Mia as she bled, and the light drained from her eyes.

He blinked, and suddenly Mia was standing in Tyrell's arms. She smiled up at his brother, and Tyrell brushed a curl from her upturned face. He leaned in. Kissed her.

And Mia kissed him in return.

A scorpion stung Grayson in the heart, and he fell. His father laughed—or was he yelling? His mother smiled—or perhaps she was sneering. Imara was there, talking to him, but he couldn't hear a word.

Then Desfan glared down at him. "You betrayed me."

Grayson was on his knees before the ruler of Mortise. *I'm sorry*, he tried to say, but his tongue wouldn't work.

Liam stared at him from the shadows, silent and inscrutable.

Desfan twisted away from Grayson, and there was Mia's lifeless body, her throat cut from Carter's knife.

Desfan roared. He dropped to his knees and cradled Mia in his arms as he sobbed, her crimson blood covering them both.

Grayson just knelt there, burning. Unable to move. Unable to even go to Mia's body.

Tyrell thrust a knife between his ribs. "This is what you deserve," he hissed, hatred in every word. "You got her killed. *You* killed her."

Grayson fell, and he didn't care that he was dying.

Mia was gone, and nothing else mattered.

But he didn't die.

He continued to fall, and he continued to burn.

When Grayson finally opened his eyes, he knew too much time had been lost. He'd been vaguely aware of time's passage; he knew he had been in and out of consciousness for a long period, and that Mia was usually beside him. He'd known that, even if he couldn't make his eyes open. He could *feel* her, even when she hadn't been touching him.

His head ached unbearably, but he knew that his fever was gone. What he did *not* know was why a young boy with large green eyes stared down at him.

"Why does your face look like that?" the boy asked.

Grayson blinked, slowly pushing himself up.

Blankets slid down his chest to pool in his lap. He wore a loose black shirt—the only change of clothes he'd packed—and from the light that poured in from the small window on the far wall, he knew it was the middle of the day. His stomach rumbled.

The unfamiliar boy stood beside his bed, his lean face smudged with dirt. He couldn't have been more than seven years old, and he stared at Grayson unabashedly. "Garrett says you were probably tortured by the Black Hand. Or maybe the king. Does it hurt? It looks awful."

Grayson eyed the boy. He made no sense. His *presence* made no sense. Grayson had no idea where he was. He was supposed to be in the forest with—

Mia.

Panic knifed him.

Mia wasn't in the room.

Terror shot painful pinpricks throughout his body. He shoved the blankets aside, and the young boy scrambled back as Grayson lurched to his feet. He swayed and had to grab the nearest bed post to steady himself. His feet were bare against the wood floor, which was smooth and cold. The pain in his head spiked, and each pound of his heart sent a new throb of agony through his temples. Nausea swirled in his gut.

"You're not supposed to get up," the boy said.

He swallowed hard, fighting to keep down bile. "Where's Mia?" he demanded.

The boy's brow furrowed. "You mean Rena?"

Rena? Grayson frowned. Rena *Fletcher?* That wasn't possible—the woman wasn't with them. He needed Mia.

He gritted his teeth. "Where's the young woman who traveled with me?"

"That's Rena," the boy said, and the way he peered at him made it clear he doubted Grayson's lucidity. "She's gone. Timothy took her outside."

Grayson didn't know who Timothy was, but if he'd touched Mia, he was dead.

He gritted his teeth and moved for the door, stumbling a little over the smooth floor.

The boy easily trailed him. "Rena told me to watch you while she was gone. She said you'd probably just keep sleeping, but if you *did* wake, you were supposed to stay in bed."

Grayson ignored him. He braced a hand against the doorframe to keep from falling over. His vision swam, and the room spun.

"You don't listen very well," the boy said, his tone as conversational as ever.

Grayson tried to breathe without throwing up or falling over. "Who are you?"

His thin chest puffed out. "Keegan."

That told him absolutely nothing. Irritation flared, hot and sharp. "Where are we?"

"Your room."

Fates give him strength . . . "This isn't my room."

"It is. Rena bought it. With a *lot* of gold coins. Papa thinks she's a runaway noblewoman who's never had to buy a thing in her life. Timothy says she's pretty. Garrett says she's pretty too, but that you probably abducted her. Timothy thinks that's stupid, because she's taking care of you. Papa says you're probably her bodyguard, or a criminal she ran away with to marry against her papa's will. Are you a criminal?"

Grayson stared at the boy. There was far too much to decipher there, so he ignored most of it. "We're at an inn?" he surmised.

Keegan bobbed his head.

Grayson's uneasiness grew. "How long have we been here?"

"Three days."

That didn't make him feel any steadier on his feet, but he'd paused long enough. He grasped the door handle and pushed into a small hallway. A staircase on his left descended into a common room, filled with empty tables.

He hadn't thought to grab any of his weapons, but he didn't want to take the time—or effort—to go back for them. He needed to find Mia. *Now.*

Keegan's light footsteps paused on the last stair. "Timothy said it wouldn't take long. They'll be back soon."

Before Grayson could demand where they'd gone, the front door swung open.

A tall young man entered, and Mia was right behind him. She spotted Grayson and her eyes widened. "You're awake!" She darted across the room and grasped his arms with cold fingers. "Fates, you should be in bed."

He grabbed her waist. Touching her steadied him in more ways than one; he couldn't ever remember feeling so weak and lightheaded. He studied her face, taking in every detail. She looked tired, but otherwise unharmed.

Mia stared at him just as intently. "How are you feeling?"

"Better." He wasn't about to admit how frail he felt, or how badly his head ached. Not when Timothy watched them so closely.

"Thank the fates. I was so worried about you."

"Where did you go?" he asked, still holding onto her.

"To look at a horse the village blacksmith might consider selling us." Mia glanced at Timothy. "Could you heat some soup, please?"

The young man dipped his chin and strode from the room.

Keegan had edged closer to Mia, and she sent him a small smile. "Thank you for watching over him."

The boy blushed—not that Grayson could blame him. He'd been around that age when Mia had thoroughly enthralled him with one of her smiles.

"I told him to stay in bed," Keegan told her. "He didn't listen."

Her smile twitched. "That's all right. Why don't you get back to your chores? Your father will want them done before he returns."

The boy sighed, but scampered off.

Mia focused back on Grayson, and her expression softened. "I'm so glad you're awake." She took his hand and led him up the stairs. "You really shouldn't have gotten out of bed. Tobin says you need to give your body time to recover."

"Tobin?"

"He's a physician. He's been treating you." She glanced at him as they reached the top of the stairs. "You were very sick. You had a fever from the infection, and the powder Devon gave you was dangerous. Tobin said you can't take any more of it—it contained something called olcain. It's very addictive."

Grayson said nothing, just squeezed her hand. They walked into their rented room, and Mia closed the door.

She lowered her voice. "Grayson, that olcain kept you moving past the pain, but you pushed your body too far. You almost died." The last word cracked.

He leaned in and brushed a soft kiss against her lips. "I'm all right," he assured her.

Moisture gathered in her eyes. "I was so scared. I thought I was going to lose you."

He hated seeing her fear; hated that he hadn't been able to do anything to help her. What if he *had* died? She would have been alone in a hostile kingdom. He hated everything about that. "I'm sorry," he whispered.

"Just promise me you'll never take something like that again. That you'll never push yourself so far."

"I won't." He meant it, too, even though there was a small part of him that craved the blissful numbness the olcain had given him. It had smothered his pain so he could function—helped keep him strong. Without it, he wouldn't have gotten Mia out of the castle.

He wondered how much of the medicine was left—if it was still in his pack. He didn't dare ask, though. Not with the way she was looking at him.

"Tobin gave you another drug to help you sleep, so you were unconscious for the worst of the withdrawal." Mia bit her lower lip. "He said you might have a terrible headache when you woke, and that you'd feel very tired."

He nodded once, the pain in his skull spiking. "How long has it been since we left the castle?" he asked.

"Six days."

Nearly a week. Making it to Porynth before Zadir left was going to be nearly impossible, now.

He swayed a little, and Mia wordlessly guided him to the

bed. They sat on the edge, their hands still locked. Grayson didn't know if he was currently capable of letting go.

"I didn't know what else to do," Mia said, her voice quiet. "I know you wanted to avoid being seen, but I had to get help. I gave them false names; I told them I was Rena, and that your name was Alun." She winced a little. "They were the first names I could think of."

Using Rena and Fletcher's names when they didn't know their fates was a bit unnerving, but Grayson couldn't fault Mia for choosing them. Or for doing all she had while he was unconscious. She'd kept him alive.

"I'm sorry I took the risk of coming here," Mia said, clearly reading his residual fear. "But I didn't have a choice."

He brushed a loose curl and tucked it behind her ear. "You did everything right," he reassured her. "Thank you for saving my life."

Relief flickered in her brown eyes. Then she spoke in a rush. "We're in Edgewood. It's a small village, and I've mostly stayed in the room with you. I haven't seen any soldiers. I've paid Jon well to give us privacy—he's the innkeeper. He has three sons, and they've all seen you. So has Tobin. None of them recognized you."

That was an unexpected blessing from the fates. He had come through Edgewood before, though it had been years ago and he'd looked quite different. Especially now, with his ruined face.

Grayson exhaled slowly. "We can leave tonight, when everyone is asleep."

She shook her head. "You're not ready. Tobin said once you woke, you'd probably need another few days in bed."

"We've delayed too long as it is. We're still too close to

Lenzen, and if we don't reach Porynth in time, we'll lose our fastest way to Duvan." Not only the fastest, but the most secure. They'd be safe on Zadir's boat; much safer than traveling by road.

Mia's eyes narrowed. "I'd rather take a year to reach Duvan than lose you. Despite what you seem to think, you're not invincible, Grayson. You need time to heal—not just from what your father did, but from what that horrible olcain did to your body. You at least need to have Tobin check on you." Her voice lowered. "Please don't make me go through any of this again. I . . . I truly thought you were going to die." The pain in her voice knifed him.

Grayson cupped the nape of her neck, bringing her forehead to rest against his. He closed his eyes, his long fingers sinking into her hair. "All right," he acquiesced softly. "But we can't stay too long. We can't afford to lose any more time."

He feared they'd already lost too much.

CHAPTER 24

IMARA

"I DON'T THINK I SHOULD LEAVE YOU," HANNA SAID, her features drawn with concern.

Imara waved an impatient hand at her maid. "I'm perfectly fine, and Clare needs your help down at the beach. Go. Please."

Reluctance made Hanna's movements slow, but at last she left.

Imara settled back against her pillows, silently cursing her bed. She was itching to move, and not just because she wanted to attend the party on the beach for the children in the palace. No, she was restless with a lethal mix of boredom and fear. Boredom, because her days seemed endless, even though Desfan and Clare both visited every day. Fear, because Jekem hadn't yet been found.

She plucked up her book, a novel she'd been attempting to read for days, though distraction made progress difficult. She cracked it open, but she didn't look down at the page.

She thought about ringing for Kaz and asking him to carry her to the balcony. She didn't know if she'd actually manage to hear anything of the children's party, but in her irritable state, their laughter would probably only make her more upset at missing it.

Imara forced her eyes to the book, only reading a handful of words before there was a knock on her bedroom door—which meant whoever it was had been allowed past Kaz and whatever Mortisian guards stood in the hall.

Curiosity prickled. Clare would already be down at the beach, and Desfan was in a council meeting. Those were her usual visitors, so she couldn't imagine who was at her door. "Come in," she called.

The door pushed open and Desfan strode in, his hands behind his back.

Her stomach fluttered when he smiled, flashing that fates-blasted dimple of his. "Good morning," he said.

She straightened in her bed. "What are you doing here? Don't you have a council meeting?"

"Not anymore. I took a vote first thing. I asked them if they'd like to attend a party on the beach, or carry on with the meeting. It was almost unanimous."

"Almost?"

He shrugged. "Ser Anoush and Ser Sifa must not like the beach—or children." He stopped beside the bed. "Now it's my turn to ask: what are *you* doing here?"

Imara stared at him, then gestured to her outstretched legs, tucked under her quilt. "I can't exactly be anywhere else."

"Clare told me you refused to have someone carry you down to the beach—even though the physician said it would be all right."

"There's really no point in all that hassle."

Desfan's brow furrowed. "You helped organize the entire thing. You should be there."

"I'm perfectly fine here," she lied. "I have my book, and—"

He snatched up the novel with one quick hand and eyed the lettering on the spine. "This is the same book you were reading last week." He angled the volume to note the placement of her marker, then sent her a look and deadpanned, "It must be riveting, to hold you in the same place for so long."

She rolled her eyes, even though she was surprised he'd paid so much attention to something as trivial as her book. "Very witty of you, Serjan." She snorted. "If you're even the serjan—you still haven't shown me your crown."

His lip quirked. "I'm the serjan," he assured her. "I just didn't think a crown was necessary for a day at the beach."

He had a point. She gestured to the book he still held. "Will you give it back, please?"

"I have a better idea." He dropped the book on the bedside table, and from behind his back he drew out a cane.

Imara's eyes widened, because it was no ordinary cane. It was made of a beautiful light wood and decorated with blue khalmin, the intricate designs twisting along the entire length. The Zennorian art was breathtaking. The fact that Desfan had commissioned it for her after they'd merely joked of such a thing . . .

Her breath caught. "Desfan . . ." With slow-moving fingers, she touched the finely carved wood, her lips parted in shock.

"I took your advice about the khalmin," he said. "And you were right, it was less expensive than decorating it with jewels."

She peered up at him, her fingertips still laid on the cane he held. "But, blue is your color." It was a silly thing to say, but she couldn't find other words. Staring up at his perfectly sculpted face, she wanted nothing more than to kiss him. Which would be a horrid mistake, she firmly reminded herself.

Desfan's eyes lowered to the cane, where his thumb rested very near her fingers. "I think blue suits you."

Calm. Steady. Fair. Strong. She'd told him that blue embodied those attributes. That *he* embodied them. And he was telling her the same.

Her heart squeezed. Fates, what was she supposed to say to that? Staring up at him, all she could think was blue suited her far too well; she couldn't think of a single aspect of the man before her that didn't suit her.

Desfan set the end of the cane on the floor. "The physician assured me that you could try standing with the cane, if you'd like."

Her pulse stuttered, and sudden dread swelled. She'd been anxious for this moment, but she also feared it. What if her leg collapsed beneath her? What if she would never walk again?

Inhaling deeply, she pushed aside her quilt and carefully eased her legs over the side of the bed. Her bare feet brushed the braided rug, and she took hold of the cane.

Desfan's palm cupped her elbow while his other hand slid over her back, preparing to brace her as she stood. This put his body far too close. The heat of him warmed her, and her heartbeat quickened.

"Just take it slow," he said.

Forcing herself to focus on the task at hand, Imara stood with Desfan's help. Her grip on the cane clenched when she wavered, and her heart pounded erratically. Once upright, her good leg took the majority of her weight, and the cane gave her balance. Slowly, she let her injured leg straighten.

Pain flashed in her knee, and she knew instantly it wouldn't be able to support her. But the cane was her anchor, and Desfan remained close—another anchor—ready to catch her if she faltered.

Slowly, she took an awkward step forward, leaning heavily on the cane. Her limp was terrible, but the cane kept her from falling. She would be slow and cumbersome, and she would tire quickly; a fine tremble was already in her braced arm and leg. But she was standing.

She took another halting step. Then another.

Desfan flashed her a grin. "You'll be walking circles around Yahri in no time."

She huffed a laugh and gently elbowed him in the stomach. It was supposed to be a simple gesture between friends, but feeling the solidness of his abdomen made her stomach tighten. Her shoulder brushed his chest, and she had to swallow before meeting his gaze.

Pride shone in his eyes, along with an emotion she was afraid to name.

So, she ignored it. "Thank you, Desfan."

His hand pressed gently against her back. "You're welcome. Now. I think we're due on the beach."

<hr />

Imara sat on a blanket spread over the sand. She was on the edge of the party, but she didn't mind at all. Desfan had carried her most of the way, though she still had her cane. He'd settled her on this blanket, but he hadn't remained with her for long.

The Serjan of Mortise was in high demand. He currently stood in the shallow waves that lapped the beach, his laugh deep and full as the children shrieked and splashed him. He splashed them in return, the impromptu game far more entertaining for those children than she would have expected.

Then again, watching a shirtless Desfan play in the water with a group of children had *her* fully mesmerized. And she wasn't the only one.

The parents had all been invited as well, and while some were undoubtedly still too injured to leave the physician's ward, many of the nobles had accompanied their children to the beach. Many of the men and women openly stared at Desfan—the women with an edge of appreciation Imara thoroughly understood. Not everyone from the council was in attendance, but those who had come looked surprised to see Desfan playing with the children.

Imara decided they must not know him well, because Desfan taking time to make children smile was perfectly in his character.

Clare was farther up the beach, helping some of the younger children make castles in the golden sand. Bennick—as always—was never far from her. He sat on the ground beside her, helping a couple of boys build their sand palace, while also managing to praise a young girl's seashell collection. She kept thrusting each new piece under his nose, but his smiles were sincere and endlessly patient.

Despite the proverbial clouds that hung over them, Imara felt peace. She wished Serene were here, though. Her cousin should be seeing Desfan like this. If the fates had been kinder,

Imara would be the one headed to Zennor now, and Serene would be here.

A selfish part of her thought that maybe this *was* a kindness of the fates. Because wrong or not, Imara knew she would always treasure this memory of Desfan.

Karim stood near the water's edge, one eye on Desfan even as he monitored the rest of the beach. Surprisingly, when Razan joined him, Karim didn't tense. They spoke in low tones, but the fact they were speaking at all seemed a small miracle. Just another testament to the peace that had settled over this stretch of beach.

All too soon, a luncheon was declared ready. While servants and parents collected their children and made their way to the provided blankets to sit and eat, Desfan strode from the water, his dark hair wet and dripping. A servant handed him a towel, which he drew over his face and neck. His eyes found Imara, and he moved toward her.

Imara straightened her spine. By the time he landed on the blanket beside her, she had almost convinced her heart to stop pounding.

Desfan grinned and shook a hand through his wet hair. "Well, that wasn't the plan, but it was fun."

"Words you've no doubt said before," she quipped.

He laughed. "More than once, much to Karim's chagrin." The towel was in his hand, but he seemed to have forgotten the need to dry. His bare feet were encrusted in sand and droplets of saltwater clung to the grooves of his chest and muscled abdomen. Her attention was drawn to a tattoo over his heart. It looked like a sun, but there were intricate designs and an artistic Mortisian script she couldn't quite decipher from this angle—and one section had fresh bruising.

Desfan noticed her stare. His fingers tapped the mark. "I got this after the shipwreck."

Understanding dawned. The decorative script wove the names of his mother and sisters into the image of the tattooed sun. "You added your father," she realized, her eyes lingering on the newest part of the tattoo.

"It seemed right." He let his hand fall. "Not that he approved of me getting this in the first place."

"I think he would approve of it now. It's beautiful."

Desfan glanced at her. "Tattoos aren't popular in Zennor, are they?"

"They are in the clans." She noticed the tattoo on his bicep; this one looked like a knotted rope. "What is that one for?"

He stretched and angled his arm so he could look at the mark; the muscles beneath his brown skin flexed and shifted in a distracting roll. "It's a popular symbol among sailors, especially those bonded by friendship or a life-debt. It means, *my life tied to yours*." He relaxed his arm and flashed her a small smile. "Karim and I each got one when I was fifteen."

It was a beautiful story, but something in his tone made her frown. "Is everything all right?"

Desfan glanced toward Karim—who was still standing with Razan. "He's dealing with a lot right now."

"His injury?"

"No, that's healed well." He sighed. "He has some family issues to sort through. I wish I could help him, but I honestly don't know how."

"He knows you care. Sometimes, that's enough. In fact, sometimes it can be everything."

Desfan considered this, then his head tipped to the side. "I've said this before, but you're very wise."

"Why thank you," she said with mock graciousness.

He laughed. It was a beautiful sound—rich, full, and warm.

Her lips eased into a smile. "You're a good friend, Desfan. To everyone lucky enough to become yours."

His eyes heated.

Her stomach tightened, and the air was suddenly harder to breath.

"Imara—"

"Serjan?"

They both looked up at the guard who had spoken over Desfan.

The older man shifted his weight, looking a little uncomfortable "Apologies for the interruption, but Ranon Sifa is asking for a moment of your time."

Desfan and Imara both craned their necks, and she quickly spotted the young nobleman standing near another guard at the entrance to the private beach. She didn't know Ranon Sifa well, but she knew he'd been a friend to Grayson.

Desfan expelled a heavy breath. "Thank you. Tell him I'll be over in a moment."

The guard nodded and took off back up the beach.

Imara eyed Desfan. "You don't seem eager to talk to him."

"I'm not. He's been asking for an audience for weeks now, but I've been avoiding him." He scrubbed a hand against the mark over his heart, the motion distracted. "I bet his father told him about the cancelled meeting, and Ranon hurried over here, hoping to catch me. I think he wants to discuss Grayson."

"And you don't want to discuss him?"

"Not particularly." He glanced at her, his voice dropping lower. "I know they became friends. I assume Ranon wants to see him, and obviously that can't happen."

True; only a handful of people knew Grayson had gone to Ryden.

"What will you tell him?" Imara asked.

"I don't know."

She sighed. "I suppose peace never lasts."

"That seems to be the way of things."

It was unfortunately true. In fact, now that Imara thought about it, it seemed odd that there had been relative peace in Duvan since Desfan's coronation—except for Jekem trying to kill her, of course. It made Imara wonder what waited for them in the shadows—what new threat was coming.

For so long, everything had seemed to be about the treaty signing between Mortise and Devendra. Now that it was done, what would come next?

War seemed the obvious answer.

Desfan set the towel aside, his movement pulling her from her depressing thoughts. He reached for his discarded shirt and shot her a look. "Would you like to stay here, or are you ready for me to take you back to your room?"

After inadvertently memorizing every hard plane of his chest, the last thing she needed was be held against it for any period of time.

"I'll stay," she said. Besides, she wasn't ready to go back to her bed.

Desfan tugged the loose white shirt over his head. "I'll return as soon as I can, but others might catch me on my way back. If you tire, any of the guards can assist you back to your room."

"Thank you. For everything," she added, indicating the cane beside her.

His answering smile made her heart skip.

When he stood, Karim joined him almost instantly, and Razan offered to get Imara a plate of food. She gratefully accepted the woman's help, and she watched as they all walked across the sands.

Off to her right, a group of men were gathered close in quiet conversation. They were comprised of noblemen, and many had visible bandages in place. She'd dismissed them earlier as uninteresting, but in the silence left by Desfan's absence, words floated toward her, low and tinged with unease.

". . . so many of them. That's what concerns me."

"It does seem suspicious. The timing of it, I mean."

"Yes. First their princess comes, and then all these refugees follow. I don't trust it."

"Do you think it could be a coordinated attack?" the first man asked, his voice more worried than before.

"I think it's possible. Newlan might think he can sneak in refugees, but they could actually be soldiers lying in wait to strike."

Imara nearly turned toward them, but caught herself. She didn't want them to realize she could hear their words.

"Did you know the serjan sent supplies to that Salvation camp?" one of the men asked, sounding torn between affront and disgust.

One of the men scoffed. "He should have dismantled the place. The Devendrans have no right to create a stronghold here."

"This is the sort of thing that worries me about his rule. He isn't protecting Mortise; he's just doing whatever fates-blasted thing strikes his fancy. There's no plan to any of it."

"I think he's afraid. He doesn't want to make a wrong move,

so he makes no real moves at all. Take the Kaelin princes for example. They're just sitting in their cells, when we should have sent their heads back to their father ages ago. Make a bold statement, that's what I say."

"It's the only way to gain the respect of the other nations," another man readily agreed. "Especially in these troubled times."

"Did you hear about that village on Dorma? All those people, sickened and dead, with no explanation."

"In Madihr?" someone asked quickly.

"No, it was a smaller village on the other side of the island. But it happened soon after the late serjan's death, and that feels like a sign."

"Desfan seems to be cursed."

"Or he's *our* curse," one of them muttered.

There were several grunts and other sounds of agreement.

Anger bubbled up in Imara, along with a rising desire to tongue-lash them all.

Before she could decide if that would only make Desfan's image worse in the eyes of his court, a new voice spoke. "He's had a harsh hand dealt to him. He had to step in as regent, negotiate with Devendra for Princess Serene's hand, and then suffer an underhanded attack from Ryden. Not to mention the betrayals from within the council and the trouble with the olcain in Duvan. Then he lost his father, became our serjan, and now faces calamitous times. You have to admit, Eyrinthia itself hasn't seen such turbulence since the last war with Ryden. I do not envy him."

Imara peeked from the corner of her eye to identify the speaker. He was middle-aged, and he had a bandage that pinned his arm to his chest.

The other men looked at him, and there was a beat of silence before one of the men cleared his throat. "Of course we don't envy him. Still, he's the serjan, and his first duty is to us—Mortise."

"Of course," Desfan's defender said. "But I think it would be better for us to stand with him, rather than stand over here tearing him apart. *That* is what will build a stronger Mortise."

Imara could have applauded, though the other men didn't seem as impressed by the man's speech. "You've spent too much time on Dorma, Kashif," one of them said. "Things in the world are turbulent."

"I'm well aware," Kashif said, his voice firmer than before. "I nearly died from the injuries I sustained at the attack the night before the coronation. An attack that was organized by Amil Havim—a man who should have been loyal to Desfan and Mortise. He—in his hatred of our serjan—killed his own people. He allied with Devendran rebels, emptied our prison of dangerous prisoners, and he allowed the royal treasury to be raided. The damage he caused to Mortise is still being calculated, and he was one of *us*." He paused, then said emphatically, "I believe that bears thinking about."

The air bristled with tension, but before anyone could speak, a lovely Mortisian woman approached the group. Her elbow was looped with Clare's, and Venn trailed them.

The Mortisian woman smiled at the men. "I hope we're not interrupting, but I wanted to introduce the princess to my husband, if I might steal him."

"Of course," one of the men said at once. "Kashif—we'll speak later, I'm sure."

Kashif tipped his head, though his mouth was tight as the men walked away. Still, he managed a smile as he faced his wife and bowed to Clare. "Princess Serene, it is an honor."

"I'm relieved to see you're well," Clare said, adopting Serene's tone and air so well, Imara could almost believe it *was* her cousin standing there. "Your wife kept me informed of your progress every time I visited her."

Kashif's wife beamed. "The princess has been most kind. And Sidrah adores her, of course. And her bodyguards." She shot a quick look back up the beach, where Bennick was admiring yet another shell from the small girl.

Much of Kashif's tension melted away as he looked lovingly at his daughter. "She is a marvelous judge of character, so that speaks highly for you and your guards, Princess."

"Thank you," Clare said. "Ilah told me Sidrah can be quite shy."

"She is at ease when among friends," the woman—Ilah—said. She focused on her husband, her eyes going serious. "I was surprised to see you speaking with Faqir and the others."

Kashif grunted. "They weren't my first choice for company. As soon as we can be away from Duvan, the better. I miss the peace of home."

Ilah brightened. "I was just telling the princess about Dorma, but you're right—there is no other place so peaceful." She turned to Clare. "Princess, you must come visit. And you'll stay with us, of course."

"That's very kind of you," Clare said. "I'm not sure when I'll be able to make the trip, however."

"The invitation is open," Ilah said. "Whenever you're able, we'd love to host you. I can introduce you to all the nobles on the island. They would be good allies for you to have, I think. They don't have as much political sway as the members of court here, but they are strong families."

"Thank you," Clare repeated.

"Serjan," Kashif called out.

Somehow, Imara had missed Desfan's approach. He looked a little preoccupied—perhaps from his conversation with Ranon—but he offered a pleasant smile as he angled toward the small group. "Ser Hassan, is it?" he asked.

Kashif bowed. "I'm honored, Serjan."

Desfan smiled a little. "I don't know if you remember, but when I was a boy, my family dined with yours during one of our trips to Dorma."

"I recall," Kashif said. "Though I'm surprised you do. You were young, and you must have had many dinners on Dorma."

The corner of Desfan's mouth twitched. "Yes, well, not all of those dinners included such fabulous desserts."

Kashif chuckled. "I think my mother found the best baker in Eyrinthia to work for her. I miss those delicious creations . . ."

The conversation continued for another few moments, though Imara caught Desfan glancing at her more than once. Finally, the Hassans excused themselves, leaving Desfan and Clare standing together.

Desfan lowered his voice; if Imara hadn't been sitting so close, she would have missed his words to Clare. "You're very impressive. You do so well with all of this."

Clare's eyes widened slightly. "Thank you, Serjan. And thank you for allowing this." She gestured to the children, who were mostly still eating.

"Of course. It was an inspired idea." Desfan twisted to face her completely, his voice lowering further—Imara had to strain to catch each word. "I haven't had a chance to tell you, but I'm sorry about your brothers. You have my deepest sorrow."

The Mortisian phrase was clearly uttered with full sincerity; Desfan was one who knew too well the grief of loss. Imara's heart tugged, feeling pain for him and Clare. But she also felt a stirring of pride. Desfan didn't know Clare well. He didn't need to take the time to offer comfort and empathy—but that was exactly who he was.

"Thank you," Clare whispered, her voice thicker than before. "I appreciate that. It has been . . . difficult."

He tipped his chin. "I remember how lost I felt. How painful every new day felt."

"I've experienced loss before," Clare admitted. "My parents, when I was a child, and then my older brother more recently. But Thomas and Mark . . . they were so young. Their loss feels different—worse."

Desfan's eyes were full of compassion. "Fates. I didn't realize how many people you've lost."

She cracked a pained smile. "I know you understand what it's like to lose your family. I'm sorry you do, though."

"I'm sorry for both of us."

There was a short pause. Then Clare sighed. "It feels like I should be better at this by now."

"I don't think mourning ever gets easier. Every loss is so different. But we learn ways to cope—and ways not to." The corner of his mouth lifted in a self-deprecating smile. "I could give you a long list of things *not* to do."

Clare met his smile, and there was undisguised admiration in her eyes. "You've survived, though."

"I have. And so will you." He reached out and touched her arm. To any onlookers farther up the beach, it might appear like an affectionate gesture between two people betrothed to marry. What Imara saw was so much deeper than that. It was a sign of compassion, strength, and understanding between a man who had once lost his entire family, and a woman who was currently wading through that same unimaginable anguish.

"Your grief will always be there," Desfan said. "I know you know that, from losing your parents. But you get to choose how you carry that grief. It can overwhelm you, or you can accept it as a part of you and continue to live." He paused, and when he spoke again, his voice was a little rougher than before. "I went through a time when I was sure the weight of my grief would kill me. I'm sure you've experienced the same. But those moments don't have to last forever. You can walk through them. And you don't have to walk through them alone."

Tears stung Imara's eyes, and she didn't care if anyone noticed. Those words—spoken from Desfan's soul—were beautiful. Powerful.

Clare seemed just as affected. Her breathing hitched thinly, her eyes shining with moisture. "Thank you, Desfan. I needed to hear that."

The corner of his mouth lifted. "We all need reminders from time to time. And if you ever need someone to talk to—or someone to listen—I'm here."

"Thank you," she said again. She wiped quickly at her eyes. "And thank you for allowing Latif to go to Devendra for me. I know that must not have been easy."

"It wasn't. But I think it was the right decision. If the man can bring you any measure of peace, that matters more than anything. In any case, I would prefer to concentrate my revenge on King Henri." The darkness in his eyes and the hardness of his jaw left little to the imagination on that score. The serjan was interested in blood.

Imara couldn't blame him. If someone had taken one of her little sisters and locked her away, Imara would *destroy* the Rydenic king.

"I was so relieved to hear that your youngest sister is still alive," Clare said, her voice so soft it barely reached Imara. "It's a blessing from the fates."

"Yes," Desfan said. "It will feel more real once she's home, though."

"I hope she returns quickly and safely."

"Thank you." He glanced toward Imara, and she tried not to look like she'd been blatantly listening to them.

She was sure she failed.

Clare followed his gaze and sent Imara a small smile before excusing herself. She moved back up the beach—toward Bennick—and Desfan came to sit beside Imara.

"I trust you've been enjoying yourself?" he asked.

"It's amazing the things one overhears when stuck in one place." She nodded toward the Hassans. "You can trust them, I think. Ser Hassan defended you among his peers. They were less kind in their opinions about you."

"I believe that. Despite being serjan, I'm not a very popular figure in Mortise."

A stray hair tickled her cheek, but before she could lift her hand to swipe it away, Desfan leaned in, his knuckles brushing the swell of her cheek as he moved to tuck the errant strand behind her ear.

Her skin tingled from the innocent touch.

Fates, she *hoped* it looked like an innocent touch to anyone who might have witnessed it. Thankfully, most everyone had moved up the beach so they could eat, so she didn't think anyone even noticed.

When Desfan pulled back his hand, Imara thought his breath thinned. His tone was unaffected as he asked, "Did you overhear anything I should be worried about?"

"I don't think so. Your nobles were concerned about the Devendran refugees, but it's all prejudiced nonsense."

"Nothing new, then. Let me know if you overhear anything I should know."

She drew back with false shock, a palm pressed over her heart for good measure. "Are you asking a princess of Zennor to be your spy?"

His brown eyes danced. "Yes. Daring of me, isn't it?"

"Or brilliant."

"Strange. Those exact words have been used to describe me all my life. Among others, of course."

She chuckled.

Gulls cried overhead and the waves crashed against the shore in frothy swells. While she studied the glistening sea, she could feel Desfan's eyes on her.

Her cheeks warmed. "How did the conversation with Ranon go?" she asked.

Her mission to distract him was accomplished; he leaned back with a long exhale. "As expected. He wanted to visit Grayson, and I denied his request."

Imara studied Desfan. She knew exactly where his thoughts had wandered. "You can trust Grayson," she reminded him softly.

"Maybe." His shoulders tensed as he met her gaze. "Even if I can trust him, though, the Kaelins are going to do everything in their power to keep Mia. Grayson is highly skilled, but he's only one person. What can he do against an army?"

Her stomach tightened. "Let's pray we never have to find out."

CHAPTER 25

CLARE

CLARE STOOD AT DESFAN'S SIDE AS HE DELIVERED a speech in front of Duvan's primary orphanage. He thanked Devendra for their example in how to better fund the orphanages of Mortise, and he thanked the nobles who had already become patrons of orphanages in their cities.

She had already given the princess's speech—thank the fates Serene had known about this appearance and had written something for Clare to memorize—so now she was free to focus on the large crowd gathered in the street.

She was looking for James.

Bridget had received a brief message from the rebel last night. He said he would be at the orphanage today, and that he'd find a way to speak with her. She wasn't sure how he would, since Bennick and Venn were both standing behind her, and neither one looked inclined to let her out of their sight.

"Because of our combined efforts," Desfan said, his voice ringing out along the packed street, "the vulnerable children of Mortise will be safer. They will no longer have to rely on the empty promises of drug masters and thieves for protection. They will no longer have to make alliances with dangerous gangs or engage in bloody street fights in order to eat. The benefits of these changes are already being seen in Duvan, and in other cities across our great country. Crimes have been reduced, and the streets are safer. If you have not already pledged your support for your local orphanage, I encourage you to do so. Your coin will go to a truly charitable endeavor, and you will change the lives of children in desperate need. Not only that, you will be aiding in creating a safer, brighter Mortise."

Applause broke out, but Desfan wasn't done.

His expression became harder, his dark eyes more intense. "To any drug masters, gang leaders, or anyone who would abuse, endanger, or misuse a child, I have one message: you will be found, and you will face retribution. As your serjan, I will not tolerate any deliberate harm to any child."

Clare noticed Serai Yahri—who was the only council member in attendance—blink once.

So, Desfan was not following a planned speech. He was speaking from his heart.

Clare admired him all the more for it. And for his next words.

"I have known too many children who have suffered because of evil or neglectful men and women, and it cannot continue. I will do everything within my power to make sure every child within Mortise is safe. Creating these havens for the orphaned is simply the first step in my lifelong vow to protect the children of Mortise. I urge you to stand with me and make the same commitment."

Clare was the first to clap, though others quickly followed. Some faces in the crowd were surprised, but most seemed pleased with Desfan's bold words. The serjan scanned the cheering crowd, and Clare could see the firmness of his resolution.

One of the orphanage's attendants stepped forward, and the applause dissipated as she said, "Thank you, Serjan Desfan and Princess Serene for coming to visit us. We appreciate all your efforts to create a safe place for our children. We would love to provide a tour of the orphanage, if you'd like."

"Please," Desfan said. He took Clare's hand. It felt a little strange to hold another man's hand—especially with Bennick right behind her. But Desfan's long fingers wrapped reassuringly around hers; the grip of a friend. She had admired Desfan from the first moment she'd met him, but after the conversation they'd shared that day on the beach, she considered him a friend.

Fates. In less than a year, she'd gone from being a kitchen maid in Devendra to befriending the serjan of Mortise. The reality of her life's drastic changes made her reel.

She held Desfan's hand a little more securely as they followed the woman inside and began their tour. They met many of the children who lived at the orphanage, as well as the staff who cared for them. Clare completely adopted Serene's small, pleasant smile, and she didn't let it waver—even when she saw a little boy who looked to be Mark's age, and her heart fractured.

Their tour ended in the dining area. Long tables and benches spanned the length of the room, and many were filled with children who ate or played games. The room was overcrowded with visitors eager to receive a tour, and conversation hummed throughout the room.

Desfan had released her hand as he was pulled into a conversation with some of the nobles who were patrons of the orphanage, and Clare stood nearby, unsure of where she was needed next.

"Princess? Might I trouble you for a moment?"

She turned to see a man who was slightly bent and wearing basic Mortisian garb. Not a noble, but probably someone who worked in the orphanage. He spoke in halting Devendran, and he had a long beard that obscured the lower half of his face. When his eyes lifted, Clare jolted with recognition.

James.

Conscious of Bennick and Venn hovering behind her—and beyond grateful neither of her bodyguards had ever seen James before, so they had no chance of recognizing him—she gave the rebel a nod. "Of course."

"Do you mind if we sit? I'm afraid my back isn't what it used to be."

"Of course," she repeated. She allowed him to lead them through the crowded room. Though Bennick and Venn followed, the level of noise in the room was such that James's low words reached only her ears.

"We won't have long," he whispered. "Tell me the most important things first."

She ducked her head a little closer to him—as if she were trying to catch an old man's wavering voice. "Serene left for Zennor."

He shot her a look. "Fates, I didn't realize . . . Clare." Relief crossed his features, and she was surprised by the sincerity of his tone as he whispered, "I'm so glad you're safe."

"Thank you." She glanced over her shoulder.

Venn was scanning the room as they sidled through the crowded walkway, but Bennick was watching her intently. The skin around his eyes tightened; he couldn't hear her—or James—and he didn't like it.

She sent him a small smile, hoping that would put him at ease.

His eyebrows only drew more tightly together.

She focused back on James. "Serene entrusted me with a letter for you. It's in my pocket."

"I'll retrieve it in a moment," James said. "If I were to stumble into you just now, I think your guards would tackle me."

"They're overly protective."

"Unfortunately, they're very justified." James sighed. "Why has Serene run off to Zennor? She's supposed to be preparing to marry Desfan."

"She has her reasons. I assume she'll explain in her letter."

James made a low sound in his throat. "She does like to improvise. But it can be inconvenient for the rest of us."

They edged around a group of children playing a game Clare didn't recognize, using dice and some small, colored glass balls that they rolled between them.

James's voice was even quieter than before. "Bridget's note only told me we needed to meet. Is there anything else you need to report?"

"I'm one of you now," she shared.

James's eyes lit up. "Welcome to the rebellion." He gestured to a couple of chairs set against the wall. Naturally, they were near the playing children—who were boisterous and growing more so—and also near a group of women who talked loudly in order to be heard.

A perfect place in plain sight to meet and discuss traitorous things.

They sat, and since Bennick and Venn couldn't stand right behind her—and the children played in front of them—they had to step to the side.

The lines in Bennick's face grew deeper, but he didn't intervene—yet.

Clare angled toward James. "Do you have anything to report?" she asked softly. "Serene gave me the names of some contacts in Zennor who can be trusted with messages."

"Well, I think the biggest concern right now is Salvation."

"The refugee camp."

James dipped his chin, and the false beard touched his chest. "Exactly. It explains much of how our people have been disappearing—both the refugees, and our fellow rebels. Grandeur has been busy with the Hunt."

"Venn and Vera just returned from the camp. They said the Hunt is no longer in control, and Desfan has sent aid."

"That's good, but I'm afraid there are still issues. Many in our network are being slaughtered or arrested, because those who were tortured in Salvation gave up names."

Clare's stomach turned. "What can be done to protect them?"

"I'm going to travel to Salvation and make contact with any of the rebels there, and learn the extent of the damage to our network. Meanwhile, I'll send word to our people in Devendra to be extremely careful. We can't have them all abandon their posts, but they need to be prepared. I hope to make contact with a man named David Holm. He was coming to Mortise, so he might have gone to Salvation. If I find him, I'll probably send him here to be your main contact in Duvan. If I can't find him, I'll send someone else . . ." His words faded as he stared at her wide eyes. "What?"

"David Holm was at Salvation," she told him, unable to keep the excitement from her voice. "Venn and Vera met him—and his children." Vera had told her much about the Holm children, and there had been true love in Vera's voice, as well as longing. It was clear she missed them. Clare hoped David Holm came to Duvan. It would be wonderful for Venn, Vera, and the children to be reunited.

James looked relieved. "Was David all right?"

"I think so. Vera mentioned that he'd been detained by the Hunt and tortured, but he was recovering at Salvation and helping a man named Lord Zander Fellnor to keep Salvation safe."

James's shoulders relaxed. "Thank the fates he's alive. I must hurry to him and get a full report. Once I take care of things in Salvation, I'll either follow Serene to Zennor, or return to Devendra. But whoever I send to Duvan, I'll have them get a message to Bridget, so you'll know who to contact if you have need."

"Is there anything else I can do?" Clare asked.

"Continue as you are," James said. "Be Serene. It will help keep her safe in her travels, and further solidify the alliance with Mortise." He paused, then muttered a low curse. "Carrigan is going to be upset."

A frown tugged at her mouth. "Ivar Carrigan?" He was infamous in Devendra. Years ago, he'd risen up against King Newlan—his cousin—and he'd started a civil war. The uprising had only been quelled after many deaths on both sides.

Clare's own father had been executed for siding with Carrigan.

Just before everything had crumbled, Carrigan had escaped Devendra, and he'd been a fugitive ever since. Serene had mentioned Carrigan before, when she'd told Clare about her family's history. When a marriage was negotiated between Newlan and Aren—a Zennorian princess—Newlan had sent Carrigan to Zennor to escort his future bride to Devendra. Carrigan had done so, but he'd fallen in love with Aren on the journey—and she him, though she'd still married Newlan.

According to Serene, Queen Aren had been the one to help Carrigan escape after the failed civil war. Newlan had found out, and in retribution for her betrayal, he had slowly poisoned his wife until she died. Grandeur had known and done nothing to save his mother.

Serene's family was a tangled mess.

"Yes," James said, and it took Clare a moment to realize he wasn't agreeing with her thoughts, but confirming her earlier question.

"How is Carrigan a concern?" Clare asked. She'd never met the man, but she hated him. He'd spoken the words that inspired her father to rise up against Newlan, and he'd run away as soon as the uprising collapsed, leaving men like Duncan Ellington to be killed in the street. She thought of Carrigan as a coward, and she'd grown up resenting him just as much as she resented Newlan for giving the execution order. Both men were responsible for her father's death, as far as she was concerned.

"Not many know this," James said slowly, "but I feel you should know. Carrigan is an ally of Serene's."

Her eyes widened. "He's a rebel?"

"Yes. When Serene first formed the rebellion, she relied

heavily on Carrigan's old contacts. That's how I was brought on, actually. Carrigan was friends with my father."

Clare frowned. She wondered why Serene had never told her that—in fact, hadn't she once claimed to barely know the man at all? In the next breath, she realized there were probably many things Serene kept secret in order to protect herself and her rebels.

The thought of being part of the same rebellion as Carrigan made Clare's stomach knot. She had to remind herself this was Serene's rebellion, not his. Still, she knew her feelings would remain complicated. Ivar Carrigan had led her father to his death—and he'd run away while his men were slaughtered. That was not something Clare could easily forget.

Wrapped up in processing the revelation about Carrigan, it took a moment for James's words to sink in. "Wait. If Carrigan is an ally of Serene's, why would he be upset with her?"

James sighed. "The alliance with Mortise . . . Well, Carrigan was the one who helped Serene see the necessity of it. He was part of a failed rebellion once, so he knows what we need to do differently in order to win now. He wouldn't want Serene to take the risk of traveling to Zennor." He snorted. "Then again, Carrigan is *in* Zennor, so they'll probably see each other soon enough."

"Maybe that's one of the reasons she wanted to go to Zennor," Clare said. "To speak with him."

"Maybe." James's eyes flicked over her shoulder—presumably to check on Bennick and Venn. "I think I've pushed them as far as they can bear. We'll both stand, and when I fumble my bow and bump into you, I'll grab the letter. Which pocket is it in?"

"My right."

"Thank you, Clare," James said, deep sincerity in his tone. "For everything you've done for Serene, and all of us. Be safe."

Clare nodded once and rose.

James did as well, and when he bowed, he stumbled and rocked into her.

She instinctively grasped his upper arms, barely feeling the glide of the letter leaving her pocket.

In the next instant, Bennick was there. He grasped James's shoulder, bracing the man to keep him away from Clare. He stood so close to her, the heat of his body warmed her.

"Apologies, Princess," James said, once again using a strained accent for his stilted Devendran words. "I am an old man, unsteady on my feet."

"It's no trouble," Clare said at once. "Bennick, please let him go."

Venn was now on Bennick's other side, eyeing James with a slight frown.

Bennick's fingers uncurled slowly, but he released his hold.

James tipped his head and ambled away, melting effortlessly into the chaotic room.

"Are you all right?" Venn asked her.

"Yes," Clare said at once. "He was harmless."

Bennick touched her elbow. It was a simple gesture, one hidden from the rest of the room by his body, but awareness coursed through her whole body at the contact. "What did you talk about?" he asked. "I couldn't hear a thing."

"He wanted to tell me about his family," Clare lied. "His daughter works in the kitchens here."

Bennick's jaw was tight, but there was no distrust in his gaze, only mild irritation. "I don't like how crowded this place is."

"I know." She touched his arm this time, and his tensed

muscles relaxed slightly beneath her fingertips.

Venn cleared his throat, but he was smiling as he said, "If you two need a moment, I can make myself scarce."

Clare's cheeks warmed.

Bennick rolled his eyes. "Stay where you are, Venn. We have a job to do."

Venn's grin only widened. "It's just nice to be able to tease you openly about this. Or, you know, carefully amongst ourselves—you can't have everyone knowing, of course. Especially not when you're in public like this. A princess in love with her bodyguard? The scandal."

"Are you done?" Bennick asked, one eyebrow cocked.

"Not even close. The moment you finally admitted to me that you loved her, we had to go our separate ways. And times were dire, so there wasn't sufficient time to needle you. Now, though—"

"Also not an appropriate time," Bennick cut in, looking pointedly toward the rest of the room.

Venn waved an errant hand. "No one can hear us."

"A little caution wouldn't go amiss," Clare interjected. "Especially considering the fact *no one* outside our small circle can know, or Bennick and I would both face the king's retribution."

"True. But he's all the way in Iden—who's going to tell him?"

Bennick muttered something under his breath.

Desfan sidled up to them. "I hope I'm not interrupting."

"Not at all," Clare said at once. "Are you ready to go?"

"Yes, but I have an errand to run with Karim, so I'll leave you the use of the carriage."

"Thank you." She was curious about where he was going with Karim, but didn't pry.

Desfan seemed grateful for that. "I can escort you to the carriage, if you're ready."

Clare took his offered arm, and everyone in the room bowed as they made their farewells and moved for the door.

Out in the street, the carriage was waiting. Desfan handed her up into the conveyance, and Clare's mouth opened to deliver a thank you, but her heart seized and her blood ran cold.

Sitting on the bench was a single, long-stemmed rose.

CHAPTER 26

BENNICK

BENNICK STARED AT THE ROSE IN HIS HAND, trying not to crush the thorny stem between his fingertips. The velvet petals were partially open and such a deep crimson they almost looked like blood.

Standing in the street outside the orphanage, his ears rang. His heart hammered.

Zilas.

"Where did this come from?" Venn demanded of the driver.

The Mortisian man gestured toward the crowded street. "A child carried it over. He wanted to leave it for the princess. I saw no harm—it's only a flower."

Clare was pale. She'd nearly jumped from the carriage, and she still looked a little unsteady as she stood by the open door, one hand braced against the doorframe, the other fisted against her stomach. She looked to Bennick, and all he saw was her fear.

His gut knotted.

Karim's low voice cut through the tense silence. "It's from the Rose. Isn't it?"

"Yes," Venn said tersely. "It has to be."

Desfan's face was grim. "Would he truly use a child to deliver a taunt?"

"He would," Bennick answered without hesitation.

Karim's eyes narrowed. "What *is* the message?"

"The rose itself is the message," Clare said, her words trembling slightly. "He's still hunting. And he's here, in Duvan."

Bennick lowered the rose, the back of his neck prickling. The street was still crowded, and though Mortisian guards had coaxed them back from the carriage, they were staring. A sea of faces, but Bennick couldn't find the one he searched for.

"Get into the carriage," he ordered Clare.

She climbed in at once, Venn right behind her.

Bennick turned to interrogate the driver, but nothing helpful was revealed. The child had come a half hour ago, and hadn't given a name. The driver couldn't remember anything significant about him, and he didn't know if he was one of the orphans.

Desfan returned to the orphanage to ask questions there, but Bennick didn't believe the serjan would learn anything useful.

Surprisingly, Karim remained with Bennick, sending two Mortisian guards to accompany Desfan.

Bennick wanted to tear through the crowd and find Zilas, but he refused to leave Clare. Or give his half-brother the satisfaction of seeing his panic—if he was even still here, watching them.

He couldn't feel him. Wouldn't he feel him?

"You should return to the palace," Karim said. "There's nothing more to be learned here. And despite how it looks, it could have been an innocent gesture."

Bennick's first instinct was to argue, but Karim might have a point. Other children had thrown flowers at Clare's feet when they'd arrived at the orphanage.

But none had been a rose.

He looked down at the petals, artfully arranged at the end of the green stem. His fingers tightened around it, and then he looked out over the crowd. Some were staring at the carriage—wondering what the delay was about, no doubt. Bennick scanned every face he could see, peered into the shadowed alleys. He didn't know if Zilas was there. But if he was, he wanted to make sure his brother understood *his* message.

Bennick snapped the blossom from the stem. He tossed both pieces of the rose under the carriage, and he joined Clare inside.

The drive back to the palace was tense. Bennick sat beside Clare, and he didn't hesitate to take her hand. With the curtains drawn, no one could see them.

Venn sat on the cushioned bench across from them, his expression hard. "If he really did leave that . . . I don't know what to tell Vera."

"We can't keep her in the dark," Clare said at once. "She

needs to know."

Of course Vera had to be told. The Rose had murdered her sister.

And yet, with every moment that passed, Bennick began to wonder if Karim was right. Maybe the rose had been an innocent gift after all. If the rose *had* been from Zilas, he wasn't following his usual pattern—there had been no note. No body or other horrific thing. Just the single red rose.

Clare's fingers tightened around Bennick's. "Are you all right?"

"I should be asking you that."

"You've been quiet," she said, ignoring his concern.

He squeezed her hand. "I'm fine. I'm actually wondering if we overreacted."

Venn's brow furrowed. "Either way, I'm telling Vera."

"Of course," Bennick said. "But instead of letting fear rule us, I think we simply take some added precautions—especially until we know for sure if it was from him."

Venn and Clare both nodded. Their tension remained, but it relaxed a little. They were trusting him. Fates, he hoped he was handling this the right way. But he truly didn't know what else to do.

When the carriage slowed, Bennick brushed the curtain aside to check their position. They were at the castle, but still outside the main gate. Another carriage was ahead of them, and from what he could tell, the guards weren't ready to wave it through. Since Desfan had increased security at the gates, it wasn't a surprise to see a stalled carriage there, awaiting admittance.

"What is it?" Venn asked.

Before Bennick could say anything, one of the guards spotted their carriage and hurried over. He looked concerned.

Not a good sign.

Bennick released Clare's hand. "Stay with Venn," he said, reaching for the door.

Clare and Venn both frowned, but said nothing as he stepped out. He closed the door before the Mortisian guard reached him. "Captain Markam," the man said, relief drawing across his face. "I'm glad you're here." He started back toward the main gate and the carriage waiting there.

Bennick quickly fell into step beside him. "What's going on?" he asked.

"I'm not sure what to do," the guard confessed. "There's a man here, claiming to be—"

"Claiming to be?" a familiar but unexpected voice snapped from inside the unmarked carriage. "I *am* Prince Grandeur Demoi, heir to the Devendran throne."

Bennick stiffened as Grandeur pushed open the carriage door and stepped down. He wore fine clothes, though they were travel-worn, and an irritated scowl twisted his normally handsome features. Captain Dervish, Grandeur's lead body-guard, was right behind him.

Bennick despised Dervish. The man was insufferable, but more than that, he'd manipulated circumstances and stolen Wilf's position when Wilf had been at his lowest after his wife's death. Dervish was a snake. But then, Grandeur had turned out to be a snake as well.

Once, Bennick had thought the Crown Prince of Devendra to be a calm, kind man. Grandeur had befriended Clare when she'd first become Serene's decoy, and he'd never shown any tendency toward the fits of temper Serene sometimes displayed, or the dark sourness King Newlan had a reputation for. Now, Bennick knew *that* Grandeur was a lie.

Even if the man standing before him had nothing to do with the deaths of Clare's little brothers, he was in charge of the Hunt. Bennick's pulse suddenly thudded harder and faster.

Grandeur's gaze sliced to Bennick, and his shoulders drew up. "Captain Markam. Good. Tell this man who I am."

Bennick's throat tightened. Grandeur was the future king of Devendra. Until Bennick had irrefutable proof of his crimes, there was nothing he could say or do. He faced the guard. "This is Prince Grandeur Demoi. You may admit him."

The Mortisian guard dipped his chin and moved for the gate, ordering for it to be opened.

Grandeur tugged at the cuffs of his sleeves. "Thank the fates you showed up. The man was an imbecile, and disrespectful. Not what I'd expect from a supposed ally."

"He was doing his job," Bennick said, his tone hard despite the voice in his head that urged caution. "You weren't expected."

"Expected or not, that's no way to treat a royal." Grandeur tracked the guard as he wandered back to them, careful to lift his voice so his next words would not be missed. "Especially the brother of your future queen."

The guard came to a halt beside Bennick. "Apologies, Prince Grandeur," he said firmly. "Security measures have been heightened since recent events. I only asked that you remain out here until Princess Serene's return."

Grandeur's mouth tightened. He glanced back at the carriage behind his own, but before he could speak, Bennick said, "You should get back inside the carriage and go up to the palace. I'm sure you must be tired after your travels."

"Indeed." The prince lifted his chin. "I would prefer to speak to my sister after I've had a chance to recover from the journey."

Bennick didn't want Clare coming face to face with Grandeur at all, but he knew that was inevitable. The best he could do was attempt to put it off.

Grandeur turned to re-enter his carriage. Unfortunately, that's when Clare stepped out of her carriage.

One hand remained curled around the edge of the open door as she stilled, her gaze locked on Grandeur. Her expression was surprisingly blank, though a myriad of emotions flashed in her eyes. Shock. Anger. And, finally, hatred.

Bennick's stomach dropped. He darted a look at Venn, who had emerged to stand just behind Clare. Unfortunately, his friend didn't look inclined to hold her back. Not when his own dark eyes were trained on the prince.

Silently cursing, Bennick hurried toward them, the back of his neck prickling under the stares of everyone watching—Grandeur, Dervish, the prince's other guards, and the Mortisian guards.

He stopped right in front of Clare, blocking her view of Grandeur.

Her eyes cut to his, and the pain there hit him solidly in the chest.

"Easy," he cautioned, his tone low. "This isn't the time or place."

Her breathing was tight and shallow, and she trembled. Tears gathered in her beautiful blue eyes, heated and full of grief.

He ached to touch her, but he held himself back.

She was still clearly struggling with her emotions, but she straightened her spine. He knew reason had won out, at least for the moment.

Footsteps scuffed the cobblestones behind Bennick. He tensed as Grandeur stopped beside him, his attention fastened on Clare.

It was obvious when he saw through her disguise. He exhaled slowly, a strange light entering his eyes. "On second thought," he said, "I'd like to talk with my sister now. We clearly have much to discuss."

CHAPTER 27

DESFAN

DESFAN SAT ON A STONE BENCH IN THE SMALL garden of Duvan's asylum. He had no guards with him, because he'd wanted to ensure Karim's privacy.

Karim had argued this point, but Desfan had won; partly because Avao had sided with him, citing the security measures at the asylum were sufficient so long as Desfan remained inside the grounds.

When they'd arrived at the asylum, Karim had insisted on going to his mother's room alone. So, Desfan waited in the inner courtyard, praying to the fates this visit would help heal his friend, not tear him further apart.

Desfan scanned the garden, though calling it that was perhaps a bit generous. It was a simple inner courtyard within the walls of the asylum. Sandstone columns ringed the small yard, and it was open to the sky. There was a fountain in the center, with four paths leading to that single point. Desfan sat in one of the four quadrants, surrounded by green fronds and shaded by olive trees. The silver-green leaves rustled gently in the breeze, accompanied by the trickle of water from the fountain. Vibrant flowers of yellow, orange, and red bloomed all around, scenting the air with their fresh fragrance.

Down the path he could see a couple of people standing near the fountain, studying the bright turquoise and gold tiles that lined the basin. They were the only other people in sight.

He should probably make use of this solitary time to puzzle through the rose that had been left at the orphanage for Clare—or Serene, he supposed, since the princess was the assassin's actual target. He could also think on Liam's cryptic words about the olcain mystery, or even sort out a good response for Yahri's imminent scolding about the deviation in his speech at the orphanage.

Instead, his thoughts turned to last night.

He'd been struggling to sleep since Imara had been attacked by her bodyguard, and last night had been no different. Instead of lying abed uselessly, he'd begun sorting through crates the servants had moved into his new suite. The rooms still didn't feel like his; even without all his father's things, the walls and furniture remained the same. This was a place Desfan had gone to for comfort as a child. The rooms of his mother and father had always made safe, full of laughter, warmth, and love. Until Farrah Cassian died and Saernon Cassian became hollow.

By the light of a glowing lamp, Desfan had sat on a rug that had lain on the sitting room floor since long before his birth, and he'd rifled through the crates. He'd found trinkets from his youth, long-forgotten in the dusty corners of his old room. He'd found a collection of drawings from Tahlyah and Meerah. The sight of those images, drawn by hands so small and precious, clawed his insides. He'd set them gently aside, though he trailed his fingers over the curling corner of one. He didn't remember receiving these drawings. He hoped he'd thanked his sisters before tossing them in a trunk.

More boxes. More memories. Forgotten moments, now remembered. The pain was sharp at times, but Desfan didn't stop. As much as it hurt, this was his past. The remnants of his family. They deserved to be remembered.

He'd found a small jar of sand, collected one day on the beach with Tally.

His fingertips brushed over the leather cover of a blank journal, stamped by an artisan with the image of a ship cresting a rolling wave. His mother had given it to him many years ago. She'd told him to write down his thoughts and dreams. He never had.

He found a note from Mia, written in faltering letters—some of her first. *I love you, Des.*

Then he found a letter from his father. A letter he'd almost forgotten.

His father had written this soon after sending a fifteen-year-old Desfan away on the *Phoenix*, though Desfan hadn't read the words until much later. Regret was heavy in father's tone, and Desfan found himself feeling an echo of that regret himself. For all the harsh words that had passed between them. For the relationship they might have had, if they'd each tried harder. Because, even though they'd lost nearly everything, they'd still had each other.

He lingered on certain phrases, unable to look away from his father's script.

Desfan, I am so sorry . . . I hate that my regret will not reach you sooner. That you will go so long without knowing how deeply I love you . . .

Then—

I know you probably hate me right now. Rest assured, you could not hate me more than I hate myself. I allowed myself to become lost in my own grief, when I should have been there for you. If I could reach you right now, I would beg your forgiveness, even though I do not deserve it.

Desfan's heart clenched in his chest. "I forgive you," he whispered. He'd never said those words to his father. Not when he could hear him. Not when it would have mattered. But he said them now in a shadowed room, with pieces of his life scattered all around him.

He read the next words more slowly.

I lost your mother and sisters in an instant, but I have been losing you for years. You, who I had a chance to save. And yet I still let you fall. The blame is entirely my own. I never want you to carry that weight . . . I am the one who failed you.

In that moment, his mind flashed to Mia. His little sister, whom he'd failed for years. He hadn't known she lived, but that didn't feel like an excuse. Not when she'd been suffering and alone.

Too long, his family had been broken. Too long, they'd *all* been alone.

I promise you now, I will never let you be alone again.

They were his father's words—a promise to Desfan made in ink—but in this moment, he swore the same to Mia.

Now, sitting in the garden, he wondered if that promise was enough. Not for the first time, he wished he'd been able to go to Ryden and rescue her himself. But he wasn't like Serene; he couldn't be in two places at once. All he could do was pray that Grayson fulfilled his promise.

He spun the black ring on his forefinger, his forearms braced against his knees, his head bent. He heard a whisper of movement, saw the flash of a long pink skirt against the stone walkway. He lifted his head and blinked when he saw Razan.

"May I join you?" she asked.

Shaking off his surprise, he shifted on the bench to make room for her. "What are you doing here?" he asked.

"Avao told me Karim decided to come." Razan sat, her back a little too straight. Her fingers twitched in her lap, revealing her nerves. "Karim told me about his mother a long time ago," she said. "Back on the *Phoenix*. And he told me about her illness the other night, in the garden."

The corner of Desfan's mouth lifted in a faint smile. "Things seem more comfortable between you since that night."

Color touched her cheeks. "Yes, thank the fates. I've missed him."

"I think he's missed you, too. Not that he'd ever admit it."

She smiled faintly, but concern rose in her eyes as she said, "I had hoped he'd take you inside with him."

"He knows I'm here. It was nice of you to come," he added.

"I hope I'm not overstepping."

He didn't think she was. Where Karim was concerned, a little push seemed necessary.

In an attempt to distract her—and perhaps himself—he asked, "How are your cousins?"

"They're well. Fivol still talks of the night the serjah and his bodyguard saved his life." Her eyes dropped to his ring, which he hadn't realized he'd resumed spinning. "You wore that ring when we first met," she recalled. "It must mean a great deal to you."

Desfan looked down, the edge of his thumb brushing over the smooth obsidian ring. His first instinct was to give a simple answer, but he found himself saying, "A long time ago, my sister Tahlyah found three identical rings in the treasury. We each took one. We thought we'd all grow into them."

Razan's lips pursed, compassion softening her expression. "I'm sorry your sisters didn't get that chance. But they would be proud of the man you've become, Desfan."

His throat cinched, suddenly feeling too hot. Clearing his throat, he said, "I remember worrying at the time that our mother would be upset about us taking them, but she never cared."

"It probably made her happy to see the three of you so united."

"It's not like it made a dent in the treasury, either." He snorted. "Nothing like the mess I've made of it now."

Razan winced. "About that . . . I've overheard some of the other council members talk. A couple of them are worried we won't have the resources to keep debts paid and the country functioning. They were critical of your decision to send supplies to help the Devendran refugees in Salvation."

He expelled a slow breath. "Ser Sifa?"

"And Anoush."

He wasn't surprised. Those two were fast becoming his loudest critics—except when Yahri thought he was being an idiot, of course.

"Serai Essa worries more about debts being called in, but Sifa has some valid concerns about keeping the military funded, if it comes to a fight with Ryden."

It was a valid concern, unfortunately. Once Desfan was given a list of what was missing, he might have a chance of tracking the more unique pieces. He wasn't very optimistic, though.

Razan met his gaze. "War is coming, isn't it?"

Desfan didn't answer at once. Yahri had cautioned him to not speak of war until after his reign as serjan was secure. For his part, he didn't want to entertain open war until Mia was safely home, and Serene had a chance to discuss the situation with King Zaire Buhari. Until now, Desfan and Yahri had sidestepped all talk of attacking Ryden. But Sifa—and others on the council, to be fair—had been calling for war since Liam and Grayson's betrayal.

"War is coming," he admitted. "It's inevitable. But I'm hoping for a little more time."

He prayed the fates were kind enough to give him that.

Karim joined them a while later.

Desfan and Razan stood to greet him, and it was obvious

from his red-rimmed eyes that tears had been shed.

Karim's voice was low and a little rough as he said, "It was good. She knew me, after a while. We talked."

Razan reached out and took his hand. "I'm glad," she said.

Karim's fingers threaded through hers, then he looked to Desfan. "I may arrange a guard to relieve me a couple of mornings each week. Her physician said she usually does better in the mornings."

"Of course," Desfan said instantly. "Take whatever time you'd like."

"Serjan?"

He twisted to face a man with wide eyes who stood just down the stone path. He wore loose clothing and his long hair brushed his shoulders. Silver touched his temples, and he had deep lines around his eyes. Desfan guessed he was probably in his fifties, though something about his presence seemed older. Heavier. It was also clear the man wasn't a physician or attendant. His attire was similar to what other residents of the asylum wore.

The man snapped to sudden attention. His shoulders went back, his hands locked behind him, and he bowed deeply. "Serjan Saernon," he said, firmly now, without a hint of question. "Thank you for granting me this audience."

Something in Desfan's chest tightened. The man thought he was his father.

He glanced briefly around them, but there was no sign of an attendant, or an escort for the man. A quick look at Karim and Razan showed they were just as unsure as he felt.

The man was still bowing.

Desfan cleared his throat. "Thank you. You may—"

The man's head jerked up. "I've been waiting to give my

report," he interrupted.

Desfan heard more than saw Razan drift away—to get assistance, he hoped. He didn't want to upset the man, so he didn't bother correcting him. He simply prompted, "Your report?"

"Yes." Tension bunched in his shoulders. "You were right to send me. But no one could have guessed the horror I found."

The man was clearly not stable, but something in his terse words made Desfan's scalp prickle. "What did you find?"

The man's eyes narrowed. "Her."

The hairs on the back of Desfan's neck lifted. His mind jumped to the first conclusion he could imagine. "Meerah?" he asked softly.

The man scowled. "No. No! She's dead. *Both* seraijahs died. Don't you remember?"

Desfan set his jaw against the man's harsh tone. "Yes, I remember. But who are you talking about?"

"*Her*," he said again, more insistent than before. "You know. You *suspected*. That's why you sent me!"

Certainly not Meerah, then; his father had suffered a seizure after learning his youngest daughter still lived. He hadn't had time to send anyone to investigate—least of all this unstable man. Besides, if this man thought Desfan was his father, he probably hadn't seen the serjan in many years—if he'd ever seen Saernon Cassian at all, of course. This man was in an asylum for a reason.

"Apologies," Desfan said, hoping to soothe the man. His agitation was visibly growing. He was breathing harder, and his frame vibrated. His hands now twitched at his sides. Desfan gestured to the bench he and Razan had recently vacated. "Why don't you sit?"

"I can't sit," the man huffed. "Not when I must give my

report."

Desfan bit back a sigh. "Very well, then. Give me your report."

The man glared. "I'm *trying*. You won't listen!"

Desfan lifted a placating hand. "I'm listening."

"Good!" he snapped. Then his tone lowered. "It was horrible. I can still feel the fear and panic. I can still hear the screams and cries. So many bodies . . . they burned them. Burned them all."

From the corner of Desfan's eye, he could see Karim looked unnerved.

In that, they were matched.

He focused back on the man and dared to ask, "Where were you?"

"Far away. In the mountains." The man's breath caught. His words were more strained as he said, "You told me to go and I went, but I won't go back. I *won't*. I barely escaped with my life." He lifted one shaking hand and pressed his fingers to his left temple. "I fell. I . . . I don't remember . . . I don't know how I . . . But I did. I came back. I couldn't give my report." His hands trembled, more violently than before. "You needed to know. You *need* to know. It will be horrible. It will be a waking nightmare. What was done to them will be done to us—worse, even." His eyes sharpened and his hand dropped. "You must protect us. *Please*."

"I will," Desfan said. "I'll protect you."

The sound the man made in his throat was torn between a pitiable whine and a formless curse. "Not just me. Everyone. *All* of us. Please!"

Desfan stepped forward. Karim tensed, but didn't stop him from catching the man's trembling hands in both of his. He met the man's manic gaze with steadiness and calm. "I will protect everyone," he promised. "You have my word."

The man's breathing remained pinched. Frantic. "Your word as serjan?" he gasped.

Desfan dipped his chin. "Yes."

The man's shoulders sank and the panic fled his eyes, replaced by a sheen of tears. His fingers squeezed Desfan's. "Thank you," he breathed out. "Thank you . . . Don't let her evil touch us. You must watch us . . . guard us . . . guard well . . ."

Rapid footsteps hurried toward them.

Desfan looked past the man to see Razan and two attendants approach. The first was a woman, the other a young man.

"I'm so sorry, serjan," the woman said. "Vakesh wanders sometimes."

The male attendant gently took hold of Vakesh's arm. "Come now. Let's go back to your room."

"Guard," Vakesh repeated weakly, still peering at Desfan as the attendant eased him away and back down the path. "Guard well . . ."

"I assure you, he's harmless," the woman said quietly, pulling Desfan's gaze away from the retreating men. "He usually doesn't even speak."

"Who is he?" Desfan asked.

"Vakesh Kazzo. I'm truly sorry he bothered you."

Desfan ignored that. "He thought I was my father. Did he know the late serjan?"

She blinked. "Well, I . . . I don't know. I think he may have worked at the palace, before his accident."

"Accident?" Karim asked.

The woman pursed her lips. "We prefer to keep our patients protected here. I'm sure you understand—"

"I do," Desfan said. "But this could be important. Can you please tell me everything you know about him?"

"I . . . suppose I can find his records," she said, reluctance pulling every word. "It may take a while for me to fetch them."

"We'll wait," Desfan assured her.

CHAPTER 28

CLARE

A FINE TREMOR SKATED THROUGH CLARE'S BODY, making her vibrate with a tension she couldn't force away. Grandeur—the man she suspected had killed her little brothers—was sitting in the chair across from her. His hands were steepled in front of his thinned lips, and his eyes were sharp as he regarded her.

Nothing in the prince looked like the man she'd once called friend, and she had to wonder if that first persona he'd shown her at the castle in Iden had been a lie. Or perhaps his paranoia and anger had twisted him into this harsh-looking man. He certainly seemed harder than he had the last time she'd seen him in Halbrook.

Dervish, the captain of his guard, stood behind him. Their presence made the princess's sitting room seem much smaller and darker, despite the sun that filtered through the tall windows.

"Leave us," Grandeur ordered.

Bennick and Venn didn't move from their places behind her.

"You don't command us here," Venn said, his tone inflexible. "You have little power in Mortise. But perhaps you've forgotten that." The barb was not well-masked.

Grandeur's expression sharpened. "What are you insinuating?"

"You won't be speaking to Miss Ellington alone," Bennick cut in, speaking before Venn could. "She is ours to protect, as I'm sure you can understand."

"She's in no danger from me."

"Regardless, we won't be leaving her."

Grandeur's irritation was obvious, but he dropped the matter and focused on Clare. "Where is my sister?"

"She's not here," Clare said. She didn't want to tell Grandeur where she'd gone, but she knew she didn't have a choice. "She went to Zennor."

His eyes rounded slightly. "Why?"

"She wanted to visit King Zaire. I don't know all her reasons." It probably wasn't a lie; it wasn't Serene's way to share everything.

"Why are you here?" Bennick asked the prince.

Grandeur leaned back in his chair. "I don't have to explain myself to you."

"No," Bennick agreed. "But if we know why you're here, we might be able to offer assistance." His voice was a little too tight, but Clare thought he was handling this meeting well. Far better than she was, if the roaring in her ears was any indication.

"I have several issues to discuss with Desfan," Grandeur said.

"Do any of your issues involve the Hunt?" Venn asked.

Bennick threw his friend a piercing look.

Grandeur's eyes narrowed. "Grannard, if there's something you'd like to say to me, do please get on with it."

Clare glanced over her shoulder at Venn. His face was hard as stone. His anger came from his experiences with the Hunt, and all that had happened to him and Vera, and the Holm children. Clare knew they'd suffered a great deal because of Grandeur's unchecked actions against anyone he thought might be a rebel.

Bennick cleared his throat. "Perhaps it would be best if we delayed this conversation. You must be tired from your journey, Your Highness, and—"

"No," Grandeur said. "I wish to know exactly what you all think of me. I won't tolerate any conversations behind my back. Not anymore." He focused on Venn. "Do you think the Hunt has gone too far, perhaps? That what I'm doing is unjust?"

"You're terrorizing innocent families," Venn said between his teeth. "You're forcing our people to flee their homes and their kingdom because they fear for their lives—"

"If they fear the Hunt," Grandeur interrupted, "they must have something to hide."

"They fear the Hunt because you've given them unchecked power," Venn snapped. "On your orders, the Hunt is making wrongful arrests, torturing innocents, and killing indiscriminately."

"You're wrong," Grandeur said firmly. "You don't know what's been happening in Devendra. The rebels have escalated their activity, which forced me to escalate my methods of finding them. The Hunt is thorough, but not vicious. You've been misinformed."

"I've seen the Hunt's actions with my own eyes," Venn argued. "I've seen what you're doing in Salvation."

Something flashed in Grandeur's eyes. Panic? As quickly as it came, it was gone, replaced by a flat mask. "I have heard tales of that camp since I arrived in Mortise, but I'm afraid I don't know why you'd think I have anything to do with it."

"You're lying," Venn gritted out.

"Careful," Grandeur said coolly. "To call your prince a liar is treason."

Clare's spine stiffened at the threat.

Venn continued to glare. "I know you sent the Hunt to Mortise. You—"

"Venn," Bennick said, his voice hard. "Get out."

Venn shot him a look. "But—"

"Go. Now." Bennick's steeled tone brooked no argument.

Venn bristled, but he strode into the princess's bedroom, where Vera and Bridget were working.

As soon as the door closed, Dervish let out a grunt. "A man under my command would never say such things."

Bennick didn't acknowledge the weak slight. His focus was on the prince. "What else do we need to discuss?"

Grandeur's hands landed on the arms of his chair, reclining as if it were his throne. "I want to know everything that's been happening here. I want to know about Desfan Cassian, and my sister, and my cousin—if Imara is still around, that is. Did she go to Zennor with Serene?"

"No," Bennick said. "Princess Imara was wounded in an attack the night before the serjan's coronation. She's still healing."

"I'll have to pay her a visit." Grandeur's chin lifted. "Now. Tell me everything."

Bennick began to share the basic facts of recent events. Clare listened, but the words didn't penetrate. All she could see was Grandeur sitting there, perfectly at ease, listening to Bennick as if this report was his due. Sitting in front of her, not even looking at her, when he had probably murdered her brothers. And for what? Because he was angry at her? Because he thought she'd betrayed him?

Her blood simmered. Her pulse roared in her ears, and her throat was so thick with swallowed anger and grief that she could barely breathe.

Bennick was still talking. Grandeur was still listening.

Her chest burned, the pressure of unspoken words building until—"Did you kill them?"

The room quieted, and every eye turned to her.

She only had eyes for Grandeur.

The prince stared at her, his expression smooth. "What?" he asked. As if he hadn't heard her, when clearly he had.

Bennick set a hand on her shoulder. His touch was a warning, but she ignored that. She also ignored the way Dervish's attention sharpened on Bennick.

For Clare, Grandeur was the only person who existed right now. "Did you kill my brothers?" she asked pointedly.

Grandeur didn't blink. Perhaps he should have—it might have hidden his flash of guilt.

His guilt could have been a blade, it cut her so deeply. It was a silent admission: he'd killed Thomas and Mark.

Something deep inside her snapped. She didn't remember throwing herself at him. She didn't remember screaming, though her throat suddenly burned.

She didn't remember who shouted first—Bennick, Grandeur, or Dervish.

Her nails raked for Grandeur's face, but never made contact. Dervish shoved her back.

She slammed into Bennick's chest, and his arms came around her—protective, but also caging.

She strained against him, desperate to tear Grandeur apart.

Then Venn was there, and Bennick pushed Clare into his arms. "Get her out of here," Bennick ordered, tension riding his words.

Clare knew she'd made a grave mistake in attacking Grandeur. Fates, if she wasn't Serene's decoy, he probably would have demanded her head. But she couldn't stop. She couldn't do *nothing*.

In the end, she was no match for Venn. Despite her struggles, he pulled her to the bedroom. The last thing she saw before the door closed was Bennick squaring off before an irate Dervish and Grandeur.

Clare sat on an iron chair on the balcony, watching the sun descend toward the horizon.

That's where Bennick found her. He sank in the chair beside her, his eyes squinting toward the distant sun.

"I'm sorry," she whispered.

He exhaled slowly. "We have no proof, Clare. Until we do . . ." He trailed off.

She understood, though. Prince Grandeur was far too powerful to accuse without irrefutable proof. It was why she'd sent

Latif to ascertain the truth.

But she knew, now. Even without proof, she knew Grandeur had killed her brothers. "I can't be around him," she said, her voice cracking. "I can't . . ."

Bennick twisted in his chair, his crystal blue eyes intense. "I know. I can't, either. Just now, watching him walk away . . ." He shook his head, a muscle in his jaw feathering.

Clare swallowed hard. "He's going to seek retribution."

"There's nothing he can do. Not while you're acting as Serene." He looked at her firmly. "And I'm not going to let him touch you."

His promise was absolute, and she didn't doubt it.

She let out a wavering breath. "I shouldn't have attacked him."

Bennick said nothing.

She looked down at her hands, which rested in her lap. Her wrists still carried faint marks from her time as Salim's captive. Some of her fingers were slightly crooked. And all she had to do was close her eyes to see perfectly the scars on Bennick's body from where he'd been run through, and Wilf had had to burn his flesh to save him.

She thought of Vera, who had suffered alongside her at Salim's hands. Who had buried her sister, after the Rose had killed her as a taunt.

She thought of Eliot, her older brother, who had died to save her life at the border.

She thought of Serene, who fought silently in the shadows for her people.

Imara, who might never walk unaided again, but still thought selflessly of others.

Desfan, who persevered no matter what fate threw at him.

Dirk, who had died for a chance at peace with Mortise.

Too many people had sacrificed too much to bring them to this point. She couldn't throw all of that away because of her own need for revenge.

Justice would come to Grandeur—she would make sure of it—but tearing him apart now would do nothing, except maybe throw her into a fight she couldn't win.

Still, she knew her limits. She couldn't trust herself in the same room with him.

She looked up, and as soon as she saw the sea, she knew. "We should go to Dorma."

Bennick's brow furrowed. "What?"

"Dorma," she repeated. "Serene was invited by the Hassans, and they'll be leaving for home tomorrow. We could go with them. I'm sure Desfan will appreciate our efforts to get to know his people better—whether here, or on Dorma." And he'd already said he was willing to help her in any way he could. She knew he would let her go, if that's what she needed.

And she needed to get away from Grandeur.

When Bennick remained quiet, her confidence faltered. "Do you think it's a bad idea?" she asked.

Bennick's face gentled. He reached out, twining his fingers around hers. "I think it's an excellent idea. Frankly, I don't think I'm capable of holding back you, Venn, *and* Vera from attacking Grandeur again."

"I'm sorry," she repeated.

With his free hand, he skimmed his knuckles across the curve of her cheek. Her breath caught as it always did when he touched her, and tingles broke out over her skin. When his hand fell, his eyes settled on hers. "He will pay for what he's done. I swear it."

She believed him. Completely. She showed that by leaning forward and pressing her lips to his.

The kiss was gentle. Sweet. An expression of deep love and unending gratitude. Bennick returned the same, but it wasn't long before their kiss firmed. Escalated.

He shifted on his chair, drawing closer to her as he tilted his head and changed the angle of the kiss. His hands moved, too. One curled around her waist and the other delved into her hair, which was loose today, thank the fates.

Her scalp tingled from the contact with his fingers. Strange, how such a small and simple touch could have such an overwhelming impact on the rest of her body.

Her palms landed on his chest, and she could feel his heart beating against the heel of her hand. The rapid tempo matched her own, and their breaths mingled—growing sharper. His tongue brushed her lips, and heat flashed through her.

Her hands glided over his shoulders and up the strong column of his neck, until her palms found the sharp bristles that covered his hard jaw. She framed his face with her hands, keeping him close as she continued to explore his mouth. His hand fisted in her hair, tugging pleasantly. She let out a short gasp, and then his lips reclaimed hers.

She never wanted this moment to end. She wanted to lean into his warmth and strength. Curl into him—lose herself in him.

She didn't know what their future could be—not with the oaths they'd both sworn—but, fates, she wanted this forever. She wanted *him*.

His fingers dug into her side and his mouth eased away from hers, breaking off their kiss. "We need to stop," he rasped.

Never. She didn't think she actually managed to say the word. It sounded more like a groan.

Bennick's forehead tipped to rest against hers, both of them struggling to catch their breath. "Venn, Vera, Bridget—they're just in the other room."

"They know about us," Clare argued.

"Bridget might not."

Clare drew back so she could shoot him a look.

He chuckled. Color was high on his cheeks, and his blue eyes shone in the light of the setting sun. "All right, she's probably guessed. But we can't afford to let anyone else know, so we need to be cautious."

Abruptly, she remembered the way Dervish had eyed Bennick when he'd touched her shoulder. She sobered and drew back, though Bennick's hand around her waist didn't let her retreat fully. "Dervish looked . . ." She couldn't find the right words.

"He's made speculations," Bennick said. "Most of them silent. He doesn't know how to mask his thoughts—every single one plays over his face."

"But he might tell Grandeur. And *he* might tell Newlan."

Bennick nodded once. Hand still wrapped around her side, his thumb skated against her abdomen. The Mortisian fabric of her dress was thin, so she felt every bit of his heat. "Grandeur will no doubt be at dinner, so you'll eat in the suite tonight. We'll talk to Desfan about traveling to Dorma as soon as he's available to meet with us."

She hoped arrangements could be made quickly, because she wanted to travel with the Hassans tomorrow.

She couldn't stand to be in the same place as Grandeur for longer than that.

CHAPTER 29

DESFAN

Desfan strode down the corridor, Karim at his side. The sun would be setting soon, but preparing for dinner was the last thing on his mind.

They reached Yahri's apartment and Karim knocked on the door.

The councilwoman answered promptly. She leaned on her cane, the wrinkles by her eyes deepening as she frowned at Desfan. "I suppose you want to discuss our newest issue."

"Can you lecture me about the orphanage speech later?" Desfan asked. "I have some questions—"

"I'm not talking about your speech," Yahri interrupted. "I'm talking about the fact that Prince Grandeur is here."

That froze him. "He is?"

"Yes. And he'll be at dinner, so we really need to discuss your strategy for dealing with him and his alleged activities in Mor-

369

tise, without creating any political problems with Devendra."

Fates, this complicated things. Yahri was the only one on the council who knew everything Grandeur had been doing in Mortise, but he wasn't sure how the other council members would feel about having the Devendran prince here.

Regardless, that problem could wait. The questions he'd come to ask Yahri could not. "I need to speak with you," he said.

"It's almost time for dinner."

"This won't take long."

Yahri sighed, but waved them in.

Desfan and Karim took seats on the long settee in her sitting room, while she dropped into a cushioned chair that was so clearly her favorite, it carried a permanent indentation of her.

"Now then," she said, planting her cane in front of her, both hands draped over the top. "What urgent questions take precedence over Prince Grandeur's unannounced arrival and you changing into a proper outfit for dinner?"

Desfan might have once taken offense, but he was quite used to Yahri's manner by now. "I want to know about Vakesh Kazzo."

A furrow grew between Yahri's silver brows. "Who?"

"Vakesh Kazzo," he repeated. "He used to be a scribe for my father. He's currently living in the asylum in the city."

The lines on her face deepened. "I'm sorry, I don't know who . . ." Her words drifted. Then her eyes widened. She straightened in her chair. "Vakesh Kazzo—I'd nearly forgotten about him."

"We met today," Desfan told her.

Yahri glanced at Karim, but she didn't say anything. Considering how warmly she and Avao had interacted at the coronation, Desfan gathered they were close enough that Yahri knew about Karim's mother.

Yahri swallowed and focused back on Desfan. "I'm sorry, sometimes my mind isn't as sharp as I'd like. But I haven't heard that name in easily ten years. Likely more. It took me a moment to recall him."

"He thought I was my father," Desfan said. "I asked for his records at the asylum, but there wasn't much information about him. He has no family, so the palace pays for his care at the asylum."

"Your father made those arrangements many years ago," Yahri said, almost distractedly. "But Vakesh wasn't a scribe."

Desfan frowned. "He wasn't?"

"No. He was a spy."

Karim coughed. "That man was a spy?"

"Yes," Yahri confirmed.

"Why do his records say he was a scribe?" Desfan asked.

"Your father thought it would be best to keep his official appointment a secret. Spies thrive, after all, with anonymity."

"He's not thriving," Desfan felt compelled to say.

Yahri sighed and leaned back in her chair. "He had an accident. We still don't know if he was attacked while returning from his last mission, or if something else happened. But he struck his head and lost many parts of himself. His memory, his ability to communicate—even his grasp on reality. Your father saw to his care, naturally, but there was nothing else for it. The last I heard, Vakesh was barely cognizant."

"He seemed aware of things today."

"He thought you were your father," Karim said blandly.

Desfan sent him a look.

He shrugged, unapologetic. "He was raving. Nothing he said

made actual sense. He's clearly trapped in the past; anything he tried to tell us, our current spies will have a better understanding of."

He had a point.

That didn't dispel Desfan's curiosity, though—or drive away the memory of the man's desperate, almost manic words.

Desfan turned back to Yahri. "Do you know the details of his last mission?"

"No. And I'm not sure you'll find any good records," Yahri warned. "Your father was very careful about any written reports from his spies. You can speak with the current spymaster, of course, but I don't know how much help he'll be. Vakesh served the crown long ago." She nodded to Karim. "I would take Karim's advice and let it rest. You have more current problems. Like Prince Grandeur and preparing for dinner."

"I won't create a political incident by accusing Prince Grandeur of crimes in Mortise," Desfan assured her. "At least not until my investigation of Salvation is complete."

"Thank you." Her head tilted. "Have you chosen an heir yet?"

The unexpected question caught him off guard. Yahri had delivered a list of candidates to him over a week ago—he hadn't even looked at it.

"No," he said.

Yahri pursed her lips. "I know you don't want to consider anyone but Meerah. But—"

"She's my heir. If something happens to me before she returns, that's my will—you and Karim are my witnesses."

"There are other factors to consider," Yahri said, almost as if he hadn't spoken. "Meerah faces a dangerous journey. Even if she makes it back, she may not want the responsibility of the throne."

That made Desfan pause. Yahri had a point, and he felt like an idiot for not considering it sooner. After all, *he* hadn't wanted this crown—at least not in the beginning. And considering all Meerah had been forced to do, he refused to make her wear a crown she didn't want.

Yahri's expression grew somber. "There is another factor to consider. Meerah may not be *able* to rule. We don't yet know the extent of what she endured in Ryden. We don't know what state she'll be in—emotionally, physically, or mentally." True pain sparked in her eyes. "Desfan, she may not even speak our language anymore. And the last formal education she received was when she was seven years old."

A strange dread had settled on his chest. "It doesn't matter. She's alive—that alone is a fates blasted miracle."

"It is," Yahri agreed. "Which is why I don't think you should hope for more. She may not be the sister you remember—or she might be frozen in many ways, just exactly as she was."

She's fine. Perfect. That's what Grayson had said—quite defensively—when Imara had asked about Mia's condition.

Desfan's throat felt horribly dry. "This is all speculative. Until she returns, we won't know anything for certain."

Yahri's eyes were unreadable, but she dipped her chin. "You're right, of course. We can continue this discussion later and discuss our options."

Discuss our options. He hated how that sounded. As if Mia—his precious little sister—was a problem that needed to be solved.

"Don't let this trouble you now," Yahri said, surprising him. He didn't think she'd ever looked so gentle—so compassionate. "There is nothing to be done about Meerah just yet, and you have more immediate concerns."

Desfan let out a slow breath at the reminder. Grandeur. Dinner. Fates, there was always something. He pushed to his feet. "Thank you, Yahri."

"You're welcome, Desfan." He and Karim had nearly made it to the door when Yahri called out, "Wear your crown to dinner. It won't hurt to remind Grandeur—and everyone else—that you're the serjan."

Desfan tossed a thin smile over his shoulder. "If I wear it, will *you* remember I'm your serjan and stop pestering me so much?"

She snorted. "If you manage to make it through one day without needing my pestering, I might."

After an exhausting dinner, Desfan headed toward Serene's suite. Bennick had approached him at dinner and asked if he could visit with him and Clare before he retired for the night. Desfan imagined the impromptu meeting had something to do with Grandeur's appearance—especially because Clare never came to dinner, and he caught Bennick shooting a hard look at the Devendran prince as he strode from the room.

Two guards trailed Desfan as he walked down the empty hallway. Desfan had already dismissed Karim for the night, since his friend had had such an emotional day. Fates, he wished *he* could be dismissed for the night. His crown dangled in one fist at his side, his head aching too much to hold it up.

Prince Grandeur was *not* his favorite person. The man

smiled too thinly, and his gaze was scheming. And then had come his requests . . .

I heard about the camp, Salvation. I would like to help you solve the problem. I would like to instate one of my men to run things . . .

Desfan had managed to put off any commitments, but he knew the prince would be asking again soon, and he needed a good answer.

He wondered how Serene would handle her brother, if she were here. She'd probably manage effortless diplomacy, or a satisfying snap at her brother; with Serene, either was possible.

When he turned down the corridor that led to Serene's suite, he spotted Imara's door. He didn't want to keep Bennick and Clare waiting, but after the long day he'd had, he needed to see Imara.

Taking a slight detour, he approached Kaz, who was standing guard outside the door.

The man bowed at Desfan's approach. "Serjan."

"Is she awake?" Desfan asked.

A crash sounded beyond the closed door.

Kaz shoved open the door, Desfan right behind him as they tore into the room. His heart raced and his palm itched for a weapon. He hadn't yet allowed weapons to be worn at palace dinners, but he had a knife hidden in his boot.

He didn't bother slowing so he could retrieve it.

He darted through the sitting room and into Imara's bedroom, almost taking Kaz down in his haste to reach Imara.

The princess was sprawled on the floor, near the window that had been repaired after her would-be-assassin had jumped through it.

But Imara wasn't under attack. She was alone. One hand

was planted against the wall, and the other strangled the cane Desfan had given her. When she looked up and their gazes clashed, he saw the sheen of tears that made her dark eyes glitter.

At once, he knew what had happened; she'd tried to walk on her own, and she'd failed.

His pulse still pounded, the adrenaline rushing through his body not understanding that there was no threat to fight.

Kaz's voice was quiet. "Do you need the physician, Princess?"

"No," Imara said, her voice wavering just enough to make Desfan's heart clench.

Kaz took a step forward, but Desfan gestured for him to retreat.

The bodyguard bowed and left, closing the door gently behind him.

Desfan stepped forward. "Would you like to return to your bed?" he asked softly.

"No." Imara sniffed, avoiding his gaze. "I wanted to study the floor over here. It looked fascinating."

Despite everything, the corner of his mouth tugged up. His legs folded, and he sat in front of her, turning the crown over in his hands. "There's a corner in the throne room that I've always found highly fascinating," he said. "If floors are of particular interest to you, I'll have to point it out."

She exhaled heavily and shifted on the floor. Her grimace as she eased her leg out made him cringe. Once she had one shoulder propped against the wall, she finally looked at him. "How was dinner?"

"An absolute joy," he drawled. "Your cousin Grandeur is wonderful."

She curled a tendril of loose hair behind her ear, her shoulders low. "When Clare told me he'd come . . ." She sighed. "He wasn't always as he is now. Losing his mother . . . it changed him."

For a moment, Desfan felt pity for Grandeur. Fates knew losing his mother had changed *him*. But if even half of what Serene believed Grandeur had done to his people was true, that pity didn't stretch far.

"He's more like his father, now," Imara said. "Sometimes I wonder if he might become worse than him." There was a short silence, then she exhaled. "What are you doing here, Desfan?"

He lifted his crown. "You've been begging to see this, and Yahri finally convinced me to wear it tonight, so it seemed like the fates had spoken."

She rolled her eyes. "You don't need to cheer me up."

"I'm not. I'm hoping you'll be very jealous. It's a beautiful crown, after all."

Her eyes trailed over the intricate details etched into the gold, and the many sparkling jewels. "It's lovely."

"It looks even better when I wear it." He winked and set it in place, ignoring the spike in his headache.

Seeing her lips twitch made any pain worth it. "You're hopeless," she told him.

"All my tutors claimed the same." He grinned and lifted his shoulders, trying for an impressive pose, even though he was still sitting on the floor. "Well? What do you think?"

She studied him for a short moment, and he couldn't quite read the emotions in her eyes. She almost looked . . . sad. "You look like a perfect serjan," she finally said.

It was an echo of something she'd said once before, when

they'd hidden in the kitchen pantry. *You will make an incredible serjan.*

She'd sounded sad then, too. He still didn't fully understand why. He tried to recall what else they'd spoken of that night. Sacrifices made for the good of a kingdom. Putting his people first, as her father did. He hadn't minded the comparison to her father that night, but now . . . it left him oddly unsettled.

Desfan plucked the crown from his head and set it aside. "You don't need to walk alone, you know. Not yet, I mean. Give your body time to heal."

"What if I don't heal?" As soon as the words were out she looked away, her throat flexing as she swallowed.

He reached out and touched her chin, slowly turning her back to face him. "You *will* walk again," he told her. "Until that day comes, you can walk with me."

She stared at him, and he realized she wasn't breathing.

Fates, now *he* wasn't breathing. Her skin was soft and warm beneath his fingertips, and he couldn't help but smooth the pad of his thumb against her cheek.

She sucked in a breath, then tensed.

He dropped his hand before she could pull away. Knowing she was going to, though . . . that was a punch to his gut.

"I need to return to Zennor," she said, her voice firmer than before. "And if I have to stay in that fates-blasted bed for one more day . . ." Her voice cracked.

His spine straightened. "It's settled, then."

Confusion crossed her face. "What's settled?"

He tapped his chin and frowned, exaggerating the expression as he stared at a spot above her head. "I'll have to make some arrangements, of course, and see if I can afford another person on my staff. What with my treasury being depleted, it could be—"

Her palm clapped over his mouth, stopping his words and forcing him to meet her gaze. She leaned in, her eyes intent. "What are you blabbering about?"

He grasped her wrist and tugged her hand away, though his lips tingled from feeling her touch, innocent as it was. "I'm hiring you," he said.

She blinked. "You're . . ."

"I need another advisor—just ask Yahri—and I have a particular job for you, if you wouldn't mind digging into a mystery. I need someone I trust to review some old spy records."

Her eyes lit up at that, but she still frowned. "I'm a princess of Zennor. *Can* you hire me?"

"You have a brilliant mind, and your skills in forgery are unmatched. I would very much like to hire you. You can have the office next to mine, and in between meetings I can consult with you. I'm sure there's a comfortable settee that can be brought, and if ever you grow tired, you can take most of your work back here."

She bit her lip. "I don't want to be carried through the halls."

He knew instantly what she didn't say; she didn't want to be seen by his people as weak.

Still holding her hand, he skated his thumb over her inner wrist. "I'll come early every morning to get you," he said. "We'll walk as long as you'd like, and if you ever tire, I can carry you through the servant passages. I think you'll enjoy discovering the secrets of the palace."

Intrigue colored her eyes once more, and it was so much better than the shame and tears that had lived there too recently.

Still, she teased him with a long sigh. "My skills *are* legendary," she said. "I hope you can afford me."

He cracked a smile, feeling her words more deeply than she surely meant them. Because of that, he didn't verbalize his reply.

If there's any way to keep you, Imara, I'll find it.

CHAPTER 30

MIA

MEERAH CLUTCHED THE QUILT CLOSER TO HER chin as she pressed into the corner of her bunk. The whole world rocked violently as the ship was tossed on the sea.

Tahlyah was in bed beside her, also fisting the blanket. Her older sister looked pale.

Darkol—the bodyguard Mia had shared with Tally and Des all her life—had left a long time ago to check in with the captain, and he hadn't returned.

On the other side of the cabin, Mother snatched up her cloak. "I'll be right back," she said. "I just need to speak with the captain."

"Don't go," Meerah begged. Darkol hadn't come back, and neither had the seraijan's guards. While Mother said it was because they must be helping the crew, Meerah didn't want her mother to vanish, too.

The ship lurched, and Mother stumbled. Her hand slapped against the wall to keep her from falling.

Thunder boomed, and Meerah screamed.

Tahlyah wrapped an arm around her shaking shoulders. She was nine years old, and not afraid of anything. Not like Mia, who was barely seven and *terrified*.

Mother looked at them. Shards of moonlight made it through the storm clouds and the cabin's window, revealing a rare hint of panic in her beautiful brown eyes. Her long dark hair was in a messy braid that trailed over her shoulder, and she wore a long white nightgown. She threw the cloak around her body, her face smooth and her mouth set. "Stay here," she said. "I'll be right back. I promise."

Meerah's gut dropped along with the ship. She wanted to scream for her mother to stay with them, but the seraijan was already out the door.

In the distance, Meerah could hear the frantic shouts of the sailors. The creak of the ship, and the snapping of the sails.

Tahlyah held her close. "We'll be all right," she said. "And we'll tell Des how brave we were. Father, too."

"I'm scared," Meerah said, clutching the black ring that hung on the delicate chain around her neck. Tahlyah had the same ring, and so did Desfan. The rings tied them together, even when they were apart.

A deafening crack of thunder rattled Meerah's clenched teeth. Flashes of lightning followed, lighting every corner of the cabin.

Then came the loudest crack of all.

Tahlyah jerked, and above them, men shrieked.

Tears rolled down Meerah's face. "What was that?"

Tahlyah's jaw stiffened. "We need to find Mother."

"She said to stay here."

Her sister grasped her shoulders. "That was the ship, Mia. It's breaking. We need to find Mother and the captain. They'll keep us safe."

Terror closed off her throat, so she jerked out a nod.

They didn't bother finding their shoes or cloaks. The ship rocked beneath them and they stumbled, but made it to the door. Tahlyah glanced back at Meerah and took her hand. "Don't let go."

"I won't," she promised, even though her chest burned with fear.

Tahlyah led the way into the narrow corridor of the ship. With every lurching step they bumped into the walls, but they kept going. Water pooled at their feet, and Mia's stomach churned.

On the deck, chaos reigned. One of the towering masts had snapped and fallen across the deck. Sails flapped madly, ropes were flying, and men ran in the storm. Other men had been crushed by the felled mast. Some were crying out—alive, but pinned.

Fates, those screams . . . She'd never heard anything so horrible.

Across the deck, their mother stood clutching a taut rope that helped keep her upright as she stood beside the captain. As if she sensed them, she looked over her shoulder. Meerah had never seen such raw fear on her mother's face. Not *ever*.

Thunder ripped the night, and lightning fractured the sky. A wave slammed into the ship, rolling it. Meerah thought she heard her mother scream.

The planks of wood beneath their feet buckled. Tahlyah's hand was torn from hers, and Meerah was falling, falling . . .

Plunged into the sea, everything was dark. Wet. Cold.

Tahlyah was gone. So was the obsidian ring she'd been clutching; the necklace must have fallen off.

Meerah clawed at the water, the salt of it burning her eyes. Desfan had told her if she learned to swim, she wouldn't be afraid of the water anymore.

That was a lie. She'd learned to swim on her own on Dorma, but she was terrified now.

Swimming in a roiling sea was no more than useless thrashing. She was swallowed by the water, dragged under the waves and pulled into the dark. Bodies knocked into her. She didn't think they were alive, because they weren't fighting the water like she was. When lightning stabbed through the darkness it illuminated the people around her, and all she saw were blank faces and empty eyes.

Inside, she was screaming.

The next boom of thunder was muted underwater. The screams of dying men and the horrendous snapping of the ship breaking were also distant. The deeper she fell, the calmer the water became—and that seemed wrong. Her hair floated around her, loose strands escaping from the braid her mother had gently weaved earlier that night.

Something bumped her.

Lightning streaked somewhere above, and wide eyes appeared in front of her face. She nearly swiped her arm at the floating body before her, but her mind caught up with her fear and labeled the person—*Tally*. Her sister was stretching out her hand.

Wanting to sob in relief, Meerah grabbed for her sister. With joined hands, the two of them kicked. Meerah didn't know which way to swim, so she let Tahlyah guide her.

Suddenly, something snagged her waist. She twitched around, her movement slowed because of the water.

A sailor had grabbed her. She didn't recognize him, but he must be one of the crew. He propelled her up through the water, much faster than she and Tahlyah had been swimming. Soon, she was above her sister, and as she looked down at Tahlyah, she could see the fear in her eyes.

Meerah tried to hold on, but Tahlyah's fingers slipped away. *No!*

Her sister sank, falling into the darkness as Mia was propelled upward.

The sailor broke the surface, and Mia gasped for air, her small lungs burning. The violence of the storm surrounded them, and rain slashed down painfully.

"Tally!" Meerah cried as she coughed and spluttered. "She's still down there!"

The sailor shoved Meerah onto a piece of driftwood and pressed her fingers almost painfully around the rough edge. "Hold on to this," he ordered.

"Get her—*please!*"

The sailor dove back into the water.

Meerah clung to the piece of wood beneath her, soaked and shivering. Thrown and dropped by the waves, hammered with rain and shuddering with each crash of thunder, she could barely see anything of the wreckage around her. Disoriented and deaf to everything but the raging storm, Meerah held on.

"Mia."

She gasped and clutched the driftwood tighter. She had not been able to hold onto Tally, but she would hold onto this piece of wood. She would grip it until her fingers bled or fell off. She would not let go. Because that sailor would save Tahlyah, and the captain would have saved the seraijan. If Mia could just hold on and survive the storm, she would see them both again.

"*Mia*." Fingers curled around hers, and the urgency in that deep voice tugged at her. "Mia, wake up."

NO! a voice deep inside her cried. If she woke, she would lose them again.

Thunder cracked, and Mia jerked against the bed.

Bed. She was in a bed. In the small village of Edgewood, at the inn.

The dream shattered, but panic clutched her chest when she realized the storm was real. Rain lashed the side of the inn. Lightning flashed, blinding her. She was lying on her stomach, clutching the bed as if it were that piece of driftwood. She couldn't breathe.

Grayson was wrapped around her, one arm braced against the mattress at her side so he could lean over her without crushing her. His other hand was wrapped around hers, gripping tight.

"It's all right," he whispered in her ear. "You're all right. It was just a dream. You're safe. You can let go."

She couldn't. Her fingers were frozen. *She* was frozen.

Not a dream, but a memory. A nightmare she could never wake from, because it was real.

Tally's hand, slipping through hers. Her wide, terrified eyes as she was swallowed by the sea.

Mia shuddered.

Grayson made a sound in his throat, and then he was moving. He swung over her and knelt on the floor beside the bed, putting their faces closer. His hand never left hers.

His callused fingertips brushed her wet cheek, and though she couldn't see his expression clearly, she could feel the force of his gaze. "I'm right here," he breathed. "You're with me. I promise, you're safe."

A sob cracked in her throat, and finally Mia released her strangling hold on the bed. She wrapped her arms around Grayson's neck, slipping from the bed and falling into his lap. He gathered her close, tugging the quilt from the bed and wrapping it around her. His back settled against the wall and she buried her face in his neck.

The storm raged outside, and Grayson never stopped holding her. And she never stopped holding him.

When the thunder grew more distant and the rain slowed to a quiet, steady fall, Grayson asked softly, "Do you want to talk about it?"

Mia tightened her hold on him. They were still curled on the floor, tucked in the corner of the room, though her arms had shifted to wrap around his waist. Beneath her cheek, she could feel the steady beat of his heart. "I held on," she whispered. "All through the storm . . . I held onto a piece of driftwood."

Grayson pressed a kiss to the top of her head, his hand rubbing up and down her spine. "I will always thank the fates you survived that night."

Mia pinched her eyes closed, shame knifing her. "You don't understand. I held onto that fates-blasted piece of wood, but I couldn't hold onto my sister."

"Mia . . ."

"I hate it," she breathed, her words choked by tears. "I hate that I wasn't strong enough to save her. And Desfan . . ." He would hate her, too.

"Desfan is not going to blame you for what happened,"

Grayson said, clearly following her line of thought. "It wasn't your fault."

It felt like her fault.

In the darkness, something she'd never said aloud came out. "I'm afraid to go home," she admitted softly. "I'm afraid of seeing Desfan because, even if he doesn't blame me, what if I'm not what he expects? What if I'm not enough?"

You're broken, Meerah. Iris's words, but they voiced what Mia feared.

"You're his sister," Grayson said. "You're *you*. Fates, Mia— you will always be enough." He pulled her closer. "No one else survived that night. Not even the grown men who had sailed all their lives. You were a little girl, and you lived. That's a gift—a fates-blasted miracle. And that's exactly how Desfan will see it."

"How can you be sure?"

"Desfan has spent all these years thinking he lost you. Getting you back . . . Can you imagine what that means to him? He loves you. And he wouldn't want you torturing yourself with this any longer."

She didn't know how to respond. But something deep inside her settled, and for that she was grateful.

There was a long moment of silence. Then she said softly, "After the storm passed and morning came, I'd drifted away from a lot of the wreckage. I still thought my mother and Tally might be alive. It's what gave me the strength to keep holding on. And when the rescue ship came . . . I didn't realize it *wasn't* a rescue. The man who pulled me from the water . . . he was kind. I thought we were heading home. I thought everything was going to be all right."

Instead, she'd been taken to Ryden. Sold to Henri. Imprisoned.

Grayson's breathing thinned. "I'm sorry, Mia."

Mia. It was the name she'd clung to during the beatings. The name she'd embraced when she couldn't be Meerah anymore, but she couldn't bear to lose herself completely. Mia was what her family had called her. It was her last tie to them, and she'd refused to sever it, even if she'd had to stop thinking about them all the time.

She hadn't thought about that in years, but she couldn't stop thinking of it now. Yes, she had been Meerah once, but she'd also been Mia—even then. Perhaps that meant a part of her was still Meerah, too. Maybe something of who she used to be had survived, even after all this time.

Maybe she wasn't broken, but rather made whole by all the different pieces of herself.

Too many thoughts filled her mind, bringing too many feelings to process. She pulled back from Grayson, just enough so she could face him. There was just enough silver light from the window that she could see the furrow between his dark brows. She touched his cheek. "Thank you. You're always exactly what I need. I want to be the same for you."

He smiled very gently. "You are everything I need, Mia. Always."

Her heart thrilled, but she let her face turn serious. "I've been pushing all of this—everything about my past—out of my mind for so long . . . I think that's why the nightmare came. It's because it won't be pushed away any longer."

He watched her almost cautiously. "That makes sense."

She nodded. "It does. Because no matter how hard I tried to force it away—all the pain and loss and guilt—it never really left." She exhaled slowly as she met his gaze. "Do you want to talk about Carter?"

Grayson stiffened. He drew back slightly, the back of his head bumping lightly against the wall. His scarred jaw worked. "What I did to Carter . . . that's not even close to what happened with Tally."

"I think the guilt can feel the same. Whether it's right or not, I blame myself for Tally's death."

"But you were blameless. I actually killed my brother."

"You were saving me."

"I don't regret that," he said at once.

"Do you regret killing Carter?"

Grayson glanced away, his dark hair falling over his brow. "Yes." Against her back, his hand fisted. "I don't remember making the choice to kill him. If I'd been thinking clearly, maybe . . ."

Mia twisted toward him and pressed one palm against the unmarred side of his face, coaxing him to look at her. "The situations are different, but please hear me—shoving this aside, not feeling it . . . it will continue to tear you up, unless you lay it to rest."

He scanned her face, his expression tight. "I don't know how."

Mia almost smiled, though it was pained. "Neither do I. But trust me, ignoring it for years isn't the way."

Grayson's throat worked as he swallowed. "I crossed the line no one else in my family has ever crossed. Not even Peter or my parents."

"That doesn't make you worse than them."

"That's not how it feels."

Mia's thumb swept over the serious line of his unmarked jaw, which was rough with dark stubble. Grayson rarely shared his deepest thoughts, and even more rarely would he share his fears. Every time he allowed her in, she treasured that show of trust. Slowly, she leaned in and pressed her forehead to his. "I understand what it's like to feel something, even if some part of you knows it's not true. But you are so much better than you believe, Grayson."

He said nothing for a long moment. Then his chin lifted, and one hand moved to cradle the back of her head as his mouth brushed hers. His lips were warm, firm, and comforting, but he ended the kiss too soon. "I don't think I'm ready to talk about Carter."

"That's all right. Just know I'm ready to listen, whenever you're ready."

"Thank you." Grayson's gaze dipped, coming to rest on her necklaces. His pebble, and Tyrell's black queen. His finger traced over the wooden piece. "Tyrell gave this to you."

Mia couldn't discern the emotions in his soft words, but she knew he didn't understand. She didn't know if she'd be able to explain, but this quiet moment seemed like the place to try. She touched the Strategem queen, her finger hovering near Grayson's. "He made it, years ago."

Grayson frowned. "He did?"

"Yes. He learned to carve when he was a boy. He made a whole Strategem set, and he'd play with it in his room, alone. Until Iris found out and burned it all. Everything but this piece, because Tyrell hid it in his fist." She met his gaze. "Wearing it reminds me there was a piece of him that she never managed to destroy. There's a part of him no one could break." She bit the inside of her cheek. "Tyrell told me that you used to play cards together in secret."

His brow furrowed. "We did, for a while. When we were very

young."

"I'm sorry you were forced to become rivals. Enemies. It's so horribly wrong. And I know you have reasons to hate him, but there's goodness in him. That was the Tyrell who became my friend."

Grayson sighed. "Mia, you don't know him like I do. You never saw the relish on his face when he hurt someone. He *enjoyed* their pain."

Her stomach twisted. "He had to protect himself. I think he did so by embracing what your parents wanted him to be, and that's what you saw."

Grayson shook his head. "I'm grateful he protected you, but I can't ever trust him as you do."

She fingered the black queen, and then the smooth pebble. "He only sees you as the Black Hand," she said, her voice soft. "But you're so much more than that. Why can't he be more, too?"

He didn't say anything. Mia hadn't really expected him to; the hatred between these two brothers ran deep.

She let it go for now, and gave him a small smile. "Once we're out of Ryden, you'll be free. You won't have to be the Black Hand anymore. You can be whoever you want to be."

And she would no longer have to be his weakness.

Instead of looking excited—or even relieved—Grayson merely nodded once.

For some reason, her heartbeat quickened. "Have you wondered what things will be like for us in Mortise?" she asked.

"No. I haven't given it much thought."

Her heart still beat a little too fast, but she forced a smile. "That's all right. We'll be together—that's all that matters."

He studied her face, his eyes strangely somber. "Mia, I'd like you to promise me something."

"Anything." Fates, her heart was pounding, and she still wasn't sure why she felt this sense of trepidation.

Grayson's tongue darted out, wetting his lips. It was the only sign of his nerves, since his voice and expression remained smooth. "If you ever doubt yourself, or blame yourself, or feel trapped or afraid . . . promise you'll tell me. I don't want you to torture yourself about things that aren't your fault."

She wasn't sure what she'd expected him to say, but it wasn't that. "I . . . I will. I promise. But only if you promise the same."

His lips pressed into a line, but he nodded.

As the storm continued to rage outside, Mia settled against Grayson and finally felt peace.

CHAPTER 31

GRAYSON

"IT'S BEGINNING TO SCAB," TOBIN SAID, EVEN AS the physician leaned in for a closer look at Grayson's jaw. "That's a good sign of healing."

"He hasn't been feverish since he woke three days ago," Mia said quickly. She sat beside Grayson on the bed, holding his hand. He didn't actually know if it was for his benefit, or for hers. Mia had always craved physical contact, and he'd stopped resisting her years ago. Besides, after what they'd shared during the storm last night, he was feeling a stronger than usual desire to keep her close.

The physician was only a handful of years older than Grayson—maybe in his late twenties. He had a long, narrow face, an intense gaze, and a somewhat brusque manner. This was Grayson's first time meeting the man who had been caring for him since their arrival in Edgewood, since he'd been unconscious the other times Tobin had visited.

The man straightened, his attention still riveted on Grayson's newest scar.

Grayson tried to ignore how that made his skin itch. Tobin hadn't asked Grayson any questions about the injury, but he knew the physician had prodded Mia for information the first night he'd come to tend Grayson. Mia had told Grayson that she'd managed to sidestep any specifics, though she had divulged the use of Flame's Breath, which was just rare enough to denote Grayson had been tortured—probably at the castle. Thankfully, Tobin hadn't pressed for more information after eagerly pocketing his coins.

"The infection seems to be gone," the physician concluded. "The fevers should be behind you as well. Is your pain manageable?"

For a brief moment, he considered lying. If he said he was in pain, Mia might insist he take more of the olcain powder. He knew the medicine was in his pack; he'd checked the other day, when Mia had briefly stepped out of the room. He hadn't taken any, but he'd replaced the packet carefully.

He wanted it, but he hesitated to take it. If Mia asked him to, though . . .

No. She wasn't going to ask him to take more. She'd made it clear when he'd first woken that she hated what the olcain had done to him. And if he told Tobin he was in pain, the man would just give him some weaker medicine.

Mia and Tobin both stared at him, waiting for him to answer.

He cleared his throat. "Yes, the pain is manageable."

"Any headaches?" Tobin asked.

They were mild now, hardly worth noting. "No."

"Good." Tobin glanced at Mia. "You've done well in caring for him."

She squeezed Grayson's fingers. "Is he well enough to travel?"

"I would advise waiting until the wound is fully scabbed over. That should be just a few more days. The infection and your dependence on olcain both took a toll, so you should be careful not to push your body too far." He looked to Mia. "I'll be traveling to a couple of other villages nearby, so it may be a few days before I can return." The physician handed Grayson a healing balm, and Mia paid him.

Grayson didn't miss the flash of greed in the man's eyes as he pocketed his payment.

"I'll return when I can," he said as he left.

Grayson closed the door behind the physician and twisted to face Mia. "We're leaving tomorrow."

Mia bit the inside of her cheek. "Tobin said you needed a few more days."

"He only wants us to stay so he can get more coin. I'm well enough, so there's no point in losing any more time." It had been nine days since they'd escaped the castle, and he was anxious to move on and reach Porynth before Zadir sailed away—even if that was less likely with every day that passed.

He also didn't particularly like Jon, the innkeeper. He was a man of few words with a watchful gaze Grayson didn't trust. He'd only interacted with Jon a few times, since he and Mia had kept mostly to their room, but something about the innkeeper made Grayson's instincts flare.

He'd learned from the talkative Keegan—who brought them their meals—that his mother had died two years ago. Jon left the care of the inn to Timothy and Garrett during the day so he could work in the nearby logging camp, where most of the men from the surrounding villages worked in order to afford the king's heavy taxes. He came home smelling of pine and covered in wood dust. Whenever he and Grayson were in the same room, Jon stared at him, distrust in his suspicious gaze. Thank the fates there was no sign of recognition.

Still, they'd lingered too long. The only reason a patrol hadn't been through here searching for them was because Henri would be focused on the larger cities along well-travelled roads, and Edgewood was little more than a hunting village on the edge of the forest. But it was only a matter of time before soldiers made their way here, or someone in the village visited a larger city and heard about Grayson's desertion.

Unless Henri would try to keep that quiet. Grayson didn't think the king would enjoy sharing the fact that his enforcer had run away.

Mia chewed her lip and glanced to the window, which revealed a sky full of thick gray clouds. The storm last night had lasted for hours, and it looked like they were going to get another one before nightfall. "All right," she finally conceded. "We'll leave tomorrow."

He breathed out in relief. "Thank you."

Her dark eyes pinned him. "We can try to move quickly, but I need you to promise me that you won't push yourself like that again."

"I promise." He truly was feeling much stronger. He took a step toward her. "Let's not tell anyone we plan to leave; we'll pay Jon in the morning, and then go."

A question rose in her eyes, but before she could ask about his motives for secrecy, there was a knock on the door.

Grayson moved to open it, a hand hovering over the hilt of one of his belted daggers.

It was Keegan, the innkeeper's youngest son. The boy grinned up at Grayson. "Hello, Alun. Can I talk to Rena?"

Mia slid beside Grayson, and the smile on her face was soft. "Hello, Keegan. How are you?"

"Good," the boy said at once. "Want to pick the garden with me?"

From further down the hall, Garrett yelled out, "Leave her be and get down here!"

Keegan's shoulders slumped.

Mia stepped forward. "I'd love to."

In an instant, the boy was beaming again.

Grayson frowned. "It's going to be muddy and cold."

"We'll only work until it starts raining again," Keegan said. "Please?"

The innkeeper's sons had obviously taken a liking to Mia; Grayson had discovered that when he'd first woken after his fever. Keegan was always asking her to come with him during his chores, and Garrett—though he echoed the words of his father and older brother about leaving their only guests alone—hung on Mia's every word. Timothy was the oldest, but certainly not immune. Whenever Mia smiled at him, his cheeks pinkened.

Grayson couldn't blame any of them. Mia was special. He'd known that since their first meeting eight years ago.

Mia took Keegan's hand, then looked to Grayson. "Would you like to join us?"

Biting back a sigh, Grayson grabbed their cloaks.

Keegan was back to a full grin. "We'll have to pick a lot of potatoes and onions, because the inn will be full tonight."

"Why?" Mia asked before Grayson could.

Keegan didn't seem to notice the tension in that one word. He just kept leading the way down through the hall and down the stairs. "Whenever a big storm hits during the day, most of the village comes here, since they can't work on their farms or other things."

Garrett was waiting for them in the empty common room with a couple of large bowls in hand, but some of his impatience faded as he caught Keegan's words. "Izac always brings his flute," he said. "There's music, dancing, and sometimes stories."

"Mama used to tell the best stories," Keegan said, his voice quieter than Grayson had ever heard it.

"My mother used to tell great stories, too," Mia shared.

Keegan stared up at her. "Is your mama dead, too?"

"Yes."

"Sorry," Keegan said. His tattered boot scuffed against the floor. "Papa says if we remember her and her stories, she's not really gone."

"I think he's right," Mia said softly.

"I still miss her."

Grayson watched as Mia wrapped her arm around Keegan's narrow shoulders and squeezed. "It's all right to miss her. I think that shows how much you loved her."

Timothy appeared across the room, a stained apron around his waist and a scowl on his face. He paused when he saw Mia hugging his little brother, and any annoyance immediately fled his expression. "I need those vegetables, boys."

"We're going," Garrett said. He stepped forward and clapped Keegan on the shoulder. "I'll race you."

Keegan shot off and Mia chuckled as her arm fell.

"You don't need to help them," Timothy said. "They can do their chores without you."

"It's all right," Mia said. "I enjoy it."

During their stay, she'd taken every opportunity to spend time with the boys, whether it was stacking wood or helping in the garden. She'd even helped Keegan wash dishes after meals. Grayson thought she just enjoyed *doing* something, but perhaps she liked the company, or even just the freedom to experience new things. She'd been robbed of so much during her imprisonment. Half her life she'd been shut away in a cell, and now that she was free, she couldn't seem to take in enough. He'd caught her watching the clouds drift across the sky like it was a captivating painting, and she listened to the morning birdsong like it was a breathtaking symphony. Watching her fascination with the world took his breath away.

Timothy shifted his feet. "Well, all right. Just know that you can tell him no."

Mia nodded and reached for Grayson's hand, walking them both to the back door.

And that's how Grayson found himself kneeling in the mud of a sparse garden, digging up potatoes. In this moment, he didn't think anyone would believe he was the Black Hand, which made him recall what Mia had said last night.

You can be whoever you want to be.

He couldn't really be anything, though. Once they reached Mortise, he would be a prisoner. And—most likely—executed. But Mia would be free. More than that, she would be with Desfan, and fully restored to the life she should have had before she'd been stolen away to Ryden.

Before she'd met him.

We'll be together—that's all that matters.

Fates, she was going to be upset. But how was he supposed to tell her the truth? If she learned about his imminent arrest, she'd probably refuse to go home.

On the ship, he decided. He'd tell her once they were aboard the *Seafire*. She'd be angry, he knew that. But he could handle her anger. He just never wanted her to blame herself. Which is why he'd asked for that promise last night.

I don't want you to torture yourself about things that aren't your fault.

Like his imprisonment in Duvan.

His depressed thoughts matched the dark cloudy sky, but Keegan's chatter filled the silence. He couldn't seem to stop talking about the anticipated party at the inn tonight, and Mia listened with obvious longing as he described it.

"You have to come," Keegan finally said. "Please?"

Mia shook her head. "I'm afraid we—"

"We'll be there," Grayson said.

Mia shot him a look.

Keegan's eyes rounded. "Really?"

Grayson nodded, his eyes on Mia. "I'm feeling much better," he said. That had been their excuse for being so sequestered during their stay. The last thing he wanted to do was be in a crowded room, but Mia clearly wanted to go, and this was something he could give her.

It was also a memory of her that he could take to his cell, or wherever else the fates decided to send him.

Keegan hadn't been exaggerating. That evening, the common room was filled with men, women, and children. Their clothes were damp with the rain they'd encountered on their walk to the inn, and most of the material was worn and faded. But Grayson had never seen any group in Ryden look so . . . alive.

They danced, cheered, and stomped their feet as an old man named Izac played a trilling melody in the corner. They ate the hot onion and potato soup Jon and his sons served, and they talked and laughed with each other. A fire roared in the wide hearth across the room, warming the entire space.

Mia and Grayson sat side-by-side at a corner table. He'd chosen to keep to the shadows on the edge of the room, to avoid attention. No one had recognized him, though. And even if someone was suspicious of the quiet travelers, they were leaving in the morning, so it hardly mattered.

The slight nervousness Mia had visibly carried as they'd made their way into the common room had melted almost immediately, and she hadn't stopped smiling since. The crowd didn't seem to overwhelm her at all. The atmosphere was boisterous and the space was filled with music and laughter. The room was so crowded, they were forced to share a table with a middle-aged couple who sat on the bench across from them. Grayson learned it was the village blacksmith and his wife, whom Mia had met when she'd gone to inspect the horse they had for sale.

Their eyes flickered to Grayson's jaw, taking in the red scarring, but they didn't stare. Mia asked them about their children, four of which danced as Izac played his flute, while the youngest—only a year old—was held in her mother's arms.

Grayson felt a bit like an observer as he watched Mia smile and talk with the blacksmith and his wife. She interacted with others so naturally, and she listened genuinely as they spoke. It was a gift. One he was grateful her imprisonment hadn't driven away.

The flickering candles and lanterns that dotted the room revealed Mia's grin as the music picked up, and she clapped along with the rest of the room when Izac finished his song and told them he needed to warm his fingers by the fire before he played more.

Grayson was torn between watching Mia and staring at everyone else. These same faces he'd spied from the window over the last few days looked completely altered. They were no longer worn-down and wary. They were laughing openly. Even Jon, the innkeeper, smiled. It was a startling change, and it made Grayson wonder just how much life his family had managed to stamp out of an entire kingdom.

Mia leaned closer, her smile soft, but her eyes bright. "Thank you," she whispered.

His lips twitched into an answering smile. "You don't need to thank me." Fates, he was grateful he could give her this—that he could witness her joy.

Mia reached over and threaded her fingers through his.

"A story!" someone called out. "Lyda, tell us a story!"

An older woman with graying hair stood, and a man helped her take a seat on top of one of the tables, so everyone could see her.

Parents called for their children to settle. Since there weren't enough chairs, they sat at their parents' feet.

One of the blacksmith's daughters—a girl of maybe three or four—rubbed her eyes and reached for Mia.

After a quick look to gain the mother's reassurance, Mia lifted the girl onto her lap. The small child instantly sank against Mia's chest, her eyes sliding to catch Grayson's stare.

He didn't know what to do, so he gave her a small smile.

She just blinked up at him, a thumb in her mouth.

"Listen well," Lyda said, her voice a little roughened with age, but still strong enough to fill the room. "I have a special tale to tell tonight."

Keegan—who had edged through the crowd to stand near Mia—let out a low snort. "She always says that."

Timothy, who stood beside his younger brother, gently slapped the back of his head. "Quiet," he muttered.

Keegan rolled his eyes, but he obeyed.

Lyda's gaze wandered the crowd. "Once," she began, "long ago, in a time before kings, the rains stopped coming to Ryden. The drought was terrible and lasted years. Fields dried up, rivers vanished, and the animals died. And as Ryden withered, people cursed the fates, believing they had abandoned this land."

The entire room listened raptly. Grayson himself couldn't look away from the woman as she continued her story. "In a small village very much like ours, there was a young woman named Elena. She was known for her great compassion and kindness, but her heart was heavy as she saw the suffering of those around her. She decided to seek out the fates and ask them why the rains had stopped falling on Ryden. She did not know how to find them or speak to them, for everyone knows the fates listen and watch as they will, and they cannot be commanded. But Elena was determined to help her village. So, armed with little more than a kind and determined heart, she embarked on a quest to find the fates."

Mia shifted on the bench beside Grayson, her shoulder brushing against his arm. Her attention was fixed on Lyda as she held the blacksmith's small daughter on her lap.

"Elena traveled for many weeks," Lyda said. "She asked every stranger she encountered if they knew where the fates dwelled. No one knew, but Elena did not stop her search.

"One day, she came across a young man who stood in the center of a crossroads. He had sharp eyes and dark hair, and when Elena approached him with a smile, those sharp eyes narrowed."

Tension pulled the air in the common room taut.

A thin smile played at Lyda's lips; she knew she had entranced them all. "When Elena drew close to him, she greeted the sharp-eyed man kindly, as she did all strangers.

"In return, he frowned. 'I rarely see travelers these days,' he told her. 'Especially those with cause to smile.'

"'There is always cause to smile,' Elena argued. 'You just have to know where to look.' She studied him a short moment and said, 'You look weary.'

"The young man did not deny this, for he was, indeed, weary.

"'Here,' Elena said. 'Share of my bread and water.'

"Her generous offer surprised him. 'No one has ever shared their food and drink with me,' he said.

"This saddened Elena. 'Everyone should receive kindness,' she said, handing him some of her bread.

"Together, the two strangers sat and began to eat. The young man eyed her curiously, for he had never met anyone like her. 'What is your name?' he asked.

"'Elena,' she answered. 'What is yours?'

"'I have been called many things, but I have never liked any of them.'

"'I will call you Raven,' Elena decided, 'because your hair is as black as a raven's wing.'

"The man liked this name. 'Where are you bound?' he asked.

"'I am on a journey to find the fates,' she told him.

"This seemed to puzzle Raven more than anything else. 'Why?' he asked.

"'I wish to ask them why the rains have stopped.'

"'Many say the fates have forsaken this land,' he said.

"'I cannot believe that to be true,' Elena returned. 'For the sun arrives every morning to chase away the darkness, and as long as that is true, the fates must be watching over us.'

"Raven was intrigued by Elena's answer, though—in truth—he was simply intrigued by her. And it had been a long time since he had been intrigued by anything. 'There is a mountain peak in the north,' he told her. 'It is the highest place in all of Ryden. From there, the fates will surely hear your cry.'

"Elena thanked him gratefully, then asked, 'Will you journey with me?'

"Raven drew back. 'I cannot,' he said. 'I travel alone.'

"'Why?' she asked.

"'Because I always have,' was his simple answer.

"His words brought an ache to Elena's kind heart. 'Change is not to be feared' she told him, 'but embraced.' Then she took his hand, and the moment she touched him, something unexpected happened to Raven. Warmth spread throughout his body, and for the first time in a very long time, he smiled. In an instant—with only one touch—Raven knew he could not bear to be parted from her."

Grayson was wholly absorbed by the story, but something about Raven and Elena's meeting reminded him of when he'd met Mia. They'd been mere children, but he'd been instantly intrigued by her. Fates, it had done something to his very soul to see such innocent beauty, when his life had only been ugliness and pain. The first time he'd touched Mia, he'd known his life would never be the same.

His heart clenched, and he wasn't entirely sure why. A strange dread curled in his gut, a whisper of warning that he may not want to see himself and Mia in this story.

"And so," Lyda continued, "Raven and Elena traveled together for many days, talking and laughing and growing ever closer. Raven had never known such joy, but as their journey continued, he noticed that Elena often grew tired. When he asked if she was well, she insisted she was. But he worried for her.

"Finally, they reached the base of the tallest mountain and began their climb. Elena moved slowly, as if each step cost her greatly. Raven urged her to stop and rest, and she waved aside his concerns. 'We're nearly there,' she said. 'We must save Ryden.'

"And so they continued their arduous hike, until finally they reached the summit.

"The view was beautiful, but Raven had eyes only for Elena. Her skin was ashen, and her footsteps slow. When she stumbled, he caught her.

"Raven cried out her name, but Elena did not answer. Her eyes were closed as if in sleep, and her breaths were shallow—fragile.

"Panic clutched Raven's heart as he held her in his arms. 'Elena?' he cried out. 'Elena!'

"But again, she did not answer."

Grayson's lungs were frozen. He didn't think anyone in the room was breathing.

Lyda's voice went softer. "Raven clutched Elena to his chest so tightly, he felt the moment she exhaled her last breath. And when she stilled in death, Raven's heart broke, and thunder rumbled for the first time in years.

"Raven screamed at the sky, calling on the fates to come to him. And they did come. For you see, Raven was one of the fates. One of his better known names was *Death*."

Gasps sucked the air from the common room. Several exclamations of shock rang out.

Grayson's mouth was utterly dry.

Lyda nodded at the room, looking more like a sage than a mere storyteller. "Death's brothers and sisters stood around him in his grief. His older brother, Life, came closer and touched his shoulder. 'I did not think you would ever befriend a mortal,' he said, 'or I would have warned you. Any who walk with Death will surely die.'

"Death could not stand this. His anger was lightning in the sky, a violence unchecked. 'Bring her back,' he ordered his brother.

"'I cannot,' Life said.

"Death could not accept that. 'Bring her back and I will let her go,' he tried to bargain. 'I will never visit her again, just let her live.'

"But Life shook his head. 'She is already gone. She is no longer in this realm that you and I have dominion over.'

"Tears rolled down Death's face, and rain began to fall all over Ryden. For Death knew his brother's words were true. He was Death, but he had no power beyond the mortal realm. He could not follow her. His Elena was lost to him forever.

"He held her body and he wept, and a fierce storm raged across Ryden. Rain watered the fields and filled the rivers.

"The fates were all moved by their brother's mourning, but

it was Death's sister Balance who knelt beside him. 'I cannot bring her back to you,' Balance said. 'But I can make her death a sacrifice for her mortal kin.'

"And as Balance decreed, so it was done. In that moment, a promise was made to Ryden. Because of Elena's sacrifice, the rain would never again be taken from the land. However, it would always come with the thunder and lightning of Death's heartbreak for the mortal woman he'd loved and lost.

"So, when the rains come and you hear the rumble of thunder and see the flash of lightning, think of the fates who can know grief, and of Elena, the girl who saved Ryden and loved even Death."

Lyda bowed her head, signifying the end of the story.

The room was quiet for a long moment, the only sound the crackle of the fire and the rain that hit the roof. There was a distant roll of thunder, and someone began to clap, the others soon joining in.

Grayson's jaw was tight, his hands fisted on his knees.

"Why are you crying?"

He glanced at the little girl curled on Mia's lap, but she wasn't talking to him. She was looking at Mia, who was brushing a tear from her cheek. Mia smiled gently at the girl, her eyes shining. "I'm crying because that story was beautiful and sad."

Grayson stared at Mia. He saw no beauty in that story. Only tragedy.

Across the room, people called for Izac to start playing again, and the old man did so. The lilting flute music soon overtook the heaviness in the room, and the dancing resumed. Some clapped along with the beat, while others stomped their feet.

Mia gently bounced the little girl in her lap, though she stilled when Keegan tapped her shoulder. "Dance with me?" the young boy asked with a lopsided grin.

"Oh." Mia shot a look at Grayson before she focused back on Keegan's eager face. "I'm afraid I haven't danced in a long time."

Keegan shrugged. "That's all right. I'm not very good at it, either."

Mia's lips twitched. She passed the young girl back to her mother, and then she took Keegan's hand.

The young boy tugged her away from the table, talking all the while. Giving her instructions, Grayson guessed, though he couldn't make out the words over the lively music.

He knew Mia well enough to see she was nervous. Her shoulders were tight and her motions a little stiff at first, but it didn't take long for her to adapt to the rhythm of the dance. And as she danced with Keegan—both of them stumbling occasionally—Mia threw back her head and laughed.

Grayson couldn't take his eyes off her. Her beauty was undeniable, but it went so much deeper than her skin. Everything about Mia was beautiful, and he knew he wasn't the only man in the room to notice her. Garrett soon asked her for a dance, and then Timothy approached and took a turn spinning her in the space between tables.

Grayson had danced with Mia once, when he was twelve and she was eleven. The memory was so strong, perhaps because he'd recalled their dance while he'd been in Mortise. It made him think of the pearl necklace he'd bought at the market in Duvan, when Imara had forced him to accompany her. He wondered if the necklace was still tucked away in the room he'd had in the palace, or if it had been thrown out. He wished he had it with him, so he could give it to her.

He'd probably never have the opportunity to give it to her.

Fates, his mood was as black as that fates-blasted story. And he didn't want it. For once—even just for tonight—he wanted to leave the shadows behind.

He may not have forever with Mia, but he had this moment.

Grayson pushed to his feet and rounded the table. He reached Mia and Timothy just as the song ended, and the room clapped. Mia's flushed face turned toward him and she smiled, her eyes shining as he extended a hand. "Would you dance with me?" he asked.

Mia took his hand, her thumb brushing over his skin. Everyone around them melted away as her brown eyes met his gray ones. "Always," she said.

A new song trilled, filling the room.

Grayson set a hand on her waist, easing her closer.

Her free hand settled on his shoulder with the lightest pressure, but he still felt her touch all the way to his bones. His skin heated, and his fingers tightened around hers. "I should warn you," he said, his tone serious. "My skills haven't improved since the last time we danced."

The corner of her mouth lifted. "You remember that?"

"I remember everything about you."

Her gaze warmed. She lifted her chin and pressed a kiss against his lips. As she drew back, she admitted, "My skills haven't improved, either. But that's all right—we've always found our way together."

She was right. With Mia, he'd always found his way.

Holding onto each other as the music flowed around them, Grayson smiled, and they danced.

CHAPTER 32

GRAYSON

GRAYSON AND MIA WERE REPACKING THEIR BAGS in the gray light of early morning when there was a knock on the door. Grayson opened it, unsurprised to see Jon, the innkeeper. He didn't look half as pleasant as he had during the village party last night.

"I've come for tomorrow's rent," Jon said, just as he did every morning before he left for his shift at the logging camp. His eyes slid over the packs on the bed, and he frowned. "You leaving?"

"Yes." Grayson shifted slightly, putting himself in front of Mia. Shielding her was an instinct he didn't think he'd ever lose.

Jon grunted. "Very well. Your payment is settled, so long as you leave before tonight."

Grayson nodded, still holding the handle on the door. He

was ready to close it, but Jon hadn't backed out yet.

Mia's voice drifted from behind him. "Thank you for giving us a place to stay," she said to the innkeeper. "You've been very kind."

The man blinked, clearly surprised by her words. "You've paid well," he said simply. Then his expression relaxed a little. "And you've treated my boys well. Thank you for that."

"They're good boys," Mia said.

"They are." There was a short pause, then Jon dipped his head. "Safe travels." He turned to go.

"Wait." Mia came to stand beside Grayson, halting him before he could close the door. As if she could feel his sudden tension at having her come closer to Jon, she laid a comforting hand on Grayson's arm. "Jon, you need to keep a close watch over your sons."

The innkeeper's eyes narrowed. "Why?"

"We've heard stories . . ." Mia looked to Grayson, silently asking for his help.

He wouldn't have chosen to take this risk, but now that she'd started, all he could see was Keegan and his brothers being dragged into the king's child-army. He forced his stiff jaw to loosen and focused on Jon. "The king is taking men and boys from their homes. He's training them to be soldiers. Boys even younger than Keegan."

Jon's expression darkened. "Is this rumor, or fact?"

"Fact. I've seen it."

Fear, shock, anger—it all flashed through the man's eyes. "Thank you for the warning," he finally said, his voice a little hoarse.

"Perhaps you could flee Ryden," Mia said.

"As you're doing?" When they didn't answer, he shook his

head. "Even if I had the means, there's nowhere to go. No other kingdom wants us. They—"

Footsteps pounded up the stairs and Timothy skidded into view. "Papa!" he hissed. "Soldiers are riding into town!"

The already tense air became thick.

Jon cursed. "The tax collectors are early. Find your brothers—I'll hide the chest."

Timothy darted off obediently, and his father was right behind him.

Grayson strode to the window, which overlooked the village's main street. In the pre-dawn light, he spotted the horses riding toward the town's center. He counted quickly; fifteen soldiers, but sixteen men.

Tobin, the physician, was riding with them. And as Grayson watched, he lifted an arm to point at the inn.

Fates.

"Mia, get the bags."

She didn't hesitate to shove their items into the packs, all thoughts of organization gone.

Grayson palmed some of his daggers, hurrying to sheathe them. "We'll go out the back," he told her.

"Maybe—"

"They're here for us. Tobin is with them."

Mia's eyes rounded, but she lifted her bag without a word. He shouldered his pack as well, and then he took her hand and tugged her from the room. The stairs led to the common room, which was deserted. Jon was somewhere hiding his gold, and hopefully Timothy had found his brothers.

Grayson could hear the soldiers outside, their voices muffled as the leader called for everyone to dismount. He pushed open the door at the back of the common room and closed it more gently behind them.

The early morning air was cold, the sun not yet peeking over the mountains, though it was close. Long shadows stretched over the yard, and through their joined hands, Grayson felt Mia shiver. The forest was on their left, but a small copse of thick trees was closer, and to their right. He tugged her right, guiding them through the inn's garden, past the logs that were only half chopped, and to the trees at the edge of the yard.

As soon as they reached the shelter of the trees, Grayson crouched behind a large boulder and raised a finger to his lips.

Mia nodded once. Her fear was evident, but so was her trust in him. Her palm braced against the stone that hid them, and they waited.

It didn't take long for soldiers to shove through the back door of the inn, the captain in the lead. They all scanned the yard, and the captain swore. "You men, into the forest. Find them!"

Six men broke off, running toward the edge of the woods—the logical place for Grayson and Mia to have fled.

Despite the still-present danger, Grayson's muscles loosened slightly.

The captain kicked a stone, sending it skittering into the mostly depleted garden. "Bring them out here," he snapped.

The small hairs at the back of Grayson's neck lifted.

Tobin was the first to be shoved into the yard. Right behind him was Jon, who looked thunderous. Too soon, Grayson saw why.

Mia inhaled sharply as Timothy, Garrett, and Keegan were pushed into the yard.

Tobin was pale and wringing his hands. "It's not my fault they're gone. I reported them to you as soon as I realized who they—"

The captain backhanded the physician.

Mia jerked beside Grayson, her breathing strained.

Tobin's shoulders rolled inward, and he kept his head down.

The captain turned to Jon. "Did they say where they were headed?"

"No," the innkeeper said, his voice deep and tight.

"There were no clues?"

"No."

The captain's lip curled, and he cursed again. Grayson didn't blame him; the king would take a personal interest in the men who lost Grayson's trail. The captain glared at Jon. "You harbored fugitives. That's a serious crime."

"Didn't know who they were," Jon said tersely. "They paid. That's all I cared about."

"I don't think the king will see it that way."

The threat hung heavy in the air, strengthening the tension in the yard.

Jon folded his arms across his chest, his shoulders stiff. "You can search their room, but I don't know what else you expect me to do."

The captain straightened. "Bring them all to the street."

The soldiers shoved Tobin, Jon, and the three boys to start moving. Keegan tripped, and Garrett had to steady him. They all disappeared around the corner of the inn.

Mia shot Grayson a frantic look. "What's going to happen to them?" she asked in a bare whisper.

Grayson's gut clenched. The captain was preparing a demonstration. One that wouldn't end well for anyone in the village, but especially not for Jon and his family. He knew this, because he'd been a part of these demonstrations before.

Guilt soured his stomach. Memories flashed, haunting him. But it was the realization that something horrific was about to happen again—to Jon and his family, including the young, talkative Keegan—that stiffened his resolve.

In the past, he'd been trapped. Unable to do anything.

He wasn't trapped now.

Mia gripped his hand. "We can't let them be hurt."

Grayson was already shrugging off his pack and reaching for the Syalla-coated blades inside. "Stay here," he said quietly, belting on the long daggers.

Indecision hovered in her eyes, and for a moment he thought she'd insist on helping. Instead, she pursed her lips and nodded. Trust lined her voice even as she said, "Be careful."

He picked up his longsword, which was still in its scabbard. On impulse, he leaned in and touched his mouth to hers. "I'll be right back."

It was a promise he fully intended to keep.

He felt Mia's eyes on him as he rose and ghosted through the trees, heading into the inn's back yard. As he went, his fingertips brushed over the throwing daggers on his belt. *Four.*

There were nine soldiers in the street, so he would need to make those four blades count.

He paused at the front corner of the inn and peered around the worn wooden planks.

The entire village was being forced into the street. Grayson recognized nearly every face from the inn last night. Izac, without his flute. Lyda the storyteller, clutching her hands in front of her. The blacksmith and his family; the wife held their smallest daughter, who hiccupped on a tired cry. Many in the village still wore their sleep-clothes, obviously forced from their beds.

They would all play witness to whatever the captain had planned. Grayson didn't know if the man intended to actually execute the innkeeper's family, when he no doubt knew Henri was gathering soldiers, but whatever happened, it wouldn't be good.

Grayson's fingers tightened around his sheathed longsword, then he eased back a few steps, glancing at the sky. The light was coming faster now.

He slung the sword over his shoulder so the blade crossed his back, and he hurried to secure the buckle against his chest. It was rudimentary, but it would do. Using the nearest window ledge, he began to scale the side of the inn.

He heard the murmurs of the crowd, and the soldiers barking orders for silence.

When Grayson reached the roof of the two-floor building, the captain's voice rose. "King Henri is searching for the Black Hand, who vanished from the castle the same night Prince Carter was murdered."

Gasps punctuated the air.

Grayson didn't let himself feel anything except the hum of a coming fight. But he did wonder why his father hadn't just blamed him for Carter's death; unless it was a way for Henri to protect himself. He needed Grayson found, but he didn't want everyone to know his enforcer was that out of control.

Grayson kept low on the roof as he crept to the front of the inn, moving as silently as possible.

"The Black Hand is wanted by the king," the captain continued. "He abducted a young Mortisian woman from the king's court. Her name is Mia, and I have been informed that both of them have been staying in this inn for days."

"I reported them as soon as I realized who they were," Tobin burst out, his voice a little higher than usual and pinched with panic. "The small villages never get news quickly, but when I went to—"

Guttural choking replaced his words, and a woman cried out.

Grayson reached the edge of the roof just in time to see Tobin collapse, his hands wrapped around a bleeding throat. As the physician toppled forward, the captain twisted to face Jon, a bloody dagger in his hand.

Jon tensed, but didn't draw back as the captain took a step toward him. "The king doesn't tolerate failure," the captain said, his strong voice projecting down the street. "Nor does he tolerate excuses." He glanced at Jon, taking in the man's clenched fists and thick arms. "You're a strong man. You'll make a decent soldier." He glanced around the gathered crowd. "In fact, most of you will. And the king needs women to cook and care for the army, so this entire village will be marched to Northland Barracks." The captain looked back to Jon. "If you resist, I'll kill your youngest. He'd make a rather pathetic soldier, anyway."

Keegan was pale as he clung to Garrett. Timothy stood near them, vibrating with fury or fear—maybe both.

Jon's eyes narrowed on the captain. "If you think the king will forgive *your* failure by offering us to him instead of the ones he actually wants, I think you'll be disappointed."

The captain glared. "I haven't lost them yet. My men will find their trail."

Jon scoffed. "Do you think six men stand a chance against the Black Hand?"

The captain backhanded Jon, the harsh clap ringing down

the street.

Jon's eyes blazed, but he didn't strike back.

The captain grinned. "It seems you've learned to hold your tongue. Good. You might live to see another dawn."

The first golden light touched the world, warming Grayson's back. He straightened from his low crouch and threw the first dagger.

The blade sank into the captain's back, piercing a lung.

The soldiers shouted and whipped around, but the rising sun was at Grayson's back, blinding them. While they squinted, he threw the next dagger.

The crowd scattered. Screams broke out, a child's wail rising shrilly. Grayson saw Jon leap for his children as a soldier turned his sword on them.

That soldier was Grayson's next target.

"On the roof!" one of the soldiers yelled. "He's on the roof!"

With only one more blade and six soldiers on the ground, Grayson chose the man closest to Timothy. When he fell, Timothy snatched up his fallen sword.

The remaining five soldiers were moving. Two ran to the tethered horses, presumably to get the crossbows Grayson had noticed earlier. The other three men ran inside the inn—probably to find their way onto the roof.

Grayson ran across the roof, feeling the dull throb of each footfall in his jaw. But it wasn't pain so much as discomfort, and he wasn't going to let it stop him. He reached the end of the roof and leaped onto the thick branch of a nearby towering oak. He dropped and swung, his palms sparking with mild pain that he shoved aside. His boots hit the ground hard, but he was already drawing the Syalla blades as he tore after the two guards running for the horses.

The movements of this fight were so practiced, they were fluid. He felt the stretching of his burned, scabbed skin, but it was a relief to move without agony.

The poison-coated blades made this fight end even faster; the soldiers dropped their guard with pained cries as the Syalla entered their blood, and he killed them quickly.

The remaining three soldiers poured out of the inn, long-swords drawn.

Their captain was lying near the steps, his body shaking, that blade still buried in his back. "*Get him*," he hissed.

Grayson sheathed the poisoned daggers and tugged his longsword from its sheath. It came out with a long hiss, and Grayson spun it once as he started forward. "You can run," he told the three uniformed men.

The soldiers chose to attack.

Grayson dodged, parried, and twisted around their three blades. They were locked in a dance that all of them had practiced, but Grayson may as well have invented. He used their moves against them; turned their ingrained motions into openings he could exploit.

He was aware of their audience, watching as the blades whirled. Most of the villagers had fled indoors, but some remained in the street. Jon stood in front of his boys at the corner of the inn, all four of them staring with rounded eyes.

Grayson made the soldiers' deaths as painless as possible. He regretted taking any life, but he'd chosen to protect the people of Edgewood who had unwittingly sheltered him and Mia. He couldn't afford to leave any of the soldiers alive.

He jerked his blade out of the last soldier and surveyed the street. A total of eight men were now dead, felled by his hand. The captain was still breathing, though raggedly. He had one elbow on the lowest step of the inn, and he was looking at Grayson with unmistakable horror.

Grayson didn't drop the captain's gaze as he slid his long-sword across the uniform of one of the dead men, cleaning both sides of the blade before he shoved it back into its sheath. Then he stepped toward the captain, his approach slow and measured.

"They'll find you," the captain rasped, his wide eyes fastened on Grayson. "The king will find you."

Grayson crouched before the man and grasped the handle of the small blade embedded in his back.

The captain tensed with a pained gasp.

"You shouldn't have killed the physician," Grayson said. "He might have been able to help you." He jerked the knife free and the captain cried out, crumpling against the steps. His face was carved with pain, his breaths ragged and shallow. He paled as Grayson leaned in. "Answer my questions, and I'll make your death faster. Where are the patrols searching?"

"E-Everywhere," the captain said, his voice hitching pain-fully. "They're searching everywhere for you. Prince Tyrell leads the effort."

It wasn't an unexpected revelation, considering the fact Tyrell thought himself in love with Mia, but Grayson still didn't like it. "Where do they think I'm headed?" he asked.

"Vyken," the captain rasped. "They think you'll—take a ship to Mortise."

He wanted to curse. If Henri thought he'd take a ship, he might send orders to increase the guard in every port city. He couldn't worry about that right now, though.

Grayson kept his word; he made the man's death as quick as he could. When the captain slumped, Grayson wiped the blade on his uniform and sheathed it.

As he stood, he caught movement from the corner of his eye.

Jon was still staring at him, and so were the boys, but Mia stood with them now, her eyes wide.

His stomach dropped. He hated that she'd seen him kill. That she could see the bodies that littered the ground.

Everything felt horribly still. Frozen. Then Mia ran to him.

He caught her around the waist and she threw her arms around his neck. "Thank you," she said, squeezing him hard. "Thank you for saving them."

Thank you for saving them.

Her words rang in his head, not making sense. Then it hit him: she didn't see the lives he'd taken—only the lives he'd saved.

His arms tightened around her.

Over her shoulder, he watched Jon approach slowly. He didn't wait for the innkeeper to speak. "You should leave here," Grayson said. "Those soldiers won't be searching the forest for long, and anyone still in Edgewood when they return will be in danger."

Jon's throat bobbed as he swallowed. "All right."

That's all he said.

Grayson pulled back from Mia, but she laced her fingers through his, keeping hold of one hand. She faced Jon and the boys. "I'm sorry for the trouble we caused you. We never meant for this to happen."

Keegan peeled away from Garrett and moved to stand before his father. His attention was fastened on Grayson, his eyes holding a mixture of shock and awe. "You're the *Black Hand*?" he gasped, incredulous.

Grayson glanced down at his ungloved, scarred hand. His fingers curled into a tight fist—but only for a moment. His hand loosened, falling open at his side. He wasn't sure *who* he was anymore, but he knew he was no longer his father's puppet.

"He's Grayson," Mia said. So simple. So . . . Mia.

He squeezed her fingers. "We need to go."

"Wait." Jon glanced across the road, looking to the black-smith. "They need a horse."

Grayson shook his head. "We can't afford—"

"You saved us," Jon cut in. "*All* of us." He focused back on the blacksmith. "Get that horse."

The blacksmith hurried toward the stable.

Grayson looked to Jon. "Thank you."

The innkeeper nodded once, then glanced at Timothy. "Grab some food they can take with them."

The young man darted off.

The street was silent. Grayson looked around them, at the villagers who still stared at him.

They didn't stop staring, not even when the blacksmith returned leading a saddled horse, or when Grayson secured their packs, along with the bag Timothy brought out. They all watched as Grayson lifted Mia into the saddle, swung up behind her, and gathered the reins.

With a final nod at Jon, they rode out—the eyes of an entire village following them.

CHAPTER 33

SERENE

THE MOMENT SERENE STEPPED ONTO THE cobbled streets of Zoroya, she breathed a little easier. She hadn't been to Zennor in far too long. It was her mother's homeland, and her uncle's kingdom. Even though her heart belonged to Devendra, Zennor was in her blood.

The trip from Duvan had taken ten days on the *Phoenix*, and they'd just said their farewells to Captain Seveh. They would stay at an inn tonight, and in the morning they'd begin their trek to Kedaah, the capital city of Zennor.

She couldn't wait to meet with her uncle, King Zaire. There was much to discuss.

On their way from the harbor, they spotted a stable. Wilf had disappeared inside to purchase horses, leaving Serene and Cardon to wait on the street.

Mist curled up from the cobblestones, which were slick

427

from a brief downpour that had hammered the port city only half an hour ago. The rains in Zennor were unpredictable this time of year; sporadic, heavy, and frequent. Looking at the churning gray clouds above them, Serene expected another spill of rain before nightfall. Premature darkness was already creeping in over the city, thanks to the thick clouds.

Serene glanced over at Cardon, trying to ignore the flutter in her belly that seemed to always rise whenever she stood close to him. He wasn't touching her, but he might as well have been. The warmth from his body heated her side, even though there was a little space between them. He was on guard, searching the busy street for any threat.

At thirty years old, Cardon had a maturity she admired and a goodness that had always called to her. He had a few gray hairs at his temples—which he blamed on her, of all things—and the strong line of his jaw almost begged for her touch. The thin scar on his cheek curved slightly, adding a ruggedness to his otherwise perfect soldier-like appearance. He was only missing the uniform, since they'd agreed to travel in anonymity.

In truth, she could probably travel as herself and be perfectly safe. Zennor was a relatively safe kingdom anyway, and no one here wanted her dead. Here, she was known as Princess Aren's daughter. The kingdom still mourned their beloved princess, even years after her death.

Three years ago, Serene had come to Zennor to mourn her mother. Her heart had been aching for Cardon as well, who had emphatically rejected her confession of love. She'd arrived at her uncle's home with too much grief to carry, and a widow's braid that she still wore hidden in her hair.

Serene resettled her cloak over her shoulders, and her arm

brushed Cardon's.

He instantly shifted to avoid any further accidental touches.

She bit her lower lip, hating the strained awkwardness that had been between them since leaving Duvan. To be fair, things had been difficult for a while—especially after that night on the beach, when they'd both confessed their feelings for each other. She still dreamed about the kisses they'd shared.

She probably always would.

She wanted to tell him about her conversation with Desfan, but their intention to find a way out of their arranged marriage was a delicate thing. She didn't want to get her hopes up, only to see them shattered. She didn't want to torture Cardon with maybes and wishes. Until things were secure, they would continue as before—a princess and her bodyguard. Friends. Nothing more.

It had been easier in Duvan. Remembering their roles while in the palace surrounded by their obligations was one thing, but traveling in anonymity through Zennor was quite another.

Wilf emerged from the stable and strode over to them. "They'll have three horses ready for us at dawn."

"Excellent," Cardon said, stooping to lift the packs he'd set aside earlier. "We should make our way to the inn Captain Seveh mentioned. We can procure rooms and turn in early so we can leave at first light."

"I'd like to go to a tavern," Serene said.

Cardon and Wilf twisted to look at her. Wilf seemed confused. Cardon looked almost wary.

Fates, he knew her too well.

"Why?" Cardon asked.

Serene lifted one shoulder, trying to appear naturally spontaneous. "I would like to catch up on news in Zennor, and there's no better place for that. Imara shared that things have been strained due to deteriorating relations with the clans, and I want to see if that's still the case."

Before the monarchy existed, there were only rival clans in Zennor. The tribes fought battles for generations before one man had managed to unite most of them. Not all of the clans had wanted a monarchy, so some had continued their nomadic lifestyle. Over the years, those clans often felt slighted by the monarchy, or disliked not having a stronger voice in how Zennor, as a whole, was run. King Zaire had tried to remedy this in the past, with mixed results. Thus, Imara's betrothal to Eilan Skyer, the leader of the Kabu Tribe—the largest and strongest of them all.

If Serene was going to have a chance at convincing her uncle to break Imara's engagement, she needed to better understand the current situation. She also needed to determine how Zennor's people felt about Mortise, if she had a chance of brokering a peace between them. It was an alliance she needed to succeed, not just because it might help end her engagement to Desfan, but also because war with Ryden was inevitable. Eyrinthia needed to unite against Ryden, or the bloodshed would be worse. If Mortise, Zennor, and Devendra could firmly unite, perhaps they could stop a war with Ryden entirely. Surely Henri Kaelin wasn't so foolish as to think he could combat the combined forces of three kingdoms?

Of course, Serene had another reason for wanting to go to a tavern. A specific one, at that.

Cardon frowned. "We can mingle with people at the inn's common room. Won't that suffice?"

She shook her head. "We need to find a place that's guaranteed to be filled with locals, not other travelers. With lots of people and drinks flowing, we're bound to hear more than at an inn."

Cardon looked at Wilf, who shrugged. "I see no harm in it," the large man said.

Serene smiled. "It's decided, then." She snatched up her pack before Cardon could grab it. "We're to look the part of simple travelers, Cardon," she reminded him, shouldering her bag. "I should carry my own things."

His mouth tightened—from the use of his name or her insistence on carrying her own bag, she wasn't sure. They'd decided not to use any titles while they traveled. So, instead of *Sir Brinhurst*, she'd been calling him *Cardon* ever since they boarded the *Phoenix*. He still hadn't adjusted to her casual use of his name; each time she said it, he reacted. And every time, she felt a thrill.

Naturally, she used his name often.

Wilf used his chin to gesture down the street. "I think we passed a tavern back there."

That was not the tavern she needed. She gestured up the street with her free hand. "Let's go this way instead." She started walking, heading deeper into the city.

Cardon and Wilf were quick to follow, and she wasn't really surprised when Cardon stepped around her so he could lead and protect her from the front. "Tell us when you find a tavern you like," he said, a hint of sarcasm in his voice.

Serene only hoped she'd remember where the Fiddler was.

While they walked, she strained to overhear anything that might be useful. Men, women, and children shopped, chatted, worked, and walked together. The topics she heard in their conversations were many and varied. Laments about the price of corn. Complaints about the early rains. Murmurs about the tribes. The last caught Serene's attention, but there was no point in lingering to listen further; it was two women, and they quickly switched to discussing Imara and Skyer's upcoming wedding, with a debate of what customs the couple would incorporate into the marriage ceremony.

They passed several taverns, but none was the Fiddler. Serene could feel Wilf's growing impatience, even though he said nothing. Cardon just kept glancing at her, a furrow between his brows.

The city slowly darkened around them, and Serene was nearly ready to give up and choose a random tavern when, suddenly, there it was.

"That one," she said, pointing.

Cardon studied the outside, probably trying to discern what made the Fiddler stand out for her. It looked as crowded as the others they'd passed, and the same style of pipe music drifted through the open door.

She didn't wait for him to question her. Striding across the street, Serene led the way into the large, crowded great room. Lamps glowed on the assorted tables and along the bar against the back wall. The atmosphere was boisterous and loud.

Perfect.

Serene stepped up to the bar, where a harried-looking bar-keep threw her a glance. "Three ales, please," she requested, aware of Cardon and Wilf pressing in on either side of her.

The man hurried away to fetch the drinks.

Serene sat on one of the tall wooden stools, her hands folded atop the stained bar. She hoped she looked innocent of any conspiring. "Perhaps we should split up," she said, her tone mild. "We'd learn more that way."

Cardon sighed and spoke over her head at Wilf. "I'll stay

with her."

Wilf only grunted.

Serene hadn't expected Cardon to leave her, but it would have made things easier. She needed to talk to the barkeep alone.

Wilf remained standing on her side, clearly waiting for their drinks.

Cardon claimed the stool beside her. "We shouldn't stay long," he said. "I want to reach the inn before full dark."

"No more than an hour," Serene promised.

The barkeep returned with their drinks. While Cardon handed over the requisite coins, she studied the man. The barkeeper was a little younger than she'd expected, but it was possible he wasn't the owner of the Fiddler—and that's who she needed.

Before she had a chance to ask, he darted away to fill another order. She'd have to wait for him to come back.

She lifted her mug and took a sip. The ale was strong, making her cough a little. Wilf and Cardon both looked at her, so she hurried to clear her throat. "It's good," she assured them. "You should try it."

"I don't drink," Cardon said.

"You don't?" she asked, surprised.

He shook his head. "Not really. I'll occasionally buy a drink with the other guards, usually when we're celebrating something, but I never finish it."

Serene stared. Fates, she hadn't known that.

Wilf didn't seem surprised by the revelation. He leaned around her and plucked up Cardon's mug. "No use wasting it," he said.

Concern prickled Serene's skin. She knew Wilf had struggled with drunkenness after losing his wife, and she didn't want him to over-indulge now. But she shouldn't have worried—Wilf was on-duty, whether he was in uniform or not. Lifting both drinks, he nodded across the room. "Those men in the corner seem the drunkest. I'll share some ale and see if they know anything useful."

He slipped away, leaving her with Cardon.

His eyes on her made her feel flushed, so she took another drink, deeper this time. It burned, but it went down easier this time.

"What are we really doing here?" Cardon asked.

The deep cadence of his voice made the fine hairs on her body rise to attention. She couldn't tell him the truth, so she shot him a smile over the rim of her mug. "I'm drinking, Wilf's gaining information, and I imagine you're about to lecture me."

His full lips twitched, though his jaw remained firm. "What exactly am I going to lecture you about?"

"Possibly the risks of being in a crowded, chaotic place like this?" As if to emphasize her point, there was a shout from the corner—two men were arm wrestling, a crowd circling them.

Cardon glanced their way, then settled his gaze back on her. "I wouldn't be wrong."

"Perhaps." She took another swallow of the potent ale. She could feel it swimming in her blood. It heated her body and relaxed her muscles. "I didn't know you don't drink."

He shifted on the stool beside her, and his knee brushed her leg since he was angled toward her. "It's not something that would have come up during our usual interactions."

True. Still, she'd known Cardon since she was thirteen years old. She knew him—his laugh, his smile, his loyalty, his goodness. It was with a pang she realized there were things she'd never asked. They'd had thousands of conversations over the years, but Cardon had always managed to turn the conversation back to her. There was so much she didn't know, and that seemed wrong. She was in love with the man; she should know him better.

Her thumb slid down the handle of the wooden tankard. "Why don't you drink?"

"I won't do anything to limit my ability to protect you."

That sounded like Cardon. However, it wasn't a full answer. Her eyebrows pulled together. "What about when you're not on duty? Or before you became my bodyguard? Have you really never been drunk?"

"No." He paused. Then, "Once."

There was a story there. She wanted to ask, but something in his tone made her hesitate. "I've never been drunk," she admitted. "Imara and I once speculated on what manner of drunks we'd be, though."

Amusement sparked in his eyes. "Why?"

She shrugged. "It was entertaining. We decided Imara would stand on tables and sing. Terribly off-key, of course."

He chuckled. "I think that's a fair guess. And you?"

"Imara thinks I'd become insufferably morose. I think I'd be more likely to lecture everyone in sight." She eyed him over her mug. "What sort of drunk are you?"

He rubbed the back of his neck. "This is a strange conversation."

"You're avoiding the question. Is it because you sing?"

His mouth curved. "Terribly off-key."

She had a hard time looking away from his lips. She busied herself with taking another drink, then cleared her throat. "For a man who doesn't drink, I find it odd that—in the event of my death—you said you'd become a drunk."

Cardon's eyes grew hooded. Clearly, he remembered the conversation they'd had so long ago in Serai Tamar's home. The admission had stunned her then, but it made no sense now.

She bit her lower lip, awaiting his response.

It never came.

Disappointment lodged in her throat, and she was once again struck by the dissonance of knowing him so completely, yet not knowing such simple things about him and his life. She took another pull from the tankard—longer this time—and determination settled in her shoulders. "Where did you grow up?"

Cardon pulled back a little, clearly caught off-guard by the unexpected question. "A small village south of Iden. You wouldn't know it; it doesn't appear on any map."

It was a vague answer, but she wasn't sure how hard to press for more. She took another drink of ale. "You told me once you didn't have any siblings."

"I don't."

"Are your parents still living?"

The scar on his cheek pulled as he frowned. "Why all the questions?"

"I'm just curious about you." She gestured to the ale in front of her. "You don't drink, and I didn't know that."

"And that bothers you?"

"Yes. Not that you don't drink, of course. I'm just bothered that I didn't *know* you don't drink."

His eyes dipped to the ale. "How potent is that?"

She shot him a defensive look. "I'm not drunk."

He lifted one eyebrow. "You're not as eloquent as usual."

Her cheeks warmed. "You think I'm eloquent?"

He sighed and reached for her mug. "I think you've had enough."

She clutched it to her chest. "No I haven't. And you're avoiding my questions."

Cardon rolled his eyes, one arm braced against the bar as he turned toward her. "I don't know if my parents are alive or not."

She hadn't expected *that*. "You don't?"

He shook his head, his eyes fastened on her. "No. I have no idea who my father was, and I have a name for my mother, but not much else. Soon after I was born, she left me with her parents. She never returned."

Her chest squeezed. "Cardon, I . . . I'm sorry."

"It's in the past—it doesn't matter." His tone was even enough, but old pain threaded his words.

"I should have asked you before now," she said quietly. "I'm sorry I never did."

"I would have evaded your questions. I don't like to think about my childhood, let alone talk about it."

It hadn't been good, then.

At the thought, she cursed herself. Of *course* it hadn't been good—he'd never known his father, and he'd been abandoned by his mother. But there was something else there, some other demon that haunted him. She could feel it.

Before she could ask, Wilf returned to the bar and ordered four tankards. While the barkeep left to fetch them, Wilf glanced down at them. "Their tongues are loosening. Apparently, they have some complaints against Buhari and the clans."

"Drunk men like to complain," Cardon murmured.

Wilf nodded, then jutted his chin toward the corner. "You should join the arm wrestling. The men who make a profit betting on you might feel friendly and buy you a drink."

Surprise lit through Serene. "You arm wrestle?" She didn't doubt his strength, but Cardon didn't have a competitive spirit or a gambling nature.

He dipped his chin. "I was one of the best in my barracks when I first joined the army."

"He's stronger than he looks," Wilf grunted. "He's beaten me before."

Serene's eyes rounded.

"You were drunk at the time," Cardon said, waving a dismissive hand.

"True." The drinks Wilf had been waiting for arrived. He lifted all four mugs, two in each fist, then looked to Serene. "If you want to make a few coins, place a bet on him."

As Wilf walked away, Serene twisted on her stool to face Cardon. "I'm learning so much about you tonight. How long have you been a champion arm-wrestler?"

Cardon snorted. "I'm no champion. Although Dirk would often pit me against people so he could make enough to buy the night's drinks at the Arrow."

Hearing Dirk's name made her chest tighten. Fates, she missed him.

Cardon rose from his stool. "Stay close to me."

She stood as well, bringing her half-full tankard with her. Cardon eyed the mug, but didn't say anything.

Still, she asked, "Does my drinking make you uncomfortable?"

"No."

She believed him, yet it was clear something bothered him. "Would you rather I didn't drink?"

He met her gaze. "Drink if you want to. I'll always make sure you're safe."

That promise made her heart squeeze. Attempting to hide that, she took another sip as she followed him through the crowded tavern. They joined the ring of spectators who watched the two men currently arm wrestling at a small table.

Cardon slid partially behind her.

Keeping her voice low, she asked, "Do you really think taking the position of a guard is the best way to avoid attention?"

He shifted to her side with a sigh. "Better?"

His elbow brushed her arm, and she smiled. "Yes."

She was feeling a little heady. Maybe from the ale, or perhaps it was just spending time alone with Cardon.

There was a dull thud against the table. Cheers pierced the room as a victory was made. Some of the men around them grumbled at their loss, and coins changed hands.

The loser at the table demanded an immediate rematch.

Serene watched, sipping carefully from her mug. Now that she was used to the potent brew, she'd decided she liked it. She enjoyed the warmth spreading through her body, though she should be careful—it wouldn't do to *actually* get drunk.

Another fleshy smack as the man's hand hit the table—again. The crowd roared. The hooting of the winner was loud as the loser stalked off. Another man stepped forward to take his place, and bets were called.

"When are you going to join in?" Serene asked.

"Soon," he said, not looking away from the men at the table, his eyes assessing. "I just want to watch them a little longer."

Serene glanced back at the bar. The barkeep was fully absorbed. She'd need to sneak her way back, if she had a hope of delivering her message without Cardon overhearing anything.

Two more rounds were played at the table, and the same man won both. He'd been undefeated for at least four rounds, now.

Serene nodded to the large man. "He's good."

"He's not bad," Cardon allowed.

She was a little surprised by the humble boast in his words. "You might be able to beat him, then?" she teased.

His arched eyebrow was his only reply.

The winner's gaze swept the spectators. "I need another opponent!" he called with a somewhat savage grin. "Who dares to challenge me?"

Serene snatched Cardon's wrist and pulled his arm up. "Here!"

Cardon scowled down at her, even as spectators cried out their approval.

She grinned. "Don't lose. I'm putting a few coins on you."

"Only a few?" He tugged his wrist free. "Stay close." With that final admonishment, he approached the table.

Serene placed her bet, then held her mug with both hands.

Cardon sat at the table with his sleeves pushed up, leaving his forearms bare. His opponent was larger, his arms thicker, but the corded muscle of Cardon's arms could not be ignored. Final bets were made, then the crowd hushed. The air was more expectant than before. Perhaps because Cardon was a stranger—an unknown.

Cardon and his opponent clasped hands, their elbows braced on the table. The man across from Cardon looked eager.

Cardon's expression was calm.

The signal for the match was called, and the clasped hands on the table barely wavered as both men engaged in the fight. Every roped muscle in Cardon's body seemed to tense, though his face remained smooth.

The longer their hands remained locked together, unmoving, the more the crowd began to stir. Muttering turned to cheering.

Cardon's opponent clenched his teeth.

A vein in Cardon's temple lifted, and he truly began to push. The reigning victor's lip curled as he attempted to resist the mounting pressure.

He failed three heartbeats later, when his knuckles slammed against the table. Cardon pulled back, a small, satisfied smile playing about his lips.

Groans and shouts of victory warred in the crowd, and the gathered men and women begged them to go again. Cardon placed his elbow on the table, his hand open and ready.

His opponent took a deep breath, flexing his hand once before he grabbed hold. The rematch lasted slightly longer, but the outcome was the same.

Serene clapped along with the rest, and when Cardon's eyes lifted to find her, she gave him an impressed grin.

More men in the crowd wanted to try their luck against Cardon, and he obligingly stayed at the table.

Serene could have watched him for hours, but he was as distracted as he was going to get; she needed to move.

She eased back, letting the eager crowd press closer to the table and shield her from view. She started back to the bar, catching Wilf's eye as she went. She lifted her mug in silent explanation, though the tankard wasn't empty.

Wilf didn't rise to follow her, but he continued to track her.

At the bar, Serene waved down the barkeeper. She passed him the mug and asked if he owned the tavern. He shook his head. "My father does."

"Is he here?" she asked.

He pointed to the end of the bar, where an older man was eating.

Serene thanked him and the barkeep nodded, already moving to help another patron.

She moved toward the older man, who sat alone, slightly hunched. Serene took the stool beside him. "Why the *Fiddler* and not the *Piper*?" she asked.

His eyes widened slightly, but he answered, "A pipe is fine, but a fiddle is better."

It wasn't the most creative code, but it did the job. Serene lowered her voice. "Do you know me?"

He shook his head slightly. "Just know who must have sent you. And if you have Carrigan's trust, you have mine."

Many people in Devendra might curse Carrigan's name, but in Zennor, many believed he'd fought Newlan to protect their beloved princess—Serene's mother. For Carrigan's attempts to save Aren all those years ago, he had a network of loyal followers in two kingdoms, and he'd turned them over to Serene when she'd decided to rebel against her father. Without him, Serene wouldn't have been able to form her rebellion so quickly or so well.

Long ago, when Clare had asked if Serene thought Carrigan was involved in the rebellion in Devendra, Serene had lied to protect her mentor and ally. She would lie again, in an instant, to guard him. But even though she preferred to keep Carrigan in the shadows, she needed his help. Things in Eyrinthia were too dire, and his help would be invaluable. Despite being a criminal in Devendra, he managed to stay well-connected with the goings-on in all the kingdoms. He was the one who had opened her eyes to the truth about her mother's death. Newlan had poisoned his wife, and Grandeur had found out and done nothing. Carrigan had shown the proof to Serene, but more than that, he had helped her plot her revenge.

"I need you to get a message to Carrigan," Serene told the old man. "Tell him Serene Demoi is in Zennor, on her way to the capital. Tell him to meet her there as soon as he's able."

She could see the moment understanding dawned. The man's eyes flew wide. "Serene?" He sucked in a breath, moisture clouding his eyes. "Fates, you . . . you're as beautiful as your mother. I saw her once—years ago."

Serene's expression softened. "Thank you. Can you get this message to him?"

His crooked spine straightened a bit. "Of course."

"I could also use a contact along my way." She considered briefly. "Have someone meet me in Danjuma." It was about halfway to the capital, so it should give the rebels time to gather a solid report.

"I'll see it done," he said. "There's an inn there owned by a sympathizer. It's on the north edge of the city—the Panther's Den, it's called."

From the corner of the tavern, men cried out in disappointment.

Serene looked over, unsurprised to find Cardon pushing through the ring of spectators. He'd noticed she was missing, and he'd abandoned the game.

His narrowed eyes searched the room for her, ignoring the men behind him who begged him to go back to the table.

"I have to go," Serene told the owner of the Fiddler.

The old man grasped her hand. "Go with the fates, Princess," he whispered fervently. "And may they protect you. Not all is well in Zennor—or Eyrinthia, for that matter."

She frowned. "What's wrong in Zennor? Is it the clans?"

"That's only part of it," he said.

From the corner of her eye, she saw Wilf notice Cardon. He rose and moved toward her, and she knew Cardon would be right behind him.

Serene leaned closer to the man. "What else can you tell me?"

"People are vanishing," he said. "Especially in the north, along the border."

Serene's scalp prickled, thinking of the Devendran refugees that had gone missing near the border. The Ivern River created a natural barrier between Zennor and the other kingdoms, but there were plenty of places for boats to cross. "Do you know where the Devendrans are disappearing?" she asked the man.

The lines on his face grew more wrinkled. "I don't know about any missing Devendrans. I was talking about the missing Zennorians."

"*Zennorians* are vanishing?"

He nodded, still gripping her hand. "Entire households. Men, women, children. No one knows why, but some suspect the clans are killing them, but I've seen clan violence before. They leave smoking ruins, and bodies. This, though . . . this is eerie. Empty houses discovered by neighbors. Some people are abandoning the smaller villages along the jungle's edge. Not safe, they say."

Serene wanted to press for more, but Wilf and Cardon

arrived.

Feeling their tension, she tugged her hand from the older man. "Thank you," she told him with false cheer. "I hope you have a lovely night."

The man's tongue darted over his lips. He viewed the two hulking men and cleared his throat. "You as well."

Serene slid off the stool, and Cardon instantly grasped her elbow. Keeping her close to his side as he pulled her toward the door, he said, "I told you to stay close to me."

"I finished my ale and wanted another. While I was waiting, I thought I'd strike up a conversation."

"You shouldn't have approached him alone," Cardon said tersely. "He could have hurt you."

"He was harmless. And he looked lonely—I thought he might like to talk. And since we came here for information . . ."

Wilf grunted from behind them. "He grabbed your hand."

Cardon's hold on her flexed minutely, but tellingly.

She'd scared both of them.

She sighed. "I was perfectly fine. He said I reminded him of someone. I was never in any danger." As they passed the swollen crowd of spectators around the arm-wrestling table, Serene paused. "I didn't get the last of my winnings."

Cardon tugged her toward the door. "You forfeited them when you walked away—consider it your punishment."

That didn't seem fair, but she decided not to argue. She'd pushed her guards far enough tonight, and she was anxious to know what they'd learned.

She had a sinking feeling that things in Zennor were even worse than she'd thought.

CHAPTER 34

IMARA

IMARA SAT IN HER NEW OFFICE, HER INJURED LEG propped up on the settee that crowded the small room. Light poured in from the sole window, and she could smell the salt on the air. She'd asked Kaz to open the window for her today, though in truth she felt rejuvenated just being in a different space—and having a unique puzzle to solve.

Desfan had told her everything he recalled Vakesh Kazzo saying that day at the asylum. He'd also given her access to all of Vakesh's old reports, though she hadn't learned much about the former spy's last mission. Yet. The notes were all so fascinatingly complicated, even after days spent going through them. The current spymaster had been quite apologetic when asked about the reports. His predecessor had often used inconsistent codes to mark his reports, which made many of them unreadable.

Desfan visited her throughout the day, and even though she rarely had any findings to report, she always looked forward to seeing him. She was extremely grateful to him for giving her this space and this task. Being useful after feeling helpless for so long made her feel much more like herself. It was especially timely, since Clare had left for Dorma and Imara missed her friend. She was glad Clare could step away from Duvan for a while, though. Fates knew she deserved a little reprieve after everything she'd endured.

A knock on the door made Imara's eyes lift from the papers she studied. "Come in," she called.

Kaz opened the door, and Imara was surprised to see Ranon Sifa standing beside him.

Ranon was probably a little younger than Imara's eighteen years. The first time she'd met him, she had been struck by the kindness in his brown eyes. Even though she hadn't interacted much with him during her time in Mortise, she'd instantly liked him. It helped that he'd befriended Grayson.

Ranon followed Kaz into the room, and Imara didn't have the heart to dismiss her guard. He'd been especially protective since Jekem's attack, and since the man was still missing, Imara didn't mind a little extra protectiveness.

"Ranon," Imara greeted with a smile. "This is a surprise."

Ranon stopped a few paces away and bowed deeply. "Princess Imara, I hope I'm not bothering you."

"Not at all. Please, sit."

He took the chair she indicated, which put him directly across from her. His fingers knotted. "I was hoping I could speak with you. About Prince Grayson. I know he was your friend as well, and that you spoke in his defense after the attack. You said he saved you."

"He did. Grayson was forced to help Prince Liam, but in the end, he betrayed his brother and defended us."

Some of the tension in Ranon's shoulders eased. "It's good to hear you say that. I mean, I knew, but . . ." He shook his head. "I've asked the serjan to allow me to see Grayson, but he won't permit it. Have you seen him?"

"Yes." She hadn't seen him *recently*, but Ranon didn't need to know that. "He's well," she added, hoping that was true.

"I'm glad to hear it," Ranon said. "Is there anything we can do for him? My father says he will stand trial, and once he does, he'll be found guilty."

"I'll speak for him," Imara said. "And I think Desfan will as well." As long as Grayson returned with Mia. Imara tilted her head, studying Ranon. "Your loyalty to him is admirable, but . . ."

Ranon cracked a smile. "Surprising?"

She lifted one shoulder. "Grayson has many talents, but making friends isn't exactly one of them."

Ranon chuckled, the sound a little edged. "To be honest, I judged him harshly at first. I didn't want any Rydenic guests in the palace. Ryden . . . well, that kingdom has taken much from my family." He swallowed hard. "It's a grudge my father still carries."

"But you don't?"

"Not in the same way my father does. Do I want justice? Yes. But turning against Grayson—against the chance for the peace he represented—no. I came to the conclusion that future peace was more important than past wrongs."

"You're very wise."

"My father thinks I'm a fool." He sighed. "What can I do to help Grayson?"

"For now, I think we both must simply wait," Imara said. "As difficult as that is."

Ranon didn't look satisfied with her answer, but he also didn't seem surprised. "Very well. But if there's anything I can do, will you tell me?"

"Of course."

With that promise, he stood. "Thank you for your time, Princess." He bowed again and turned for the door.

Before he could walk away, Imara called, "Ranon?" She waited until he looked back at her. "I know Grayson will be grateful to hear of your continued friendship."

Ranon's gaze warmed. He dipped his chin and left.

Before Kaz could close the door, Imara had her next visitor—her cousin, Grandeur. In truth, she was surprised he hadn't sought her out before now. She supposed every reprieve must end eventually.

Grandeur left his bodyguard in the hall, and after a pointed look at Kaz, Imara sighed. "You can leave us, Kaz."

Her guard did not appear thrilled, but he obeyed.

Grandeur eyed her leg as he took the chair Ranon had just vacated. "I meant to visit you sooner, but I must have been given the wrong impression of your injury. I thought you were still bedridden."

"I can move around well enough," she said. It might have been a lie, but with Desfan and Kaz, she managed.

Grandeur inclined his head. "I'm glad to hear it, cousin."

His tone wasn't overly sincere, but at least he wasn't openly mocking. She released a slow breath. "What do you want, Grandeur?"

"I want to know why Serene went to Zennor. She acted against our father's orders, so she'd better have a good reason for it."

Ah, that was the arrogant, demanding Grandeur she knew. "Mortise is on the brink of war with Ryden," she said. "Serene wants to secure my father's help in any coming conflict."

"She's trying to broker a treaty between Mortise and Zennor?" Grandeur snorted. "She has no right to represent either side."

"She's half-Zennorian, and she's Desfan's future wife." She tried to ignore how those words stung her throat.

"She isn't Desfan's wife yet," Grandeur said. "And her first loyalty should always be to Devendra. By excluding Devendra in these talks, she's turning against her own people."

"You know she's not," Imara responded firmly. "Stop making her out to be some kind of traitor. She came to Mortise to marry Desfan—for the good of Devendra. She's protecting all of us by trying to formalize a treaty before war comes." Her head cocked to the side; after a brief debate, she decided to push him. "Perhaps you're just feeling jealous you didn't think of doing it first? You've always been second to her—even in birth."

Grandeur's gaze darkened. "Your hatred of me is misplaced."

"Is it? We've been annoying each other for years."

"That's because you're endlessly irritating."

Imara's eyes narrowed. "What by all the fates happened to you? You and Serene used to be close. Then you became . . . *this*."

"I grew up," Grandeur said. "I learned that life can be cruel, and no one can be truly trusted." He leaned back in his chair, clearly settling in. "We are family, Imara—regardless of our personal feelings. And I came to ask a favor."

She snorted. "You certainly broached the topic with delicacy."

He ignored that. "You have a friendship with Desfan. I would like you to suggest that he give me authority to oversee Salvation. They are Devendran citizens, and I would like to look after them."

"They fled Devendra," Imara pointed out. "And they live on Mortisian soil now."

"Do you think Desfan would be more amenable to me relocating them, then?"

A chill swept down her spine. "You would force all those people back to Devendra?"

"I would help them get back home, yes. It would require a contingent of my guard, naturally, but they could be summoned from the outpost at Lythe quite easily."

"Desfan won't allow you to bring even a fraction of your army into Mortise."

Grandeur's expression hardened. "Blunt as ever, Imara."

"I'm only speaking the truth. Stop wasting your time and Desfan's. He's not going to allow a foreign prince to take over any part of his lands. If that's the only reason you came to Mortise, you might as well leave."

"Oh, I don't see any reason to leave just yet." He folded his arms across his chest. "I'm learning a great deal. For instance, the fact that Ryden seems especially fixated on Mortise. Sending the Rydenic princes here, and learning the details of their attack . . . Perhaps we were too hasty in allying with Mortise and promising the use of our army, in the event of an attack on *our* lands. I think my father would be interested to know about this, and some of the other nuances I've been picking up."

Imara tensed. "The treaty was signed. You can't nullify it now."

"Can't we? Every promise in there is contingent on Serene marrying Desfan, and she's not even here. If she decided not to return . . . well, the treaty could be voided."

She stared at her cousin, trying to guess his game. The fact that he was telling her this told her one thing—Devendra wasn't seriously considering pulling back from their alliance with Mortise. No, he was trying to intimidate her. Scare her. Or—more likely—he expected her to run to Desfan and tell him everything.

He was trying to get Desfan to fear him.

Her voice was soft as she said, "You truly want control of that refugee camp, don't you?"

His eyes went flat. "I don't see how that has anything to do with what I just said."

"Oh, I think it has everything to do with what you just told me." She set her jaw. "Whatever your plans for Salvation are, I can assure you that you won't achieve them. Desfan won't let you. Cleverer men than you have tried to manipulate him, threaten him, or even destroy him, and they haven't succeed-ed."

Grandeur studied her, the air between them tense. "You're a staunch defender of him," he finally said. "I certainly hope your betrothed never finds out. Men from the clans are very possessive, aren't they?"

The corner of Imara's mouth tipped up. "Are you done?"

Grandeur shook his head, but he pushed up from the chair. "Good day, Imara."

She didn't bother to return the same.

Desfan joined her later that afternoon, bringing a light luncheon with him. While they ate, Imara informed him of her morning's visitors. His frown was actually quite impressive as she detailed Grandeur's visit—and she hadn't even told him her cousin's parting words, since they'd been aimed at her.

"I should send extra guards to Salvation," Desfan said. "I don't think he would dare attempt anything, but I would prefer to take precautions anyway."

"I think that's wise. Though, as you say, I don't think he would dare try anything so blatant."

They were all quite locked in this political box; none of them could risk making accusations without proof, but proof was hard to come by.

Desfan popped a purple grape into his mouth and nodded to the papers beside her. "Have you learned anything more about Vakesh?"

She embraced the change in topic eagerly. "There's still a lot to decipher, but I did learn his last mission was in Ryden." She lifted a small piece of parchment and passed it to Desfan.

He took it, and his eyes widened. "This is my father's handwriting."

She nodded. "He wrote it after Vakesh's return." She quieted then, letting him read the words she'd already memorized: *Vakesh Kazzo was found near the Rydenic border. He was badly injured and cannot tell us anything of what he learned in the north.*

When Desfan lowered the page, Imara said, "It's not much more than we already knew, but it at least gave me an idea of where he was." She gestured to the stack of papers. "Some of these were written by the spymaster at the time, and some are notes in Vakesh's hand. His last mission was perhaps a dozen years ago. There's no exact date to go by, but I think that's the timeline. And I think Vakesh had gone to Ryden before—it's implied in the way the spymaster made his reports."

"*Don't let her evil touch us,*" Desfan mused. "That's what Vakesh said to me. He was very focused on a *her.* Do you think he might have been investigating Queen Iris?"

Imara frowned. "I haven't found anything that indicates he ever got as far north as Lenzen, and I haven't seen any mentions of the royal family. According to your current spymaster, they've never succeeded in getting spies deep within Ryden—certainly never in the castle."

Desfan grunted. "I don't suppose he might have crossed the Poison Queen's path at some other place?"

"It's possible, but I doubt it. At least from what I've heard of Iris Kaelin, she rarely leaves the castle."

Desfan passed back his father's note and straightened in his chair. "Well, I can't think of any other *hers* in Ryden that would inspire that level of fear. Vakesh was quite panicked."

"Well, this was years ago—perhaps she moved around more back then." Imara paused, making a brief calculation. "Twelve years ago, Grayson would have been . . . six?" Fates, what would a six-year-old Black Viper have looked like? She had a hard time imagining. "He may not remember anything going on in Ryden at the time," she continued. "But we could always ask him when he gets back."

"Or we could try asking Liam. As the spymaster of Ryden, he might have a better idea."

"He probably would," Imara agreed. "But even still, this all happened a long time ago. It truly might not be relevant anymore. I'll continue to pick through these codes and notes, though."

"Thank you. It's more a matter of curiosity at this point. If I could learn a little more, I might be able to put some of these questions to rest."

"Thank you," she said softly.

Desfan's brow furrowed. "For what?"

She waved at the papers. "For this. For sitting with me the other night and saying exactly the right things, even though I didn't even know what I needed in that moment. Just . . . thank you."

His eyes softened. "You're welcome."

Under his stare, her heartbeat quickened. Needing an excuse to look away from him—even for a moment—she reached for her glass and took a swallow of wine.

"Imara?"

Hearing her name in his deep, rich voice made her belly flutter. She glanced up at him, still holding her glass.

His gaze was direct. "I think we should talk about the kiss we shared."

Her chest constricted. "I don't think that's a good idea."

"I disagree." He leaned forward, his arms braced against his knees. "I was willing to let it rest once, but not anymore."

"Nothing has to change," she said quickly, trying to fend off his words. "We're friends, Desfan."

"I don't kiss my friends."

Warmth flooded her cheeks. "It was hardly a kiss. It was a moment of high emotion, that's all."

"It was a kiss," Desfan argued gently. "And I've been dying to kiss you again."

Imara's heart leapt. But just as quickly, her gut twisted. "We can't," she whispered. "We're both betrothed—"

"Serene wants to end our engagement."

Desfan's words halted her breath; they stilled the very air in the room. "What?" she breathed.

Determination lined his face. "Serene is going to see if there's any political way out of our marriage. With war coming from Ryden and a strong alliance with your father, she and I may not have to marry. If I were free, would you want me?"

She stared at him. Her pulse thudded in her ears, and something in her heart cracked. "Desfan, even if you were free, I wouldn't be. I'm—"

"Imara, I love you."

Her lungs locked. Her heart leapt, even as her stomach dropped.

Desfan Cassian had just told her that he loved her. It was a dream and a nightmare—impossible, extraordinary, perfect—and terrible. He loved her, but she could never be his.

Desfan rubbed the back of his neck, color high on his cheeks. "Fates, I didn't mean to just say it like that—I wasn't planning on saying anything quite yet. I don't want to put you in a difficult position, but . . . I can't keep pretending to ignore what's between us."

She struggled to find her voice; even when she found it, her words came out hoarse. "There is nothing between us—just friendship."

"Imara Buhari, I've been falling in love with you since the moment I first saw you. I think you know that."

Silence permeated the room, the only sound their strained breaths.

Tears stung her eyes, and she begged the fates to have a shred of mercy. If she started crying in front of him, she would die. *Please don't let him see my broken heart.*

Her throat was tight and hot, but she forced it to loosen. "Desfan—"

Raised voices in the hall cut through the closed door. She and Desfan shared a look, and he was quick to stand as the door was pushed open by a harried-looking Mortisian guard.

"Apologies for the interruption, Serjan—Princess." He offered an abbreviated bow to them both. "I'm afraid he was quite insistent about being shown up immediately."

Desfan's brow furrowed. "Who?"

Imara heard a deep voice rise above the others in the hall. Her heartbeat quickened, and shock held her immobile as a tall man strode into the room, ignoring the guards who argued behind him.

His broad shoulders filled out the doorway. His skin was dark and his brown eyes were fastened on her. His head was shaved, and khalmin swirled across his skin in red, black, and silver ink—on the backs of his hands, his bare arms, up his neck, and even on his face. They marked his kills, his station, and his fierce reputation. Not that there was any mistaking who he was.

He stared at her, his jaw set and his tone dark. "Imara."

Her lungs were frozen, but she had enough breath for one word. "Skyer."

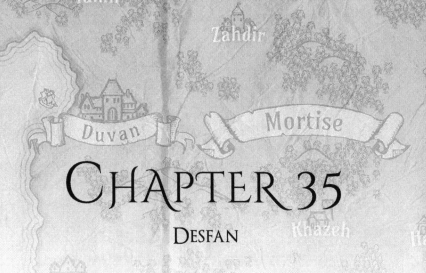

CHAPTER 35

DESFAN

DESFAN STARED AT SKYER. THE ZENNORIAN CLAN leader was larger than Desfan; taller and thicker, with heavily muscled arms inked in swirling designs. His hard expression was locked somewhere between disapproval and menace. His dark piercing eyes turned to Desfan, and the challenge in that stare made Desfan's spine stiffen.

He'd never particularly wanted to meet Imara's betrothed, but he certainly didn't want to meet him unexpectedly—and right after he'd just bared his heart to Imara.

"You are?" Skyer asked shortly. He used the trade language, and for some reason that felt like an insult; as if he didn't think Desfan could speak Zennorian.

Desfan's shoulders went back. "Serjan Desfan Cassian," he said, his voice a little harder than it probably needed to be.

Recognition flared in Skyer's eyes, but his terse expression didn't alter. The intricate lines of ink on his face and skin made him look even harsher, somehow. "Serjan," he greeted firmly. "I do not know your Mortisian customs, but among the clans it is considered rude for a man to be alone with a woman who does not belong to him."

Desfan's hands fisted. Every nerve grated at Skyer's possessive words.

In the corridor, the argument between their guards had settled into an annoyed silence. Desfan could see one of Imara's guards glaring at one of Skyer's men, and one of Desfan's own guards was visibly seething, a hand on his belted dagger.

The agitated guard in the doorway hovered, clearly unsure of how to handle the situation. To be honest, Desfan felt some of that himself. He wanted Skyer thrown out of the palace, but he couldn't do that. Skyer may not have a crown, but he was a powerful man who held a strong position in Zennor. Not just as the Kabu Clan leader, but also as the man who was currently poised to marry into the royal Buhari family. It was the only reason the guards would have allowed Skyer to get this far into the palace; attacking him would have risked issues with Zennor.

That didn't make it easier for Desfan to address the distressed guard caught in the doorway. "Thank you for showing him up. You may wait outside."

The guard dipped his head at once and slipped from the room. He tugged the door closed behind him, sealing Imara, Desfan, and Skyer inside.

Silence strained the air. Imara looked to be in shock, so Desfan asked, "What are you doing here?" His voice was just rude enough that Yahri would have probably hit him over the head with her cane, if she'd been present.

"I have come to fetch my bride." Skyer's attention slid to Imara. "We will go. Now."

Imara shifted on the settee, and for a brief moment Desfan thought she truly would stand and go to him. Instead, she reached for her cane and lifted it demonstratively. "I'm afraid I'm not able to travel just yet."

Skyer's eyes narrowed. "What happened?"

Desfan noted no concern in the man's question—only irritation.

Imara's chin lifted fractionally. "I was injured. Clearly, I'm still recovering."

Skyer's attention slid back to Desfan, censure in the set of his mouth. "You allowed harm to come to her?"

Desfan's spine stiffened.

"It wasn't Desfan's fault," Imara said quickly. She rocked to her feet, leaning heavily on the cane. Standing didn't increase her height all that much—not before Skyer's towering form—but something like challenge flashed in her eyes. "Did my father send you?"

"No. I sent myself." Skyer's gaze lingered on the cane. His lip curled. "You should not have run away."

"I wasn't running," Imara said. "I was visiting my cousin."

"You picked an unfortunate time to do so."

"Why?" Imara asked. "Has something happened?"

Skyer shot a look at Desfan, though his words were directed at Imara. "Perhaps we should speak of these things in private."

Desfan's entire body went rigid at the thought of leaving Imara alone with Skyer. The man was domineering and rude; he didn't seem to even *like* Imara.

"There's no need," Imara said. "Serjan Desfan is a friend."

The skin around Skyer's eyes tightened. "I see."

Desfan didn't falter under the man's piercing stare.

Imara sighed. "Skyer, please. If you have something to tell me about what's happening at home . . ."

The man finally looked away from Desfan so he could focus on the princess. "Tensions have escalated between the clans and the monarchy."

The color drained from Imara's face. "Have there been any attacks?"

"There have been demonstrations," Skyer said. "Some of the clans—not Kabu, of course—have set fires to fields, orchards, and manors. Nothing too violent, yet, but it must end. This can only happen once we are married, so we must return home with all haste. Your father has insisted we marry as soon as possible."

Desfan's stomach plunged.

Imara's expression was horribly smooth as she said, "Very well. But I'm afraid I won't be able to travel just yet."

"How soon?" he demanded.

"I don't know," Imara said. "It could still be a few weeks."

Skyer's scowl deepened, and he muttered a curse in a language Desfan didn't recognize—maybe a clan dialect?

Desfan's jaw ached, he was clenching it so hard.

"The first part of the journey is by ship," Skyer said. "Surely you can manage to sit on a ship just as well as that couch."

Imara stiffened.

Unable to stay silent any longer, Desfan interceded. "Imara needs to remain here until the physician deems her well enough to travel. Surely you don't want to risk endangering the health of your betrothed?"

Skyer's head twisted slowly back to Desfan. There was a long, taut silence. Then, "I would speak to my woman alone,

Serjan. Leave us."

Desfan's chin lowered. "I'm afraid that won't be possible."

Imara sucked in a breath.

Skyer's nostrils flared. "What?"

"Imara has an appointment with the physician now," Desfan lied, latching onto the first thing he could think of. "She can't be late. You'll have to talk later."

Imara didn't refute his claim. The fact that she so readily took the excuse made Desfan feel even more protective of her.

Fates, was her father blind? How could he not see how Imara sank into herself in Skyer's presence? How the domineering man treated her with almost impatient disdain? Or was Zaire Buhari perfectly aware, and simply desperate for the alliance with Skyer and the clans?

Desfan didn't like either option. Because, either way, Zaire Buhari was not a man Desfan could respect. If Desfan had a daughter, there was no fates-blasted way he'd marry her off to a man like Skyer. He would sooner die.

All things considered, Desfan hoped the Zennorian king was simply blind. Because if he was this desperate for peace with the clans, Serene would have a hard time ending this arranged marriage.

And it needed to be ended.

Skyer let out a scathing exhale. "Fine." He looked to Imara. "I will go with you and speak to this physician myself."

"No," Desfan said.

Imara tensed.

Skyer blinked once, then turned his entire body to face Desfan. "*No?*" he repeated, the question spiked with low fury.

Before Desfan could answer the man's clear challenge, Imara spoke. "You must see to settling your men, Skyer. Desfan will help make arrangements for all of you, I'm sure."

Fates, no, Desfan wanted to growl. He didn't want this man in his home. But he knew he had no choice but to provide accommodations.

The one consolation was that Skyer didn't look pleased with how things had turned out, either. Frustration dug lines in his hard expression, but he lifted his chin. "Very well. Imara, we will talk later." He angled toward Desfan. "You and I will talk now."

From the corner of his eye, Desfan could see Imara wince. Obviously *that* hadn't gone as she'd planned.

Desfan met Skyer's gaze and smiled thinly. "I think that's a good idea."

Desfan left Imara in Kaz's care. He hated to leave her at all, but he wanted Skyer away from her. If the cost was keeping Skyer close to him, so be it.

From the moment Skyer had entered that room, Imara had seemed like a shadow of herself. And Desfan hated everything about that. No one should have the power to dim Imara's bright, beautiful spirit.

And anyone who did shouldn't be allowed near her.

Skyer walked at Desfan's side. Two men who looked almost as dangerous as Skyer trailed them, along with Desfan's two guards. Karim hadn't returned yet from visiting his mother at the asylum. He'd gone with his grandfather this morning, so Desfan wasn't surprised things were taking longer. Honestly, it was probably for the best. Karim wasn't as impulsive as Desfan, but he was fiercely protective. He probably wouldn't have remained silent during that scene in Imara's office.

Desfan's own rage still simmered, and it took everything he had not to snap at Skyer and create a political incident. Offending Skyer could alienate Mortise from Zennor; something they couldn't afford to do, with war on the horizon. Not to mention, Serene wouldn't thank him for upsetting things with the clans while she was trying to convince Buhari he didn't need to marry Imara to Skyer.

"Your palace is impressive," Skyer said.

Desfan glanced over at the man walking beside him, caught off-guard by the compliment. "Thank you," he said, a bit grudgingly.

"Your ancestors were strong to build such a fortress," Skyer continued. "Strong lineage is a gift bestowed by the fates, but it is not a gift all men end up honoring."

Desfan was pretty sure there was an insult in there, but he decided to ignore it. "I'm surprised you were admitted. Security measures have been increased."

"One of Imara's guards was in the yard. He spoke for me."

Desfan nearly asked which guard, but he didn't want to draw undue attention. He intended to find out, though. He needed to know if the bodyguard could still be trusted with Imara's safety. If Skyer had recognized the man and forced him to speak for him, that was one thing. If the bodyguard had done so voluntarily, Kaz needed to know.

Every instinct Desfan had screamed that Skyer was a threat to Imara. Maybe some of that was an overreaction on his part, but he trusted his instincts enough to take heed of the warning.

"How many men do you have with you?" Desfan asked. When Skyer shot him a look, he added smoothly, "I need to know how many rooms should be prepared."

"Ten," he said. "I left most of them outside."

As they neared a maid, Desfan gestured her over. The woman eyed Skyer and his men with mild apprehension. "Work with the steward and see that rooms are prepared at once for our Zennorian guests," Desfan said. "Ten guards, one ser." It was a term she would understand. Even though Desfan didn't want to give Skyer any measure of respect, he needed to do at least that much. "Make arrangements in the north wing," he added impulsively. That would put Skyer's room as far as possible from Imara's. "Send someone to join us in the yard as soon as they're ready."

She bowed and hurried off.

"Ser?" Skyer questioned.

"The Zennorian equivalent is *lord*," Desfan said, resuming their course.

Skyer grunted as he fell into step beside him. "I am not a lord. I am a Warrior. I earned my place through skill, not an accident of birth."

This time, the slight to Desfan was obvious. "I thought you claimed ancestry was a gift," he said, a bit wryly.

"Strong ancestry *is* a gift, but it only has true merit if we live up to it. I know far too many Zennorian lords who grow fat and lazy from the exploits of their ancestors. I am not one of them. I will *never* be one of them."

The man was arrogant, condescending, and just about every other negative trait Desfan could think of. Imara had claimed not to know Skyer well, since she'd only met him a handful of times. But it had only taken a brief moment for Desfan to know Skyer all too well. Perhaps Imara's positive nature had tried to convince her there was more to Skyer than his rough exterior.

Desfan was far less optimistic.

"Where is Imara's room?" Skyer asked. "I would know where she sleeps."

He forced his voice to remain even. "I'll arrange for you to receive a full tour of the palace."

"That will suffice. Now, tell me how she was injured."

Desfan did so, trying not to reveal too many details. He didn't have a strong reason to keep Skyer in the dark, other than he didn't like the man, but that seemed reason enough not to inform him of all that had been happening in Duvan recently.

When he finished, one dark eyebrow arched. "She saved your life?"

It was not the detail he'd expected Skyer to fixate on. "Yes, she did."

The man barked a short laugh. "She's a tiny thing. Admitting she protected you in battle is not something a member of the clans would ever do."

"I'm not of the clans," Desfan returned thinly. "I'm Mortisian, and I believe in honesty. Imara is brave and fierce."

Skyer laughed again. "Words I would not use to describe her, but perhaps I have yet to know her fully. Maybe one day she will show me her bravery and protect me so fiercely." He snorted, clearly discounting the idea.

Desfan stopped walking.

Skyer made it another two steps before he realized Desfan had halted. He twisted, his brows lifting. "Is something amiss?" he asked.

Desfan's jaw worked. "You will not disrespect her again."

"I do not disrespect her," Skyer said easily. "I only speak the truth. And even if I *did* show her disrespect, I do not see how it is your concern. She is mine. Not yours."

Desfan could almost feel the tension among the four guards playing witness to this, but they didn't have his focus—Skyer did. "She is not yours yet," he said slowly.

Skyer smirked. "She is my betrothed."

"And she is also my friend, a princess of Zennor, and an honored guest of Mortise."

"Perhaps. But we will marry as soon as we return to Zennor, and then the only title she need concern herself with is *wife*."

Desfan's skin felt too tight. He had a thousand scathing responses, and one emphatic denial. But for now, he kept his voice level as he said, "For as long as you stay in my palace, you will treat her with respect. Is that clear?"

Skyer's eyes were inscrutable, though the corner of his mouth remained slightly quirked. "Extremely clear, Serjan. In fact, I think I begin to see everything clearly."

Desfan met the man's stare easily. Frankly, he didn't care what Skyer saw in him, or if he assumed Desfan had feelings for Imara. He may not be able to make those feelings public, but he wasn't about to tell Skyer they didn't exist. "Good," he said, keeping his reply simple.

Still wearing that aggravating smirk, Skyer huffed shortly; it conveyed a strange mix of irritation and humor. "As long as we understand each other, Serjan. That is all that matters."

CHAPTER 36

IMARA

IMARA'S HEART POUNDED AND HER EARS ROARED as she stood outside the dining room. Sweat coated her palms, making her cane harder to grip.

Every hour since Skyer's arrival earlier today had almost felt unreal. Panic threaded through her, and her thoughts jumbled. His appearance had been so unexpected. And, fates, she'd forgotten how overwhelming he was. He walked into a space and demanded control of it. Watching Desfan's reactions to Skyer had only aggravated her mounting dread.

She wanted to scream. She wanted to run. She'd done both of those things once, but she couldn't do them again. Zennor needed her. She had to be strong. She would not run from Skyer again.

She *did* let Desfan lie for her, though. When he'd said she had an appointment with the physician, she hadn't countered

469

him. She'd let Desfan and Skyer walk away together, and she'd remained in her office and fought to calm her ragged breaths.

When her hands finally stopped shaking, she'd called for Kaz to take her to her room. She'd kept expecting Skyer to come barging in, but he hadn't. Hanna helped dress her for dinner, and still Imara expected Skyer to appear.

He had not.

So, she had Kaz escort her to dinner.

It was a large affair, as it always was in Mortise. The council members were all there, along with many of their family members and any other visiting nobles. Music drifted from the corner as a lute was strummed, and conversation rumbled in the great stone room. The meal smelled delicious, but Imara's curdling stomach rebelled against the very notion of food.

Skyer wasn't in the room. Somehow, that was worse than seeing him again. It prolonged the dread, and made her worry about where he was.

Desfan was seated at the head of the table. His expression was tighter than usual, and his eyes narrowed when he spotted her in the doorway.

Using the cane he'd given her, Imara limped rather ungracefully to the nearest empty chair. The fates might have been with her after all, since it placed her safely between Serai Yahri and Razan.

Glancing up the table, she wasn't surprised to see Desfan still staring at her. She couldn't read his hard expression.

Imara Buhari, I've been falling in love with you since the moment I first saw you. I think you know that.

His words echoed in her mind, making her skin feel too hot. She reached for her glass of wine.

"How is the cane?" Yahri asked.

Imara was used to the woman's brusque manner by now, so the sudden question hardly surprised her. "It's lovely. My skills with it, however, could use some polish."

Yahri cracked a smile. "The skill comes with practice. You'll probably master the art just in time to no longer need it."

If that day ever comes. Imara tried to banish the negative thought as she took a sip of the red wine. Flavor exploded on her tongue. It was Zennorian, which provided a much needed taste of home. It gave her strength, and helped steady her nerves.

Yahri's voice lowered. "Desfan has informed me of our newest guest. He has asked me to appoint someone to give Warrior Sky Painter a tour of the palace."

"I'm sure Skyer will appreciate that." Just as he'd appreciate the use of his formal title, if he'd been around to hear it.

"I plan to give the tour myself," Yahri said. "My old bones may need to stop and rest frequently, but I think I'm the one best equipped to give him a most *thorough* tour." Her lips twitched. "It will last hours—potentially the greater part of the day."

Imara's throat tightened as she realized what Yahri was offering her. She was going to keep Skyer from her tomorrow, for as long as she possibly could. Gratitude sparked in her chest, but reality descended. "You don't have to do that," she said softly. The man was going to be her husband, after all—she couldn't avoid him forever.

"I know," Yahri said simply. "But I will."

Extremely touched, Imara set a hand against Yahri's rather bony one. "Thank you."

Yahri tipped her head and returned to her meal.

Imara glanced at Razan, who sat on her left. She was a little surprised the woman hadn't joined in their quiet conversation, but it was obvious Razan was distracted. And upset. Her knife flashed sharply as she cut her fish with more force than necessary.

Habit had Imara looking for Karim, and—yes, he looked angry, too. Standing behind Desfan's chair, his hands behind his back, Karim's dark gaze was on Razan.

Imara sighed. "Dare I ask?"

Razan stopped sawing at her fish, her knife and fork still clutched in her hands as she looked to Imara. "What?" the councilwoman asked, clearly distracted.

Imara nodded toward the head of the table. "Karim's grinding his teeth; you're abusing your dinner. Dare I ask what's happened between you?"

Razan's lips pressed firmly together, her eyes flickering to Karim. Then she lowered her utensils and twisted slightly to face Imara. Her voice was extremely low. "I sometimes think I hate him."

"I thought things were improving between you."

Razan snorted, but there was pain in the sound. "I thought things were better, too. Then, without warning—when I think the fates-blasted man might actually kiss me—he throws all my past mistakes in my face and storms away."

Imara couldn't keep from looking to Karim, and she startled when she locked gazes with him. He stared at her with intensity, but that earlier darkness was gone.

"What does he want from me?" Razan breathed, even quieter than before.

Imara didn't have an answer. "Men are complicated," she said.

Razan huffed. "And stupid."

"Yes," Imara agreed at once. "Definitely stupid."

A sudden chill scraped down her spine, painful and unnerving. She looked over her shoulder and spotted Skyer. He prowled into the room, like a panther scanning a clearing for weaknesses. He found her and stared.

Her breath seized in her lungs. She prayed he wouldn't make a scene. That he wouldn't demand she move and sit beside him—

Grandeur stepped up to Skyer, extending a hand as he no doubt offered an introduction. Imara couldn't hear her cousin's words over all the other sounds in the room, but it was an obvious deduction. While Grandeur had never met Skyer, whispers carried gossip quickly through the palace. No doubt everyone knew who Skyer was. His presence was large, and the khalmin markings on his body were unique.

Skyer shook Grandeur's hand, his face too stone-like to read. After a brief conversation, Grandeur gestured for Skyer to join him at the other end of the table, near Sers Sifa and Anoush and their sons—Ranon and Arav.

After Skyer joined Grandeur, Imara relaxed a little.

Razan noticed. The skin around her eyes tightened as she viewed Skyer. "Your betrothed, I presume?"

"Yes."

"He seems . . ." Her voice drifted, struggling to find any appropriate word.

Imara sighed. "Yes. He is that."

Razan frowned. "Are you safe with him?"

"Of course." She managed to sound wholly confident, when inside, some deep part of her trembled. Skyer had never hurt her, though—and he never would. He wanted this alliance far too badly to risk her father's wrath. He was rude. Overbearing. Dominant in a way that made her spine stiffen. But he would not dare harm her.

Razan set a hand on Imara's arm. "Princess, I know you and I haven't had a chance to truly become friends, but if you ever need anything, please don't hesitate to ask."

For the second time at this table, Imara struggled to keep her emotions in check. "Thank you," she said. "I truly appreciate that."

The meal continued. Imara managed to eat a little, but it wasn't long before she excused herself. Skyer's plate was still quite full, since he'd just loaded it with more rice and fish, but that wasn't the reason she hurried out now. No, she wasn't running. She was just tired.

She almost believed her own lie.

She half expected Desfan to follow her, but he was locked in conversation with one of the council members. Maybe she'd planned that, too; she didn't think she could summon up the energy for a conversation with him right now. It didn't matter what he wanted to discuss—Skyer, or his admission of love. Both were topics Imara ardently wished to avoid.

She made it to her room with Kaz helping her along, and when he wished her goodnight and closed the door, some of the tension in her body drained.

She called for Hanna, but she hadn't made it to her bedroom before there was a loud knock on her door.

The hairs on the back of her neck lifted. She knew who it was.

Twisting back to face the door, she gripped her cane in both hands and raised her chin. It was a gesture Serene used to convey strength, and fates knew she needed that. This conversation needed to go differently than their last one. He had caught her off guard before, but she was Imara Buhari. She was no quaking woman.

"Enter."

Kaz prodded open the door, and Skyer stalked in. "We must speak," he said without preamble. "Privately."

Imara nodded once. "We should."

Kaz's mouth was a tight line, but he obeyed her silent command and closed the door—keeping himself in the corridor. Hanna also retreated back into the bedroom she'd just emerged from.

Imara faced Skyer, both of them standing on opposite ends of the large braided rug that dominated the sitting room.

Skyer broke the short silence. "You can walk."

"Not well. And not for long distances."

"I will speak with your physician tomorrow," he declared. "I want to know how soon we might leave."

"I'll introduce you to him." It was easier than arguing, and what was the point? She needed to go home, even if she didn't want to. "Do you have any messages from my father?"

"No formal ones." He strode toward her, stopping only two paces away. His gaze was direct. She barely knew the man, but she knew that about him. "He was disappointed that you left. Hurt. Embarrassed."

Shame cut her. She tried to shove that aside. "He will forgive me."

"Will he?" Skyer's voice lowered. "Imara, you have no idea what's been happening in Zennor. The demonstrations I mentioned earlier are only a small part. Our people feel the tension. Your father feels it even more than most. His health is declining."

Shock jolted her. Zaire Buhari was a giant. The strongest man she knew. "My father is ill?" she asked.

"He eats little and sleeps rarely. This I am told by your mother, as your father would not admit weakness."

No, he wouldn't. Imara's shoulders sagged, and she leaned more heavily on her cane. "I didn't mean to hurt him."

"You were selfish," Skyer said. There was no true insult in his tone—only fact. "This will be remedied when you return and do as you promised." He turned from her and sat on the center of the settee. His long arms stretched over the back, nearly covering the whole thing. Relaxed in a reclining sprawl, he studied her. "Tell me of your cousin, Prince Grandeur."

The question surprised her. She shifted her weight with the cane, trying not to reveal the building strain of simply staying upright. "I'm not sure what you'd like to know. He's the crown prince of Devendra, and we're not close."

"Why?"

Imara sighed. "We don't have a good relationship, that's all."

"Hm."

Imara's good leg shook. She limped toward the nearest chair, but Skyer's words halted her. "Sit beside me."

"I would prefer to sit in the chair."

"And I would prefer it if you'd sit beside me." Skyer smirked. "Stand or sit with me, Imara—it is your choice."

He was trying to exert power over her. He wanted her to cave and sit beside him. Or perhaps he thought she'd try to sit elsewhere, and he could have grounds—however weak—to accuse her of disobedience. Disrespecting him was something she couldn't overtly risk; he could hold that against her and her father.

The one thing Skyer didn't expect was for her to stand her

ground.

Her hold on the cane tightened, and she remained standing. "Grandeur may not look physically impressive to you, but he has teeth. You should be careful."

"You worry for me?" Skyer asked.

She ignored that. "That's all I can say about Grandeur. The rest you would no doubt find boring. Childhood spats."

He tipped his bald head, the muscles along his dark arms flexing as he shifted into a deeper recline. "Tell me about Desfan."

Warmth infused her cheeks, and she prayed Skyer wouldn't notice in the flickering lamplight. "He is a new ruler, but a strong one."

"He is your friend."

"Yes."

"More than a friend?"

Her throat cinched. "No. Of course not. He is engaged to marry Serene, and I you."

"Yes. But that does not always stop a man from dallying." He glanced at her cane, which trembled a little. "Are you sure you would not rather sit beside me?"

"I would rather go to bed. It's been a long day."

"Soon," he said. "I have a few other questions. I heard of Prince Liam and Prince Grayson's attack during the treaty signing. Are they still in prison?"

"Yes." There was no way she would share Grayson's mission to Ryden with Skyer.

Something flashed in Skyer's eyes, gone too quickly for Imara to interpret. "What can you tell me about the Rydenic princes?" he asked.

She truly didn't know what he wanted to hear. She kept to

basic facts, answering shortly any of his additional questions.

Her injured knee was screaming. Her good leg was quivering, desperate for relief after taking her weight for so long. Sweat beaded along her spine. "I would like to retire," she said firmly.

"Not yet." Skyer's arms dropped from the back of the settee as he leaned forward, his eyes fixed on her. "If we are to be stuck here for weeks, I would know everything that has been happening in Mortise. If I learn that you left anything out, I will not be pleased."

"Can't we speak in the morning, Skyer? I'm tired." Impatience infiltrated her words, hardening her tone.

"No. This is important. I wanted to speak earlier today, but you were unable to accommodate me. Now, you will."

Her teeth clenched. Challenge flared in his dark eyes—a challenge she would meet, fates blast it. "Very well," she said, grinding her teeth.

Skyer's head dipped. "Good. But before you do, I have one more request. As my future wife, you will call me *Eilan* from now on."

Her skin prickled at that, but she had no good reason to deny him.

We need this alliance, her father had told her, desperation in every word. *Please, Imara. Please . . .*

Imara swallowed thickly. "Of course, Eilan."

Skyer's lips curved. "Very good, Imara. Now, tell me everything."

Sitting in her office the next day, Imara's entire body ached. Her legs were so stiff she had difficulty moving around, even with her cane.

She didn't know how long she'd stood facing Skyer last night. An hour? Two? Hanna had peeked in on them three times, and each time Skyer had waved her back.

Pure, stubborn pride had kept Imara standing. That was all. And it had snapped the moment he'd strode from the room. As soon as the door clicked shut behind him, she'd collapsed on the colorful rug.

She told Hanna and Kaz that she'd tripped, but they knew it was a lie. She could see it in their faces.

She'd been drenched in sweat, and her muscles spasmed painfully as they'd helped her to her bed. Her muscles still twitched, even now, taut and strained beneath her skin.

Hanna had suggested she stay in the suite today, but Imara couldn't tolerate the prospect of staying in bed, and she refused to sit on that settee—or look at it. So, Kaz had carried her to her office first thing this morning.

The old spymaster's notes were sitting beside her, but she didn't have the energy to pursue the puzzle that had absorbed her so much only yesterday.

A light rap on the door gave her only a brief moment to straighten her shoulders before Desfan walked in. His expression was oddly cautious. "Good morning," he said.

"Good morning." A flutter in her stomach made her breath hitch.

He closed the door and crossed to the chair he'd occupied yesterday. "I went to your suite. I was surprised you weren't there."

They'd established a routine; he always walked with her or

carried her to her office each morning before going to his.

"I didn't sleep well," she said. "I was anxious to get an early start."

His eyes grew more serious. "Are you sure you weren't avoiding me?"

That's precisely what she'd been doing. She wasn't going to admit it, though. "Of course not."

He didn't look like he believed her.

Imara picked at her turquoise skirt, before smoothing it over her knee. "I heard Yahri is giving Skyer a tour of the palace today."

"Yes," he said, his tone a little too even. "It should take them a good long while."

She peeked up at him. "You don't need to protect me from Skyer."

Desfan stiffened slightly. "I don't like him."

A half-laugh escaped her. "He's not the most likable person. At least not at first. He has a . . . strong personality."

A furrow grew between his brows. "I didn't like how he spoke to you. Is it always that way with him?"

"No." The first time she'd met him, he'd barely spoken to her at all, choosing instead to speak with her father. She sighed. "He was irritated. Rightly so, considering I *did* sort of run away from him when I left home. And he's frustrated by my injury, because that delays things. I'm frustrated too, as you know. I'm anxious to return home."

Something flickered in Desfan's eyes. An emotion she couldn't name. "You didn't seem comfortable with him," he finally said. "At all."

"He caught me off guard, that's all. I assure you, I can handle Skyer."

Desfan frowned. "Imara—"

The door opened without warning and Karim pushed in, followed closely by Razan.

The relief Imara felt at the interruption was probably wrong. But if Desfan had spoken of what he'd said yesterday—of things that could never be between them—it would only torture them both.

Karim's expression was severe. "Sorry for interrupting. Des, this is urgent."

Razan sent Imara a small, apologetic smile before she handed Desfan a folded note. "This was delivered to me this morning."

Desfan flipped it open and scanned the message.

Curiosity pulled at Imara. Before she could ask what the note said, Desfan finished reading and passed it to her.

She was careful not to let their fingers brush as she took it.

"I assume you read it?" Desfan asked Karim.

"Yes," the bodyguard said tightly.

Imara scanned the scrawled words.

Give this message to the serjan at once. Tonight, I will meet with the serjan, his bodyguard, and you. No one else must come. At midnight, find me in the market district, in the northernmost alley. You must come. Please.

—Fang

She glanced up. "I feel like I know the name, but . . . who is Fang, exactly?"

She got three simultaneous responses.

"An old acquaintance," Desfan said.

"A drug master," Karim huffed.

"A criminal." Razan blinked at Karim. "Look at that. We agreed on something."

His expression hardened.

Imara handed the note back to Desfan. "Why would he send this message to Razan and not you?"

"I don't know." Desfan studied the note again. "Fang might know we're friends, and that Razan could reach me easily when he obviously couldn't—my messages are closely monitored these days. But he clearly wants Razan at the meeting, so there may be an ulterior motive for involving her."

"Which is not an issue," Karim said, "because there will *be* no meeting."

"But—"

"No," Karim said, cutting Desfan off. "The last time you sought Fang out, he abducted us for ransom."

Razan's eyes widened.

A memory rose in Imara's mind; Desfan had told her about Fang when he'd told her about the olcain issues Duvan had recently faced. If she remembered correctly, Fang had vanished after failing to ransom Desfan and Karim. Why would he be reaching out now?

"True," Desfan said to Karim, his response pulling Imara back into the conversation at hand. "But in all fairness, we *did* show up uninvited." He lifted the note. "He's asking for us this time. He even said *please.*"

"How exactly does him luring us to an alley in the middle of the night make things better?" Karim demanded.

Desfan shrugged. "It's different, at least."

Karim muttered something under his breath.

Imara frowned. "If Fang knows you won't trust him, why did

he sign the note? Wouldn't you be more likely to show up if you didn't know who sent it?"

"That's a good point," Desfan murmured, his gaze thoughtful. "If he meant me harm, he probably would have left his name out of it."

"Maybe he's an idiot," Karim said. "Or arrogant enough that he doesn't think he'll get caught."

Desfan shook his head slightly. "He successfully vanished from our attention after the failed ransom. Why show himself now? He must have a reason. A strong enough one to risk revealing his name, and calling a meeting with me. Not just that, but he's chosen a place outside his usual domains—not his warehouses or the Red Cobra, his favorite haunt."

"Fang can't be trusted," Karim said shortly. "He's proven that. He probably sent this note thinking he can lure you out by exploiting your insatiable curiosity. It's a trap, and it's too dangerous for you to go."

"He's right, Desfan," Razan said. "You can't risk going to this meeting." Her shoulders went back. "But I can."

Karim's face went red. He spun on her. "Absolutely not."

She folded her arms across her chest, her expression mild. "I don't know this Fang, other than by reputation. I'm curious as to why he wants to meet me."

"Fates blast it," Karim growled. "You're not going."

"You have no right to dictate to me," Razan shot back, suddenly less calm. "You've made that perfectly clear the last few days."

Karim's eyes narrowed. "You're not going. That's the end of this discussion."

"It's really not," Desfan said. "I'm serjan. And I say the three of us are going—with guards nearby to assist, if the need arises."

Karim threw his hands in the air. "You're both reckless idiots!" He twisted toward Imara. "You can't think it's a good idea."

She winced. "It's not a *terrible* idea."

Karim cursed again.

Fates, she'd never heard him swear this much.

"Karim," Desfan said, almost gently. "How else are we going to learn what Fang wants? He sounds desperate. He may have some vital warning for us."

Karim did not appear swayed.

Desfan sighed. "You know we're going. Just accept it."

The bodyguard's eyes narrowed. "You are the fates-blasted serjan. If you were in my place, what would you advise?"

"I would remind you of the facts—that as serjan, it's your duty to protect your people." Desfan lifted a hand, stalling Karim's response. "And I would also advise you to be careful—which I will be." The corner of his mouth lifted. "That's why I'm taking you."

Once again, Karim swore.

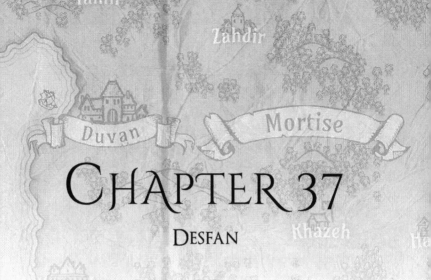

CHAPTER 37

DESFAN

KARIM REFUSED TO STEP INTO THE ALLEY BEFORE Fang arrived, so they waited inside an empty candle shop just down the street. Men were on the roofs of all the surrounding buildings, as well as waiting near the alley. They'd been in place for hours, at Karim's insistence, just in case Fang tried to come early and set his own trap.

Karim still wasn't thrilled they were here, though Desfan had stopped trying to convince him to see the benefits. After all, it *was* Karim's job to focus on the risks.

As for his own part, he was eager for this. Adrenaline hummed through his veins, awakening his reckless side that hadn't stretched its wings in far too long. Ever since Skyer's arrival yesterday, he'd been burning with the need to *do* something. A midnight meeting with a drug master was safer than indulging the impulse to punch Skyer in his smirking face—or kiss Imara again, which would definitely be a mistake.

Fates, he hated feeling helpless. And that's exactly how he felt when it came to Skyer. He hadn't even been able to get upset at Imara's bodyguard for identifying Skyer at the palace gates, because the man hadn't had a choice; Skyer had recognized him and demanded the bodyguard identify him to the Mortisian guards.

At least Desfan was reassured that Imara's remaining bodyguards were loyal to her; her guard had looked miserable when Desfan had questioned him, and Kaz—who had been standing nearby—looked just as distressed about Skyer's sudden appearance. It made Desfan wonder once again why King Zaire would arrange such a marriage for his daughter—Skyer was immediately and thoroughly distasteful.

He needed to stop thinking about Skyer. It was only making his tension rise, and there was nothing he could do at this point but wait and pray Serene succeeded in nullifying Imara's betrothal.

Forcing his attention to the present, Desfan glanced around the darkened shop they stood in. Candles of all shapes and sizes covered the counters in the room, the smell of wax and various spicy scents filling his nose.

Razan was wrapped in a light-weight cloak with the hood pushed back. Her dark hair was in a long braid that trailed over one shoulder, and she was pointedly not looking at Karim. Desfan assumed they'd had a private fight before coming here, because their walk to this part of town had been unbearably strained.

They stood near the window, so they could get the benefits of the meager moonlight. This close to midnight, the streets were nearly empty, but for a few skirting shadows that darted along their way.

"Do you have daggers?" Karim asked Razan, his voice stiff.

"Yes," she said curtly.

He made a low sound in his throat. "Now, if only you knew how to use them."

Her eyes narrowed.

Desfan barely held in a sigh. "Maybe we should—"

"Tomorrow morning," Razan bit out at Karim. "Training grounds. You and me."

"Fine," he snapped. "Your arrogance could use some diminishing."

Color burned her cheeks. By the way her spine straightened, Desfan knew it was with anger, not embarrassment. "You have *no* idea what I've learned since we were sixteen," she hissed. "You don't know me anymore, Karim."

He laughed, the sound dark and hard. "I didn't know you even *when* we were sixteen."

Razan's teeth clenched. "You are such a *srik*."

Desfan's eyes flew wide. "Let's not—"

"Call me anything you want, if it will make you feel better," Karim cut over Desfan, his gaze sharp on Razan. "Everything is always about you, after all."

"I think this conversation should wait," Desfan said quickly. "Perhaps after—"

"No," Razan said, her eyes flashing. "I think this is the perfect time. Karim's annoyed, so he's more likely to actually speak his mind."

"What's that supposed to mean?" Karim demanded.

"It means you only communicate when we're fighting—the rest of the time you hold it all in and just glare and grunt!"

Desfan rubbed a hand across his brow. "I suppose this *is*

happening now."

He was ignored as his friends continued to glare at each other.

"Fates," Karim swore. "You are the most aggravating woman in Eyrinthia."

"As if you're not the most aggravating *man* in Eyrinthia?" Razan's hands clamped onto her hips, her boots planted firmly on the wooden floor of the shop. "The night of Eyrinthia's Ball was the first time you truly talked to me since I came back. Do you remember what you said while we danced?"

Karim was visibly seething. "I told you to leave."

Desfan's eyes widened, but when Karim shot him a glower, he plucked up the nearest candle and pretended to study it intensely.

"Yes, you told me to leave," Razan said, her tone hard. "But do you remember why?"

"Of course I do," Karim flung at her. "Anyone who knows *anything* about our past knows why I don't want you in Duvan."

"No," she argued. "If our past was the reason you wanted me gone, I might have left. But on the dance floor you said, *I can't have you around me.* That's not the same as saying, *I can't ever forgive you,* or, *I can't stand the sight of you.*"

Karim's jaw worked. "It all means the same thing."

Razan actually stomped her foot. "No it *doesn't*, you unbearable man!"

"Your relationship is so confusing," Desfan muttered, setting the candle aside.

Two glares found him this time, though their annoyance was so clearly for each other, all he did was put up his hands and back away.

Razan twisted to Karim. "I know you've had a lot to sort

through—not just with me, but with Desfan, your changing role, and your mother."

Karim's eyes narrowed dangerously.

Razan ignored that and plunged ahead. "I think I've made my position clear. I want to be a friend to you. But if you don't feel the same—if you don't want me in Duvan anymore—then tell me that right now. Tell me you want me out of the palace and out of your life forever, and I'll go."

Karim said nothing, just scowled.

Razan laughed once—harsh and edged. "You can't even do the decent thing and just tell me what you want." She shook her head, and when she spoke now her voice was threaded with pain. "You've changed, Karim. You used to be compassionate. Kind. That's what I loved most about you. When I met you, I was trapped in a world not of my making, surrounded by men who did nothing but scheme and take and hurt. You were the complete opposite of that. You saved me in ways you don't even know. But now you're angry, bitter, and uncompromising. You have no compassion. And you're cruel." Her voice broke on that final word.

Karim's scowl deepened, but he didn't say anything, just listened as Razan continued with tears shining in her eyes. "You know exactly where I stand, yet you keep hurting me. Hate me if you must, but please just *hate me*. Tell me that you hate me and let that be the end of it. Don't stare after me. Don't dance with me and touch me like you care. Don't give me the security and warmth of your arms, only to tear them away. Don't give me glimpses of the man who stole my heart, only to shatter me with this harsh version of him."

Karim stared.

Desfan wasn't breathing, and he didn't think Karim was,

either.

The shop was silent in the wake of Razan's flood of words, and it was unbearable. Desfan's skin burned, and he didn't know what to do. How to intercede. Then—

"I *have* changed," Karim said tensely. "But you haven't changed at all."

Razan flinched as if he'd struck her. The tears that had threatened in her eyes now dashed down her cheeks. She hurried to swipe them away, angling her head away from him. "Fine," she said, the single word gnarled with emotion. "I suppose that's my answer." She moved to step around him, but Karim caught her wrist, halting her.

Gilded in the moonlight that shone through the window, Karim stepped closer to Razan, invading her space. "You haven't changed," he repeated, his voice rougher than before. "You haven't, because you still have me wholly snared—just like you did from our first meeting."

Razan inhaled sharply. Her wrist was still held in his grasp, and Karim didn't look like he had any intention of ever letting go.

He peered down at her upturned face, his jaw flexing once before he said, "As much as I try to hold on to the sting of your betrayal, it keeps slipping away. Because you're standing here in front of me, and all I can see is *you*. Not what you did. Not what I swore when I left you on Dorma. I just see you. And you are the most frustrating, fascinating, and beautiful woman I've ever known."

Her throat visibly clenched, and those silent tears were still sliding down her cheeks. "Then why?" she asked, her voice trembling. "Why have you kept pushing me away?"

Lines dug across his brow. "At first, I think I *was* trying to punish you. But mostly I've been punishing myself. I shouldn't want you—not after I swore to never forgive you. How could I hate what you'd done, but love who you are? It didn't make sense. The only thing I knew was that I couldn't let myself have you."

She blinked up at him, the tearstains on her cheeks glistening. "Aggravating man," she breathed. She grasped his face in both hands and pulled his mouth to hers.

Karim's arms banded around her shoulders, tugging her impossibly closer as he returned her kiss.

Desfan glanced away, though a smile played at his lips. Fates, they both deserved this.

After a long moment, Desfan heard them pull back.

"Stop grinning," Karim growled at him.

Desfan's smile widened. "I can't," he said as he twisted back to face them. "This is just so fates-blasted romantic."

Razan beamed, her cheeks still wet as she clutched the front of Karim's shirt.

Karim had one arm locked against the small of her back, keeping her close as he eyed Desfan. "Can you please not ruin the moment?"

Desfan shrugged, still grinning.

A shadow moved outside the window as a man stepped up to the door. Three short taps; the signal that Fang was in place.

Karim looked down at Razan, but before he could speak, she laid a finger over his lips. "No," she whispered. "We do this together, as planned."

He frowned.

She dropped her hand and rose on her toes to place a quick kiss at one downturned corner of his mouth. "I love you, Karim Safar," she said with a gentle smile. "Every overprotective, loyal, aggravating part of you."

Karim made a sound in his throat. Desfan wondered if he would have said something if they'd been alone, or at least not about to meet a drug master at midnight.

As it was, Karim leaned in and pressed a kiss to her forehead. "Just stay close to me," he said, before grasping her hand and tugging her toward the door.

<hr />

The alley was dark and Fang wasn't alone. Two large guards flanked him, and all three men looked surprisingly nervous.

Desfan strode forward with confidence. "Hello, Fang. I'm surprised you reached out, considering our history."

Fang's jaw tightened. "Believe me, I had no other choice."

Desfan stopped several paces away as Karim had previously ordered. His best friend was on his right, and Razan was on his left.

Fang glanced at Razan. "Serai Krayt; I wasn't sure if you'd come."

"I was too curious to stay away," she said, her tone perfectly controlled, betraying no unease. "Why did you write to me?"

"I needed to make sure the serjan got my message," Fang said. "And I asked you to accompany him, because I'd like a witness to this—one who isn't the serjan's bodyguard." He glanced at Karim's stony expression, then focused back on Razan. "I chose you because I've heard good things about your character. And I knew your uncle, Gaizl."

Razan's smile turned sharp. "I hate my uncle."

The corner of Fang's mouth rose. "So do I. Since everyone knows you helped get him thrown in prison, I figured you and I might see eye-to-eye on other matters as well."

"What matters?" Desfan asked Fang.

The man crossed his arms over his chest. "I would like to state, in front of our witness, that I have not been guilty of any crime, so this isn't a confession. You've caught me in nothing."

Desfan sighed, exaggerating the sound. "Yes, we all know you're a criminal, but we're not here tonight to judge. Is that the assurance you're looking for?"

Karim sent him a look that clearly said, *Do you really need to aggravate him?*

Desfan flashed his friend a smile.

Karim's sigh was unfeigned.

Fang didn't seem to even notice their exchange. "I know you have men asking more questions about the olcain in Duvan. I can assure you that the market is still here, even though Jamal is gone."

Omar Jamal was a former member of the council who had turned into a drug master for the coin. Desfan's eyes narrowed. "Are you now admitting to being involved in the olcain trade?"

"No."

When he didn't elaborate, Desfan lifted one eyebrow. "Why don't we bypass the show of reticence and get to the point of this meeting?"

Fang glanced at his men, then sighed. "I've come to you for aid and protection."

Desfan lifted both brows. "Do go on."

The man gritted his teeth. "I run a profitable business. I know what is within my capabilities and what is not. I have been very careful to avoid too many entanglements with the olcain trade, so I thought I was far removed from the entire venture. A few days ago, I received a summons I couldn't refuse." His jaw was clenched so tightly, a muscle ticked. "They took my daughter, her husband, and their infant boy—my grandson."

Desfan's spine stiffened. He'd met Fang's daughter during his more rebellious phase. When he thought of Ayma, he pictured a pretty girl with large eyes and an easy smile. Even though she'd had no part in her father's illegal enterprises, she'd been dangerous to Desfan by mere association. That had been an intoxicating draw for him, back then. Fang had caught them once, kissing in her bedroom.

The man hadn't liked Desfan since.

Desfan hadn't seen Ayma in years, and he had no idea if she and her husband were involved in Fang's business now, but he hated to think of anyone being abducted—especially an innocent infant. His eyes narrowed. "Who has them?"

"A Zennorian named Sahvi," Fang said tightly.

Sahvi. A name Desfan kept hearing—from Jamal, from the kivs who continued to investigate the olcain, and even Liam.

"He's the one who brought olcain to Duvan on such a large scale," Fang explained, though Desfan had already known that.

"I think it's time I met this Sahvi," Desfan muttered.

Fang shook his head. "You can't go against him just yet. He's hiding somewhere in Duvan—even I don't know where. But I know where he'll be in ten days."

"Where?"

"My warehouse. His men took control of it, along with my home. It took a great deal to arrange this appointment with you; I'm watched constantly." For the first time, Desfan saw fear in Fang's eyes. "Sahvi controls all I have and he'll continue to manipulate me as long as he has my family."

"Why did he do this?" Desfan asked. "What does he want from you?"

Fang shifted his weight, obviously debating how much to share.

Desfan's eyes narrowed. "I can only help you and Ayma if you tell me everything."

The criminal scrubbed a hand through his hair, his exhale sharp. "For the last several weeks, many of my associates have gone silent, only to eventually go missing entirely. At first, I assumed they were fleeing due to your tightening security in Duvan. Now, I suspect Sahvi used them as he's attempting to use me, and then—when he got what he wanted—he killed them."

"What does Sahvi want from you?" Razan asked, repeating Desfan's earlier question.

"He wants me to smuggle goods from Duvan to Zennor." Fang hesitated, shooting a look at Desfan. "According to the men I overheard, it's a portion of the treasure stolen from you, Serjan."

Shock rippled through him. "How did a drug master from Zennor end up with my treasure?"

"I don't know," Fang said. "But if you want to reclaim it—and capture Sahvi, so you can ask your questions—then help me." Desperation tinged his next words. "Help me save my daughter and her family. Please."

Desfan looked at Karim, then Razan. Finally, he focused back on Fang. "Tell us everything you know of Sahvi's plan."

CHAPTER 38

CLARE

CLARE HAD ONLY BEEN ON DORMA FOR TWO DAYS, but she'd already fallen in love with it. The island was breathtaking. It was larger than she'd expected, with lush jungle surrounding the sprawling main port city of Madihr, and the other smaller cities and villages she hoped to visit one day.

Madihr was even more colorful than Duvan, which was no easy feat. Clare was used to the cities of Devendra, which were all varying shades of gray stone, and mostly dark woods. In Mortise, buildings were made of golden sandstone, or painted in vibrant shades of crimson, indigo, emerald, and coral. On Madihr, Clare had yet to see a door that was plain, or a fountain without exquisitely patterned tilework. Once, the chaos of the varying colors might have overwhelmed her Devendran tastes. Now, they made her feel alive.

She was grateful Desfan had been so understanding of

497

her need to leave Duvan. He'd helped make all the arrangements so she could leave with the Hassans, the very day after
Grandeur had arrived at the palace.

The Hassans were wonderful hosts. Their estate was private
and beautiful, and Ilah especially relished showing Clare—or
Serene, as she thought of her—every beautiful thing Madihr
had to offer. They had attended a play last night, and a tea
this afternoon with some of the local ladies. Ilah planned to
host a ball, to welcome the princess properly to Dorma and
introduce her to all the influential families of Madihr.

She never would have dreamed to visit a place like this. The
foods, the markets, the sights, the smells. Thomas and Mark
would have delighted in all of it. Sometimes, Clare felt a stab
of guilt for the joy she was experiencing. But Desfan's words
that day on the beach kept floating back to her: *Your grief will
always be there. But you get to choose how you carry that grief. It can
overwhelm you, or you can accept it as a part of you and continue to
live.*

She would miss her brothers for the rest of her life. Sometimes, the pain of missing them would be excruciating. But
she would survive, just as Desfan had survived. That meant
facing each new day as it came. It meant reaching out for Bennick, Vera, or Venn when she needed them, and not isolating
herself. It meant feeling her grief, but not succumbing to it.

So, when Ilah asked if Clare wanted to visit one of Madihr's
museums, she hadn't hesitated to accept the invitation.

As she wandered the galleries, she wished she knew a little
more about art. But even with her untrained eye, she could
see the paintings were masterful. There were stunning landscapes, depictions of old battles, and portraits of previous
royals—including a portrait of Desfan, when he was only a

couple of years old. But while the paintings were stunning, it was the sculptures that completely staggered her.

Clare had never seen such works of art. The outdoor statues in Devendra were weathered and crude compared to this protected stonework. The marble had been molded to look like living flesh, and the emotions that had been captured in their poses and expressions held *her* captive. She couldn't look away from the carved hands—with details as minute as fingernails—or the veined throats that somehow looked real, despite the striations in the stone.

Bennick trailed behind her at an expected distance for a bodyguard. Venn was with him, though his focus was on Vera, who had lingered on the other side of the room to study a painting of a jungle.

When Clare had asked Ilah if Vera could accompany them today, the Mortisian woman had eagerly acquiesced. Ilah was a woman who did not stand on ceremony, and she was proud to show her island to everyone, including a princess's maid.

Ser Hassan had elected to stay home with Sidrah, so Clare had had Ilah's unwavering attention during most of their tour of the museum's many wings. She'd pointed out her favorite pieces and answered many of Clare's questions, and she'd introduced her to many of the people they encountered. She'd only excused herself a moment ago to speak with a friend she'd spotted on the other side of the gallery.

Alone, Clare studied the statue in front of her. It was a man seated on a bench, his posture slightly hunched. One hand was balanced on the empty spot beside him. From one angle, his face looked sorrowful. Heartbroken, even. It spoke of loss and grief. But when she shifted to the other side, he almost looked nervous, or anxious. As if he was anticipating the moment he would be joined on the bench, rather than already abandoned on it. Somehow, the artist had captured a moment between moments. The breath between expectation and rejection. Excitement and mourning. Hope and loss. Something in his tipped head and that empty hand on the bench filled her with longing.

Warmth brushed her back, and Bennick's voice was low at her ear. "I think I'm getting jealous."

A thin breath escaped her—almost a laugh. She peeked up at him, surprised to find him so close.

The novelty of her presence at the museum had run out at least an hour ago. Patrons were admiring the art, now, not the Devendra princess they thought she was. No one seemed to be watching her at all—except Bennick.

His crystal blue eyes were locked on her, and that—along with his nearness—made it difficult to breathe.

"He's made of stone," she pointed out. "There's no reason to be jealous."

He ducked his head beside her, his breath teasing the sensitive skin of her ear. "Anything that claims this much of your attention makes me jealous."

Warmth infused her cheeks, and she fought to stop her blush. The way they stood was innocent enough—there was space between them, regardless of how thin, and a bodyguard whispering in the ear of his charge wouldn't be unexpected. He might be asking her when she planned to leave, or telling her something he'd observed.

Nothing in this moment felt innocent, however.

Heat curled low in her belly and a shiver skated down her spine when Bennick leaned in just a little closer, the tip of his nose skimming against the curve of her cheek. "Tonight, there's somewhere I want to take you," he whispered. "After dinner, excuse yourself as soon as you can."

Curiosity flared, along with excitement. She peeked over at him. "I assume you're not going to tell me anything else?"

He smiled his heart-stopping half-smile. Fates help her if he ever found out what that simple quirk of his lips did to her. "No," he said. "You'll just have to wait for tonight."

"Are you going to tell me where we're going yet?" Clare asked, her voice hushed in the darkness.

Bennick's hand tightened around hers, gently tugging her forward. "No."

Despite her raging curiosity, his response made her mouth twitch. Anticipation hummed inside her as Bennick led her further up the moonlit path, which wandered away from the mansion they'd left behind.

Clare still wore her dress from dinner. The long, silvery blue skirt just brushed the ground, covering the Mortisian sandals that wrapped her feet. The rippling fabric was soft and lightweight and gathered at her waist, the bodice looser than she was used to. Mortise had different styles, but she was growing to love them. Silver pins with decorative twists in the delicate metal secured the dress atop her shoulders, leaving her arms bare. Silver bangles circled her wrists, hiding her scars. The bracelet that meant the most to her was on her right arm—the hidden garrote Bennick had given her.

Before sneaking out of the manor, Bennick had snatched up

a light cloak for her, but he only held it over his arm as they walked. The night air was warm—something that felt wrong, considering that, in Devendra, the leaves would be turning as they prepared for the coming winter.

Bennick, of course, wore his dark blue uniform. Except on the hottest of days, he had continued to wear the jacket that fit his frame perfectly. Clare didn't mind, since it outlined the breadth of his strong shoulders, the strength in his long arms, and the well-defined lines of his chest and tapered waist. His sword was belted to his side, and he carried an assortment of knives on his belt. He walked easily with the weapons, fully comfortable with their weight.

She understood, since she wore a knife strapped to her leg. After carrying it for so long, she felt more balanced with the weapon than she ever had without it. It was another example of just how much her life had changed since becoming Serene's decoy.

The path they walked was made of packed earth, the soil dark and rich. The earthy smell was accompanied by the light fragrance of sweet-smelling flowers, and the faintest trace of the sea in the distance. The foliage was thick here, hemming the path and creating a sense that they were the only two people on the entire island.

She knew they must still be on the Hassan's property, since they hadn't yet reached the stone wall that surrounded the estate. They'd passed through the beautifully cultivated gardens, and then followed this meandering path. Clare hadn't noticed a single branching trail; wherever they were going, it seemed to be the only destination this pathway offered.

She threaded her fingers with Bennick's. "Since you rarely leave my side, I'm curious how you found this place—whatever it is."

"I'm still not telling you where we're going, no matter how creatively you try to ask. But to answer your question . . . I've found moments to explore."

"You mean when you should have been sleeping?"

He tossed her a casual smile. "Maybe." His steps slowed so he walked beside her, rather than slightly ahead. "I've been searching for a place like this since we arrived."

"You're trying to be cryptic."

"Is it working?"

"Annoyingly well."

He chuckled.

She shook her head, her ears straining to pick up any sound that might give her a hint of what waited around the next bend in the path. All she heard was the chirp and buzz of insects, and low croaks of frogs. Then, she heard a trickle of water.

They rounded the corner and Clare's breath caught. A small clearing had opened at the end of the path, and a stream of crystalline water cut through the clearing and disappeared into the thick foliage beyond. The water glistened in the moonlight as it rolled over the smooth stones in the winding creek bed, the soft burbling sound incredibly peaceful. A stone bench was positioned near the water's edge, and wild, tropical flowers brought bursts of color even in the dim light of the moon. It was secluded, beautiful, and absolutely perfect.

"Bennick," she breathed. "This is . . ."

He squeezed her hand. "I know." He leaned in and pressed his lips to her temple.

Her heart swelled and she smiled up at him. "Thank you for this."

"You're welcome. Though I have to admit, I had selfish

reasons for wanting to find a place we could escape to."

Clare looked around the clearing once more, and she slowly shook her head. "It feels like a place from a dream. It's too beautiful to be real." She twisted to face him fully, which put her back to the stream. Peering up at his moonlit face, seeing the love in his eyes, made her own sting. "I don't know how you're mine."

His eyes softened. His fingers touched her chin, keeping her eyes on him. "I wonder the same thing every time I look at you, Clare."

Those words melted her. She set a hand against his chest to steady herself, and it was instantly covered by his own.

Pinning her palm against his heart, she felt his heartbeat quicken just before his head angled down and he kissed her.

His lips against hers were firm but gentle, and her pulse skipped as she returned the kiss. Her fingers curled into his jacket, urging him closer, her free hand untangling from his so she could cradle his bristled jaw. It felt harder than the stone statues she'd admired all afternoon, yet this man was real—warm and strong and hers to touch.

The cloak draped over Bennick's arm slipped to the ground, but neither of them spared the pool of fabric a glance. His free hand drifted up her spine and she leaned into him, her fingers on his jaw moving to grip the back of his neck. His sandy blond hair felt like silk beneath her fingers.

He kissed her like she was air—something he needed to survive. Her blood rushed and every part of her heated. Their bodies were pressed together and they shared every breath. Their mouths gave and took, explored and remembered. Every touch from Bennick was like a brand on her soul. Everything about him called out to her.

Her skin tingled from his touch. Her heart pounded against his body. Her fingers tangled in his hair, his clothes—she couldn't stop touching him.

She had no idea how much time had passed before he groaned and pulled his lips from hers. Immediately, he buried his face in the curve of her neck, holding her close. "Fates," he rasped. "This is torture."

"Torture?" That was certainly not the word *she* would have chosen.

His laugh was short and strained. "Fates, yes. Every time I stop kissing you, it kills me."

Her arms shifted to wrap around his shoulders, and she felt every heavy breath he took. "Perhaps you shouldn't ever stop," she whispered.

Hot breath huffed against her neck, lifting all the fine hairs on her body. "I don't want to. But we've been gone too long. Venn will worry."

"Venn is probably enjoying his time alone with Vera," Clare pointed out.

"You're probably right," he said. But he didn't resume kissing her.

It was probably wise of him, since she seemed to forget everything when she kissed him. And there were some things she couldn't afford to forget—like why they needed to be careful, even when they were alone. Some lines could not be crossed. Not when they were already walking a treasonous line.

She rested her forehead against his shoulder, her breaths gradually steadying as they just held each other and breathed.

"I have an odd request," he said suddenly.

Intrigue sparked in her chest. "What?"

He gently pulled back so their eyes could meet. "I know this isn't the best place, but . . . Clare Ellington, will you dance with me?"

A surprised chuckle escaped her. "What?"

"I want to dance with you," he said. "I've had to watch you dance with other men for far too long, and I want my chance. It might help me keep my sanity at the Hassan's ball."

The corner of her mouth twitched. Her hands slid down his arms and stopped behind his elbows. "I would love to dance with you, Captain Markam."

A grin split his face, and they danced together in the moonlight, with no music except for the sounds of the night around them, and the soft rush of the stream.

Clare could not think of a more perfect, peaceful moment. And after everything they'd been through, they deserved a little peace.

CHAPTER 39

SERENE

SERENE HUNCHED HER SHOULDERS AGAINST THE battering rain. It was early evening, but the dark clouds above made it pitch dark. She gripped the reins and guided her horse to follow Wilf's. Cardon rode behind her on the narrow street. Danjuma wasn't a large city, so it shouldn't take long to find the Panther's Den.

She hoped her rebel contact would be there. After nearly three weeks since leaving Duvan, they were finally in the midlands of Zennor, and Serene was more than ready to get a full report on what had been happening in this kingdom.

The whispers they'd heard in their travels were many and varied, but all were distressing. People vanishing in the north. Fields and crops burned by raiding clans. Drug masters flexing their hold on cities. An increase in olcain. A shortage of steel and other metals.

Sometimes Serene overheard people talking about Desfan. A young serjan taking over Mortise was looked upon as a good thing by some, while others only saw his inexperience.

Imara's name was also whispered, along with fears that she had run away to avoid marrying Eilan Skyer.

"What will the clans do if Skyer is insulted?" a woman had whispered fearfully just the other night. "The Kabu Tribe has been fighting for peace, but . . . what if they decide to make war instead?"

Serene was decidedly unsettled by everything they'd overheard so far—and she'd felt Wilf and Cardon's tension rise with every day. She was hoping the rebel contact she met tonight would put her mind at ease, or at least lay out the dangers more specifically.

Exhaustion pulled at her body. She was tired, drenched, and sick of traveling. The rapid pace had taken a toll on all of them—including the horses. So when she spotted the Panther's Den just ahead, she praised the fates.

She'd mentioned the inn to Cardon and Wilf yesterday, naming it as the place she'd like to stay in Danjuma. She wanted to meet her contact, of course, though she obviously didn't tell them that. She'd simply said that Imara had mentioned it was a charming place the Buhari family had stayed at once.

The place looked a little worn from the outside, but warm light glowed in the windows, beckoning them inside.

Wilf was the first to dismount, though Cardon swung down from his horse a moment after. Serene held in her wince as she slipped from the saddle. Fates, she was sick of riding. Especially since this animal was not Fury, and she missed her horse.

"I'll take care of the horses," Wilf offered. "You get rooms."

Cardon nodded and grabbed his pack. Serene lifted hers down as well, jolting a little when Cardon took her arm. His touch was casual, but she felt it to her core. Despite the downpour, her skin heated.

Traveling in anonymity had its advantages, but the one she enjoyed most was the informality between her and Cardon. True, he still treated her with deference, but he did not treat her overtly as a princess.

It was probably a good thing Wilf was with them. If not for him, Serene might fall completely into the illusion. While she and Desfan had reached an understanding, they had agreed not to tell anyone yet. She didn't know how Cardon would react to her possibly ending her engagement with Desfan. In truth, she was a little nervous to tell him. Cardon was nothing if not practical, and he'd already made it clear that she was a princess, and he was a guard. There could be nothing between them.

She was determined to change that.

Until then, she would simply enjoy this time with him. She would keep calling him *Cardon*. She could keep thrilling at the frequent touches between them, and the cadence of his voice as he called her *Serene*. Soon enough they would reach the capital, and this would end. While she was anxious to finally speak with her uncle—and Ivar Carrigan, whenever he managed to arrive in Kedaah—she would miss this.

Cardon shouldered open the door to the inn. The rain continued to fall loudly against the roof, the hammering dampening the music in the corner and the conversations that hummed throughout the great room. The bad weather must have driven people indoors, because the common room was filled with people. Lamps burned brightly, banishing the shadows. There was no fireplace; they were rare in the great rooms of Zennor, since even during the worst storms it rarely grew cold.

Cardon caught the attention of a passing maid, who was quick to tell them there was only one remaining room. Cardon's mouth tightened, but he didn't hesitate to pay for the room. The woman showed them upstairs, and promised to direct Wilf to the room once he finished with the horses. She opened the door for them, handed Cardon the key, then headed back down the stairs.

Serene stepped into the room first. Fates, the space was small and cramped—and there was only one bed.

Her heartbeat sped up.

Cardon moved in behind her. "Wilf and I will take the floor," he said.

Serene eyed the close-set walls. "Will Wilf even fit in here?"

Cardon chuckled and stepped up to the room's small window. He peered out, and Serene couldn't help but admire his strong profile. The lamp the maid had left with them highlighted the sharp angles of his face.

When he twisted toward her, she hurriedly looked away. Plucking the ties of her cloak, she freed the knot at her throat and draped the wet material over the back of a simple wooden chair. "Perhaps we should give Wilf the bed. It's the widest space in the room."

"You're not sleeping on the floor, Serene."

She peeked over her shoulder at him. "Where else is Wilf going to fit?"

Cardon cast his eyes around the room. "In front of the door."

That would take up every bit of floor space they had. She folded her arms over her chest. "Where exactly will you sleep, then?"

He nodded to the corner. "I'll fit there."

"Standing up?"

He snorted. "Stop fussing. We'll all fit."

"I'm not fussing, I'm being practical."

"You're hungry," he argued. "That makes you irritable, and the first stage of your irritability is fussing. So, let's hurry and get you some dinner."

She stared. "I do not get irritable when I'm hungry."

"You most assuredly do." Cardon removed his own cloak and dropped it over hers. She tried not to get distracted by the wide expanse of his chest, covered by a dark blue shirt. Even with the cloaks protecting them, their clothes were damp, and his molded tightly to his body.

"We should change into dry clothes," Cardon said.

Her eyes darted to his, her heart skipping a beat. "What?"

He gestured to her pack. "Find something to change into. I'll wait in the hall."

Ah. Of course. She mentally shook herself, though her cheeks heated.

Cardon double-checked his belted knives, then stepped out of the room. When the door clicked behind him, Serene reached for her pack.

Changing didn't take long. She hadn't brought many clothes, so there weren't a lot of options to choose from. She smoothed the simple blue skirt down, then called for him to return.

As he did, she brushed strands of wet curling hair away from her face. The hood of her cloak hadn't been deep enough to protect her from the driving rain. She caught Cardon watching her, but the moment he realized she'd noticed, he glanced away.

She cleared her throat. "Would you like me to step out so you can change?"

"No, I'll wait for Wilf."

Her lips twitched. "You don't trust me on my own?"

"Not at all." He leaned back against the door and folded his arms over his chest. "So. Zaire Buhari stayed here with his family?"

"Yes."

He glanced at the peeling paint around the window sill, the faded rug, the worn wood. "A king chose this place to stay the night?"

"Yes," she repeated. "It's charming."

He lifted one brow. It was a gesture she was known to use—something she'd learned from him. "He stayed here with all seven of his children?"

"Well, I doubt they all stayed in this very room," she quipped. Since she couldn't explain her reasons for insisting they stay at the Panther's Den, she changed the subject. "I'm the smallest. If anyone is sleeping in the corner, it only makes sense for it to be me."

"There is no world in which that makes sense," Cardon disagreed.

A rap on the door, then Wilf pushed in. He paused, taking in the small room. "Fates," he muttered. "Maybe I'll sleep in the hall."

Something curled low in Serene's gut. Maybe anticipation. What would it be like, to sleep in the same room as Cardon? Just the two of them, breathing together in the dark?

Her cheeks grew warmer.

"Serene thought you should take the bed," Cardon said to

Wilf, amusement threading his words.

The large man drew back, clearly affronted.

Serene threw her free hand up, halting the tirade before it could start. "I don't think I'm the only one hungry and irritable. You two need to change so we can eat."

Wilf's eyes narrowed, but he didn't argue.

Cardon's eyes fairly glittered with triumph. "You admit I was right, then."

She rolled her eyes and marched for the door.

———◆———

Serene would never tell Cardon, but she did feel much better after eating. The flatbread was divine, the braised chicken and roasted vegetables even better. They each leaned back in their chairs, relaxing as the food settled.

Wilf's attention was on a game of dice two tables away, where a group of men had gathered. "I may try my hand," he said. "They seem talkative. Maybe I can learn more about those disappearances, or about the other rumors we've heard."

Serene and Cardon both nodded, watching in silence as he left.

The rain had stopped its merciless pounding, so the music from the corner filled the room. A group of people had even begun to dance to the fast tempo, while onlookers clapped.

"The mood is better here," Cardon noted.

"Still not as bright as usual, though."

Zennorians were usually friendly, even toward strangers. But since leaving Zoroya, they had noticed men watching each other with wariness. Mothers kept their children close, and no one seemed to linger in the streets like they used to. It was not the same place Serene had known, and that saddened her.

It seemed all of Eyrinthia was being thrown into shadow. She wanted to know what was casting it—or who.

Serene searched the room, but she didn't know who she was looking for. She would need to locate the inn's owner and see if he knew who her contact would be.

If her message had even reached someone in time.

"Maybe we should stay here for a couple of days," Cardon said. "The horses could use the rest, and so could we."

"I thought you disliked the place?"

"I'm beginning to see its charm," he said, his eyes fixed on her.

Her pulse quickened. They'd become relaxed around each other, yes, but that had been utterly flirtatious.

She glanced at his glass of water. "How much have you drunk tonight?"

He exhaled a short laugh at her thin joke. "Would you like to stay?" he asked.

It would give her contact more of a chance to reach her. And it would lengthen this time they had together. She dipped her chin. "I think that would be nice. Though we should try to get another room for tomorrow night."

"I am a little old for sleeping on floors," he conceded with a smirk.

"You're not old, Cardon."

"I *feel* old." What he didn't say—at least in this moment—was, *I'm too old for you.*

Before she could answer, she heard someone at the table

beside them mention Duvan. She strained to hear the rest.

". . . Nasty business. Olcain keeps making its way in, and the serjan doesn't seem able to stop it."

"Who do you think is selling it? Chizumbo?"

"He's got the biggest empire these days, but who knows. Could be anyone."

"I want to know how they're hiring ships," another man complained. "I've got crates of wine from my vineyard, but my brother says the warehouse in Zoroya is full, and not to send any more on the barges. He says there aren't enough merchant ships to go around."

"Why is that?"

"Who knows. More goods have been shipping to Ryden, he says, and the journey takes longer. Maybe that's all it is."

"What ever happened to that Mortisian merchant? The one with the fast ships?"

"Rahim Nassar. He's been absent a while, hasn't he?"

The conversation devolved, and Serene turned her focus back to Cardon. He was looking at the men, frowning. Probably thinking along the same lines she was. More ships going to Ryden didn't sound good. Was King Henri purchasing food, weapons, and other supplies for his war from Zennor? More olcain in Duvan wasn't good, either—Desfan had enough problems. Fewer merchants, not enough ships . . . none of it felt right.

Serene straightened in her chair. "I'm going to get an ale and mingle. See what else I can learn. You do the same. You don't have to drink it," she quickly added. "Just hold it to make the others feel more comfortable."

His eyes narrowed. "I'm not leaving you alone."

"I won't go far. But I may be able to talk to some of these

women as long as you're not hovering and looking so . . ."
Distracting. "Intimidating," she said instead.

He sighed. "You have your knife?"

"Of course."

"Stay in sight of me. And don't drink too much."

Him and drinking; she still wanted that story.

Perhaps she was feeling a little bold after his flirtation, because she leaned forward to whisper, "Or maybe tonight we should find out what sort of drunk I am."

His expression was frozen, but she saw something in his eyes flare.

She threw him a smile and made her way to the bar, where she ordered an ale from—as the fates would have it—the innkeeper. "Do you know the Fiddler?" she asked.

Realization struck him, just before excitement lit his face. He smiled. "I do. And you're traveling to the capital?"

"I am."

He grabbed a tankard and filled it from the keg behind the bar. His voice went low. "Lord Dakaar has been here every night for the past three days waiting for you." He nodded across the room, and Serene studied the man who meticulously cut the chicken on his plate.

Lord Dakaar was tall—Serene could see that, even with him sitting at the table—and he was dressed in plain clothes, probably to blend in. His tight curls were cut close to his head, and he looked to be in his thirties—maybe a year or two older than Cardon. Dark skinned, dark haired, and dark eyed, he appeared regal and handsome. She easily believed he was a lord.

With Cardon watching, she couldn't walk straight up to Dakaar. She needed a moment to speak with the women grouped on the edge of the gaming table, where Wilf was just tallying points from his latest roll of dice.

Serene focused on the innkeeper. "Would you discreetly go to Lord Dakaar in a few moments and point me out to him? Tell him to ask me to dance."

Cardon would surely love that, but she could think of no other way to get a semi-private moment with Dakaar.

She drifted over to the women with her tankard, feeling Cardon's eyes on her while she sipped. She spoke a little with the women, and not just for appearances. She was anxious to know their opinion of affairs in Zennor. But they were reticent, and she didn't press.

Finally, she saw Dakaar approach.

She had to tilt her head back to look him in the eye, he was so tall. He smiled down at her, warmth in his gaze. His voice was a low, pleasant rumble, his Zennorian accent thick and proud. "My lady, might I beg a dance?"

She readily agreed, setting her tankard on a nearby table as she took his offered arm. She couldn't help but shoot a glance toward Cardon.

He watched her with hooded eyes, his expression unreadable.

Dakaar led her to the cleared space in the room that served as the dance floor, then twisted to face her.

Other couples danced around them, the music loud enough that Serene didn't fear anyone overhearing their quiet words. "Lord Dakaar, it's a pleasure to meet you."

"The pleasure is all mine." His voice dipped to a bare whisper as he added, "Princess."

Fates. Clearly, the old man in Zoroya had shared her identity with Dakaar. Hopefully he'd *only* told the Zennorian lord.

"You look younger than your years," Dakaar told her. "It makes what you've done all the more impressive."

"There's still much to do."

"True. Due to my position so far north, James has kept me informed of events in Devendra and Mortise. I was surprised to hear you were in Zennor."

"I didn't have a chance to speak with James before leaving Duvan," she admitted. "But I'm glad I came. Things in Zennor are . . ."

"Unsettled," Dakaar supplied.

"Yes. Please, tell me everything you can."

"I'm afraid I don't have much news from the capital," he confessed, his expression tightening. "Information from the castle itself has been non-existent for weeks."

She frowned. That was unlike her uncle. He was normally very transparent, allowing nobles and commoners alike to enter his court. "Why?"

"I don't know. Meetings have been cancelled, and court is not in session. A week ago, I received a notice that cancelled my annual summons to report on my lands. It's all very strange. And more tribesmen walk the streets of the capital than ever before, which has made people uneasy."

"Are they from the Kabu Clan?"

"Mostly." Clearly he followed her trail of thought, because he added, "Which makes sense, since Skyer is their leader and he's been negotiating with Buhari. But rumor has it Skyer is no longer at the castle."

"Where is he, then?"

"No one seems to know." He spun her once, then pulled her back in. "Also troubling is the fact that King Zaire has not been seen among his people for months now."

Her stomach clenched. "*Months?*"

His expression tightened. "Yes. Soon after he sent Princess Imara to attend you in Devendra, on your journey to Mortise, in fact."

Well, Imara hadn't actually been *sent*. But her father must have claimed the lie in order to keep the peace.

"The rumor is that the king is sick," Dakaar continued. "Though his advisors assure everyone he's in perfect health. They say he's simply busy negotiating with the tribes."

"What of the queen?" Serene asked.

"No one in the royal family has been seen in that time. They don't leave the castle at all. Some speculate the entire royal family has been cursed by the fates for trying to make peace with the tribes, and they're trying to hide the sign of the curse."

That was indeed troubling. Not the superstition, of course, but the facts.

"People have been disappearing," Dakaar continued.

"I've heard this, but I don't know details. Is there a pattern?"

"Not one I can discern. Sometimes it's a noble family, though it's been mostly common folk. Entire households simply vanish. No blood left behind, or sign of a fight. No messages or ransoms. From the oldest man to the smallest babe—all of them, gone. People disappear from the roads as well; they leave one place, but never arrive at their destination. Many of the disappearances happen near the jungle's edge—tribe territory, which of course rouses ire and suspicion. But people have vanished from the capital, the midlands, the coast—everywhere, really. The latest I heard happened last week. A whole shift of vineyard hands just disappeared. Their replacements came on schedule, but all twenty men were nowhere to be found."

One of her tentative theories dissolved. If families had left without a trace, it was possible they were simply seeking a quiet escape from the kingdom. But not on this scale. And not unrelated vineyard workers.

"How long has this been going on?"

Dakaar shook his head. "It's difficult to say. At least several months, but there have been more lately." He leaned closer. "You need to be careful, Princess. I don't know what you'll find at the castle, but there's bound to be trouble of some sort. If you need assistance, you may call upon me at any time. And when you manage to meet with the king, please send word to my manor so I do not continue to worry. It's near Vibba."

"I will. Thank you for your help."

A hand touched Serene's shoulder, stilling their dance. "May I cut in?" Cardon asked. His stance was firm, but his voice was harder. He was clearly not prepared to be declined.

Dakaar stepped back, a wide smile sliding into place. "But of course." He bowed deeply to her, then retreated, melting into the crowd.

Serene faced Cardon, who had yet to take her hands.

The music bounced happily around the room, and couples spun beside them.

She arched one eyebrow. "Were you actually planning to dance with me? Or did you dismiss my charming dance partner for no reason?"

The skin around Cardon's eyes tightened. "I had reasons."

CHAPTER 40

SERENE

THE MUSIC CONTINUED TO PLAY, AND THE ALE Serene had drunk made her feel overwarm as she stared at Cardon. Her stomach fluttered from his answer, but she wasn't sure what to say; nothing seemed quite right for this tentative dance they'd been doing since leaving Duvan. The lingering glances and touches they'd shared could only communicate so much.

When the silence stretched, she cleared her throat. "So you're *not* going to dance with me, then?"

Cardon watched her for a brief moment before stepping closer, still not touching her. "I will if you want me to."

"Do *you* want to dance with me?"

He stared at her, silent. The tension, the anticipation—it was killing her. Her heart pounded wildly in her chest as she awaited his reply.

"Yes," he whispered.

Her pulse skipped. The breathlessness in her voice did not come entirely from the dancing she'd done with Dakaar. Eyes locked on Cardon, Serene said, "Dance with me, then."

Without breaking eye contact, one calloused hand slipped around hers, his other palm cupping her waist. His throat bobbed. "Perhaps this isn't a good idea."

She eased closer, settling her free hand against his shoulder. Beneath his sleeve, his roped muscles tensed. "I think it's an excellent idea," she whispered.

Cardon's hold tightened, then he pulled her into the first step of their dance.

The tempo of the music was fast, but it might as well have been a sweeping waltz. The common room could have been a grand ballroom, and she and Cardon might have been the only couple on the floor.

She had never danced with Cardon before. Imagined it, yes. Dancing with him had been a favorite of her girlhood fantasies. Her love for him had been real even then, and though she had gone through a long period when she had barely dared to dream something like this could happen between them, reality overpowered every daydream.

She was not in a gorgeous ball gown, and he was not in his dress uniform. She knew this dance would not end in a kiss, like so many of her old fantasies did. They would not exchange words of love or devotion. But no dream could compare to feeling Cardon's strong hands against her body. No dream could come close to the thrill of having him so near, his body only a breath away. And even if the words she longed to hear remained sealed inside him, his deep brown eyes conveyed everything she needed to know. What he'd said on the beach that night in Mortise rang through with every glance, every breath, every press of his fingertips against her body.

I love you, Serene. No one deserves you. Least of all me. And yet, no man will love you as much as I do.

She was breathless when the song ended, unable to look anywhere but at him.

Cardon tugged her even closer—her skirt brushed against his legs. "You're flushed," he murmured.

She imagined she was. "Probably from the ale."

The corners of his eyes crinkled slightly; he was fighting a smile, trying to look firm. "How much did you drink?"

"Not much," she admitted.

"You listened to me?"

"No need to sound so surprised; it's not such a novel thing."

"Trust me, it is." His thumb skated over her knuckles; he was still holding her hand.

The bodice of her dress felt too constricting. Her lungs strained, and she tightened her hold on his shoulder. They weren't dancing anymore, but they stood like they were.

The next song started.

Serene cleared her throat. "Cardon?"

"Yes?"

She wet her bottom lip.

His eyes darted to follow the motion, his attention lingering on her mouth. Tingles wound down her spine. "Maybe we should take a walk outside," she said. "Get some air."

Be alone. A dangerous idea, but deliciously tempting.

For a brief moment, she worried he'd say no. That he would shield the emotions shining in his eyes, like he'd done so many times since their kiss on the beach in Duvan.

Instead, his grip on her hand flexed. "Let's tell Wilf."

A thrill shot through her, continuing to spark when he released all of her but one hand.

He'd never held her hand like this.

He pulled her through the crowd and spoke briefly to Wilf. The large man was still playing with the loud group of men, and though he noticed their joined hands, he didn't say anything; merely nodded.

Cardon tugged her toward the door, threading their way through the common room until, finally, they were free.

The night air was muggy, due to the earlier rains, but still cooler than inside the inn. The ground was muddy, but flat stones wound a path around the back of the inn. Cardon continued to hold her hand as they navigated the stepping stones, which led them toward the stable.

"Did you learn anything interesting tonight?" Cardon asked.

She'd learned that dancing with Cardon was one of her favorite things—but that probably wasn't what he meant. "Not especially," she said. If she gave too many of the details Dakaar had shared, Cardon might want to find the man and question him. Then again, she hadn't noticed him in the common room—maybe he'd left. "There was more talk about those disappearances," she said. "Not just families, but lone travelers, and even twenty men who work a nearby vineyard."

Cardon frowned. "I think that was the discussion at Wilf's table just now. Twenty grown men. Laborers, at that. They wouldn't have been taken without a fight."

"Who would take them? And where? *Why?*"

"I'm hoping Buhari might have some answers for us."

She thought of her uncle, who hadn't been seen in months. Better not to share that, though; he would certainly question Dakaar about any possible trouble awaiting them at the capital.

They reached the barn, but instead of going inside, Cardon led her around the side, still following the stepping stones.

"You're a good dancer," Serene said.

"Surprised?"

"A little."

The corner of his mouth quirked. "I suppose that's fair. I took lessons after becoming a bodyguard."

"Why?"

"I never knew if an occasion would call for me to dance, but I wanted to be prepared."

That sounded very much like Cardon. He was always prepared and unruffled. "Your easy confidence has always impressed me," she admitted.

He glanced over at her, his surprise evident. "You're the most confident person I know."

"I don't feel very confident these days."

He squeezed her fingers. "It doesn't show."

Considering her responsibilities, that was a good thing. A princess couldn't afford to show vulnerability; certainly not one who also led a rebellion.

Silver moonlight peeked through the thinning clouds, and she could make out some glittering stars. They reached the end of the stones, which had led them to a large well. Cardon slowed, but Serene wasn't ready to go back. Not now that she and Cardon were finally alone.

She looked across the yard, over the long grass to a sturdy wooden fence. A pen for the horses, she guessed. She took a tentative step; the ground was soft, but the long grass kept her from sinking in the mud.

Cardon hesitated, but she pulled at him. "You're not afraid of a little mud, are you?"

He grimaced slightly, but followed her into the yard.

As they walked, Serene glanced at his profile. He was always so confident and self-assured. It made her wonder what he'd been like as a child. Her mind flashed with images of a little boy with a soft face, eager eyes, and tousled brown hair.

"What are you smiling about?" Cardon asked.

She hadn't realized she was smiling, but her lips lifted higher now. "I was imagining you as a child." She tossed him a grin. "You were adorable."

An emotion she couldn't quite read ghosted in his eyes. His smile was a little wry. "I wasn't a child you would have noticed, Princess."

"I doubt that very much." There was something about Cardon that had always drawn her in, always made her feel comfortable and happy. And that was before she'd fallen in love with him.

The skin around his eyes tightened.

Looking at him as she was, she didn't notice the sudden dip in the ground. She tripped. Cardon attempted to stop her fall, but she still dropped to her knees, her free hand flashing out to catch her. Mud squelched beneath her palm, and she let out a shaky laugh. "I suppose I should watch where I'm going."

He pulled her to her feet, and Serene swept back tendrils of her hair. She could feel the smear of mud on her cheek her fingers left behind, but she was determined to ignore it. She'd already ruined the quiet moment with her ungraceful stumble, and she wanted to return to their conversation.

Cardon twisted her to face him, his brow lined. "Are you all right?"

"Perfectly fine."

Her skirt was a little tangled; he bent to straighten it, his hand scraping some of the mud away.

She touched his shoulder. "Cardon, it's fine."

Still crouched, he looked up at her, and something in his eyes made her pause. It wasn't concern, exactly. At least, it wasn't *just* that.

Her smile died. "Cardon?"

He swallowed and stretched to his full height. His thumb skated over the streak of mud she'd left on her cheek, gently removing it. Her pulse rushed faster, but she kept her focus on him.

"I used to live in the mud," he said.

Serene stared. She couldn't read his expression—couldn't understand the words he'd said, nor the flat way he'd said them.

Cardon's mouth twitched up at one corner, but it was not a happy smile. "Not literally, of course. We had a hovel. But I could never get the mud and dirt off me from working in the fields with my grandparents. We grew onions for a noble lord who paid us just enough so we wouldn't starve. That's why you never would have noticed me, Serene. I was nothing."

Her entire soul rebelled against that.

She opened her mouth to protest, but he spoke first. "It's all right. I've made peace with my past. And I left it behind a long time ago." His thumb still stroked her cheek, attempting to clean the mud away. "I could never get clean," he whispered. "I hated that."

An ache settled in her heart. She grasped his hand, stilling the insistent motion. "I'm sorry, Cardon. I didn't know."

His eyes drifted to hers. "Of course you didn't know. And you have no reason to be sorry."

But she was. She hated that he'd lived in such poverty. That he'd had to work so hard, even as a child. She hated that children still worked fields in Devendra.

Her voice softened. "Will you tell me more?"

Cardon glanced away. At first, she thought he just wanted to avoid her question, but then he pulled her gently to the nearby fence. Grasping her waist, he lifted her with ease and settled her on the top rail of the fence. Once he was sure she was secure, he hoisted himself up beside her.

He gripped the fence rail on either side of him, bracing his shoulders as he took a breath. "My grandparents raised me," he said, the words coming slowly. "They were onion farmers—just like their parents before them. Apparently, my mother hated her life." His jaw tightened. "My grandfather wasn't a kind man in the best of times, but especially when he drank—which was almost all the time. I imagine my mother's life was hell, so I don't blame her for running away when she was fifteen. She had no siblings still living, and my grand-mother was a timid woman who never stood up to her hus-band. Especially when he hit."

Serene's stomach dropped. She didn't know if she was strong enough to hear the rest of this story. But Cardon had been strong enough to live it, and he was strong enough to tell her—she would be strong enough to listen.

She took his hand again, and she was grateful when his fingers locked around hers.

"My mother returned home about a year after leaving, pregnant with me. She didn't know who the father was. At least, she never told her parents. They hid her to avoid the shame. Shortly after I was born, my mother handed me to my grandmother, walked out the door, and never returned. I know nothing else of her, or her fate." He stiffened beside her. "According to my grandmother, leaving me behind was a kindness. My mother was a wayward soul, she said. Too young and selfish to be a mother. My grandfather called her worse." He glanced over at her, but couldn't quite hold her gaze. "That was my life, Serene. That's where I came from."

Still holding his hand, she used her other palm to rub his tense arm. "I admire you more for it," she said.

He choked weakly. "How?"

She studied his profile—a profile she had memorized years ago, but which she viewed with new respect. "Cardon, you are the kindest, gentlest man I know. Fiercely protective and loyal. Filled with honor. You were dealt a terrible hand, and yet you became the man you are today. That is incredible."

He shifted, self-conscious, but at least he didn't pull away from her. "I tried to protect my grandmother," he said. "But I was small, and my grandfather hit hard. When he'd grab me . . . the reek of ale and onion is all I'd smell."

Serene's teeth clenched. That anyone would hit a child was reprehensible. That someone would hurt their own blood—a child in their care—was unforgivably monstrous. But the knowledge that a man had abused Cardon made her vision haze. "Is your grandfather still alive?" she asked.

"No."

"Good."

He exhaled a thin laugh. "You shouldn't sound so vengeful. The fates don't favor such a thing."

"I can't be sorry he's dead."

"Neither can I," he admitted.

Silence stretched, before she asked, "What about your grandmother?"

"I was eight years old when she died of a fever."

Her stomach turned. "You were left alone with your grandfather."

"Yes. I stayed with him until I was thirteen. Sometimes I wish I would have left sooner, but I was afraid. I didn't want the world to swallow me, like it had my mother."

"Thirteen is so young." She hated to think of him, alone and afraid. Desperate to find a place of safety.

"I wasn't alone," he said.

That snared her curiosity. "Who were you with?"

His shoulders straightened, but he didn't answer her right away—at least, not directly. "I hated working in the field, but I liked going into the village. We went whenever it was time to sell the harvest. I'd always managed to sneak away and play with the other children. We were all essentially farm hands, but in the market we felt like children. We played games, and I loved eating something other than onions."

He paused, gathering his thoughts. "When I was thirteen, we went to the village and I saw something I never had before—soldiers. I couldn't stop staring. They looked so . . . perfect. Their uniforms were clean, and everyone showed them respect—even my grandfather. I yearned to be one of them; strong, and confident. So, I followed them into the tavern and asked where I could go to become a soldier. Most of them laughed, and I can't blame them. I was strong from working the land, but I was still scrawny and dirty. Certainly unimpressive. But one of the men told me where the nearest barracks was located, though he told me I was too young to go. I didn't care—I left right then. I lied about my age so the soldiers at the barracks wouldn't reject me, and I never went home. Never looked back." He glanced at her. "I received a letter when my grandfather died, but I never went to visit his grave."

"He wouldn't have deserved it," Serene said. "He didn't deserve *you*."

"Thank you." His expression gentled. "It was at the barracks that I met Dirk. He was the one who recommended me to become a bodyguard. He's the only one I ever shared the entirety of my story with. No one else knows all of it." He tucked an errant strand of hair behind her ear. "Except you."

That warmed her, even though she still ached for him. "Thank you for trusting me with your story."

"I trust you completely."

Her heart swelled. She lifted his hand and placed a soft kiss against the back of it. "I'm sorry for what you had to suffer."

"It's in the past," he said. "That helpless boy I was . . . he no longer exists."

He was smiling faintly—reassuring her, she knew—yet his words hollowed out a part of her. She could picture that boy too easily. The dirt. The bruises. She wanted to hold him. Shelter him, and defend him. Assure him that one day he would be safe. That someday, a princess would love him more deeply than he could ever know.

"He's the reason I don't drink," Cardon explained softly. "My grandfather was always miserable, but when he drank, it was so much worse. He would lose all semblance of control. All hints of humanity. Sometimes, he'd look at my bruises the next day and ask where I got them—as if he didn't even remember giving them to me. I swore I'd never let myself be like him. That I'd never drink and lose myself. I couldn't understand why anyone would do that to themselves. My grandmother excused it by saying drinking made living easier for him. It helped him forget his pains, at least for a moment."

He frowned, the motion pulling at his scar. "That's why Wilf did it. Though I think I can almost understand that. When he lost Rachel, he lost his world. He lost an essential part of himself." He looked to her. "That's why I would become a drunk if I lost you, Serene. I would have nothing else to lose at that point."

Her heart beat too loudly in her chest. Fates, she hadn't even thought of that during his story, but knowing his past and the promise he'd made himself . . . it all meant so much more now.

She looked at him, her heart beating a little too fast. "You told me you got drunk once."

"Yes." He studied her. "It was the day your father decided you'd marry Desfan. It was no longer just a possibility, but a certainty. And you were miserable and afraid, and . . ." He swallowed. "I thought I'd see how effective drinking really was at blocking out pain."

She was trapped by the intensity of his gaze. Thrown by the vulnerability he'd revealed. Overwhelmed by everything he'd shared with her tonight.

She was far too breathless when Cardon sighed and withdrew his hand. "Apologies. None of this is appropriate. I promised you in Duvan that I wouldn't—"

She cut him off with a kiss, her mouth finding his with an ease that spoke of a thousand past kisses. Could imagined kisses make her an expert in kissing Cardon? She didn't know, but it came so easily. Effortlessly.

His hand settled against her cheek, but he did not push her away. His fingers drifted into her hair, keeping her close as he changed the angle of the kiss. His other hand curled around her side, coaxing her closer, his thumb tracing the line of her ribs through the fabric of her dress.

She didn't know how they didn't fall off the fence. Her balance was completely shaken, even though she had never felt more grounded than when she kissed him.

When their mouths finally broke apart for air, he rested his forehead against hers. His breathing was thin and ragged. "Fates, we can't do this."

"Why not?"

He pulled back, though his hands remained blessedly in place—one buried in her hair, the other firmly at her hip. "We've already discussed this. It's not right. You are promised to Desfan."

Her lips pursed. "Cardon, I—"

A muted scream rent the night.

Serene jerked. Cardon's fingers dug into her body, keeping her close as he stiffened. He scanned the night, and she did, too.

She didn't see anything. But the scream turned sharper. Agonized. Terrified. And it was quickly joined by others.

The screaming came from inside the inn.

Cardon dropped to the ground, pulling her with him. "We need to hide."

"What about Wilf?"

Cardon's lips parted, just as the back of the inn crashed open. Men and women flooded out into the yard, frantic and screaming.

Serene spotted Wilf's bulk easily. He had a knife in his hand and he scanned the darkness. When he saw them, there was no relief in his worried gaze. "*Run!*" he bellowed.

Serene's breath caught when she saw at least a dozen men barrel around the side of the inn, weapons drawn.

Chapter 41

Bennick

Bennick stood near the side door of the Hassan's manor, his gaze sweeping the torch-lit yard as guests arrived for the ball. He couldn't see the entirety of the grounds, due to the large trees that screened much of the yard, but he could see the eagerness of the guests as they prepared to meet who they believed was Princess Serene.

Bennick should have already joined Clare in her room, but he'd warned her and Venn that he might have to meet them in the ballroom. He'd needed to check in with the guards at the gate, and he insisted on looking over everything brought into the mansion for the Hassan's ball. That included last-minute flowers from Serai Jabar's personal garden.

The woman was extremely old, mostly deaf, and though Bennick had only met her once at a tea party yesterday, he knew her greatest passion was flowers. While the other ladies in the room had chatted about sending supplies to a village on the other side of the island that was suffering with illness, Serai Jabar talked only about the healing capabilities of cheerful flowers.

Tonight, Serai Jabar had arrived in a carriage with a cart full of flowers just behind her. After Bennick inspected the cart, Serai Jabar had shouted orders to the servants—both her own and those who served the Hassans—and insisted they carry her precious flowers gently and respectfully.

Apparently, that meant only one basket at a time.

"The Drammins can't be carried in with the Sunset Blooms —put them down at once, young man! Do you want to crush the souls of those Drammins? No? Then don't put them next to the *one* flower that can outshine them!"

Despite the itch to return to Clare's side, Bennick was amused by the woman's critical instructions.

The Hassan's servants looked less amused and more harried. Serai Jabar's men seemed used to it. They carried the large baskets carefully, and Bennick watched to make sure nothing more than flowers entered the manor—and that every man who entered returned, so no one was unaccounted for.

Serai Jabar also watched things with a sharp eye, though once the servants complied with her particular orders, she picked up a large bouquet and carried it over to Bennick. "You're Princess Serene's bodyguard, correct?" When he nodded, she thrust the flowers into his hands. "These are for her," she said, her volume overloud. "I'm giving it to you now so she doesn't have to carry it in the ballroom."

"Thank you, Serai Jabar. The princess will love them."

Her face scrunched. "What?"

He repeated his words, louder than before.

The woman nodded, and the dangling pearl earrings she wore wavered beside her short neck. "I did promise to bring my finest to honor her first ball on Dorma. That ballroom will outshine any in Duvan!"

He was only half listening as he kept an eye on the passing baskets of flowers. "This was a very kind and generous gesture."

"What?"

Before he could speak again, one of her men approached. "That's everything unloaded, Serai Jabar."

He must have gauged his tone correctly, because she beamed. "Wonderful! Please pay the driver and his men."

The servant obediently tugged a coin purse from his pocket as he walked to the head of the cart, where the driver stood beside his dusky gray horse. The man hadn't wandered from the animal since they'd arrived. His hand rubbed soothingly against the animal's long neck; the horse seemed rather impatient to be on his way.

Bennick could relate. But no matter how eager he was to return to Clare, he took the time to re-count all the servants in view, just to make sure none had slipped away.

"Will you escort me inside?" Serai Jabar asked of him loudly. "I've never been through the side entrance, and I'm not sure where to go."

"Of course." Bennick offered his arm, glancing back at the cart in time to see two men climb into the back. The driver hopped up onto his seat and steered the horse back toward the main gate. He lost sight of them quickly because of the thick trees.

Serai Jabar tugged at his arm. "Is anything wrong?"

"No." In fact, things on Dorma had been perfectly peaceful. He was grateful; fates knew Clare deserved a little peace. He and Venn hadn't relaxed their guard, of course—that's why he was personally overseeing the Hassan's security tonight. But the Mortisian guards were vigilant and committed to protecting the princess, which made Bennick's job easier.

Bennick led Serai Jabar to the brightly glowing ballroom, then continued on his way toward the second floor. The bouquet the older woman had given him was still in his hand, and he couldn't help but feel relief that there wasn't a single rose in the arrangement—or in the cart she'd had delivered. Perhaps they didn't grow on the island, or maybe she'd heard of the infamous assassin who had stalked the princess, and she'd avoided them purposefully.

He hadn't thought much about the rose left outside the orphanage in Duvan. With Grandeur's arrival and their rush to come to Dorma, the incident had been far from his mind. He knew a confrontation between him and Zilas was inevitable. Someday he'd find a taunting note and know that Zilas was back, and he'd have to face his half-brother. But for now, he enjoyed the reprieve.

He reached the suite on the second floor that had been given to Clare—or *Serene*, as the Hassans thought of her—and he greeted Walters, who was stationed at the door. The Devendran guard returned the greeting, and Bennick stepped into the room, nearly running into Venn.

His friend glanced down at the bouquet between them. "Oh, Bennick—you shouldn't have."

Bennick snorted as he kicked the door closed with the heel of his boot. "They're for Clare. From Serai Jabar."

"That's the old lady who wouldn't stop talking about her

flowers the other day, right?"

Bennick lifted one eyebrow—and the flowers. "Astute of you."

Venn chuckled. "I just wanted to make sure." He glanced at the flowers. "Clare's clearly made a good impression on the Mortisians here. She really handles this part of being the decoy well; the mingling and creating friendships . . . To be honest, it makes me want to stay on Dorma indefinitely. Everyone here adores her, so she's safer here."

Bennick couldn't disagree with his observations; in fact, he completely agreed. If it were possible, he'd keep Clare here forever. Her spirits were higher, and they'd managed to steal more time together than he'd dared hope for. They'd managed to visit their place beside the secluded stream nearly every night.

"Do you think we'll get any word from Serene?" Venn asked suddenly.

"I asked Cardon to send a message once they reached the castle," Bennick said. "Just so we know they arrived safely."

Venn didn't look fully satisfied. "It feels wrong, not knowing exactly where she is. Not being with them while they face the unknown in Zennor."

"I know. But Serene wouldn't be dissuaded."

"Her stubbornness is aggravating, yet impressive." Venn shook his head, and his voice was quieter as he said, "Devendra would have a brighter future with her on the throne."

Bennick didn't disagree, especially after the things Grandeur had been doing lately. Still, he cautioned, "Be careful who you say that around."

Venn's eyes rounded. "Are you going to report me, Captain?"

Bennick rolled his eyes. "How about we leave the politics to the politicians?"

He snorted. "Oh yes, because they've done such a *marvelous* job."

Bennick's mouth twitched, and Clare entered the room.

She wore a dark purple gown in one of the popular Mortisian styles that left her arms bare. Her dark hair was piled up on her head and pinned into place, making her graceful neck look even longer. Gently curling locks brushed her high cheekbones. A delicate gold chain with a glittering diamond rested at the hollow of her throat, and she wore thick gold bracelets and a matching circlet on her head. Her visible skin was tinted to better match Serene's deeper tone; the long-lasting stain had worn off during Clare's captivity, but Bridget had re-applied it once they'd arrived in Duvan. Bennick missed her natural warm skin color. But even though she'd been made to look like Serene, Clare's beauty was undeniable.

She stole his breath. Every thought in his head. And when she saw him and her red lips curved, she stole his heart all over again.

Vera walked in behind her, and Venn plucked a white flower from the bouquet Bennick held. He walked up to Vera, extending the flower with a bow. "My lady."

Vera's cheeks pinkened, but she smiled as she took the offered flower. "You're ridiculous," she told him mildly.

Venn grinned. "And yet you love me."

"I do." She rose on her toes and kissed his cheek. "Thank you," she said, lifting the flower so she could smell it.

A spark of envy caught Bennick. He was grateful his best friend and Vera had found their way to each other, but it was a little difficult to watch them. It reminded Bennick that

King Newlan didn't care if a bodyguard and a maid had a relationship, but it would be akin to treason for the captain of the princess's guard and her decoy to fall in love.

He knew he could kiss Clare, and Venn and Vera would say nothing. But Bridget was in the suite somewhere, and it was better not to take risks.

Bennick stepped forward, holding out the colorful bouquet to Clare. "A gift from Serai Jabar."

She took the flowers, their fingers brushing.

He might have been pathetic for feeling that simple, glancing touch so deeply.

Clare smiled. "They're lovely."

"You're breathtaking," he told her softly.

A blush colored her cheeks, and her eyes glittered.

Fates help him survive this night of watching her dance with other men. "Tonight," he whispered. "After the ball. Save a dance for me."

Her expression softened, anticipation in her gaze. "I can't wait."

The Hassan ballroom was packed with people and lined with flowers from Serai Jabar's garden. Lamps blazed, laughter rolled over the music, and the smell of perfume was overwhelming.

Bennick stood on the edge of the dance floor with Venn, watching as Clare was spun gently through a Mortisian waltz. Her laugh reached him, sounding genuine. Her partner—a handsome nobleman only a couple of years older than her—grinned.

"I can't imagine what that feels like," Venn said quietly.

Bennick exhaled slowly. "It doesn't feel good."

"You know," Venn said, his eyes still on Clare, "I once thought it was impossible for me to be with Vera, but we found a way. And I've never been happier." He glanced at Bennick. "I want you and Clare to have that."

"So do I." Bennick's brow furrowed—the Mortisian had snatched her hand and kissed it, before spinning her again. His voice was a little rougher as he said, "I don't know the way forward."

"You'll find it," Venn said. "Of that, I have no doubt."

Before Bennick could respond—not that he had a reply—Ser Hassan stepped up beside him. The man was dressed in his finery for the ball, but his expression showed concern, the fine lines on his face betraying his stress. "Captain Markam, may I speak with you for a moment?"

Curiosity—and sudden wariness—had Bennick nodding. "Of course." He left Venn watching Clare, confident his friend would keep her safe.

He walked with Kashif Hassan to the nearest exit, shouldering through the crowd until they reached the empty corridor. Once there, Ser Hassan's stride increased, and Bennick hurried to keep up. "What's happened?" he asked, his voice low even though they were alone in the hall.

Kashif's shoulders tensed. "There's been an incident. My men found Serai Jabar in the library. She's suffered a blow to the head. She hasn't come around yet, but I thought you'd want to question her personally."

Bennick's gut tightened. Fates, he couldn't imagine anyone

striking the old woman. "Has a physician been sent for?"

"Yes. And my wife is with her." His fingers twitched at his sides, betraying his anxiety. "I'm sorry, I didn't know what else to do."

"How long ago was she discovered?" Bennick asked.

"Not long—minutes, only."

Bennick frowned. He should send a message back to Venn. This didn't necessarily mean Clare was in danger, but it increased the risk.

Before they passed a servant or guard he could send back to the ballroom, they reached the library.

"I need you to send someone to Sir Grannard," he told Kashif. "Just to advise him of the situation."

The man nodded, rubbing his forehead. "Of course. I'll do that at once."

Bennick pulled open the door and strode into the room.

Bookshelves lined the walls, and a settee and chairs were gathered in the center of the room. The library was shadowed, with only one lamp burning near the settee.

Serai Hassan was seated on the end of the couch, facing away from the door. She twisted to look at Bennick over the back of the settee, fear clearly outlined in her pinched expression. "Captain Markam," she said, her words tangled with emotion. "Please help us."

Her terror—and her husband's anxiety—made sense when Bennick remembered they'd lived through the brutal attack in Duvan. The panic they felt now might be an echo of what they'd suffered then. Old attacks could haunt a soul for years.

"Everything is going to be all right," Bennick reassured her, keeping his voice calm and even.

He came around the settee and saw Serai Jabar lying on the

cushions, her head in Serai Hassan's lap. Blood congealed at her temple, clumping her hair. The sight of such an injury on an elderly woman made his blood boil.

He crouched beside the settee, studying the wound. "Has she stirred?" he asked.

Serai Hassan shook, tears now rolling down her cheeks. "I'm so sorry, Captain."

Bennick's scalp prickled. He shot the woman a look. "What?"

"We had no choice," she rasped, crying harder. "He has Sidrah."

The library door clicked shut.

Bennick straightened, his hand on the hilt of his belted sword as he eyed Kashif, who now stood in front of the closed door.

"I'm sorry," he whispered brokenly. "I wish this hadn't happened."

A blade pressed against Bennick's back—right on the scar where he'd been run through.

He stilled.

From too close behind him, a familiar voice said, "For all the flowers that old woman grows, can you believe she doesn't grow roses? I had to get them in the city."

Anxiety flared, but instinct took over. Bennick rammed his elbow into Zilas's gut, ignoring the rasp of the assassin's blade as it sliced harmlessly over his uniform. He shoved Zilas back, creating space to draw his sword.

Serai Hassan cried out and her husband jumped in front of Bennick, his hands outstretched as he gasped, "Don't! He'll kill Sidrah!"

Bennick leveled his sword at the Mortisian nobleman, his breathing tight.

Zilas chuckled, safe behind Kashif. "It's true. I have a friend holding the girl's neck right now. Such a pity she's missing the ball. Her pink dress is so pretty."

Serai Hassan sobbed. "Please let her go."

The Rose met Bennick's glare with a smirk, ignoring the distraught mother on the settee. "You knew I wasn't gone forever. You said it yourself—our fates are intertwined. You knew I would come back."

"You made that clear before you betrayed us in Krid," Bennick gritted out.

"It was more of an abandonment than a betrayal," his brother reasoned. "I'm glad you and Clare survived, though."

A deep rage rose to the surface, causing Bennick's hand to shake. "I lost her that night because of you."

Zilas's smile tipped higher. "You'll lose her tonight because of me, too. But this time will be much more permanent."

"You're not leaving this room alive," Bennick growled.

"Oh, I like my chances." Zilas flipped the dagger in his hand. "Have you been looking over your shoulder for me, all this time? Searching the shadows? I certainly hope so. I've thrilled at the thought."

Bennick's ears roared as his pulse pounded. "You're not touching her."

"We'll have to disagree on that score, little brother." Zilas shifted, and the light from the lamp lit only half his face, casting the rest in shadow. "I considered killing her in front of you. Making you watch as I take her life. There's something delicious in the thought of you being in the room—*right there*—while she dies. So close, but unable to save her. But then I imagined killing her when she's alone. How you won't even be there when she takes her last breath. You won't see the light leave her eyes. The knowledge that—up until the moment she stills in death—she'll think you're coming to save her. The idea of you finding her body . . ." He closed his eyes briefly, a grin stretching his lips. "*Fates*, it feels good."

The twisted evil that stood before him made Bennick's stomach churn. "You don't need to do this."

"I really do, though. If I take away the thing you love most, I destroy you—and that will destroy our father." Zilas's eyes gleamed. "Especially when his precious son rages against him for bringing this—*me*—upon him. Remember, this is all his fault. I am what he made me, and Clare would still breathe if not for him."

"I hate him too," Bennick said. "But what you're doing is worse than anything he's done."

Anger flashed over the assassin's face. "No. That man deserves his own hell, and I'm happy to create it for him." He nodded to Bennick's sword. "Drop it."

He only clenched his hold.

Zilas glanced at Serai Hassan. "Take his sword, or your daughter dies."

The woman swallowed a sob. Bennick didn't turn to watch her stand, but suddenly she was beside him. "Please," she begged, her tears falling faster now. She reached for his sword, and he retreated, lifting the blade threateningly.

His heart thundered. He didn't want to attack a defenseless woman, but he refused to surrender his weapon. He just wasn't sure how to get them all out of this alive.

Zilas sighed. "Cooperate, Bennick. Or do you want that girl's death on your hands?"

Serai Hassan covered her mouth with her hands, her shoulders shaking.

"Where is Sidrah?" Bennick demanded.

"I'm afraid I have little patience for questions tonight." Zilas grabbed Ser Hassan and laid the knife over his exposed throat.

Kashif closed his eyes, a cringe twisting his face.

Serai Hassan wailed.

The Rose smiled thinly at Bennick. "Perhaps we should make Sidrah fatherless. Fathers are only disappointing, so why not do her the favor?"

Gritting his teeth, Bennick dropped his sword, kicking it when ordered. "You won't get close to her," he told Zilas. "She's too well guarded."

"By Venn and a handful of guards?" Zilas scoffed. "Honestly, the only bodyguard that ever gave me pause was Wilford Lines; I stabbed that bear so deep he should be a corpse, but somehow he lived. That's unnerving. But he's gone—protecting Serene, perhaps? Speaking of the real princess, I haven't forgotten her. Will you tell me where you've hidden her, or will I need to hunt her down? I do have a reputation to uphold, and I *did* promise to kill her." He glanced at Serai Hassan. "Maybe you can host the real princess sometime, and not just her decoy."

Bennick shot a look at Serai Hassan, but she didn't look confused—just terrified.

Zilas's eyes widened mockingly. "Oh, I'm sorry, Bennick. I know you've been protective of that little secret. But I wanted to explain things to the Hassans." He patted Kashif's shoulder, and the man flinched. "I've reassured them that their actions aren't really treasonous, since they're only helping me kill the princess's decoy."

Fates. In his panic, Bennick hadn't even realized that Zilas had been talking openly about Clare. Not that her secret truly mattered right now.

Zilas's chin lifted to indicate Bennick's belted knife. "Toss that, too. And the one you no doubt have in your boot."

Tension rode him, but Bennick complied. "Did you leave that rose in Duvan?" he asked. "Outside the orphanage?"

"So it *did* reach you. Good. I couldn't resist leaving you a little reminder of my existence."

"How did you get Sidrah?"

"You're stalling, Bennick."

True. But if he didn't return soon with a report, Venn would grow worried. He'd send someone after him and Kashif—or bring in more guards for Clare.

Bennick glanced at the unconscious Serai Jabar. And some-how, he suddenly knew why she was here—why she was ever in Zilas's sights at all. "You were the driver." The man who had kept his head ducked or his back turned to Bennick the entire time. He muttered a curse. "You made sure she hired you. That was your way in."

"You're mostly accurate, Bennick. I *was* the driver. But I didn't make sure she hired me—I simply killed the men she hired and replaced them. She never noticed. When I spotted you, though, I worried you'd recognize me. I didn't expect you to be there, personally overseeing a flower delivery. But then, you have good reason to be paranoid. And luckily, your focus was on the men carrying the flowers."

Bennick's mind raced. He remembered the cart driving away. Fates, he should have made sure it actually left.

Memory stirred. Two men had climbed in the back of the cart. Did that mean Zilas had two allies, then? If one was with Sidrah, where was the other?

Zilas cracked a smile. "As entertaining as all of this is, I'm afraid I have places to be."

Bennick tensed, readying for a fight. It didn't matter that he didn't have a weapon. The moment Zilas moved for the door, Bennick would tackle him.

He was *not* getting close to Clare.

The attack didn't come from Zilas, though.

"Serai Hassan," Zilas called softly.

Bennick looked down just as the lady jabbed a needle into his bared wrist. Dizziness hit him like a boulder, making him stagger. Serai Hassan cried out an apology as he stumbled back a step.

Zilas strolled forward. "You'll wake in a few hours and find Clare surrounded by roses. It will be beautiful. I'll take extra care with the setting, just for you."

Bennick's world spun and darkened at the edges. He didn't know what drug he'd been given, but he was losing consciousness—fast. He crashed to his knees, his hands braced against the carpet to keep from toppling. "Zilas," he gasped. "Please."

The Rose stopped before him, but Bennick was too weak to attack. He slumped lower, his arms trembling to hold his weight.

"I didn't know Markams could beg," Zilas mused. "Do you think Father will beg for your forgiveness?"

Bennick collapsed, his head knocking against the rug. He barely felt it.

Zilas bent close. His voice was quieter, his tone containing an emotion Bennick couldn't name. "I always hated you. He chose you, and I couldn't stop hating you for that. But the things you said to me in that alley in Krid made me realize he failed you, too. Not as badly as he failed me, but . . ." He shook his head—the image blurred, making Bennick feel sick.

"If we'd been raised together, we might have been friends. Instead, he shoved me away and made us enemies. How different our lives would have been if he'd accepted all his . . ."

Blackness enfolded him, and Bennick heard no more.

CHAPTER 42

SERENE

"RUN!" WILF SHOUTED AGAIN, CHARGING TOWARD them across the darkened inn yard.

The dozen or so attackers held weapons that gleamed in the moonlight. The weak light also revealed the khalmin markings on their skin. The clan warriors were rushing to head off the men and women who were attempting to flee the inn.

Serene could hardly believe her eyes. She didn't understand what was happening. She was frozen, caught in shock. Why was a clan attacking the Panther's Den? It didn't make sense.

Unlike her, Cardon wasn't frozen. He grabbed her middle and all but threw her over the fence. She stumbled in the mud, turning just in time to see him plant a hand on the top rail and vault over it. "Run," he hissed, snatching her hand. He jerked her forward and they bolted across the field, headed for the treeline of the encroaching jungle. Cardon didn't bother to draw a weapon; the goal was to lose their pursuers, not fight them.

They were outnumbered—if it came down to a fight, they would lose.

They'd abandoned their packs, their horses—*Wilf.* Serene's gut tightened, but there was no choice except to keep running and pray Wilf was somewhere behind them, also running.

They were almost to the edge of the jungle when darts sliced through the air around them. Serene cringed and ducked, one dart sailing right beside her ear. Cardon shoved her in front of him, using his body to shield her back.

They reached the trees. Undergrowth forced them to slow down, but the lush foliage and thick vines might be enough to camouflage their escape.

Serene chanced a look back and the sight chilled her blood. Wilf had whipped around and now charged the host of warriors with his sword in hand. She stumbled to a halt, gasping out his name.

Cardon's hand clamped around her arm, dragging her forward. "He's giving us a chance," he gritted out. "Don't waste it."

Tears stung her eyes, blurring the image of Wilf swinging his longsword. A death cry went up, but she forced herself to look away. He would escape.

If any man could take down a dozen enemies and survive, it would be Wilf.

Clinging to that hope, Serene ran as quickly as she could with Cardon. They didn't stay on any trail. The thicker the terrain, the more likely Cardon was to dive through it. They hopped over the debris of the jungle, dodging past the towering trees and leaping over boulders.

Serene's lungs burned and her head spun. She didn't know

how long they'd been running, but it had felt like hours when Cardon finally trotted to a stop. He peered around them, then gestured toward a natural hollow in the mossy earth. They could hunch behind the low ridge, hidden from the view of anyone who might have followed their serpentine path.

Serene dropped to the ground, breathing too heavily. Cardon crouched beside her, peering up over the lip of the crevice.

The jungle was alive with night sounds. Insects hummed and chirped. Birds cried mournfully, and leaves rustled with the movement of unknown predators.

Her eyes darted everywhere, but her thoughts ran even faster. She hadn't been able to discern the colors of the khalmin markings, so she didn't know which tribe had attacked. But an attack by any clan wasn't good.

She hadn't been the target. At least, she didn't think so. The whole inn had been attacked—possibly the whole city of Danjuma. Was this one of the acts of random violence some of the clans had been guilty of lately, or was this something else?

The stories of the disappearances drifted through her mind, though she dismissed them. This attack would leave signs of a struggle, while those who had vanished usually did so without a trace. It couldn't be the same thing. Could it? Dakaar had said the disappearances had become more frequent lately. Maybe they were changing in the manner they were carried out, too.

Dakaar. Had he still been inside the inn, or had he left? She had no idea if he was safe or not. Or . . . had he been the one to summon the clans? She dismissed the thought at once. James trusted Dakaar, and she trusted James.

Silence reigned. Her tension increased. If their attackers didn't show themselves, did it mean Wilf had somehow stopped them? Or did it simply mean Cardon's route had confused them? And how was Wilf supposed to find them?

She rubbed her forehead, her breaths slowly evening out. Her legs ached. She desperately hoped they would not have to take off running again.

Cardon finally eased back, shooting her a look. "Are you all right?"

She nodded. "What now?"

His face tightened. "We can't risk going back to Danjuma."

Which meant they had no supplies. She swallowed. "Which direction did we run?"

"Northeast, I think."

She envisioned a map of Zennor and cringed. "We'll have to veer south again if we're going to hit Matanona." That was the next city they'd planned to stop in. She swallowed. "We have to go there. That's where Wilf would go to find us."

"If he's able, yes."

Her stomach turned. She tried to think past her fear for Wilf. If they didn't meet up in Matanona, then she had to believe he would find them in the capital. Because if she considered the possibility that he was dead, she couldn't breathe.

She forced herself to speak. "It will take a full day or two in the jungle without horses."

"You're right." Cardon stood. "Let's make up some of that distance now. We have too much adrenaline to sleep, anyway."

That was true. Every nerve hummed as she pushed to her feet. She glanced around the dark jungle. "I'm not sure I can get my bearings here."

Cardon pointed. "We'll go that way." As he lowered his arm, he grimaced.

She stepped closer. "Are you all right?"

"Fine." He stretched his limb. "Just pulled something when I went over the fence."

Her own body ached, so she understood.

They started walking, but they hadn't gone far when Serene noticed the eyes in the trees watching them. A closer look revealed a host of brown-mane monkeys looking down on them. "That's unnerving," she muttered.

Cardon grunted beside her. "I hate the jungle. It makes me feel caged."

"It's the creatures we're caged *with* that worry me." She thought she heard a low growl in the distance and imagined a panther stalking them. She sidled closer to Cardon. "Do you think we were the targets?" she asked, needing a distraction.

"I don't know. It doesn't seem likely. Few people know we're here."

True. Although she now wondered if she'd made a mistake in contacting the man at the Fiddler. He might have betrayed her. Or the owner of the Panther's Den could have been to blame. Or Dakaar, as much as she didn't want it to be him.

There really was no way of knowing at this point.

"The tribes haven't been this aggressive in years," she said. "I can't believe things have gotten so bad."

"It certainly doesn't bode well." He brushed a vine aside, holding it as Serene stepped past. "It makes me worry about the situation in the capital."

"What situation?" She hadn't told him what Dakaar had told her—that the capital and castle were all but sealed to outsiders and the royal family had not been seen in months.

Cardon shrugged. "Who knows what we'll find there. I think it's safe to say at this point that something is terribly wrong in Zennor. I'm beginning to think the castle won't be the safe haven we were hoping for."

"I'm glad Imara is safe in Duvan." She was oddly grateful for her cousin's injury; she didn't want Imara anywhere near this place.

Cardon snagged her elbow, halting her. He raised a finger to his lips, urging her to remain silent.

Other than her thundering heart, she complied.

The entire jungle had quieted. Even the clicking chatter of the monkeys had stopped. She turned back to Cardon, and in his eyes she saw a reflection of her own anxiety.

A twig snapped.

Cardon whirled, drawing his longsword as he barked at her to run.

A dart flew out of the bushes, barely missing Cardon, and then two tribesmen attacked.

Cardon lifted his sword, stopping the downward swipe of the first attacker.

The second warrior raised the bamboo pipe to his lips, his focus on Cardon's exposed back.

Serene lunged, knocking the man aside before he could shoot the blow dart. He growled and dropped the bamboo weapon, then tried to grab her wrist.

Serene palmed her knife and sliced his grasping palm.

He hissed and drew his own knife; she ducked around his angry slice and came at him from the side.

Her knife sank in to the hilt, catching him between his ribs. He cried out and buckled. Serene heaved out her dagger, bile climbing her throat at the sight of blood. Her body trembled as she gripped the blood-streaked knife. She watched as the tribesman fell, his body going still.

She had trained for years to defend herself. She'd even killed before, in defense of herself and others, but the actual reality of taking a life never ceased to rattle her.

Still shaking, Serene turned—and her heart stopped.

Cardon was on the ground, his sword beside him. The warrior he had presumably slain was curled on his side nearby.

"*No*." Serene gasped and darted forward. "No, no, no—Cardon?" She knelt, her hand going to his face. "Cardon, look at me."

His head rolled, his eyes only half-open. He was breathing, but shallowly. "I told you to run."

She ignored that. "Where are you hurt?" She spread a hand over his chest and ran her fingers over his sides. He had a thin slice on his arm, but nothing serious. She touched his shoulder and he hissed.

Her lungs froze. She tugged at his shirt until she bared his shoulder, but confusion washed over her. There was no gaping wound, or horrible flow of blood. There was nothing but a small puncture mark. The skin around it was lividly red.

At first, it didn't make sense—then everything clicked into place.

The darts, from when they had first tried to run. He'd been struck. The darts were too small to be dangerous on their own, which meant they carried poison.

Cardon had been poisoned.

Her chest constricted, and her hands shook. "You said you were fine."

He made no response. His pulse was erratic, his eyes barely open now.

She pulled his arm closer to study the shallow cut that leaked blood, and she could feel the throbbing heat coming from his flesh. His arm was stiff. Too stiff.

He'd been poisoned *twice.*

"You've been poisoned," she said, shocked and horrified.

He peeked up at her, his breathing thready. "I know."

She clenched her teeth. The fates-blasted man had known the dart was poisoned. "Why didn't you tell me?"

He blinked slowly, his eyes opening to mere slits now. "I didn't want to alarm you."

She cursed and clenched his hand in hers. "I don't know what to do."

He winced when he tried to move. "My entire arm is numb. I don't know what this poison is, but I think it spreads faster the more I exert myself. I'm quite dizzy." His eyes fluttered closed.

Serene grabbed his face in her hands. "Don't close your eyes."

The lids of his eyes pulled open, but barely. "Keep going south," he rasped weakly.

Her stomach clenched. "You're a fates blasted fool if you think I'm leaving you here."

"It will spread to my legs soon enough," he said quietly. "My heart." His eyes slipped closed again. "I need you to go. Keep going. Wilf will find you."

Her pulse pounded. Panic gripped her. Her fingertips pressed against his cheeks, and he managed to look at her again. Her voice wavered, desperation and fear twisting together in her words. "Cardon, please. Don't leave me."

He slowly lifted his right hand and laid it over hers, his thumb smoothing weakly over her knuckles. "I'm sorry, Serene."

Her breathing hitched, but she refused to give in to the tears flooding her eyes. She didn't blink as she glared down at him. "No. You get up. *Now*. You're not dying. I need you."

"I'm sorry," he murmured again.

Serene clenched her jaw. "Don't apologize. Just don't leave me. That's an order, Sir Brinhurst."

She thought his mouth twitched. "Hate that name," he muttered. His eyes fell closed. "Go. Be safe."

"I'm not going anywhere without you." Her breathing hitched as she fought against the flood of tears. "Cardon, please—Cardon?"

His eyes did not open.

Horror choked her. "Cardon."

Nothing. He was barely breathing.

"*Cardon!*"

It didn't matter how many times she screamed his name.

His eyes never opened.

CHAPTER 43

CLARE

THE MUSIC SWELLED AND THEN DIED. AS THE FINAL note faded, Clare curtsied, answering the deep bow of her latest dance partner.

Clare glanced toward Venn, who stood on the edge of the dance floor. She'd glimpsed Bennick slipping away with Kashif Hassan nearly half an hour ago. Anxiety fluttered in her stomach. Where was he?

Venn stepped forward, and in his slight frown she read an echo of her own nervousness. "I've sent someone to track down Bennick and Ser Hassan," he said, his voice pitched low so no one around them would hear.

Clare nodded, grateful for the update.

"The musicians are taking a short break," Venn continued. "I think it would be fine if you did, too. I'll feel better having you in the suite under guard until Bennick gets word to us of

561

what's going on." He gave her a gentle smile that didn't quite warm his eyes. "I'm sure nothing's wrong, I just want to be cautious."

Clare didn't protest. She took his arm and they walked to the nearest door. She nodded and smiled to those who greeted her as she passed, but no one questioned where she was going. With the lull in dancing, many were stepping out onto the terrace for fresh air or converging on the food-laden tables.

Once in the hall, Clare pursed her lips. "Ser Hassan looked upset."

"He did," Venn said. "But if it was a true security risk, I'm sure we would have heard something by now."

That was true. If she was in danger, Bennick would have returned immediately. The fact that he hadn't should put her at ease.

It didn't.

She sighed as they started up the staircase to the second floor. Her feet ached from dancing, and she was looking forward to putting them up, if only for a few moments. "Ser Hassan may have been stressed because of the large crowd," she speculated. "Ilah said he doesn't care for socializing."

"That could have been it."

She lightly elbowed Venn's side. "Or maybe you're just looking for an excuse to return early to Vera."

He laughed. "Can you blame me?"

"No. She's incredible."

"She is. I can't wait for my family to meet her. My sisters will adore her."

Clare smiled. "You have two sisters, don't you?"

"Yes, one older, one younger. They're both married to good men, and I have three beautiful nieces."

"You must miss them."

"I do. But I spent a lot of time away training to be a soldier, like my father, so they're used to it."

"I didn't know your father was a soldier." She hadn't heard Venn talk about his father at all, actually.

"He was. I don't have any solid memories of him, though. He died when I was two years old."

Her heart squeezed. "I'm sorry, Venn."

"Thank you." He smiled faintly. "I'm just grateful my mother didn't return to her family in Zennor when he died. If she had, I never would have met Bennick—or Vera, or you, or the other bodyguards."

They had reached the guest wing. The Mortisian guard on duty bowed as they walked past, entering the private hall that led to her suite. "I would love to meet your family one day," Clare said.

"I'd love that, too. When we return to Iden, I'll make arrangements." A shadow swept over his face. "I hope they're safe. Just knowing what Grandeur has been doing there—the Hunt, and all their crimes . . . It doesn't really sound like the home we left."

Clare agreed. Thinking of Devendra itself was strange. The kingdom felt so distant. Devendra—more specifically, Iden—had been her entire world before becoming the decoy. Knowing her brothers were no longer there only added to the feeling of dissonance. Without them, she wasn't sure where home was, now.

Venn frowned as they reached the unguarded suite. "I wonder where Walters is."

"Perhaps he's inside."

Venn's steps slowed, urging Clare to hesitate as well. "Let me go first," he said.

The tang of the air changed. Clare stiffened, a sense of warning spiking. "Venn . . ."

"Just stay out here," he said quietly. "It's probably nothing." But he drew the dagger at his belt as he opened the door. He moved in slowly, and Clare remained where she was for half a beat before following.

The sitting room was empty, the lamps glowing weakly. There was no sign of Walters, Vera, or Bridget.

Venn glanced at Clare, exasperation in his gaze, but he didn't order her back. He remained silent as he moved toward the small bedroom Vera used. He prodded the door open with his fingertips and peeked inside.

Clare peered around him, but there was nothing to see—the room was empty.

Venn's brow furrowed, his tension obvious as he walked to the main bedroom. He paused at the door, and Clare soon realized why.

The door was mostly closed, but wasn't actually latched.

The small hairs on the back of her neck lifted as Venn nudged the portal open. He instantly stiffened, and Clare sucked in a sharp breath.

Vera was laid out on the bed, staring at the ceiling. Red roses were placed all around her, and her blonde hair had been carefully combed out across the pillow. One red blossom was in her mouth, crimson petals open, mimicking an open mouth, silently screaming.

Grief tore through Clare. Her knees trembled, and her stomach lurched. Images of Ivonne's body flashed over what she currently saw. Fates, Ivonne—now Vera.

Venn was like stone, frozen and hard. Then, with an agonized cry, he flew forward and grabbed Vera's arm.

Clare gasped when Vera's hand flashed up, wrapping around Venn's forearm.

She was still alive.

Clare staggered as relief hit her like a crashing wave.

"I told you not to move, Vera."

Clare spun at the words, flinching when she saw Zilas emerge from behind the door. But even though her body reflexively retreated, her training took over. This wasn't an enemy to run from.

This was an enemy she needed to fight.

She shoved the door into him. It connected harshly and Zilas grunted, but the blow didn't do more than rock him. His hand flashed out and he snagged her elbow, wrenching her into his arms. She struggled, until Zilas's blade pressed into her side.

Stilling, she looked up to see Venn—still clutching Vera's arm, but angled toward Clare, that dagger still clutched in his hand.

The smile in Zilas's voice was clear. "I told Vera we'd play a little game. If she holds still and keeps that rose in her mouth, I won't kill her. And I won't kill you, Venn, if you don't try to stop me from taking Clare. So. Are we all going to play the game, or is everyone going to die tonight?"

His chest rose and fell calmly against her back. Clare shuddered in his hold.

Venn's grip on Vera was desperate, his eyes dark as he glared at the Rose.

Zilas chuckled. "No grand words, Venn? No useless promises? I think Bennick would be disappointed in you."

Venn's knuckles were white as he clutched the dagger. Indecision tore his expression; he was poised to fight, but unable to act. Not with Zilas holding a knife to Clare's side. His eyes darted beyond Zilas, through the partially opened door.

"Looking for Bennick to help you?" the Rose asked. "I'm afraid he won't be helping anyone tonight."

Clare's heart tripped. "What have you done?"

Zilas ignored her, still focused on Venn. "Clare is dying tonight. There's nothing you can do to stop that. If you attack me, I'll kill her here and now, then I'll kill you and Vera, just like I killed her sister. And of course, poor little Sidrah would have to die as well."

Clare sucked in a breath. "Sidrah?"

The knife in her side pressed deeper—a warning to keep still. "She's a pretty thing. Far younger than I usually terrorize. I actually feel a little bad for scaring her."

Clare's ears rang. "Where is she? Have you hurt her?"

"No. But I'm prepared to." His attention shifted back to Venn. "It's your choice. Either everyone dies, or you let me leave with Clare."

Vera was shaking on the bed, her fingers digging into Venn's arm.

Venn's brown eyes flashed to Clare. Muscles in his arms rippled beneath his uniform, but he didn't move.

"It's all right, Venn," Clare said, a tremble riding her words. She fought to steady her voice. "Stay with Vera."

His dark eyebrows drew together, his body tensed.

The Rose sighed. "I suppose you might need a little more persuasion. Don't worry, I came prepared." With a short whistle, a Mortisian man entered the bedroom. He held a small crossbow loaded with a dart, and he aimed it at Vera's chest.

Venn ground his teeth. "Don't do this, Zilas."

The assassin huffed a short laugh. "First Bennick begs me,

and now you do the same. It makes me wonder why men even bother fighting wars. Simply find the thing your opponent loves, and they'll be on their knees—victory is simple." Zilas tightened his hold on Clare, still speaking to Venn. "Do me a favor, won't you? When you see Bennick, tell him how you gave me Clare without a fight, all to save the woman *you* love."

Clare's pulse skipped, and hope surged. *Bennick was alive.*

"He's going to hate you, Venn," Zilas continued. "I hadn't realized how much that meant to me until this moment, but it's fates-blasted perfect."

Venn's nostrils flared, but otherwise he remained still. One eye remained fixed on the crossbow, still leveled at Vera.

Zilas looked to his hired man. "Keep them here for a quarter hour. That's all the time I'll need." He dragged Clare into the sitting room, his knife still held against her side.

As they crossed to the door, Clare caught sight of Bridget. The maid was crumpled behind the settee, easily hidden from the view of the suite's main door. Bridget wasn't moving, and Clare could see blood at her temple. She prayed it hadn't been a killing blow, and that the woman was only unconscious.

"Keep cooperating, and no one else has to die," Zilas told her. "If an alarm is raised, Venn, Vera, and Sidrah will be killed."

She gritted her teeth. "What did you do to Bennick?"

"He's currently battling the effects of a rather potent Rydenic potion that will leave him unconscious for several hours."

The reassurance that he would be all right loosened some of the tightness in her chest, but her fear remained. Bennick had fallen into the Rose's trap. He was unconscious, Venn was pinned, and Walters was missing—dead?

Clare had no choice but to face this demon alone.

Panic swirled, but resolve steeled her spine. She would not die without a fight, even if she couldn't fight yet. She didn't know where Sidrah was, and she would not risk Venn and Vera's lives. She had already lost one family—she would not lose the only one she had left. Once Zilas led her far enough away, she would strike.

Zilas pulled her into the empty corridor, forcing her toward the south end of the manor—away from the main staircase. This section of the house was dark, and farther from the ballroom.

"The island of Dorma suites you, Clare," Zilas said. "You look lovely."

She didn't bother summoning a response. The man was only taunting her.

The corner of his mouth twitched. "I think it's suited Bennick as well. He's been much more relaxed here. It made it all too easy to keep an eye on you. I got fairly close a few different times, but you never saw me. Not at the theater, or the museum—certainly not at your special meeting place by the stream."

Chills skated over her skin. The thought of this man watching her—watching *them*—made her sick.

They reached the end of the hall and Zilas pulled her into a musty bedroom that clearly hadn't been used in some time. Zilas moved confidently toward the corner of the room. "Did you know," he said conversationally, "years ago, Dorma was constantly being raided by pirates? These older manors were built with that in mind." He kept hold of her, but his other hand—still wrapped around the hilt of the knife—moved as he ran his fingertips along the side of some wooden paneling. "Each wing had an escape route so residents wouldn't be trapped on the upper floors in the event of an attack. It was quite ingenious." There was a click, and a thin door jumped open from the paneling, revealing a narrow staircase. Zilas moved his grip to her shoulder. "After you."

Clare ground her teeth as she picked her way slowly down the narrow staircase. All was dark, but Zilas's knife prodded her down the steep stairs.

"You don't need to torture Bennick like this," Clare said. She didn't know if she'd be able to persuade someone like the Rose with logic or emotion, but she was willing to try. "You are brothers."

"Ah. Bennick told you the truth, then."

"Yes. I know your father abandoned you and your mother. That's awful, Zilas, and I'm sorry that happened to you. But it wasn't Bennick's fault." Her heel caught on an uneven step and she pitched forward.

Zilas's hold tensed, keeping her from falling. His tone was a shade harder when he said. "True. And the commander was a terrible father to both of us. But between Bennick and me, it's clear who had the better life."

"Punishing Bennick for that isn't fair."

"Maybe not. But it feels good."

The hairs on her arms lifted, and she knew there would be no reasoning with this man.

They reached the base of the staircase. "There's a latch on the door in front of you," he told her. "Unlock it."

Clare's fingers splayed over the smooth wood as she searched blindly in the darkness. As long as they remained in the walls of the manor, she didn't dare fight him. When she found the latch, she unlocked the door and forced it open. The creak was terrible, the hinges stiff, but fresh air and moonlight reached them.

They stepped outside and Zilas once again shifted his hold on her, grasping her upper arm with one hand, his knife held almost gently against her side. He nudged her forward, and they moved across the grounds, heading away from the manor. She stiffened as soon as they stepped onto a familiar path.

The assassin chuckled. "Since it didn't work out to kill you in your bed like I usually do, this intimate place seemed the next best thing. I think Bennick will eventually think to find you here, don't you?"

Clare continued to walk, forcing herself to relax so she wouldn't give away her intentions. She knew this path, and she knew the best place to make her strike. She tried to breathe regularly, even though adrenaline hummed through her body.

They turned a corner in the winding path, and Clare could hear the gentle rush of the stream ahead. The boulder she'd been waiting for came into view, sitting just on the edge of the path.

She took a steady breath. Another. Then, when she was close enough, she planted a foot against the rock and shoved back against Zilas's hard chest.

He cursed and stumbled, struggling to hold onto her and the dagger, which she grabbed and tried to wrestle away from her side. She didn't dare run—he'd catch her. She couldn't afford to reach for her own knife, because he'd strike the moment she released his blade. And he was too tall for the garrote to work well, so getting his knife was her best option.

Falling into the training Bennick had given her, she fought

for her life. She kicked, hit, and twisted. She nearly fell when he shoved her, but she managed to keep her feet. Her fingers strained to yank the knife away from him. If she could get it, she could stab him, and—

A small, pinched cry pierced the night.

Clare's head snapped in the direction of the soft, anguished sound.

Zilas's fist slammed into her cheek.

Blood filled her mouth and she staggered, crashing to the ground. Dazed, she panted against the dirt, her vision sparking. Pain bloomed across the side of her face.

Zilas dragged her to her feet and hauled her around the final bend. The glistening stream came into view, and so did Sidrah. The little girl was bound with a length of rope and secured to the iron bench. A sharp cry came from the girl when she saw Clare, her tear-streaked face shining in the moonlight. She sounded hoarse. Fates, how long had she been out here crying?

"How could you?" Clare gasped. "She's only a child!"

"She'll be fine, as long as you don't struggle." The assassin threw Clare to the ground beside the bench. She almost knocked over a basket full of roses. The velvet petals were all she could see for a moment. The strong floral scent filled her lungs, and nausea swam in her gut. Her cheek throbbed from where he'd hit her.

The assassin smiled at Sidrah, who cowered against the bench. "Sidrah knows to be a good little girl and not say a word. If she listens, she'll see her parents again. As long as you're a good girl too, Clare."

"Please, let her go," Clare begged. "I won't fight—just let her go."

"Considering what you just tried to do, I think it's better if she stays until the end. Lie on your back."

Clare trembled, but she did as he ordered, her fingers curling in the dirt.

He towered over her. "Sooner or later, being the decoy was bound to get you killed. At least I'll kill you gently. Other assassins might not be so kind."

"Fates rot you."

He only smirked at her curse. "Not such a horrible threat, really—I don't believe in the fates."

He knelt beside her, the blade spinning once in his hand.

Clare glanced at the little girl. "Close your eyes, Sidrah."

She did, scrunching her entire face as she bowed her head.

Zilas plucked up a rose from the basket. "I'll give you the choice I try to give all my victims: do you want me to kill you first and then arrange your body, or will you hold still?"

Her first fistful of dirt hit his eyes. The second she kept in her palm, and it helped dull the slice of the blade as she caught the descending knife and shoved it aside.

Zilas snarled.

Clare rolled, snatching the small dagger strapped to her calf as she moved to the bench. Sidrah's eyes were wide and she screamed.

Clare swiped her blade at the rope tying Sidrah to the bench, but her shaking hand missed. She tried again, but Zilas tackled her.

His weight crushed her, but she managed to keep a grip on her knife.

He grunted as he straddled her back, pressing the aching side of her head against the ground. "You've made your decision, then," he grunted. His fingers knotted in her hair, ripping at the pins as he jerked her head up, exposing her throat.

She could already feel the phantom swipe of his blade. The end of her life.

Desperation choked her. With him behind her, she couldn't stab him effectively. But her knife wasn't useless. *She* wasn't useless.

She drove the blade into the only part of his body she could reach—his leg, braced firmly against her side.

He howled and jerked away from her.

She kicked, knocking him off her. She'd lost her knife—it was still buried in his leg—but she snatched up a fist-sized rock. She twisted around, still crouched on the ground, prepared to strike him with the stone. But when her eyes locked on Zilas's they were wide. Shocked. Pained.

Not quite seeing her.

He was rigid, crouched on his knees. Then Bennick rose from behind him, gripping Zilas's shoulder. Bennick's other hand jerked back, removing the dagger he'd shoved into his brother's back.

Clare trembled, still holding the rock. Her recently-healed fingers burned with the pressure, and she tried to loosen her hold. Only, she couldn't. She couldn't let go of the cool stone, even as she watched Bennick release his hold on Zilas, and the assassin slumped to the ground.

He landed on his side, gasping for air. He glanced at her, then his gaze flicked up to Bennick, who knelt over him. "You," he croaked.

Bennick said nothing. Just stared at him, bloody knife in hand.

Zilas's face clenched. "I . . . I'm not the only one . . . I'm not . . . the last . . ."

His breath rattled out, and his body stilled.

The smell of roses hung heavy on the air, mixing with the scent of blood.

Bennick's throat worked. Still kneeling, he reached for Clare.

She pushed up from the ground and threw her arms around him, clutching him to her. His arms came around her, weaker than normal. Shaking. Fates, he'd been incapacitated by some horrible poison. How was he even here?

Behind her, Sidrah burst into fresh tears.

Clare pressed a quick kiss to Bennick's jaw before she pulled back. She hated to leave him, but the little girl needed her.

She retrieved her small knife from Zilas's leg, grimacing as it pulled free. She shoved aside her nausea and hurried over to Sidrah. Murmuring soothing assurances, she cut the girl free, then wrapped her in her arms and stood.

Bennick's fingers were pressed against the side of Zilas's neck—checking to make sure his brother was truly dead. When his hand fell away, Clare couldn't quite read the emotion that sparked in his eyes.

With Sidrah's face buried in Clare's neck, she kept her words soft. "Bennick? Are you all right?"

He blinked slowly, his eyes sliding to her. "Yes. Are you?"

They were both alive. "Yes," she whispered.

His gaze sharpened. He pushed to his feet, that bloody knife still in his hand. He stepped forward, his fingertips brushing the edge of her throbbing cheek. It burned, and she imagined he could see the redness. Her palm stung from the cut of Zilas's knife, only partially shielded by the handful of dirt she'd held.

"He said you would be unconscious for hours," she said.

Bennick's fingers curled away from her cheek and dropped. His voice was stronger now—more sure. "I should have been. The Hassans were helping him." He glanced at Sidrah, who was clinging tightly to Clare. A muscle in his jaw ticked. "They didn't have a choice. But after Zilas gave Serai Hassan the drugged needle, she wiped off as much of the poison as she could when he wasn't looking. I was only knocked down with the residue. As soon as Zilas left to get you, the Hassans worked to revive me. They didn't dare go after Zilas on their own—especially because he'd left a guard in the hall."

Clare didn't blame the Hassans for their part in this nightmarish night; they'd been trapped the moment Zilas had taken Sidrah. While she wished they'd dared do more to warn Bennick of the threat, they'd done what they could.

She didn't have to ask what had happened next; Bennick would have fought Zilas's hired guard, even though he'd just been drugged. He would have rallied more men, and he would have run to the suite, expecting to find Clare on the bed.

Her heart squeezed. "Venn and Vera? Bridget?"

"They're all fine, just worried about you." Bennick swallowed hard. "Venn didn't know where Zilas had taken you. He always tries to kill his targets in their bedroom. If not there . . . We were looking everywhere." He eyed the small clearing around them. "I thought he might have known about this place, since he was watching us. I couldn't be sure, so I told the others to keep tearing the manor apart, and I ran here."

He looked almost lost. He was in shock, and still clearly feeling the effects of the drug. The terror he'd obviously felt—mixed with the reality that he'd just killed his half-brother—was clear on his lined face.

Her heart hurt for him.

She reached for his hand and squeezed his fingers, still holding Sidrah easily against her chest. "Let's go back," she said, her voice soft. "We need to get Sidrah to her parents and let the others know we're all right."

Bennick nodded once, the motion a little slow. With one last look at Zilas's still body, he gripped Clare's hand and they walked out of the clearing together.

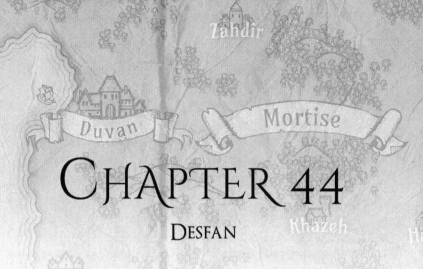

CHAPTER 44

DESFAN

DESFAN RAN HIS FINGERS OVER THE SMOOTH edge of the table. The air was chilled in the upper level of the prison, where he and Karim waited for the guards to bring Liam.

"Is this really necessary?" Karim asked.

"He knows more about Sahvi and his partners than we do," Desfan pointed out. "He might be able to tell us something that helps us capture him."

Ever since meeting with Fang in that alley nine days ago, Desfan had been thinking about what Liam had told him during his interrogation weeks ago; that Sahvi was just one enemy in Zennor, and that following the trail of olcain was the only way to understand the full threat against Mortise. The Shadow of Ryden had been cryptic, but that seemed to be Liam's way. Especially because he wanted Desfan to learn the truth on his own, so he wouldn't think Liam was manipulating him. He wanted them to have the same enemies so Desfan would end them.

Actually, that felt a bit like manipulation.

But there wasn't a lot of time to debate his decision to talk to Liam now. Fang's meeting with Sahvi would take place tonight, and if the Rydenic prince could help them, it was worth the time for this conversation. Frankly, he would have come sooner if he hadn't been so fates-blasted busy with council meetings and the like.

The door opened and three guards escorted Liam into the holding room. Chains clinked as the prince shuffled forward, his ankles and wrists both manacled. His hair was a little longer than last time, his beard more unruly, but his clever eyes seemed exactly the same as he scanned the room.

"No Captain Markam today?" Liam drawled. "I almost feel slighted."

"He's otherwise engaged," Desfan said, dropping his hand from the table. He watched as Liam lowered into the chair across from him, then his eyes flicked to the guards. "You may wait outside."

They bowed and retreated. The door closed heavily behind them.

Liam reclined as much as the chains would allow. He almost looked fates-blasted comfortable. He was certainly more self-assured than he had been during their last visit, at least in the beginning. It made Desfan think that Liam's previous concern for Grayson had been unfeigned—not that he truly knew what to do with that knowledge. Did Liam actually care about Grayson's welfare? It seemed so unlikely, it was almost laughable.

The prince of Ryden smiled. "What can I do for the serjan

and his guard today?"

"You can answer some questions." Desfan briefly told him about their meeting with Fang in the alley. When he mentioned Sahvi, the skin under Liam's left eye twitched.

"Sahvi is in Duvan?" the prince clarified.

"Yes. But he wants Fang to help him leave tonight. We obviously aren't going to let that happen."

"What's your plan to capture him?" Liam asked.

Desfan glanced at Karim, who stood beside him. His friend was not happy about this plan, though he was resigned. "Members of the city guard—along with Karim and myself—will be disguised as Fang's men. We'll be in the warehouse when Sahvi arrives. We'll wait to spring our trap until the warehouse is surrounded by my men, and Sahvi has revealed where Fang's family is—and possibly why he's in possession of my gold, why exactly he's been bringing olcain into Mortise, and who in Zennor is giving him orders. Of course, if he doesn't confess on his own, we can always secure a confession later."

Liam pondered this. "That plan isn't utter rot."

Desfan snorted. "Thank you."

"It could be improved upon, of course." Liam resettled his shoulders against the back of his chair, making the wood creak. "You should use members of the palace guard, not the city guard. Sahvi and his men may have taken note of some faces on the streets and recognize them."

Karim grunted, the sound a little too gruff to be considered appreciative.

Desfan tipped his head. "A good recommendation. Thank you."

"Of course, by that same logic, you shouldn't be there," Liam said. "If Sahvi has been in Duvan for a while, then he might have glimpsed you at one of your public appearances."

"I will be there," Desfan said—quickly, so Karim couldn't throw in his argument as well. "The light will be imperfect, and he won't expect me. I'm not worried."

Liam shrugged. "It's your neck, Serjan. Of course, there are a few other issues with your plan."

His brow furrowed. "Like what?"

"The fact that Sahvi is slippery as a serpent, for one—you're not likely to actually catch him. Not unless you have a blade to his ribs when you spring your trap. You'll need someone to get close to him, and that will be virtually impossible for all of you."

"What would you suggest, then?"

Liam arched one brow. "Allow me to hold the knife."

A laugh burst out of him. When Liam's calm expression didn't falter, Desfan's eyes widened. "Fates, you're serious, aren't you?" He laughed harder, the sound ringing against the stone walls.

Liam sighed. "I'm glad I amuse you."

Desfan still shook with laughter. "Fates! As if I'd trust you to just walk out of here and give you a knife?"

The spymaster's lips pressed into a line. "I'm the only one who has a chance of getting close to Sahvi."

"Why?" he asked, mirth still heavy in his voice. "Does *he* trust you?"

"No," Liam said blandly. "But he'll be surprised to see me, and that has its advantages."

"Why would he be surprised to see you?"

Liam's hand lifted so he could scratch his bearded chin. "We have a history. Not a good one. The last time we were in the same room together, I thought he was dead."

Desfan folded his arms across his chest. "Were you the one who tried to kill him?"

"Not at that exact moment, no. But I assure you, the moment Sahvi sees me, he'll be thrown off-guard. He'll allow me close, and I can get a blade on him before his men can react."

Desfan shook his head. "No. I'm not bringing you with us."

Liam exhaled slowly. "I assure you, you'll regret your choice."

"I'll cope. In the meantime, is there anything else you can tell me about Sahvi or why he might have some of the gold from my treasury?"

The prince frowned. "Well, that's an interesting turn. I didn't think Zennor was involved in that attack against you."

"I thought the same. Do you have any idea why Sahvi would involve himself in raiding my treasury?"

Liam's mouth quirked. "For the gold, I'd imagine." Before Desfan could roll his eyes, the prince continued. "However, it's worth remembering that Amil wasn't working alone that night."

Desfan's eyes narrowed. "Go on."

"Amil coordinated the attack because he wanted you dead. At least, that's my understanding of events. I wasn't up there, of course, but from what I've gathered, that was his main goal. He needed help, though, and he was fine with the added chaos of having your treasury raided and your prison invaded—but those weren't *his* goals. So, whose were they?"

Desfan felt his brows pull together. "The Devendran rebels came to the prison." He'd heard the story of Clare's encounter with the rebels—one in particular, who had tried to kill her. "They were probably looking specifically for their own people, but anyone who might be an enemy to Mortise was worth freeing."

Liam tipped his head. "Right. Which is why they were giving me a guided escort out of the prison."

"You know," Desfan said, "there's a part of me that wondered if somehow you'd schemed the whole thing as an escape."

Liam's eyes shined. "If I'd planned the escape, Serjan, I wouldn't still be here."

Instinct told Desfan that Liam wasn't merely boasting. He cleared his throat. "So, if the Devendrans wanted the prison emptied, and Amil wanted me dead and my court terrorized . . . Who wanted my gold? Like everything else that night, all of them would have benefited from stealing from me, but who would have made that their primary goal?" He eyed Liam. "The last time we spoke, you told me to follow the trail of olcain beyond Sahvi. You said it would lead me to other enemies—to Zennorians allied with your father. You said they were a mix of nobles, clan members, and criminals like Sahvi. If all of this is tied together, then the attack on my treasury could be tied back to Ryden."

"No," Liam said at once. "I would have known about a plan like that."

That was probably true. But Liam could be lying. "It's well known that Ryden is not a wealthy kingdom," Desfan said. "And war is expensive."

"True," Liam acknowledged. "But what few people realize is that the people of Ryden are poor because my father—and my grandfather before him—have taxed the people ruthlessly in order to make this war a reality. Weapons, armor, soldiers, food, training—all of it has already been paid for. My father doesn't need your gold."

A chill swept down his spine. "Fine. Then what other explanation do you have for Sahvi having my gold?"

"Criminals tend to be a greedy sort. Perhaps Sahvi simply took an opportunity offered to him by Amil."

"Do you truly believe that?"

Liam lifted one shoulder. "Without speaking with him, I'm not sure what more you want from me. Sahvi would steal from a starving child; stealing from you would have been an easy choice for him. Now, what he intends to do with that gold, I can't say. He's already in the business of olcain, which is extremely lucrative. Not only is it the most expensive drug in Eyrinthia, it's also highly addictive. You know personally what that feels like. From the first taste, your body craves it. That want never fully goes away, which means the sellers benefit greatly. By selling once to a man, they sell a thousand times."

Desfan's jaw tightened. "As fascinating as your views on olcain are, I think it's time you gave me more names. I want to know who is working behind Sahvi in Zennor."

"I can't just tell you. You must discover the truth for yourself."

Desfan exhaled, long and hard. "You're extremely irritating."

Liam flashed a smile. "I've been called much worse."

Karim shifted, his voice low as he spoke for the first time. "This has been useless. We would have more luck asking a Zennorian."

"I don't think Imara knows much about the criminal goings-on of her kingdom," Liam said easily.

"No," Karim said. "But Skyer might."

Desfan instantly rebelled against the idea, but if the Kabu Clan leader could shed any light on—

"Skyer is here?" Liam hissed, cutting into Desfan's thoughts.

One look at the Rydenic prince, and Desfan almost flinched back in his chair. Liam looked . . . *terrifying*. There wasn't another word for it. His eyes—tinged with humor only a second ago—were black as pitch and blazing hotter than the sun. His harsh expression was deeper than rage. Sharper than shock. Far more than simple hatred.

Wariness thinned Desfan's breath.

Karim must not have felt the same, because he snorted. "I suppose the guards aren't talking as freely around you anymore."

Liam's gaze snapped to Desfan. "You must tell me everything. Immediately. Why is Skyer here? When did he arrive? Where is he *right now*?"

The edge in his voice made the fine hairs on Desfan's body rise. "Why?" he asked. "Is he a threat?"

Liam laughed once, the sound harsh and cold. "Skyer is one of the most ruthless, bloodthirsty men I have ever known—and I'm the spawn of Henri Kaelin. You can't trust Skyer. Not for an instant."

Karim angled toward Desfan, his voice pitched low. "You can't believe him. As much as you might want to—"

"You don't trust him," Liam interrupted, his focus solely on Desfan. "You can feel it. That instinct that screams he's your enemy? Trust it."

Karim set a hand on the table, leaning toward Liam before Desfan could speak. "As the future husband of Princess Imara, Skyer is a protected ally of Mortise. We can't cast him out. You telling us to do so could be your way of creating a rift between Zennor and Mortise."

"Or I could be trying to save your stupid lives." Liam craned his neck, eyes locking on Desfan. "You care for Imara."

The unexpected words jolted him. So much, he wasn't sure what his expression revealed.

Liam's mouth set in a grim line at whatever he saw. "Desfan, listen to me. Do not let Skyer near her."

Karim growled in his throat. "You're playing on our fears to get what you want."

"Your fears are valid," Liam said, his tone a little sharper. More desperate. "Skyer came here for Imara, didn't he?"

"An easy guess," Karim said.

"You can't let him take her." Liam looked once more to Desfan. "Even *I* don't know everything Skyer plans, but he wants this marriage to Imara. Badly. And that doesn't bode well for any of us—least of all Imara. If you care for her at all, you can't let Skyer take her."

"They're not going anywhere yet," Desfan said. "Imara is still recovering from her injury and can't travel."

"That buys you time and little else." Liam's features tightened. "Skyer and Sahvi are allies."

Surprise cut him. "Do you have proof?"

"No. Nothing that could touch a man as powerful as Skyer, anyway. But I can get a confession from Sahvi, and he'll have proof."

Karim barked a laugh. "So we're back to that. You only want to get out of this cell."

Liam glared at the bodyguard. "I believe the serjan and I want the same thing right now—Skyer's downfall. And if I'm at that meeting with Sahvi, I can make that happen."

Desfan stared at the prince, his thoughts whirling.

Karim stood beside him, fuming. He hated that Desfan was considering this.

It was a risk. A stupid risk, possibly. But if it could free Imara from Skyer . . .

It wasn't really a choice.

"I can't believe you're taking Liam Kaelin with you," Imara said, her voice clearly communicating her shock.

Desfan slid another dagger into the sheath at his hip. His biggest regret with their plan was the need for a disguise. It meant he couldn't bring his dual blades; they were too distinctive. "He was persuasive," he said to Imara.

He hadn't told her anything else that Liam had said this morning; that Skyer was allied with Sahvi, and that even Liam Kaelin seemed to take the threat of Skyer so seriously. Desfan didn't want to scare Imara. Especially when—if all went well tonight—he could arrest Skyer for his crimes before she truly had to fear him.

He was in his suite, preparing to go to Fang's warehouse. And though Imara stole his focus, he hadn't hesitated to invite her in when she'd knocked on his door.

The Zennorian princess sat on the end of the settee in his sitting room. It was the seat his mother had always favored. The thought entered his mind, but didn't sting like thoughts of his mother often did. Instead, warmth settled in his chest.

He liked seeing Imara there.

"I can't believe Karim is allowing this," Imara said.

"I *am* the serjan," Desfan reminded her. "I outrank him."

"He must get tired of hearing that."

He chuckled and grabbed another knife.

Imara's white teeth worried her bottom lip as she watched him. "Do you always have to be the one to take risks?"

He flashed her a smile. "You sound like Karim."

"The meeting with Fang was one thing, but you being there to take down Sahvi is quite another."

He twisted to face her fully. "You're worried about me."

"Of course I am." She shook her head with a sigh. "Just promise you'll come tell me the moment you get back so I know you survived."

"Consider it done." Desfan moved to sit beside her on the settee, his voice gentling as he said, "I'll be fine."

"How can you know that?"

He shrugged. "Because I always am."

Her eyes narrowed. "That only lasts until it doesn't."

"That's fair." He bit the inside of his cheek, choosing his next words carefully. "I would prefer it if you avoided Skyer while I'm gone."

Confusion crossed her face. "Why?"

"Just . . . please, Imara. Don't be alone with him tonight." He'd been watching the man as closely as he could, without risking detection. Guards reported his movements—which were many. The man didn't seem the type to sit still. He spent hours in the training yard, he conversed with Grandeur at least once a day, and he took trips into the city.

"I'm not even sure what his plans are tonight," Imara said. "But I'll be in my suite with Razan."

Desfan cracked a smile. "Will you both be fretting together over Karim and me?"

"We're more likely to be cursing you, actually," Imara said dryly. "But we might squeeze in a prayer or two."

This time his grin was full. "That's very kind of you."

Seriousness filtered back in her dark eyes, and she surprised him when she took his hand. "Please be careful."

His body heated at her simple touch. Just feeling her fingers against his made his heart pound. A spark deep inside him lit.

She cared.

No matter what she said, or how she avoided him . . . she cared.

He would do everything in his power to free her from Skyer. Even if that meant trusting Liam Kaelin.

Desfan squeezed her fingers. "It will all be over soon."

CHAPTER 45

MIA

AFTER WEEKS OF UNRELENTING TRAVEL, THE CITY walls of Porynth loomed before them. Mia sat in front of Grayson on the horse they'd been given in Edgewood. They'd been pushing hard to make up for lost time, and Mia was exhausted. She could tell Grayson was, too. She was desperate for a bath, for a warm place to sleep—for a meal that would actually fill her aching belly, since they'd been rationing their meager food for the last few days. Seeing the towering walls of Porynth brought her relief, but also a flash of terror.

They'd reached the port city, which meant she would be expected to get on a ship—if the pirate Zadir was even still waiting in the harbor, since they were nearly a week past his deadline. She was desperate to escape Ryden, but now, looking at Porynth . . . Mortise had never seemed closer, and the reality of returning home brought out so many mixed emotions. Despite all of Grayson's assurances, she still felt an edge of panic whenever she thought of reaching the palace she'd once called home. She was aching to see Desfan again—she could admit that, now—but she didn't know if she was ready to face him. Maybe she never would be.

The gray stone walls of Porynth were painted by the vibrant colors of sunset, and the salty sea air was almost painful to breathe. Familiar. Frightening. It was a scent that meant home, but also reminded Mia of death.

The sea glittered in the distance, seemingly going on forever. As did the line to enter the port city. Grayson guided their mount so they joined the twisting queue, and slowly, they inched toward the city gate.

All around them, Mia saw the faces of the desperate. She wondered if many of those seeking admittance into the city hoped to flee Ryden. She could not imagine there were enough boats to hold them all.

A cold wind blew in from the north. Each day had gotten increasingly cooler; the ground was covered in shimmering frost every morning, and Mia had gotten used to a perpetual chill in her bones. She and Grayson had their hoods pulled up, which helped obscure their identities as well—not that anyone in the crowd seemed intent on watching them. In Ryden, Mia was learning, everyone preferred to remain aloof. Separate. Closed off. It was no doubt safer that way.

They ambled closer to the gate, Grayson's grip on the reins tight. Their horse shifted a bit restlessly. Or maybe he was nervous.

Mia kept her voice low as she asked, "Is it normal for Porynth to be so crowded?"

"I don't know. I've never been here. But something

doesn't feel right." Grayson suddenly tensed against her back. "They're searching everyone at the gate."

Mia craned her neck, hoping to see the still-distant gate. The crowds were so thick, she couldn't see much of anything. But she began to hear the whispers around them.

"*That's* what's holding up the line?"

"They're looking for a scarred man traveling with a woman."

"Are they criminals?"

"The right side of his face will be burned . . ."

Mia's heartbeat quickened. "Is there another gate?" she asked Grayson.

"Yes," he answered quietly. "But there will be guards at every one."

She glanced over her shoulder at him, urgency tightening her words. "We need to leave. We can find another way to Mortise."

His mouth was a firm line. "If Zadir is still in port, he's our fastest and safest way to Duvan. We need to get to that ship."

"How?"

He studied the high stone wall. "It will be dark soon. We could scale the wall and avoid the patrols."

Her stomach pitched. "Grayson, I can't climb that wall." She wasn't strong enough for such an endeavor.

He frowned, clearly realizing she was right. "I can take you back to the treeline. You can hide there while I sneak in and see if Zadir is even still here."

Concern bloomed. "You'd have to sneak back out to tell me."

"I can do it."

She was sure he could, but it increased the risks he was taking by making him climb that wall twice. She exhaled slowly. "If I go alone, I can get through the gate."

His eyes narrowed. "No."

"They're looking for both of us together," she pointed out. "And it doesn't sound like they have a description of me. They'd let me in."

"Mia, I'm not letting you out of my sight."

She made sure to keep her words muted. "We don't have time to argue. Besides, we're close enough to the front of the line that I think the soldiers would notice if we suddenly rode off."

His expression soured. Obviously, he hadn't thought about that.

Mia set a hand on his arm, which was wrapped loosely around her. "I'll be fine. You can disappear into the crowd, I'll go through the gate, and we'll meet at the harbor. Or we can find another way to Duvan," she added, rather hoping he'd take that option.

Grayson stared down at her, his jaw working as he debated. She knew what he'd choose, though—fates knew he wanted them on that ship.

He exhaled sharply, muttering a curse. "I'll watch and make sure you get past the guards. Once you're in the city, keep your head down and make your way to the harbor. Find the *Seafire*, and ask to speak with Syed Zadir."

Nerves danced inside her, but she nodded.

Tension lined Grayson's features, and she could see the anxiety in his gaze. "If the ship isn't there," he said. "Find a crowded tavern nearby and wait for me. I'll find you."

"I'll be all right," she said, gently rubbing his arm. "And I have my knife."

That didn't seem to calm him. He all but glowered at the gate that loomed in front of them. He growled another curse, then glanced back down at her. "If you find Zadir, you need to stay on the ship. If I'm not there by midnight—or at the first sign of soldiers—tell Zadir to leave."

Her spine stiffened and she threw a look over her shoulder. "I won't leave without you."

Grayson's hold on her tightened. "I'll find another way to Duvan. Trust me."

Nausea churned in her gut. "I trust you." And she did. But leaving him behind in Ryden? She wasn't capable of that.

He ducked his head beside hers, their temples brushing. "Everything will be fine," he said. "Just promise me that you'll stay with Zadir."

"I will." That was a vow she would keep, even if it meant convincing the pirate captain to come with her to look for Grayson.

She would not leave Ryden without him.

They were getting closer to the gate. The crowd was thick, but quieting as they neared the soldiers.

Grayson shifted behind her and swung off the back of the horse. He passed her the reins, his warm hand landing on her knee.

She looked down at him, her heart in her throat as she strangled the reins in her fists.

His gray eyes were stormy. "Don't be afraid," he said quietly. "I'll find you."

She wanted to tell him she wasn't scared, but the lie would be obvious. As he disappeared into the crowd, she couldn't stop a shiver from shaking through her. But even though she soon lost sight of him, she knew he was watching. She sat straighter on the horse and didn't resist the press of the crowd that forced her closer to the soldiers.

There were four men guarding the gate, and they seemed just as cold and weary as those waiting to be searched. Two peeled back the cowls from grumbling faces, and the other two peered into the crowd with bored expressions. When it was Mia's turn at the gate, she was told to push back her hood. She did so, letting them stare at her. Her scalp prickled under their scrutiny.

"What's your business in Porynth?" one guard asked.

"I . . ." Fates, her tongue wouldn't move. She cleared her throat. "I'm hoping to purchase some things in the market."

"Traveling alone?" one guard asked.

"Yes."

The man nodded, already looking away as he waved her through.

Her heart pounded, but she gently heeled the horse forward.

She'd barely made it two steps before another guard stepped forward, hand raised. "Hold for a moment," he called.

Mia fought to steady her breathing, but her heart still raced. She tried to keep her face smooth. "Is something wrong?" she asked.

The soldier was young, probably only a handful of years older than she was. He smiled. "Not at all. I'll be off-duty soon and I was wondering—if you don't have any plans this evening—if you'd like to have dinner with me."

She stared at him, her palms sweating and her thoughts jumbled. He was . . . asking to spend time with her? She didn't understand why. She was travel-worn, and covered in dust. Tendrils of hair hung around her face, coming loose from her braid. Grayson had always called her beautiful, and Tyrell had said the same, but she often struggled to believe it; not after

Papa and Mama had spent years telling her how ugly she was.

The soldier was waiting for an answer.

"I . . . sorry," she said, her cheeks warm. "I'm meeting a friend."

"Oh. That's a shame." He looked genuinely disappointed. He rocked back on his heels, giving her one last smile. "Enjoy your time in Porynth."

She offered a timid smile, then urged the horse forward. While she did, she also tugged her hood back over her head.

The streets of Porynth were paved, the stones rubbed smooth with years of heavy traffic. There were carts, wagons, and carriages, and those trying to make progress found it slow due to all the milling people. Mia was grateful to be on a horse, and not caught in the thick of the crowd. From her higher vantage, she could see better where she was going.

The crowd's momentum pulled her deeper into the city, and discomfort rose. She'd handled the crowd at the Edgewood inn without issue, but this city was so much larger. She didn't like being surrounded by so many people. The sights, smells, and sounds were foreign to her, but they loosened old memories of visiting other cities when she was a child. She had felt small then, too—but she hadn't been overwhelmed by it all, like she was now.

Shops lined the streets and homes were built on the floors above. Smoke curled up into the sky, which was growing overcast as the sun set, and the scent of burning wood wove around the smells of grime and sweat. She could also smell baking bread, which made her mouth water and her hollow stomach clench. Memories assaulted her.

She remembered standing in the palace kitchen as a child. She, Tahlyah, and Desfan would hang on the counter's edge and watch the cooks mix, knead, and shape the dough. They'd stick their small fists in the gooey dough, and draw letters in the flour sprinkled on the counter. They'd chatter away as they watched the bread bake. She remembered the delicious smell, and how it felt to hold a fresh slice in her small hands, golden and steaming. She could hear Tally asking for a bigger slice, and more garlic butter. She could see Desfan tugging the end of Tally's braid, telling her that Mother would know if her appetite was ruined.

Mia closed her eyes tightly, emotion clogging her throat. The sudden hunger she felt was about far more than the fact that she and Grayson hadn't been eating enough. It was a hunger for home. For the past. For something lost. Something she could never have again.

Her eyes stung with tears and she blinked rapidly.

"Papa, stop!"

Her stomach plunged at the young girl's shriek. Her head whipped to the side, her heart nearly jumping out of her chest as she searched the crowd for the little girl.

It didn't take long to spot her, and when the girl laughed, Mia knew she wasn't in any danger. The child squirmed in the arms of a tall man, trying to avoid his smothering kisses as he held her.

Other men walked around the father and daughter, all of them looking tired—as if they'd just returned from a long day's work. Most managed a smile as they were greeted by their own children. The man who held his daughter bounced her in his arms, and Mia couldn't tear her eyes away.

Emotion built in her throat as the father tucked the girl under his arm, laughing as she kicked and demanded to be let down. Another girl darted forward, slightly older than the other, and she clung to her father's hand, beaming up at him with all the adoration a daughter could have for her father. Then Mia spotted the older brother, standing at the front door of their home, the mother standing behind him, her hands on his shoulders.

Tears leaked from Mia's eyes as she watched the family move inside their home. She was happy for them. Jealous of them. She missed her family so much in that moment it took a conscious effort to keep breathing. She had once been held like that by her father. She had laughed with him. Looked at him with that same adoration. He had smiled at her like that.

He would never smile at her again. She'd never again hear his laugh, or be held by him.

Her father was dead.

Beneath her, the horse shuffled restlessly. Mia swiped a hand over her cheeks, shoving the tears away. She forgot about the bread. She wasn't really hungry anymore.

Mia tried to steer the horse as best she could through the crowded streets, heading deeper into the city. She assumed the harbor would be there, and she prayed she'd be able to find the *Seafire* without trouble. She also prayed the sun would set faster, so night would fall and Grayson could make his way into the city.

Her progress was slow. The horse seemed to grow more and more skittish. She didn't think he was used to thick crowds, either. Soon, he stopped responding to her nudges, and she gave up trying to ride him. She dismounted and proceeded on foot, pulling him along behind her.

The sun sank in the sky, and darkness encroached, deepening the shadows in the streets. When the streets began to slope downward, the smell of the sea grew stronger. The crowds thinned, then suddenly seemed to vanish. She supposed not a lot of business was done at the port at night.

Her tension was high by the time she reached the harbor. Ships were docked in organized rows, their sails tucked away as they bobbed gently in the deep water.

Mia paused at the top of a stone staircase which led down to the docks. The horse would never be able to make it down the steep steps, so she glanced around for another path down, confident there must be a path fit for horses and carts.

As she searched, she caught sight of someone just ducking out of a nearby building on the far side of the harbor—probably the harbor master's office. There was a lamp hanging near the open door, and it illuminated his face as he turned.

Tyrell.

Her breath caught, and her grip on the reins convulsed.

Tyrell shoved a hand through his dark hair, his eyes scanning the area as soldiers filed out behind him.

Then—in the mounting darkness of night—Tyrell's gaze collided with hers.

He froze. Then his lips moved, and she knew he whispered her name.

Her heart slammed against her ribs. For one suspended moment, everything around them held perfectly still. His eyes were wide, full of relief. Then his mouth tightened, and resolve firmed his expression.

Tyrell took a step forward, and the suspended moment shattered.

Mia dropped the reins and bolted back into the city. She didn't care that she was abandoning their packs or the horse. Desperation shot adrenaline through her veins and she had no other thought but escape.

She heard Tyrell shout at the soldiers with him, and she heard their pounding footsteps. She darted into the nearest alley, ignoring the horrid smells that burned her nose as she plunged through the shadows. Porynth was a massive city; surely she could lose herself in it.

The shouting continued, drawing nearer. She could imagine Tyrell leaping up the stairs. As determined as she was to get away, she knew he shared that same determination to catch her.

She had to move faster.

Traveling with Grayson these past few weeks had forced her stamina to grow, but she was exhausted, afraid, lost, and hungry. She ran blindly, dodging around men, women, and children who had sought shelter in the narrow alleys.

If she could cut through here and make it to one of the main thoroughfares, she could get lost in the sea of people—

A hand snared her wrist, jerking her body around to slam against a solid chest.

Both of them staggered from the impact, and Mia's breath flew out of her lungs on a painful gasp. Strong arms locked around her middle, keeping her chest pressed against his.

"Easy," Tyrell grunted. "I've got you."

Panic made her dizzy. She struggled against his hold, but he only clamped her more tightly.

"You're safe now," Tyrell said, grunting a little when she shoved against him.

"Let me go," she gasped.

Tyrell's arms didn't budge. "Where is he?" he asked, his voice rougher than before. "Did you get away from him?"

"Get away from—?" Mia cut herself off when she realized what he was saying. Tyrell thought she'd been in danger with

Grayson. That she'd run *away* from Grayson. "I'm fine," she said, her breaths short and tight. "Let me go."

He loosened his hold, but kept a firm grip on her wrist. It allowed her to pull back enough to actually see him, though in the dark she couldn't see much. His eyes were hooded, and his expression was hard as stone.

Her lungs squeezed harshly, her breaths ragged.

"You're having a panic," Tyrell said, his voice threaded with concern. "Are the salts in your pack?"

She wheezed out a thin, shallow breath. "You have to let me go. You can't take me back."

"Mia, you're not thinking clearly. Let me help you."

She yanked her arm, but his fingers held firm. The movement jostled her necklaces, though, and Tyrell's eyes dipped.

Heat flooded his gaze, and she knew he'd seen the queen he'd given her.

"Please," she cracked out. "Let me go."

His gaze lifted to meet her stare, and her stomach sank at the emotion she saw there. His fingers tightened against her skin. "Never."

CHAPTER 46

DESFAN

DESFAN STOOD IN THE CORNER OF FANG'S DIMLY-LIT warehouse. Surrounded by a combination of Fang's men and disguised palace guards, his muscles twitched with restlessness. He wanted Sahvi to arrive so this infernal waiting could end.

Tension thinned the air, and no one spoke above hushed whispers. Fang stood nearby; Karim had ordered the drug master to remain close to them.

Desfan fingered his belted knives and scanned the large room. The ceiling stretched loftily, and the many shelves in the room sagged with Fang's wares—both legitimate and illegitimate. Barrels as large as a man, wooden crates of every size, and heavy-looking burlap sacks were stacked all over the floor.

In all, there were twenty men in the room. Fang had urged

them not to bring any more, or else Sahvi might become suspicious.

Once Sahvi arrived, the guards outside could move in and surround the warehouse. Then, when Liam got close to Sahvi, they could spring their trap without risk of Sahvi's men fighting back.

Liam sat on the edge of a crate on Desfan's left. Karim had removed his chains only moments ago, and the prince was rubbing his wrists as he eyed the room.

Karim stood close to the Kaelin prince, along with another guard whose sole job was to watch Liam.

"You made the right decision," the prince said suddenly. "In bringing me, I mean."

"Your words put me at ease," Desfan said dryly.

Liam huffed once. "Believe me or not, it doesn't matter. Just know I will do anything to ruin Skyer."

"Why do you hate him so much?"

"I have my reasons. They don't concern you."

Desfan stepped closer, aware of how intensely Karim watched them. "I don't trust you, Liam. You're only here because I need you."

The prince met his gaze. "You know, we have more in common than you realize."

Desfan scoffed. "We're nothing alike."

"Wrong." Liam's head tipped to the side as he studied him. "Both of us were born with royal blood, which brought obligations we didn't want. I was never destined to sit on a throne, of course—but you didn't ever really want yours. We're both men of action; we can't stand by while there's something to be done. We both went through a depressive stage, in which we tried to feel alive in any way we could—risk, pain, adrenaline

... at least if we could feel that, it meant we were still breathing. And we both turned to olcain to dull that part of us that seemed to never stop screaming."

Desfan stared. He didn't know what to say to any of that, because ... it was all true. He also didn't know why Liam was revealing so much of himself; his words didn't feel like a lie.

Liam closed his eyes briefly. "Regardless of our complicated circumstances, I don't want your fate to be mine, Desfan. I don't want you to lose what I lost."

"What do you mean?" he asked, suddenly cautious.

Liam's voice lowered. "Your feelings for Imara are exceedingly obvious."

Desfan's spine stiffened. He ignored the bait in Liam's words. "You can say whatever you'd like to, but you're not here for altruistic purposes."

"True," Liam allowed. "I'm here for vengeance. But in getting what I want, I'm giving you what you want—Imara, safe from Skyer."

Before Desfan could answer, the double doors across the warehouse pushed in.

Fang straightened. The man was unusually pale, and Desfan could feel his fear as he faced the doors. Desfan and Karim moved to stand beside him, Liam and his guard falling into line as well.

Zennorians trooped in, one dressed more elegantly than the rest. Instantly, Desfan knew that was Sahvi.

The man looked to be in his fifties. He walked with the confident swagger of a man used to getting his way. He had a short dark beard, though streaks of white stood out starkly against his dark skin. Jeweled rings glittered on his fingers as he gestured for his guards to fan out behind him.

He had brought thirty men, easily outnumbering them.

Desfan breathed in slowly, embracing the flutter of nervous energy in his gut. It would keep him loose and able to react quickly.

"Fang!" Sahvi called out, his eyes firmly on the Mortisian criminal. "I trust you have made all the necessary preparations. I tire of this kingdom and long to go home."

Fang's hands twitched at his sides, but he didn't reach for his blades. "All preparations have been made. The ship is ready in the harbor."

"Good. You will just need to load the last of my things." Sahvi gestured toward the door. "I left it all out there. Send your men to pack it on the ship."

Fang cast a quick look at Desfan, who dipped his chin.

They had no choice but to comply, even if it meant dismissing a few of their guards.

Fang ordered two of his men away. They readily complied, closing the large warehouse doors behind them.

In the silence, Fang spoke stiffly. "My daughter?"

Sahvi waved a negligent hand. "She is safe. So is her husband and their brat."

Fang's hands fisted. "I want to see them before we leave."

"That won't be possible," Sahvi said. "You'll see them when you return."

Desfan smothered a curse. Not knowing where Fang's family was—if they were even still alive—made all of this more dangerous. Especially if Fang didn't keep his focus on taking down Sahvi.

The Zennorian criminal glanced around the room. As Sahvi's eyes skirted over Fang's men, Desfan lowered his eyes to avoid any chance of recognition. "Where is the olcain I left in your care?" Sahvi asked.

Fang whistled sharply. One of his men stepped forward, carrying a small crate. He set it on a nearby table. "It's all here, as you requested," Fang said, his voice tight.

"Good." Sahvi smiled and stepped up to the table, the lamp-light dancing over his face. He tossed aside packing straw before scooping up a dark pouch. "This is destined for another port," he said. "I would like your men to send it to Vyken once we're gone."

Beside Desfan, Liam shifted. Desfan shot him a warning glance, and the prince's lips pursed.

Desfan hadn't realized olcain was being delivered to Ryden. Especially not through his city.

Sahvi opened the pouch and studied the contents. "Of course, I must make sure it hasn't been tampered with. I can't send faulty olcain to my buyers. I have a reputation to uphold—something that has proved difficult recently, due to an extremely vexing rival who tried to make my empire his own." He glanced at Fang. "You know how it is, I'm sure."

Fang grunted non-committedly.

Sahvi closed the olcain pouch and tossed it to one corner of the table. His eyes landed on Desfan, who stood near Fang. "Try some," he said, nodding to the pouch.

Karim stiffened.

Desfan's stomach plunged, even as a sick desire rose. Liam was right about one thing—olcain was something an addict would always crave, even if he'd resisted for years.

"I haven't tampered with your olcain," Fang said firmly.

"Good," Sahvi said. "Then you won't mind one of your men sampling it." His eyes locked on Desfan once more. "Try it. *Now*."

Desfan met his gaze, his pulse skipping. They had no choice. They hadn't given the men outside enough time; they needed to keep stalling, or risk a fight they might lose.

Desfan took a step forward, but Karim beat him to the table. "I'll test it," Karim said. His expression was set as he snatched up the pouch.

Oh, fates no. Desfan gritted his teeth. "He's a raging addict," he lied. "He'll think any fates-blasted powder is good, even if it's no better than dirt."

Karim glared at him, but Desfan met that easily enough. His friend was *not* putting that in his body. They didn't both need the experience of an olcain addiction.

"I'll do it," Liam said, his accent vaguely Mortisian. He stepped forward and took the olcain from Karim, his ducked face in shadow as he opened the pouch. He took a pinch of white powder and held it to one nostril. He sniffed sharply, and Desfan could almost feel the burn himself.

Liam's shoulders relaxed subtly as he no-doubt felt the first rush of olcain. He cleared his throat, his fingers tight on the pouch. He took another step closer to the table and dropped the olcain onto the smooth surface. The movement put him a step closer to Sahvi.

Desfan's heart beat a little faster.

Liam's voice was wholly even as he said, "That's good olcain, Sahvi. Perhaps your best."

The drug master frowned. "What . . .?"

Liam lifted his head, finally looking at Sahvi full-on. The lamp on the table would have illuminated every plane of his face.

Sahvi's eyes flew wide as he sucked in a breath. "Rahim Nassar?"

Liam smiled, and there was nothing pleasant about it. "Hello, Sahvi."

Desfan cursed.

CHAPTER 47

MIA

MIA SAT AT THE SMALL TABLE IN THE HARBOR master's office, saying nothing as Tyrell set a bowl of thick stew in front of her.

He'd dragged her back to the harbor and into this room, leaving the guards outside so the two of them could be alone. The horse she'd abandoned had been tethered near the door, and her pack—along with Grayson's—had been thrown into the corner of the small office.

Mia hadn't said a word since they'd left the alley. Tyrell hadn't said anything, either. Not even when he'd dug through her pack and found the jar of salts, which now sat open on the table.

She hadn't needed the salts to steady her breathing. She wasn't having a panic.

She was simply desperate.

Tyrell tugged an empty chair forward, angled it toward her, then sat. "You should eat. You look half-starved."

She didn't touch the spoon. Her stomach gnawed painfully, but she couldn't make herself eat. She stared at him, forcing her voice to remain strong. "You can't take me back."

A furrow grew between his dark brows. "Of course I have to take you back. My father's been tearing Ryden apart looking for you. If I hadn't found you first . . ." He swallowed hard, then gestured to the bowl with his chin. "Please eat."

She kept her arms folded across her chest. "I'm not hungry."

The lie was blatant; especially when her stomach growled loudly.

Tyrell's expression tightened. "Did he hurt you?"

"No. Grayson would never hurt me."

"He endangered you, Mia. He never should have taken you."

"He didn't *take* me. He *saved* me."

"He abducted you."

Her eyes narrowed. "No. Your father did that to me when I was nothing more than a child, and you want to take me back to him. You want him to cage me again."

"I don't want to cage you," he gritted out. "I'm taking you back to the castle so you'll be safe. You'll be under my protection." He leaned forward, his elbows on his thighs. "You won't be punished for any of this—my father gave his word on that. And as soon as the war is won, I'll take you home to Mortise."

"After you conquer it."

A muscle ticked in his cheek. "I don't want to argue about this."

"Then let me go."

He ignored that. "Where is Grayson?"

When she said nothing, Tyrell muttered a curse. "He's a

murderer. He killed Carter." His eyes darkened. "He killed Devon."

Shock blasted her, making her mouth drop open. "*What? Grayson didn't kill Devon!*"

Tyrell's expression didn't change. "Even if he didn't kill him directly, Grayson's arrogance and idiocy got Devon killed. And unless you stay away from him, he's going to get you killed, too."

Mia only shook her head. She had no response for that—any of it.

Tyrell reached out, his fingers stretching for her cheek.

She jerked back.

He couldn't hide his flinch, though it was quickly smothered. His hand lowered, turning into a fist as it fell. "You tried to tell me goodbye," he whispered. "I've relived that conversation so many times . . . You didn't want to leave me."

She pursed her lips, regret heavy in her tone. "I didn't want to leave my friend. But it seems he's gone."

Tyrell drew back. "I love you," he said, his voice low and thick. "That hasn't changed. It will *never* change."

"If you truly love me, you'll let me go."

"You said you loved me. In your letter."

The vulnerability that flashed in his eyes cut her, and despite everything, her heart ached. "Yes. And I didn't want to leave you there. That castle is a prison for you, just as much as it was for me." She leaned toward him. "You don't have to go back, Tyrell. Come with us."

An emotion she couldn't name darted across his face. "There's nowhere else I belong."

"That isn't true. You deserve so much more than the life your parents trapped you in."

"I'm not trapped," he said stiffly. "As a prince of Ryden, I have the power to protect you."

"Tyrell—"

He pushed to his feet, and something in his demeanor changed. Hardened. And it broke part of her heart. "Where is Grayson?" he demanded again.

"If you think I would tell you that, you don't know me at all."

He ground his teeth. "If you tell me where he is, I might be able to spare him some pain. My mother wants him dead for what he did to Carter, but my father wants him alive. If I can return him before more damage is done, it will go easier for him."

Mia kept her silence.

Tyrell huffed out a breath. "Clearly, you still see him as some sort of hero. That means you didn't leave him. And I know he wouldn't leave you, unless he had to—and he wouldn't have gone far." His eyes narrowed. "He's meeting you here. At the docks. You were going to buy passage on a ship."

She fought to keep her expression neutral, but her heart beat faster.

"There are a few ships here bound for Mortise," he said. "That's what I came to check with the harbor master. I'm grateful the fates intervened and brought you directly to me. I was afraid you might be hurt during the rescue." He moved for the door and pulled it open, revealing a soldier standing at the ready. "Position men around every entrance into the harbor," Tyrell said. "Keep to the shadows and watch for him. He's coming."

The soldier nodded and hurried away.

Tyrell closed the door, and when he turned back to Mia, he smiled a little.

It wasn't a good smile.

"My brother will be in for a surprise when he shows up."

Mia's pulse thundered. Grayson was incredibly skilled—his fight in Edgewood proved as much—but Tyrell had more men, and this time Grayson didn't have the element of surprise. *He* was the one being hunted this time, and he would walk right into the trap.

Mia's fingers dug into her crossed arms. "What if I came with you?" she asked softly.

"You *are* coming with me," Tyrell said immediately.

"What if I came with you willingly?"

His focus was fixed on her. "What is it you want in return?"

Mia's tongue darted over her dry lips. "We leave now. With all your men."

A shadow passed over his face. "You want me to let Grayson escape."

"Yes." She was caught—Grayson wasn't. She knew he wouldn't abandon her, but if he avoided this trap, he had a better chance of mounting a rescue later.

Tyrell considered her offer, his eyes going back to the Strategem piece that hung around her neck.

Her breathing thinned. Fates, he was truly considering it.

She was terrified of going back to Lenzen. Terrified of seeing Henri, Iris, and Peter again. Of being a prisoner. Of being trapped, and used. But for Grayson, she'd do it. Without hesitation.

Tyrell's lips parted.

A shout shattered the night, cutting him off before he could speak. Tyrell shoved open the door, though he stayed in the doorway.

Mia pushed up from her chair and hurried toward him, her

heart in her throat. *Please, don't let it be Grayson* . . .

Tyrell's back was painfully straight as they waited, both of them peering out into the night. A slight mist had drifted in, covering the ground and making the darkness seem even thicker.

There was a yell. A scuffle. A thud.

Another shout—then eerie silence.

All Mia could hear was the creaking of the nearby ships, and the lapping of the waves against the stone walls of the harbor.

With the lamp glowing brightly beside the door, it was hard to see anything in the thick shadows. Tyrell was tense beside her. "Simmons?" he snapped. "Farr?"

No response.

The small hairs on Mia's arms rose.

Just outside the spill of light from the lamp, the darkness stirred. Mist parted as a form took shape, a single figure clothed in black, striding forward.

Grayson's hood was thrown back, his dark hair a tangled mess. His expression was carefully neutral, though his gray eyes burned.

Tyrell grabbed Mia's arm and drew a long knife from his belt.

"Let her go," Grayson said. "*Now.*"

Tyrell's hold cinched, painfully tight.

Then a new voice said, "I'd do what he says. Spewer's looking quite serious."

CHAPTER 48

GRAYSON

GRAYSON'S ATTENTION REMAINED FIXED ON HIS brother and the knife he'd drawn. Tyrell had one hand banded around Mia's wrist, keeping her close to his side. Her tension was obvious, but she seemed unharmed, thank the fates.

From his periphery, Grayson saw Zadir and his tightening ring of pirates step into the light.

Tyrell's eyes bounced around them, counting them. He was vastly outnumbered.

When Grayson had reached the harbor and seen the increased guard, fear for Mia had spiked. Then he'd spotted Tyrell outside the harbor master's office, and he'd known.

His brother had Mia.

Grayson had wanted to rescue her immediately, but Tyrell would have laid a trap. He needed reinforcements. Luckily, he'd found the *Seafire*.

Captain Zadir edged a little closer to Grayson, his crew surrounding Tyrell easily. The harsh gleam in Zadir's eye hadn't lessened since Grayson had told him about Mia's capture, but now there was an edge of satisfaction. "The seraijah is ours," the pirate said to Tyrell, his tone deceptively calm.

Tyrell didn't react. He still gripped Mia's arm, and that knife—while not held against her—remained far too close.

Grayson's insides burned. He needed Tyrell to let go of Mia. *Now.*

Zadir was on his right, Swallow on his left. Grayson recognized the other pirates as well, including his somewhat enemies Gale and Weeper. Everyone was focused on Tyrell and Mia, waiting for the prince to release her.

Tyrell's glare sharpened on Grayson. "You can't take her."

"Neither can you." His words were carefully even. "You're surrounded, Tyrell. Surrender."

"Why? So you can kill me, like you killed Carter?"

Grayson hid his flinch, but he felt the blade in his brother's words.

Mia winced, and he didn't know if it was because of what Tyrell had said, or his tight hold.

Grayson's eyes narrowed. "Release her."

"No." His hold on the knife flexed. "You may have me outnumbered, but I hold the advantage. As long as I have Mia, none of you will make a move, and it's only a matter of time before a patrol passes by."

"Oh, it might take a while," Zadir said. "I have boys in every street leading to the harbor, and they're all eagerly awaiting the first soldier that walks this way. They all have a sighting to report. Can you believe the Black Hand was seen scaling the northwall? Or maybe it was the south one." His grin stretched wide. "Your soldiers will be quite busy tonight, I assure you."

Tyrell visibly seethed.

Mia looked up at Tyrell. Her quiet words were for him, but they carried in the still night. "You need to let me go."

He glanced down at her. "I can't."

Grayson hated the desperate pang in Tyrell's voice.

"I'm sorry," Mia breathed, still looking at Tyrell. "But I'm choosing to go with Grayson. Let me go, before you're hurt."

Tyrell wasn't going to let go. Grayson knew this, because *he* would have never let go. Despite Zadir's plan to keep the guards busy, Grayson knew their time was not endless.

They needed a new approach.

Grayson took a step forward, and Tyrell's gaze snapped to him. "You and me, Tyrell," he said, his voice even. "Just us. The last one standing walks away with Mia."

"No," she said at once. She tugged against Tyrell's hold, but it didn't break.

Tyrell stared at Grayson. "To the death?"

"No. Incapacitate. Just like one of Father's matches."

Tyrell glanced at the pirates that surrounded them. "And they'll just let me take Mia and go?"

"Yes," Grayson lied. There was no way Zadir would let him take Mia. But since Grayson wasn't going to lose this fight, the lie didn't matter.

Tyrell's lips were pressed flat. He didn't trust Grayson, but his choices were limited. A fight would make noise; possibly bring the soldiers he'd sent to watch the nearby streets. Fighting Grayson was a risk, but it was a calculated one.

Grayson was just doing the only thing he could think of to get Mia away from Tyrell.

Tyrell straightened. "A fight between just us, then. No interference."

Grayson dipped his chin.

Tyrell's grip finally loosened, and Mia took a step away. "Stay there," Tyrell ordered.

She hesitated in the doorway. She shot Grayson a panicked look, and he tried to give her a reassuring smile.

Tyrell was the only brother who could occasionally beat him. Fates, he wished he was at his full strength. He might have recovered from his fever, but he hadn't been eating or sleeping well, and the long days of travel had taken their toll. But this fight was for Mia—he would win, because he could not afford to lose.

He saw the same resolution burning in Tyrell's eyes.

The two brothers walked forward, each of them with a knife in hand. Tyrell spotted the Syalla blades belted at Grayson's waist. "Maybe we should use those. In memory of the last time I beat you."

Grayson tugged one free and tossed it onto the ground in front of his brother.

Tyrell bent to snatch it up, his eyes never leaving Grayson. He sheathed his own blade and tossed the poisoned knife in the air.

Grayson rolled his shoulders and settled into a fighting stance, his fingers curling around the decorative hilt of the Syalla-coated weapon.

Zadir gave a whistle, sharp and piercing.

Mia jumped as the pirates near Tyrell surged forward, knocking the prince to the ground.

Grayson stilled, watching as Tyrell was tackled and the knife wrestled from him.

Zadir strode forward and clapped Grayson's shoulder. "I'm

sure it would have been an epic fight, lad. But frankly, we have better things to do."

Tyrell snarled, but the enraged sound was cut short as Gale punched him in the temple.

The prince slumped to the cobbled ground, unconscious.

Mia gasped, her hands slapping over her mouth.

Grayson rushed to her. "Are you all right? He didn't hurt you?" His knuckles brushed her cheek, his eyes raking over her face, looking for any sign of abuse.

"I'm fine," Mia assured him. She grasped his wrist. "Are you all right?"

He nodded.

Zadir stepped up beside him. "Will there be formal introductions, Spewer?"

Grayson cleared his tight throat. "Mia, this is Syed Zadir, the captain of the *Seafire*. Zadir, this is Meerah Cassian."

Mia's expression turned hesitant, as if unsure how to greet the pirate. "Captain Zadir, it's a pleasure."

Zadir beamed. "The pleasure is absolutely mine, my serai-jah. We'll get to know each other well on your journey home, I'm sure." He looked to Grayson, but gestured toward Tyrell's crumpled form. "Would you like me to kill him?"

Mia inhaled sharply. "You can't kill him." She looked to Grayson, fearful and pleading.

Grayson stared back at her. As long as Tyrell drew breath, he would try to take Mia back. Grayson knew that beyond a doubt. Tyrell was an enemy—Henri's personal soldier. He would return to the king, and he would come after them again.

Mia wasn't safe as long as Tyrell lived.

But how could he kill Tyrell when she was looking at him like that? Fates, how could he kill Tyrell when the thought alone made him sick? He could feel his knife cutting through Carter's throat. He could see the blood rushing out. The blood on his hands.

He didn't know if he was strong enough to kill another brother. Especially when that brother was unconscious.

Zadir glanced between them. "I'm confused. Is this truly a debate?"

"Please." Mia looked away from Grayson, turning instead to face Zadir. "Don't kill him."

One of the pirate's bushy eyebrows lifted, but he offered a sweeping bow. "As you command, my seraijah."

Mia blinked, clearly unsettled. Grayson didn't know if it was the situation, or Zadir's immediate submission that had thrown her. Perhaps it had been the bow.

Swallow stepped up beside them, the old man's frown deep. "We could take him prisoner, I suppose. The serjan would pay handsomely for such an important political prisoner."

The pain that flashed across Mia's face cut Grayson deeply. She knew too well how it felt to be locked up. Moisture gathered in her eyes as she looked to him. "He would never be freed, Grayson. I . . . I can't do that to him."

Grayson didn't know what to say. A prison was his fate in Mortise, though Mia didn't know that. It didn't seem like the right moment to tell her. She'd suffered enough. *Too* much.

Footsteps pounded behind them, and everyone whirled to see a young boy darting toward them through the mist. His hissing voice carried easily on the cold breeze. "Soldiers are starting back this way!"

Zadir straightened. "Time to go." He looked between Mia and Grayson. "Is the prince coming or not?"

Grayson's teeth clenched. They were out of time, and he

couldn't hurt Mia. "Put him in the harbor master's office." It would keep him out of view for as long as possible.

Mia's fingers wrapped around Grayson's. "Thank you," she breathed.

The pirates hurried to do as ordered. When Mia moved to follow them, he gripped her hand tightly, keeping her close. She shot him a small, somewhat weary smile. "I just want to grab our packs."

He went with her, tensing when he spotted the open jar of salts on the table. "You had a panic?"

She shook her head, but didn't offer more as she sealed the jar and lifted it.

Weeper grabbed their packs, and Swallow snatched up Mia's belt and dagger, which had been thrown in the corner. The old sailor glanced at Grayson. "Yours?"

"Mine," Mia corrected.

Swallow's smile gentled. "Apologies, Seraijah. I will carry it for you."

She nodded, still looking a little unsettled by the pirates. She glanced at Tyrell's limp body, but she didn't hesitate to take Grayson's outstretched hand.

That alone helped loosen the knot in his stomach.

They moved back into the night. Mia glanced at the tethered horse they'd ridden since Edgewood. "Do we have to leave him?" she asked Grayson softly.

Zadir answered. "I'm afraid horses hate sailing more than Spewer. Best to leave the poor creature, my seraijah. I'm sure he'll be cared for."

Mia's concern lingered, but she didn't hesitate to walk with Grayson and the pirates as they made their way toward the docked ship that waited for them.

"You'll love the *Seafire*," Zadir told Mia as they walked. Grayson wondered if he was trying to distract her from leaving the horse behind. "She's the fastest ship to ever sail these waters," Zadir added. "Which is for the best, since we'll need to sail like an entire kingdom is chasing us."

Weeper grunted. "It's like Zoroya all over again, but without the goods."

"On the contrary," Zadir said, smiling at Mia. "I think we have our most precious cargo yet."

CHAPTER 49

DESFAN

LIAM DREW A BLADE WITH LIGHTNING SPEED and laid it against Sahvi's throat. "You know what to do," he said to the Zennorian criminal, his voice dangerously soft.

Sahvi's eyes were round, his hands frozen at his sides. "Get back, you useless dogs," he barked at his guards.

The warehouse was taut with the tension of this moment; the air itself, and everyone in it. Desfan, Karim, and Fang stood frozen as the balance in the warehouse shifted. Desfan's mind raced.

Rahim Nassar. That's what Sahvi had called Liam. And the prince hadn't shown any reaction—like that truly was his name. Was Liam Kaelin *Rahim Nassar*? The Mortisian merchant and smuggler who had been impossible to locate these past few months?

Liam was the Shadow of Ryden; he must have had many

identities. Desfan had just never imagined that one of those would be so established. So complete. So *Mortisian*.

Liam hadn't told him any of this, which meant Desfan couldn't predict what the Rydenic prince would do next. With his knife against Sahvi's throat, he now commanded everyone in the room.

The Zennorian drug master's throat bobbed under Liam's steady knife. "I thought you were dead."

"I once thought the same of you." Liam readjusted his hold on the dagger and slid closer to Sahvi.

The Zennorian tensed. "Now, Nassar. There's no point in revisiting past grievances."

"I think you and I are going to have to disagree on that. Your past sins may have a very negative impact on your immediate future."

Sahvi glared. "What do you want?"

"Information. About Skyer." He leaned in. "Or should I say, *the Dawn*."

Sahvi's dark eyes narrowed. "You play a dangerous game, Nassar. You would be wise to stop."

"You must have proof of Skyer's treachery," Liam said, completely ignoring Sahvi's words. "Tell me where it's hidden."

Sahvi's chin lowered slightly. "I don't know what you're talking about."

"I'm not an idiot, Sahvi. Two years ago, I swore I saw you die. And you hid very well, especially in the beginning. It must have been a deep hole you found to crawl in to avoid Chizumbo. He took over your entire enterprise while you hid. I assume Skyer helped you then, and that he's been helping you rebuild your empire. Give me the proof I need, and you might survive this night."

Sahvi said nothing.

Liam waited, drawing out the long silence.

Desfan tensed, his eyes darting warily over Sahvi's men. They were all stiff, their hands hanging near their weapons. All it would take was one wrong breath. One wrong move.

Liam eased the blade away from Sahvi's neck, just slightly. Sahvi's shoulders loosened.

Liam sighed. "The hard way, then." In one smooth motion, he grabbed Sahvi's wrist, slammed it on the table, and stabbed the knife through his hand.

Sahvi howled.

Karim shoved Desfan back as Sahvi's men attacked. Fang's men darted forward, and so did the palace guards.

Blades hissed as they emerged from their sheaths, metal struck metal, and men yelled. The warehouse became a battlefield.

Desfan dodged a swinging curved sword and skirted the worst of the fight, heading for Sahvi and Liam. Alarm rushed through him. He needed Sahvi alive. He needed to know everything about Skyer so he could protect Imara. He needed to stop Liam—*now*.

Fang reached Liam first. His fist collided with the prince's jaw, and Liam reeled back.

Fang grabbed the knife in Sahvi's hand—which pinned him to the table—but he didn't pull the knife out. Instead, he twisted it, shouting, "Where is my daughter?"

Sahvi screamed.

Desfan swore as one of Sahvi's men jumped in front of him, daggers spinning. He jerked his own blades free, and then they fought.

He didn't know where Karim was. He caught a glimpse of

Fang, slamming a second blade into Sahvi's bleeding hand. Sahvi cried out and fell to his knees.

Fang's men surrounded him, protecting him from Sahvi's men as well as the palace guard.

A burning cut sliced the back of Desfan's hand. He nearly dropped his dagger. Fates, he needed to focus on the fight in front of him.

But it wasn't easy. Where was Liam?

"Karim will never let me hear the end of this," Desfan muttered.

The Zennorian man in front of him snarled wordlessly and struck again, his knives flashing.

Desfan retreated until the heels of his boots hit a crate. He leaped back on it, and he didn't hesitate to use the high ground. He kicked the man in the face, and the Zennorian flew back. Blood rolled down Desfan's wrist from the cut on his hand, but he forced that pain aside so he could search the room without distraction.

The extra guards hadn't arrived yet—they hadn't had time to get into position. He knew they'd run in once they were close enough to hear the commotion inside the warehouse.

Desfan looked over the room, his chest rising and falling with quick breaths.

Karim fought one of Sahvi's men.

Fang had a *third* knife in Sahvi's hand.

Liam dodged a strike from one of Fang's men, his nose bleeding, his face furious. His clear target was Fang, but only so he could get to Sahvi.

Desfan had to get there first.

He jumped off the crate and shouldered his way through the melee, ducking and leaping to avoid the whirling blades and flying fists.

He was close when one of Fang's men slid in front of him, blocking his path with bared teeth.

Beyond him, Sahvi screeched in agony.

"Tell me where she is!" Fang snarled.

Desfan cursed. "Fang!" he yelled around Fang's guard. "Let me arrest him. We'll get Ayma—I promise!"

Fang said nothing. He didn't even turn. He cut off one of Sahvi's fingers.

Desfan's stomach roiled. This had to end. "Fang—"

A blade was at his side, pressed deep enough that he hissed. A voice he didn't know spoke harshly in his ear. "Give me Liam Kaelin, or die."

Desfan shot a look to his attacker. He was maybe a couple of years younger than Desfan's twenty years, but his brown eyes looked older. His expression was uncompromising, and his hold on the knife against Desfan's ribs was steady. His hands were badly scarred—even his fingers carried marks. White lines covered his hands, perhaps from a blade—and burns?

Desfan met the young man's hard gaze. "Who are you?" He didn't think it was one of Fang's men, and he wasn't with Sahvi. Had he come from the shadows themselves?

His lips curled. "I'm the one holding the knife poised to split you open, Serjan. And I demand that you let Liam Kaelin go."

"You can't have him. Sorry."

"I think you—"

Desfan spun and kicked, and the blade sailed through the air.

Unfortunately, the young man just whipped out another. His eyes darkened, and then he struck.

Desfan engaged, because he didn't have a choice. His opponent might be younger, but he was an adept fighter—and he stood between Desfan and Sahvi.

The fight was brutal, with fast swipes and powerful jabs. Sweat beaded Desfan's brow, until finally he found his opening. The young man dropped his guard, just a fraction, and Desfan slammed his blade into his shoulder.

He screamed and jerked back from Desfan.

From across the room, there was a roar. "*Akiva!*"

Desfan's eyes widened when he saw Liam lunge for the injured young man—Akiva, apparently.

Liam snagged Akiva's good arm and yanked him away from Desfan. The prince's eyes blazed as he locked on Desfan. "Don't you dare—"

Karim came up behind them. His arm snapped around Akiva's neck and he jerked the young man back until his spine hit Karim's chest.

Akiva scratched ineffectually against Karim's arm, his eyes popping wide as he struggled for breath.

Karim's other hand gripped a knife, which rested against Akiva's side. "Get away from Desfan," Karim snarled at Liam. "Or I'll kill him."

Liam spun. A dagger wavered in his hand. Then he took a deliberate step away from Desfan. "Let him go," Liam said, his voice oddly hoarse. "Please. He has nothing to do with this."

Karim's hard expression didn't alter. "Throw down your weapon. Now."

Liam did.

The second the blade hit the ground, Desfan turned toward Fang and Sahvi—just in time to see one of Sahvi's men grasp Fang's shoulder and shove a blade in his stomach.

Fang gagged and collapsed.

Sahvi ripped the blades from his hand, cursing harshly as he cradled the bleeding mess to his stomach. "Retreat!" he bellowed. "*Retreat!*"

Desfan twisted to go after him, but he halted when a Mortisian man stepped behind Karim.

When Karim stiffened, Desfan knew a blade was at his friend's back. "Release the boy," the man rumbled darkly.

Karim's arm tightened. He looked to Desfan.

The moment felt surreal. All around them, men blurred as they fought. Guards and criminals—Fang's men and Sahvi's. Fang was on the floor beside the table, bleeding out. Sahvi was lurching toward the door, his men huddled around him in a human shield. The perimeter guard wasn't here yet. *Why weren't they here?*

In the end, none of that mattered. It couldn't. Not when Karim had a blade against his back.

Desfan glared at the man behind Karim. "If you harm him, you will suffer the pain of a thousand deaths."

"I do not fear pain," he said evenly. The man was middle-aged, and his hard face could have been carved from stone. "Release the boy."

In the strained silence between them, Liam's hands fisted at his sides. He was as trapped as Desfan; Karim held a dagger to Akiva—a person Liam clearly cared about, though Desfan hadn't known that was possible—and Desfan couldn't move, because Karim was being threatened by this other Mortisian.

Desfan ground his teeth. "Karim. Release him."

Karim didn't so much as twitch. His eyes blazed. "If I let him go, Liam will grab you."

"If you don't let him go, you're dead," Desfan gritted out.

Karim's stubborn jaw set.

Liam finally spoke, his voice tense. "We're losing Sahvi, and that can't happen. Kazim, release him."

The man—Kazim—did not step back from Karim. "He will kill Akiva."

"He won't," Liam said.

A bang echoed across the room. The double doors had been thrown open by Sahvi's men. New cries rang out, and steel clashed as they encountered the perimeter guard.

Desfan relaxed, if only a little.

Liam twisted to face him. "I will return to prison willingly if you let Akiva and Kazim go."

Akiva made a strangled sound.

Kazim growled. "Liam—"

The look Liam threw the man was hard. "You shouldn't have come at all."

"We were tracking Sahvi," Kazim snapped back. "When we saw you . . . We had to try."

Liam's gaze softened slightly. "I know. But this isn't the time." He glanced at Desfan. "Will you let them go?"

Desfan didn't have to debate; he wanted that blade away from Karim, Liam in prison, and this moment ended so he could pursue Sahvi. Agreeing would get him all of that. "Yes."

Liam faced Akiva and Kazim, but his focus seemed to be on the younger man. "You will go. You will not attempt to free me again. Do you understand?"

Moisture shined in Akiva's eyes. "Liam—"

"Promise me," he growled.

Akiva's gaze sharpened. He said nothing, but Liam must have read something reassuring in his expression, because he looked at Kazim now. "Release Karim, and do not linger. Go. Now."

Kazim's eyes narrowed, but he did as Liam said and stepped back from Karim.

Desfan nodded to Karim, and his friend released Akiva.

Karim stepped around the boy and grasped Liam's arm, though the Rydenic prince had made no move to run. He stared at Akiva and Kazim. "Go," he repeated. "*Now.*"

Kazim snagged Akiva's elbow and pulled him away, moving in the opposite direction of the open double doors. A back entrance—possibly the one they'd used to enter the warehouse in the first place.

Akiva didn't drag his feet, but his eyes didn't leave Liam. Not until both men disappeared from sight.

Karim kept a firm hold on Liam. "You betrayed us," he said.

"No," Liam argued mildly. "I improvised."

Desfan stepped away from them, moving to kneel beside Fang. His men were all dead around him, and blood drenched his abdomen. Sweat streaked his face, and his breathing was ragged.

His eyes flicked to Desfan. "Find—her," he pleaded. "Promise me."

Desfan grasped the man's blood-slick hand and squeezed. "I will," he promised.

Fang gulped, blood trickling from his mouth now. "Sorry," he rasped. "Tell her—I'm sorry."

The moment Desfan whispered he would, Fang stilled, his eyes glazing in death.

CHAPTER 50

IMARA

"I HATE THIS," RAZAN SAID.

Imara looked up from her cards. "We can play a different game."

The Mortisian woman sighed. "I don't hate Assassins, I hate *waiting*. Shouldn't they have returned by now? It's been hours."

Imara's stomach pitched, but she strived to ignore her growing unease. "Desfan said it could take hours to make the arrests, recover Fang's daughter, and everything else. I'm sure they're fine."

Razan made an impatient sound in her throat. She tossed the cards on the low table between them. "I need something more challenging than Assassins if I'm going to take my mind off things. And perhaps something stronger than wine."

Imara glanced at the bottle on the table, which they'd nearly emptied. "I'm not sure that's a good idea. But if you're looking for a more challenging game, I have a Zennorian strategy game called Yerret." She'd bought it the day she and Grayson had gone to the market in the city. The game had reminded her of home, and she'd been unable to walk past without buying it.

"The more challenging the better," Razan said. She sighed. "I thought I worried about Karim before, but now . . ."

"Now that you know he loves you, it's harder," Imara said softly, a pang in her heart as she thought of Desfan. Of what he'd admitted, and what she had not—*could* not—admit.

"Yes," Razan said. "It is harder. I don't know how, because it was already so difficult, but . . ." She shook her head, her loose dark hair shifting beside her oval face. "I need that game. Yert?"

"Yerret." Imara reached for her cane, but Razan waved her down. "I'll get it."

"I can call for Hanna," Imara offered. She felt a little guilt about doing so, though. It was the middle of the night, and she'd dismissed Hanna two hours ago so the poor girl could sleep. Her maid had only left on the condition that Imara call for her when she was ready for bed, and she hated to interrupt her for something as trivial as fetching a game.

"No need for that," Razan said quickly, already standing. "Just tell me where it is."

"The bedroom. In the bottom drawer of the dresser. It's a leather pouch full of small, half-sphere glass pieces."

Razan stood and crossed the sitting room, moving for the bedroom. When she disappeared inside, Imara took a moment to close her eyes and utter one of those prayers she'd promised Desfan. He couldn't be hers, but she needed him safe.

Please.

The memory of him sheathing his daggers and preparing for this fight made her lungs feel tight. He'd given her a re-assuring smile, but there was an intense edge to Desfan these days. She truly didn't know if it had arisen the moment he'd told her he loved her, or if it had been triggered by Skyer's arrival. Perhaps it was both.

He'd certainly wanted her to avoid Skyer, that much was clear. Luckily, that had been easy enough tonight; he'd been invited to a night of drinking and conversation with Sers Sifa and Anoush, along with Grandeur.

She knew she couldn't avoid Skyer forever. He was going to be her husband, after all. But at the moment, any time she had free of him, she cherished. Her father had promised that—in time—an arranged marriage could offer warmth and security. Maybe even love. She prayed that was so. Because if nothing changed between her and Skyer, her future would be miserable.

In the bedroom, she heard the low drag of a drawer opening, followed by rustling as Razan no doubt rooted through Imara's things.

Pulling herself from her depressing thoughts, Imara reached for the bottle of wine. It wasn't empty *yet*.

She poured some in her glass and took a long sip. Then she frowned and looked to the darkness that pooled in the open bedroom door. She couldn't hear anything, and it was too dark to see anything. Lamps were lit in the sitting room, but Razan hadn't taken a light into the bedroom. She'd probably thought she'd see well enough from the borrowed light of the other room.

"Is it not there?" Imara called out gently, moderating her

voice so as not to wake Hanna in her small bedroom.

There was no response.

Perhaps Razan hadn't heard.

Rather than calling out again, Imara set aside her wine and lifted her cane. Getting to her feet was difficult, but with one hand on the cane and the other on the arm of the chair, she pushed up and stood. She was getting used to walking with her injury.

She started forward, the cane tapping mutely against the rug. When she reached the doorway she paused, peering into the shadows. Her eyes couldn't discern anything yet. "Razan?" she whispered.

When Razan said nothing, the fine hairs on Imara's body lifted. Instinct had her taking a small step back.

"Don't," a deep male voice rumbled from the bedroom. "Do not make a sound, or Serai Krayt dies."

Imara stilled, though her heart pounded. Terror clutched her chest in a painful fist. "Jekem."

Her old bodyguard materialized from the darkness as he stepped forward. A small crossbow was in his hand, loaded with a dart that was pointed at her. Instinct told her the dart was poisoned. His breathing was steady and his eyes were frighteningly calm. "Princess," he greeted, almost softly.

Imara trembled, her grip tightening on the cane. "Where is Razan?"

He glanced behind him. "Can you not see her?"

Imara eyed the shadows, and—gradually—her eyes picked up enough details to see Razan sprawled on the floor, in front of the dresser. The bottom drawer was still open. Razan wasn't moving.

"What did you do?" Imara breathed, dread pooling in her gut.

"She is alive. Merely unconscious." Lines appeared on Jekem's forehead. "No one else needs to die tonight. Just you."

Bile stung her throat—she swallowed it back down. She stared at the dart, aimed uncompromisingly at her heart. "Why?" she asked, still whispering. She didn't know if she had enough air to scream, even if she dared.

"You cannot marry Skyer," Jekem said. "The clans cannot have a legitimate claim to the Zennorian throne. The monarchy would be ruined. Zennor itself would be torn apart. I'm doing this for the good of Zennor."

"I appreciate your loyalty to Zennor," Imara said. "But if you revere the monarchy so much, you must honor my father. He wants me to marry Skyer—"

"He's wrong. He doesn't see the danger. He thinks this marriage will stop the bloodshed, but it will only bring more death." Jekem's throat bobbed as he swallowed, and Imara saw true regret in his eyes. "I do not want to do this. But I must. I tried to make it painless, but you woke, and Kaz . . ." His voice trembled. "Did I kill him?"

"No. He's alive."

Relief flashed across his features. The crossbow wavered, then steadied, the dangerous point of the dart still aimed at her. "Good," he said firmly. "That is good."

Screaming would do no good—the dart would hit her before help could arrive. With her bad leg, Imara couldn't run. She didn't have a weapon, other than her cane. Razan was unconscious, but she wouldn't stay that way forever. And Desfan and Karim *were* coming—eventually. If she could just distract Jekem, keep him talking . . .

"How did you get in?" she asked. It was the first question she could think of.

"I'm a good climber," he said. "Once I snuck into the castle yard, it was easy enough to reach your balcony. From there . . ." He let his words trail off.

Imara eyed the dart. "It was a bit daring of you to come back to the palace." Presumably through the window he'd jumped through the last time he'd been in her room. She didn't feel any breeze, so he clearly hadn't broken the glass this time. Had he managed to lift the latch? He must have done just that—he'd been nearly silent.

"I was going to wait until you left for Zennor," Jekem said. "But Skyer arrived, and . . . I can't overpower him and all his men. This was my best chance."

"You swore oaths to protect me," Imara said, allowing the pain of his betrayal to strain her words.

Jekem winced, reinforcing the fact he had a conscience—at least of some sort. "The oaths I swore were to protect the monarchy," he said. "It is painful for me to do this, Princess. But it is the only way I can see to truly protect Zennor. You must understand."

"I really don't think I have to understand," Imara said. "And let me be clear: *I don't.* Murder is never a good answer to a problem, Jekem. If you had concerns, you should have expressed them to my father."

"He didn't listen to the others, and they were nobles in his court. Why would he listen to *me*?"

Imara noted the frantic edge in his voice. She didn't know if it showed an advantage on her end, or if it would just mean a quicker death. Unable to decide, she looked him in the eye and said honestly, "I don't want to die."

Jekem grimaced. "I'm sorry. But it will be virtually painless. Just hold still."

Imara's pulse hammered in her ears. Her fear was real as she asked, "Is there poison on the dart?"

"Yes. It only needs to break your skin. One prick. That's all, and it will be over."

Imara trembled; she clutched her cane more desperately. Help wasn't coming soon enough. Razan wasn't stirring. She was about to die.

"Please," Imara breathed. "Don't shoot it. That will hurt more. Just . . . can you cut my palm with it instead?"

If he would unload the dart, she might have a chance. He would step closer—within striking distance of her cane. She could scream. Her guards would come quickly—she and Razan might both survive.

Jekem hesitated. "You won't struggle?"

"No," she said tremulously, allowing tears to show in her eyes. "I just don't want it to hurt."

Jekem's jaw flexed. The crossbow lowered slightly, but he didn't take out the dart. With his free hand, he reached into his pocket, pulling out something wrapped in soft leather. With a flick of his wrist, one side of the leather fell, revealing two more darts.

Imara's lungs froze.

Crossbow still trained on her, Jekem lifted the other two darts. "Step forward and hold out your hand," he said. "Then this will be over. I promise."

Imara's muscles locked. She couldn't even draw a final breath. She took a step forward, imagining what it would feel like for that dart to tear into her body.

She didn't have any final words. None that she could speak aloud, anyway.

I love you too, Desfan. From the very beginning, I think I loved you.

She met Jekem's stare and held out her palm.

Jekem's attention dropped to her hand.

The second his focus shifted, Imara swung her cane. Balanced on her good leg, she almost fell—but the cane struck his arm, and the crossbow was knocked to the floor.

"Help!" she screamed.

Jekem cursed and grabbed for her. She swung her cane again, but he grabbed it and tore it out of her hand. Imara staggered, her shoulder crashing into the doorframe.

Jekem threw the cane and lurched forward.

In the sitting room, doors banged open.

Imara cried out as Jekem grasped her arm, his hard fingers bruising her skin. "I'm sorry," he said, lifting the remaining two darts clutched in his hand. He stabbed downward, aiming for the exposed skin of her inner arm, right above where he held her.

She jerked against his hold—the first dart grazed skin, but didn't break it. The second scraped a little deeper, making her gasp.

Arms snared Imara from behind, yanking her back against a strong chest. One she knew far too well.

Desfan.

His harsh breath grated against her ear and he clutched her so firmly, she couldn't breathe.

Karim shot past them and wrestled with Jekem.

"The darts!" Imara gasped. "They're poisoned!"

Karim spun, barely dodging Jekem's furious swipe.

Her former bodyguard roared. "I must kill her!" he shrieked. "*I must!*"

Imara's other guards ran in, moving to help secure Jekem.

Imara clutched Desfan's arms that were locked around her

waist, her vision hazing. Relief, fear, panic—it tangled inside her, choking her.

Then Desfan cursed raggedly. "No," he rasped. "*No.*"

The raw pain in his voice—the desperate agony—made her stomach twist.

He pulled her fully into the sitting room and set her in the nearest chair. She barely got a look at his face—pale and terrified—before he dropped to his knees in front of her, his shaking hands clutching her arm. One of his hands sported a deep cut that still leaked blood, and that crimson streak was all she could see.

Then she noticed the thin trail of blood on her inner arm.

In a daze, she blinked at the light scratch marring her skin. There was pain, she realized. But it was slight. Far too slight to deliver death—except for the poison now in her blood.

Poison.

Desfan had heard her warning. That's why he trembled. He knew she was dying. He seemed more sure of it than even she was at this moment, because everything inside Imara rebelled.

She wasn't dying. She *couldn't* die. Not from such an infinitesimal wound. Dying now would be pathetic. And wrong. So fates-blasted wrong.

She hadn't told him she loved him.

Desfan's head jerked over his shoulder. "I need a physician," he thundered. "*Now!* The princess has been poisoned!"

Footsteps pounded away.

Jekem was sobbing in the bedroom. She couldn't make out his words, but she assumed Karim had disarmed him.

Desfan must have known the same. "*Karim,*" he bellowed. "I need to know what poison he used!"

Finally, Desfan looked at her.

Fates, he was beautiful. Even frantic and terrified, his brown eyes were completely arresting. Every plane of his face, every hard line and swath of brown skin, begged to be touched. His lips were set harshly, and a muscle feathered along his jaw. "Did he tell you?" Desfan asked, urgency sharpening his words. "Imara, what poison did he use?"

Imara stared at him, unable to look away. Unable to register anything but the fact that the fates had at least given her one last moment with him. "You came just in time," she breathed.

The skin around his eyes tightened. "What?"

Her free hand moved without thought, and her fingers curled around one of his trembling hands—the one that wasn't bleeding. "I love you," she whispered. "I know I can't, but I do. I need you to know that, before . . ." *I die.*

She couldn't say the words, but she knew Desfan heard them anyway.

Too many emotions flashed across his face; she couldn't register any of them. Then resolve hardened his features. "You're not going to die."

She almost managed to smile. "You may be serjan, but you don't command the fates."

His gaze darkened. "I am *not* losing you."

Tears stung her eyes, pain welling in her chest and cinching her throat. "I was never meant to be yours."

His fingers curled more tightly against her skin.

Skyer shoved into the suite. She didn't know how he'd known to come, but he looked livid, so he seemed informed on events. He cut across the room and crouched beside Desfan, one hand balanced on Imara's uninjured arm. "What happened?" he seethed. "A man in the hall said she was poisoned?"

Desfan stiffened, but didn't get a chance to reply; Karim strode into the sitting room, his focus landing on Imara. "Do you feel sick? Faint? A burning in your wound?"

Imara felt far too much in this moment. With Desfan and Skyer both touching her, both looking at her with such intensity, her entire body was burning. But . . . She glanced over at Karim. "No," she whispered. "I don't feel any of that."

Karim's shoulders dropped, though tension remained in his voice as he said, "Jekem said the spare darts didn't have the poison. Only the loaded one. He just wanted you to lower your guard."

Imara inhaled sharply. "I'm *not* dying?"

Karim shook his head. "No."

She could barely comprehend it. *She wasn't dying.* There had been no poison on that dart.

She may not be dying, but a weight still crushed her chest. Panic she didn't know how to dispel. She blinked rapidly to stop her tears from falling.

Desfan bowed his head, muttering a rapid prayer in Mortisian, his hold on her not relaxing.

Skyer pushed to his feet. "Where is this Jekem?"

Karim nodded toward the bedroom.

Skyer marched around Karim and disappeared into the room.

Imara shook a little as she looked at Karim. "Razan . . .?"

"She's fine," Karim said, his voice a little rougher than before. "He hit her temple—hard—but she'll wake soon. I put her on your bed."

Relief swelled, making it a little easier to breath. "Go to her."

Karim hesitated, but only briefly before he returned to the bedroom.

Imara turned her attention back to Desfan, just in time to see his thumb brush carefully over her small cut. There was a tremor in the motion that tugged at her heart. "Thank the fates you're all right," he breathed.

She gingerly touched the back of his bleeding hand. "You're hurt."

"Things didn't go smoothly at the warehouse."

That was hardly an answer. "Did you capture Sahvi?" she asked.

Desfan's body tensed as he glanced up at her. "No. We're still looking for him. We seized Fang's ship, though, so Sahvi will need to find another way out of Duvan."

"Is Liam secure?"

"Yes." A strange note colored his tone. "He had a chance to escape, but . . . he surrendered to save a couple of people who showed up to help him."

Imara's eyes widened. "That seems out of character for Liam."

"It does," Desfan agreed.

There was more. Imara could sense it, and her dread built. "What about Fang's family?"

"We found them," Desfan said. "That's why we were gone so long; we had to search several buildings. One of Sahvi's men that we captured told us that Fang's family was being kept near the harbor, but he didn't know where. He said the men Sahvi left with them had orders to kill Ayma, her husband, and their child once Fang's ship left the harbor."

Imara squeezed his hand. "I'm so glad you saved them."

"So am I." He paused. "Fang is dead."

Understanding swept through her; that's why he sounded so defeated. Desfan was a good man, and he no doubt blamed himself for not keeping everyone alive. "I'm sorry," she said softly.

Desfan lifted one shoulder. "He was a criminal. He didn't follow the plan. But in the end, he was just a terrified father and grandfather."

Imara had never met Fang, but her heart hurt for him—and his daughter, who was surely mourning him.

Desfan shifted before her, and one hand lifted. His knuckles brushed the curve of her cheek, coaxing her gaze to lock on his. "Imara, what you said when you thought you were dying . . . Did you mean it?" Hope burned in his eyes.

Longing burned in her heart, but she couldn't find her voice. She couldn't tell him *no* when every part of her soul screamed *yes*.

I love you, Desfan Cassian.

Shouting broke out in the bedroom. Desfan lurched to his feet, angling his body so he was between her and the open door. Peeking around him, Imara stared as Skyer returned to the sitting room. Blood was spattered across his shirt, and he clutched a bloody knife. He met Imara's gaze.

"You are avenged," he said.

Karim stormed out of the bedroom, fury twisting his face. "You had no right to kill him. He was not your prisoner."

Skyer faced Karim. "He attempted to kill my future wife. That gives me every right."

Karim's fists clenched at his sides. "He was subdued—he was no longer a threat. You didn't avenge anyone, you just committed murder."

Imara's breath caught at the dark shadow that entered Skyer's eyes. "You dare speak to me in this manner? I am the leader of my clan, and I am a future prince of Zennor."

"That may be," Karim said firmly. "But this is Mortise. You are not above our laws."

Skyer's brows slammed down.

Desfan glanced over his shoulder at Imara, and something in her expression must have conveyed her alarm, because he exhaled slowly. His voice was deceptively measured when he turned to Skyer. "We will discuss this later."

Karim glared. "We needed to question Jekem."

"He told me nothing of consequence," Skyer said. "He was working alone. There are others who believe as he does, but he did not know any names. He did not deserve to draw another breath—not when he would have stolen all of Imara's."

Karim's mouth twitched, but he didn't offer a retort.

Skyer tipped his head, just slightly. "I thank you, Karim Safar, for assisting me tonight by saving my bride." He turned to Desfan, though Imara noticed there was no respectful nod this time. "I thank you as well, Serjan. Though I am curious what brought you to my betrothed's room so quickly, so late in the night."

The innuendo was clear. Imara's face heated.

The muscles in Desfan's back tensed beneath his shirt. "I had business in the city," he said stiffly. "Serai Krayt was staying with Imara, so Karim and I came to fetch her. That is all."

"Good," Skyer said. "Now, I ask that another room be prepared for Imara, since this one is drenched in blood. While it is prepared, Imara will come with me." His dark eyes settled on her, and she fought a shiver. "We have matters to discuss."

Imara sat in Skyer's sitting room, which was smaller and more masculine than hers. She held her cane, since Desfan had retrieved it for her. His fingers had brushed hers as she'd taken it, and one look at his face assured her that he had no intention of letting her go with Skyer.

She didn't give him a choice. "Will you personally see to the arrangements for my new room?"

Desfan's expression had tightened. "Very well," he said. Then, attention sliding to Skyer, he added, "It will be ready soon. I'll come get her as soon as it is."

It was a warning. One Skyer noted, if the hardening of his jaw was any indication.

Imara had walked beside Skyer to his rooms, neither of them saying a word as her cane tapped against the stone floor. Four guards trailed them—two for each of them. Kaz looked uneasy when they finally reached Skyer's suite. Imara sent him a small, reassuring smile, even as Skyer closed the door on their guards.

"Sit."

She followed his order, mostly because her limbs were shaking.

A servant had left one lamp glowing, but Skyer moved to light another.

Imara clutched the top of her cane. "How did you know I was attacked?" she asked.

Skyer didn't turn as he lit the lamp before him. "I stationed one of my men to watch your door. When you screamed, he allowed your guards to eliminate the threat while he came to alert me."

She noted his clothing; what he'd worn at dinner, not night-clothes. "You weren't sleeping?"

"No." He didn't expound. Light flared, and he turned to face her. His face was shadowed. "You lied to me."

Imara's heart rate quickened. "What?"

"You did not tell me that Jekem—one of your own body-guards—attempted to assassinate you. You were supposed to tell me everything that has been happening in Mortise, and you did not."

Imara's spine straightened. She remembered the night of his inquisition. How she'd stood before him, because she had refused to sit. "I didn't lie," she said evenly. "I just didn't think about Jekem. You were more interested in Mortise anyway."

"I told you I wouldn't be pleased if you left anything out." His eyes narrowed. "I am not pleased, Imara."

"Skyer, I—"

"*Eilan*," he gritted out. "You will call me *Eilan*."

The anger in his voice was low but dangerous.

A tendril of fear rippled through her. Uncomfortable, Imara shifted in her chair. "Eilan, I'm sorry you're upset. I truly didn't think to tell you about Jekem. He tried to kill me, yes, but he disappeared. We hadn't heard anything in—"

"A man tried to kill you—because he doesn't want you to marry me—and you didn't think that was relevant?" His tone was softer, but no less furious.

Imara stared at him. "I . . . don't know how you wish me to answer."

He strode toward her. Her breathing thinned as his hands—one still horribly bloody—landed on the arms of her chair and his face descended to hang level with her own. "I wish you to tell me the truth, Imara. In all things."

The blood on his shirt was so close, she could smell the metallic tang of it. She wanted to sink back in the chair—anything to put distance between them. But she refused to cower. "I did not deliberately keep this from you," she said, fighting to keep the tremor from her voice.

One dark eyebrow rose. "Is there anything else you may have forgotten to tell me?"

Her thoughts flashed to Desfan. His confession, and hers. She swallowed hard. "No."

Skyer watched her too long. Too intently.

She braced herself, though for what, she didn't know. He hadn't raised his voice—not once. And he'd never lifted a hand against her.

His eyes drifted down to her lips.

Her pulse quickened.

Skyer grasped her chin with his blood-smeared hand and tipped her head back.

Her neck strained, and her stomach squirmed as his mouth descended, landing firmly on hers.

His lips were hard. Bruising. Controlling, and dominant. He kissed her like it was a punishment—or a branding reminder that she would not soon forget.

When he finally pulled back, Imara's eyes stung.

Skyer noted the sheen of moisture. She knew it, because the corner of his mouth lifted fractionally. "You will not forget me again, Imara. You will not forget my name, or the fact that you belong to me. I will make sure of it." He released her chin and took a step back.

Her heart pounded. Her skin burned from his touch, and the slickness of the blood that now clung to her chin—Jekem's blood—made her gut churn. She wanted to swipe her hand over her mouth, but she didn't dare. Not when Skyer was watching her.

649

"You left before the engagement rites could be completed," he said. "Luckily, one of my men has the skills to perform the clan ceremony. He will do so at dawn."

Panic flooded her. "But—my family should be present."

"They should have been," he agreed. "But you chose to run, and this cannot wait any longer."

Imara stared at him, hating everything about the face before her. The smugness. The arrogance. The mere fact that this man could kiss her, and she could not protest. That she effectively belonged to him, even now, before a single wedding vow was uttered.

Most of all, she hated that there was nothing she could do about it.

"You are mine," Skyer said, echoing her thoughts. "Perhaps if you look the part, you will remember that fact and respect me enough to tell me everything—always." He took another step back. "I'm going to wash this blood off. You stay here; I'll escort you to your room once it's been readied." He smirked then. "I do think it will be soon, like the serjan promised. He seems particularly attentive to your needs. That is something we might use before we return home."

Without another word, he left.

An unwanted tear slipped down Imara's cheek and splashed silently in her trembling lap. Her hand shook as she used the back of her wrist to scrub the blood off her jaw.

But even after her skin was rubbed clean, it still felt soiled. Her body didn't feel like her own, and that was the worst feeling of all.

Her future had been set for some time now. But tomorrow, at dawn, it would become permanent in a way she could no longer ignore.

Tomorrow, Eilan Skyer would be written on her skin. She would wear his mark and belong to him—forever.

There was no escape. Nowhere to run. No one to save her.

Nothing she could do to save herself.

Her chest cracked with a repressed scream, and another tear fell.

CHAPTER 51

GRAYSON

"IT TRULY IS A PRIVILEGE TO ESCORT YOU HOME," Zadir said to Mia as he led the way up the gangplank. Mia was behind him, and Grayson followed after her. He already felt a little lightheaded as the plank swayed beneath him, and his stomach churned. That didn't bode well, since they weren't even on the ship yet.

Zadir stepped onto the deck before turning to help Mia onboard. She paled as she darted a look around the ship.

Grayson suddenly wanted to curse. He was a fates-blasted idiot. How had he not considered what this would be like for her? To step foot on a ship again? Fates, she must be terrified. She'd probably been frightened from the moment he'd mentioned the *Seafire*, but she'd never said a word. If he'd known . . . But what could he have done differently? Zadir's ship was their best way out of Ryden.

He just hated that he hadn't even thought of her now-obvious fear.

Zadir still held her arm, as if assuring himself she was steady before he released her. "I do hope you'll pardon me while I get us underway, my seraijah."

"Of course." Mia glanced at Grayson, as if uncertain why Zadir would keep addressing her so deferentially.

She would have to get used to it. This was Zadir—a pirate—and even *he* was delighted to be in the presence of his long-lost princess. Grayson could only imagine what everyone in Mortise would think. What everyone in Eyrinthia would think.

It was a sudden and brutal reminder that Grayson's days with her were numbered. That her life was about to change forever—and so was his.

The other pirates slid around them, hurrying to their assigned positions so they could set sail immediately.

Zadir paused before walking away. "I forgot to mention, but were you by any chance missing an Alun and Rena Fletcher?"

Mia's breath caught. "They're here?"

"They arrived over a week ago," Zadir confirmed. "They kept insisting you'd come. I'm glad I listened."

Despite the paleness of her complexion, Mia smiled. "Thank the fates they made it."

"I gave them my first mate's cabin," Zadir said. "You, my seraijah, will of course have mine."

The ship pitched suddenly, and Grayson's stomach lurched dangerously in response. His mouth went dry, then suddenly watered.

"Excuse me," he bit out. He darted for the side of the ship and heaved.

Zadir's laughter boomed behind him. "We don't call him Spewer for nothing!"

The *Seafire* cut through the dark, foggy sea, taking them farther from Ryden with each passing moment.

Grayson had heaved up everything his stomach could offer, and though he urged Mia to leave him more than once, she'd remained beside him. He stayed draped over the railing even after he was done retching, his arms braced against the smooth wood.

Mia kept rubbing his back, his arm. "Do these pirates have a physician?" she asked him, worry tightening her voice.

"We pirates do indeed have a physician," Zadir said, drawing near. "But I'm afraid Spewer's just got the stomach of an old, sickly woman."

Grayson gagged dryly over the edge again, his face flushing at the strain of retching up nothing. At least the mist was cool against his face.

Mia gripped his shoulder. "Is there anything we can do for him?"

"Not really," Zadir said easily. "He'll get a little better as we go."

Mia didn't seem convinced, but before she could say more, the Fletchers arrived on the deck.

Rena Fletcher cried out and threw her arms around Mia, talking so rapidly Grayson could barely make out a word she said. The tears she struggled with certainly didn't help.

Fletcher hung back a little, though when he saw Grayson's gaze, he offered a short nod. A greeting, or thanks for keeping Mia alive—Grayson wasn't sure what it was supposed to convey.

Rena's rate of talking finally slowed enough that Grayson could make out her words. "Fates, you need to get out of these dirty clothes. And when did you last eat? Come, let me take care of you."

Mia resisted the woman's tug. "I want to stay with Grayson."

"You should go," he said, his voice heavy despite his best efforts. "I'll be a while. I need the fresh air."

Zadir leaned back against the rail beside Grayson. "I'll stay with him, my seraijah. Make sure he doesn't fall off." He threw in a wink.

Mia looked torn, but after Grayson managed to throw her a weak smile, she allowed Rena to guide her away. Fletcher followed close behind, a silent guard.

It felt strange to watch Mia walk away.

Grayson didn't like it.

"You look a little worse for wear," Zadir said, grabbing his attention. "But you did the impossible. You saved the stolen seraijah, just like a hero in a story." His eyes were on Grayson's profile—more specifically, his burn.

Grayson fingered the edge of his scar before he ordered his hand to drop to the rail. He recalled their conversation of heroes and adventure tales before he'd left the ship so many weeks ago. "Do I still fit the part of a nightmarish assassin?" he asked a bit dryly.

"Indeed. You're even more nightmarish now." Zadir leaned closer, unabashedly staring at his jaw. "By the fates, that *is* real, isn't it? I thought it was a trick of the shadows." He whistled lowly as he drew back. "I suppose you're more of a sacrificing hero than you thought."

Grayson didn't know what he was, but it wasn't a hero. "How worried do I need to be about Tyrell coming after us in a

Rydenic patrol ship?" he asked, changing the subject.

Zadir snorted. "He's got just as much of a chance catching us that way as by swimming himself. The *Seafire* is the fastest ship on these waters, and this fog plays in our favor."

"Good."

The captain's head tilted to the side as he studied him. "You going to tell me who did that to your face?"

"My father."

His eyebrows drew together as he muttered a long string of curses.

That seemed to say it all, so Grayson didn't bother responding.

A short silence stretched between them, then Zadir asked, "How old are you?"

Surprised by the question, Grayson answered without thought. "Seventeen." But no, that wasn't right. He'd had his birthday while sailing back to Ryden to rescue Mia. He hadn't even realized. "Eighteen," he corrected.

Zadir scratched his dark beard. "That's not many years, Spewer."

With his family, it had sometimes felt like an eternity.

"You've seen a lot of terrible things," the captain continued, as if following his thoughts. His voice was quieter as he added, "You've done a lot of terrible things, too."

He couldn't argue that.

Zadir exhaled slowly. "The fates aren't always fair. But you had her, and you saved her. That counts for something."

Grayson didn't really know what to say to that. But he didn't have to form a response, because another wave of sickness had him ducking over the edge of the ship.

Zadir straightened, shrugging off the mood between them

as he clapped him on the back. "I'll leave you to it. When you steady out a bit, come down and eat something. But wait until you're feeling a little better, or you'll just—yeah, that." He chuckled at Grayson's renewed retching. "Ah, Spewer, I think I actually missed you." He winked and strode away, even as he called over his shoulder, "I still wouldn't hire you, though."

CHAPTER 52

MIA

MIA'S HEART POUNDED TOO RAPIDLY AS SHE FELT every movement of the ship. What had once felt normal to her was now threatening. Every drop, every sway, every creak—it reminded her of the ship that had shattered beneath her feet.

Rena unknowingly distracted her by helping her clean up and change into a fresh dress, which the older woman had taken from the castle laundry. It was brown, and not a very pretty shade, either. But it was warm, with long sleeves that fell just over her wrists.

Settled in the captain's cabin aboard the *Seafire*, Mia ate the hearty soup Fletcher had brought her.

The Fletchers wanted to know everything about her escape with Grayson, but Mia was too tired to give every detail. She kept looking at the closed door of the cabin, willing it to open. She didn't like being separated from Grayson. It was almost as if her muscles couldn't fully relax until he was with her again.

While she ate, the Fletchers shared their tale of the night they'd escaped the castle.

"We were still in Lenzen, just approaching the south gate, when soldiers barred everything." Fletcher's brow furrowed. "We didn't know why, but we suspected it had to do with you, Grayson, and Devon."

Rena paled at the memory, and she clutched Mia's hand. "We thought you'd been captured."

Mia's throat suddenly burned. "We almost were. Devon . . . he was dead at the gate. And Prince Carter was there."

Fletcher's expression fell, though resignation hung in his eyes. "When I didn't see Devon with you, I feared the worst."

Mia swallowed hard. "Did you try to make it to Oland's Bridge?"

"Yes, but it was two days before the soldiers let anyone through the gates. We had to slip through with a group of people to avoid being recognized. Luckily, they were concentrating on looking for you and Grayson. And we never actually made it to the bridge—soldiers were searching that area of the forest, so it didn't seem wise. We were forced to go to Porynth another way."

"We hated to leave you," Rena added quickly. "We had most of the supplies, and we were so worried about you."

"I knew Grayson would keep you safe, though," Fletcher said. "That's why we wouldn't let this Mortisian pirate leave. We knew you would make it."

"And as long as the soldiers were still looking for you and Grayson at the city gates, we knew you hadn't been caught." Rena smiled, moisture shining in her eyes. "Thank the fates you're here safely."

She'd just finished her third bowl of soup when the cabin door opened and Grayson slipped inside. His expression was drawn, his face pale. He was clearly still struggling with his seasickness, but that didn't stop his gray eyes from settling on her. "Is there anything you need?" he asked. "Zadir is wondering."

She shook her head. "I'm fine, thank you."

He nodded and braced one hand on the doorframe as he said something to whoever waited in the hall. Zadir, presumably.

Rena stood suddenly. "Alun, we should let Mia sleep. She must be exhausted."

Fletcher rose a moment behind his wife, his gaze lingering on Grayson, who slowly turned back to face the cabin. "We can split watches," he said. "Unless you're too tired."

From the hallway, Zadir made a sharp sound of indignation. "The seraijah is completely safe on my ship! My crew would never harm her. They would die for her!"

Mia felt her eyes fly wide.

Grayson's mouth twitched. "Zadir's men are trustworthy, Fletcher. You can sleep in your cabin."

When the old guard frowned, Mia reached out and touched his hand. "Everything is all right now. I'm safe."

Safe. Fates, she was, wasn't she? After spending half her life in a prison cell, she was finally free. And against all odds, she and Grayson had made it out of Ryden. His family couldn't use her against him anymore. It felt impossible. Wonderful. Overwhelming. Tears stung her eyes, but they were tears of relief.

They were safe.

The skin around Fletcher's eyes tightened at her show of

emotion, but she blinked rapidly so the tears dissipated.

With a sigh, the old guard gave in. "I'm just across the hall," he said. "Call out if you need anything. And lock this door behind us."

More muttering from Zadir—this time, with creative Mortisian curses Mia had never heard before.

Rena and Fletcher filed out, taking the remaining soup with them. Mia almost asked them to leave the food for Grayson, but then she saw him turn a little green and hold his breath as the large pot was carried past.

Not the soup, then. But she had bread and water, and she would make him eat a little of that.

Before Fletcher left, he met Grayson's stare. "Don't keep her up long. Let her sleep."

Grayson nodded, and then the Fletchers were gone and he was closing the door, leaving them alone in the cabin.

Mia patted the bed beside her. "Come sit down."

He did, moving slowly—tentatively.

Once he was settled, she rested a hand on his knee. "Why didn't you tell me you get seasick?"

He swallowed, and she noticed the sweat beading along his hairline. "It never really mattered."

She pursed her lips. "If you knew you'd be so sick, why did you insist we travel by ship?"

"It was the fastest way to get you home."

Once again, he had put her first. As he always did.

He eyed her. "I never thought about what it would be like for you to sail again. Are you all right?"

Strangely, knowing that he hated sailing made her fear diminish. Perhaps it was her turn to be strong for him. "I'm fine," she assured him. "Truly."

He studied her intently. "Good. If that ever changes, I'm here."

Fates, he melted her heart. "I'm here for you, too."

The corner of his mouth lifted. "Thank you."

She brushed a long lock of his dark hair behind his ear. She had always enjoyed touching him. Contact with him, even when they were children, had calmed her—fed a part of her soul that had been starved during that first year of captivity.

Though Grayson didn't always reach for her, she liked to think her gentle touches fed a part of his soul, too.

"Are you still nervous to return home?" he asked softly.

"Yes. But I'm so grateful to be gone from Ryden. Just knowing I won't be used against you anymore—that I won't be your weakness . . ." Her words trailed off, because he'd stilled.

His gray eyes traced her face, and then one hand cupped her cheek. "Mia, you have *never* been my weakness. You're the fates-blasted opposite of that." The ball of his thumb skated over her skin, leaving a warm trail she felt all the way to her toes. "My father may have thought you were my weakness, but he was wrong. You are my strength. You always have been."

Her stomach clenched. She stared at his face—one side burned, and the other nicked with old scars. "You've been hurt so many times because of me. Your father has used me to force you to do horrible things."

"My sins are my own. Not yours. *Never* yours." He leaned in carefully and planted a soft kiss against her brow. "I have never blamed you, and I never will. Promise me that you won't, either."

She didn't know if letting go of her guilt was possible, but she would try. For him, and for herself.

The ship rocked, and Grayson's hold tightened.

She held him in return, her heartbeat surprisingly steady. "Is there anything you need?" she asked. "Anything that will make you feel better?"

Grayson gingerly shook his head. "It will get better in time."

His face was tight, and she knew he was struggling.

She shifted so she could reach the pitcher of water Rena had left. She poured some into a tin cup and passed it to Grayson. "Just sip it slowly," she urged.

He did, his throat bobbing as he swallowed.

When he finished, she filled the cup again.

As he drank, she told him what had happened to the Fletchers. She hoped to distract him. She also handed him a slice of the crusty brown bread left on the tray.

He pinched off a piece and chewed slowly. "I just wanted to make sure you're all right. Then I'll leave you to rest."

He spoke so easily, but she didn't understand. He was going to leave? They'd been inseparable since their escape; she'd assumed he'd be staying in the cabin with her.

Her lips parted, ready to ask him to stay, but doubt trickled in. If she asked, he would stay—of course he would. But did he *want* to? Grayson had been given far too few choices in his life, and she didn't want to take any more from him.

"Did Tyrell hurt you?" he asked. The suddenness of the question made her think he hadn't intended to ask.

She thought of Tyrell. Of the things he'd said, and the desperate way he'd held her arm.

"No. He didn't hurt me." She sighed. "He thought I was in danger with you. That *you* would hurt me."

Grayson went rigid. "I would never hurt you."

"I know." She bit her lip. "He wasn't going to let me go. He would have dragged me back there." He thought he was protecting her. From Grayson, and Henri.

He was going to be so angry—so hurt—when he woke. She wished she could give him one last embrace. Tyrell Kaelin was many things, but a part of her would always pray that he could one day be happy. That one day, he could be free.

Sending that thought to the fates, she focused on Grayson. He was barely eating, but he had to be starving.

"I can ask for something else to eat," she said. "There must be something that will soothe your stomach."

She moved to stand, but Grayson set a hand on her thigh, the touch stilling her. "I'm fine, Mia. Don't worry about me."

"I'm always going to worry about you," she said. "But once we get to Duvan, things will be better."

A muscle flexed in his jaw.

Not the reaction she'd expected—especially since *he'd* been the one trying to convince her of that, even when she'd panicked at the thought of going home.

Dread she didn't fully understand rose inside her.

"Mia . . ." His voice was guarded. Almost wary. Then, like a wall falling down, his expression softened. His head shook slightly, as if knocking aside a thought. He leaned in and brushed a kiss against her cheek. "Everything will be fine," he promised, a whisper against her skin.

There was something he wasn't telling her, and instinct screamed it was bad.

The ship rocked, and Grayson's jaw locked.

Compassion drove away her curiosity; she could question him later, when he wasn't feeling so sick. She rubbed a hand down his arm. "Lie down."

He looked like he might protest, but then the ship dropped on another wave. He paled and eased down on the mattress, lying on his back. "Just for a moment," he said, closing his eyes.

Exhaustion lined his face, so she wasn't surprised when he soon fell asleep.

She studied him for a long moment, just grateful she had him in her life. She'd had many dark moments in her sixteen—almost seventeen—years, but Grayson was a gift. One she was determined not to lose.

Whatever her fate, she knew she would be holding Grayson. And he would be holding her, too, because he loved her.

On that thought, she shoved away any niggling doubts about the future and blew out the lamp fastened to the wall beside the bed, plunging the cabin into darkness. Moonlight crept through the mist on the other side of the window, shedding just enough light that Mia could easily settle in beside Grayson. She tugged a quilt over them both. With her head tucked on the pillow beside his, the familiar scents of pine and spice surrounded her. Lying beside Grayson, she felt like she was already home.

She smiled at him, even though he couldn't see her. "I love you, Grayson," she whispered. She slipped her hand into his limp one, and his fingers curled around hers.

Holding onto her, even in sleep.

CHAPTER 53

TYRELL

TYRELL'S HEAD WAS A BLAZING AGONY, AND HIS heart beat too fast.

Mia was gone. Even without the soldier's hurried report, he knew she'd sailed away with Grayson.

The soldier who had found him in the harbor-master's office continued his report, but Tyrell barely heard him.

Fates, he should have taken her immediately out of the city. He'd been a fool to linger. He'd wanted Grayson dead—preferably in a way he could claim was an accident or necessity, so Mia and his father would both believe him. He'd stayed so he could end Grayson, and now Mia was gone.

His pulse roared in his ears. He grimaced as he shoved to his feet.

The world spun. He grasped the edge of the table, breathing too hard.

The young soldier eyed him warily. "Your Highness, perhaps you should—"

"I need a ship," he gritted out. "*Now.*"

The soldier hesitated. "Prince Tyrell, that was—"

"NOW!" he roared, ignoring the vicious spear of pain that stabbed through his brain.

The man darted out of the guardhouse.

Tyrell stared at the chair where Mia had so recently sat. The stew he'd set before her—now cold—remained untouched. He grabbed it and threw it at the wall, snarling a curse as the bowl clattered to the floor.

He'd lost her again. She'd left him—again. Grayson had taken her.

Again.

He kicked the chair and shoved the table. He yelled until his lungs burned, and then he stormed outside, stumbling once. His head was killing him, but that hardly mattered. He didn't know how long it had been since Grayson had taken the coward's way out and had those men ambush him, but their lead couldn't be too great.

Outside, the mist had thickened into a dense fog. Several soldiers hurried up to him, as well as the harbor master. The man was pale as he approached. "My prince, I'm afraid it's no use. Pursuing them, I mean."

Tyrell glared. "Why?"

The man flinched from his furious bark. "The fog, first of all. And they took Syed Zadir's ship. He's a Mortisian pirate. He docked under another name, of course, but I glimpsed his ship sailing out of the harbor. The *Seafire* is the fastest ship on the sea. You won't be able to catch him—even without the fog."

Tyrell's very bones vibrated with his rage. "I don't care. Get me the fastest ship in port."

The man winced. "It won't be enough, Your Highness. I'm sorry."

His hand fisted. He wanted to lash out at the man. Strike him down. But despite the anger flowing through him, the man's words finally penetrated.

Tyrell had been raised as a soldier. He knew when to give orders, and when to listen to the expertise of other men. The harbor master knew ships and the sea. He knew this Zadir, and Tyrell did not—other than the fact that one day, the pirate Zadir would be punished for the role he'd played in taking Mia away from him.

The truth settled on his soul like the first bitter frost. Mia was gone. He hadn't been able to stop her from leaving Ryden. He would not be able to catch her. Not by ship. Not before she reached Mortise.

Tyrell's gut clenched, and he ground his teeth. "I need a horse."

A soldier darted away.

Tyrell looked toward the sea, though he could barely discern the open water through the fog. His hand slipped into his pocket, and he fisted the silk ribbon he'd carried with him since Mia had left. Feeling it was a comfort—almost like touching her, because her fingertips had run over the length of it.

She wore the black queen around her neck. The gift he'd given her—the piece he'd carved—she kept it near her heart.

He wasn't a fool. He knew she loved Grayson. But she loved him, too.

He'd once told Mia that he wasn't afraid of anything, but that was a lie. He was terrified of losing her. She was the one person in his life who didn't hate him. The one person who made him feel even remotely redeemable. She was his air, his light—and he would do anything to get her back.

Tyrell had lost tonight, but he was not done fighting. He would go after Mia, and he would bring her back to Ryden. But first, he would return to Lenzen.

When he found Mia again, he would not lose her, and Grayson would not escape.

Next time they met, he would have an army at his back.

CHAPTER 54

CLARE

CLARE STOOD ON THE STONE BALCONY ATTACHED to her suite, overlooking the distant harbor of Madihr. The city was spread out along the shoreline, with hills and dark foliage separating the main port from the expensive manors the nobles lived in. The sea glittered in the early morning sun, stretching as far as Clare could see. A soft breeze played over her skin and teased the loose hairs that hung by her cheeks. She closed her eyes, sinking into the peace of the moment as she breathed in the tropical, earthy air.

Movement stirred behind her, but she didn't open her eyes. She knew who it was. She would always know him.

Bennick came up behind her, his arms folding around her middle. His chin settled against the top of her head, and she leaned back against his hard chest.

He joined her in her silence, his presence making this rare

moment of peace infinitely more precious.

Her sleep had been troubled last night, but that made sense. Zilas had only been dead for two days. After haunting them for so long, his death didn't seem real, even after Bennick had helped bury his body.

He would no longer hunt them. Terrorize them. The Rose was gone.

I'm not the only one.

Zilas's final words ghosted through her thoughts. She'd been turning them over in her mind ever since he'd spoken them. She remembered every detail. The way he had looked at Bennick, the struggle in his dying words and the almost desperate shine in his eyes.

I'm not the only one.

Not the only assassin who would try to kill her or Serene? That seemed an easy assumption.

Not the only discarded child of the commander? Considering Commander Markam's long line of mistresses, it wasn't hard to believe he had other children. In fact, Zilas's last words had reminded Bennick of something the assassin had said back in Devendra, when Bennick had first learned they were half-brothers.

You knew the commander sired other children. Is it really so surprising that one of them learned about you?

Bennick had been so stunned to learn he and the Rose shared blood, he hadn't truly processed the off-hand comment at the time—or thought anything of Zilas's assumption that Bennick knew he had other siblings. Now, those words took on a new and sinister meaning.

While Bennick had speculated about Zilas's final words, it was clear he didn't really want to discuss the Rose. Clare and

Vera, however, had talked late into the night.

"I thought I would feel better," Vera had confided quietly. "For so long I've wanted him dead. I'm relieved, I just . . . His death didn't heal my grief at losing Ivonne. And I'm worried something worse is out there. The Rose was every kind of evil, but we knew him. He was a demon with a face. Now . . . I don't know where the next strike will come from."

Clare felt the same apprehension. Perhaps that's why Zilas didn't feel gone. It wasn't him she felt, just an overarching danger that still hung over them.

It was harder to shake the feeling at night. But in the daylight—especially with Bennick—her fears receded. She didn't know what the future held, but in this moment, she had him. That was enough.

Bennick shifted behind her, his voice soft. "I spoke with the Hassans."

Kashif and Ilah had apologized profusely for the part they'd played in the Rose's plan, however unwillingly. They'd faced Clare as if she had the ability to call for their heads, even though Zilas had told them she was only Serene's decoy. As they'd stood before her, pale and shaking, Clare knew she couldn't blame them for doing what they felt they had to in order to save their daughter; especially since she herself had cooperated with the Rose to save Venn and Vera.

Of course, forgiveness was easier knowing everyone had made it out of that night alive, with the exception of Zilas and his hired men.

"They want to know if you wish to return to Duvan," Bennick said, bringing Clare back to the present moment.

"I'm not ready to go back," she said. After what had happened here, she supposed it was a miracle Dorma still felt safe to her, but it did. This island was an escape from the chaos in the rest of Eyrinthia, and it had helped calm the storms in her own heart as she continued to grieve her brothers.

Bennick pressed a kiss to the top of her head. "Then we'll stay."

She twisted in his arms, putting her back to the stone railing. His hands moved to her waist, and her palms settled against his chest, feeling the steady thump of his heart. "Do you ever worry about the future?" she asked.

"No."

Surprise lit through her. "You don't?"

He shook his head, though his crystal blue eyes remained fixed on hers. "No. Because no matter what happens, I know what lies ahead." His fingers flexed against her sides, fingertips pressing against her lower back. "*You're* my future, Clare."

Her heart skipped a beat. Her throat was suddenly tight. But warring with elation was reality. "How can I be your future when my life belongs to Newlan?"

"You don't belong to him," Bennick said at once, his voice edged.

"I swore oaths to him." When his mouth opened, she hurried to continue. "I'm not the only one who swore oaths, Bennick."

Intensity sharpened his gaze. "I know."

Her chest tightened. "I love you. You know I do. But the future . . . I can't even see it right now. You almost died at the border—I thought you *had* died. All my brothers are dead, and I feel like death is coming for me, too. And—"

Bennick ducked his head and captured her lips, drawing her into a kiss that made her fingers curl into his uniform and her stomach flutter. He stole her breath and her fears, giving her love and assurance. The kiss was everything she ever needed, because it was his.

When he finally eased back, her cheeks were warm and they both breathed shallowly.

His voice was low and a little rough as he said, "There will always be uncertainty. But I love you, Clare. More than anything." His eyes sharpened. "I'm going to desert."

Shock blasted through her. "But—you can't."

"I've given this a lot of thought, and I've made my decision."

"Your career . . ."

He shook his head. "Inconsequential." His voice gentled. "We won't be able to return home, and I'm sorry for that. But once Serene is safely married, I'll tell her we're both cutting ties with Devendra. If you want, I can ask if Desfan will hire me, and we can remain in Duvan. Or we can go anywhere you want. Newlan won't be able to stop us."

Her mind reeled. She didn't know what stunned her more—his words, or how methodically he had planned things. He wasn't speaking on a whim. He'd thought this through.

Her heart cracked. "Your mother . . ."

His voice was soft, and tinged with a resigned sort of pain. "I know. I can ask her to join us, wherever we settle, but she'll probably refuse. Even if she was well enough to travel, I don't think she'd ever leave my father."

Her heart burned. "Bennick, I can't ask you to give up your entire life for me."

"You're not asking. And I'm not giving up anything. Not really. Not compared to what you'll be giving me."

She stared as he drew back a step, his hands catching hers as he sank to his knees before her. His thumbs slid over her knuckles, and her chest swelled as he peered up at her. "I have made many oaths in my life, but none is as important as the one I now give to you. Every drop of blood I possess, every beat of my heart, is yours. For you, I renounce all other oaths. No king can command me. No kingdom can hold me. I am yours. Completely."

Tears pricked her eyes, but she refused to cry. She wanted nothing to cloud her vision of him in this moment. The sunlight danced in his sand-colored hair, and his blue eyes had never looked so bright.

His throat flexed as he swallowed. "Clare Ellington, will you marry me?"

Her breath hitched. Those tears she'd been fighting were unstoppable, now.

"It may not happen today or tomorrow," he continued, "but Clare . . . please be my wife."

Emotion strangled her throat, rendering speech impossible. She couldn't tell him how much she loved him, or how much she wanted him to be her husband. But that was all right—she would have the rest of their lives to tell him. Because for the first time since becoming Serene's decoy, Clare felt like she had a future. And it was with Bennick Markam.

"Yes," she finally managed, her voice wavering with tears. "*Yes.*"

He stared up at her, a grin breaking across his face. "Thank the fates," he breathed.

He shoved to his feet and cupped her face between his palms, and kissed her.

CHAPTER 55

WILF

BLOOD SEEPED THROUGH THE ROPE BINDING Wilf's wrists and sweat stuck his shirt to his back. He'd only been given minimal food and water since his capture two days ago. The clan warriors had managed to subdue him in Danjuma, but instead of simply killing him, as he'd expected, they'd abducted him, along with everyone else they'd managed to capture at the inn. Their captors didn't allow their prisoners to speak. When Wilf tried, he was struck. So, he listened and watched.

Unfortunately, the clansmen didn't speak much, except amongst themselves and in hissing whispers. They spoke in a dialect he didn't know, so he only caught a few Zennorian words. He knew they were distressed. Probably because the two men who had gone after Cardon and Serene had not returned. He assumed that meant Cardon and Serene had overcome their enemies, and that they were still alive. He had to believe they were safe. Cardon would give his life for Serene, and the princess was resourceful.

They would be fine.

Wilf and the other prisoners were bound tightly and forced to walk behind the clan horses as they traveled deeper into the jungle. More than a dozen warriors had attacked the inn, but they'd been joined by another dozen as they made their journey.

Wilf didn't attempt to escape; he was watched too closely. As the largest in the group, he was clearly the biggest threat, and so the guards always hovered nearby. That couldn't last forever, though. Their attention would slip at some point, and once he spied his chance to flee, he'd seize it.

They'd been traveling east, he thought, which was in the general direction of Zennor's capital. They were much farther north, though, and deep in the jungle. He wasn't aware of any villages in this area—he couldn't possibly guess their destination. Questions and suspicions swirled in his head, but finally—after days of walking—Wilf began to get his answers.

His jaw tightened when he and the other captives were shoved into a large clearing. His empty stomach clenched as scores of men, women, and children came into view. Fences and buildings had been constructed from the trees that had been cut down to create the clearing. It was a compound, with long outbuildings, cook fires, tents, canopies, and what looked to be a large training yard.

The perimeter was guarded by armed clansmen, who seemed to hail from various tribes, judging by the different colors of their khalmin markings. Their armed presence made it clear this wasn't a community.

It was a prison.

Wilf spotted Zennorians dressed in ragged clothing, hunched over as they carried burdens under the watchful eyes of the guards. There were many Devendrans as well, of all ages; some were caged behind guarded fences, while others skittered around camp, looking dirty and afraid.

The large clearing had to hold a thousand people—probably more.

He thought of Venn and Vera's story; the Devendran refugees who had vanished along the southern border. And he remembered the disappearances in Zennor he'd heard about since arriving here.

Wilf had a horrible suspicion he'd just found the missing.

Tribesmen laughed and talked, eating an early dinner. They seemed completely ignorant of the pain and suffering around them. Children cried. Women worked to cook and serve the assorted clansmen. Most of the camp's men were locked within the fenced areas. Despair hung heavy on the air.

Fates. What was this place?

The men who had captured him and the others from the inn reined in their horses and dismounted. One man held the rope secured to Wilf's bound wrists, and he jerked Wilf forward. An unnecessary shove at his back propelled him further.

Wilf gritted his teeth and lengthened his stride, taking in every detail he could as they led him and the others to the center of the camp.

There was a brief discussion between one of their captors and one of the camp's guards, though Wilf didn't understand what was said. The guard eyed him, and the others. More rapid words were exchanged, then Wilf was pulled toward a fenced area on his left, filled with large men. Other men from the inn were forced along with him, while the women and children were diverted in another direction. Husbands separated from their wives and children cried out, but were struck and hauled back into place.

Wilf's heart beat a little faster. They'd been sorted. But for what?

An angry shout split the air.

Wilf's attention whipped to the sound, just in time to see a large Zennorian leap to his feet, shaking out his wet arms. The khalmin on his skin marked him a tribesman—but so did the weapon sheathed at his hip. He was cursing a pregnant woman, who clutched a large bucket she clearly struggled to lift. Water sloshed over the sides, and it was obvious she'd spilled water on the man.

The woman was Zennorian, her skin darker than Imara's. She looked to be in her twenties, and judging from the roundness of her belly, she was due to give birth any moment. Her long dark hair was in a messy knot at the nape of her neck, her dress torn and muddy. Her cheeks were gaunt; she had clearly been a prisoner for a long time. She steadied the bucket and apologized.

The man seethed, shouted at her again, then backhanded her.

Every muscle in Wilf's body hardened as the woman stumbled. One hand flashed to cradle her protruding belly while the other went to her red cheek. The bucket crashed to the ground, drenching the bottom of her dress and the man's legs.

The tribesman cursed again, kicking the bucket as he drew back his hand to strike her once more.

Wilf elbowed the man behind him, knocking him back with a pained gasp. At the same time, he yanked his bound wrists, jerking the rope from the fist of the man who led him.

Men shouted in alarm, but Wilf was more or less free. With hands still tied and a rope dragging on the ground, Wilf charged the tribesman.

Before Wilf could reach him, a young boy darted in front of the pregnant woman and launched himself at the swinging man.

The boy took the hit, and the pregnant woman cried out, clutching the boy's shoulders to keep him from falling.

The tribesman roared and pulled back his foot, ready to kick the boy for interfering.

That's when Wilf slammed into him.

Shouts of alarm went up, and Wilf knew it wouldn't be long before he was subdued. To make his moment of freedom count, he drew back enough so he could smash both bound fists into the man's shocked face.

His nose snapped and blood spurted. His howl was sharp.

Harsh hands snagged Wilf, dragging him off the man and then forcing him to the ground. One cheek was forced against the hard earth, and from the crushing weight on his back he assumed he was being pinned by at least three men.

He probably shouldn't have done that. He would be less likely to take them by surprise now, because they would not underestimate him again.

Glancing up at the pregnant woman and the boy she clutched so protectively, he decided it was worth it.

The woman eyed him with a mix of gratitude and wariness, and the boy . . .

Wilf stared. Startlingly blue eyes met his. The boy's skin was caught between Zennorian and Devendran. And the shape of his face . . . so familiar.

The pregnant woman twisted the boy to face her, brushing at his reddened cheek. "Are you all right, Mark?"

The name jolted through Wilf, even though he'd already known.

Mark. Clare's youngest brother.

He was alive.

Wilf ignored the shouting above him as a commander of some sort demanded to know what had happened. He barely registered the pain as his ribs were kicked by an irritated guard.

"Mark," Wilf growled.

The boy's gaze snapped to him. The Zennorian woman held Mark a little closer, defensiveness setting her grim features as she studied him.

There wasn't time for explanations. Wilf was hauled to his feet and dragged back a step. Five men had hold of him, and at least two blades were pressed to his back. Too many to effectively fight, especially with Mark so close. Besides, if he caused too much trouble, the clansmen might just decide to kill him, and he had even more to live for now.

He locked eyes with Mark and said the only thing he could think of. "Clare sent me."

The boy's eyes widened.

Then Wilf was shoved away, and he lost sight of Mark and the Zennorian woman.

His plans would have to be adjusted. He needed to find out everything that was happening here, and then he needed to escape.

And he was taking Clare's brother with him.

THE STORY CONTINUES IN
ROYAL TRAITOR
BOOK 5 OF THE FATE OF EYRINTHIA SERIES

GLOSSARY

AKIVA *(AH-KEE-VAH)* One of Liam's Mortisian contacts. Alias: Zeph.

AMIL HAVIM *(UH-MEEL HAH-VEEM)* A Mortisian nobleman who served in Devendra with his father as an emissary of peace. Due to his father's murder in Devendra, he turned against the alliance and orchestrated an attack on Desfan's court. Deceased.

ANOUSH *(AH-NOOSH)* A newly appointed member of the Mortisian council. Father to Arav. Full name: Ramit Anoush.

ARAV ANOUSH *(AH-RUHV AH-NOOSH)* A Mortisian nobleman. Son of Ser Anoush, a newly appointed member of the Mortisian council.

ARCAS *(AR-KUS)* A kiv in the Mortisian city guard. He assists in some of the palace security now as well. Full name: Manusch Arcas.

AREN BUHARI DEMOI *(EH-RUHN BOO-HAR-EE DE-MOY)* The late queen of Devendra, mother to Serene and Grandeur. Was married to Newlan Demoi. Sister to Zaire Buhari, king of Zennor.

ASHEAR *(UH-SHEER)* A former member of the Mortisian council. He was killed before the prisoner exchange at the

Mortisian-Devendran border. Full name: Duman Ashear. Deceased.

ASSASSINS A popular Mortisian card game involving luck, skill, and bluffing. The cards are decorated with an array of royal and noble classes, as well as some peasant occupations, and the rarest card of all: the assassin.

AVAO TARN *(AH-VAY-OH TARN)* Grandfather to Karim, and a former bodyguard to Seraijan Farah Cassian, Desfan's mother. Father of Azima Safar.

AZIMA SAFAR *(AH-ZEE-MUH SA-FAR)* Karim's mother. She resides in an asylum in Duvan. Daughter of Avao Tarn. To learn more about her, read the novella *Fire & Ash*.

BENNICK MARKAM *(BEN-ICK MARK-AHM)* Captain of Serene's bodyguards. Son of Dennith and Gweneth Markam, and half-brother of Zilas. He is in love with Clare.

BRIDGET *(BRI-JEHT)* The senior maid for Serene. Also one of her rebels.

CARDON BRINHURST *(CAR-DEN BRIN-HERST)* One of Serene's bodyguards. He has a distinctive scar on his cheek. He is in love with Serene.

CARTER THELIN KAELIN *(CAR-TR THEL-IN KAY-LIN)* The second prince of Ryden. Son of Henri and Iris Kaelin, and brother to Peter, Liam, Tyrell, and Grayson. A close follower of Peter's. Also a dutiful pupil of his mother's, so he is well-versed in poisons.

CLARE ELLINGTON *(CLAIR EL-ING-TUN)* The decoy for Serene. Former maid in the castle kitchen of Devendra. Sister to Eliot, Thomas, and Mark Ellington. She is in love with Bennick.

COMMANDER DENNITH MARKAM *(DEN-ITH MARK-AHM)* A high-ranking Devendran commander. Married to Gweneth Markam, and father to Bennick and Zilas, also known as the Rose.

DAKAAR *(DAH-KAHR)* A Zennorian lord who is counted among Serene's rebels. Full name: Aadan Dakaar.

DANJUMA *(DAN-JOO-MUH)* A Zennorian city located in the northern midlands.

DARKOL *(DAR-KOHL)* A former bodyguard to the Cassian children. He died during the shipwreck that claimed the lives of Farah and Tahlyah Cassian.

DAVID HOLM *(DAY-VIHD HOLM)* Father to Finn, Sarah, and Rebecca Holm. A key member in Serene's rebellion. Currently at the refugee camp known as Salvation. To learn more about David and his children, read the novella *Shield & Blade*.

DAWN OF EYRINTHIA A two-week holiday in Mortise celebrating Eyrinthia, proclaimed goddess of the world and creator of the fates.

DESFAN SAERNON CASSIAN *(DES-ɛᴀᴡɴ SAIR-ɴᴏɴ CAS-ᴇᴇ-ᴜʜɴ)* The heir to the Mortisian throne. He has been serving as regent ever since his father fell ill. Now that the serjan has died, Desfan is set to become the new ruler of Mortise. He is betrothed to marry Serene Demoi in an effort to make an alliance with Devendra. Son of Saernon and Farah Cassian, and brother to Tahlyah and Meerah.

DERVISH *(DUR-ᴠɪsʜ)* Captain of Prince Grandeur's bodyguards. He once served under Wilf, when Wilf was the captain of the prince's guard, but Dervish stole his position years ago.

DEVENDRA *(ᴅᴜʜ-VEN-ᴅʀᴜʜ)* One of the kingdoms of Eyrinthia, ruled by the Demoi family.

DEVENDRAN *(ᴅᴜʜ-VEN-ᴅʀᴜɴ)* Relating to the kingdom of Devendra or its people.

DEVON *(DEV-ᴜʜɴ)* A physician who works in the Rydenic castle. He has taken care of Mia during her captivity.

DIRK ARKLOWE *(DIRK ARK-ʟᴏᴡ)* A former bodyguard to Princess Serene. He was the oldest of the guards and protected Serene since her birth. He was killed during the betrothal signing recently held in Mortise.

DOLBAR PASS *(DOHL-ʙᴀʀ PASS)* A mountain pass that connects Ryden and Devendra.

DORMA *(DOHR-ᴍᴜʜ)* The largest Mortisian island.

Duvan *(DOO-vahn)* The capital city of Mortise.

Eliot Ellington *(EL-ee-uht EL-ing-tun)* Older brother to Clare, Thomas, and Mark. He was a Devendran city guardsman who rebelled against King Newlan. Also known as Eliot Slaton. (Slaton was his mother's surname.) Deceased.

Essa *(EH-suh)* A member of the Mortisian council.

Eyrinthia *(AIR-INTH-ee-uh)* The name of the known world. The four kingdoms of Eyrinthia are Devendra, Mortise, Ryden, and Zennor. In Mortise (and select religions in Devendra and Zen-nor) Eyrinthia is also the name of a goddess.

Faersin *(FAIR-sin)* A poison that lowers inhibitions and compels one to be truthful. It also induces gradual, temporary paralysis.

Fang A Mortisian criminal who operates in Duvan. He has had some run-ins with Desfan, and once captured Desfan with the intent to ransom him.

Farah Cassian *(FAIR-uh CAS-ee-uhn)* The late seraijan of Mortise. Was married to Saernon Cassian, and mother to Desfan, Tahlyah, and Meerah.

Flame's Breath A powder that can burn skin with an exceeding amount of pain.

Fletcher *(FLEH-chr)* Mia's primary guard since her imprisonment in Ryden. Married to Rena Fletcher. Full name: Alun Fletcher.

GALE A pirate aboard the *Seafire*, the ship captained by Mortisian pirate Zadir.

GRANDEUR NEWLAN DEMOI *(GRAN-JER NEW-LUHN DE-MOY)* The crown prince of Devendra and heir to the throne. Son of Newlan and Aren Demoi, and younger brother to Serene. He is the leader of the Hunt, a military group designed to eradicate the rebellion in Devendra.

GRAYSON WINN KAELIN *(GRAY-SUHN WIN KAY-LIN)* The youngest prince of Ryden. He is the enforcer of his father's laws, and feared throughout Ryden for his actions. He is also known as the Black Hand. In Zennor, he is known as the Black Viper. Son of Henri and Iris Kaelin, and brother to Peter, Carter, Liam, and Tyrell. He is in love with Mia.

GWENETH MARKAM *(GWEH-NETH MARK-AHM)* A Devendran noblewoman. Married to Dennith Markam, and mother to Bennick. She is of delicate health, and rarely leaves her room.

HANNA *(HA-NUH)* Imara's maid.

HENRI KAELIN *(HEN-REE KAY-LIN)* The king of Ryden. Married to Iris Kaelin, and father of Peter, Carter, Liam, Tyrell, and Grayson.

THE HUNT A Devendran military group led by Prince

Grandeur, designed to eradicate the rebellion in Devendra.

IDEN *(EYE-DEN)* The capital city of Devendra.

IEANNAX *(EYE-AHN-AX)* A rare poison that delivers painless death. Originates from Zennor.

ILAH HASSAN *(EYE-LAH HA-SAWN)* A Mortisian noble-woman from the island of Dorma. Married to Kashif Hassan, and mother to Sidrah. Ilah and Kashif were both injured during the attack the night before Desfan's coronation.

IMARA AIMETH BUHARI *(IH-MAR-UH AY-METH BOO-HAR-EE)* The third Zennorian princess and daughter of Zaire Buhari. She is Serene's cousin.

IRIS KAELIN *(EYE-RUHS KAY-LIN)* The queen of Ryden. Married to Henri Kaelin, and mother of Peter, Carter, Liam, Tyrell, and Grayson. Also known as the Poison Queen.

IVAR CARRIGAN *(EYE-VAAR CARE-I-GUHN)* King Newlan's cousin. He led a failed uprising in Devendra ten years ago. Alive; current location unknown.

IVERN *(EYE-VURN)* A large river that divides Zennor from Devendra and Mortise.

IVONNE SMALLWOOD *(EE-VOHN SMAHL-WOOD)* A former maid of Serene's and older sister to Vera. She was killed by the Rose.

JAHNU SAFAR *(JAH-noo sa-FAR)* Father to Karim, and husband to Azima. He abandoned them when Karim was only a child.

JAHZARA *(jah-ZAR-uh)* A disgraced Zennorian noblewoman who lives in Ryden. Current mistress of Peter Kaelin.

JAMAL *(jah-MAHL)* A former member of the Mortisian council. He was recently arrested for treason and other crimes, including bringing olcain into Duvan. Full name: Omar Jamal. Deceased.

JAMES *(JAIMZ)* A Devendran commoner who is a friend to Serene and serves as one of her leading rebels.

JAYIV *(JAY-IV)* Physician aboard the *Phoenix*, the ship Desfan sailed on when he was fifteen years old. To learn more about him, read the novella *Fire & Ash*.

JEKEM *(JEH-kum)* One of Princess Imara's bodyguards.

JERSHEN *(JUR-shen)* First mate aboard the *Phoenix*, the ship Desfan sailed on when he was fifteen years old. To learn more about him, read the novella *Fire & Ash*.

JULNE *(JOOLN)* A vast network of rivers in Ryden.

KARIM SAFAR *(KAH-REEM sa-FAR)* Desfan's bodyguard, as well as his best friend. Son of Jahnu and Azima Safar. Grandson of Avao Tarn.

KASHIF HASSAN *(KUH-SHEEF HA-SAWN)* A Mortisian nobleman from the island of Dorma. Married to Ilah Hassan, and father of Sidrah. Kashif and Ilah were both injured during the attack the night before Desfan's coronation.

KAZ *(KAZ)* Captain of Princess Imara's bodyguards.

KAZIM *(KAH-ZEEM)* One of Liam's Mortisian contacts. Alias: Neev Sal.

KEDAAH *(KE-DAH)* The capital city of Zennor.

KIV *(KIV) (RHYMES WITH GIVE)* A Mortisian military title, similar to the rank of captain.

KRID *(KRID)* A city in northern Mortise.

LAMBERN LAKE *(LAM-BURN)* A lake located in northwestern Devendra.

LATIF *(LAH-TEEF)* A Mortisian man also known as Gamble, a retired sailor who played a role in taking Meerah to Ryden nine years ago. More recently, he was blackmailed by Liam Kaelin into abducting Serene, who he ultimately learned was her decoy, Clare. Though he saved Clare's life, he was arrested by Desfan for his crimes.

LENZEN *(LEN-ZUHN)* The capital city of Ryden.

LIAM KELL KAELIN *(LEE-UM KEL KAY-LIN)* The third prince of Ryden. He is the spymaster for his father. Son of

Henri and Iris Kaelin, brother to Peter, Carter, Tyrell, and Grayson. Also known as the Shadow of Ryden. Currently imprisoned in Mortise for crimes against Mortise, Devendra, and Zennor.

MADIHR *(MAH-DEER)* The capitol city on the Mortisian island of Dorma.

MAMA One of Mia's former caretakers. Deceased.

MATANONA *(MA-TUH-NO-NUH)* A Zennorian city located in the midlands.

MARK ELLINGTON *(MARK EL-ING-TUN)* The youngest of Clare's brothers.

MEERAH JEMA CASSIAN *(MEER-UH JEH-MUH CAS-EE-UHN)* The youngest seraijah of Mortise. Once presumed dead, she has spent the last nine years imprisoned in Ryden. Few know who she really is, or that she is still alive. Daughter of Saernon and Farah Cassian, and sister to Desfan and Tahlyah. Also known as: Mia.

MIA *(MEE-AH)* A prisoner of King Henri's, she has spent the last nine years in Ryden. Though her identity has been largely unknown, she is Meerah Cassian, the youngest seraijah of Mortise. She is in love with Grayson.

MICHAEL BYERS *(MY-CULL BY-URZ)* A former Devendran city guardsman and a rebel who wanted to kill Serene. He blamed Clare for Eliot's death; he tried to kill Clare to avenge his best friend's death, but was killed by Latif.

MORTISE *(MOR-TEES) (RHYMES WITH GEESE)* One of the kingdoms of Eyrinthia, ruled by the Cassian family.

MORTISIAN *(MOR-TEE-SHUN)* Relating to the kingdom of Mortise or its people.

NEWLAN DEMOI *(NEW-LUHN DE-MOY)* The king of Devendra, father to Serene and Grandeur. Was married to the late queen of Devendra, Aren Buhari Demoi. Cousin to Ivar Carrigan, who led a rebellion against him ten years ago.

OLCAIN *(OHL-CAIN)* A highly addictive drug that originates from Zennor.

PAPA One of Mia's former caretakers. Deceased.

PETER HENRI KAELIN *(PEE-TR HEN-REE KAY-LIN)* The heir to the throne of Ryden and oldest Kaelin prince. Son of Henri and Iris Kaelin, and brother to Carter, Liam, Tyrell, and Grayson.

THE PHOENIX *(FEE-NUHKS)* The name of the patrol ship Desfan sailed on when he was fifteen years old. Also the name of a legendary creature from Zennor.

PORYNTH *(POR-INTH)* A port city in southern Ryden.

RAHIM NASSAR *(RAH-HEEM NAH-SAR)* A Mortisian merchant and suspected smuggler. Believed to be involved with the olcain being brought into Duvan.

RANON SIFA *(RAH-NON SEE-FAH)* A Mortisian nobleman. Son of Ser Sifa, a newly appointed member of the Mortisian council. Ranon befriended Grayson during his time in Mortise.

RAZAN KRAYT *(RAA-zan KRAYT)* A Mortisian noblewoman recently appointed to the Mortisian council. She has a complicated past with Desfan and Karim. To learn more, read the novella *Fire & Ash*.

REEVE *(REEV)* A captain in the Rydenic army. He has served with Grayson in the past, and may suspect him of disloyalty to the crown. Grayson saved his life during a tax collection mission.

RENA FLETCHER *(RAIN-uh FLEH-chr)* Wife to Alun Fletcher. She serves as Mia's maid.

REW *(ROO)* A small city in northeastern Ryden. Iris Kaelin was born and raised there.

RYDEN *(RYE-den)* One of the kingdoms of Eyrinthia, ruled by the Kaelin family.

RYDENIC *(RYE-DEN-ick)* Relating to the kingdom of Ryden or its people.

SAERNON JARON CASSIAN *(SAIR-non JAIR-uhn CAS-ee-uhn)* The previous ruler of Mortise, recently deceased. Was married to Farah Cassian, and father of Desfan, Tahlyah, and Meerah.

SAHVI *(SAW-VEE)* A Zennorian drug master believed to be responsible for the olcain recently brought into Duvan.

SALIM *(SAH-LEEM)* A Mortisian man who led an infamous group of sadistic mercenaries. He was hired by Amil Havim to abduct Serene. He captured Clare and Vera, believing them to be the princess and her maid. Deceased.

SALVATION A refugee camp for Devendrans, located outside the Mortisian city of Zahdir.

THE *SEAFIRE (SEE-FYER)* The ship of the Mortisian pirate Zadir.

SER *(SAIR)* The Mortisian term for *lord*; title used to address noble males.

SERAI *(SAIR-AY)* The Mortisian term for *lady*; title used to address noble females.

SERAIJAH *(SAIR-AY-ZJAW)* The Mortisian term for *princess*.

SERAIJAN *(SAIR-AY-ZJAWN)* The Mortisian term for *queen*.

SERENE AREN DEMOI *(SER-EEN EH-RUHN DE-MOY)* The princess of Devendra. She is Newlan's firstborn but not in line for the throne, because in Devendra women cannot rule. Older sister to Grandeur.She is betrothed to Desfan, though she is in love with her bodyguard, Cardon.

SERJAH *(SAIR-zjaw)* The Mortisian term for *prince*.

SERJAN *(SAIR-zjawn)* The Mortisian term for *king*.

SEVEH *(SEH-vuh)* Captain of the *Phoenix*, the ship Desfan sailed on when he was fifteen years old. To learn more about him, read the novella *Fire & Ash*.

SHEBAR *(SHEH-BAAR)* A port city in northwestern Mortise.

SIDRAH HASSAN *(SID-ruh ha-SAWN)* Daughter of Ilah and Kashif Hassan.

SIFA *(SEE-fah)* A newly appointed member of the Mortisian council. Father to Ranon. Full name: Abeil Sifa.

SIV *(SIHV)* Rigging expert aboard the *Phoenix*, the ship Desfan sailed on when he was fifteen years old. To learn more about him, read the novella *Fire & Ash*.

SKYER *(SKY-ur)* The leader of the Kabu clan in Zennor. He is betrothed to Imara. Also known as *Sky Painter*. Official title in his clan: Warrior.

STRATEGEM A Rydenic strategy game involving a wooden board with checkered spaces and multiple moving pieces that include a king and queen.

SWALLOW A pirate aboard the *Seafire*, the ship captained by

Mortisian pirate Zadir.

Syalla *(SY-AL-UH)* A pain-causing posion that is often applied to blades. Generally used in Ryden.

Tahlyah Farah Cassian *(TAHL-YAH FAIR-UH CAS-EE-UHN)* One of the late seraijahs of Mortise. Daughter of Saernon and Farah Cassian, and sister to Desfan and Meerah.

Tamar Nadir *(TAH-MAR NAH-DEER)* A Mortisian noblewoman who lives near the Devendran border. A great supporter for peace between Mortise and Devendra. She had recently begun a romantic relationship with Dirk Arklowe, before he was killed.

The Rose The most feared assassin in Eyrinthia. He always leaves a rose with his victims. His real name is Zilas. He is the illegitimate son of Commander Markam and half-brother to Bennick.

Thomas Ellington *(TAH-MUS EL-ING-TUN)* One of Clare's younger brothers.

Tyrell Zev Kaelin *(TY-REL ZEHV KAY-LIN)* The second youngest prince of Ryden. Grayson's closest rival. He oversees the training of Ryden's soldiers. Son of Henri and Iris Kaelin, and brother to Peter, Carter, Liam, and Grayson. In love with Mia.

Vakesh Kazzo *(VAH-KESH KAH-ZOH)* A former Mortisian spy who once worked for Saernon Cassian. Currently in an asylum in Duvan.

Venn Grannard *(VEN GRAN-ard)* One of Serene's body-guards and Bennick's best friend. He is half-Zennorian; his father was Devendran, and his mother is Zennorian. He is in love with Vera.

Vera Smallwood *(VER-ah SMAHL-wood)* One of Serene's maids. Younger sister to Ivonne and friend to Clare. She is in love with Venn.

Vibba *(VEE-buh)* A city in Zennor, located in the northern midlands.

Vyken *(VY-ken)* The main port city of Ryden.

Weeper A pirate aboard the *Seafire*, the ship captained by Mortisian pirate Zadir.

Whistler A pirate aboard the *Seafire*, the ship captained by Mortisian pirate Zadir.

Widow's Braid A Zennorian custom for widows to mark the stages of mourning. Serene wears one hidden in her hair to symbolize the love she lost when Cardon rejected her three years ago.

Wilford Lines *(WIL-ford LINES)* One of Serene's body-guards. Former captain of Grandeur's guard, before being demoted. He nearly died from the pox five years ago. The same illness killed his wife, Rachel.

YAHRI *(YAH-REE)* The senior member of the Mortisian council and a primary advisor to Desfan. Full name: Amna Yahri.

YERRET *(YAIR-ET)* A challenging Zennorian game that is played by strategically arranging small half-sphere glass pieces of different colors. The game can be played individually or against an opponent.

ZADEN *(ZAY-DIN)* A commander in the Rydenic army. Captain Reeve serves in his ranks.

ZADIR *(ZAH-DEER)* A Mortisian pirate captain who has become an unexpected ally of Desfan's. His ship is called the *Seafire*. His full name is Syed Zadir.

ZAIRE BUHARI *(ZAIR BOO-HAR-EE)* The king of Zennor. Imara's father and Serene's uncle. Brother to the late Aren Buhari Demoi.

ZAHDIR *(ZAH-DEER)* A city located in central Mortise. The refugee camp known as Salvation is located outside the city walls.

ZANDER FELLNOR *(ZAN-DUR FEL-NOR)* A Devendran nobleman who is currently in charge of the refugee camp known as Salvation. To learn more about him, read the novella *Shield & Blade*.

ZENNOR *(ZEN-OR)* One of the kingdoms of Eyrinthia, ruled by the Buhari family.

ZENNORIAN *(ZEN-OR-EE-UN)* Relating to the kingdom of Zennor or its people.

ZEPHAN *(ZEF-UHN)* A traitor and former member of the Mortisian council. Full name: Ganem Zephan. Deceased.

ZILAS *(ZY-LUHS)* Illegitimate son of Commander Markam, and half-brother to Bennick. Also known as The Rose, the most infamous assassin in Eyrinthia.

ZOROYA *(ZO-ROY-UH)* The main port city of Zennor.

ACKNOWLEDGEMENTS

Every time I sit down to write this page, I feel so humbled and overwhelmed by the love and support for me as a writer and a person, and for this series specifically.

First, I want to express my deepest gratitude to my Heavenly Father for giving me the gift of imagination, and a love for stories. There is an indescribable joy that comes from knowing I'm using these gifts to help others, even if it's just giving them a world to escape to for a few hours when life becomes overwhelming.

Endless thanks to my family for helping me on my author journey. Mom, thank you for always encouraging me. Dad, even though you aren't on this earth anymore, I know you're cheering me on, just like you always did. Thank you to all my siblings for helping me in a myriad of ways. Special thanks to Kimberly for helping me find my courage so I could make my author dreams become a reality—and for designing such a perfect cover for Grayson—and to Kevin, for creating a beautiful map so everyone can see Eyrinthia without having to suffer through my terrible sketches.

This book would not be anywhere near as coherent and polished without my incredible beta readers and proofreaders. These early readers have the kindness of Mia and Clare, the fierceness of Grayson and Bennick, the wit of Desfan and Imara, and the critical eye of Serene and Karim—and sometimes Wilf, though the bluntness can be a very good thing. Your feedback is essential, and I'm so grateful for it. Huge thanks to: Anna Brown, Amy Cardon, Cassidy Clarke, Elyce Edwards, Cynthia Ford, Laurie Ford, Crystal Frost, Marlene Frost, Kimberly Frost, Ashley Hansen, Sarah Hill, Michalla Holt, Rebeca McKinnon, Jonnie Morgart, Amelia White.

Special thanks to my street team, Heather's Frosties—you're all amazing, and I'm so lucky to have your support and love. Thank you for helping to share my books with the world!

Thank you to all the amazing bookfluencers who will not rest until everyone has read my books. (Haha, okay, please rest, though!) I'm so grateful to you all for posting reviews, making videos, messaging me with your reader reactions and theories, and just posting about my books. Word of mouth is how good books are spread, and I'm so honored whenever I see you post about my work. Thank you!

And finally, thank YOU for picking up this book and returning to Eyrinthia again. I know there are a thousand and one things you could be doing at any given time, so thank you for choosing to spend time with my characters. I hope you enjoy this story, and that you're looking forward to the next one. And please know that I appreciate every review and every message my readers send me—it helps keep me going!

If you enjoyed Royal Rebel, or any of my books,
would you consider leaving a review?
It doesn't take long, and it makes a world of
difference in the success of a book.
Thank you!

THE PRINCESS

AND THE

NEW BODYGUARD

A FATE OF EYRINTHIA SHORT STORY

HEATHER FROST

THE PRINCESS

AND THE

NEW BODYGUARD

A FATE OF EYRINTHIA SHORT STORY

———◆———

SERENE KNOWS THINGS HAVE BEEN STRAINED BETWEEN
HER PARENTS SINCE THE CIVIL WAR ENDED. SHE HOPES A
TRIP TO LAMBERN LAKE WILL BRING HER FAMILY BACK
TOGETHER. WHAT SHE DOESN'T EXPECT IS TO GROW
CLOSER TO HER NEW BODYGUARD, CARDON.

SERENE IS ABOUT TO LEARN THAT ONE DAY CAN
IRREVOCABLY CHANGE THE COURSE OF A LIFE . . .

———◆———

SERENE

SERENE KNELT ON THE SOFT EARTH of the lakeside beach, the briny scent mixing with the smell of pine that drifted from the surrounding forest. Lambern Lake glittered as far as she could see, the sight both familiar and comforting.

Her family always visited the lake in the summer, and the area held some of her most treasured memories. Her father had never been an overly affectionate man, but he smiled most when he was away from the castle. Serene knew he felt a great deal of stress as the king of Devendra, but he hadn't always been so irritable. The civil war had changed him, and even though the conflict had ended five years ago, he had never fully lost the new edge of tension that always seemed to ride him.

Perhaps their time at the lake would help.

"Find any good ones yet?" Dirk asked as he settled onto his

knees beside her.

Serene glanced at her small pile of collected shells. She was only weeks away from her fourteenth birthday, so she knew she was too old to pick shells from the dark, gritty sand. Still, it was something she had done every summer since she was a little girl, and she never wanted to outgrow the tradition. She would only choose the most beautiful shells to add to her collection. She often shared some with her mother and her guards as well. She knew Dirk, at least, kept every one. And her mother always treasured them, too.

Fates, Serene wanted to make her smile. Queen Aren had once been bright and happy, but the civil war had left its mark on her, too. And it seemed as if things were only growing *more* strained between her parents.

Dirk was still awaiting her answer.

She shook herself from her thoughts and gestured to the pile of shells. "I've found a few good ones." They were all small, but they were pristine. Uncracked, and undamaged.

Perfect.

Dirk looked them over. "Do you have a favorite?"

"Not yet."

He cracked a smile. "Well, you don't want to be too hasty."

She shot him a scowl. "You're teasing me."

The corner of his mouth lifted higher, but he shook his head. "I'm truly not. Your patience is a good trait, Serene. It will serve you well in life." His spine straightened and he nodded back toward the lodge. "I need to check in with Captain Gates. Cardon will remain with you."

Serene looked over her shoulder to where Cardon stood. He was turned toward them, though his gaze was on the treeline. He was twenty-five years old, and her newest guard. Dirk had recommended him to the position about a year ago, and Captain Gates had accepted him even though Cardon had never been a bodyguard before. His career as a soldier had been impressive, though; at least, that's what Serene had overheard.

She enjoyed spending time with Cardon. He was rather quiet, but he was kind, and he made her laugh—even after a frustrating day with her tutors.

Dirk patted her shoulder. "See if you can find me a perfectly chipped shell."

She frowned. "Why do you want a chipped shell?"

"Because damaged things are often more intriguing."

She wasn't sure what he meant by that, but she was still struggling to understand his first request. "What makes a perfectly chipped shell? If it's perfect, it *won't* be chipped."

"Sometimes, imperfections make something *more* perfect."

She looked at him through narrowed eyes. "You're not making any sense."

He laughed. "Never fear. You'll know it when you see it." He pushed to his feet, winked at her, and strode away.

Serene watched him go, until Cardon came and crouched beside her. A small smile played about his lips. "The last time I saw Dirk look that smug was when you escaped his hold on the training field and blackened his eye."

That had been a good day. She smiled fondly. "Clearly, strange things amuse him."

Cardon chuckled and settled more comfortably on the moist ground, his eyes drawn back to the lake.

"Is this your first time at Lambern?" Serene asked. He hadn't been her guard last year, so this might have been his first time seeing the lake.

He nodded. "It's beautiful."

Serene surveyed the rippling water and tree-lined edge with new eyes, her appreciation growing. It truly was beautiful. Once, her family would have been enjoying it together. Now, they were scattered.

Her mother was back at the lodge, making final preparations for the hunt tomorrow. Queen Aren loved hunting, and they all accompanied her every year. Serene had been working with her bow and arrow for months in preparation, because she wanted to truly participate this year, rather than just ride around with the rest of the hunting party.

Her father was on the beach, but he sat in a chair a fair distance from her, his brow furrowed as he read some report. Years ago, he might have joined her in looking for shells, or might have asked her to go sailing with him on one of the moored boats.

Grandeur was in the water. The twelve-year-old prince seemed to be enjoying the sun-warmed lake, though he kept close to shore—probably at Wilf's insistence. The large bodyguard was in the water with Grandeur, keeping a close eye on him. Serene liked Wilf. He had been Queen Aren's guard before Grandeur's birth, so he'd been around the castle for as long as Serene could remember. She liked his wife, too—Lady Rachel was kind, and always made Serene feel valued, even if she wasn't destined to sit on the throne.

Serene had always known her family was different. As royals, they had other responsibilities than the normal roles of father, mother, brother, and sister. In truth, she'd never thought much about it before. But recently, she found herself longing for a simpler fate. What if her family didn't live in a castle, or bear the weight of an entire kingdom? Would the strain she felt among them now still be present?

She supposed she would never know.

She glanced at Cardon. "Did you ever take trips with your family?"

He shook his head, his eyes a little distant. "No. It seems like a nice thing to do, though."

"It is." Just not as nice as it used to be.

Cardon nodded at the pile of shells. "How many more do you hope to find?"

She shrugged. "However many catch my eye." And apparently, she needed to keep her eye out for a perfectly damaged one.

"Are you excited for the hunt tomorrow?" Cardon asked, absently picking at the dirt around a half-buried shell.

"Yes." Excitement and nerves mingled in that one word. She wanted to do well on the hunt. Perhaps that would make her mother smile, and her father proud.

Cardon must have discerned her anxiousness, even with only one word, because he said, "I'm sure all your practice will pay off."

Some of the tension in her shoulders relaxed. "Thank you."

He smiled, his brown eyes shining in the sun. Then he glanced down at the shell he'd unearthed, and his expression turned regretful. "Ah, this one has a crack."

Serene eyed the small shell in his palm. The fracture was instantly noticeable, since it cut diagonally across half the shell's surface. Despite the break, it was still in one piece. Serene imagined if she held it up to the sun, the crack would glow with light.

She wasn't sure if this was the type of broken shell Dirk wanted, but it *was* interesting.

Serene plucked it out of Cardon's hand before he could

discard it. When he looked at her questioningly, her cheeks warmed. "I think Dirk might like it," she tried to explain. "He thinks broken things are intriguing."

A smile played at Cardon's lips. "That certainly seems like something Dirk would say. He tends to value things that many others would dismiss." His expression turned musing, and Serene wondered if he was thinking about the fact that Dirk had noticed *him* in a barracks full of soldiers.

She was grateful Dirk had seen Cardon. If he hadn't, Serene probably never would have met him.

Dinner was a quiet affair. Grandeur was clearly worn out from all his swimming, and her father was entirely focused on his meal. Queen Aren sat across from her husband at the long table, and though she ate as well, she seemed distracted.

The silence was oddly strained, and Serene couldn't stand it any longer. "Is everything ready for the hunt?" she asked her mother.

The queen sent her a small smile. "Yes. We'll leave at dawn."

Her father glanced up from his plate. "I won't be able to join you."

Aren's smile fell. "Why not?"

His jaw stiffened. "I have letters to write."

"Can't they wait a day?"

"They shouldn't." His gaze flickered to Serene, who watched her parents with suddenly shallow breaths. Fates, why did they always do this? It was a fight, but not a fight. She didn't understand, and she hated it.

Newlan's throat flexed as he swallowed, and his attention returned to his wife. "You'll enjoy yourselves more without me, I'm sure."

"Newlan, please." Aren darted a look toward their children, her expression tense.

It must have communicated something more to Serene's father, because his lips pressed into a hard line. "Very well," he said grudgingly. "I'll accompany you."

"Thank you." Aren's voice was a little stiff.

Serene shifted in her chair. She was aware of their guards standing on the edges of the lodge's dining room, and she wondered if they'd noted the changes in how the king and queen had been interacting over the last few years. Did this happen to all parents? Or just those who had led a kingdom through a bloody war?

She was reminded of a conversation she had overheard years ago between her parents, soon after the civil war had ended. The memory stood out starkly, because her mother had been *furious*—and that was not something Serene had ever heard before.

She had wanted her mother's comfort after a nightmare. Dirk had walked her to her mother's suite, and the queen's guards had let her in. Her footsteps had hesitated when she reached the mostly closed door of her mother's bedroom. Even now, she wasn't entirely sure why she'd hesitated, because the room had been filled with silence.

Perhaps even at nine years old, she'd been able to hear the horrible heaviness of that silence.

"Tread carefully, Newlan," Aren had said, her voice low and hard. "There will be no going back from this accusation once you give it air."

"Perhaps you should have taken your own advice all those years ago," Newlan said harshly.

Serene's eyes widened. *No one* spoke to Queen Aren like that.

Her mother's laugh sounded wrong—strangled and barbed. "Maybe you should have come to Zennor yourself instead of sending Ivar."

"Do not speak his name," her father hissed.

Serene's fingers had knotted in her skirt. She knew that Ivar Carrigan was a traitor. He was the reason the awful civil war had even happened. She'd always liked Ivar, even though he was often away from the castle. He was the king's cousin, and he was often fulfilling responsibilities across Devendra. He'd always had a smile for Serene, though, along with a story from his travels, or some sweet or trinket. He had done the same for Grandeur, behaving almost like an uncle to them.

Then he had tried to kill her father and take his throne, and those actions had sent the whole kingdom into war.

"You're so afraid of him, even now." There was a strange note in Aren's voice. Sorrow, or a taunt? Serene couldn't decide.

"I am *not* afraid of him," Newlan snapped. "If the coward hadn't fled, I would have killed him along with all his insurgents."

"Fates rot you both! Your rivalry nearly tore this kingdom apart, and now you're letting it destroy your family."

"I've done nothing to destroy our family, Aren. Have *you*?"

That same terrible, weighted silence. Then, "If you ask me this one more time, I will leave. I swear it, Newlan. I will return to Zennor and never look back. And I'll take the children with me."

Newlan's tone darkened. "You would commit treason? You would abandon me and steal my heir?"

"To protect my children from your insane jealousy? Yes."

"*Your* children? They're not mine, then?"

"Fates!" she cried out, making Serene cringe. "I can't keep doing this with you!"

"Then give me an answer once and for all that I can believe!"

"You refuse to believe me—no matter how many times I tell you the truth. How am I supposed to convince you?"

He snarled. "You can stop avoiding me and just answer the question!"

"Or you could choose to trust me!" Aren's words were pinched, and even though Serene couldn't see her, she swore her mother was fighting back tears. "If you keep asking me this, I swear I'll never forgive you."

"Your forgiveness means little to me," Newlan retorted. "But *my* forgiveness should be your only goal right now."

Aren's laugh was cold and mirthless. "We both know your threats are empty. If you put the smallest bruise on me, my brother would annihilate you. And with your depleted army, you know Devendra wouldn't stand a chance against him."

"You dare threaten me?" Newlan's voice vibrated with terrible rage.

Serene never heard her mother's answer, because she hurried away from the door. She wanted to leave their fight behind, as if that would make it so the confrontation hadn't happened at all.

Five years later, and she still remembered every word.

Seated at the dining table, Serene tried to focus on cutting her roasted potatoes into smaller bites.

"Serene, Grandeur—did you both have a nice time at the

lake?" Aren asked.

The prince nodded, and despite the weary sag in his shoulders, his blue eyes were suddenly bright. "I can hold my breath underwater longer than Wilf!"

Wilf stood with the other guards along the wall, and Serene caught the smile that flashed across his face.

Amusement warmed Queen Aren's eyes. "That's very impressive," she said to her son. "I'm so proud of you." She turned to Serene. "Did you find any new shells to add to your collection?"

"Yes. One is especially interesting," she added, shooting Dirk a meaningful look. He grinned from his position near the back wall.

Queen Aren smiled as well. "I can't wait to see it."

Serene held Fury's reins loosely, letting the horse instinctively follow the other mounts. Their guide rode at the front of the line with Queen Aren so they could confer readily about their route through the forest. Newlan trailed behind his wife, somehow looking both pensive and bored. Serene and Grandeur rode close behind, with a handful of servants taking up the rear. It was nearly midday, and Serene knew they'd be stopping soon to eat a picnic luncheon the servants had prepared.

The bodyguards were alert, as always. The king and queen had their full guard—five men each, though only two rode directly beside them. The rest were flanking the entire company. The royal children each had two guards, and Serene was grateful that Dirk and Cardon were the ones with her. Captain Gates and the others were wonderful, but Dirk and Cardon were her favorites; her longest-serving guard, and her newest. The thought made her smile.

The forest was alive with squirrels darting up trees, birds trilling in the overhead branches, and the faint trickling of a nearby stream. The forest seemed ageless and fleeting at the same time. Permanent, because it would never change or stop brimming with life, no matter what wars were fought or what families walked among these trees. Fleeting, because every sound was new and faded quickly, and no creature lived forever.

Fates, that was a somber thought. Suddenly, Serene didn't feel much like hunting the animals that called this forest home.

A more strident birdcall made her look up from the strung bow attached to her saddle. She wasn't sure what bird made such a fierce sound—it didn't sound quite like any of the others.

From her periphery, she saw that she wasn't the only one to notice. Beside her, Dirk and Cardon both tensed.

The guide stopped his horse, his fist raised in a silent command for everyone to stop.

Newlan straightened in his saddle, any show of boredom instantly gone. "What—?"

His quiet voice was cut off by a scream as an arrow struck the shoulder of one of the queen's guards—a guard who had just shifted his horse to stand more closely to the queen.

"Ambush!" Wilf bellowed.

Serene's heart leaped into her throat, terror slashing

through her as she spotted the masked men who ran out from the trees they'd been hiding behind. Swords flashed in the sunlight that filtered through the leafy canopy, though other attackers stayed in place and took careful aim with their arrows.

They were surrounded.

Serene cried out as more arrows snapped toward the hunting party.

There were sickening thunks, and men and horses screamed and toppled. Guards drew their weapons and shouted orders. The horses panicked.

Serene clutched Fury's reins as her horse snorted madly and stomped her hooves.

Cardon grabbed Serene's arm and hauled her onto his horse, keeping her smaller body tucked in front of his own.

Dirk swung his sword at the nearest attacker, though it seemed that most of the assassins were targeting the king and queen.

Serene's fingers dug into Cardon's arm as she twisted in front of him and frantically searched for her parents in the melee. They weren't on their horses; their guards had pulled them down so they would be less of a target. But there were so many guards, servants, and attackers—she couldn't see her parents.

"To the king and queen!" one of her father's guards yelled, the frantic edge in his voice betraying his fear.

Dirk glanced back at Cardon, his usual calm replaced by fierce intent. "Guard her."

"With my life," Cardon swore.

Dirk jerked out a nod. He swung down from his horse, his sword swinging as he rushed into the fray that had swallowed the king and queen.

Serene couldn't breathe. She had been in danger before, but an attack like this was wholly different. Though she had been trained to defend herself, this felt like she'd been dropped into the middle of a battlefield. Fear froze her.

While most of the guards rushed to defend the king and queen, the remaining ones took up positions around the royal children. One of Grandeur's guards had snatched the prince off his horse, just as Cardon had grabbed Serene. But as she watched, an arrow pierced the guard's arm.

Grandeur recoiled with a terrified screech and fell off the horse, landing hard on the ground.

"Grandeur!" Serene screamed.

Cardon's hold on her tightened, keeping her in the saddle with him as he fought to calm the horse.

Wilf was suddenly there, dropping off his mount beside Grandeur. He scooped the prince into his arms, and panic swirled in Serene's gut. Her brother wasn't moving.

Then Grandeur sucked in a breath, his face pained.

Serene sagged with relief. He had only had the air knocked from his lungs.

Wilf turned with the prince and ran into the trees, not bothering with the spooked horse. In the thick forest, he would be faster on foot, anyway.

Abandoning the chaos of the attack felt like the wiser choice, even if it meant separating from the other guards.

Cardon must have had the same thought. He gripped Serene tightly as he dismounted, pulling her with him. Once on the ground, he drew his longsword. "Stay close to—" His words were cut off when an attacker sprang at them.

Cardon shoved Serene away and met the attacker's blade

with his own.

Serene's heart pounded painfully as she watched Cardon fight. The ferocity of the battle was unlike anything she had seen on the training field. But then, that made sense—this was a real battle where people lived or died based on their skill, and that of their opponent. And Cardon's opponent was brutal in every strike of his sword.

Cardon matched him blow for blow. He seemed anxious to shift the fight away from Serene, and yet he clearly didn't want to get too far from her.

Another attacker joined the fight, and that's when Cardon must have given up on keeping her in his sights. "Run!" he yelled.

She couldn't run—she could hardly even breathe. And how could she run when Cardon was fighting *two* men?

It only took a moment for her to realize this second man wasn't as skilled as his companion, though. His movements were unpracticed—clumsy, even. Cardon managed to get under his guard easily, his sword going into the man's stomach almost all the way to the hilt.

Unfortunately, the other attacker swept in at that moment, and Cardon didn't have the precious seconds he needed to drag out his sword.

He ducked to avoid a killing strike, and leaped back to avoid the next deadly swing. He drew the dagger at his belt so he could block the man's next attack.

The chaos in the clearing blurred as Serene watched the heated battle Cardon was locked in. He only had a dagger as he faced a man with a longsword.

Fates knew that wouldn't end well.

Serene darted forward, intent on pulling Cardon's sword

out of the dead man on the ground.

She hadn't made it two steps before someone grasped her braid and hauled her back against a hard chest.

From the corner of her eye, she saw his blade lift, the point aimed down at her.

Serene screamed.

Cardon whirled toward her. Without hesitation, he threw his knife; the dagger spun in the air and embedded in the chest of the man behind her.

He jerked back, and Serene managed to break away from his weakened hold and twist to face him.

The man was hardly a threat anymore. He dropped his own knife so he could clutch at the one buried in his chest, even as he fell to his knees.

Serene's stomach pitched as he slumped forward. She scrambled back, her heart in her throat as she watched him twitch once, then still in death. He . . . he was dead. A man who had tried to kill her . . .

Fates, she had almost died.

Her skin prickled with a strange burn, and tears stung her eyes.

"Serene!"

Cardon's shout ripped through her, making her flinch. She looked away from the dead man, her attention snapping to Cardon.

He was grappling with his opponent, both of them wrestling for control of the attacker's sword.

Fates. Cardon had thrown his knife to save her. He didn't have a weapon anymore. And the man he'd been fighting now pressed his advantage.

Cardon's arms shook, his face flushed as he wrestled for that blade. "Serene!" he bellowed again. "Run! *Now!*"

Her heart thudded against her ribs. The terror of the last few moments wanted to keep her frozen, but that wasn't an option.

Cardon had risked everything to save her. If he died now, she would never forgive herself. That was the only thought in her head as she ran. Not for the safety of the trees, or even Cardon's longsword—but for Fury.

Her horse was as anxious as the other animals, but she hadn't bolted.

Serene snatched up her bow and yanked an arrow from her quiver. She glanced over her shoulder and saw Cardon on the ground. The attacker was on top of him, and the longsword had been abandoned—it wasn't a weapon for close combat.

The attacker had a knife in his hand, and though Cardon had caught his wrist, the wavering blade was slowly descending.

Serene's pulse roared in her ears. She loaded her bow, settled her stance, and drew back the taut string. The muscles in her arms and across her back stretched, but she'd practiced this motion a thousand times in the past few months. The tip of her arrow didn't falter.

She aimed and released, and the arrow flew into the attacker's unguarded back.

The man fell forward, and Serene couldn't see Cardon because the attacker's body covered him.

Serene trembled, the bow clutched in one tight fist. Fates, had she been too late?

The attacker's body shifted, then was shoved aside. Cardon rolled to his knees, breathing hard. He looked at her, his eyes wide. Blood streaked his right cheek from a harsh cut, but he was alive.

His expression was impossible to decipher. Surprise, concern, admiration, and a hundred more emotions she couldn't name all mingled together. He didn't thank her, though, and she knew that was because she should have run. That had been his order, and it was what Dirk and her other guards had always trained her to do.

Not wanting to hear a lecture, she kept her stance firm as she met his stare boldly. She refused to appear rattled or afraid.

She lifted one eyebrow and said dryly, "You're welcome."

Serene knocked lightly on Cardon's door. Everyone in the lodge seemed settled for the night, but she knew she couldn't rest until she checked on Cardon.

"Come in," he said from the other side.

She nudged the door open and stepped into the room. It was small and sparsely furnished, with only a narrow bed and a bedside table tucked under the window. Dirk remained in the hall—possibly because of the tight quarters.

Cardon was riffling through his trunk, but he straightened to attention when he spotted her standing in the doorway.

She winced a little at the dark red line that cut across his cheek. The glow of the lamp did nothing to hide the mark, and it was deep enough that she knew it would leave a scar. "Does it hurt?" She instantly regretted the stupid question, though she couldn't take it back now.

"It's much better than being dead, so I won't complain."

Cardon glanced behind her, to where Dirk no doubt hovered. When he focused back on Serene, his gaze was warm. "Thank you, Serene. You saved my life."

Pride, and perhaps something else, flushed through her. She smiled. "Let's try not to make a habit of it."

Cardon chuckled. "Fair enough. I think my ego might be damaged if you were always the one saving me. It's not exactly the roles we're supposed to be playing, is it?"

"True."

His expression quickly grew serious. "As grateful as I am, you should have run. In the future, you need to listen to me."

Ah, there was the anticipated lecture. "Dirk has already gone over this with me."

Cardon arched an eyebrow. "Did you take his words to heart?"

"Not really."

Through the open door behind her, she heard Dirk snort.

Cardon's lips twitched. "At least you're honest."

Serene sighed. "If I'd listened to you, you'd be dead. As it is, we're both still breathing. Isn't that the better outcome?"

"It was a good outcome for today," he allowed. "But that doesn't guarantee a similar outcome in the future. You could have died."

"I could have died while running away, too." She folded her arms. "To be honest, I don't think running is in my nature."

The corner of his mouth lifted. "I think you might be right."

Dirk muttered something that sounded very much like *fates help us all.*

Serene decided she had pushed her guards enough for the night. She reached into her pocket and held out her fist. "This is for you."

His forehead wrinkled, but he held out his hand.

She dropped the small, perfect shell into Cardon's palm. Her fingertips brushed against his callused palm as she pulled back, and her heart beat a little faster than normal. "Thank you for saving my life today, too," she said softly.

His eyes lifted from the shell, his voice just as quiet as he said, "It was my honor, Princess."

They exchanged their goodnights, and Dirk escorted her back down the hall to her room.

Before stepping inside, she handed him a shell, too.

Dirk turned it over in his hand. "You couldn't find a perfectly broken one for me?" he teased.

Serene fingered the shell still in her pocket, the edge of her fingernail following the seam of the crack. "Actually, I did find one." Or rather, *Cardon* had found it. The memory warmed her in an unexpected but intriguing way.

"Oh, you're keeping it for yourself." Dirk smiled. "You realized I was right, then. Sometimes, imperfections can make something *more* perfect."

Still holding the shell in her pocket and thinking about the wound on Cardon's cheek that would undoubtedly scar, Serene returned Dirk's smile. "You were right," she agreed. Imperfect things could be perfect, because they were perfect to her.

And, just like Dirk had said, she knew it when she saw it.

ABOUT THE AUTHOR

Heather Frost is a #1 Amazon bestselling author who writes YA/NA fantasy romance and paranormal romance. She is the author of the Seers Trilogy, the Fate of Eyrinthia Series, and Esperance. Her books have been finalists and nominees for a variety of awards, including the Whitney and Swoony Awards. She has a BS in Creative Writing and a minor in Folklore, which means she got to read fairy tales and call it homework.

When she's not writing, Heather likes to read, travel, and re-watch Lord of the Rings. She lives in a beautiful valley surrounded by mountains in northern Utah.

To learn more about Heather and her books, visit her website: www.HeatherFrost.com.

Made in United States
Orlando, FL
27 December 2023